This book is dedicated to my father

Fantagraphics Books
7563 Lake City Way NE
Seattle WA 98115

Designed by Ted Stearn
Production by Paul Baresh
Editor and Associate Publisher: Eric Reynolds
Publisher: Gary Groth

Visit the Fantagraphics website:
www.fantagraphics.com
First printing: September 2016
ISBN: 978-1-60699-966-0
Library of Congress Number: 2016936308
Printed in China

FUZZ & PLUCK

THE MOOLAH TREE

Ted Stearn

PRESENTED THUS TWO MISFITS
WHO BELONG NEITHER HERE NOR THERE
ONE IS A DEFEATHERED ROOSTER
THE OTHER A RAGGED TEDDY BEAR

TRULY THERE NEVER WAS A STRANGER PAIR
OF CREATURES DOWN ON THEIR LUCK
THAN THE TWO VAGABONDS DEPICTED BELOW
THEIR NAMES ARE FUZZ AND PLUCK

Long ago in a garbage truck
our heroes just happened to meet
they struck up a tenuous friendship
that was not bitter, but surely not sweet

Their ordeals between then and now
were a jumble of people, places and things~
enough to fill two previous tomes
from whence this story springs

AND SO THE READER MAY WONDER
WHAT BRINGS US HERE AND WHERE ARE WE?
ALAS, THEY ARE TRAPPED ON A RAMSHACKLE BARGE
WHICH SLOWLY DRIFTS OUT TO SEA...

LOST AND ALONE BUT NOT WITHOUT HOPE
STILL YOKED TO THE FICKLES OF FATE
THEY (AND WE) CAN ONLY GUESS
WHAT DESTINY LIES IN WAIT ~

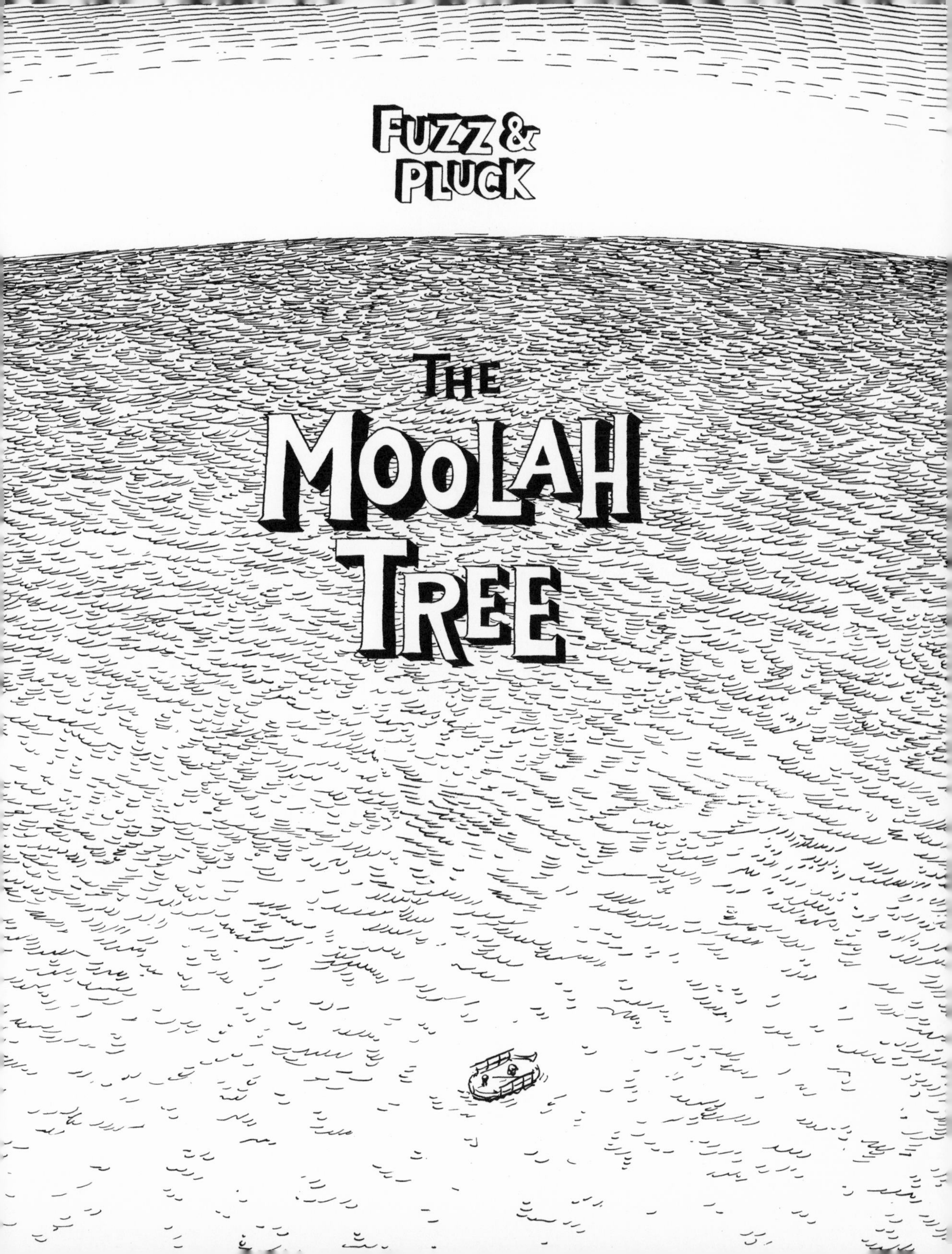
FUZZ & PLUCK
THE MOOLAH TREE

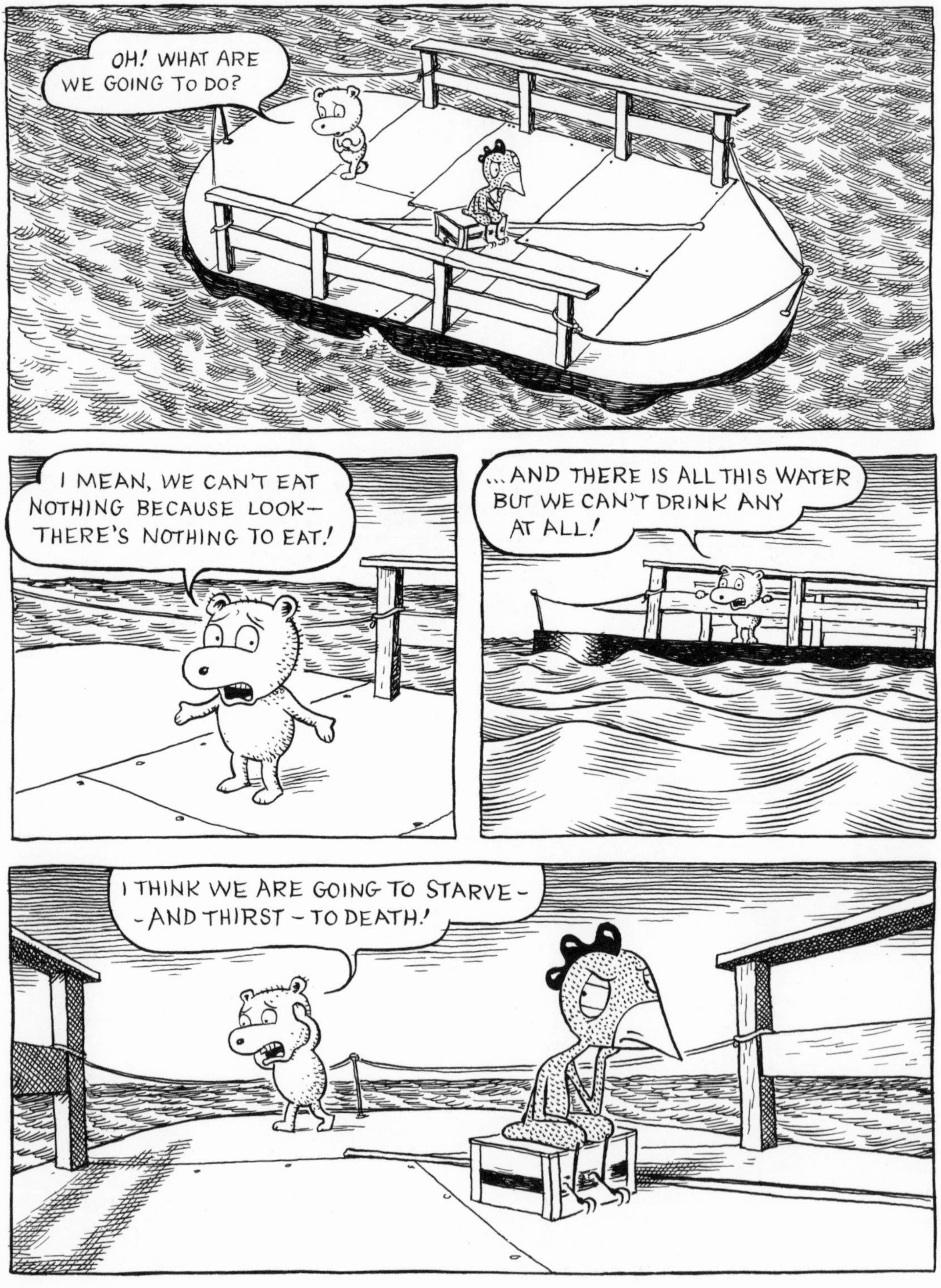
OH! WHAT ARE WE GOING TO DO?
I MEAN, WE CAN'T EAT NOTHING BECAUSE LOOK— THERE'S NOTHING TO EAT!
...AND THERE IS ALL THIS WATER BUT WE CAN'T DRINK ANY AT ALL!
I THINK WE ARE GOING TO STARVE - - AND THIRST - TO DEATH!

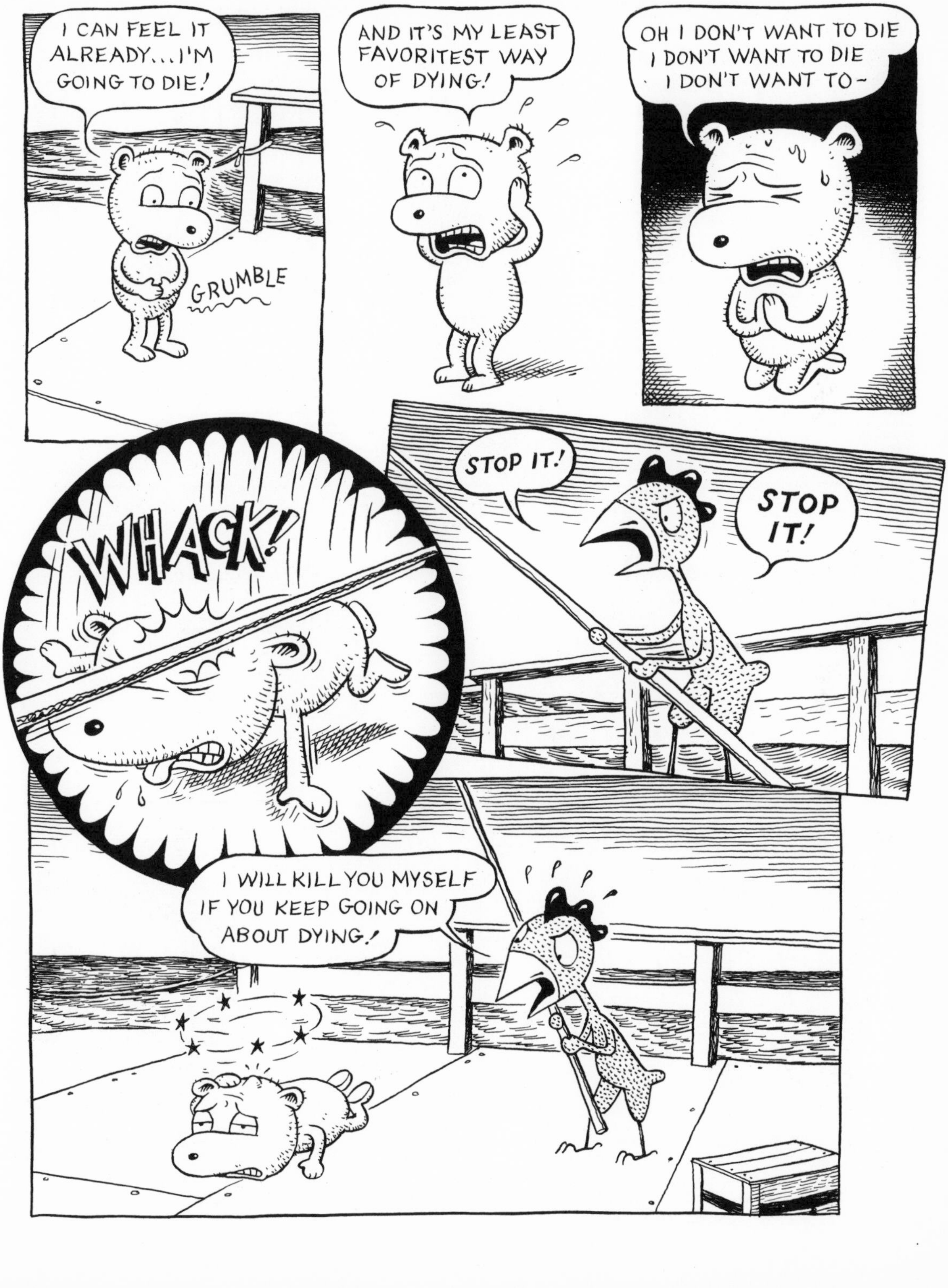
I CAN FEEL IT ALREADY...I'M GOING TO DIE!
GRUMBLE
AND IT'S MY LEAST FAVORITEST WAY OF DYING!
OH I DON'T WANT TO DIE
I DON'T WANT TO DIE
I DON'T WANT TO-
STOP IT!
STOP IT!
WHACK!
I WILL KILL YOU MYSELF IF YOU KEEP GOING ON ABOUT DYING!

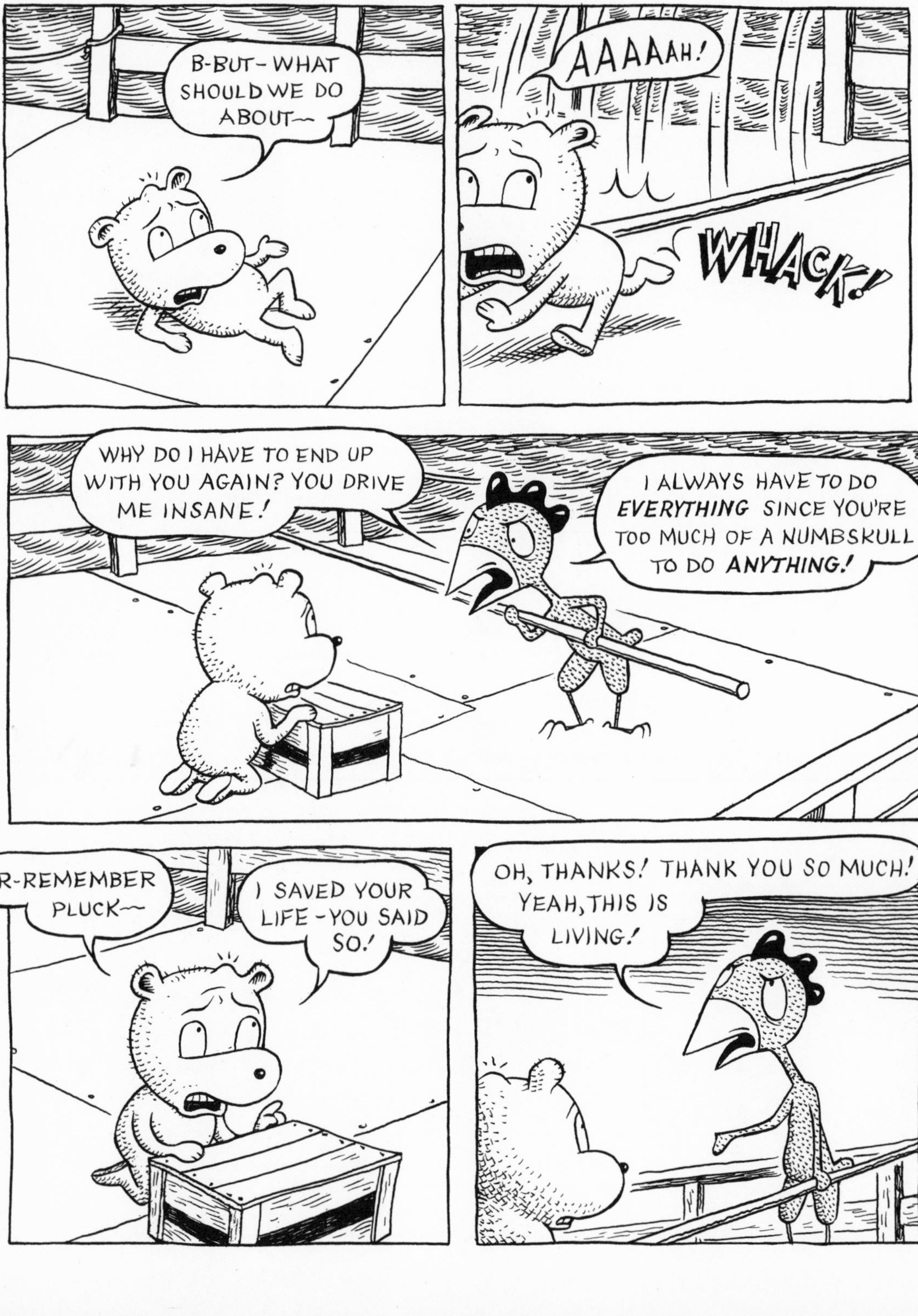
B-BUT- WHAT SHOULD WE DO ABOUT~~
AAAAAH!
WHACK!
WHY DO I HAVE TO END UP WITH YOU AGAIN? YOU DRIVE ME INSANE!
I ALWAYS HAVE TO DO EVERYTHING SINCE YOU'RE TOO MUCH OF A NUMBSKULL TO DO ANYTHING!
R-REMEMBER PLUCK~~
I SAVED YOUR LIFE -YOU SAID SO!
OH, THANKS! THANK YOU SO MUCH!
YEAH, THIS IS LIVING!

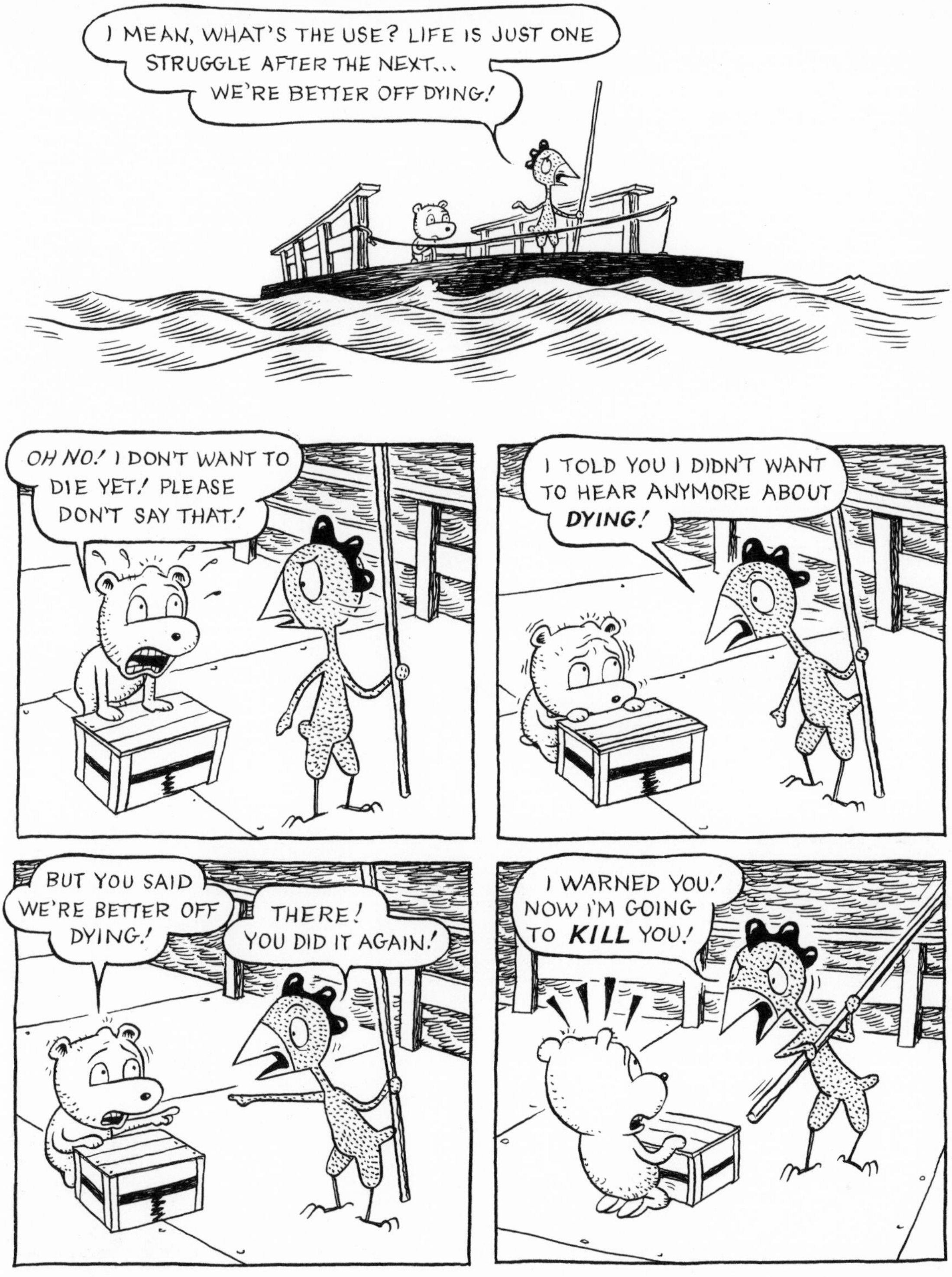
I MEAN, WHAT'S THE USE? LIFE IS JUST ONE STRUGGLE AFTER THE NEXT... WE'RE BETTER OFF DYING!
OH NO! I DON'T WANT TO DIE YET! PLEASE DON'T SAY THAT!
I TOLD YOU I DIDN'T WANT TO HEAR ANYMORE ABOUT **DYING**!
BUT YOU SAID WE'RE BETTER OFF DYING!
THERE! YOU DID IT AGAIN!
I WARNED YOU! NOW I'M GOING TO **KILL** YOU!

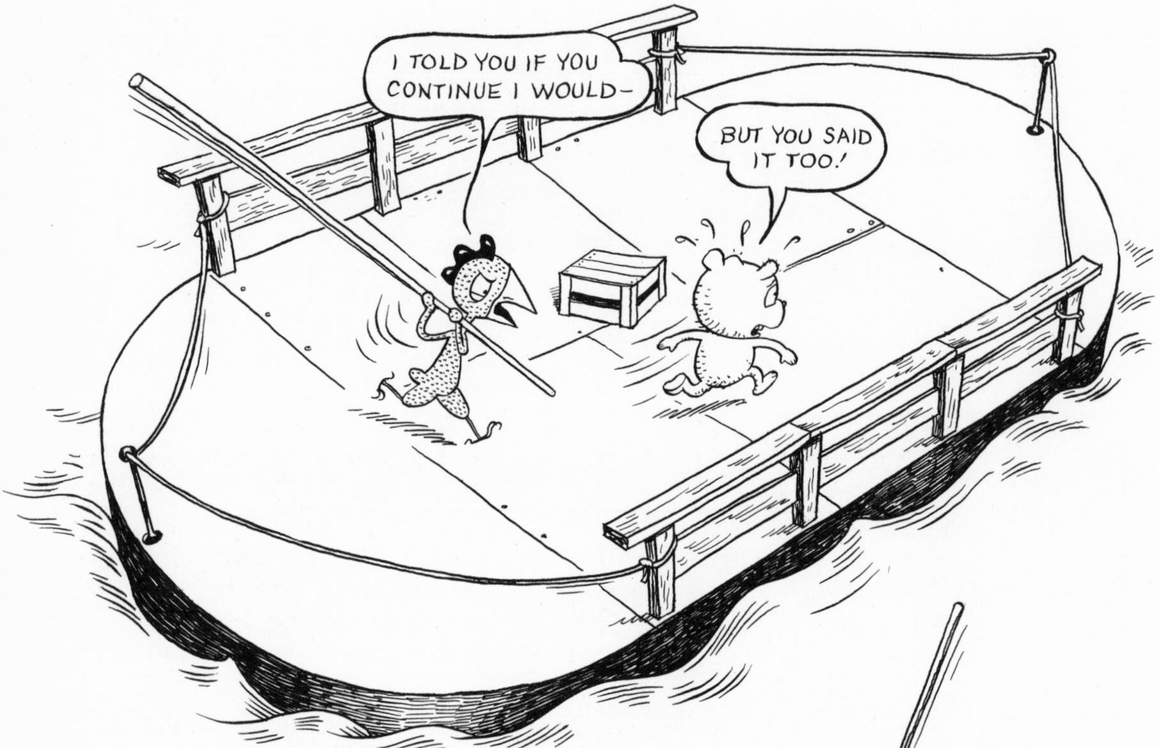
I TOLD YOU IF YOU CONTINUE I WOULD-
BUT YOU SAID IT TOO!

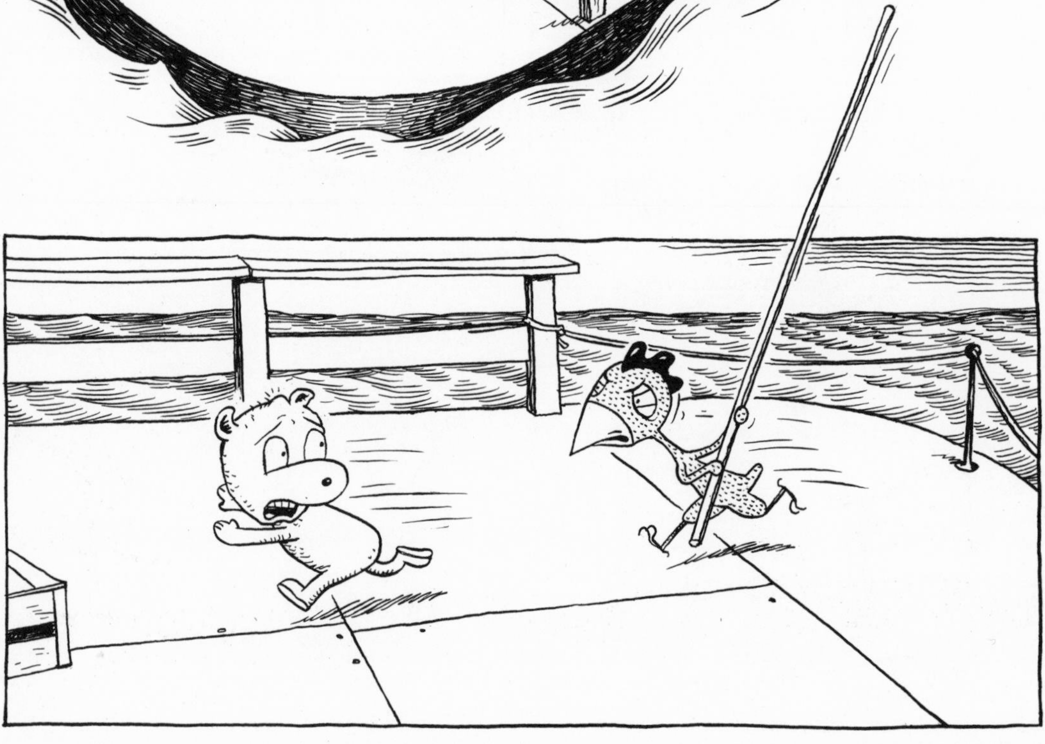

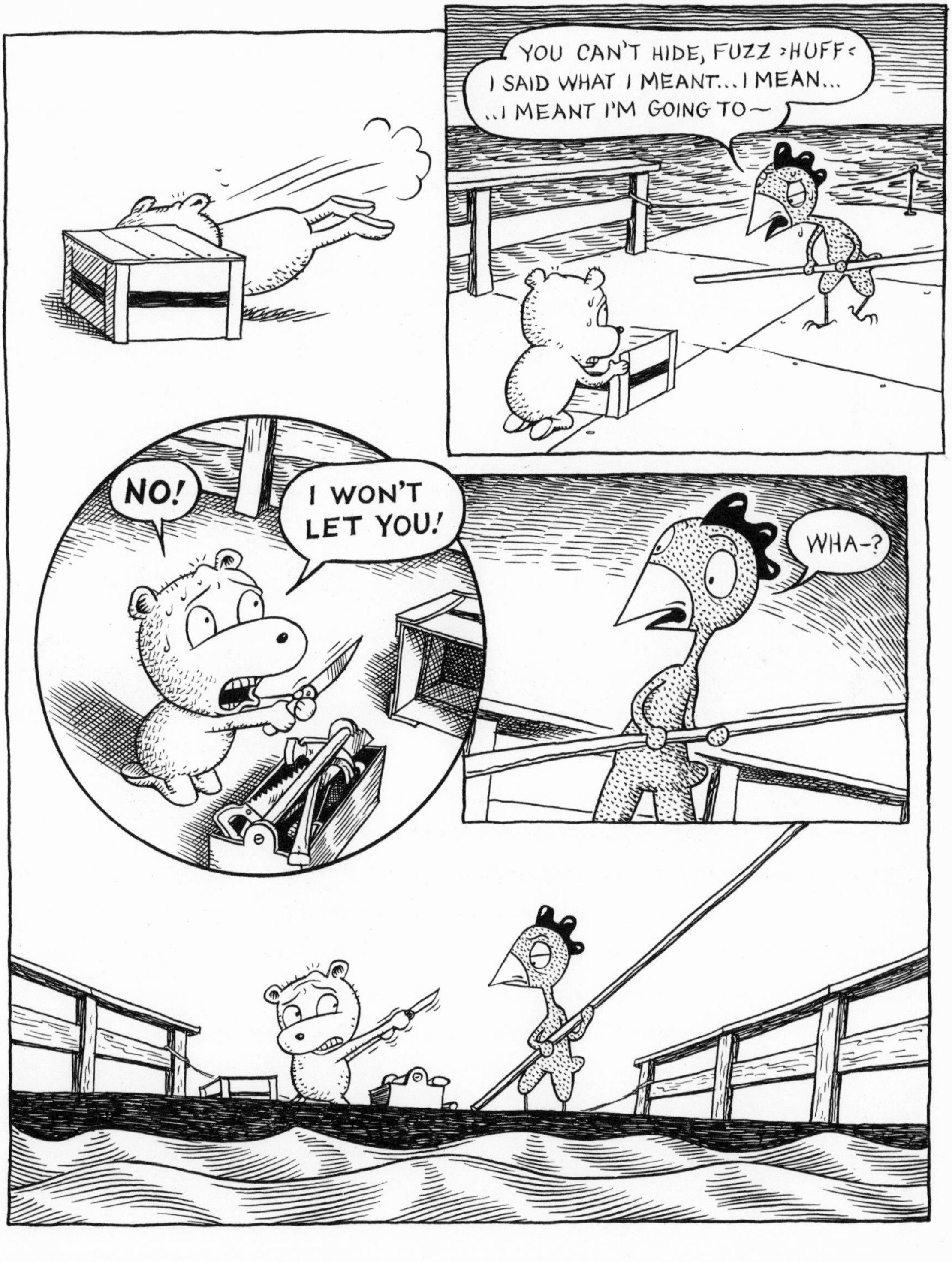
YOU CAN'T HIDE, FUZZ >HUFF< I SAID WHAT I MEANT... I MEAN... ..I MEANT I'M GOING TO~
NO!
I WON'T LET YOU!
WHA-?

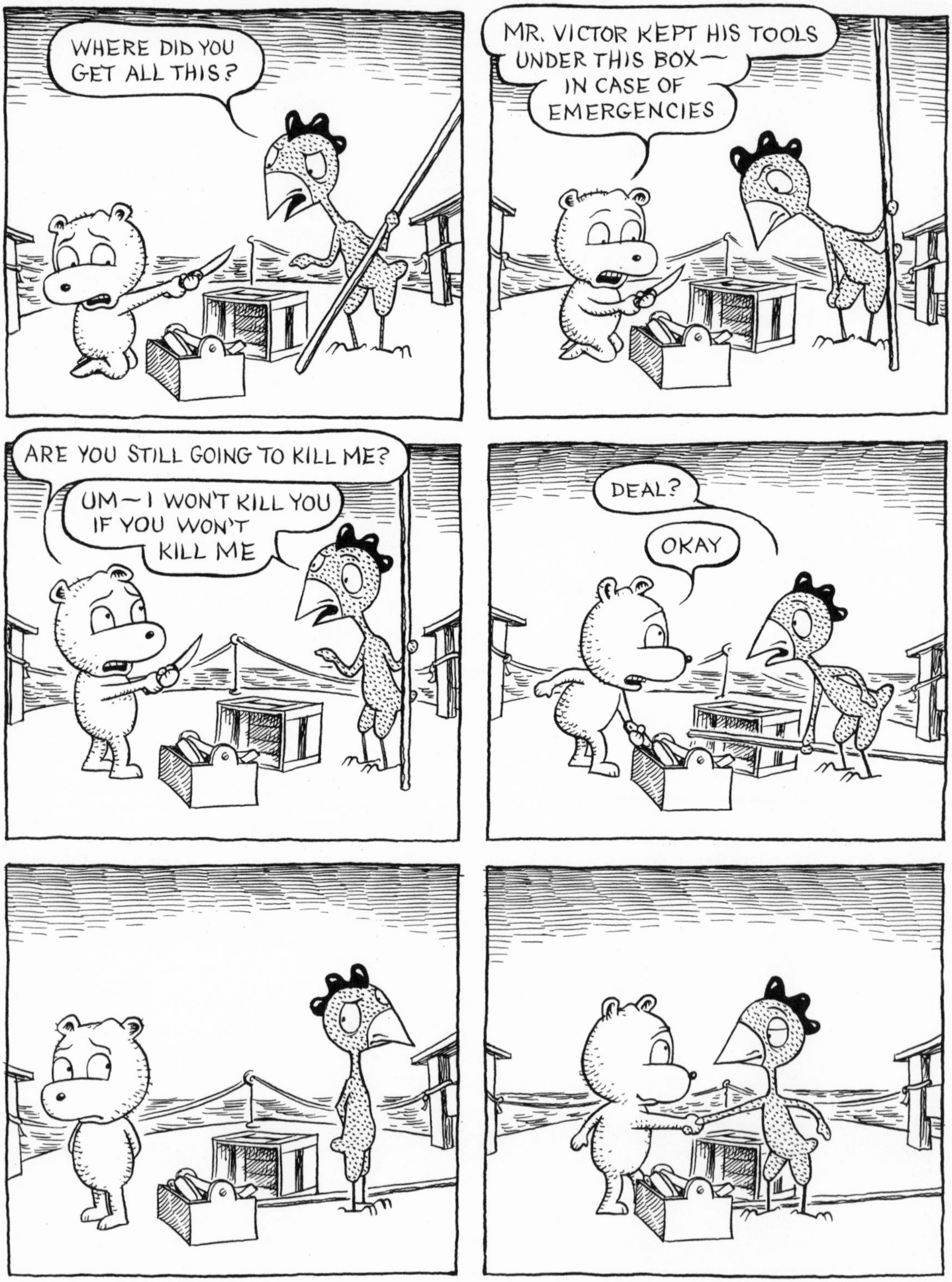
WHERE DID YOU GET ALL THIS?
MR. VICTOR KEPT HIS TOOLS UNDER THIS BOX— IN CASE OF EMERGENCIES
ARE YOU STILL GOING TO KILL ME?
UM—I WON'T KILL YOU IF YOU WON'T KILL ME
DEAL?
OKAY

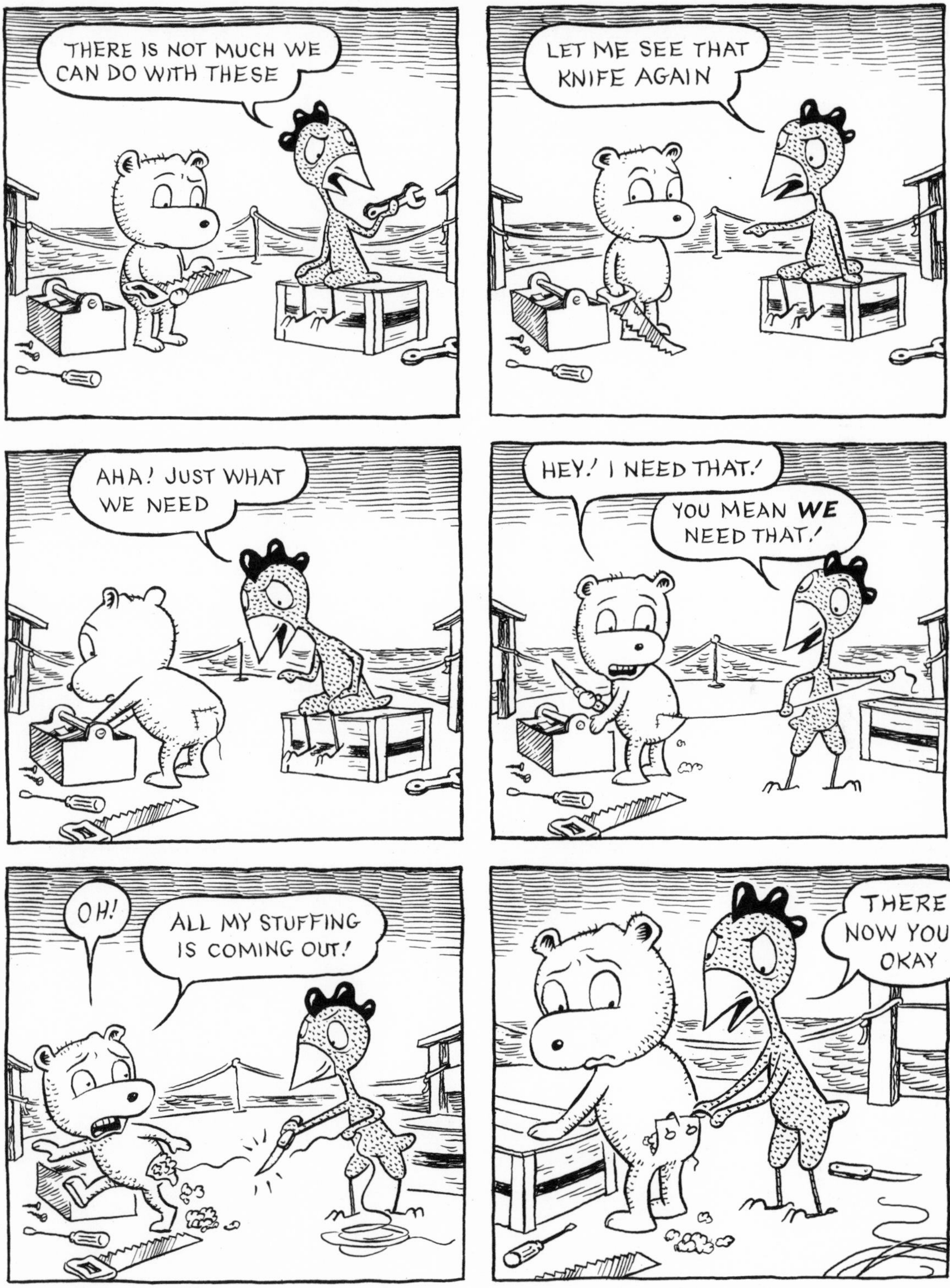
THERE IS NOT MUCH WE CAN DO WITH THESE
LET ME SEE THAT KNIFE AGAIN
AHA! JUST WHAT WE NEED
HEY! I NEED THAT!
YOU MEAN **WE** NEED THAT!
OH!
ALL MY STUFFING IS COMING OUT!
THERE NOW YOU'RE OKAY

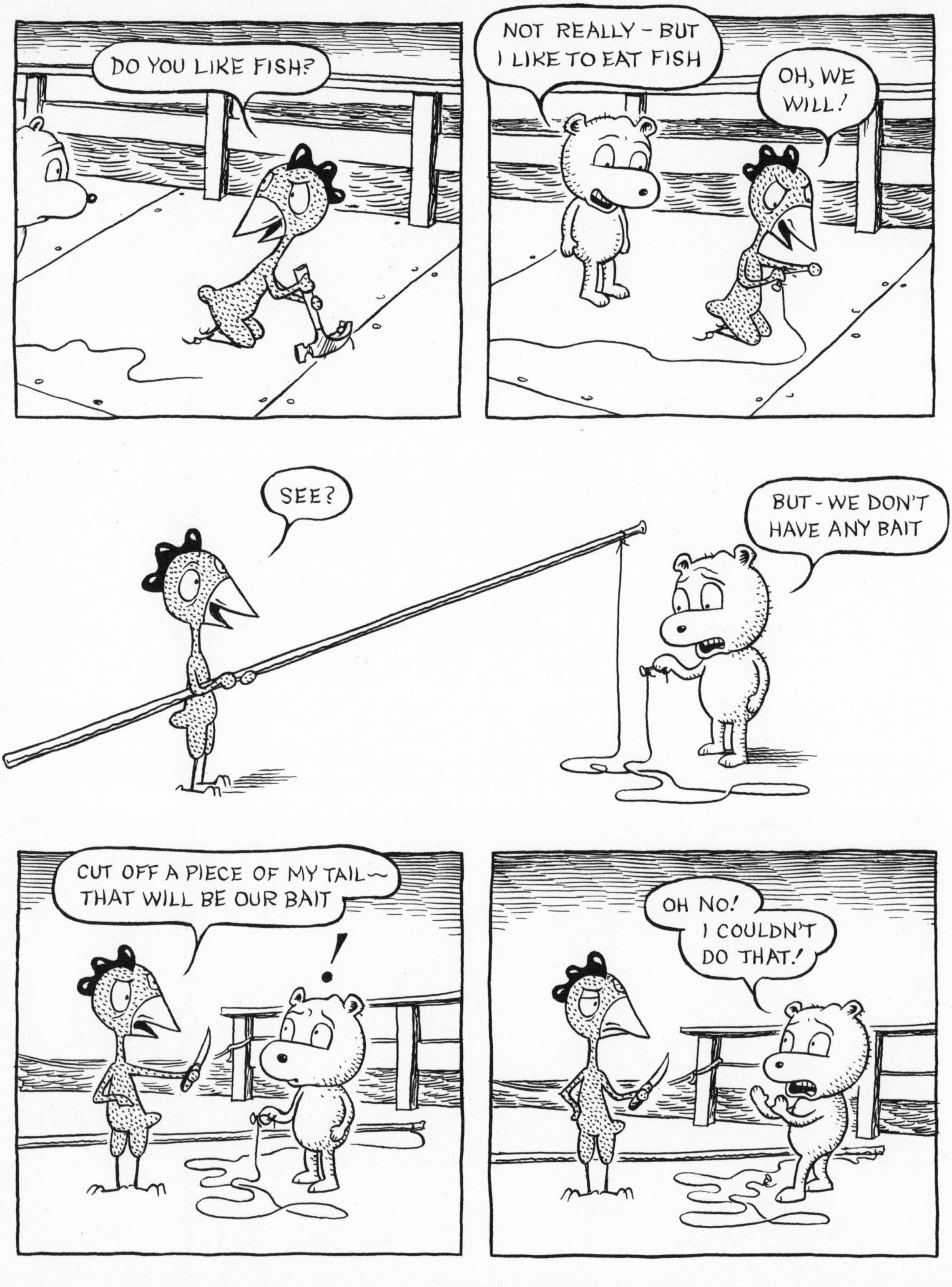
DO YOU LIKE FISH?
NOT REALLY - BUT I LIKE TO EAT FISH
OH, WE WILL!
SEE?
BUT - WE DON'T HAVE ANY BAIT
CUT OFF A PIECE OF MY TAIL~ THAT WILL BE OUR BAIT
!
OH NO! I COULDN'T DO THAT!

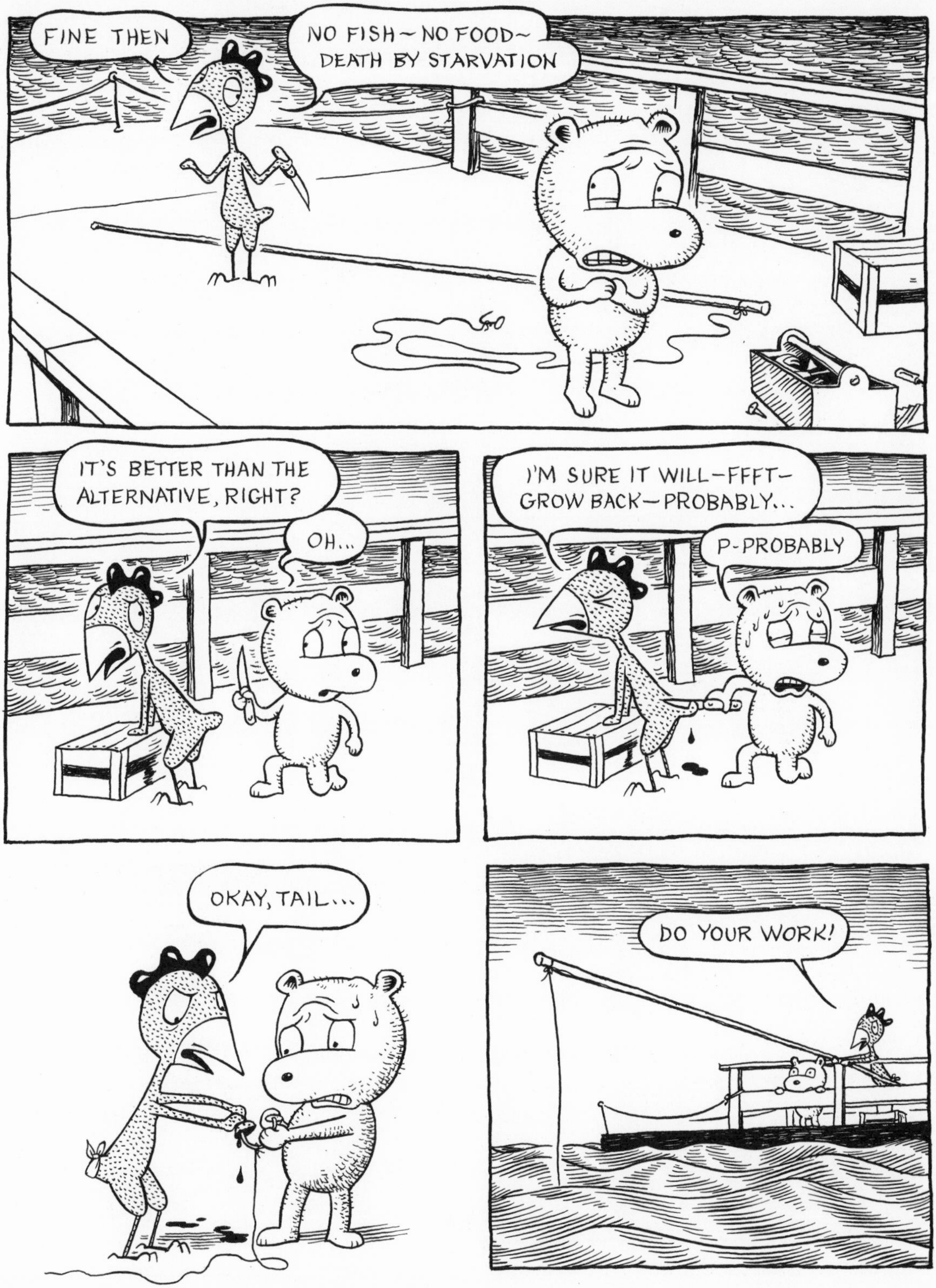
FINE THEN
NO FISH ~ NO FOOD ~ DEATH BY STARVATION
IT'S BETTER THAN THE ALTERNATIVE, RIGHT?
OH...
I'M SURE IT WILL—FFFT—GROW BACK—PROBABLY...
P-PROBABLY
OKAY, TAIL...
DO YOUR WORK!

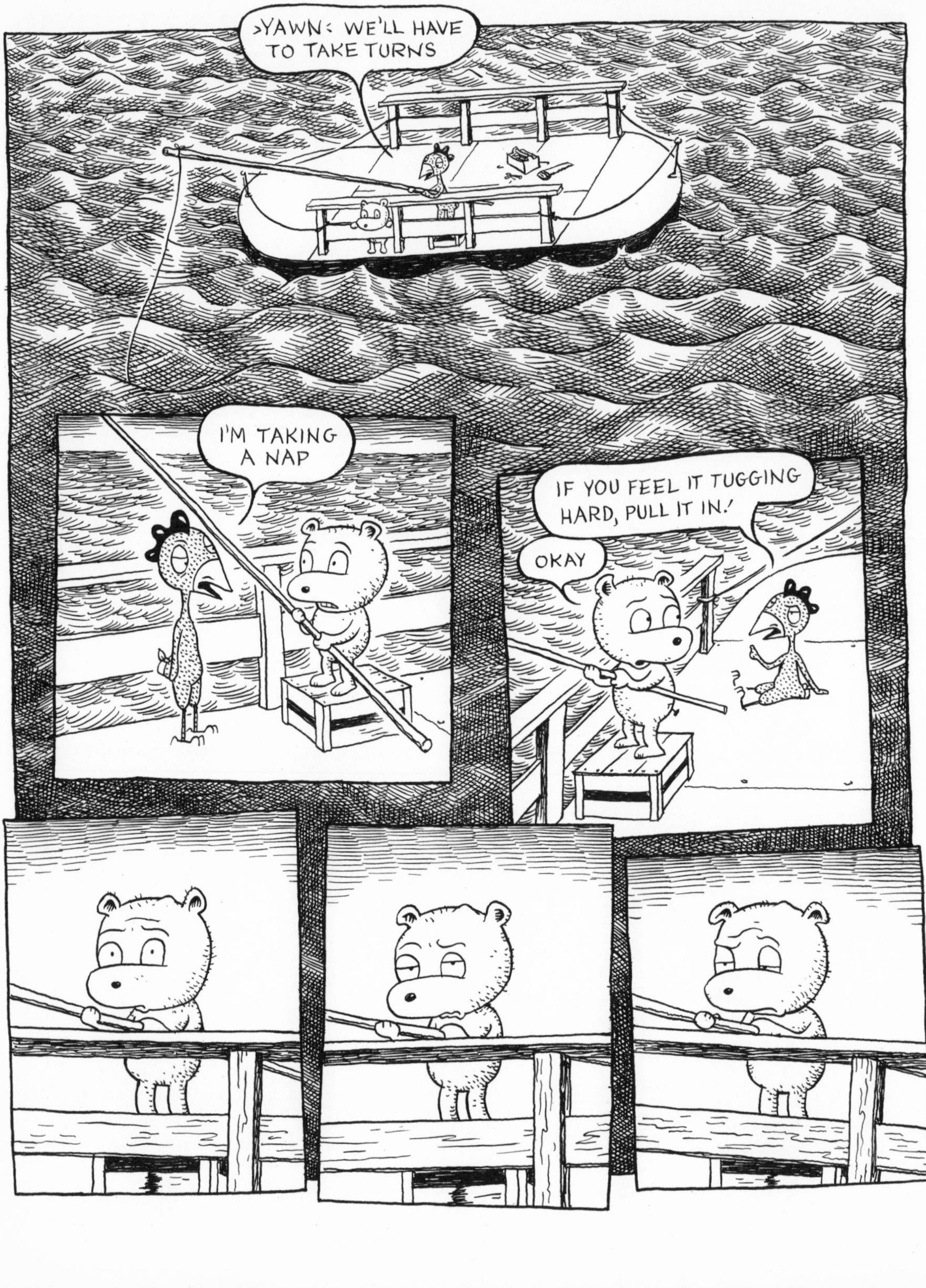

>YAWN< WE'LL HAVE TO TAKE TURNS
I'M TAKING A NAP
IF YOU FEEL IT TUGGING HARD, PULL IT IN!
OKAY

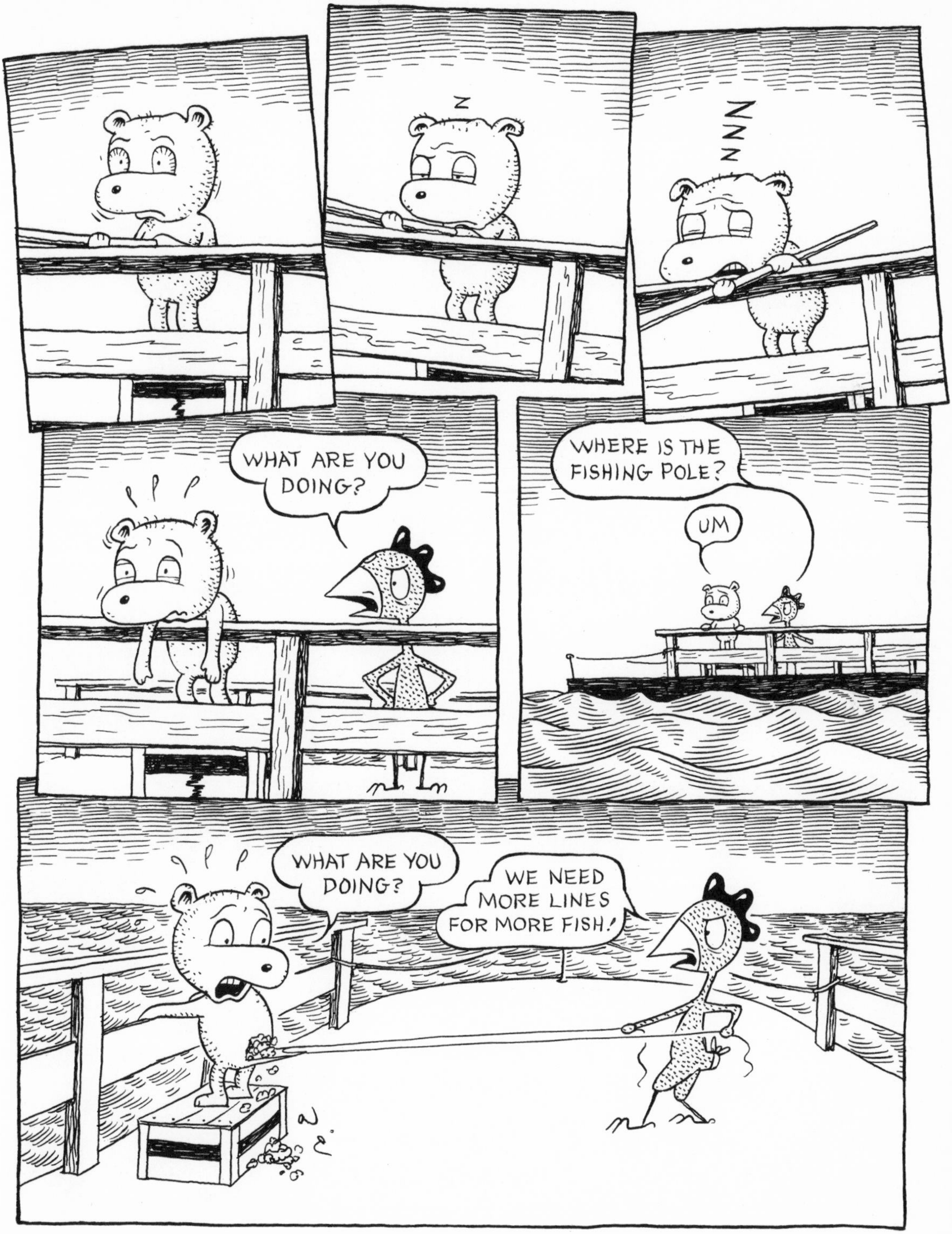
Z
ZZZ
WHAT ARE YOU DOING?
WHERE IS THE FISHING POLE?
UM
WHAT ARE YOU DOING?
WE NEED MORE LINES FOR MORE FISH!

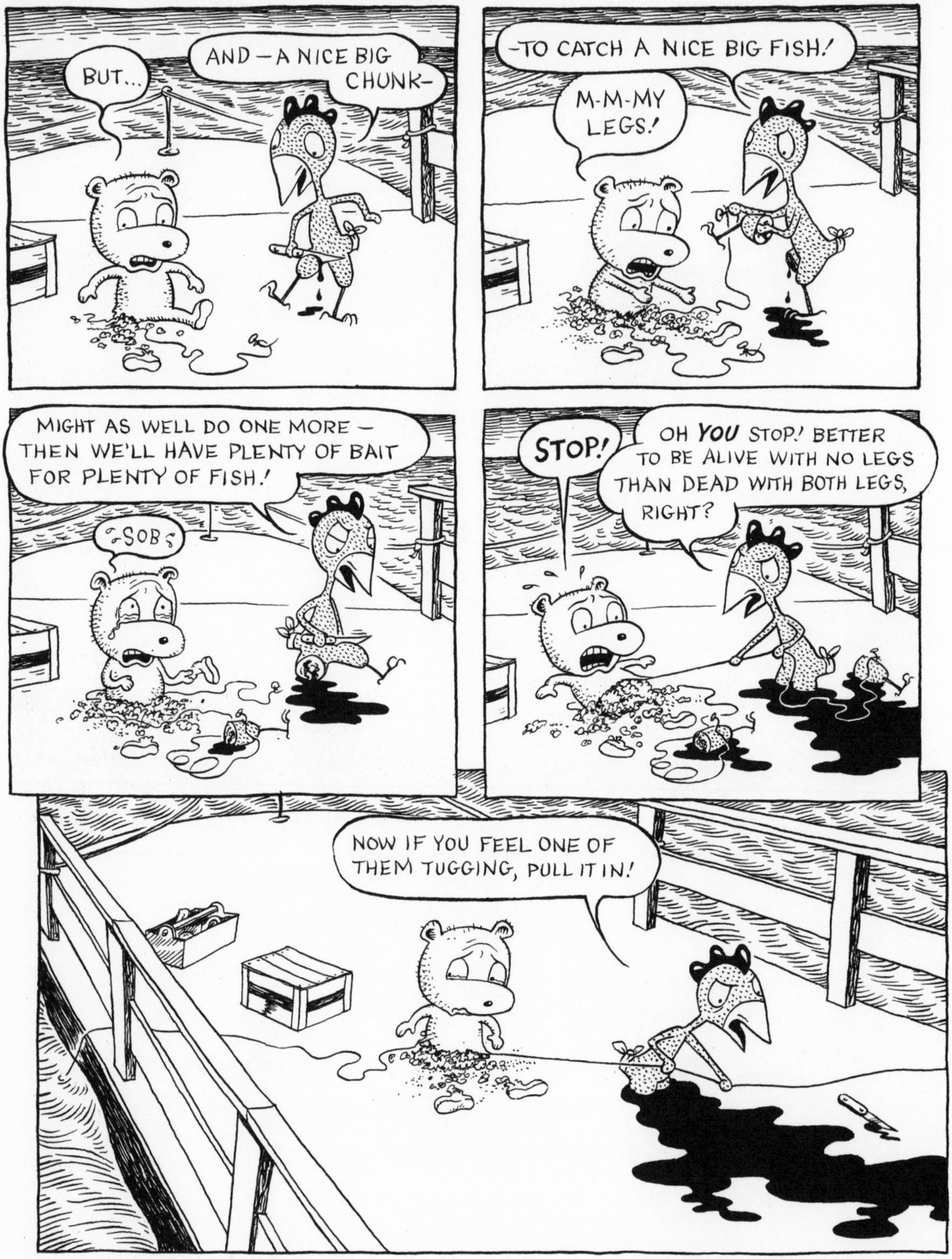
BUT...
AND—A NICE BIG CHUNK-
-TO CATCH A NICE BIG FISH!
M-M-MY LEGS!
MIGHT AS WELL DO ONE MORE— THEN WE'LL HAVE PLENTY OF BAIT FOR PLENTY OF FISH!
SOB
STOP!
OH YOU STOP! BETTER TO BE ALIVE WITH NO LEGS THAN DEAD WITH BOTH LEGS, RIGHT?
NOW IF YOU FEEL ONE OF THEM TUGGING, PULL IT IN!

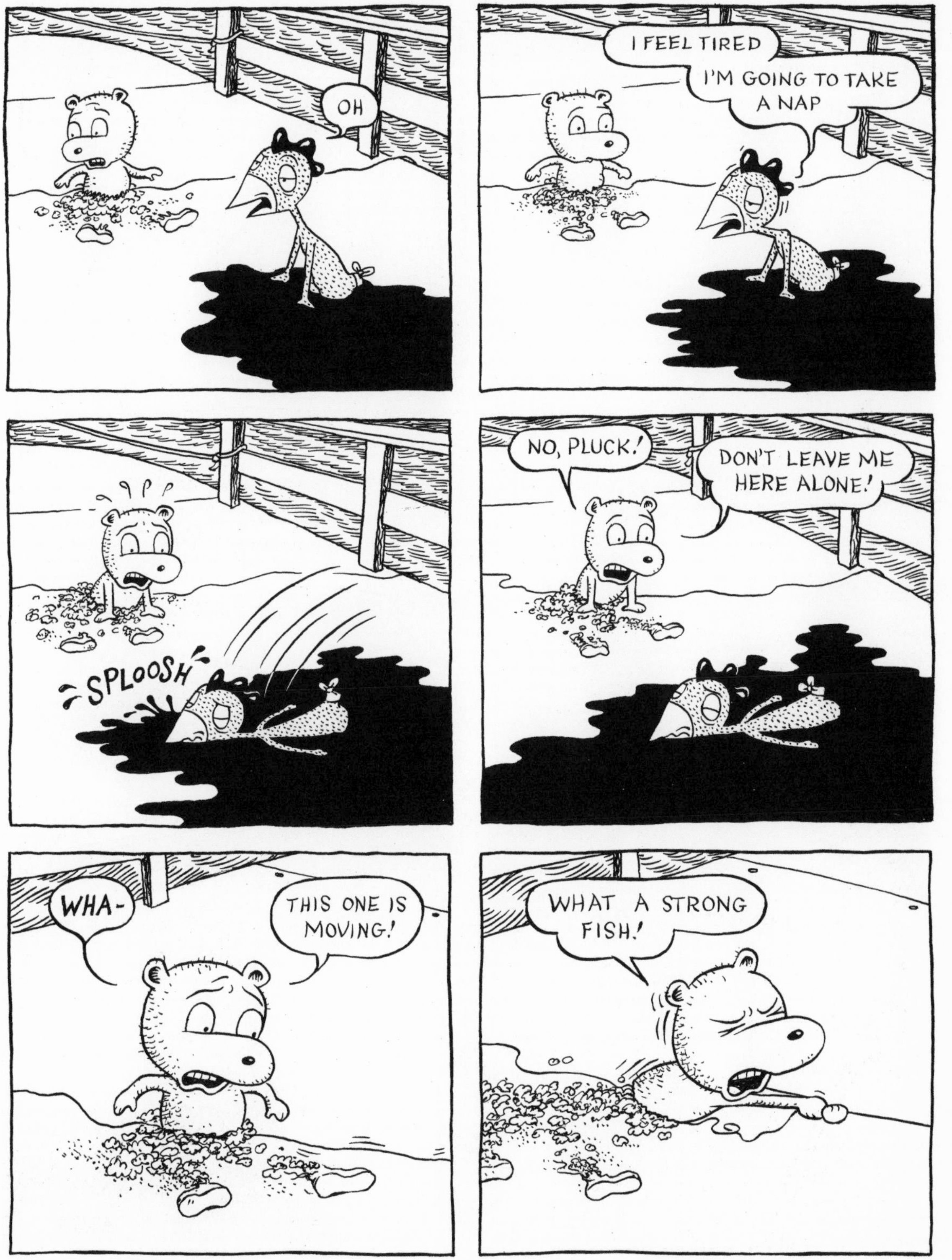

OH
I FEEL TIRED
I'M GOING TO TAKE A NAP
SPLOOSH
NO, PLUCK!
DON'T LEAVE ME HERE ALONE!
WHA-
THIS ONE IS MOVING!
WHAT A STRONG FISH!

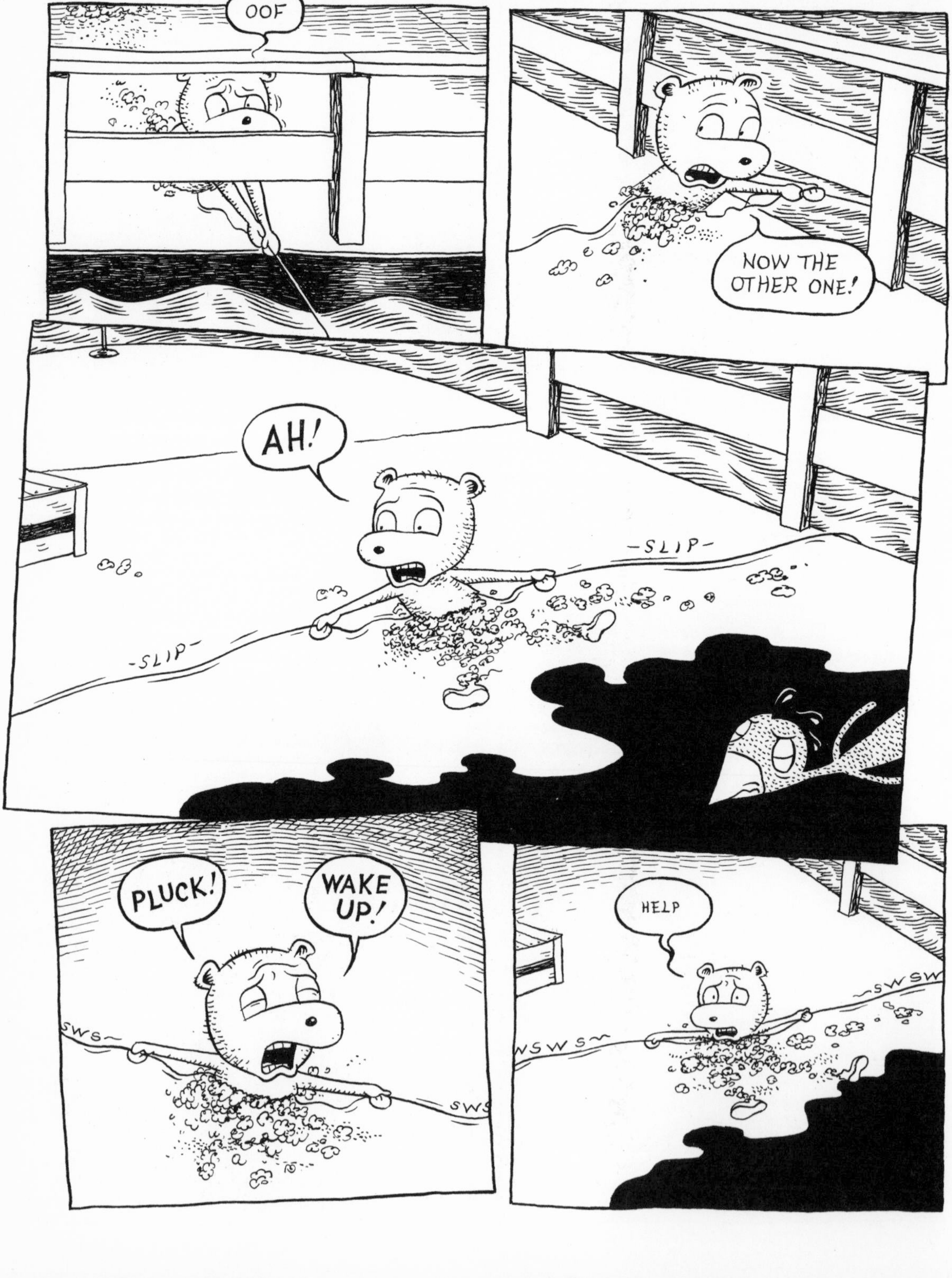
OOF
NOW THE OTHER ONE!
AH!
-SLIP-
-SLIP-
PLUCK!
WAKE UP!
SWS~
SWS
HELP
WSWS~
~SWSW

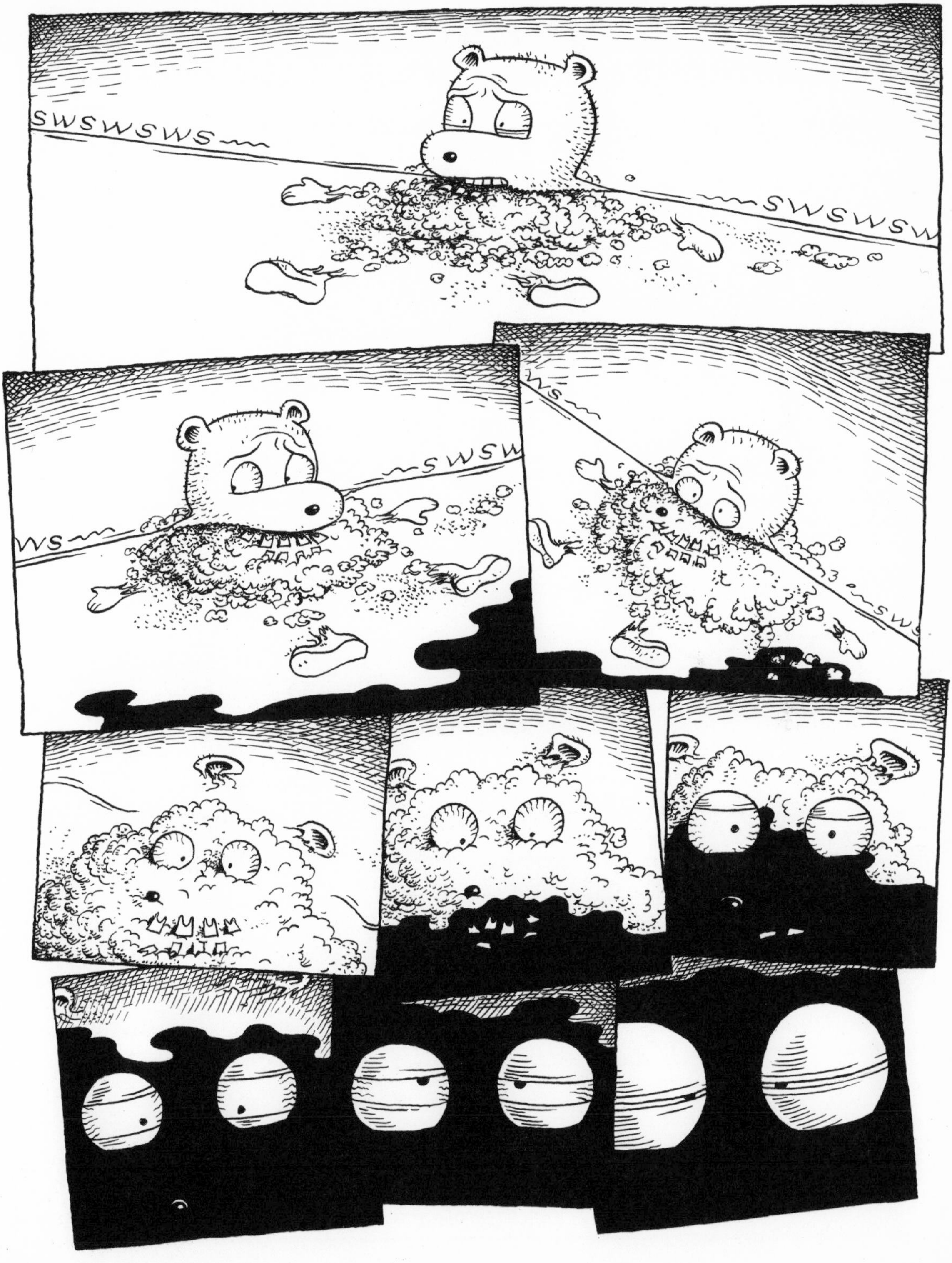
SWSWSWS
SWSWSW
SWSW
WS
WS
SWS

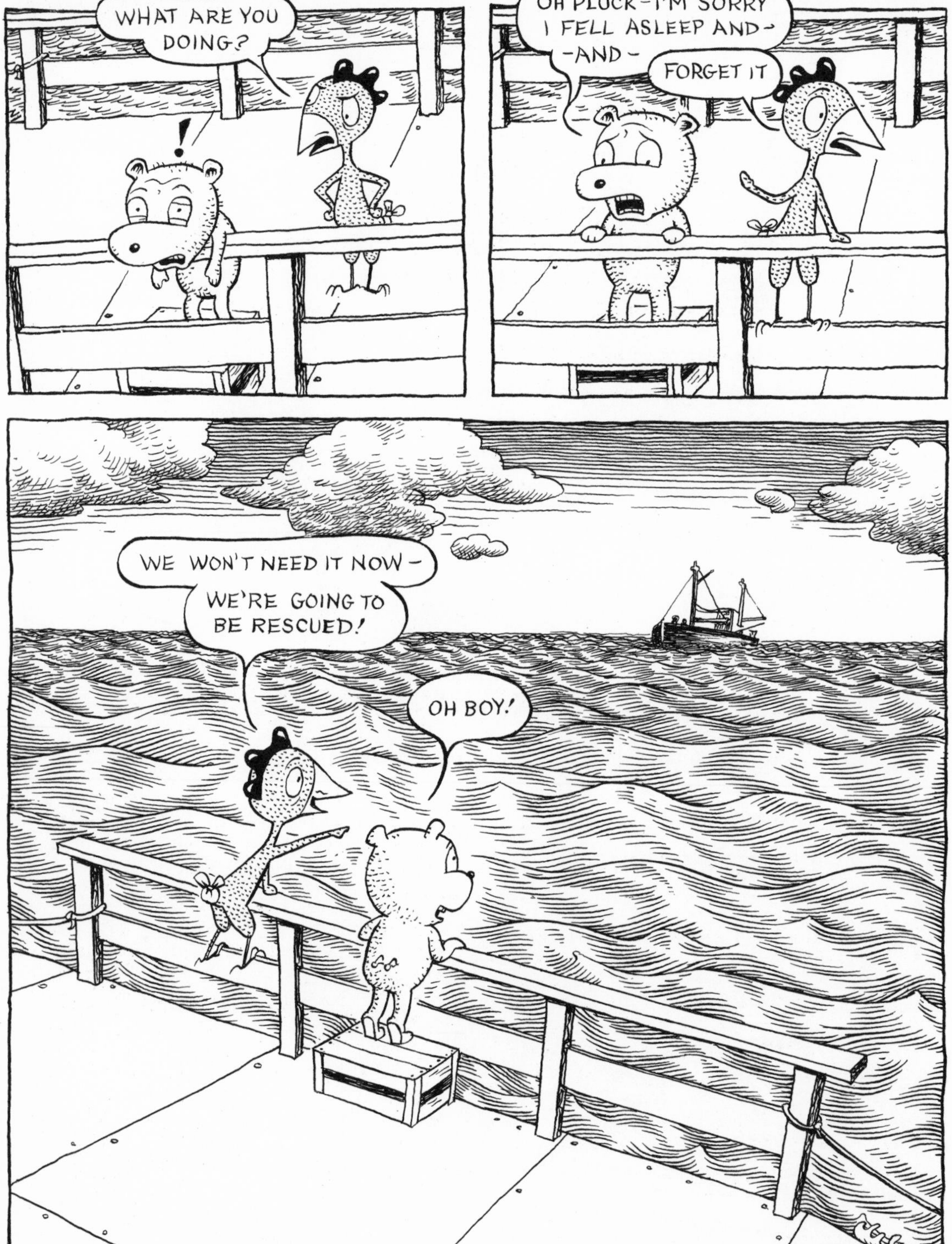

WHAT ARE YOU DOING?
!
OH PLUCK – I'M SORRY I FELL ASLEEP AND– –AND–
FORGET IT
WE WON'T NEED IT NOW–
WE'RE GOING TO BE RESCUED!
OH BOY!

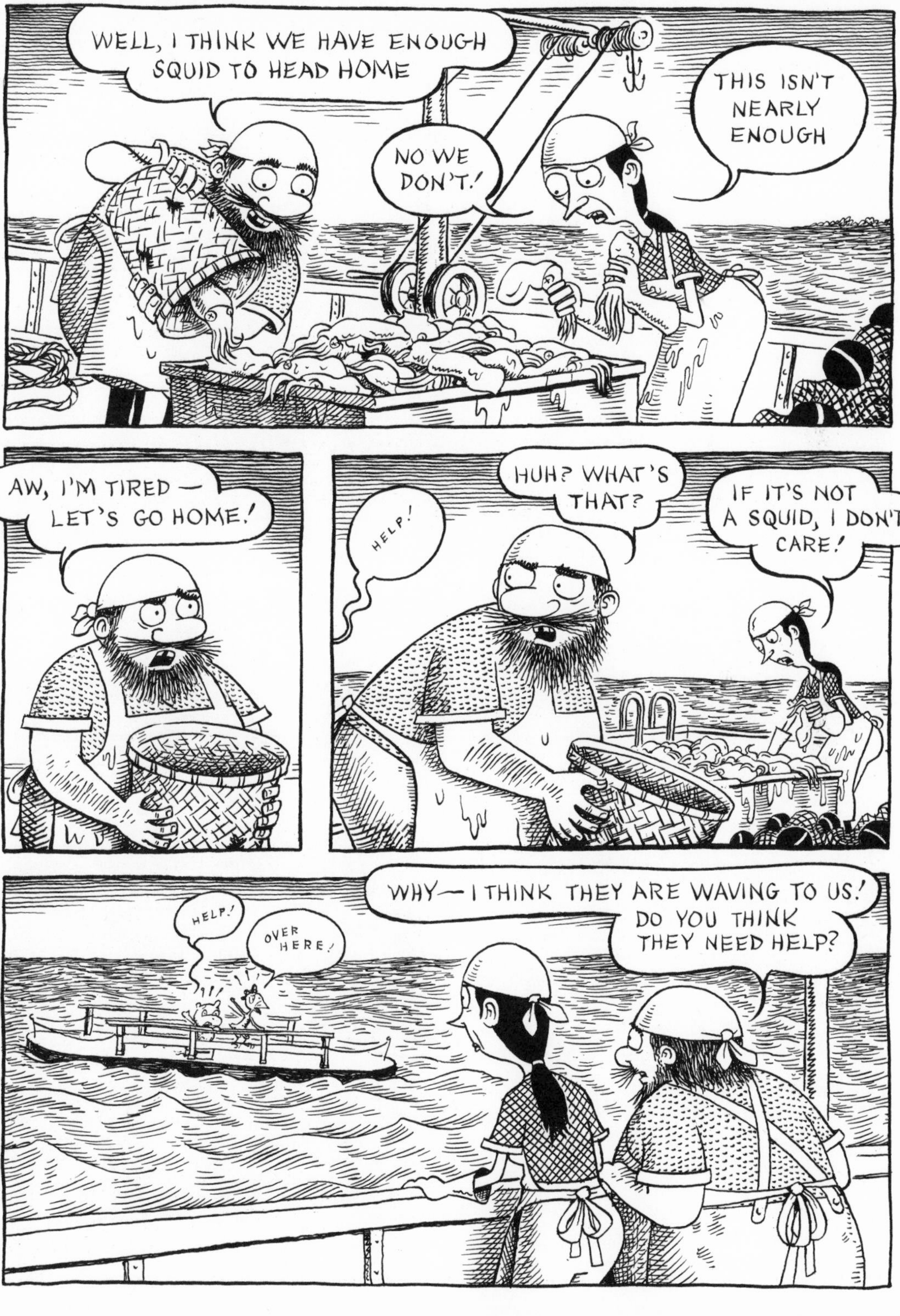
WELL, I THINK WE HAVE ENOUGH SQUID TO HEAD HOME
NO WE DON'T!
THIS ISN'T NEARLY ENOUGH
AW, I'M TIRED — LET'S GO HOME!
HELP!
HUH? WHAT'S THAT?
IF IT'S NOT A SQUID, I DON'T CARE!
HELP!
OVER HERE!
WHY — I THINK THEY ARE WAVING TO US! DO YOU THINK THEY NEED HELP?

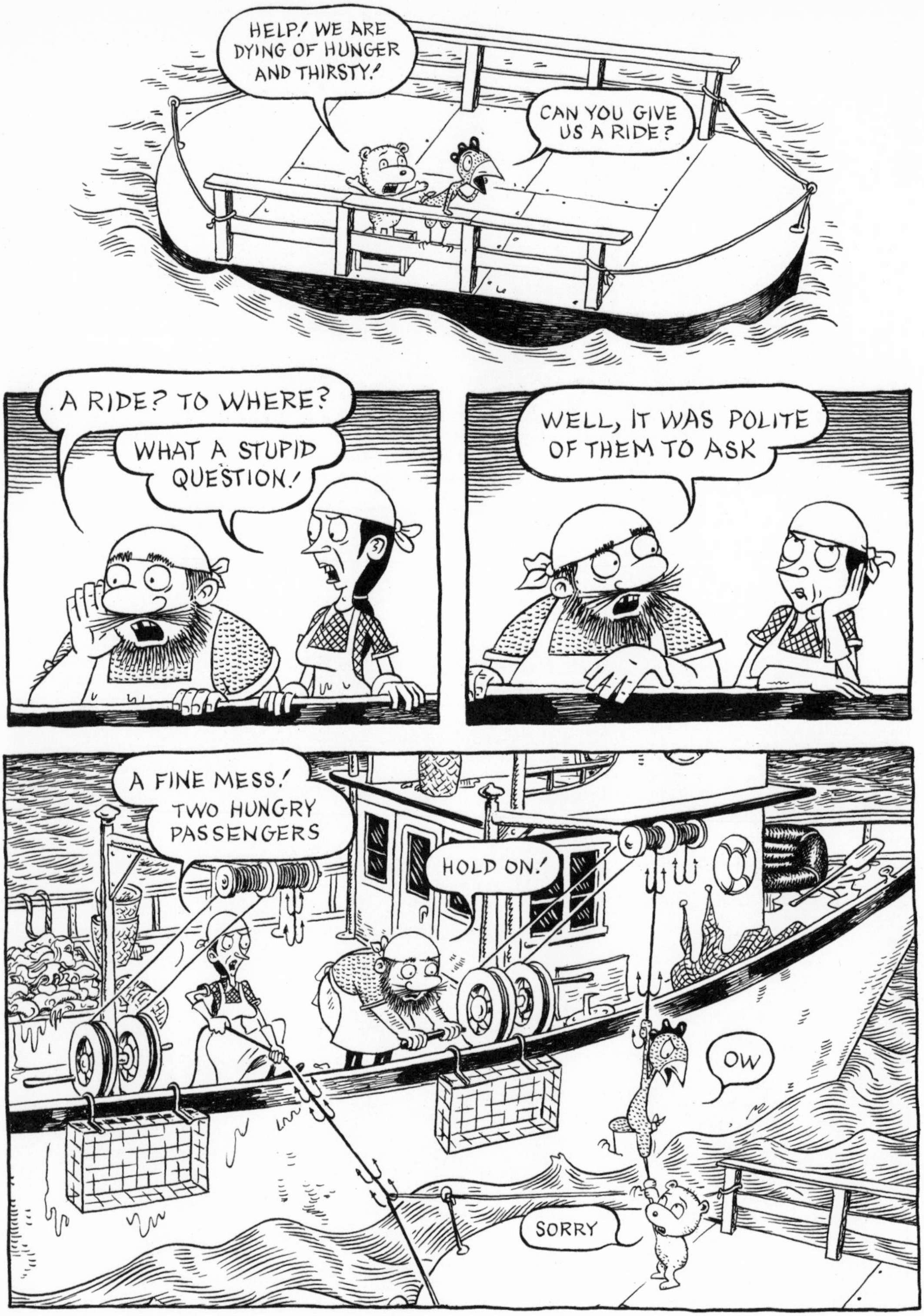
HELP! WE ARE DYING OF HUNGER AND THIRSTY!
CAN YOU GIVE US A RIDE?
A RIDE? TO WHERE?
WHAT A STUPID QUESTION!
WELL, IT WAS POLITE OF THEM TO ASK
A FINE MESS! TWO HUNGRY PASSENGERS
HOLD ON!
OW
SORRY

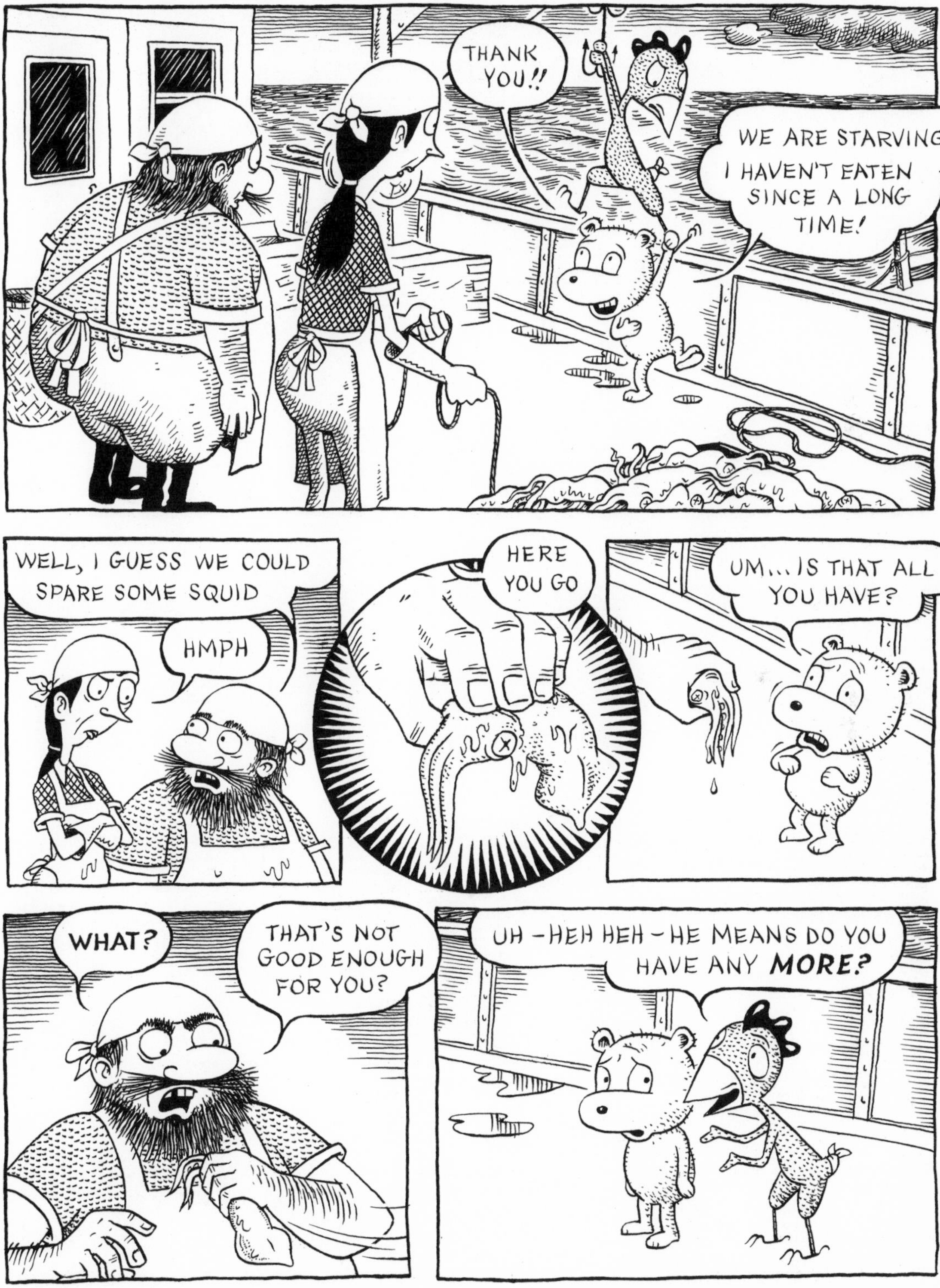
THANK YOU!!
WE ARE STARVING! I HAVEN'T EATEN SINCE A LONG TIME!
WELL, I GUESS WE COULD SPARE SOME SQUID
HMPH
HERE YOU GO
UM... IS THAT ALL YOU HAVE?
WHAT?
THAT'S NOT GOOD ENOUGH FOR YOU?
UH -HEH HEH- HE MEANS DO YOU HAVE ANY MORE?

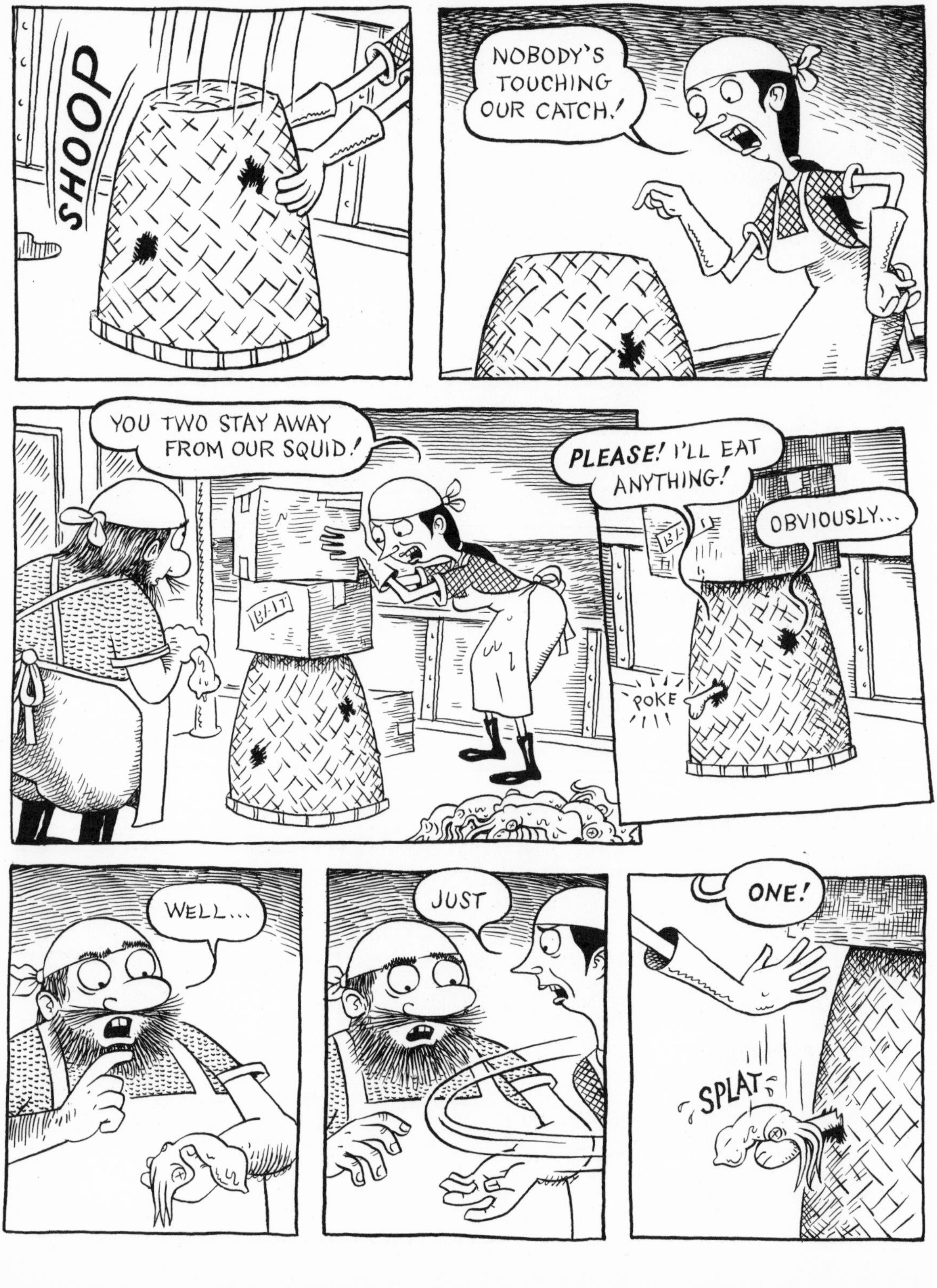
SHOOP
NOBODY'S TOUCHING OUR CATCH!
YOU TWO STAY AWAY FROM OUR SQUID!
BAIT
PLEASE! I'LL EAT ANYTHING!
OBVIOUSLY...
POKE
WELL...
JUST
ONE!
SPLAT

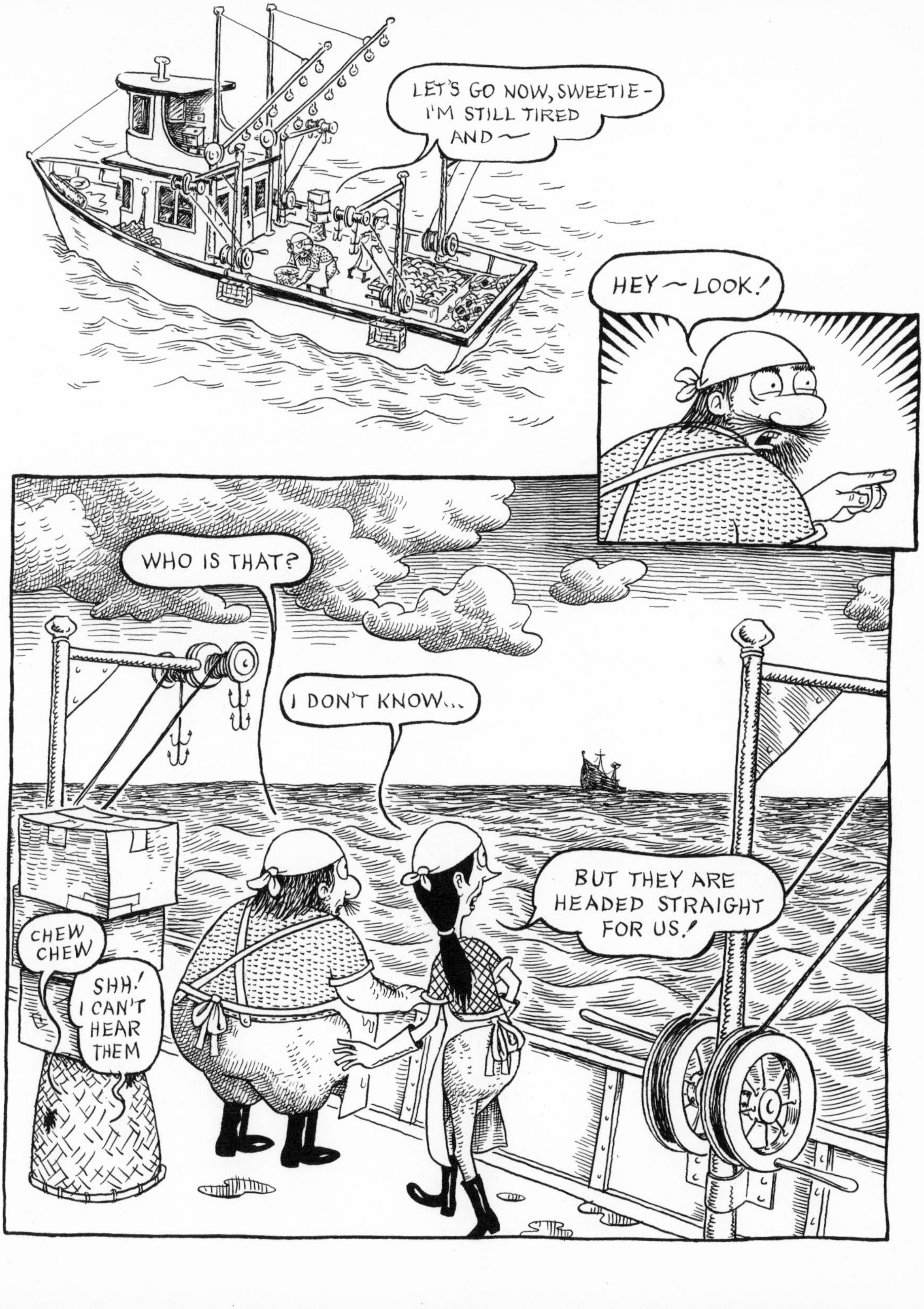
LET'S GO NOW, SWEETIE - I'M STILL TIRED AND ~
HEY ~ LOOK!
WHO IS THAT?
I DON'T KNOW...
BUT THEY ARE HEADED STRAIGHT FOR US!
CHEW CHEW
SHH! I CAN'T HEAR THEM

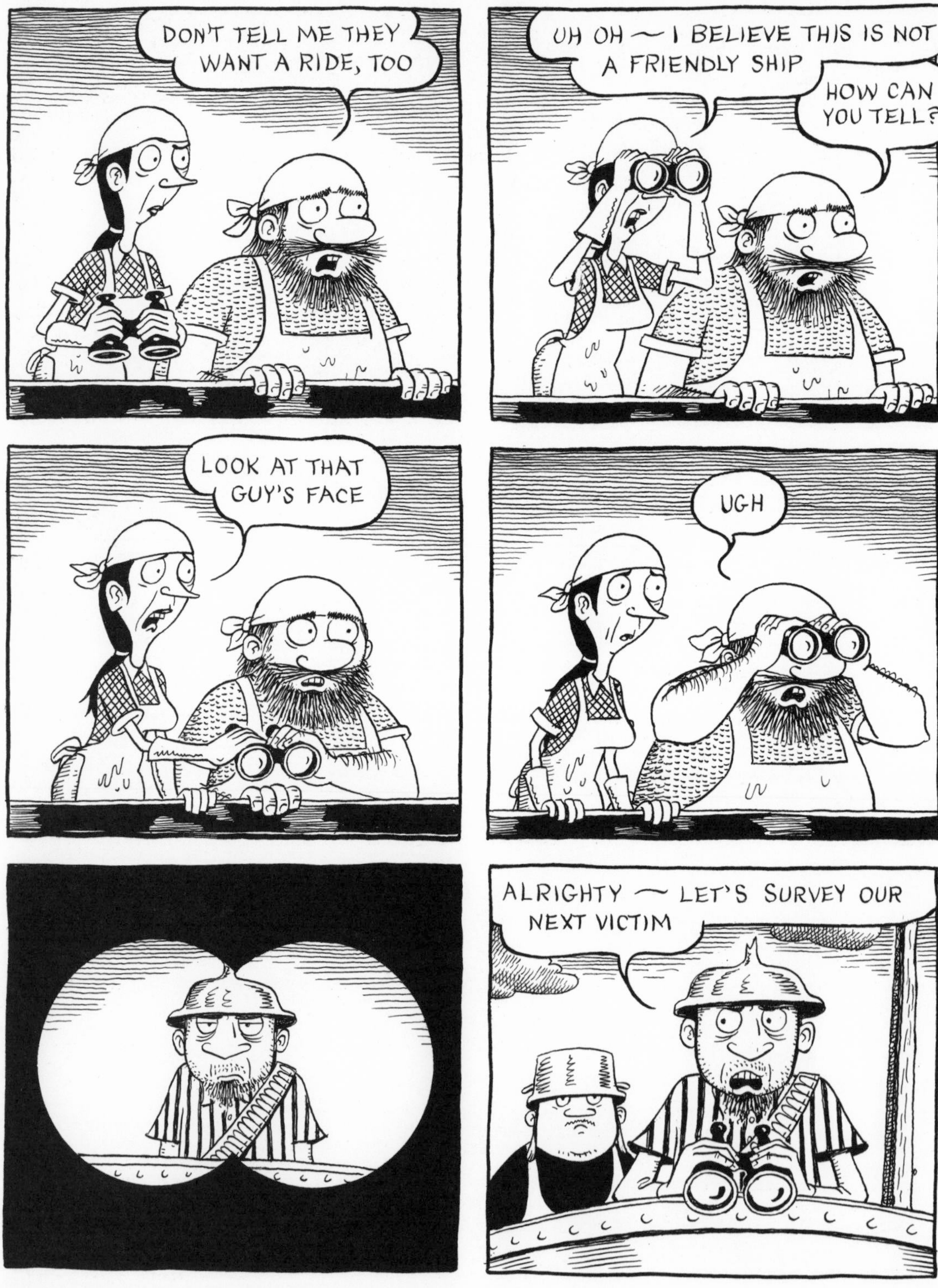
DON'T TELL ME THEY WANT A RIDE, TOO
UH OH ~ I BELIEVE THIS IS NOT A FRIENDLY SHIP
HOW CAN YOU TELL?
LOOK AT THAT GUY'S FACE
UGH
ALRIGHTY ~ LET'S SURVEY OUR NEXT VICTIM

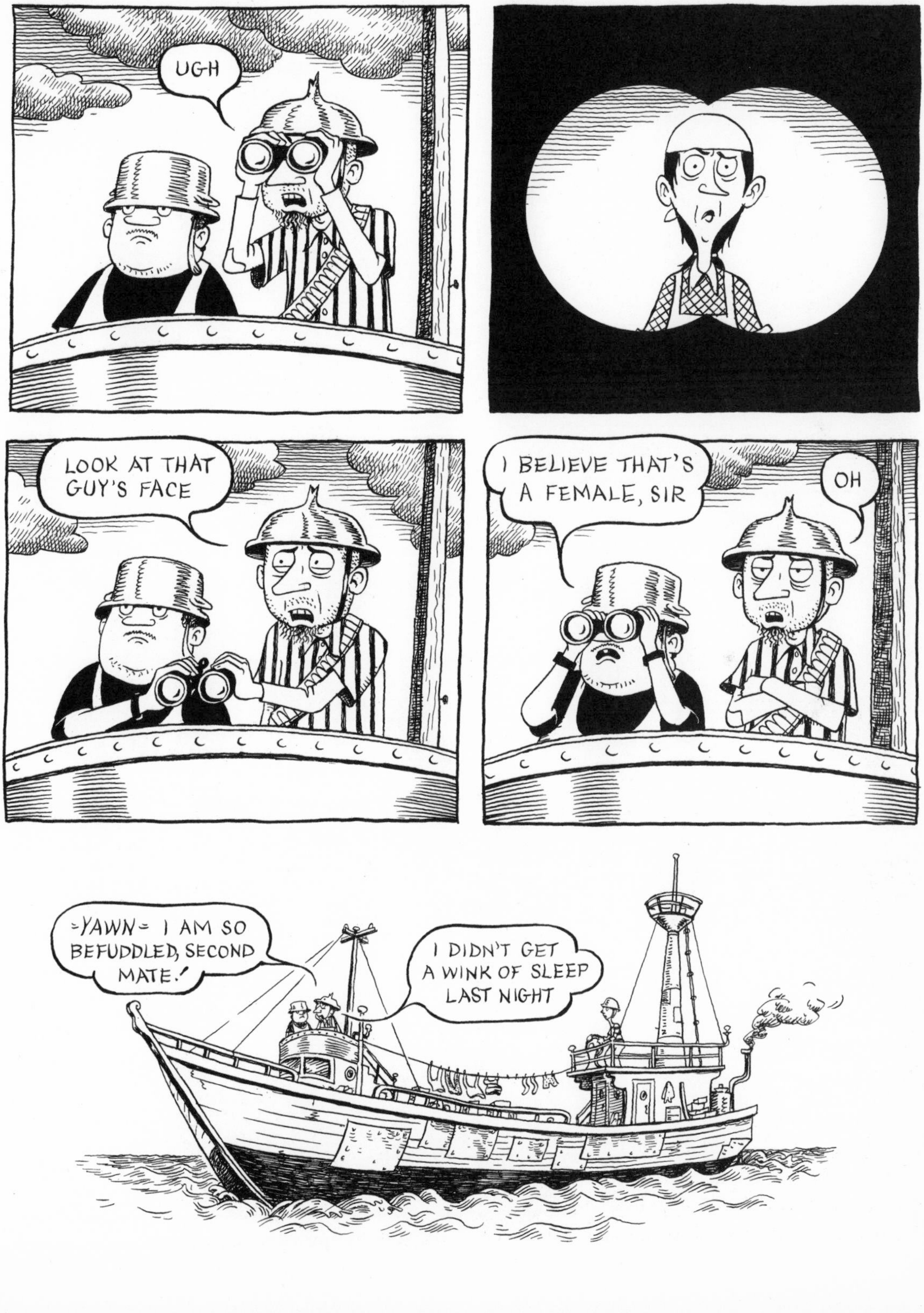
UGH
LOOK AT THAT GUY'S FACE
I BELIEVE THAT'S A FEMALE, SIR
OH
=YAWN= I AM SO BEFUDDLED, SECOND MATE!
I DIDN'T GET A WINK OF SLEEP LAST NIGHT

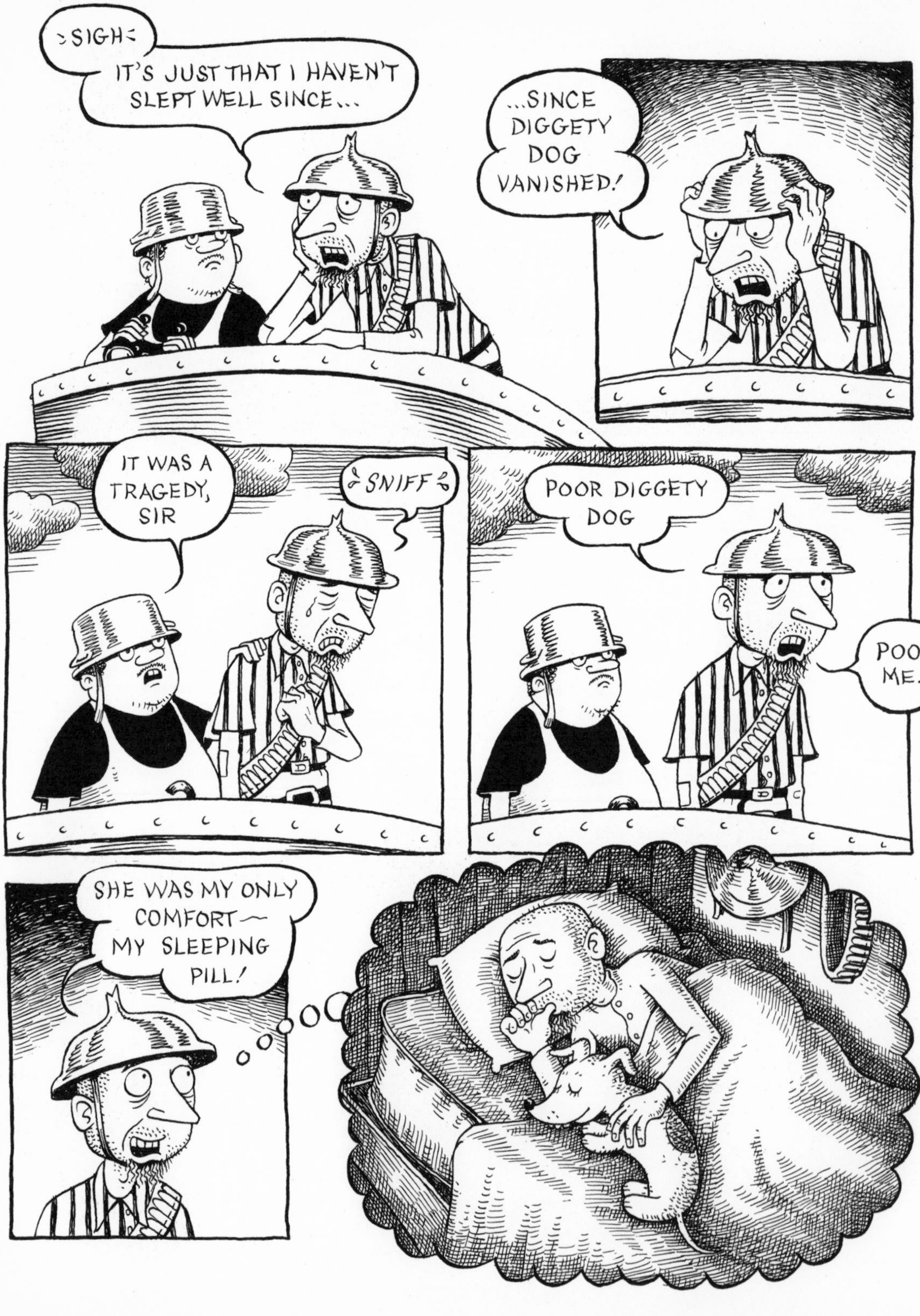

SIGH
IT'S JUST THAT I HAVEN'T SLEPT WELL SINCE...
...SINCE DIGGETY DOG VANISHED!
IT WAS A TRAGEDY, SIR
SNIFF
POOR DIGGETY DOG
POOR ME!
SHE WAS MY ONLY COMFORT— MY SLEEPING PILL!

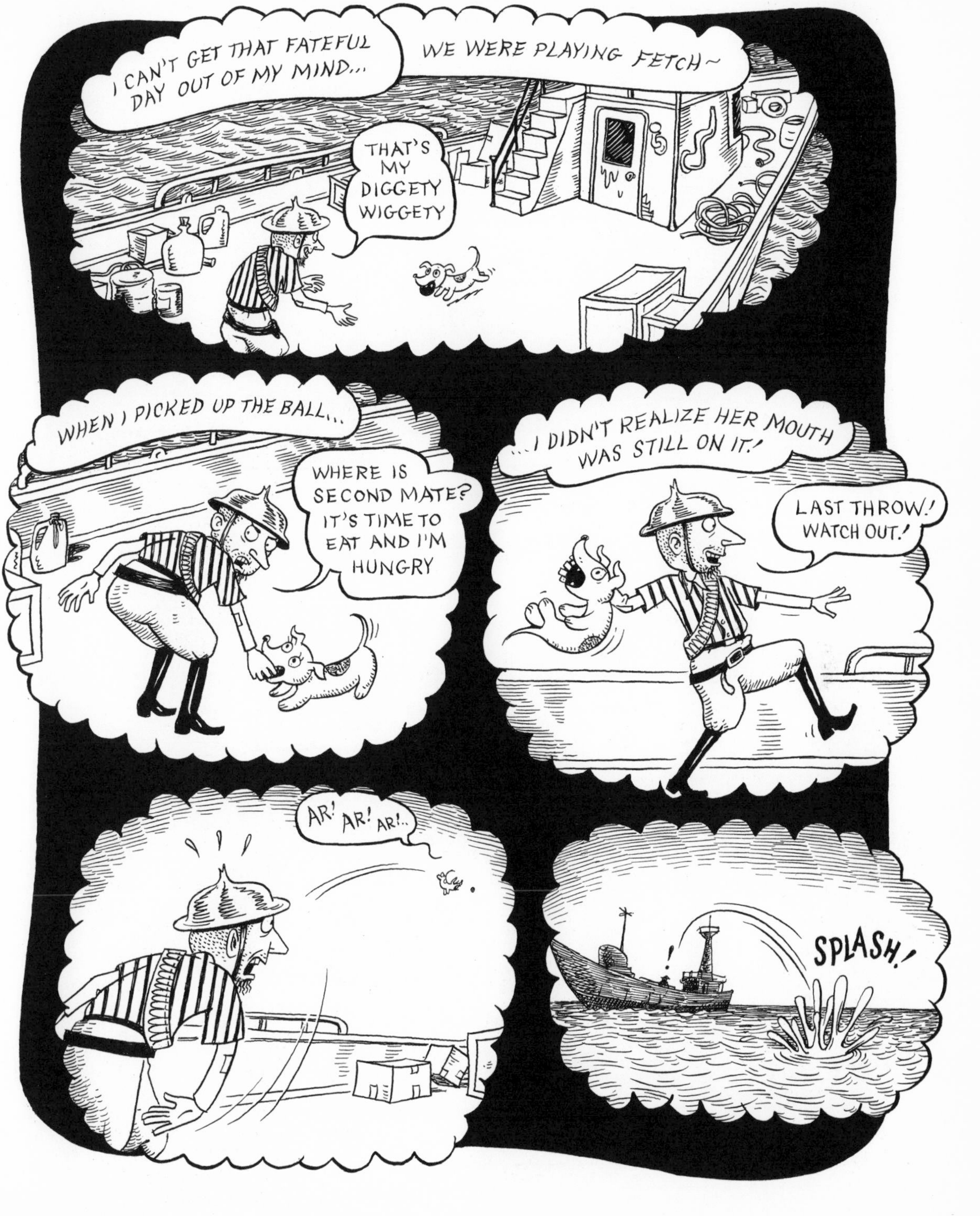
I CAN'T GET THAT FATEFUL DAY OUT OF MY MIND...
WE WERE PLAYING FETCH~
THAT'S MY DIGGETY WIGGETY
WHEN I PICKED UP THE BALL...
WHERE IS SECOND MATE? IT'S TIME TO EAT AND I'M HUNGRY
...I DIDN'T REALIZE HER MOUTH WAS STILL ON IT!
LAST THROW! WATCH OUT!
AR! AR! AR!..
SPLASH!

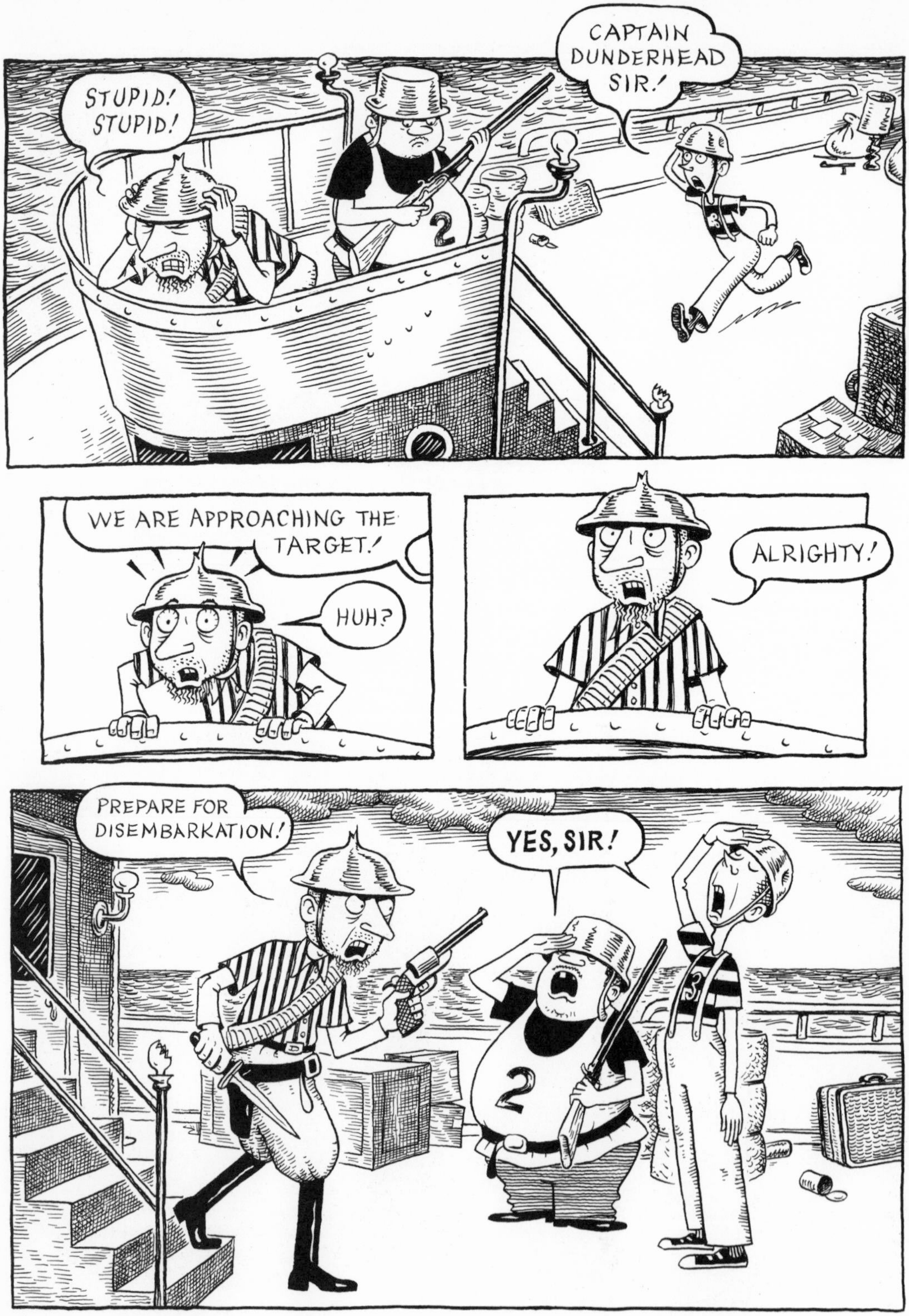
STUPID! STUPID!
CAPTAIN DUNDERHEAD SIR!
WE ARE APPROACHING THE TARGET!
HUH?
ALRIGHTY!
PREPARE FOR DISEMBARKATION!
YES, SIR!

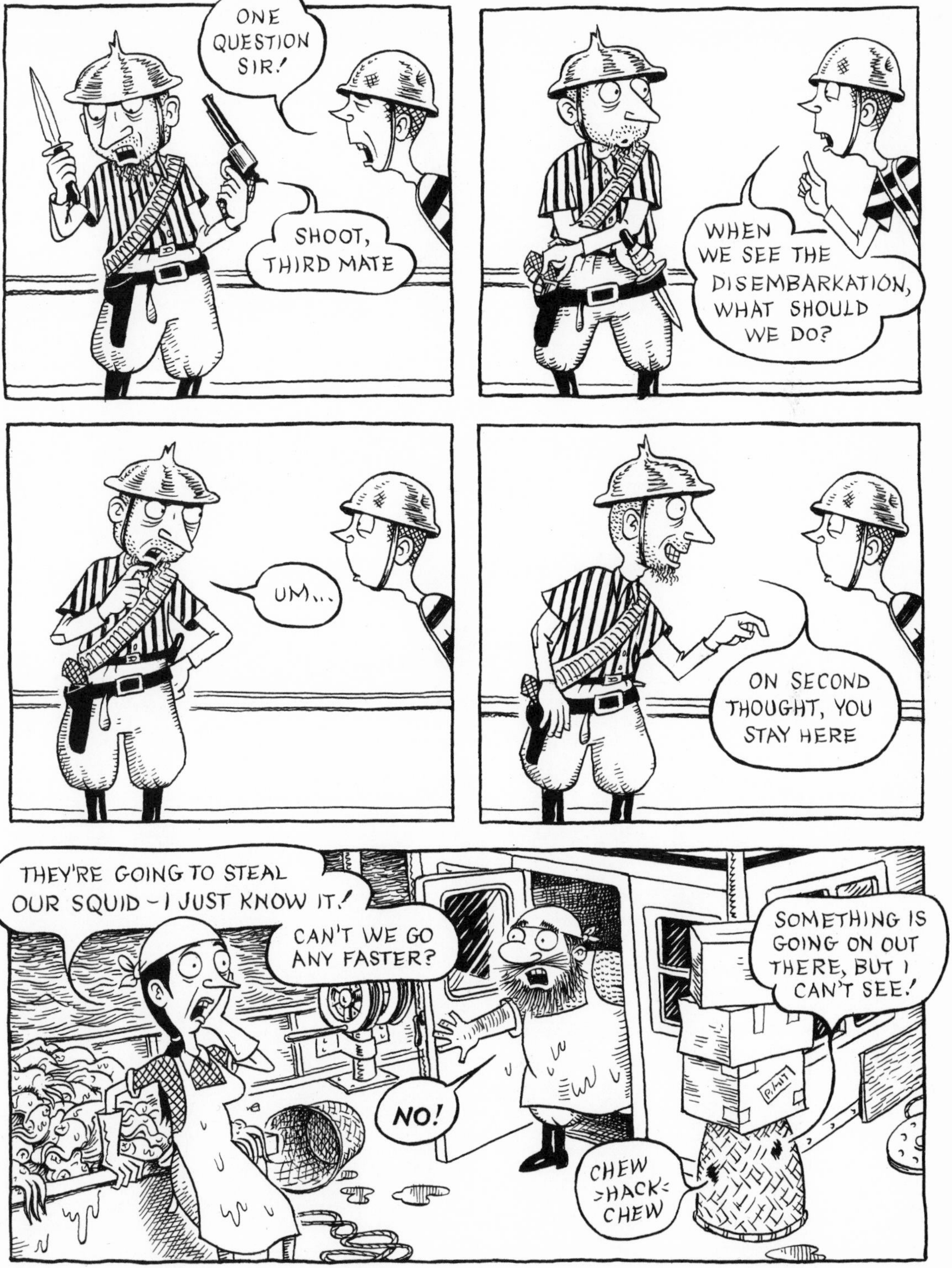
ONE QUESTION SIR!
SHOOT, THIRD MATE
WHEN WE SEE THE DISEMBARKATION, WHAT SHOULD WE DO?
UM...
ON SECOND THOUGHT, YOU STAY HERE
THEY'RE GOING TO STEAL OUR SQUID – I JUST KNOW IT!
CAN'T WE GO ANY FASTER?
NO!
SOMETHING IS GOING ON OUT THERE, BUT I CAN'T SEE!
CHEW
>HACK<
CHEW

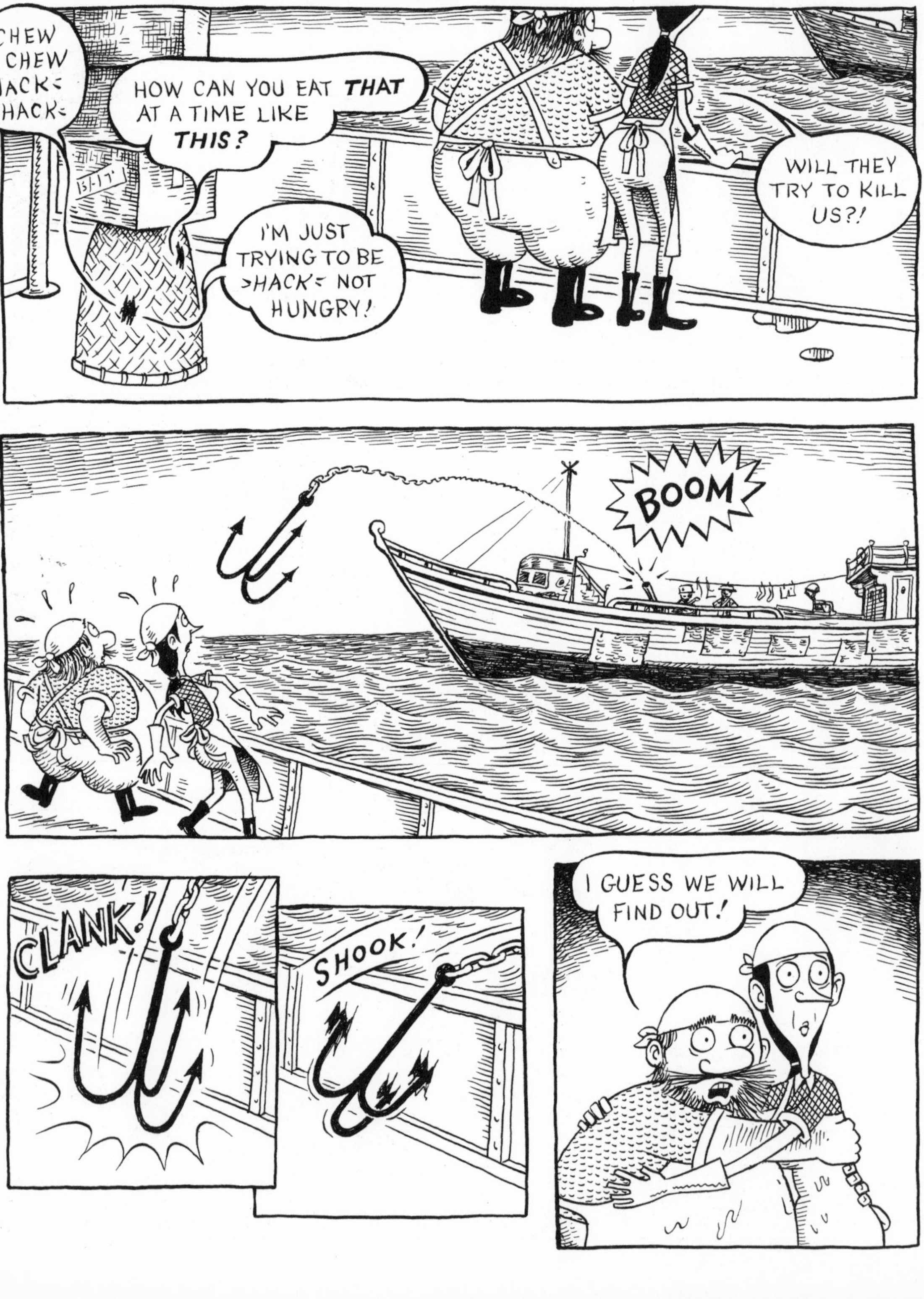

CHEW CHEW >HACK< >HACK<
HOW CAN YOU EAT THAT AT A TIME LIKE THIS?
I'M JUST TRYING TO BE >HACK< NOT HUNGRY!
WILL THEY TRY TO KILL US?!
BOOM
CLANK!
SHOOK!
I GUESS WE WILL FIND OUT!

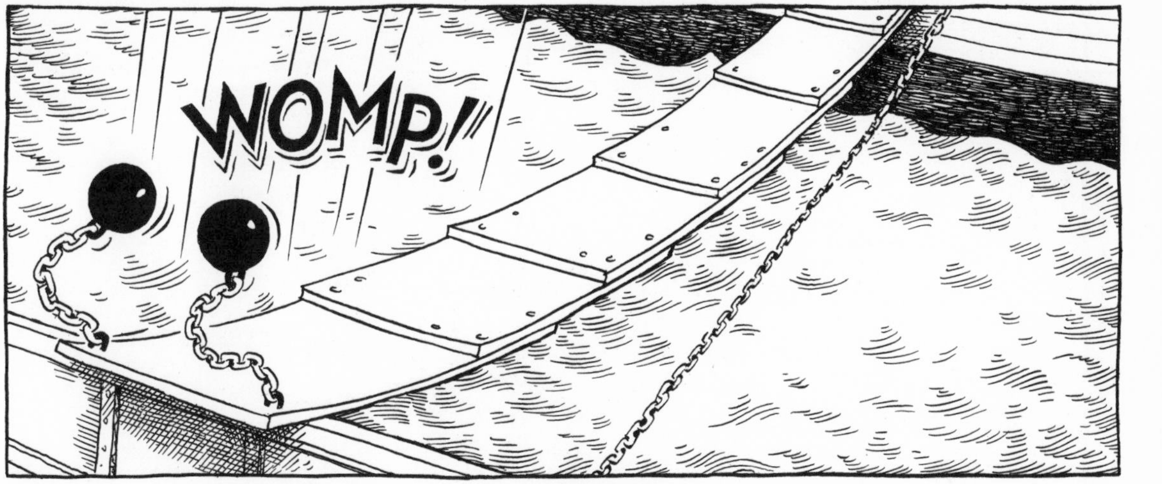
WOMP!

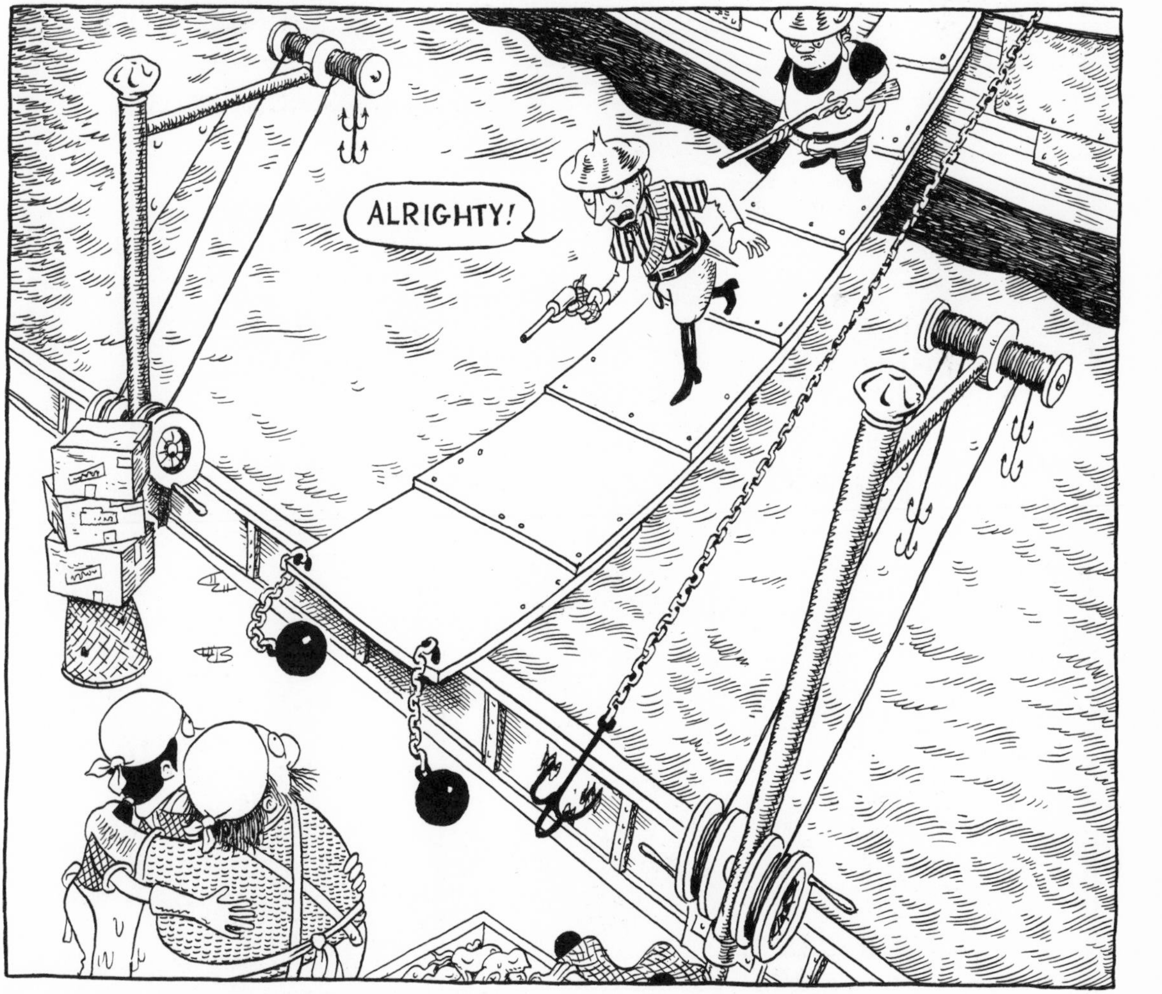
ALRIGHTY!

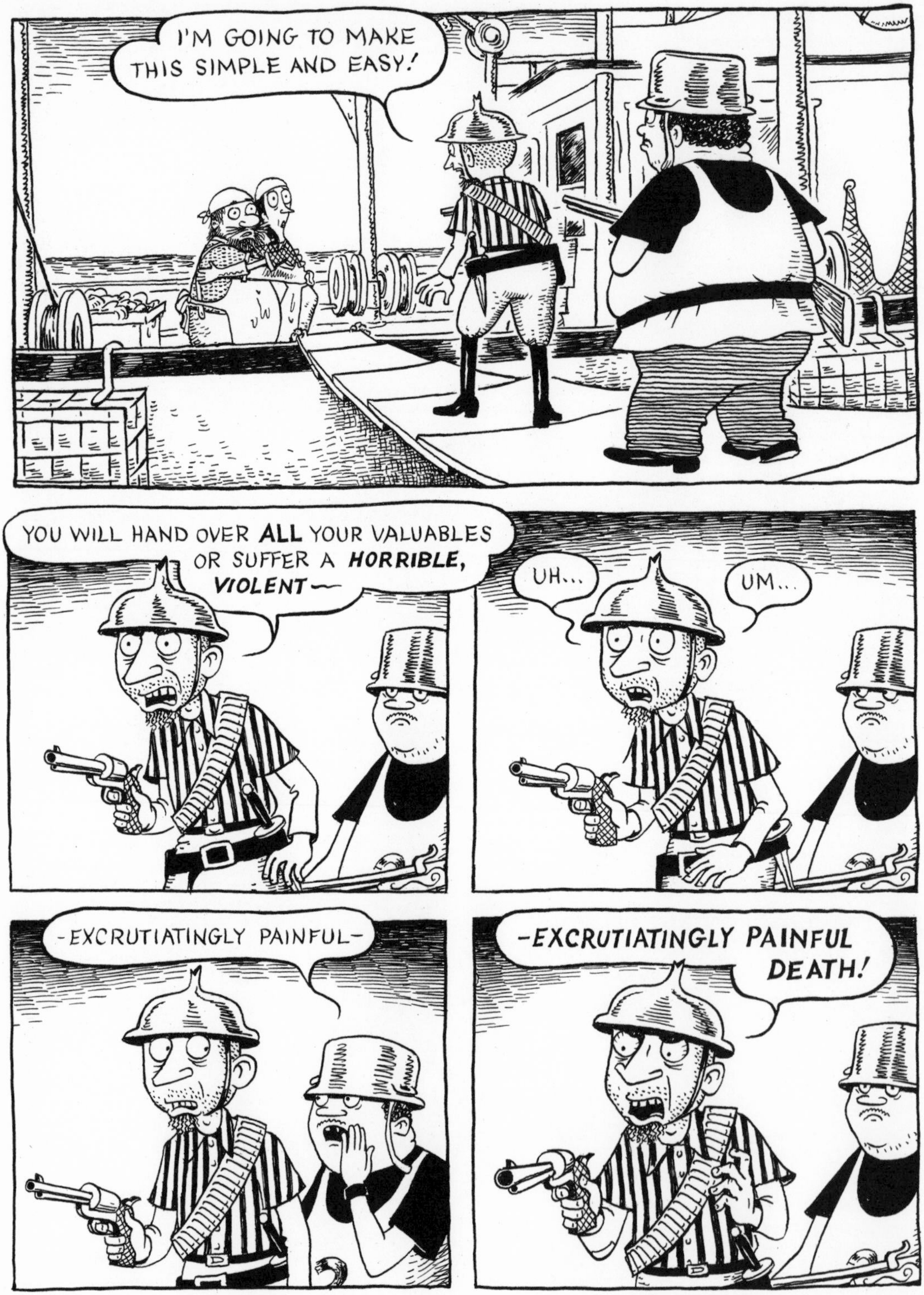
I'M GOING TO MAKE THIS SIMPLE AND EASY!
YOU WILL HAND OVER **ALL** YOUR VALUABLES OR SUFFER A ***HORRIBLE, VIOLENT***—
UH...
UM...
-EXCRUTIATINGLY PAINFUL-
-EXCRUTIATINGLY PAINFUL DEATH!

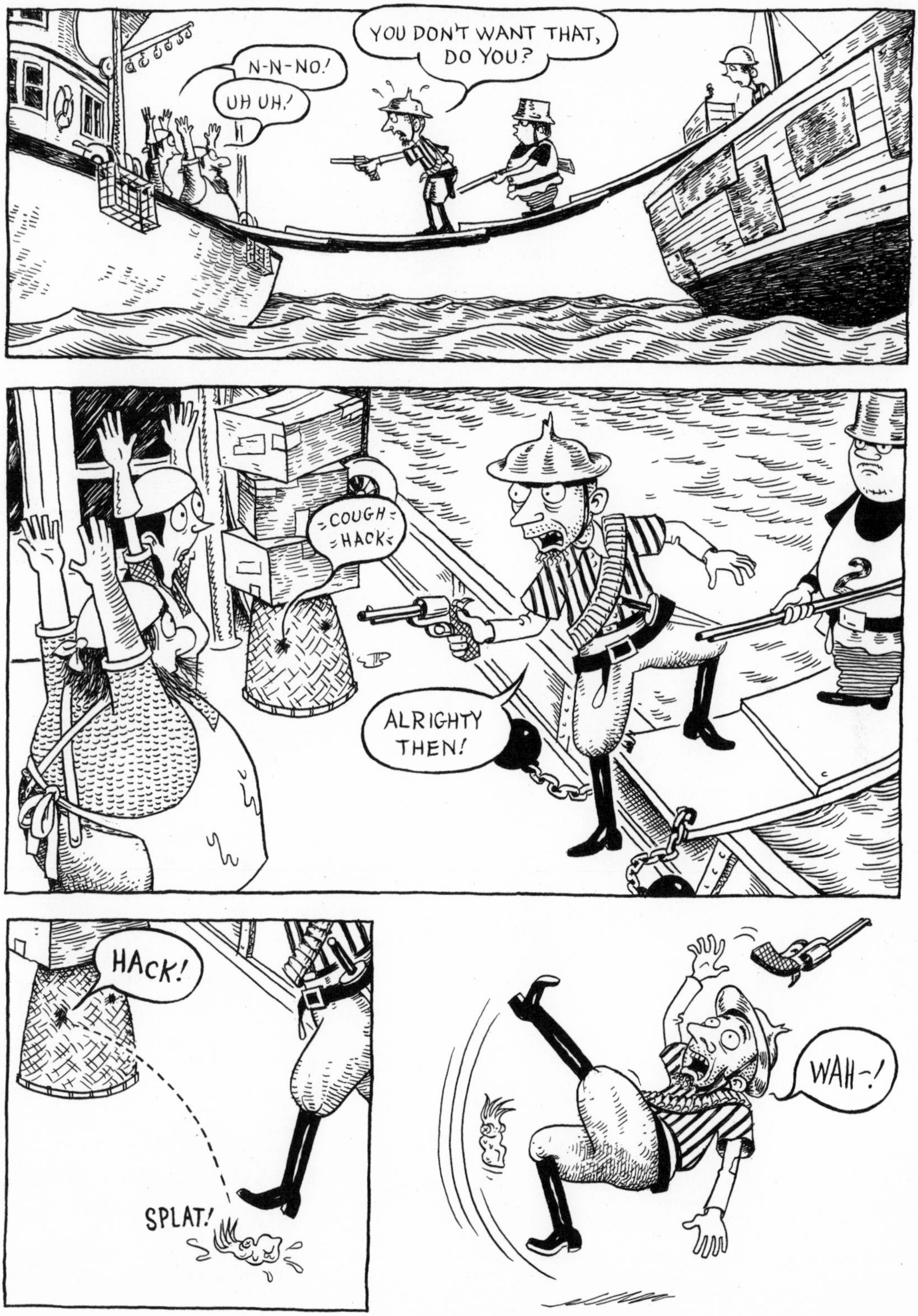
YOU DON'T WANT THAT, DO YOU?
N-N-NO!
UH UH!
COUGH HACK
ALRIGHTY THEN!
HACK!
SPLAT!
WAH-!

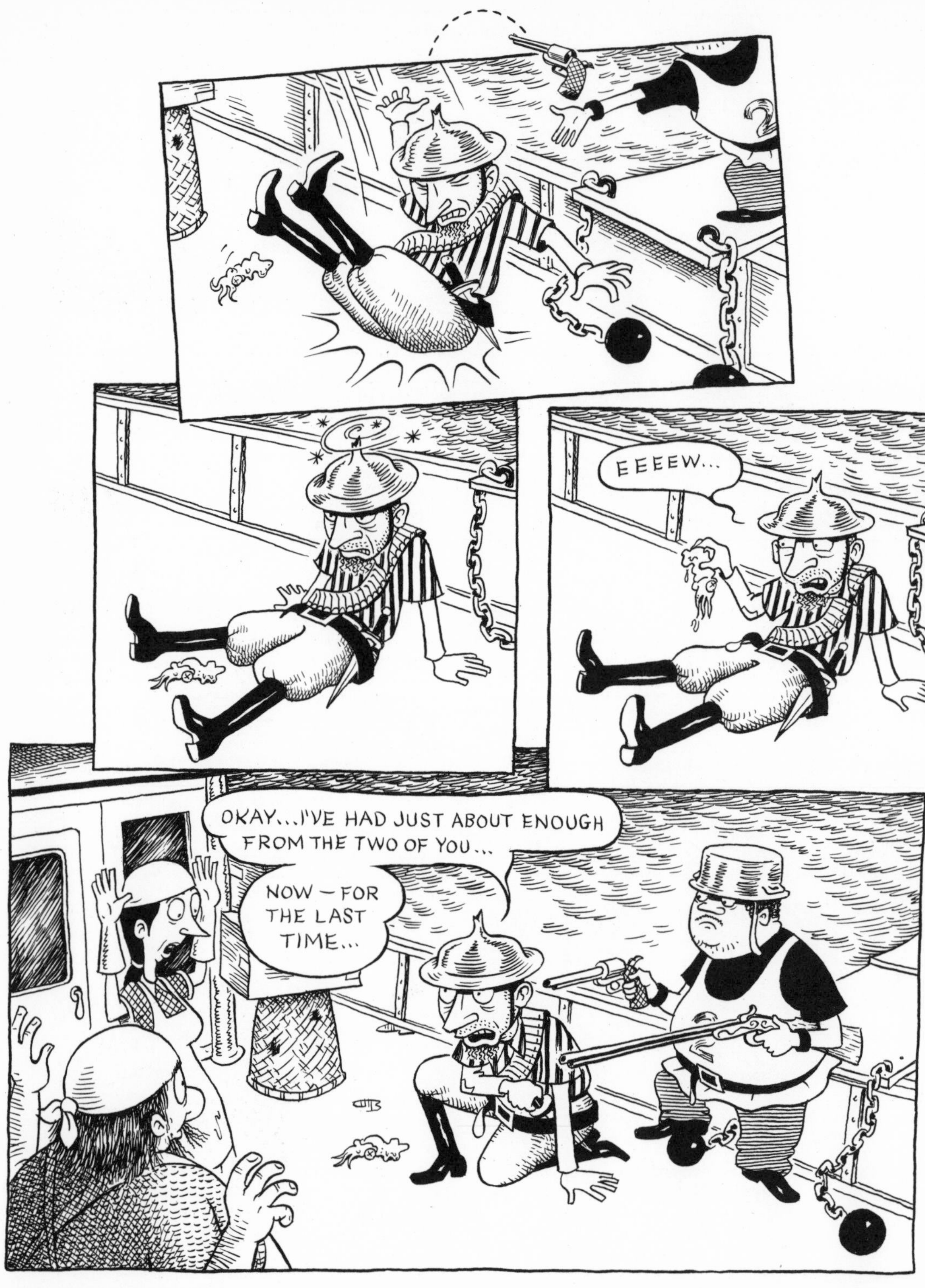
EEEEW...
OKAY...I'VE HAD JUST ABOUT ENOUGH FROM THE TWO OF YOU...
NOW — FOR THE LAST TIME...

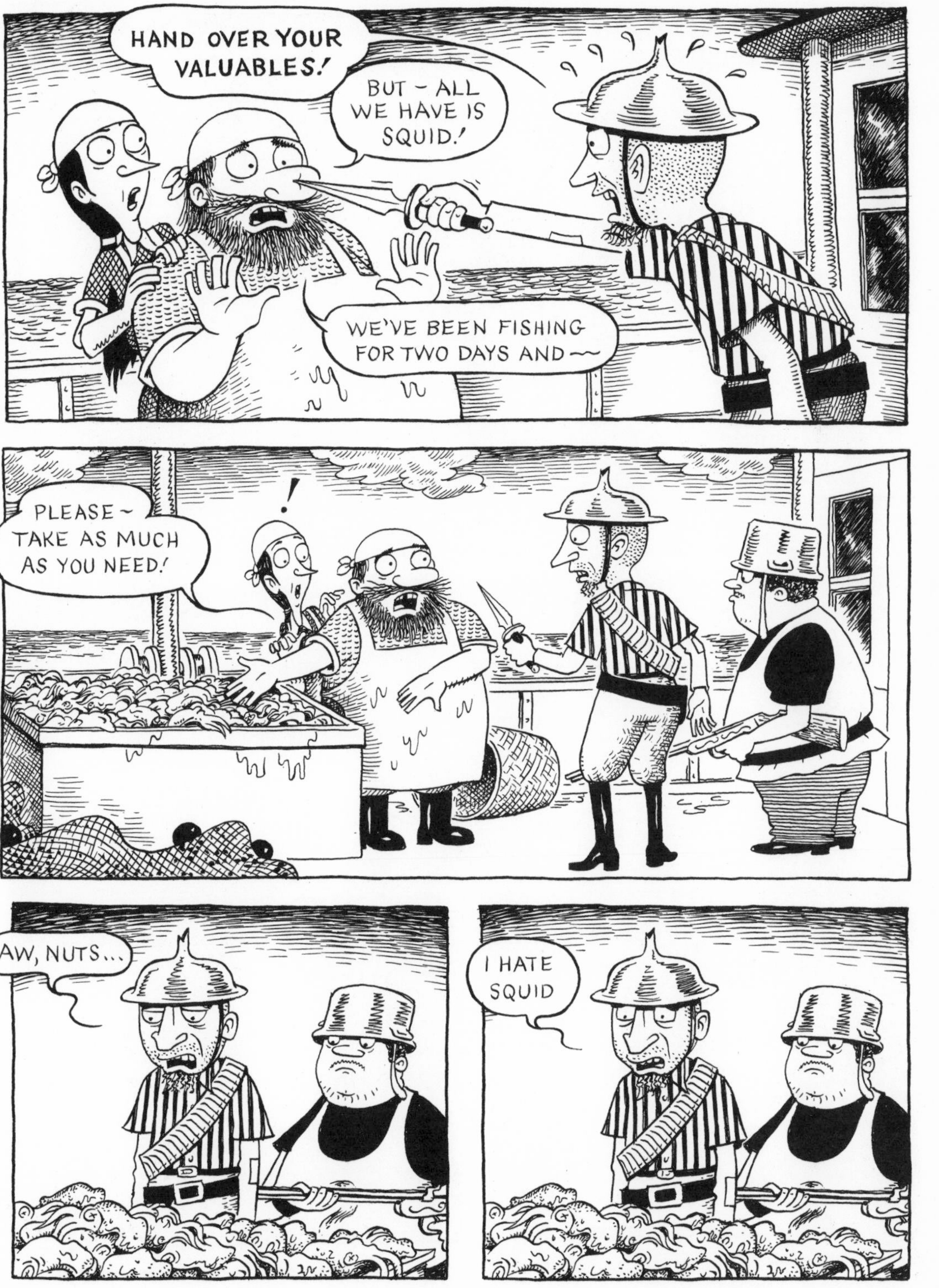
HAND OVER YOUR VALUABLES!
BUT ~ ALL WE HAVE IS SQUID!
WE'VE BEEN FISHING FOR TWO DAYS AND ~~
PLEASE ~ TAKE AS MUCH AS YOU NEED!
!
AW, NUTS...
I HATE SQUID

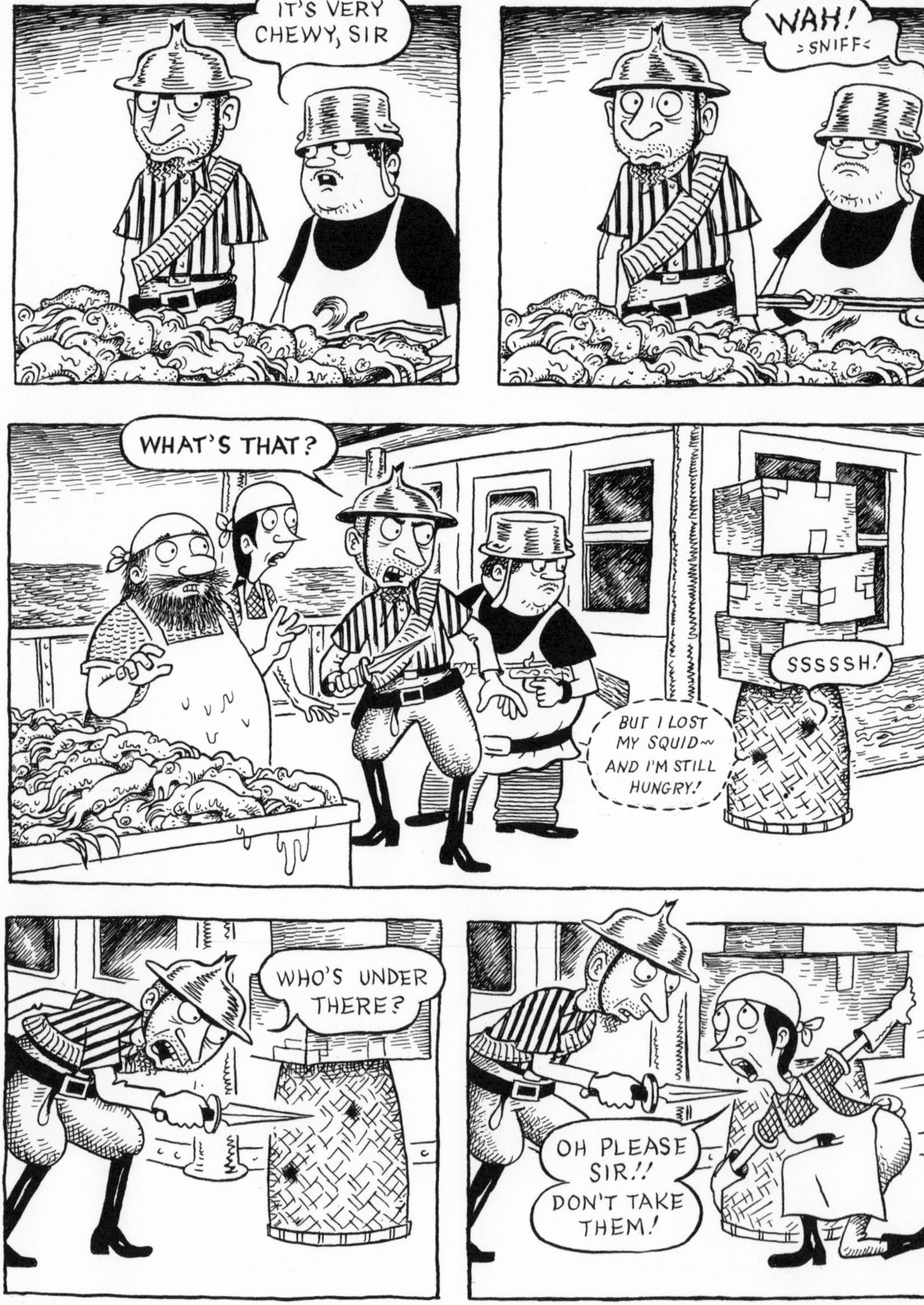
IT'S VERY CHEWY, SIR
WAH! >SNIFF<
WHAT'S THAT?
SSSSSH!
BUT I LOST MY SQUID~ AND I'M STILL HUNGRY!
WHO'S UNDER THERE?
OH PLEASE SIR!! DON'T TAKE THEM!

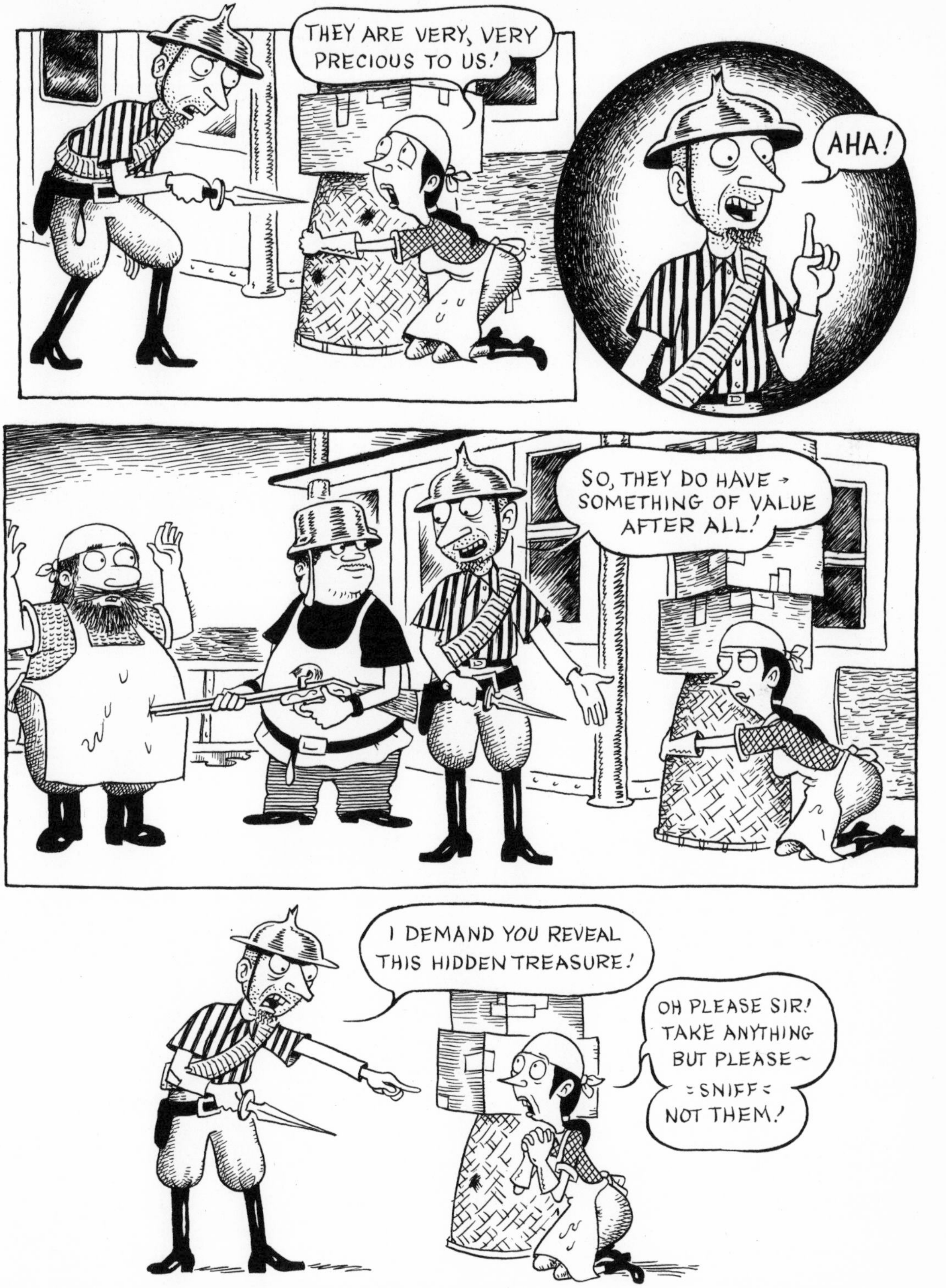
THEY ARE VERY, VERY PRECIOUS TO US!
AHA!
SO, THEY DO HAVE SOMETHING OF VALUE AFTER ALL!
I DEMAND YOU REVEAL THIS HIDDEN TREASURE!
OH PLEASE SIR! TAKE ANYTHING BUT PLEASE~
SNIFF
NOT THEM!

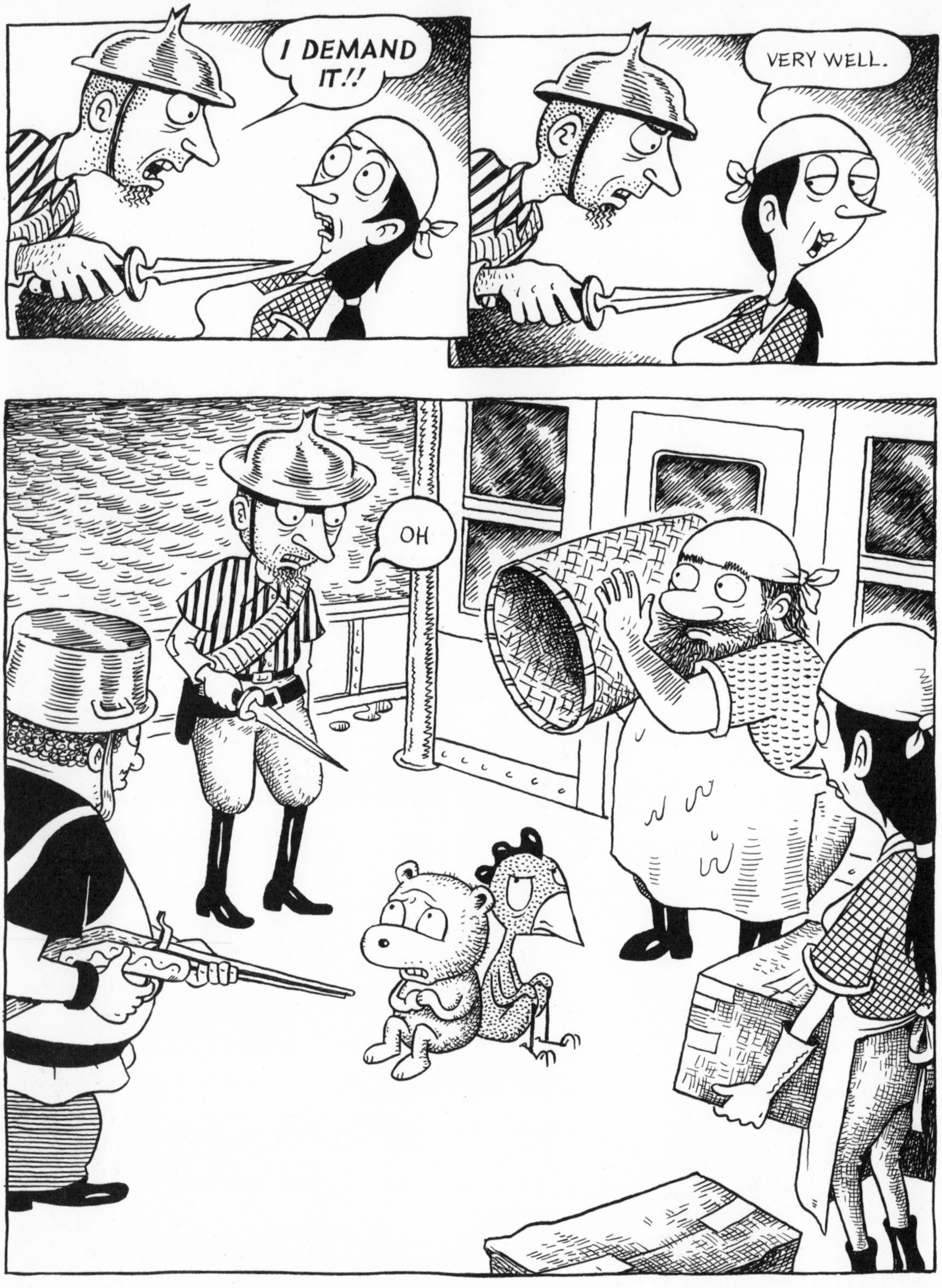
I DEMAND IT!!
VERY WELL.
OH

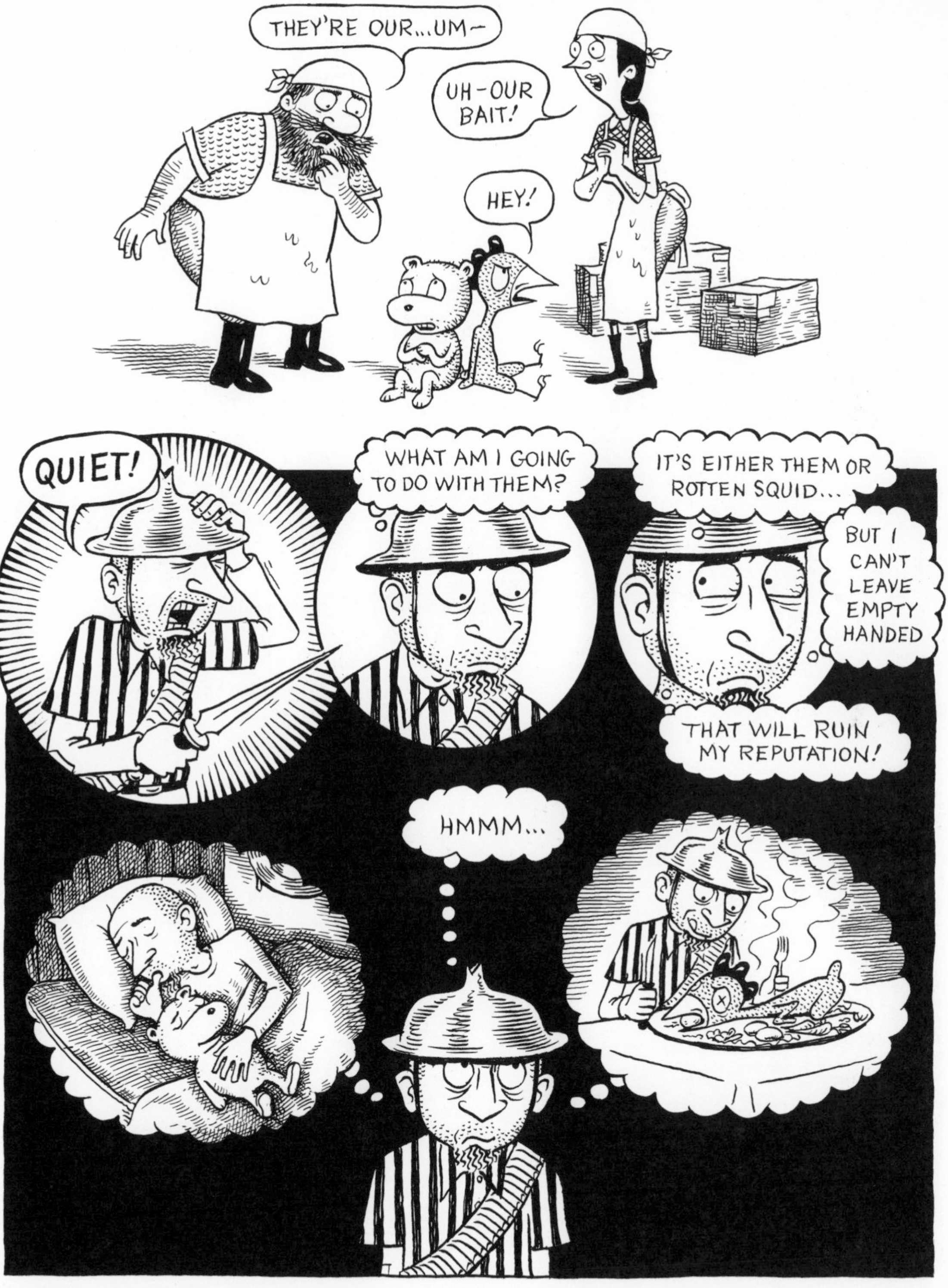
THEY'RE OUR...UM–
UH-OUR BAIT!
HEY!
QUIET!
WHAT AM I GOING TO DO WITH THEM?
IT'S EITHER THEM OR ROTTEN SQUID...
BUT I CAN'T LEAVE EMPTY HANDED
THAT WILL RUIN MY REPUTATION!
HMMM...

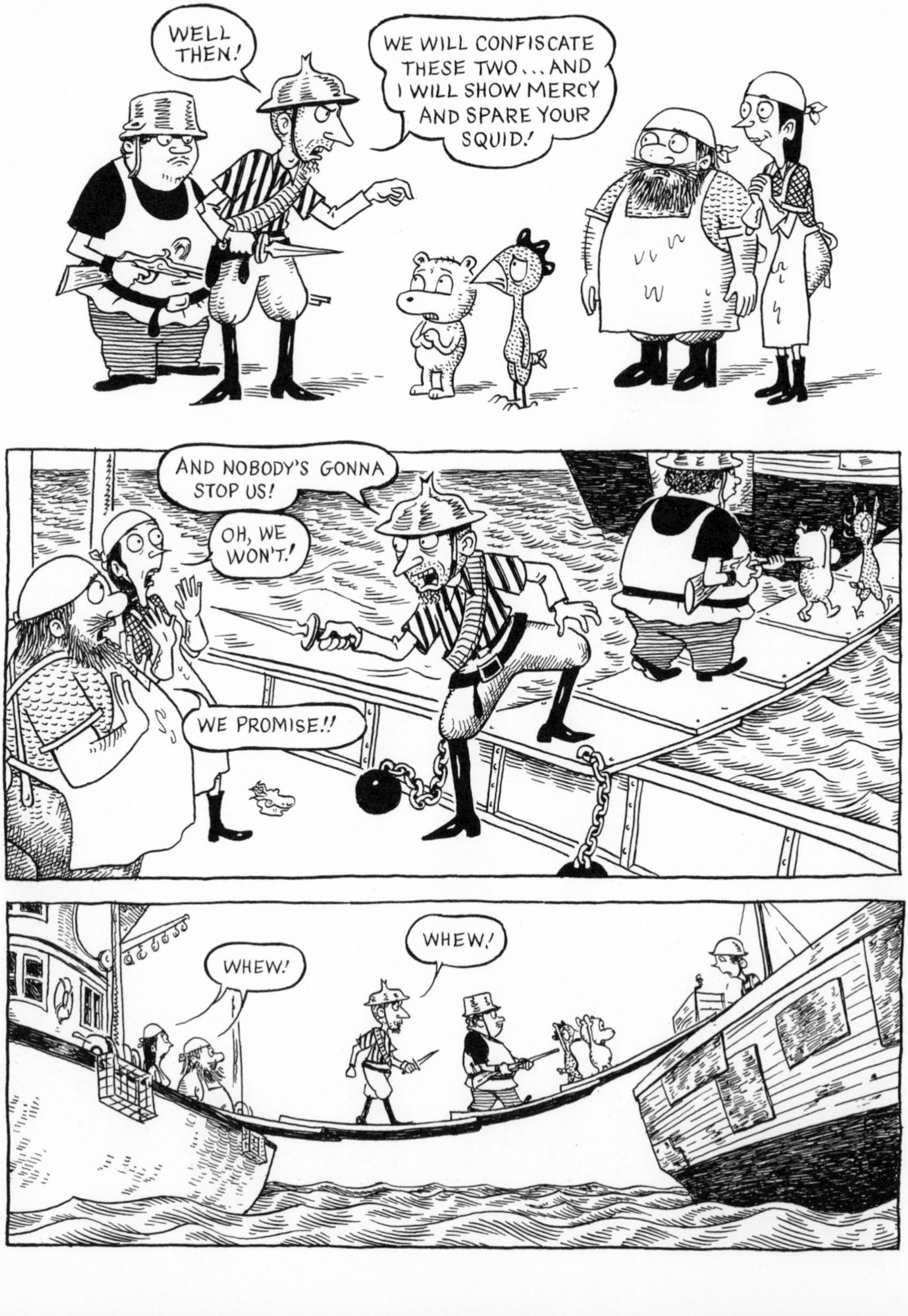
WELL THEN!
WE WILL CONFISCATE THESE TWO...AND I WILL SHOW MERCY AND SPARE YOUR SQUID!
AND NOBODY'S GONNA STOP US!
OH, WE WON'T!
WE PROMISE!!
WHEW!
WHEW!

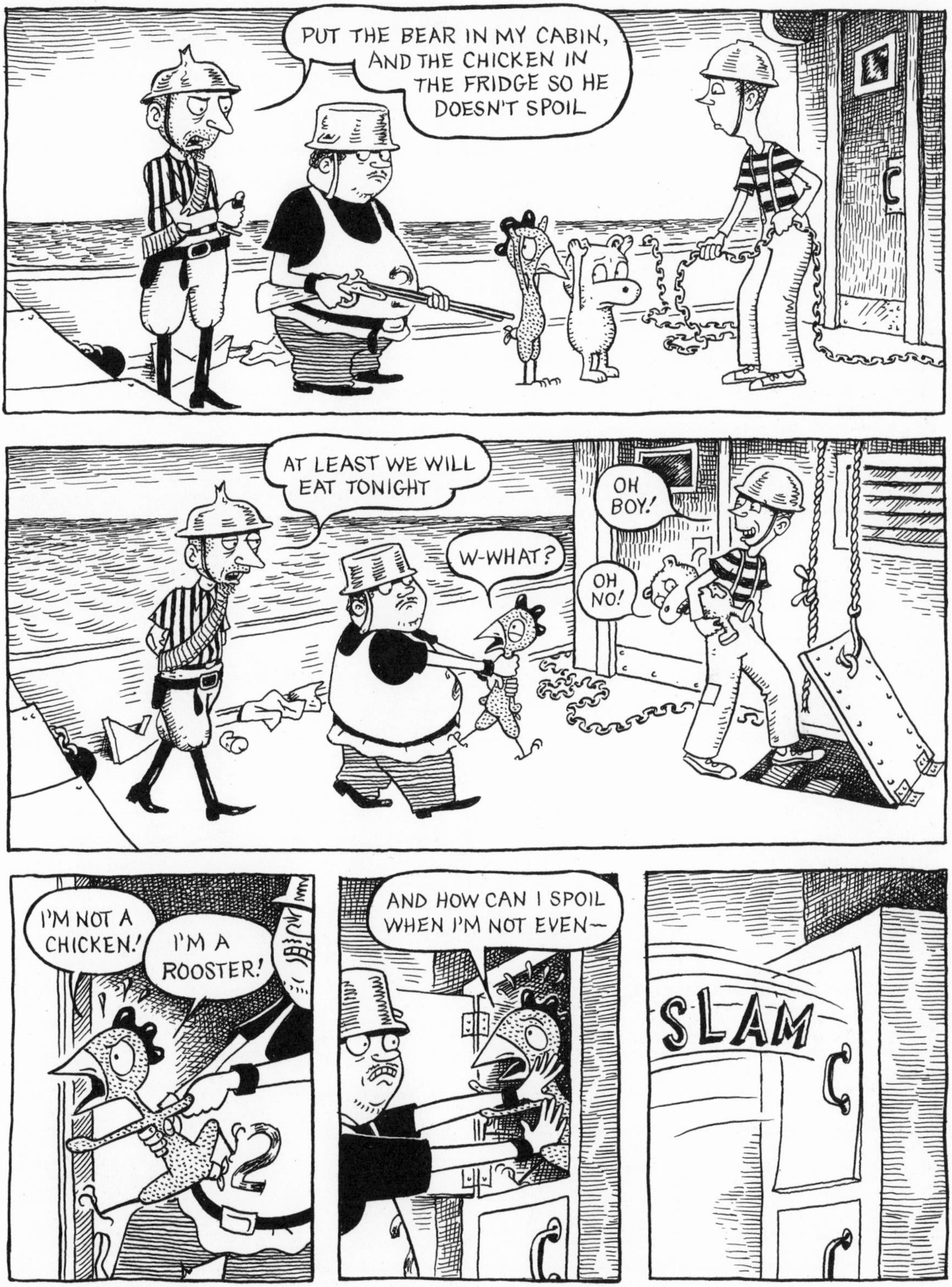
PUT THE BEAR IN MY CABIN, AND THE CHICKEN IN THE FRIDGE SO HE DOESN'T SPOIL
AT LEAST WE WILL EAT TONIGHT
W-WHAT?
OH BOY!
OH NO!
I'M NOT A CHICKEN!
I'M A ROOSTER!
AND HOW CAN I SPOIL WHEN I'M NOT EVEN—
SLAM

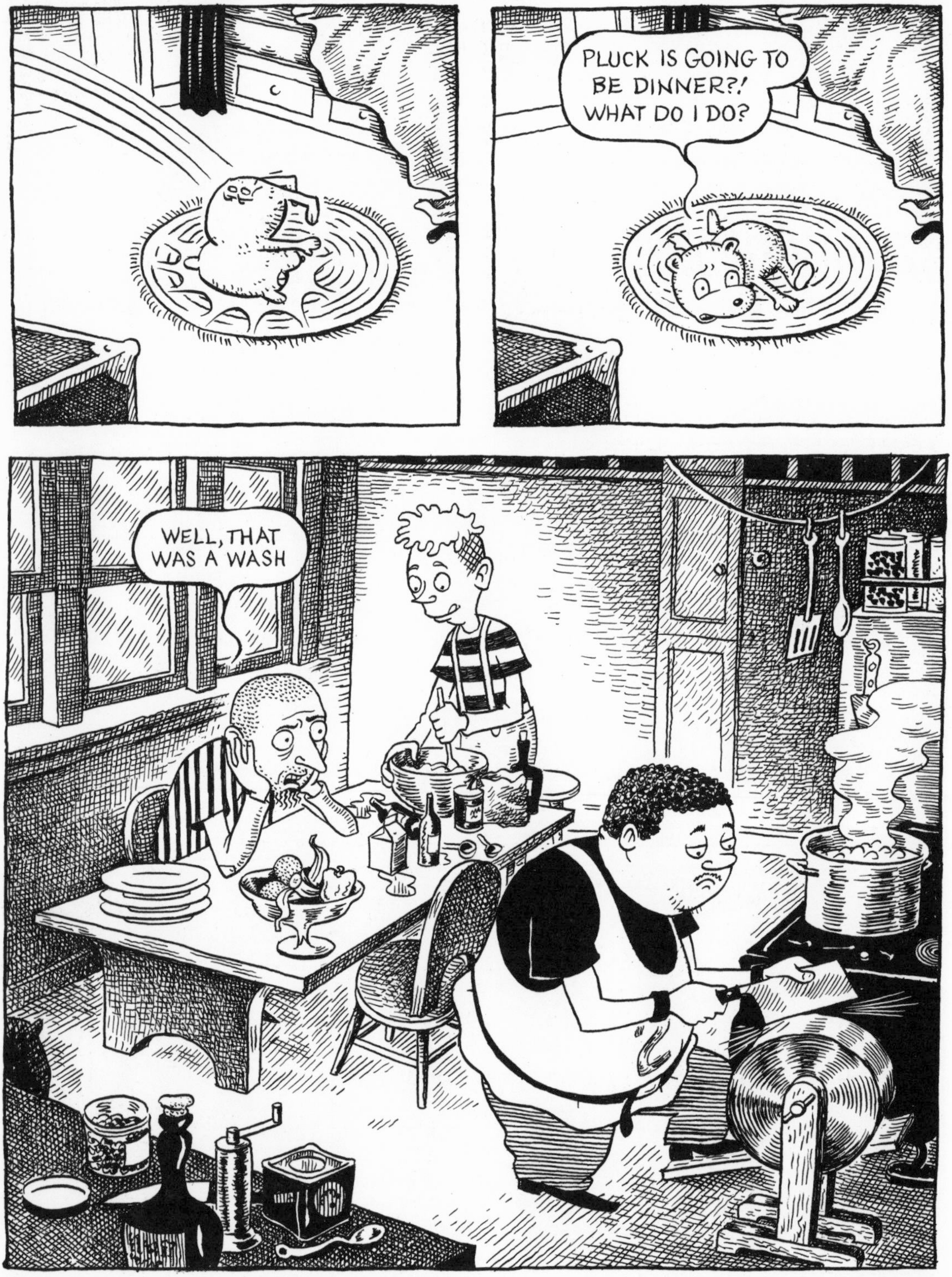
PLUCK IS GOING TO BE DINNER?! WHAT DO I DO?
WELL, THAT WAS A WASH

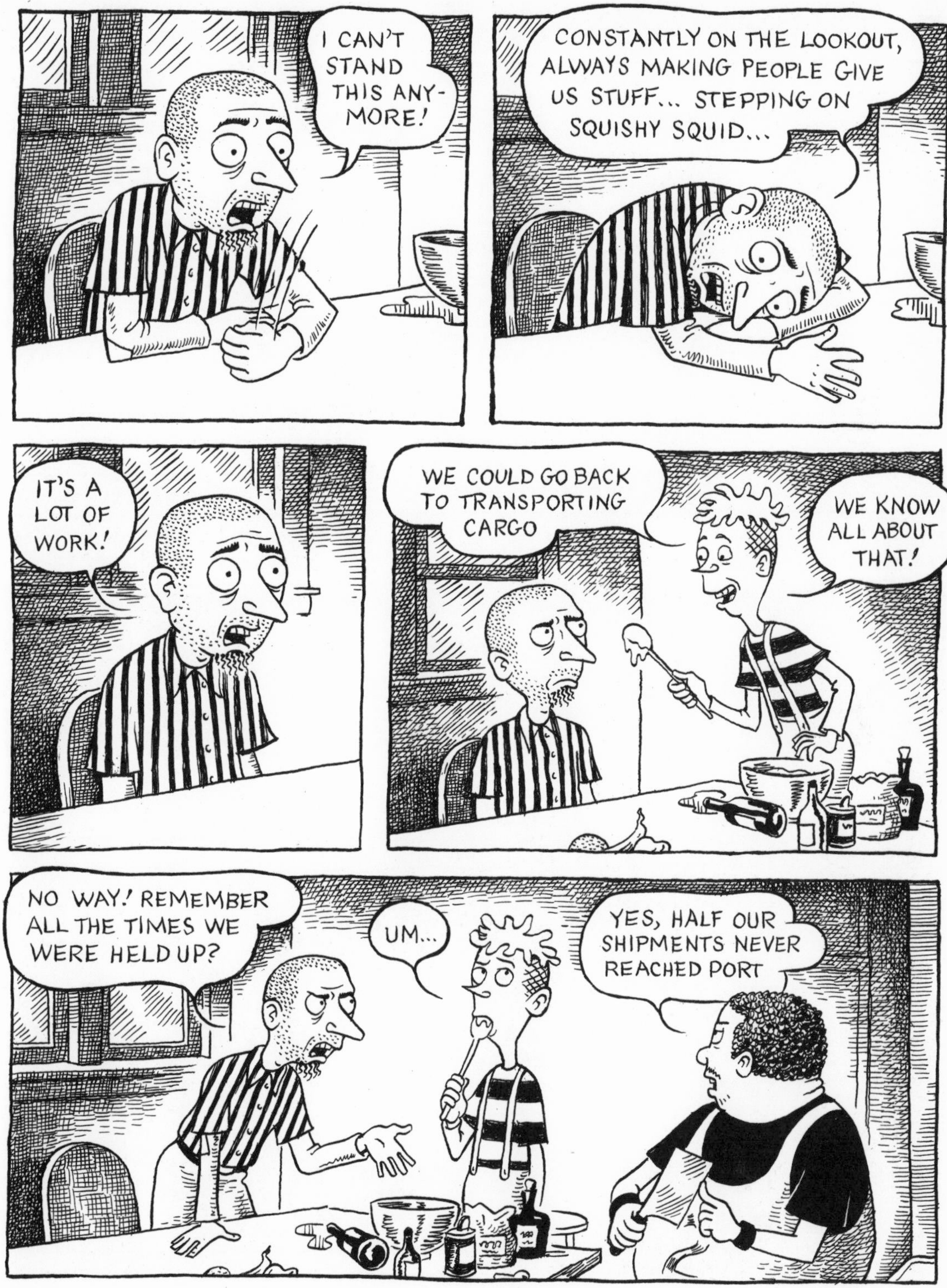
I CAN'T STAND THIS ANY-MORE!
CONSTANTLY ON THE LOOKOUT, ALWAYS MAKING PEOPLE GIVE US STUFF... STEPPING ON SQUISHY SQUID...
IT'S A LOT OF WORK!
WE COULD GO BACK TO TRANSPORTING CARGO
WE KNOW ALL ABOUT THAT!
NO WAY! REMEMBER ALL THE TIMES WE WERE HELD UP?
UM...
YES, HALF OUR SHIPMENTS NEVER REACHED PORT

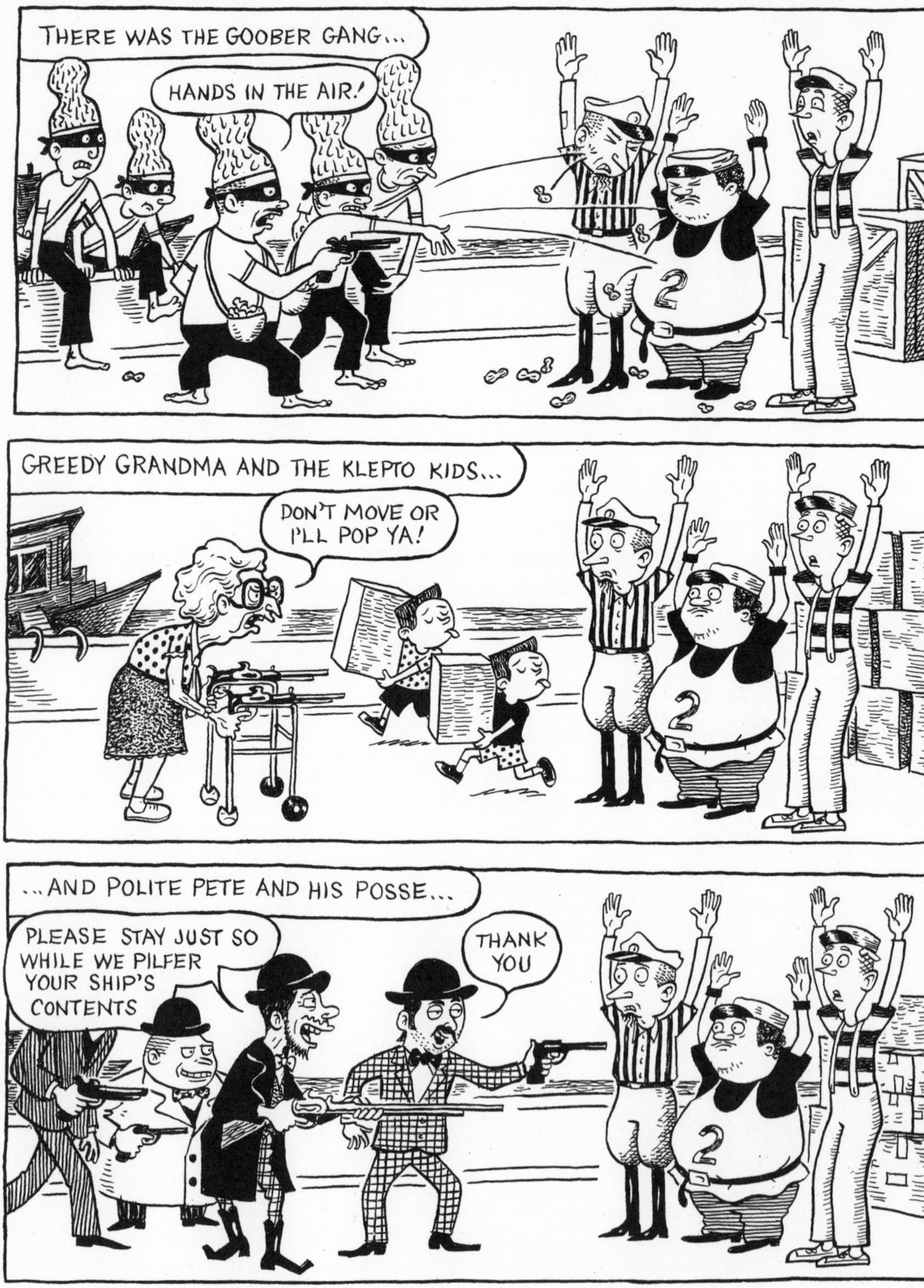
THERE WAS THE GOOBER GANG...
HANDS IN THE AIR!
GREEDY GRANDMA AND THE KLEPTO KIDS...
DON'T MOVE OR I'LL POP YA!
...AND POLITE PETE AND HIS POSSE...
PLEASE STAY JUST SO WHILE WE PILFER YOUR SHIP'S CONTENTS
THANK YOU
2
2
2

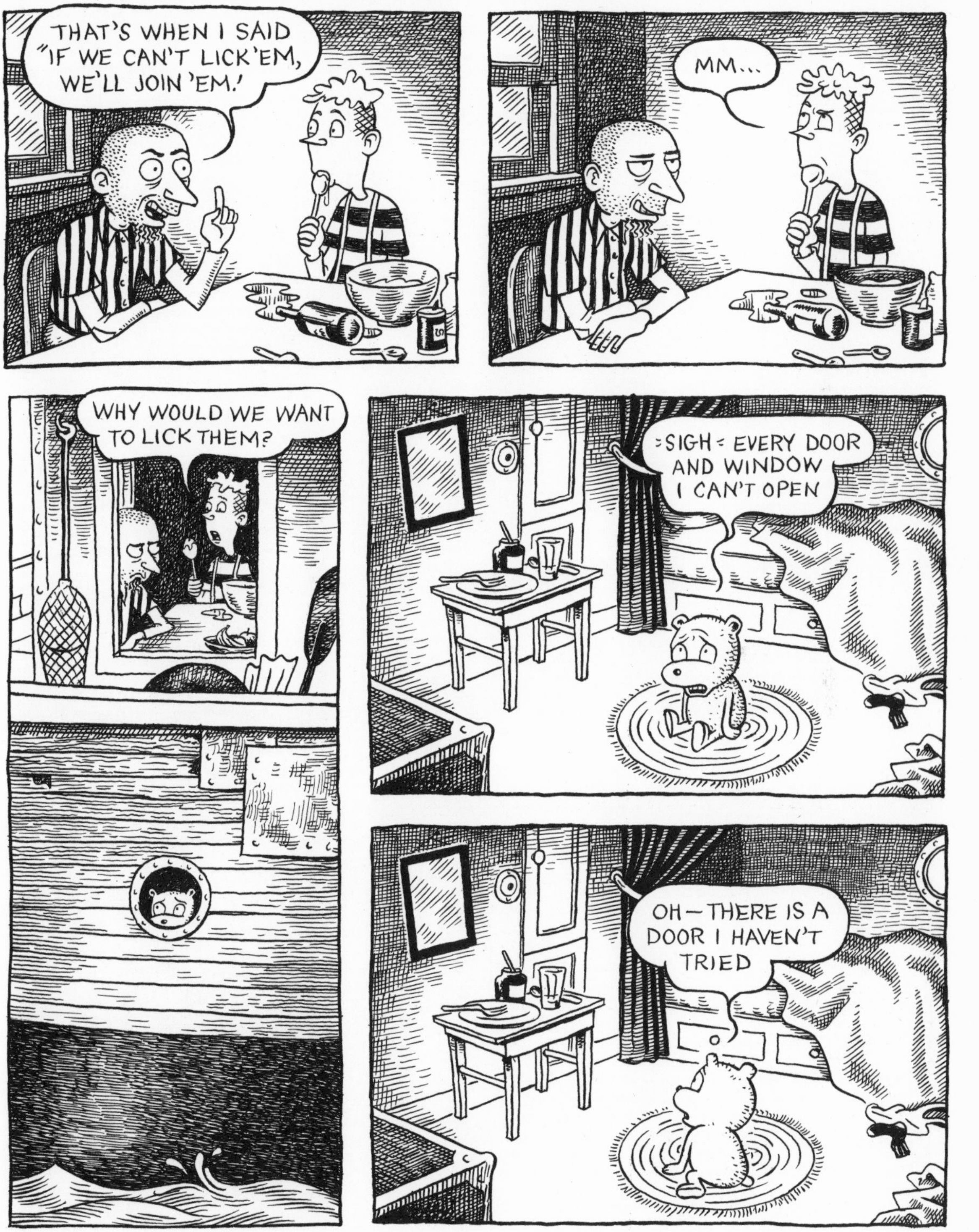
THAT'S WHEN I SAID "IF WE CAN'T LICK 'EM, WE'LL JOIN 'EM.'
MM...
WHY WOULD WE WANT TO LICK THEM?
=SIGH= EVERY DOOR AND WINDOW I CAN'T OPEN
OH—THERE IS A DOOR I HAVEN'T TRIED

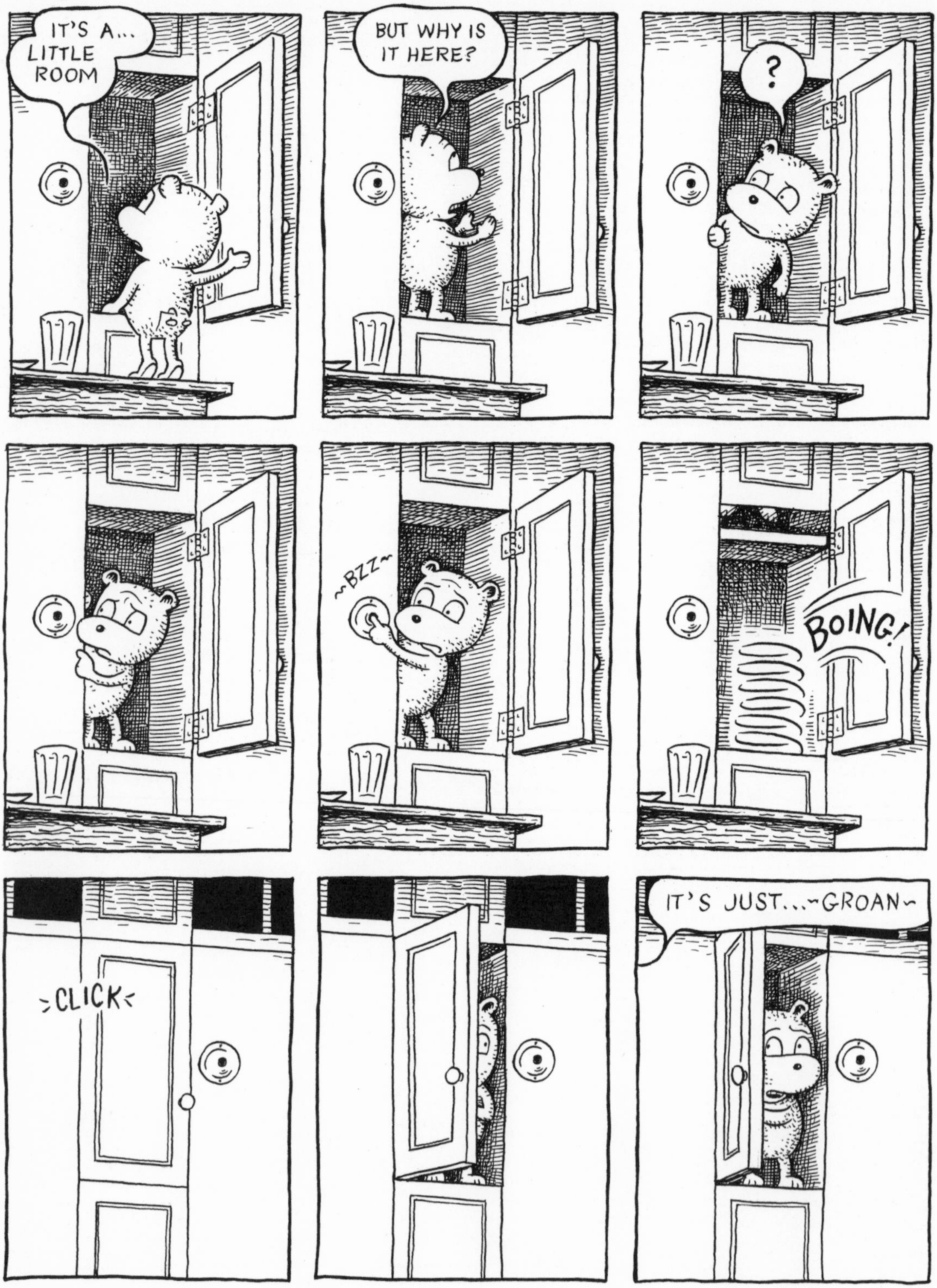
IT'S A... LITTLE ROOM
BUT WHY IS IT HERE?
?
~BZZ~
BOING!
CLICK
IT'S JUST...~GROAN~

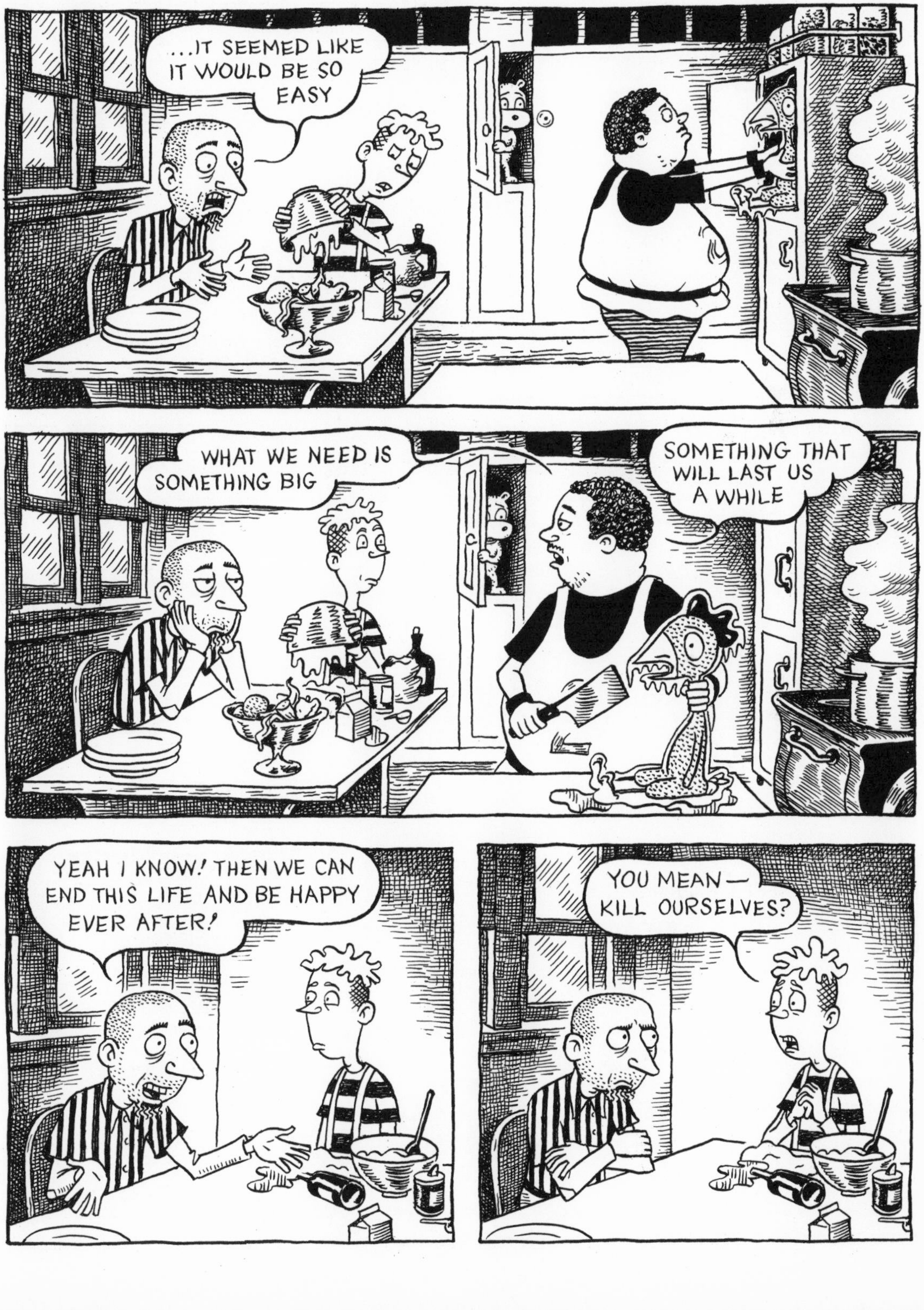
...IT SEEMED LIKE IT WOULD BE SO EASY
WHAT WE NEED IS SOMETHING BIG
SOMETHING THAT WILL LAST US A WHILE
YEAH I KNOW! THEN WE CAN END THIS LIFE AND BE HAPPY EVER AFTER!
YOU MEAN— KILL OURSELVES?

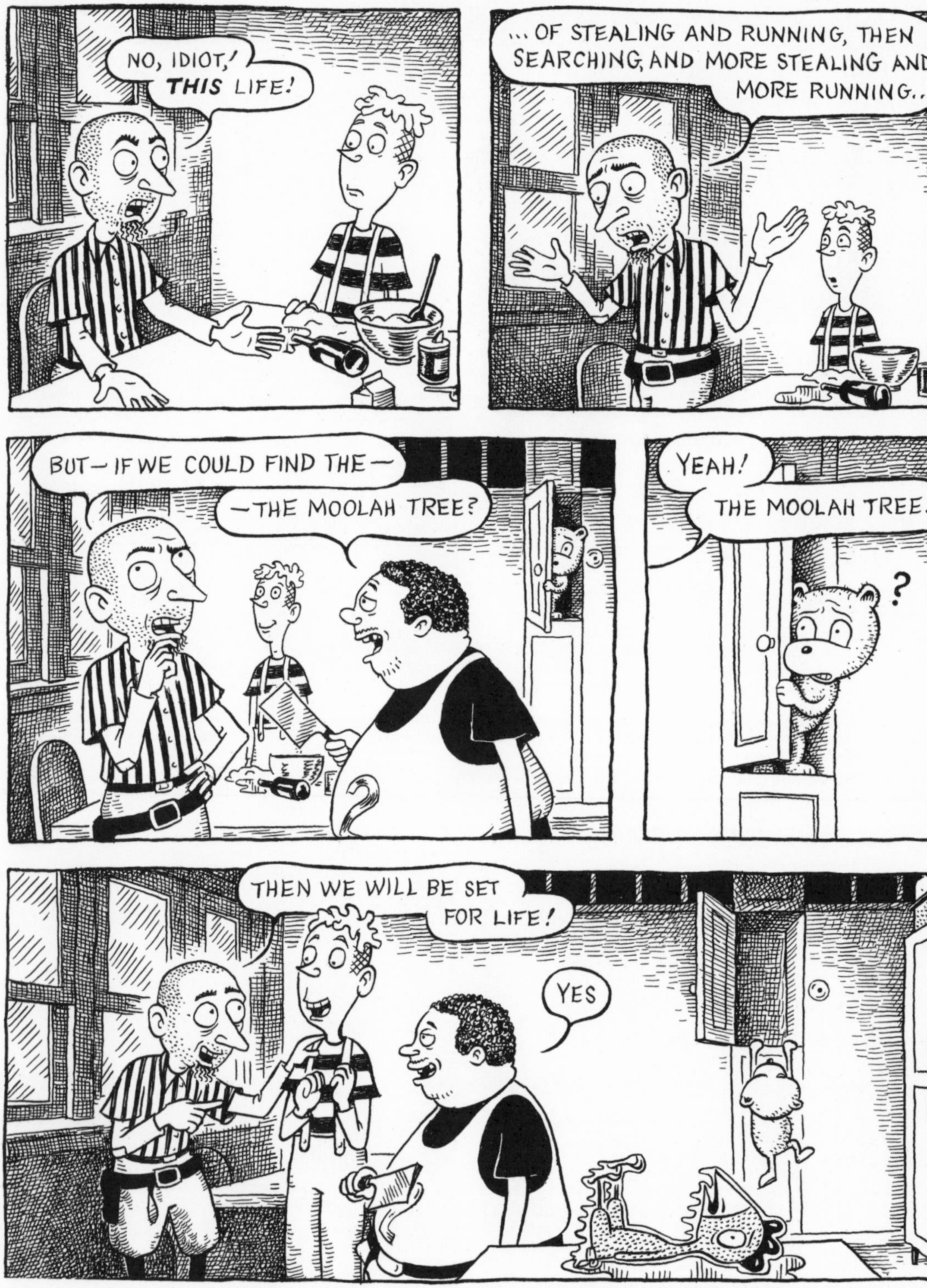
NO, IDIOT,! *THIS* LIFE!
...OF STEALING AND RUNNING, THEN SEARCHING, AND MORE STEALING AND MORE RUNNING...
BUT— IF WE COULD FIND THE—
—THE MOOLAH TREE?
YEAH!
THE MOOLAH TREE!
?
THEN WE WILL BE SET FOR LIFE!
YES

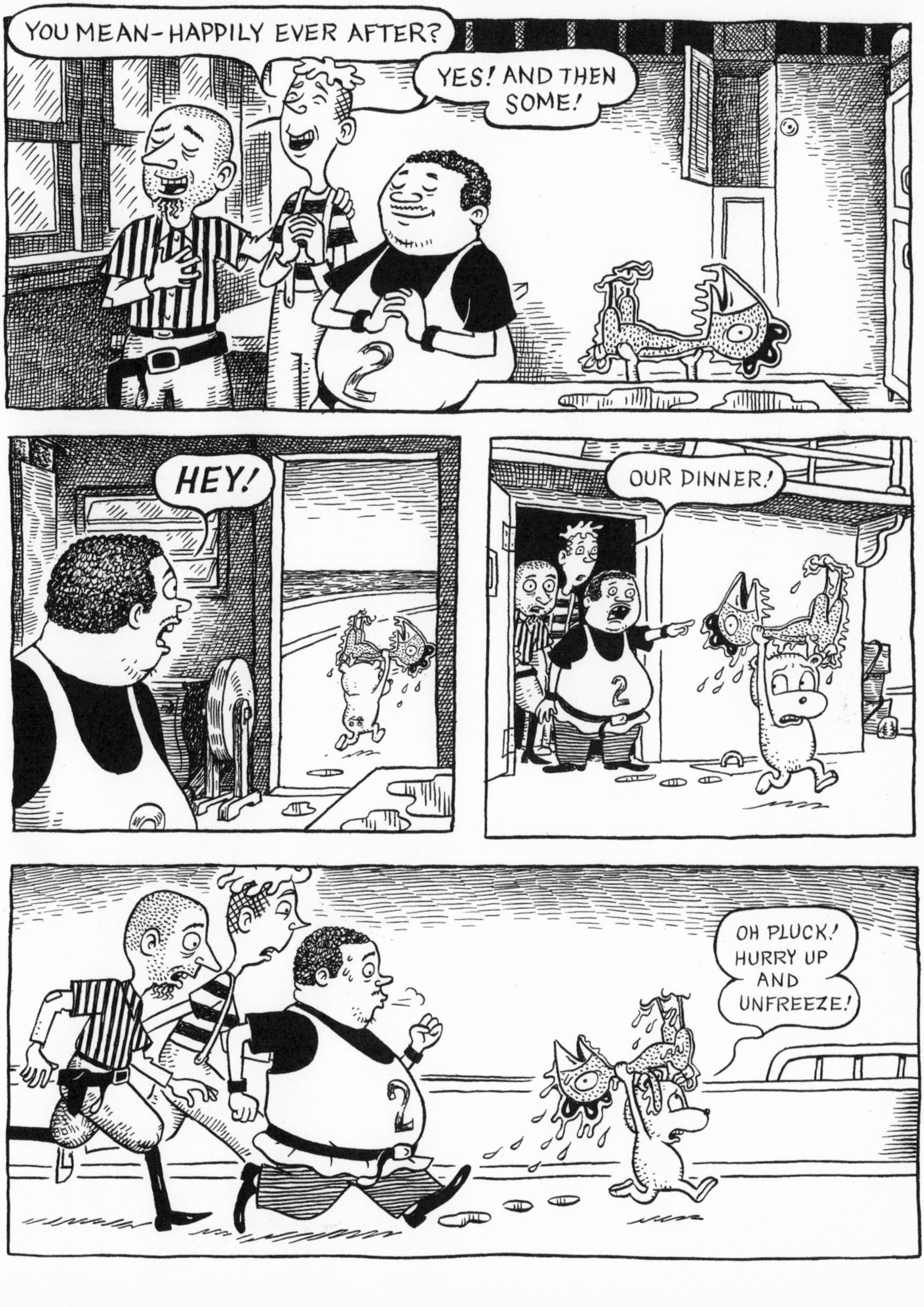
YOU MEAN-HAPPILY EVER AFTER?
YES! AND THEN SOME!
HEY!
OUR DINNER!
OH PLUCK! HURRY UP AND UNFREEZE!

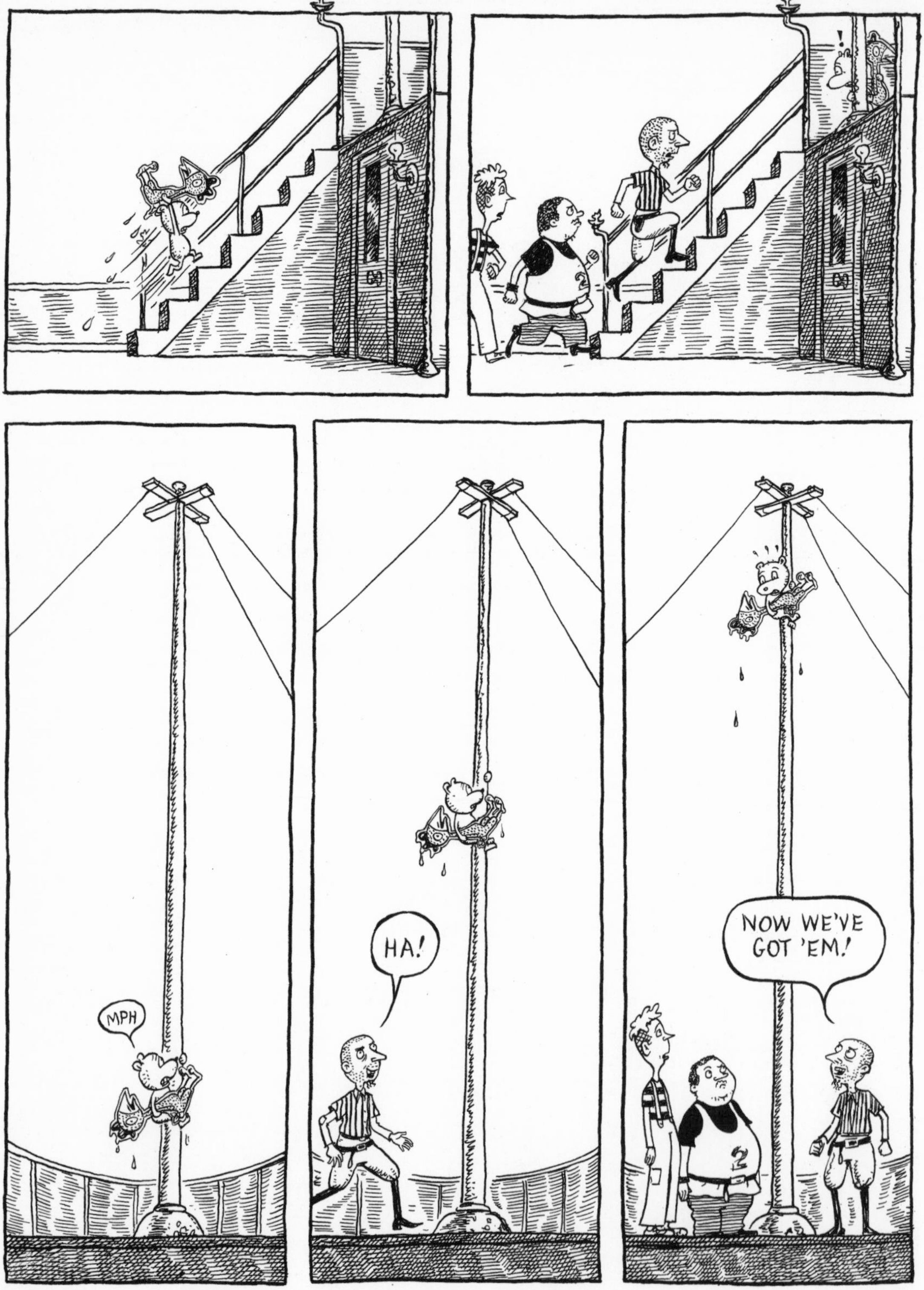
MPH
HA!
NOW WE'VE GOT 'EM!

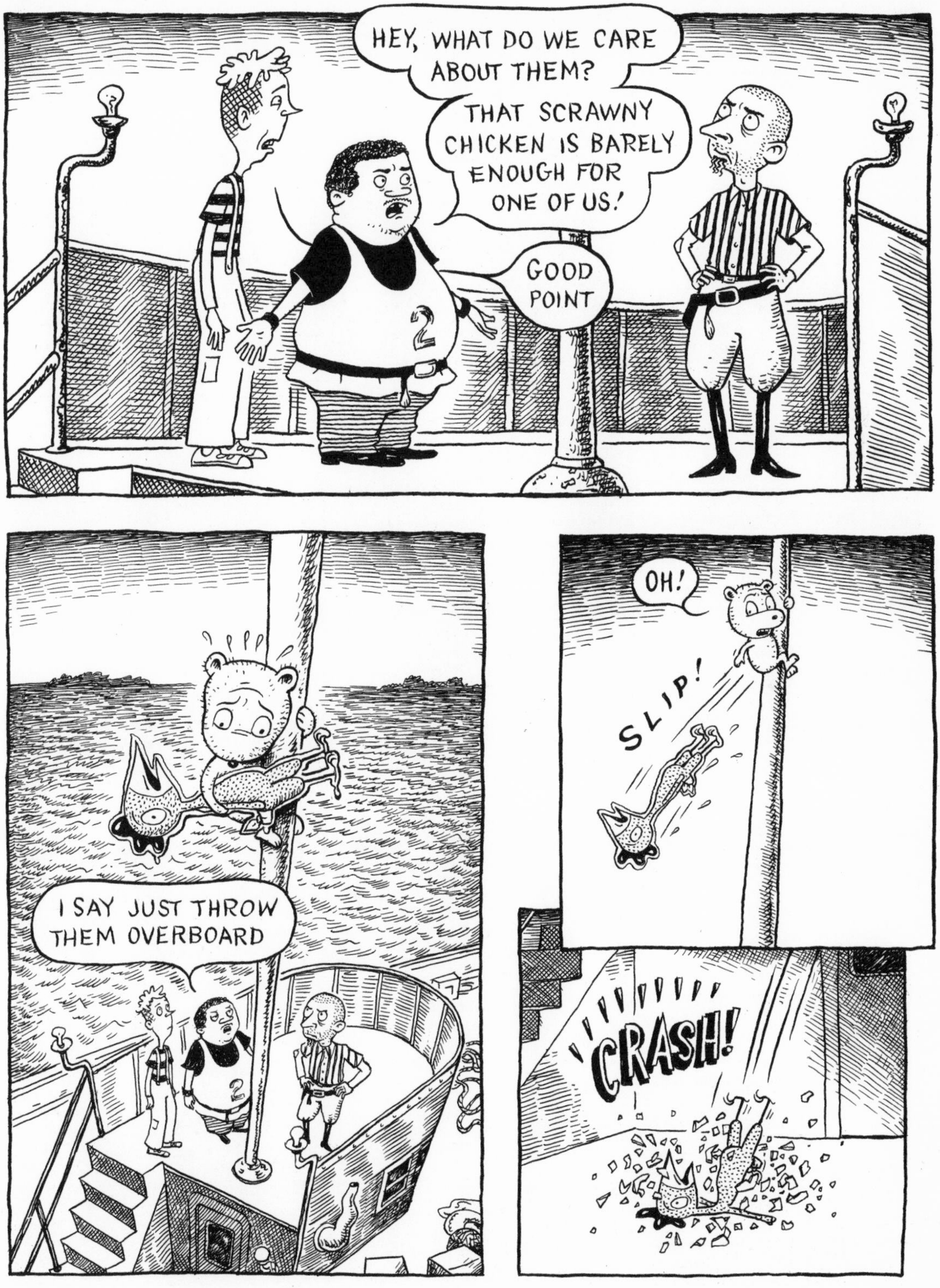
HEY, WHAT DO WE CARE ABOUT THEM?
THAT SCRAWNY CHICKEN IS BARELY ENOUGH FOR ONE OF US!
GOOD POINT
2
I SAY JUST THROW THEM OVERBOARD
2
OH!
SLIP!
CRASH!

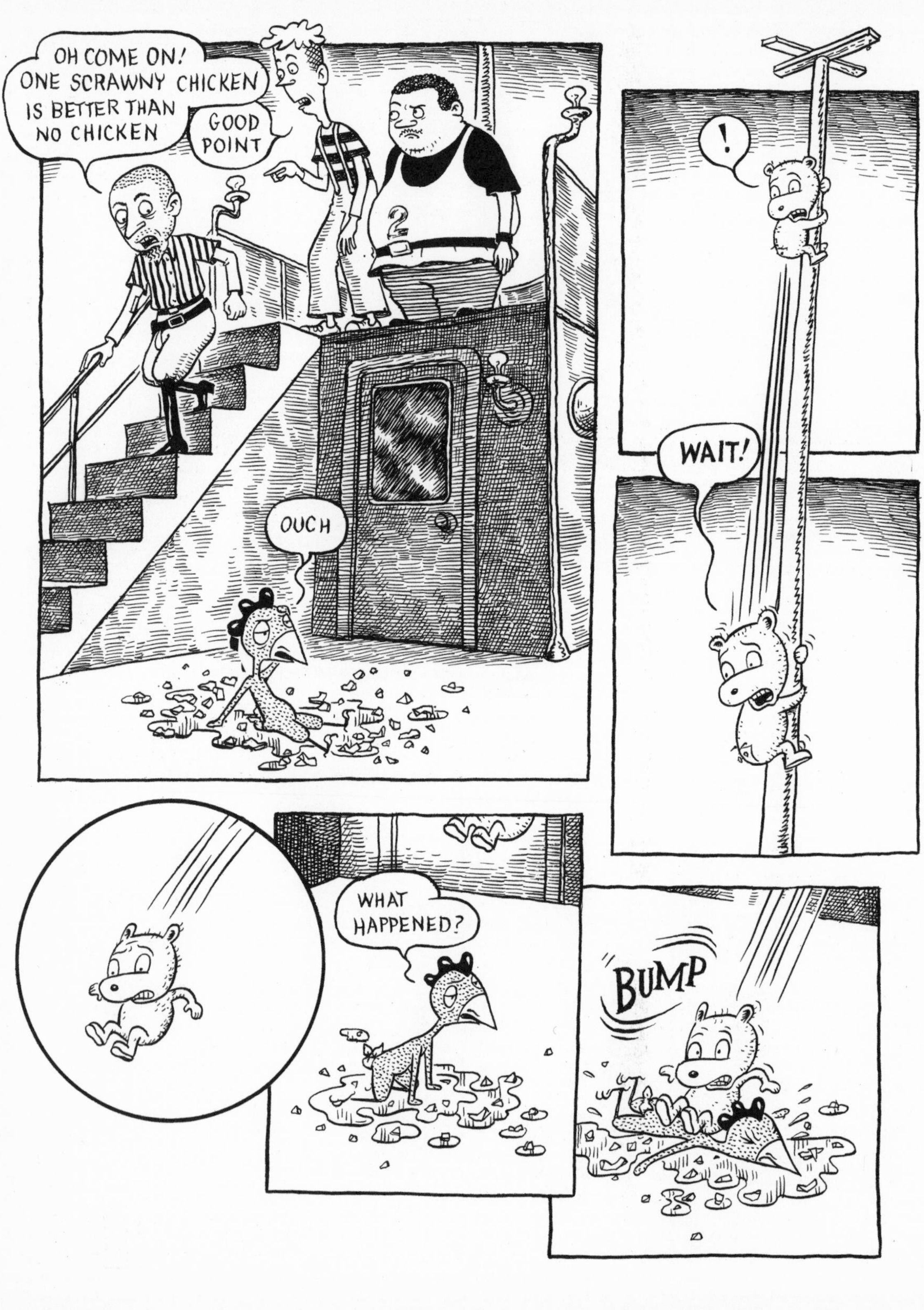
OH COME ON! ONE SCRAWNY CHICKEN IS BETTER THAN NO CHICKEN
GOOD POINT
OUCH
!
WAIT!
WHAT HAPPENED?
BUMP

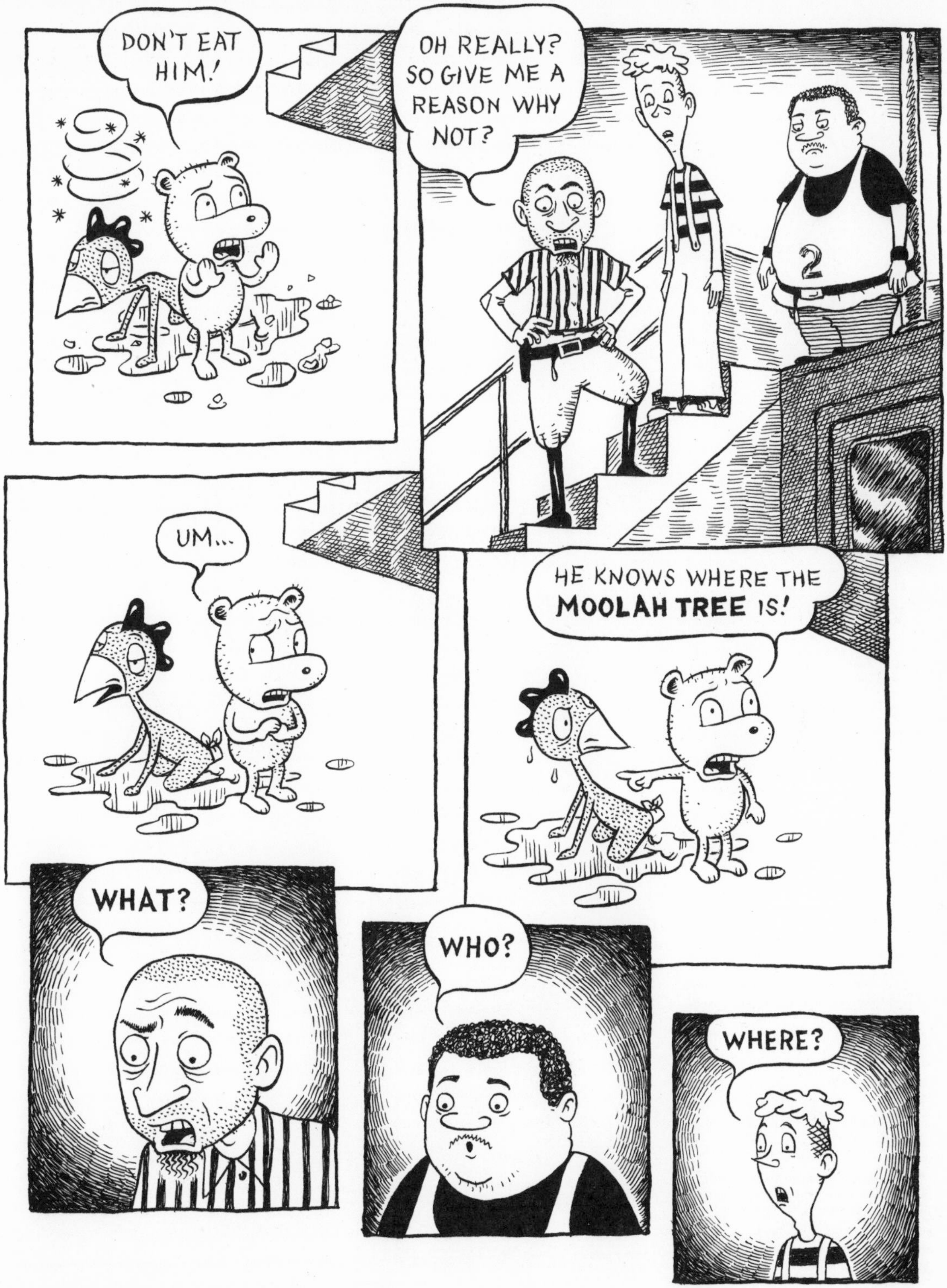
DON'T EAT HIM!
OH REALLY? SO GIVE ME A REASON WHY NOT?
UM...
HE KNOWS WHERE THE MOOLAH TREE IS!
WHAT?
WHO?
WHERE?
2

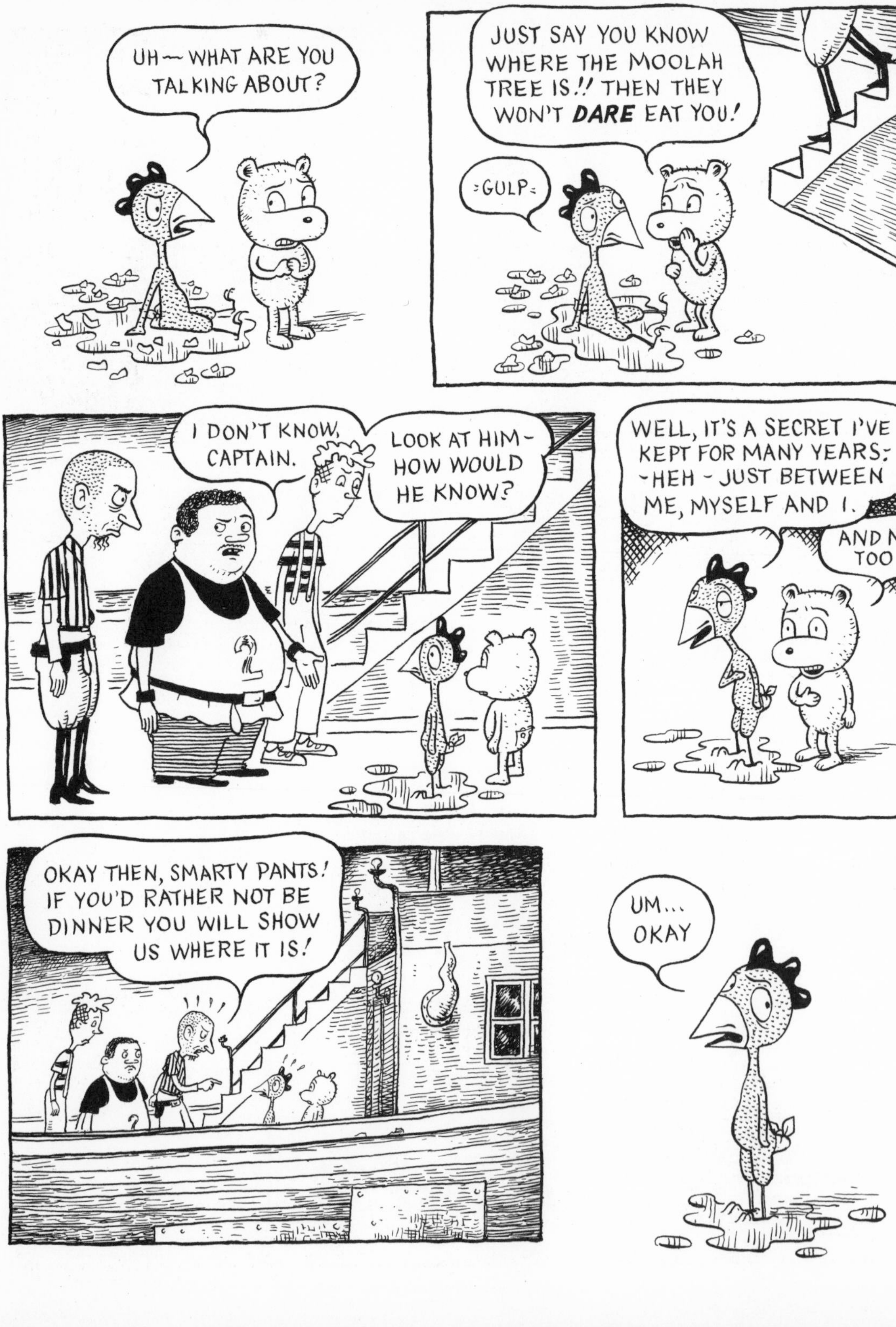
UH — WHAT ARE YOU TALKING ABOUT?
JUST SAY YOU KNOW WHERE THE MOOLAH TREE IS!! THEN THEY WON'T DARE EAT YOU!
GULP
I DON'T KNOW, CAPTAIN.
LOOK AT HIM - HOW WOULD HE KNOW?
WELL, IT'S A SECRET I'VE KEPT FOR MANY YEARS - HEH - JUST BETWEEN ME, MYSELF AND I.
AND ME TOO
OKAY THEN, SMARTY PANTS! IF YOU'D RATHER NOT BE DINNER YOU WILL SHOW US WHERE IT IS!
UM... OKAY

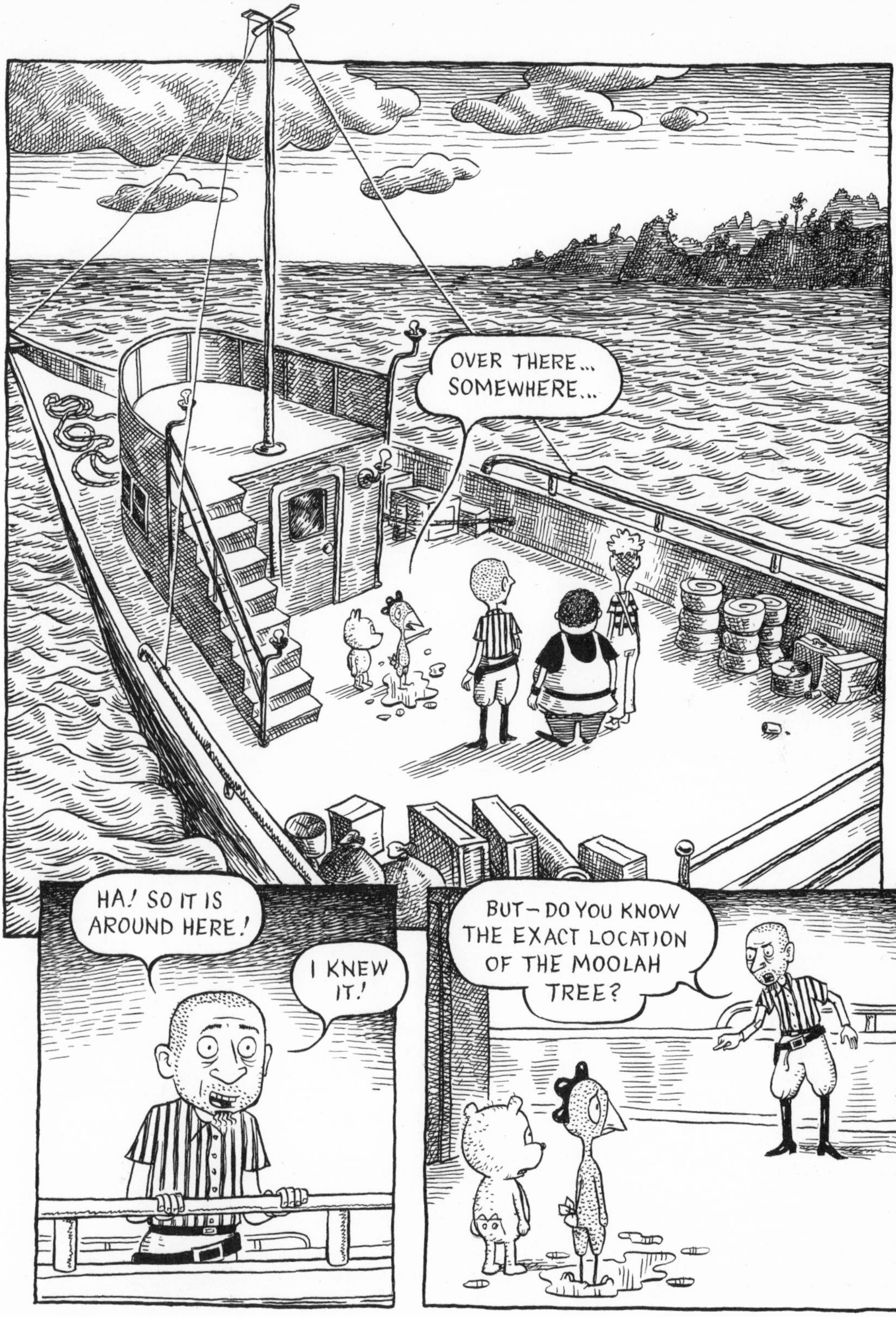
OVER THERE... SOMEWHERE...
HA! SO IT IS AROUND HERE!
I KNEW IT!
BUT— DO YOU KNOW THE EXACT LOCATION OF THE MOOLAH TREE?

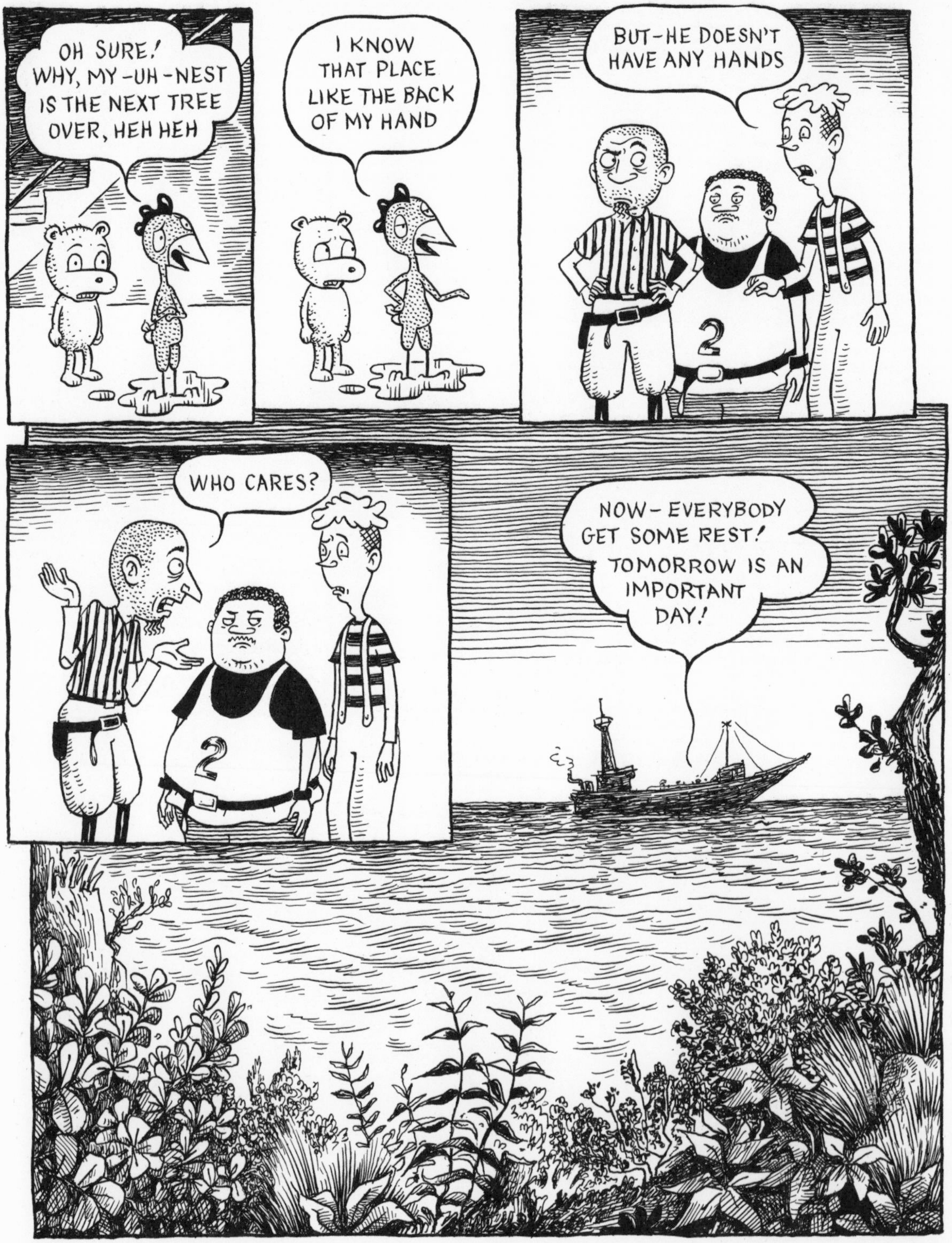
OH SURE! WHY, MY -UH -NEST IS THE NEXT TREE OVER, HEH HEH
I KNOW THAT PLACE LIKE THE BACK OF MY HAND
BUT-HE DOESN'T HAVE ANY HANDS
WHO CARES?
NOW- EVERYBODY GET SOME REST! TOMORROW IS AN IMPORTANT DAY!

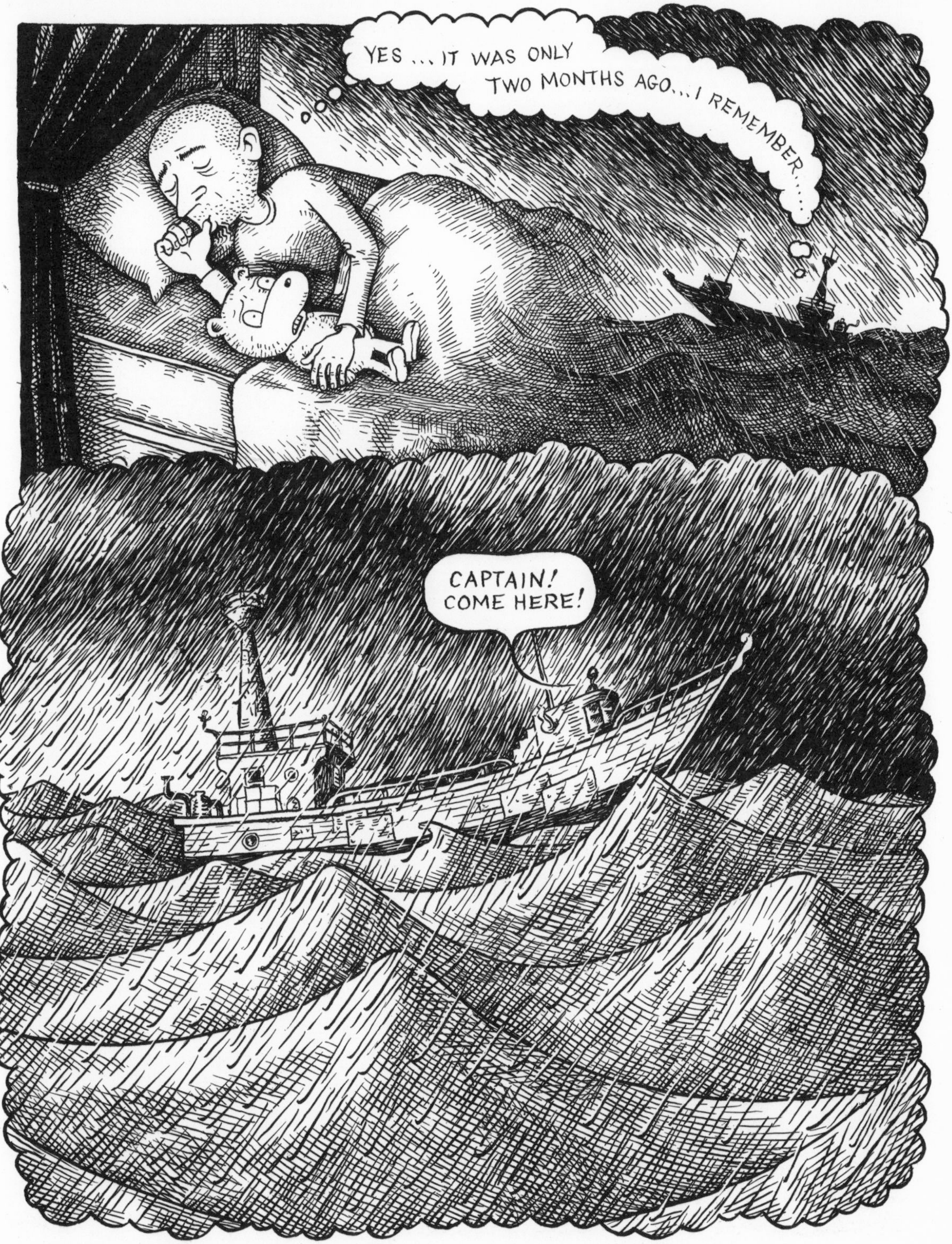
YES ... IT WAS ONLY TWO MONTHS AGO... I REMEMBER....
CAPTAIN! COME HERE!

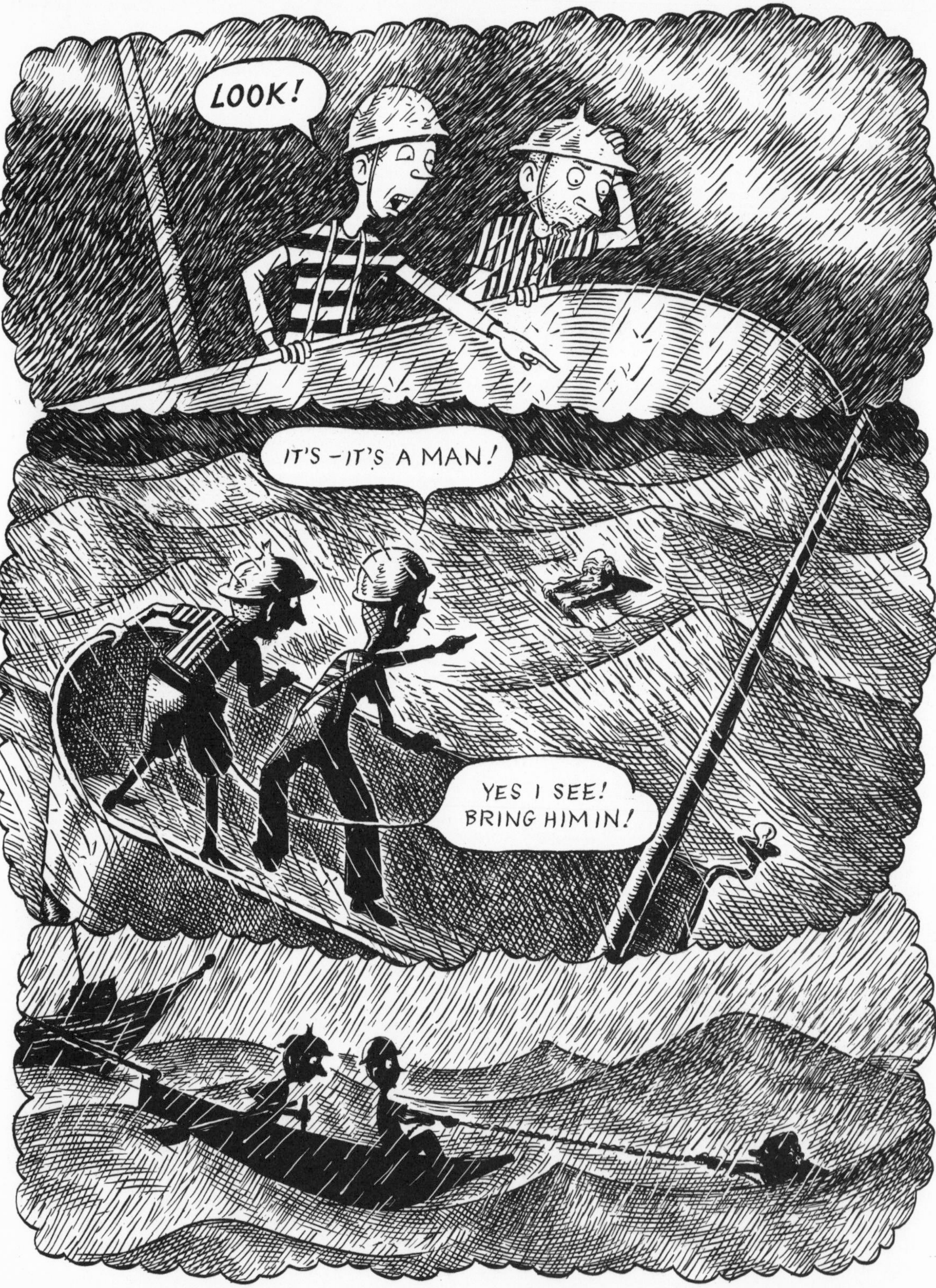
LOOK!
IT'S – IT'S A MAN!
YES I SEE! BRING HIM IN!

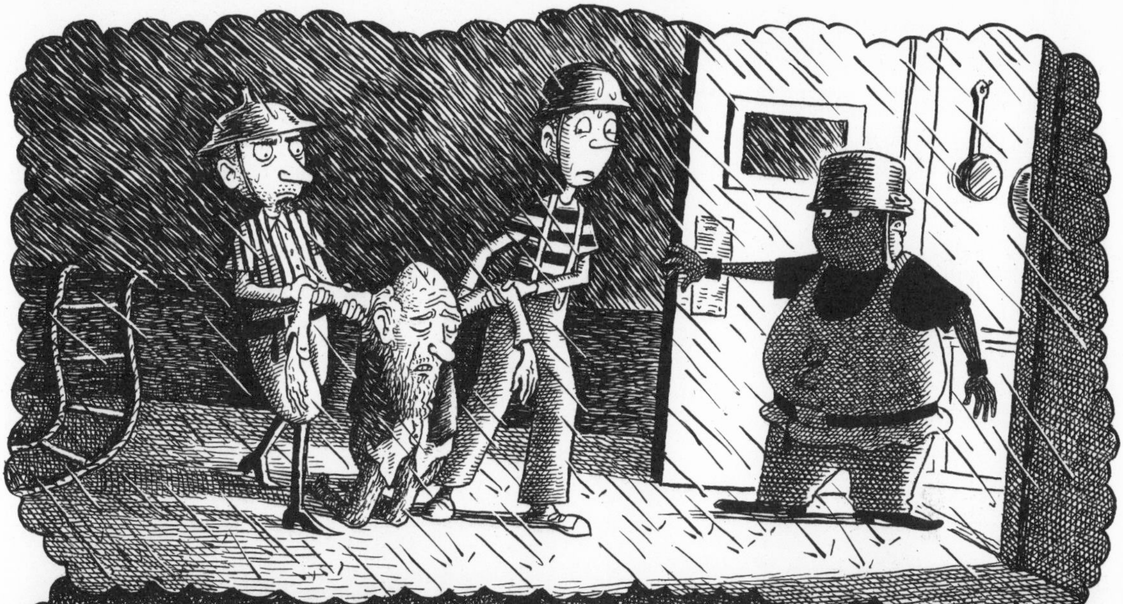
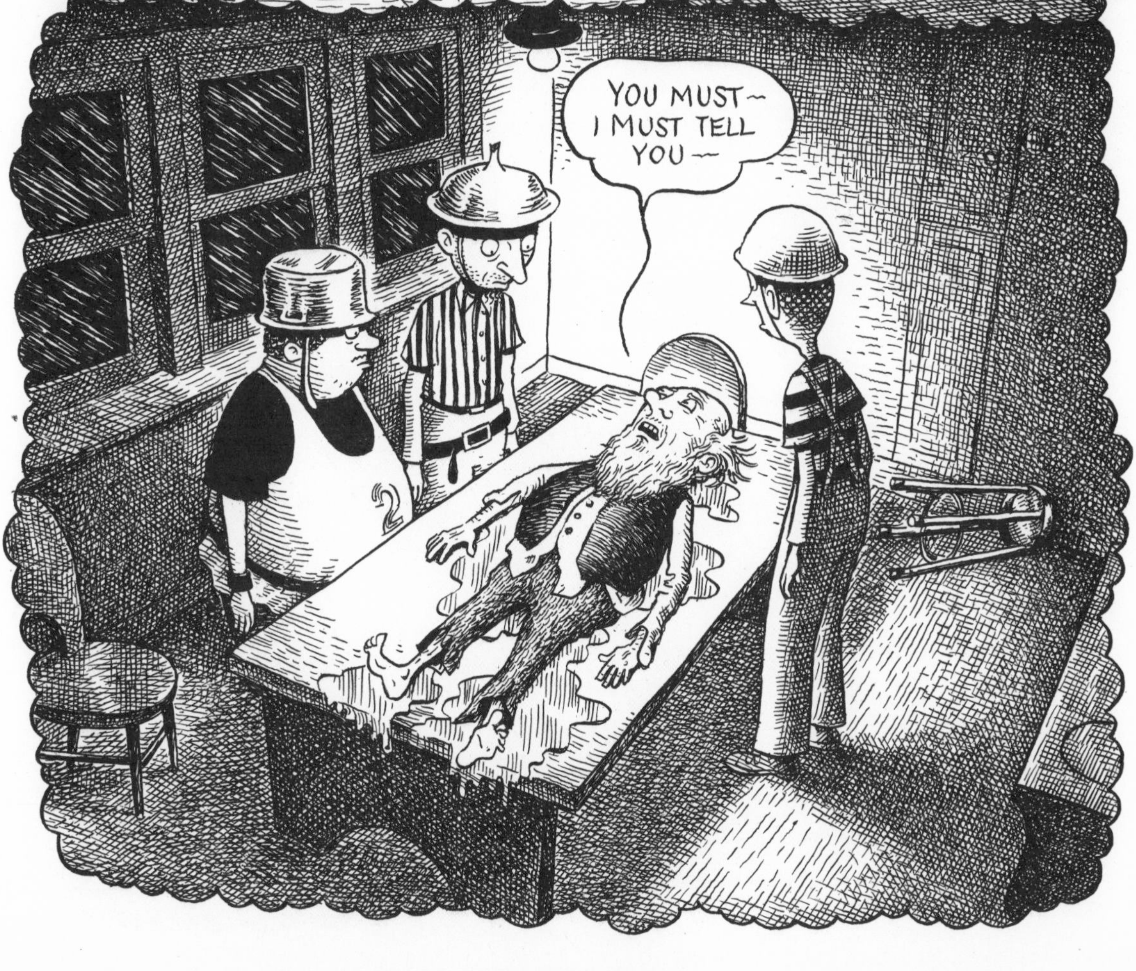
YOU MUST—
I MUST TELL
YOU—

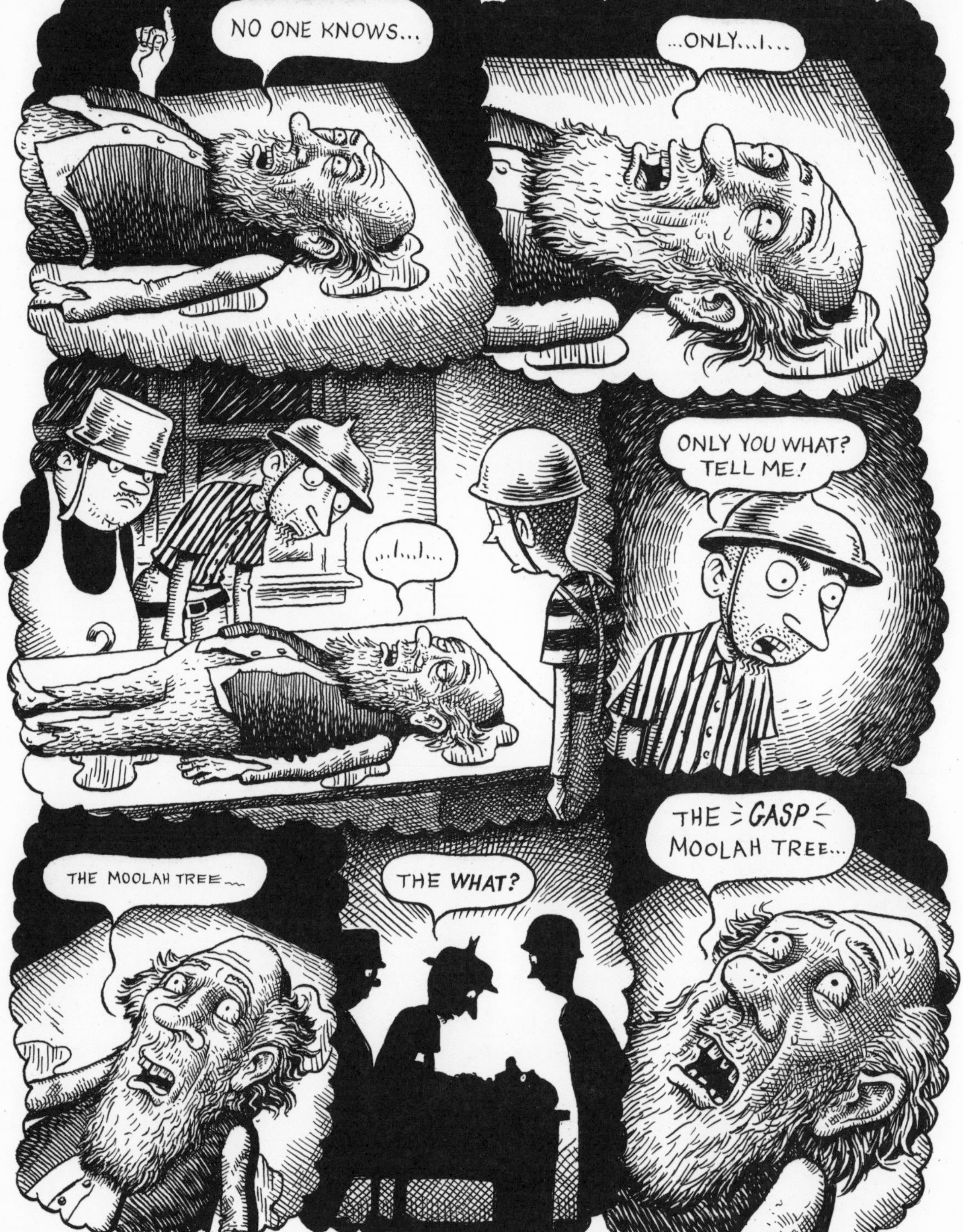
NO ONE KNOWS...
...ONLY...I...
...I...I...
ONLY YOU WHAT? TELL ME!
THE MOOLAH TREE...
THE WHAT?
THE GASP MOOLAH TREE...

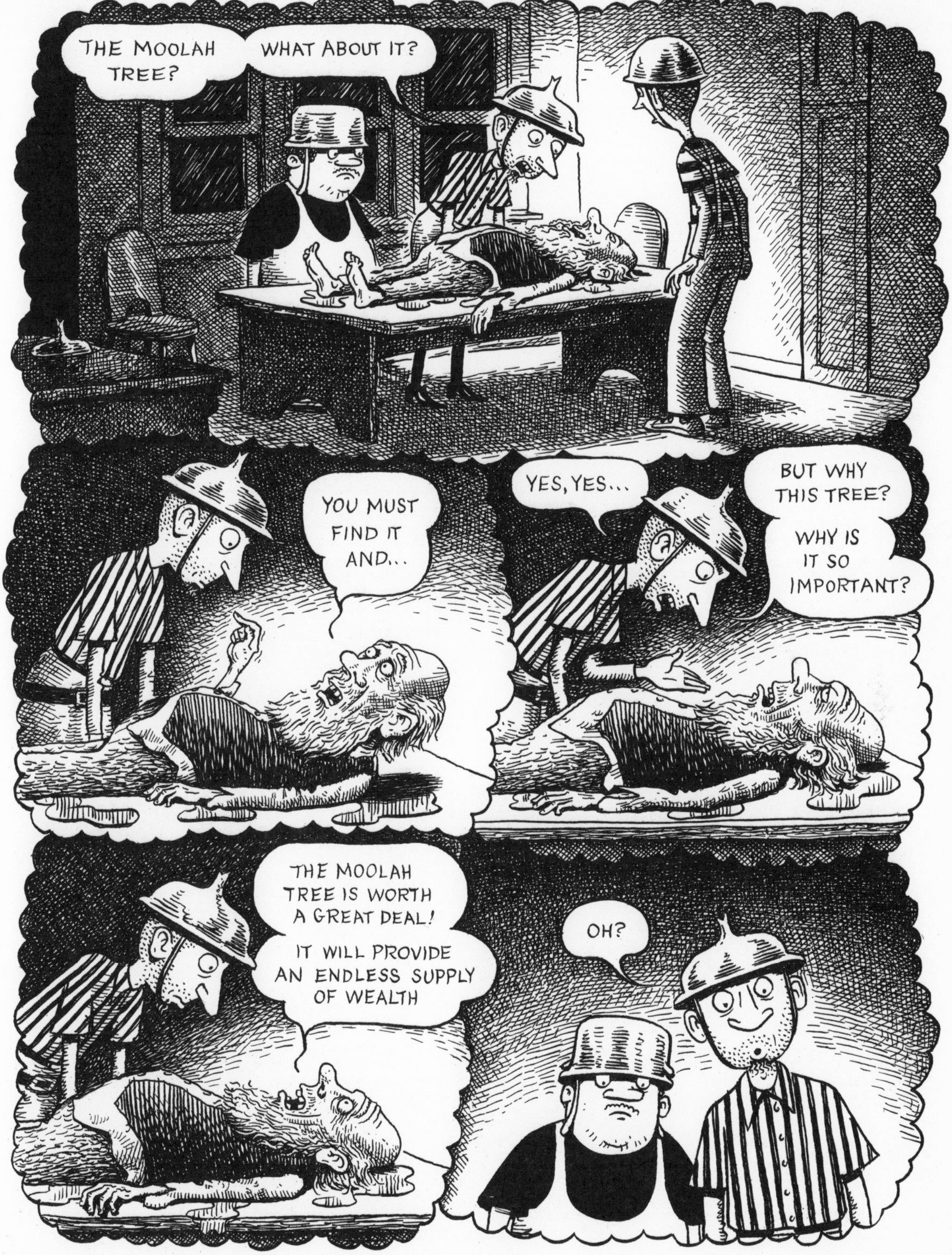
THE MOOLAH TREE?
WHAT ABOUT IT?
YOU MUST FIND IT AND...
YES, YES...
BUT WHY THIS TREE?
WHY IS IT SO IMPORTANT?
THE MOOLAH TREE IS WORTH A GREAT DEAL!
IT WILL PROVIDE AN ENDLESS SUPPLY OF WEALTH
OH?

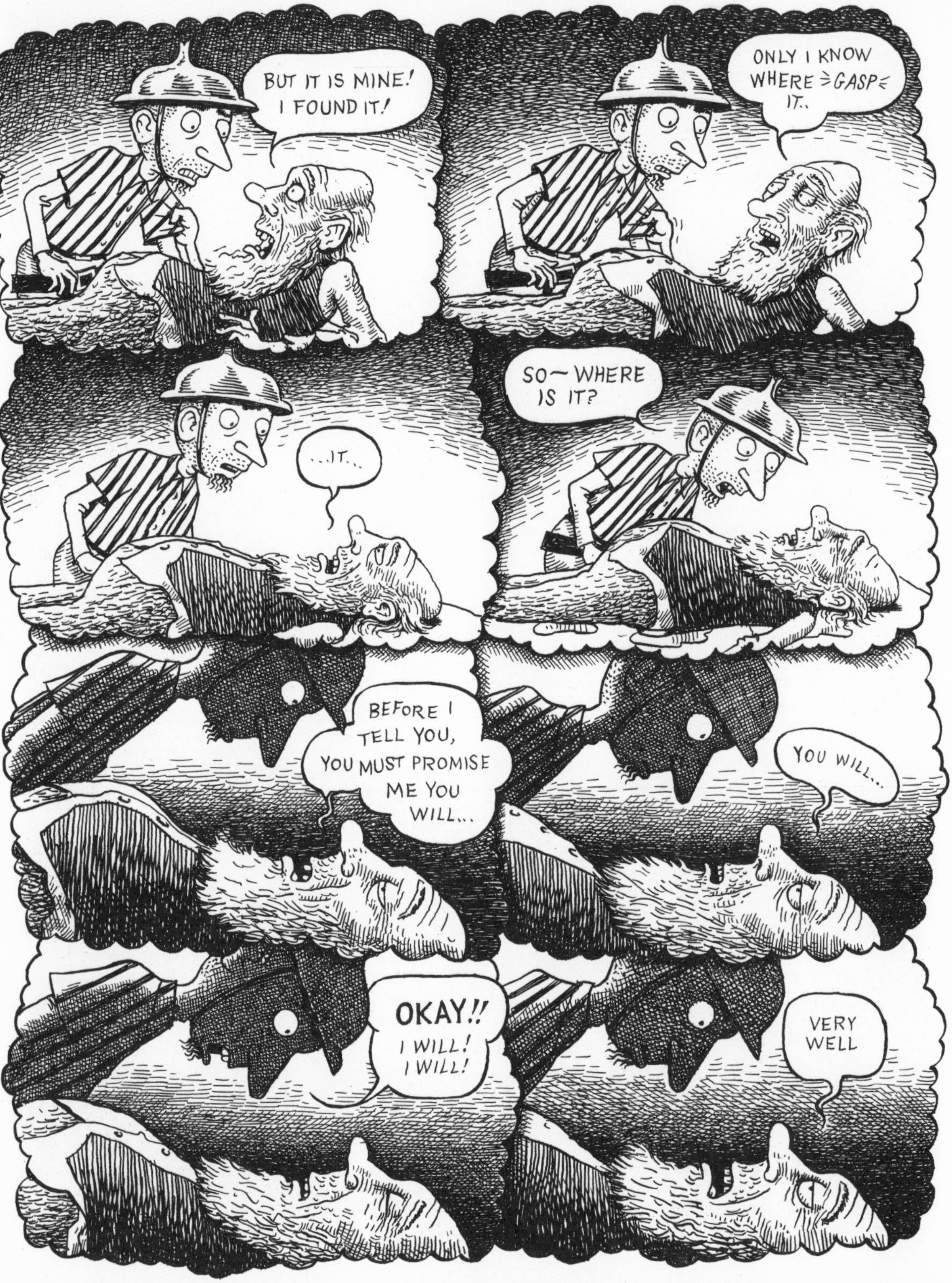
BUT IT IS MINE! I FOUND IT!
ONLY I KNOW WHERE ≥GASP≤ IT..
...IT...
SO— WHERE IS IT?
BEFORE I TELL YOU, YOU MUST PROMISE ME YOU WILL...
YOU WILL...
OKAY!! I WILL! I WILL!
VERY WELL

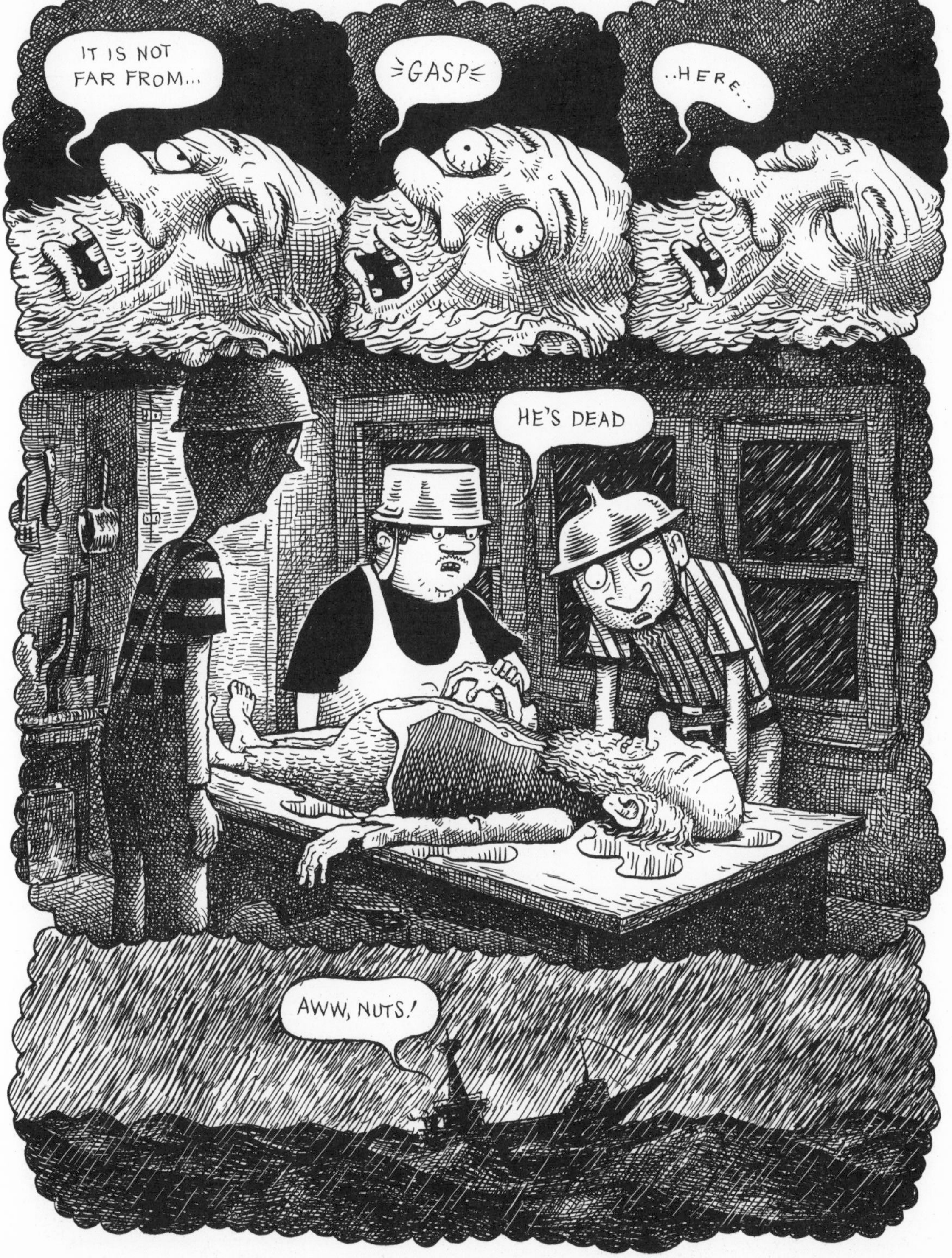
IT IS NOT FAR FROM...
GASP
..HERE...
HE'S DEAD
AWW, NUTS!

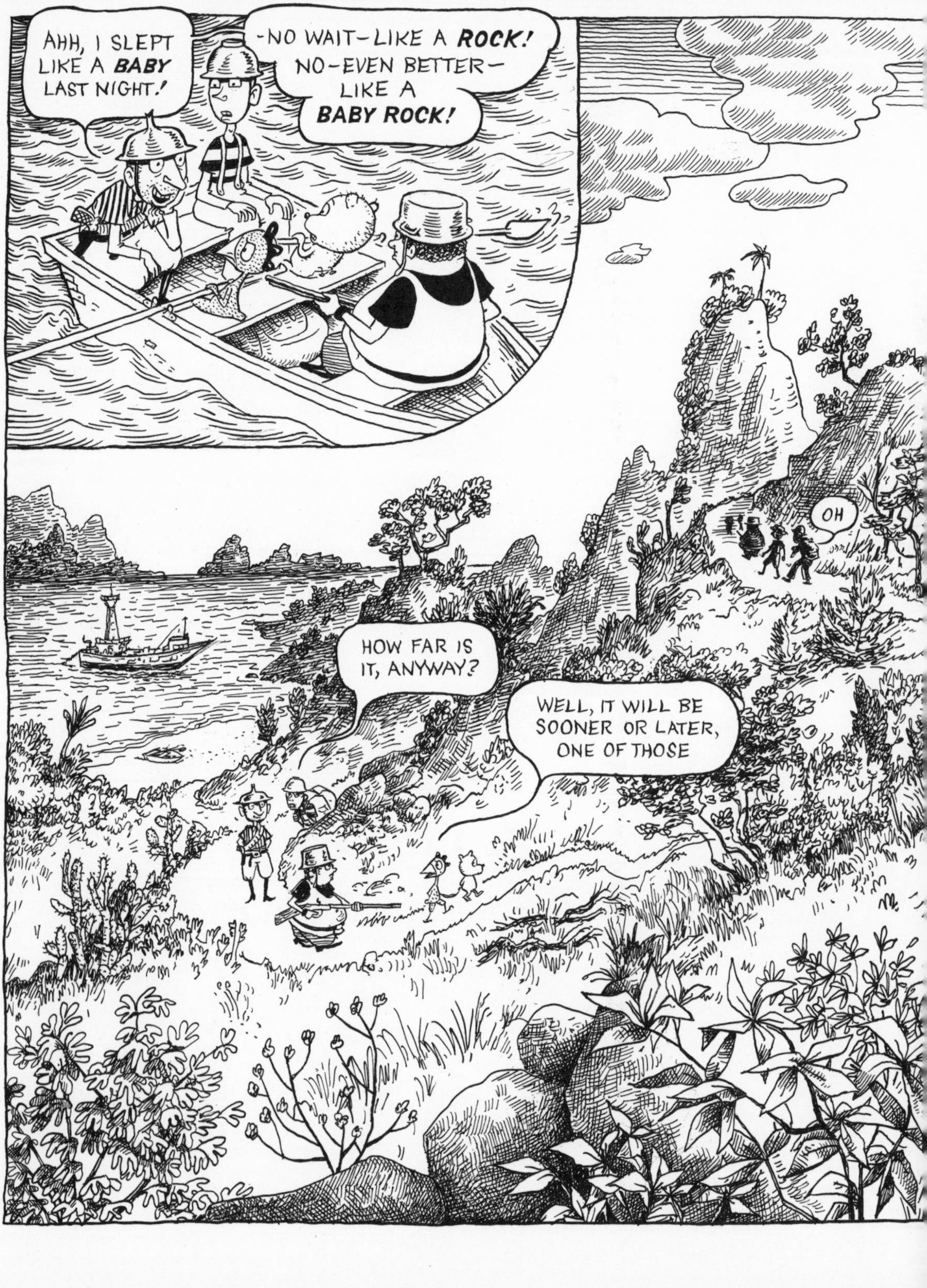
AHH, I SLEPT LIKE A **BABY** LAST NIGHT!
-NO WAIT-LIKE A **ROCK!** NO-EVEN BETTER-LIKE A **BABY ROCK!**
OH
HOW FAR IS IT, ANYWAY?
WELL, IT WILL BE SOONER OR LATER, ONE OF THOSE

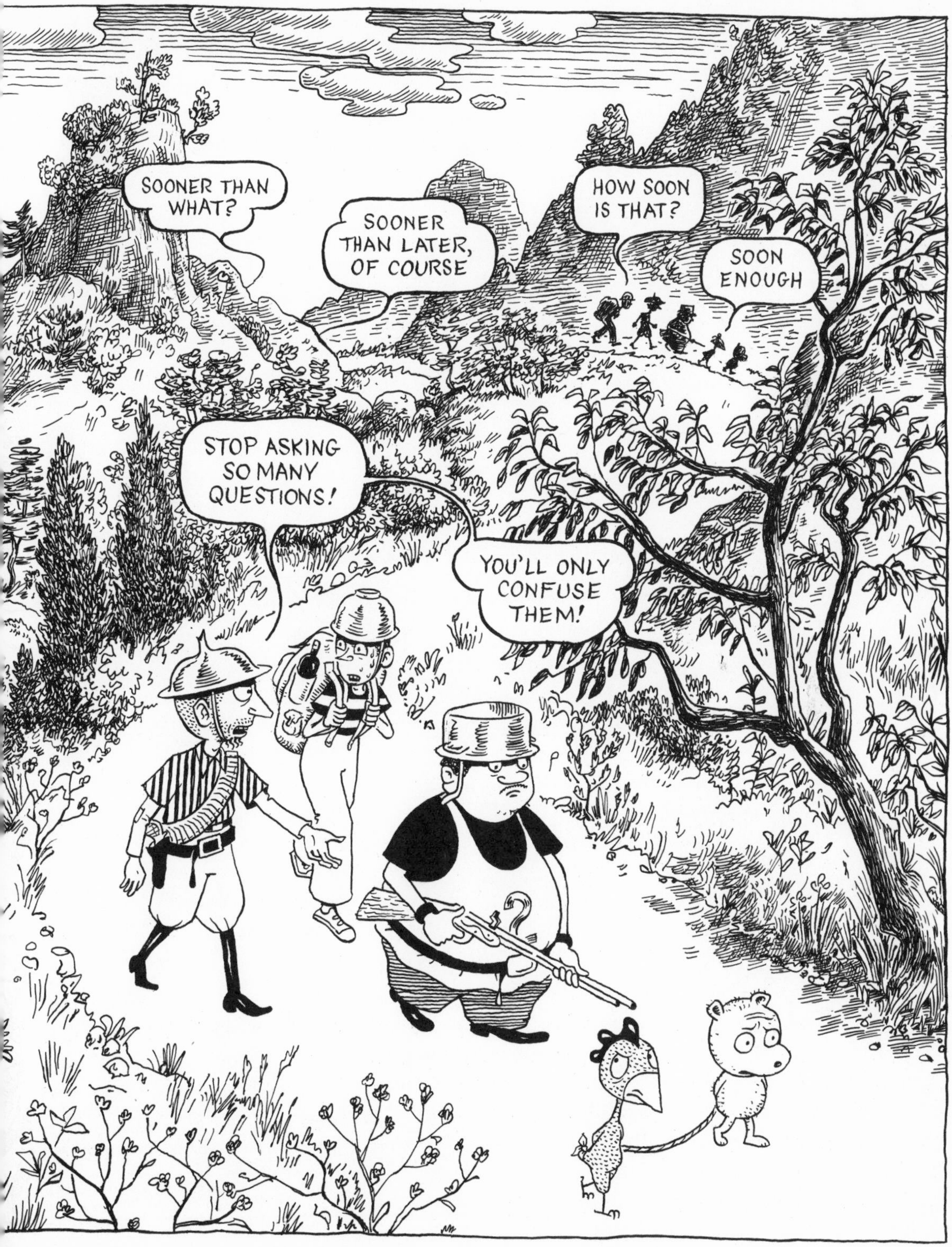

HOW SOON IS THAT?
SOON ENOUGH
SOONER THAN WHAT?
SOONER THAN LATER, OF COURSE
STOP ASKING SO MANY QUESTIONS!
YOU'LL ONLY CONFUSE THEM!

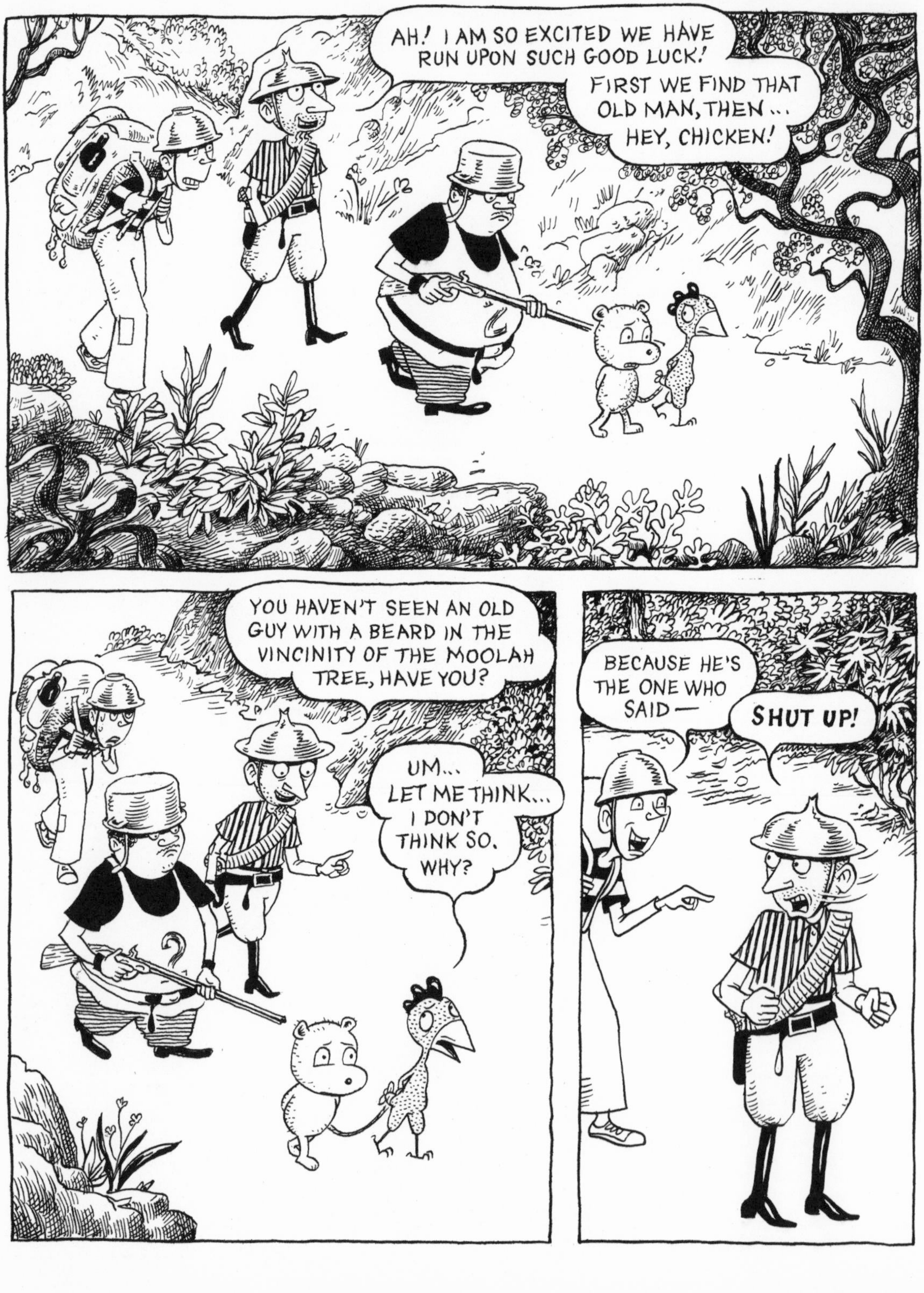
AH! I AM SO EXCITED WE HAVE RUN UPON SUCH GOOD LUCK!
FIRST WE FIND THAT OLD MAN, THEN ... HEY, CHICKEN!
YOU HAVEN'T SEEN AN OLD GUY WITH A BEARD IN THE VINCINITY OF THE MOOLAH TREE, HAVE YOU?
UM... LET ME THINK... I DON'T THINK SO. WHY?
BECAUSE HE'S THE ONE WHO SAID —
SHUT UP!

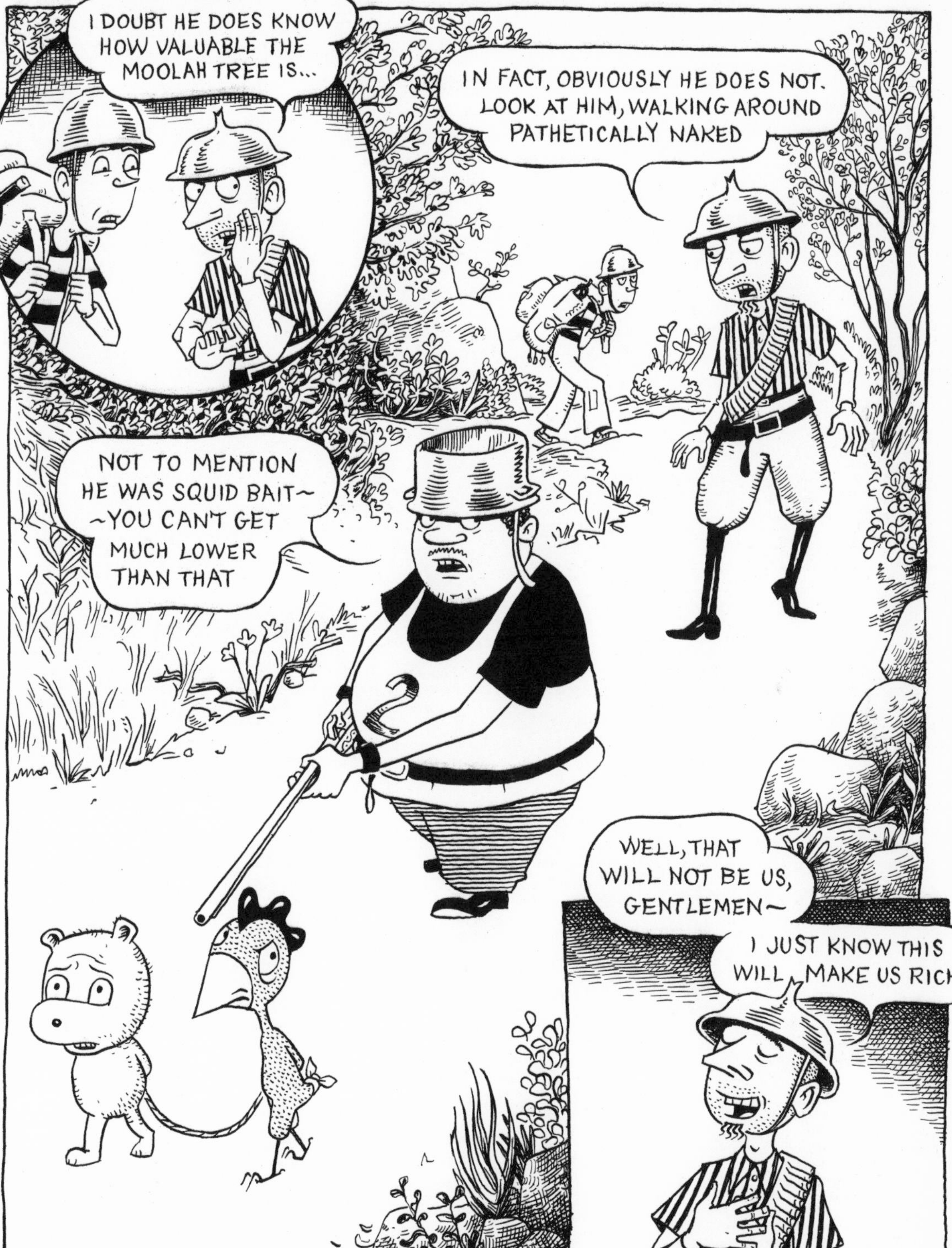
I DOUBT HE DOES KNOW HOW VALUABLE THE MOOLAH TREE IS...
IN FACT, OBVIOUSLY HE DOES NOT. LOOK AT HIM, WALKING AROUND PATHETICALLY NAKED
NOT TO MENTION HE WAS SQUID BAIT~ ~YOU CAN'T GET MUCH LOWER THAN THAT
WELL, THAT WILL NOT BE US, GENTLEMEN~
I JUST KNOW THIS WILL MAKE US RICH

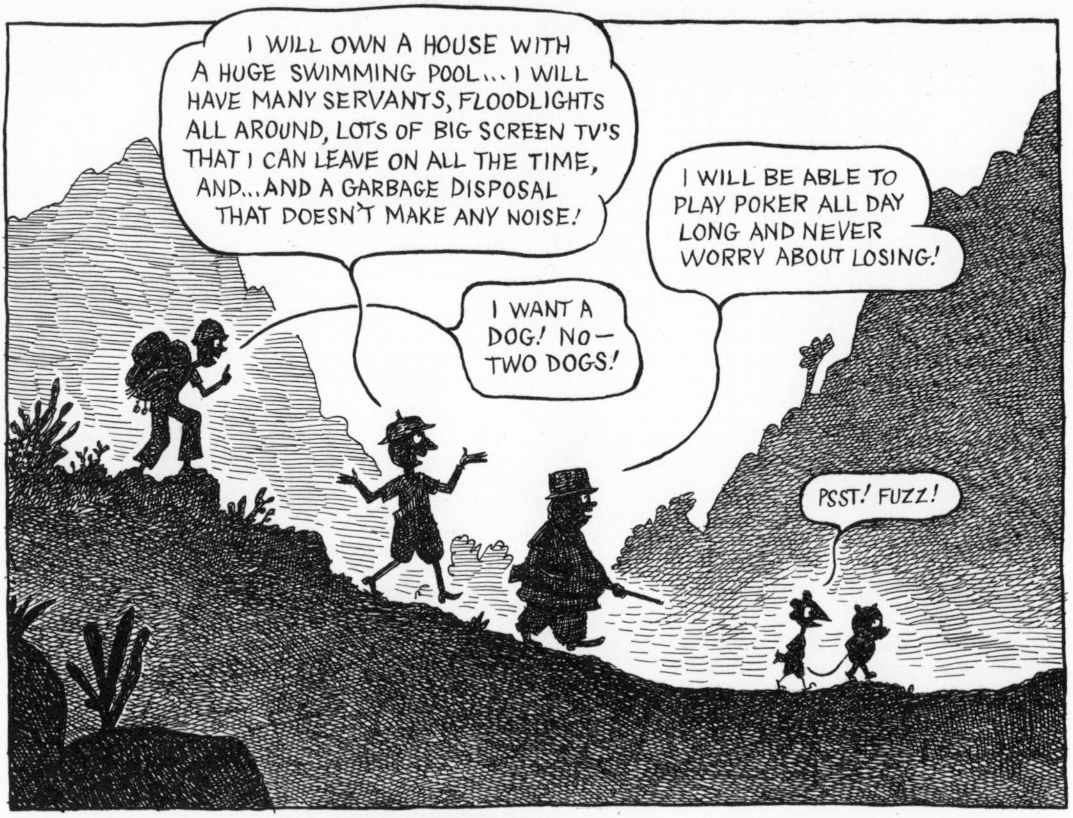
I WILL OWN A HOUSE WITH A HUGE SWIMMING POOL... I WILL HAVE MANY SERVANTS, FLOODLIGHTS ALL AROUND, LOTS OF BIG SCREEN TV'S THAT I CAN LEAVE ON ALL THE TIME, AND...AND A GARBAGE DISPOSAL THAT DOESN'T MAKE ANY NOISE!
I WANT A DOG! NO— TWO DOGS!
I WILL BE ABLE TO PLAY POKER ALL DAY LONG AND NEVER WORRY ABOUT LOSING!
PSST! FUZZ!
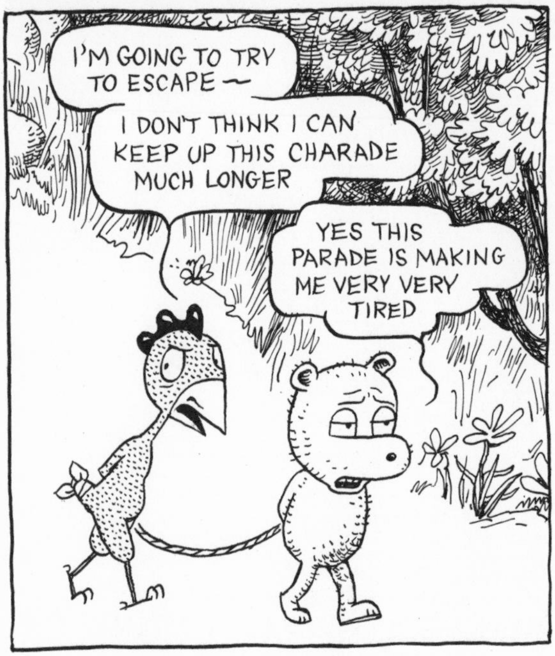
I'M GOING TO TRY TO ESCAPE—
I DON'T THINK I CAN KEEP UP THIS CHARADE MUCH LONGER
YES THIS PARADE IS MAKING ME VERY VERY TIRED
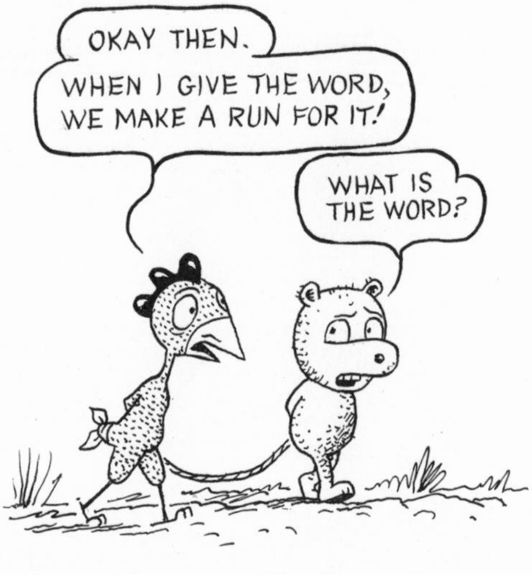
OKAY THEN.
WHEN I GIVE THE WORD, WE MAKE A RUN FOR IT!
WHAT IS THE WORD?

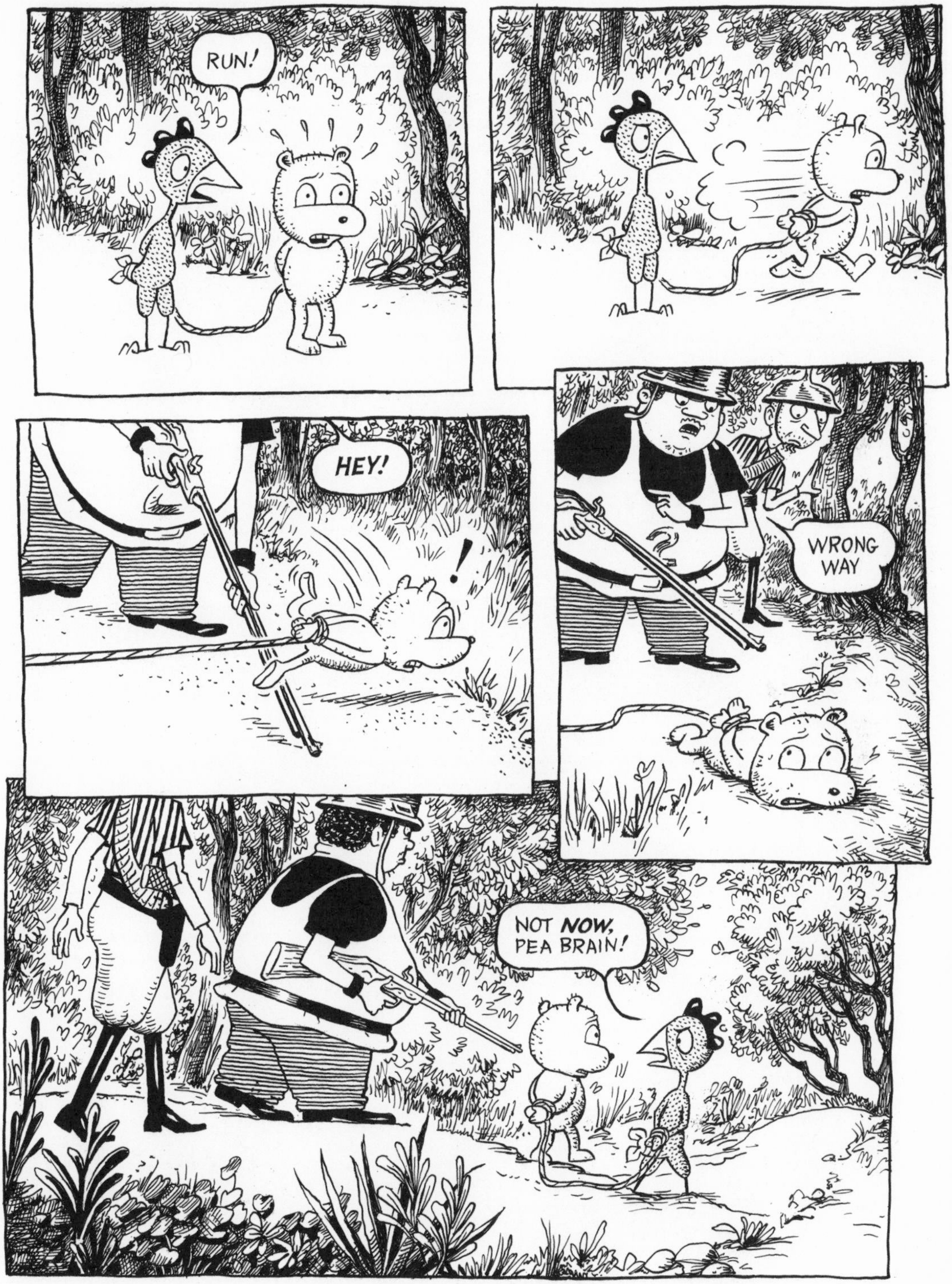
RUN!
HEY!
WRONG WAY
NOT NOW, PEA BRAIN!

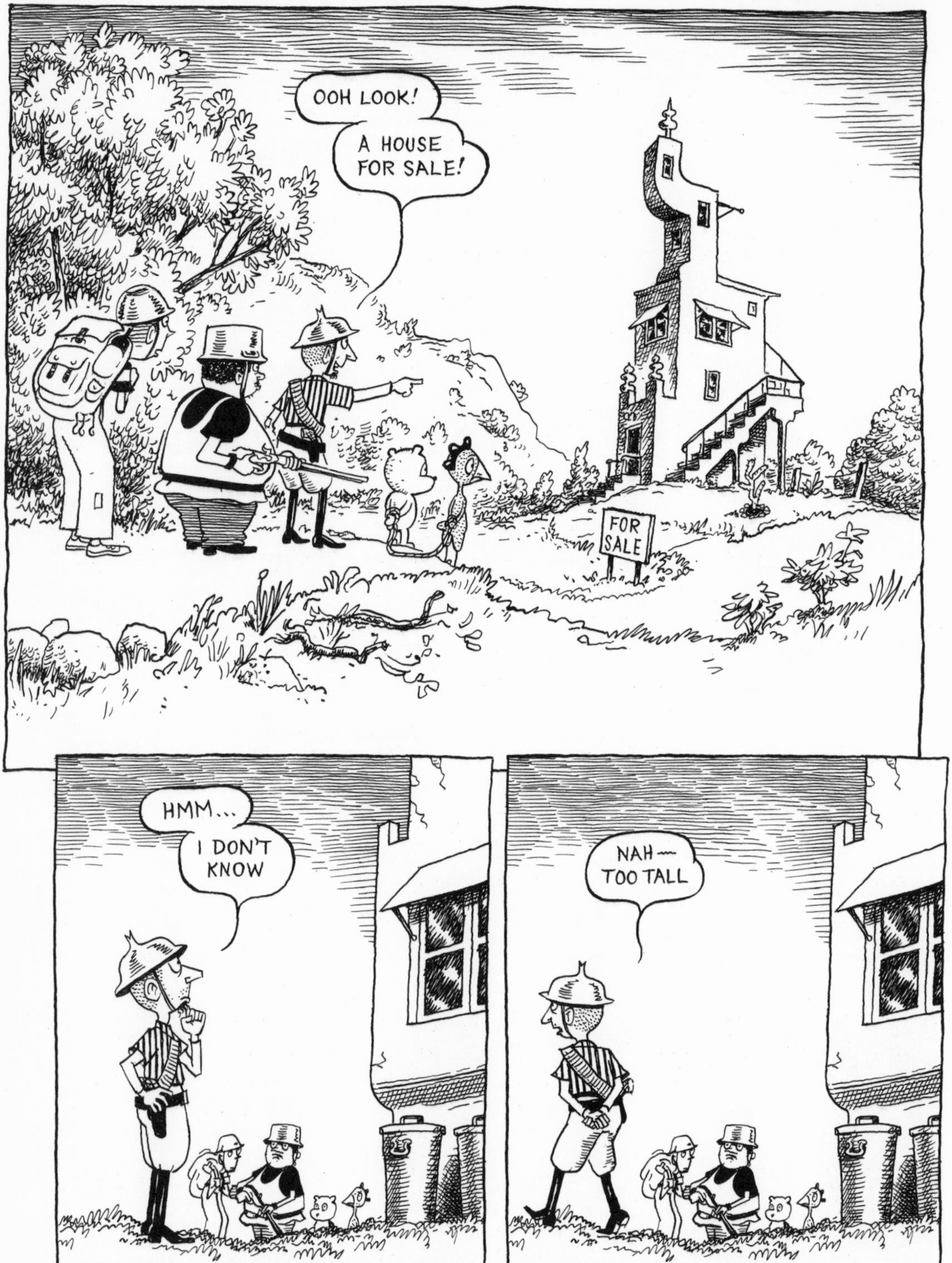
OOH LOOK!
A HOUSE FOR SALE!
FOR SALE
HMM...
I DON'T KNOW
NAH— TOO TALL

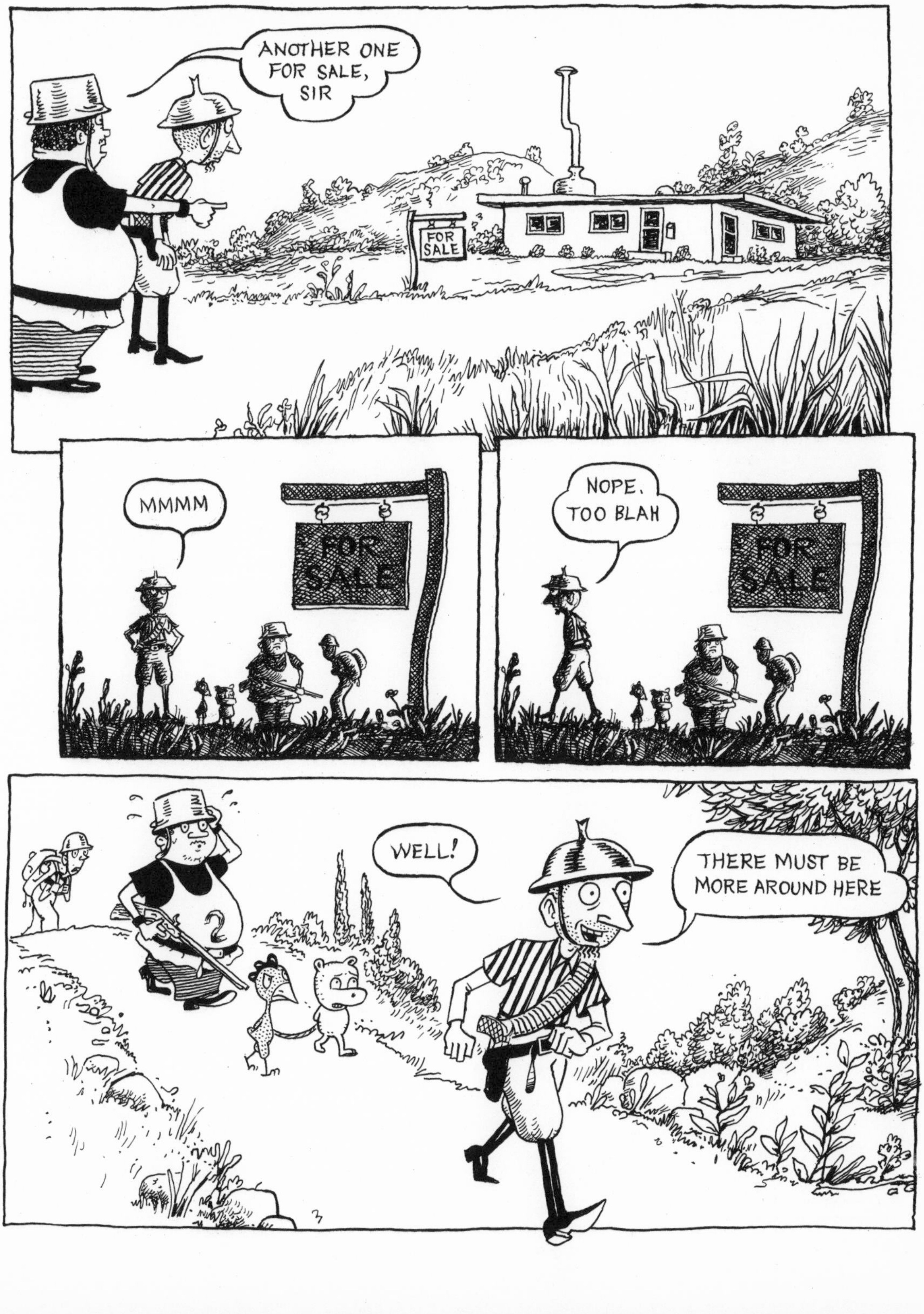
ANOTHER ONE FOR SALE, SIR
FOR SALE
MMMM
FOR SALE
NOPE. TOO BLAH
FOR SALE
WELL!
THERE MUST BE MORE AROUND HERE

AAH!
COUGH COUGH
SCOUNDRELS! YOU CAN'T TREAT US THAT WAY!

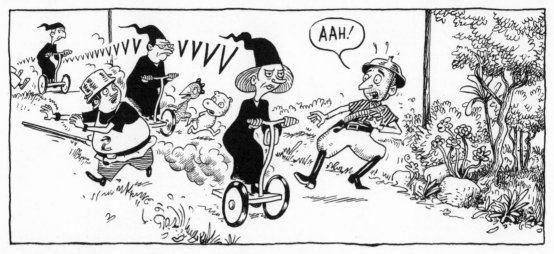

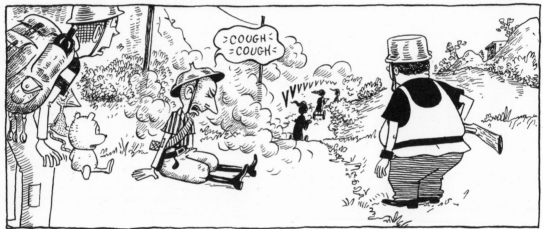

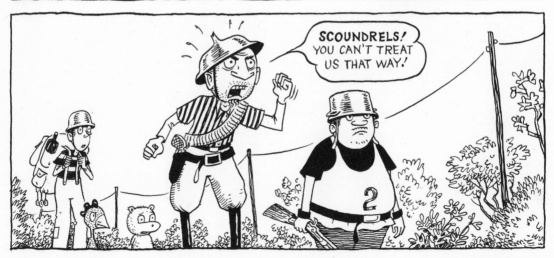

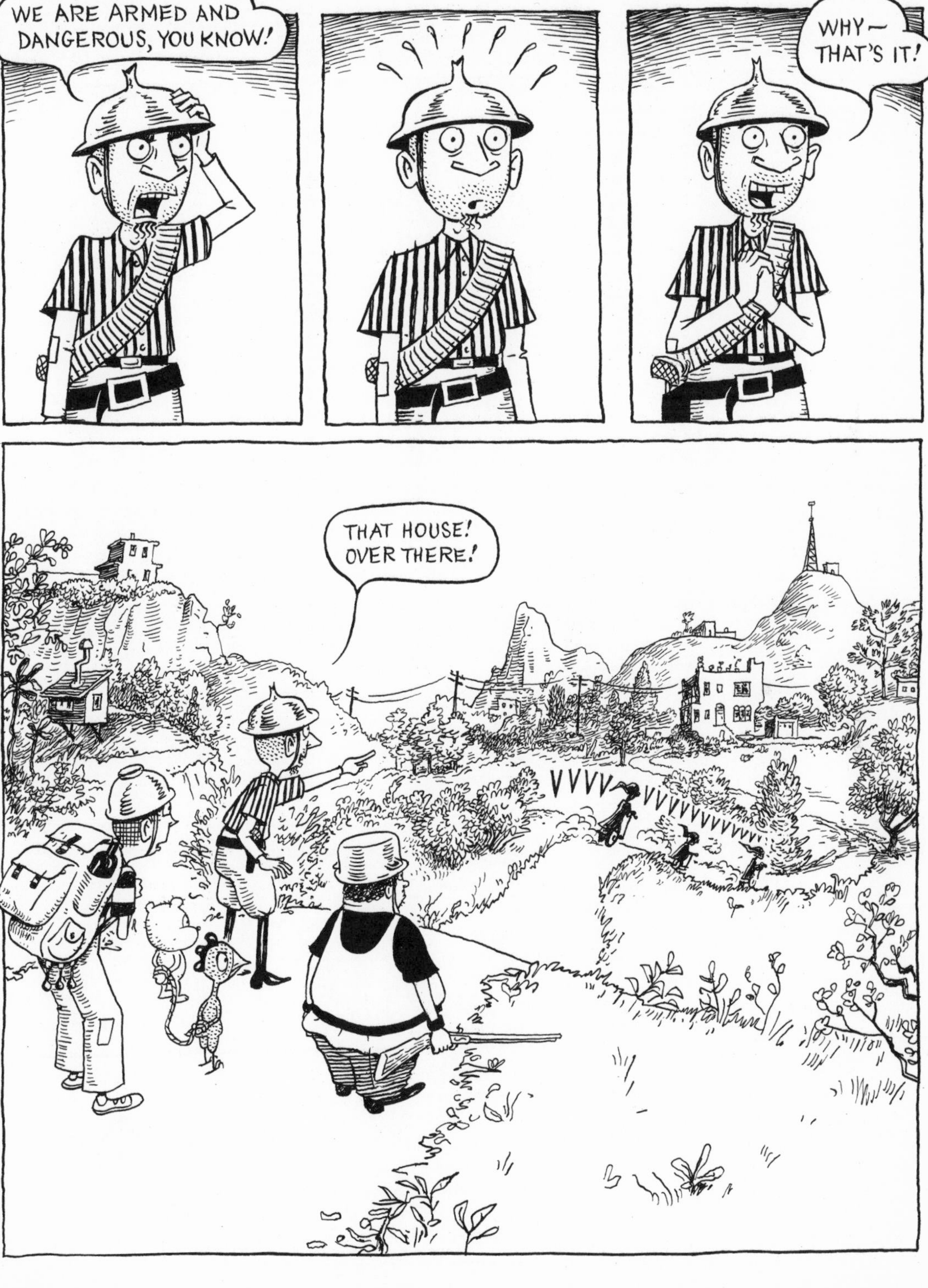
WE ARE ARMED AND DANGEROUS, YOU KNOW!
WHY— THAT'S IT!
THAT HOUSE! OVER THERE!

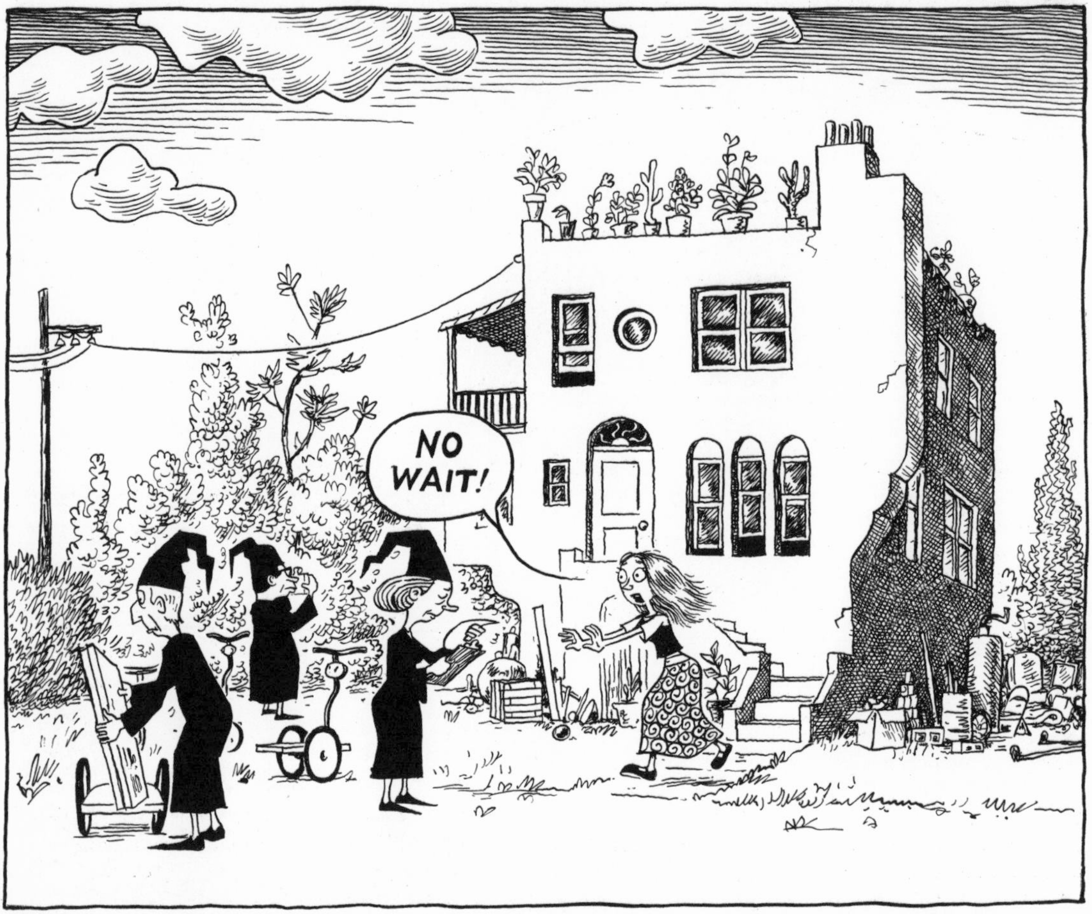
NO WAIT!

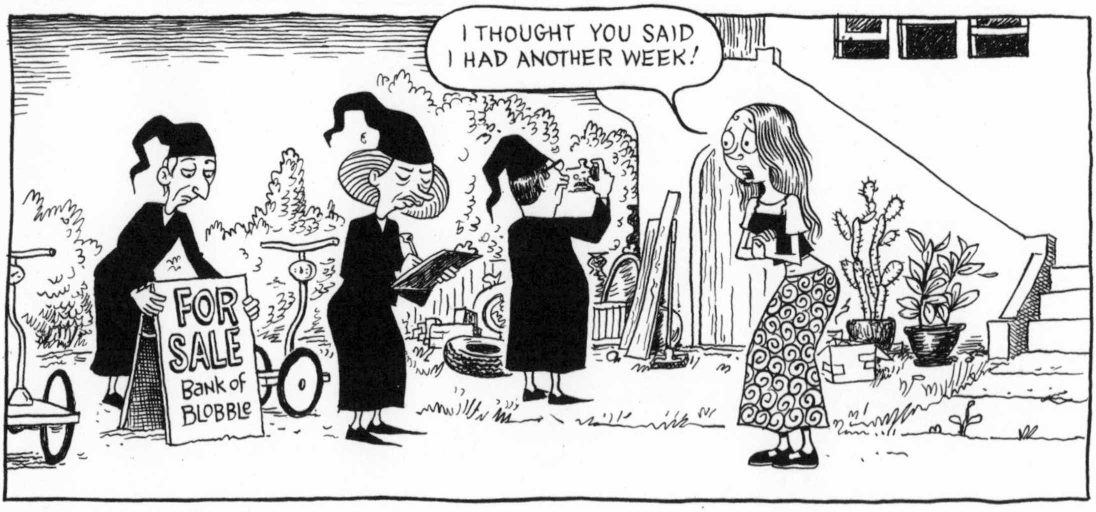
I THOUGHT YOU SAID
I HAD ANOTHER WEEK!
FOR SALE
Bank of
BLOBBLE

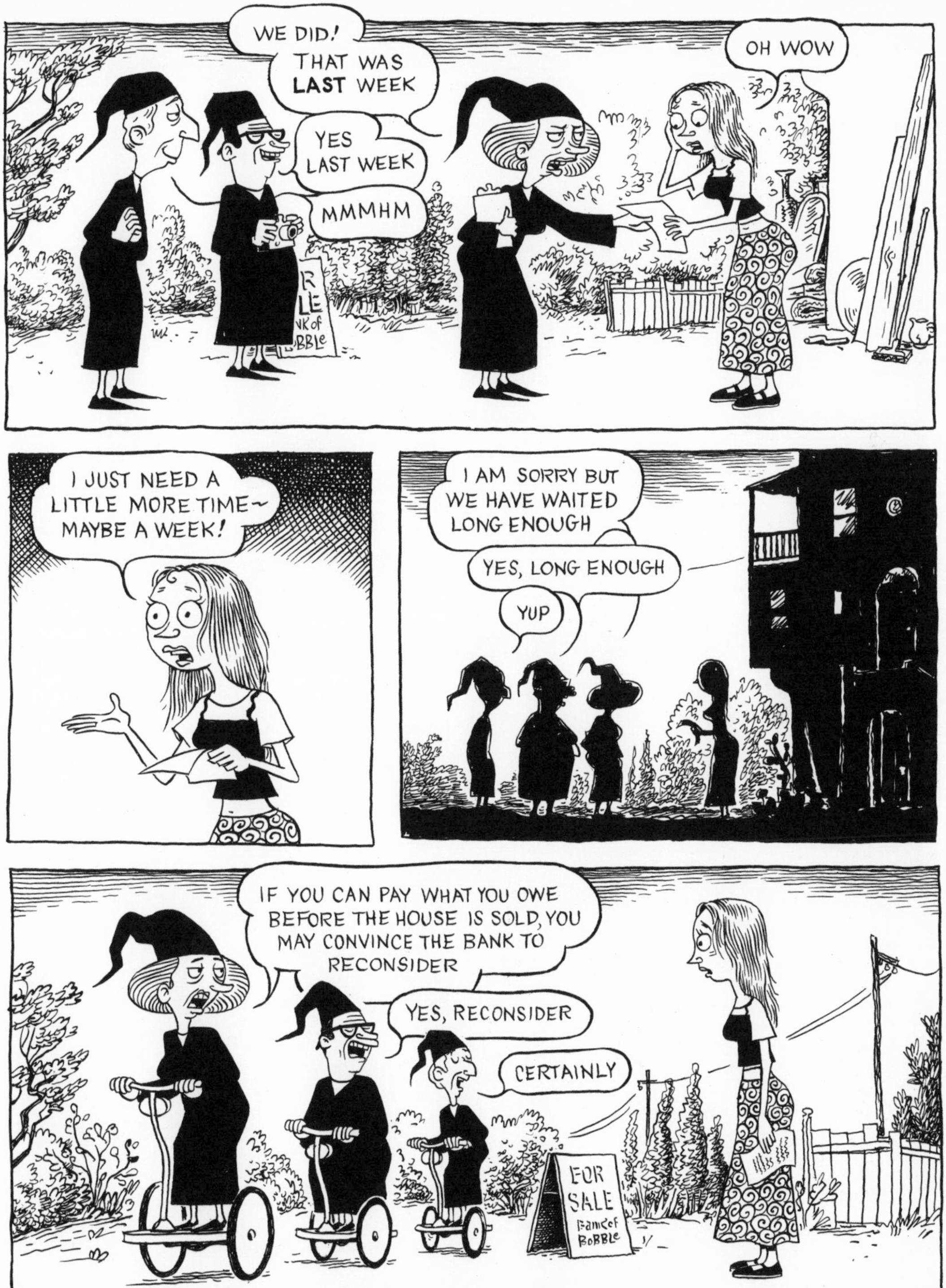
WE DID! THAT WAS LAST WEEK
YES LAST WEEK
MMMHM
OH WOW
I JUST NEED A LITTLE MORE TIME~ MAYBE A WEEK!
I AM SORRY BUT WE HAVE WAITED LONG ENOUGH
YES, LONG ENOUGH
YUP
IF YOU CAN PAY WHAT YOU OWE BEFORE THE HOUSE IS SOLD, YOU MAY CONVINCE THE BANK TO RECONSIDER
YES, RECONSIDER
CERTAINLY
FOR SALE
BANK of BOBBLE

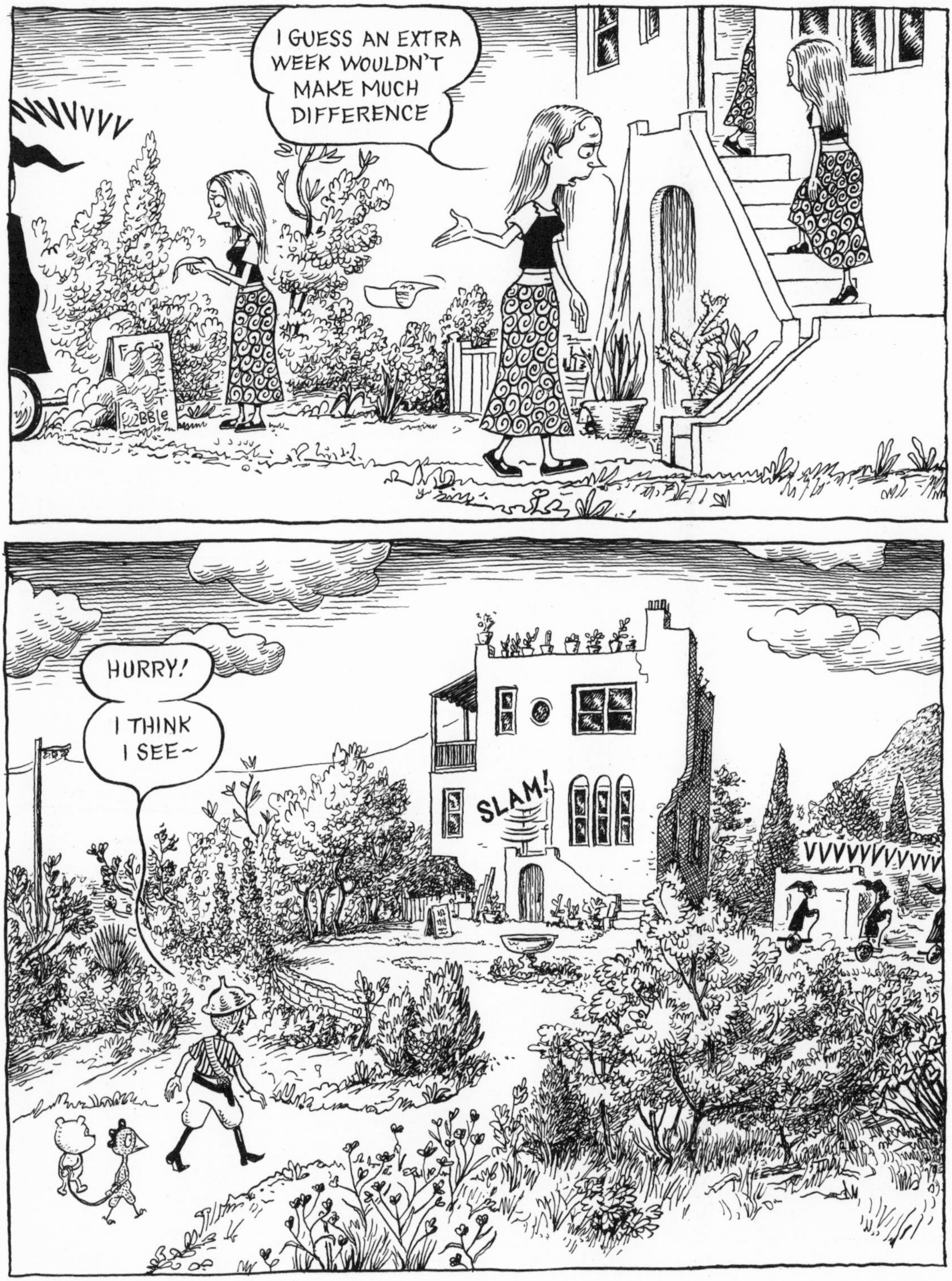
I GUESS AN EXTRA WEEK WOULDN'T MAKE MUCH DIFFERENCE
HURRY!
I THINK I SEE~
SLAM!

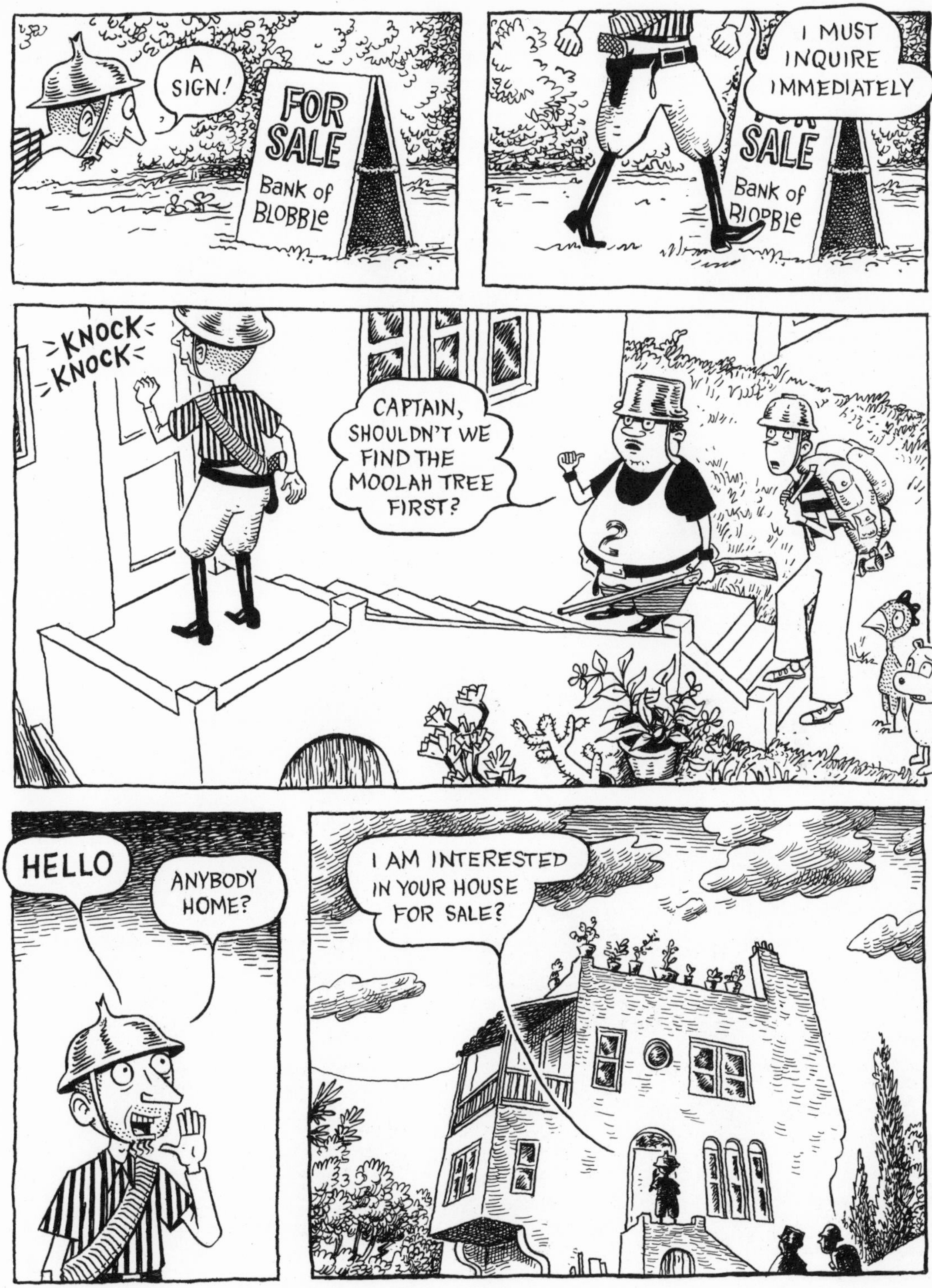
A SIGN!
FOR SALE
Bank of BLOBBLE
I MUST INQUIRE IMMEDIATELY
SALE
Bank of BLOBBLE
KNOCK KNOCK
CAPTAIN, SHOULDN'T WE FIND THE MOOLAH TREE FIRST?
HELLO
ANYBODY HOME?
I AM INTERESTED IN YOUR HOUSE FOR SALE?

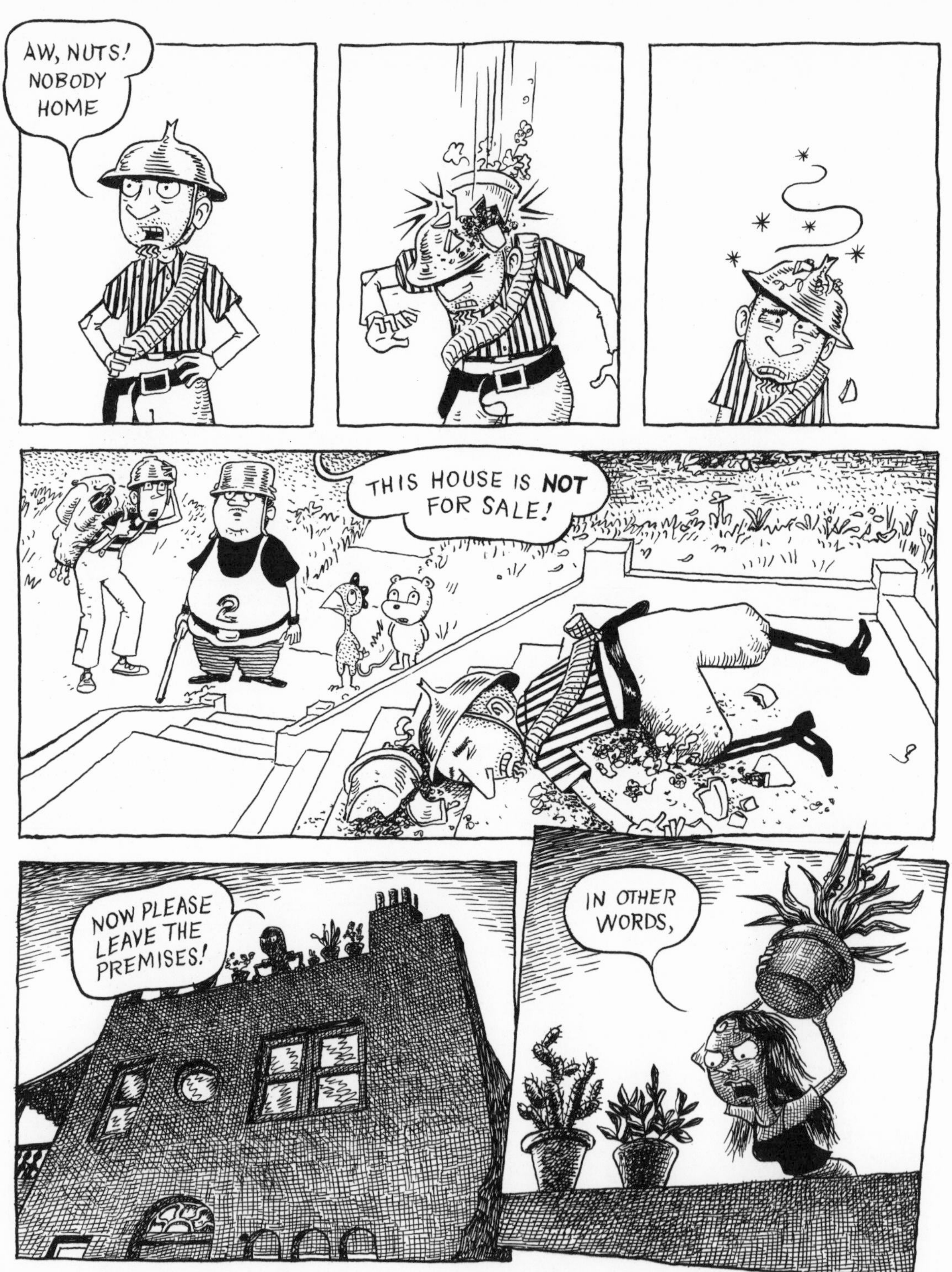
AW, NUTS! NOBODY HOME
THIS HOUSE IS **NOT** FOR SALE!
NOW PLEASE LEAVE THE PREMISES!
IN OTHER WORDS,

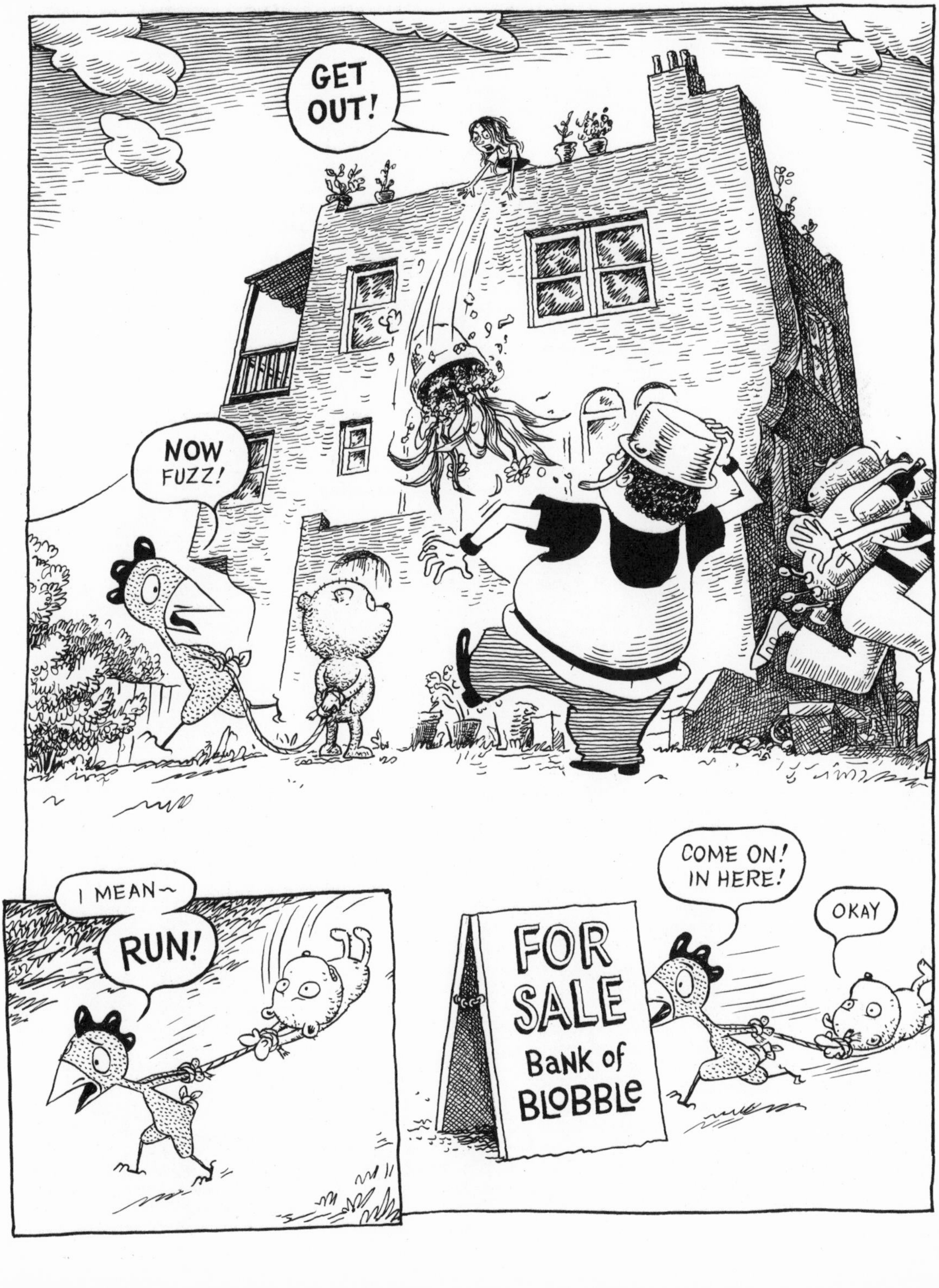
GET OUT!
NOW FUZZ!
I MEAN~
RUN!
FOR SALE Bank of BLOBBLE
COME ON! IN HERE!
OKAY

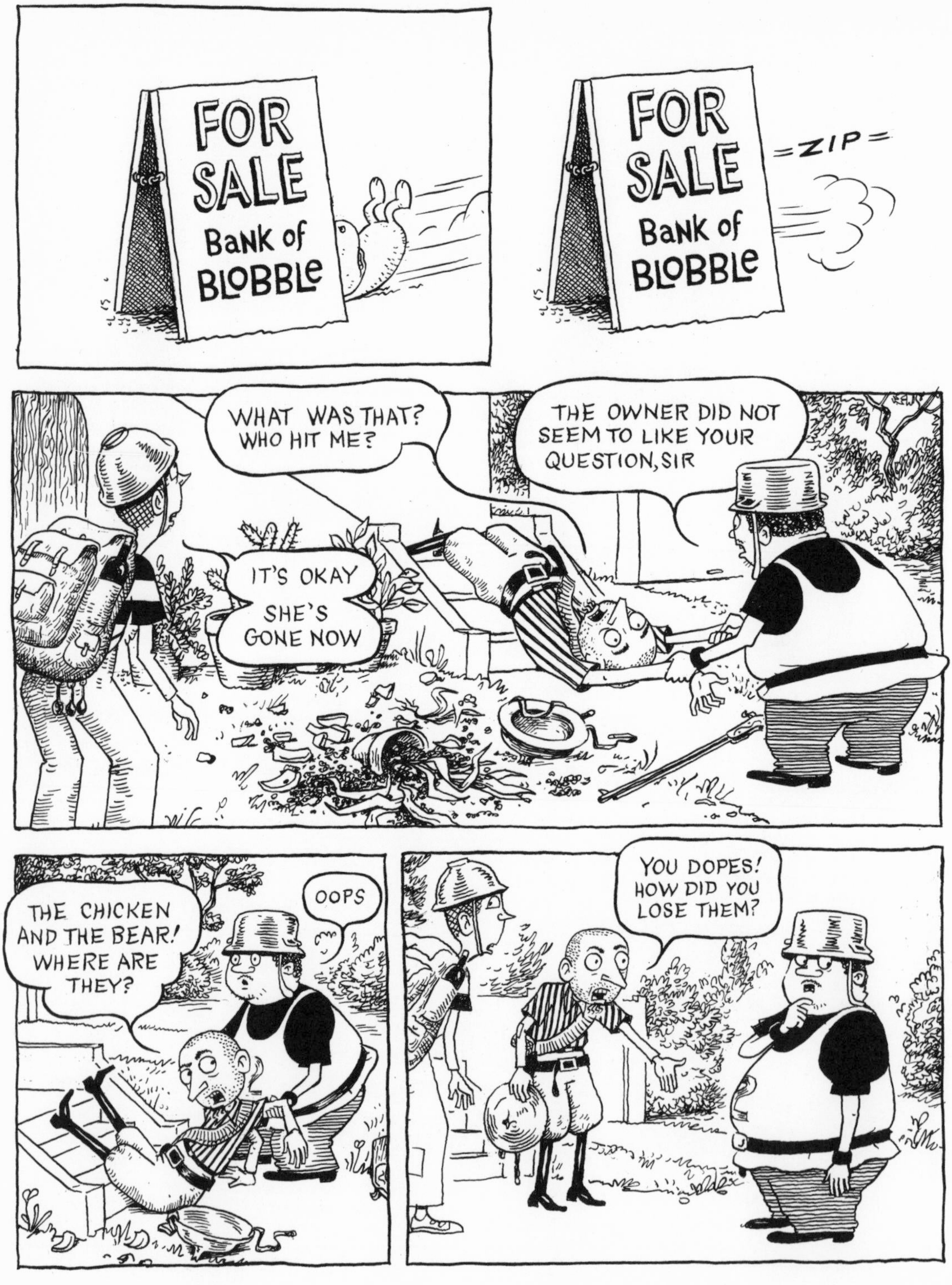
FOR SALE Bank of BLOBBLE
FOR SALE Bank of BLOBBLE
=ZIP=
WHAT WAS THAT? WHO HIT ME?
THE OWNER DID NOT SEEM TO LIKE YOUR QUESTION, SIR
IT'S OKAY SHE'S GONE NOW
THE CHICKEN AND THE BEAR! WHERE ARE THEY?
OOPS
YOU DOPES! HOW DID YOU LOSE THEM?

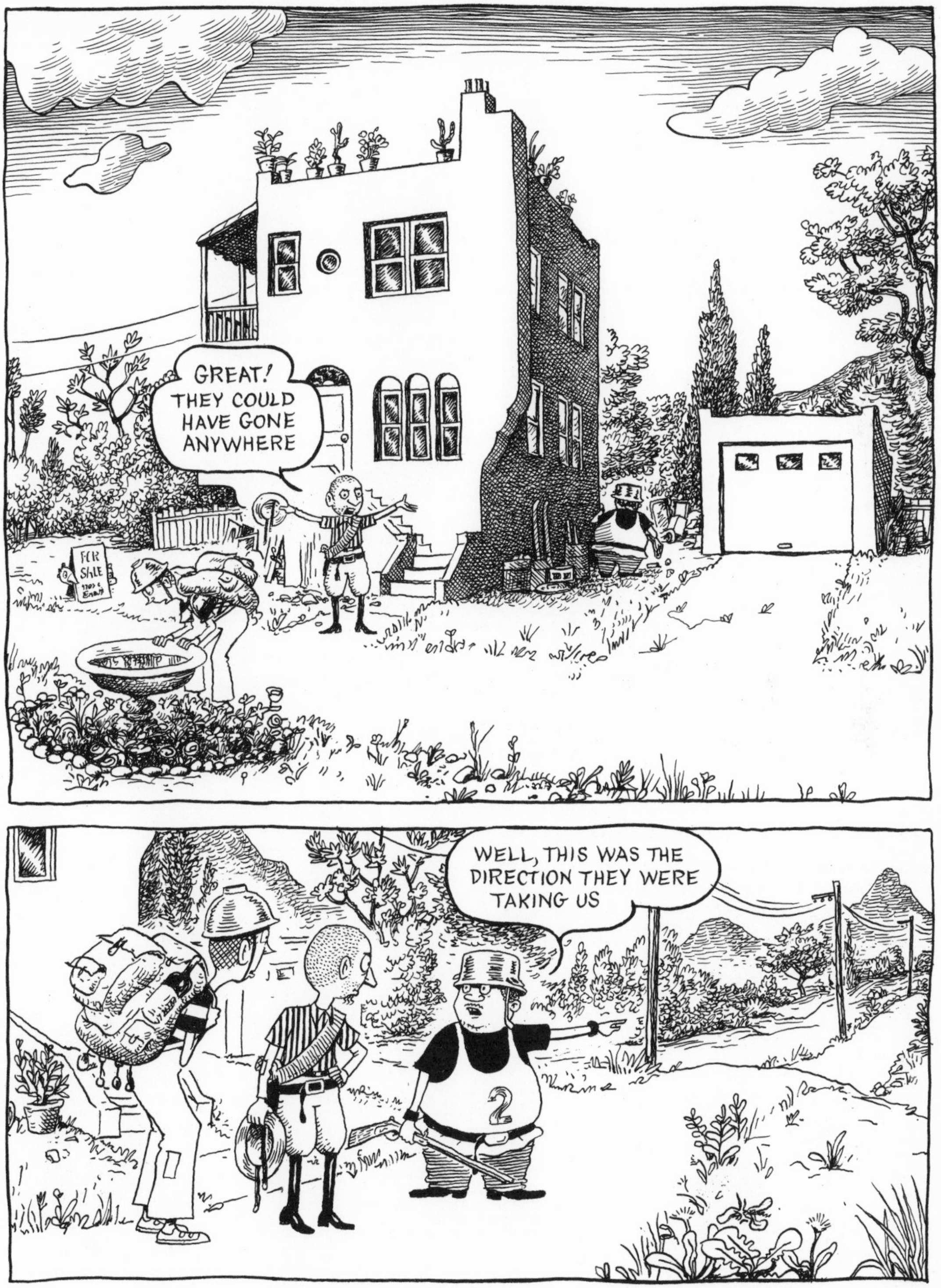
GREAT! THEY COULD HAVE GONE ANYWHERE
FOR SALE
WELL, THIS WAS THE DIRECTION THEY WERE TAKING US

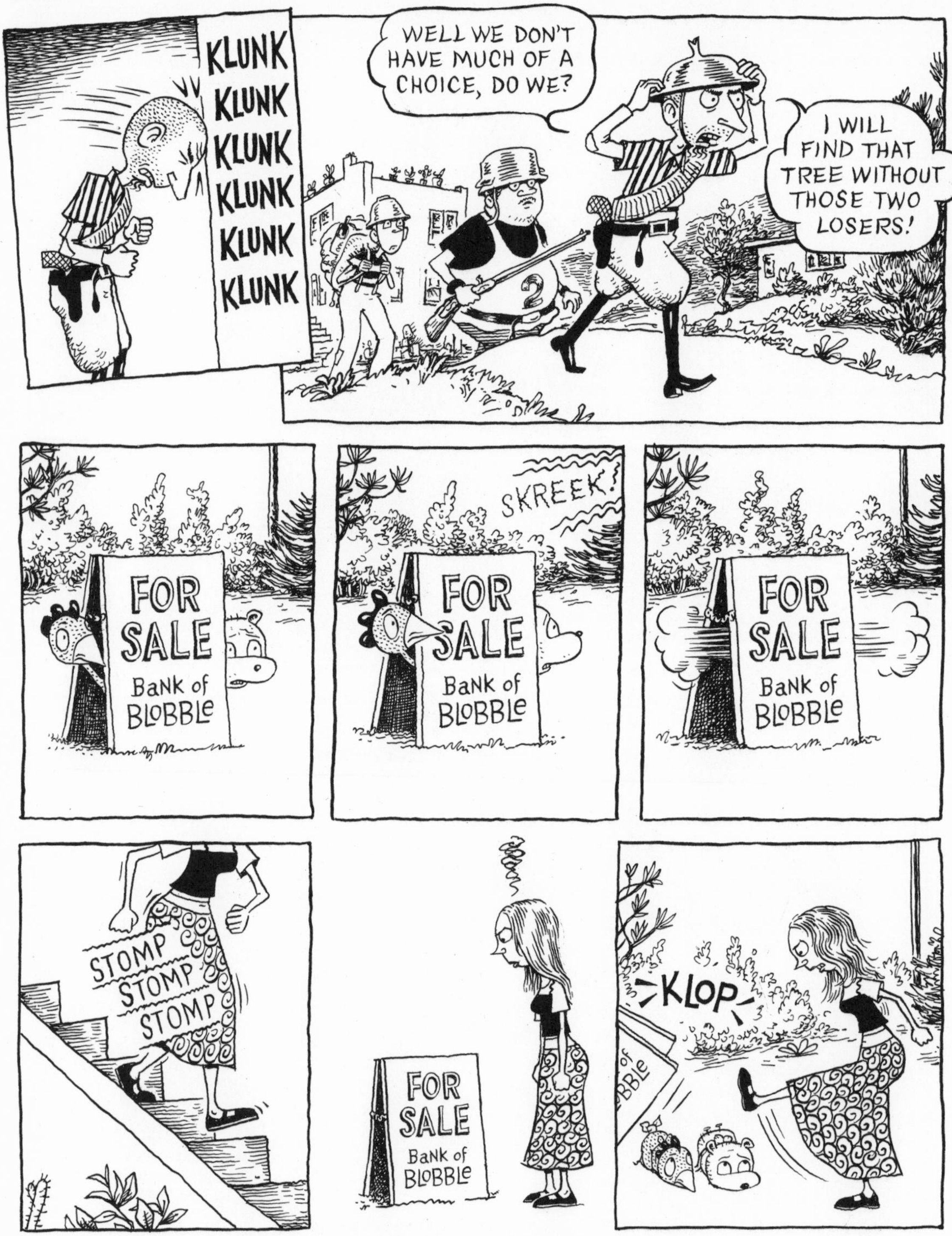
KLUNK
KLUNK
KLUNK
KLUNK
KLUNK
KLUNK
WELL WE DON'T HAVE MUCH OF A CHOICE, DO WE?
I WILL FIND THAT TREE WITHOUT THOSE TWO LOSERS!
FOR SALE
Bank of BLOBBLE
SKREEK!
FOR SALE
Bank of BLOBBLE
FOR SALE
Bank of BLOBBLE
STOMP
STOMP
STOMP
FOR SALE
Bank of BLOBBLE
KLOP

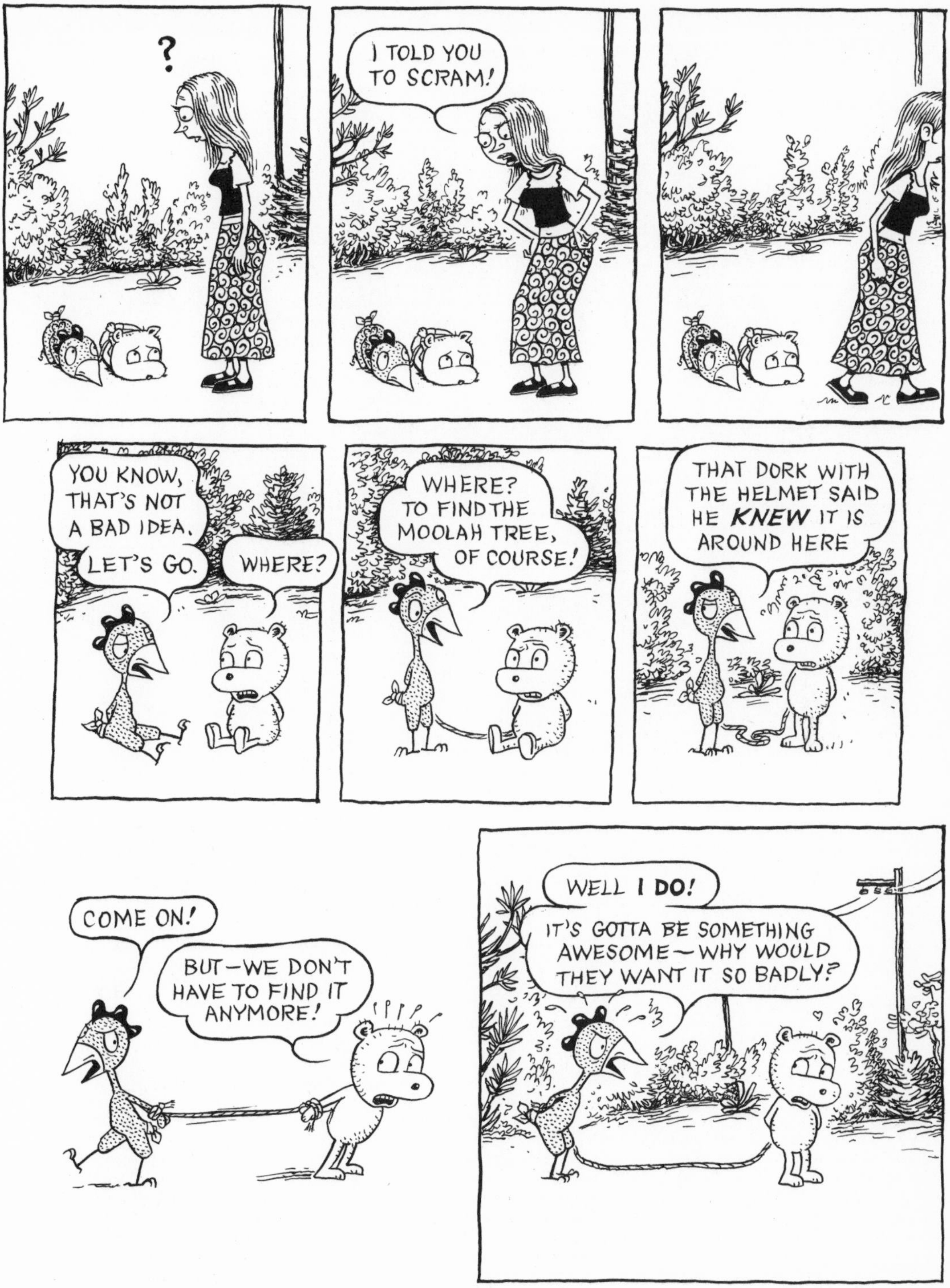
?
I TOLD YOU TO SCRAM!
YOU KNOW, THAT'S NOT A BAD IDEA.
LET'S GO.
WHERE?
WHERE? TO FIND THE MOOLAH TREE, OF COURSE!
THAT DORK WITH THE HELMET SAID HE **KNEW** IT IS AROUND HERE
COME ON!
BUT—WE DON'T HAVE TO FIND IT ANYMORE!
WELL **I DO!**
IT'S GOTTA BE SOMETHING AWESOME—WHY WOULD THEY WANT IT SO BADLY?

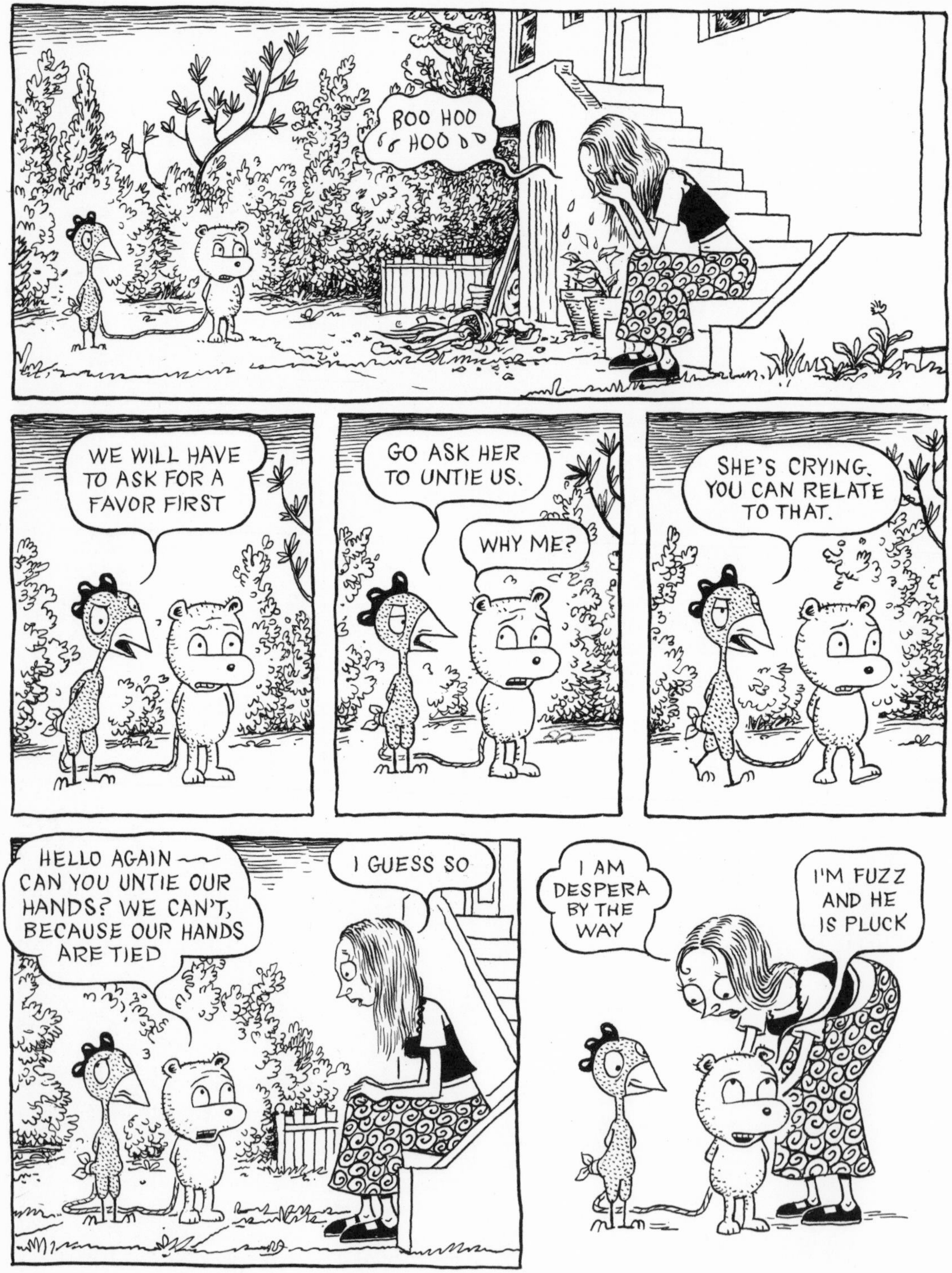
BOO HOO HOO
WE WILL HAVE TO ASK FOR A FAVOR FIRST
GO ASK HER TO UNTIE US.
WHY ME?
SHE'S CRYING. YOU CAN RELATE TO THAT.
HELLO AGAIN — CAN YOU UNTIE OUR HANDS? WE CAN'T, BECAUSE OUR HANDS ARE TIED
I GUESS SO
I AM DESPERA BY THE WAY
I'M FUZZ AND HE IS PLUCK

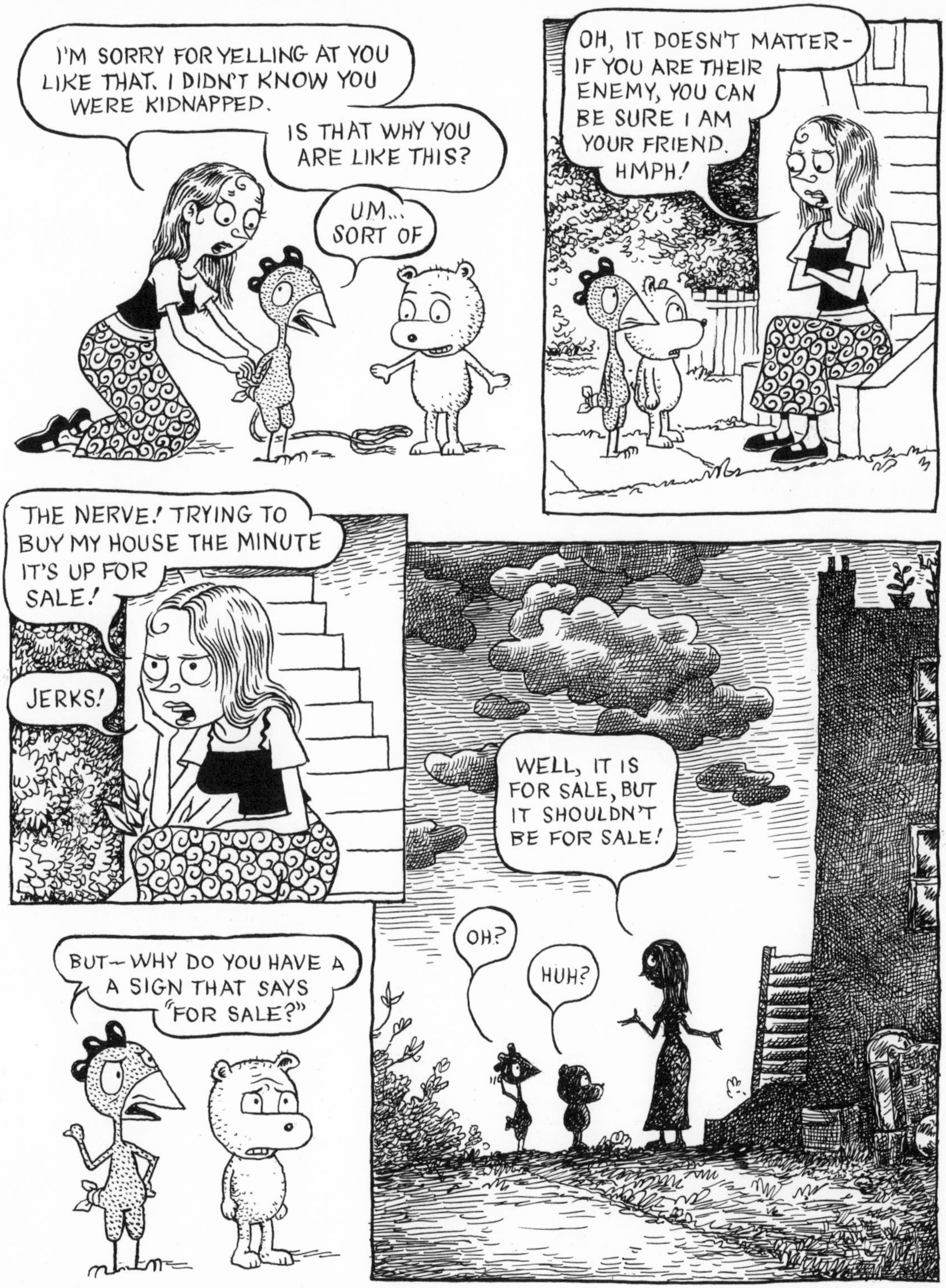
I'M SORRY FOR YELLING AT YOU LIKE THAT. I DIDN'T KNOW YOU WERE KIDNAPPED.
IS THAT WHY YOU ARE LIKE THIS?
UM... SORT OF
OH, IT DOESN'T MATTER- IF YOU ARE THEIR ENEMY, YOU CAN BE SURE I AM YOUR FRIEND.
HMPH!
THE NERVE! TRYING TO BUY MY HOUSE THE MINUTE IT'S UP FOR SALE!
JERKS!
BUT-- WHY DO YOU HAVE A A SIGN THAT SAYS "FOR SALE?"
WELL, IT IS FOR SALE, BUT IT SHOULDN'T BE FOR SALE!
OH?
HUH?

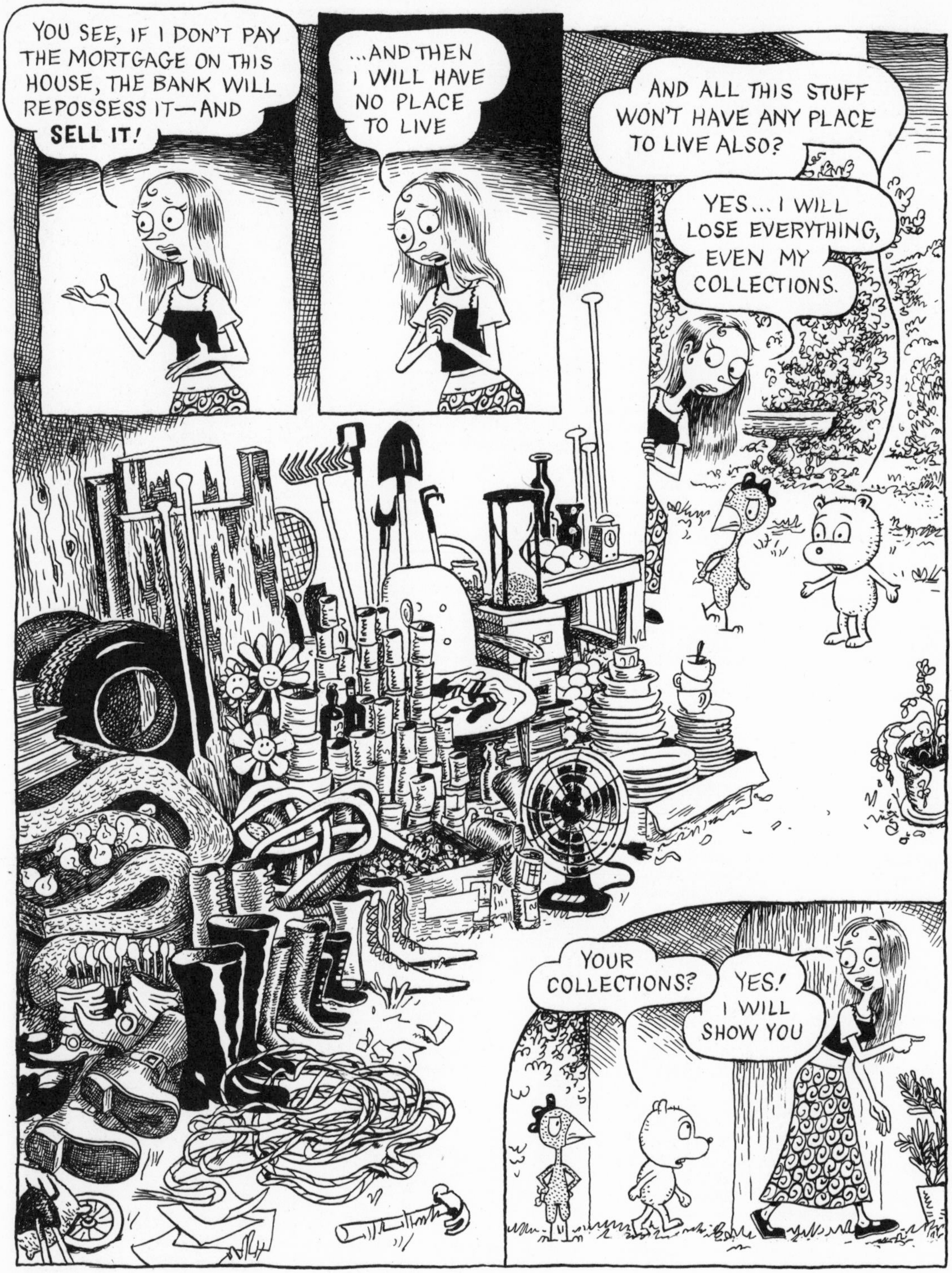

YOU SEE, IF I DON'T PAY THE MORTGAGE ON THIS HOUSE, THE BANK WILL REPOSSESS IT—AND SELL IT!
...AND THEN I WILL HAVE NO PLACE TO LIVE
AND ALL THIS STUFF WON'T HAVE ANY PLACE TO LIVE ALSO?
YES... I WILL LOSE EVERYTHING, EVEN MY COLLECTIONS.
YOUR COLLECTIONS?
YES! I WILL SHOW YOU

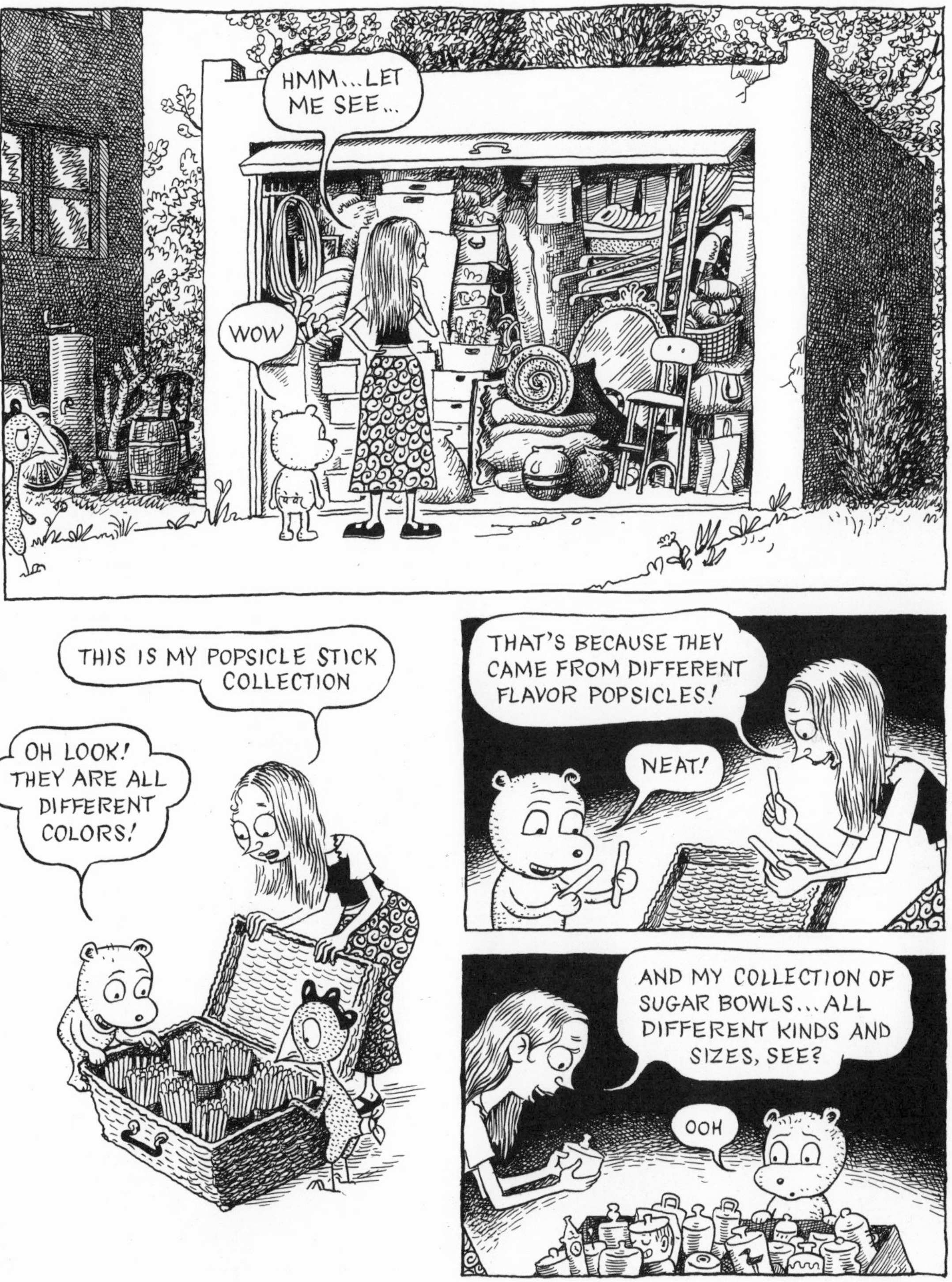

HMM...LET ME SEE...
WOW
THIS IS MY POPSICLE STICK COLLECTION
OH LOOK! THEY ARE ALL DIFFERENT COLORS!
THAT'S BECAUSE THEY CAME FROM DIFFERENT FLAVOR POPSICLES!
NEAT!
AND MY COLLECTION OF SUGAR BOWLS... ALL DIFFERENT KINDS AND SIZES, SEE?
OOH

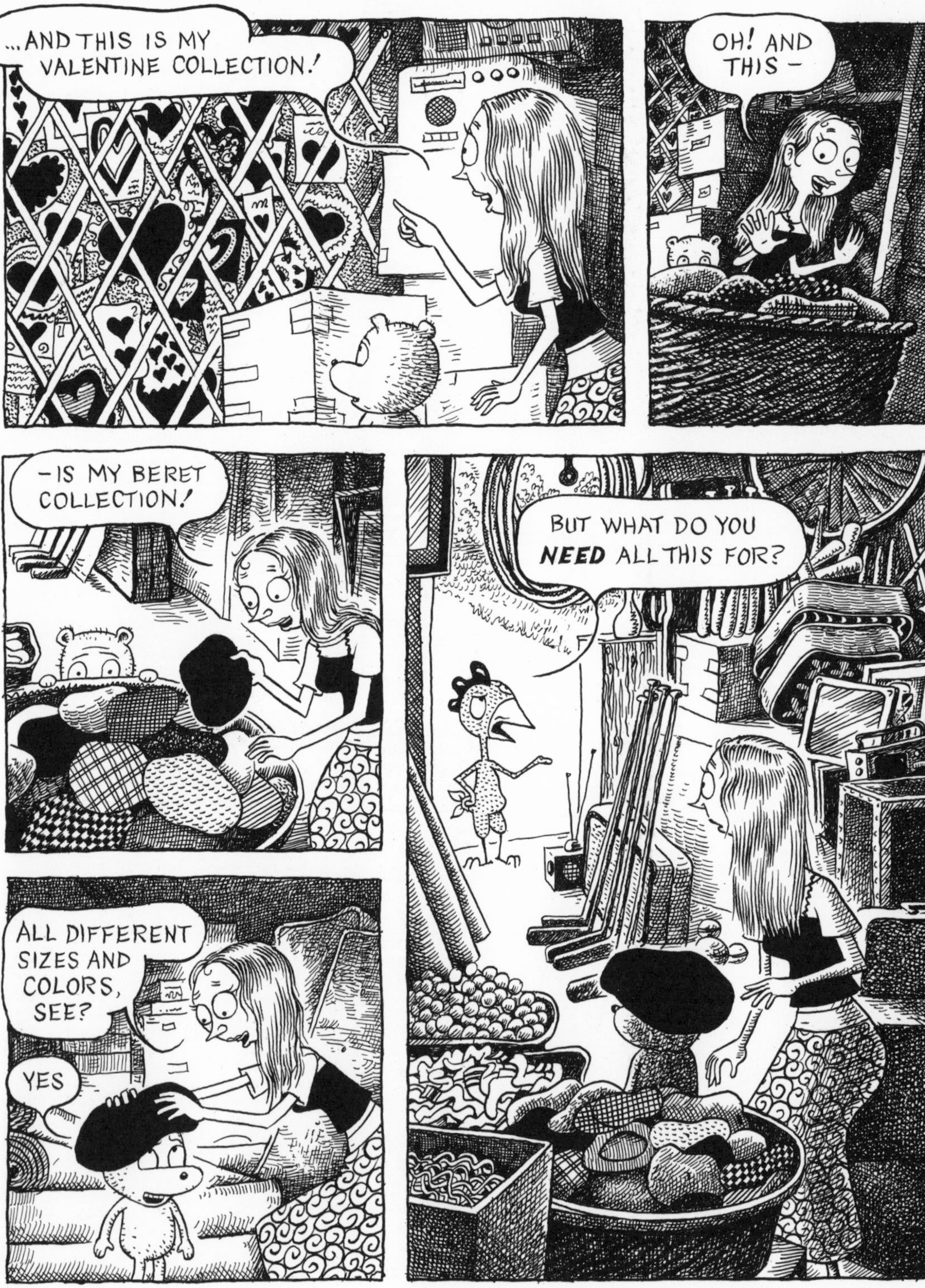
...AND THIS IS MY VALENTINE COLLECTION!
OH! AND THIS -
-IS MY BERET COLLECTION!
ALL DIFFERENT SIZES AND COLORS, SEE?
YES
BUT WHAT DO YOU **NEED** ALL THIS FOR?

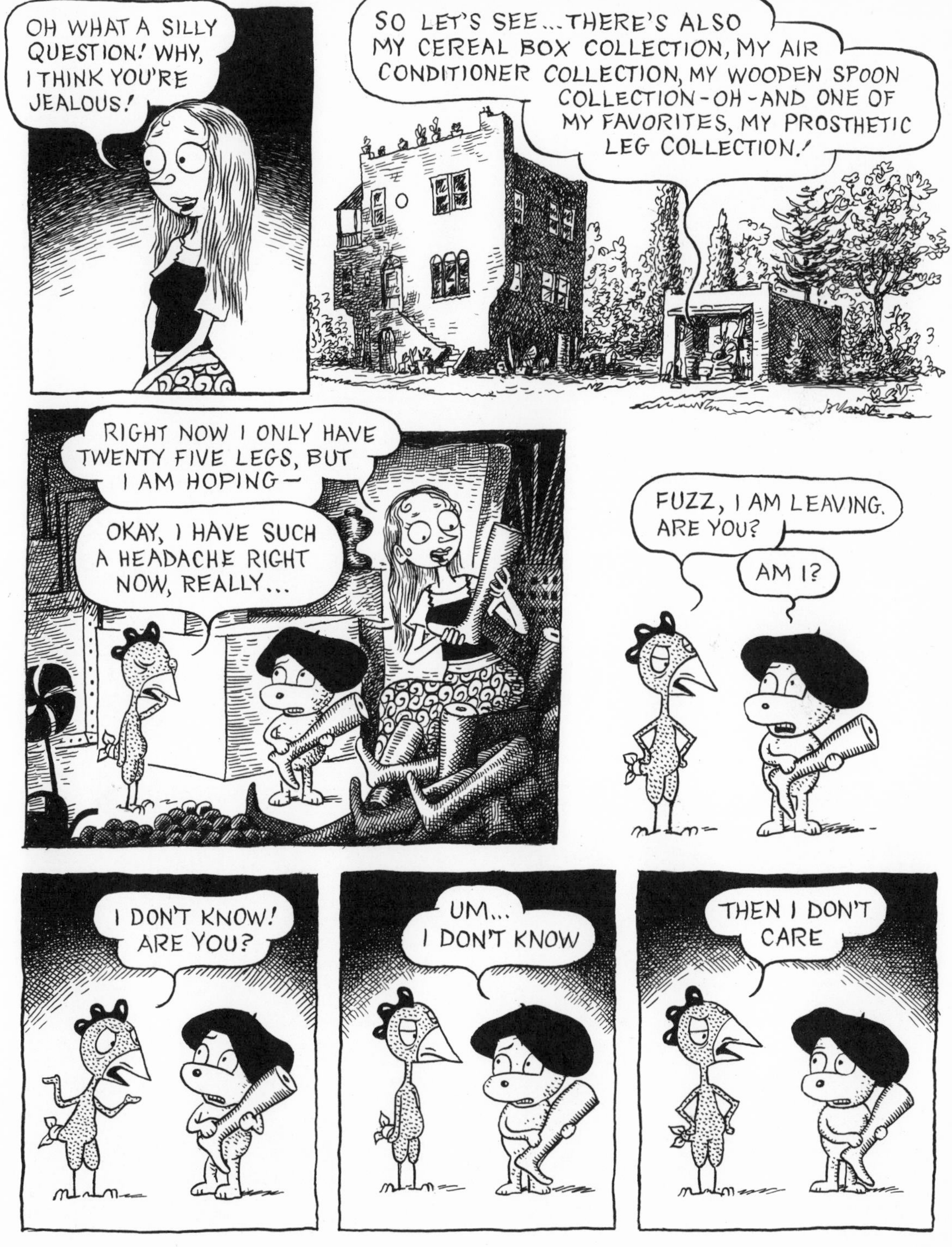
OH WHAT A SILLY QUESTION! WHY, I THINK YOU'RE JEALOUS!
SO LET'S SEE... THERE'S ALSO MY CEREAL BOX COLLECTION, MY AIR CONDITIONER COLLECTION, MY WOODEN SPOON COLLECTION - OH - AND ONE OF MY FAVORITES, MY PROSTHETIC LEG COLLECTION!
RIGHT NOW I ONLY HAVE TWENTY FIVE LEGS, BUT I AM HOPING—
OKAY, I HAVE SUCH A HEADACHE RIGHT NOW, REALLY...
FUZZ, I AM LEAVING. ARE YOU?
AM I?
I DON'T KNOW! ARE YOU?
UM... I DON'T KNOW
THEN I DON'T CARE

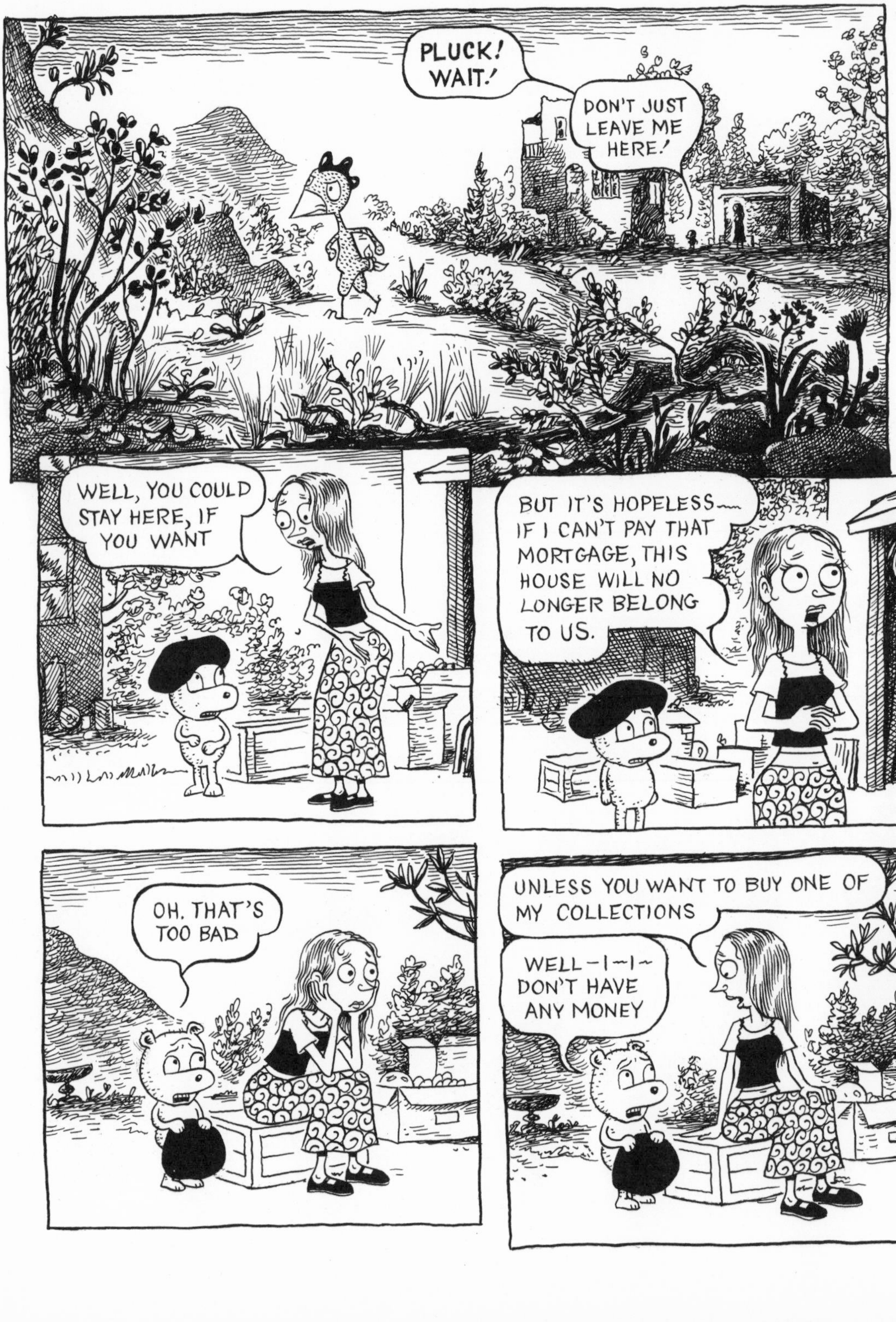
PLUCK! WAIT!
DON'T JUST LEAVE ME HERE!
WELL, YOU COULD STAY HERE, IF YOU WANT
BUT IT'S HOPELESS— IF I CAN'T PAY THAT MORTGAGE, THIS HOUSE WILL NO LONGER BELONG TO US.
OH. THAT'S TOO BAD
UNLESS YOU WANT TO BUY ONE OF MY COLLECTIONS
WELL—I—I— DON'T HAVE ANY MONEY

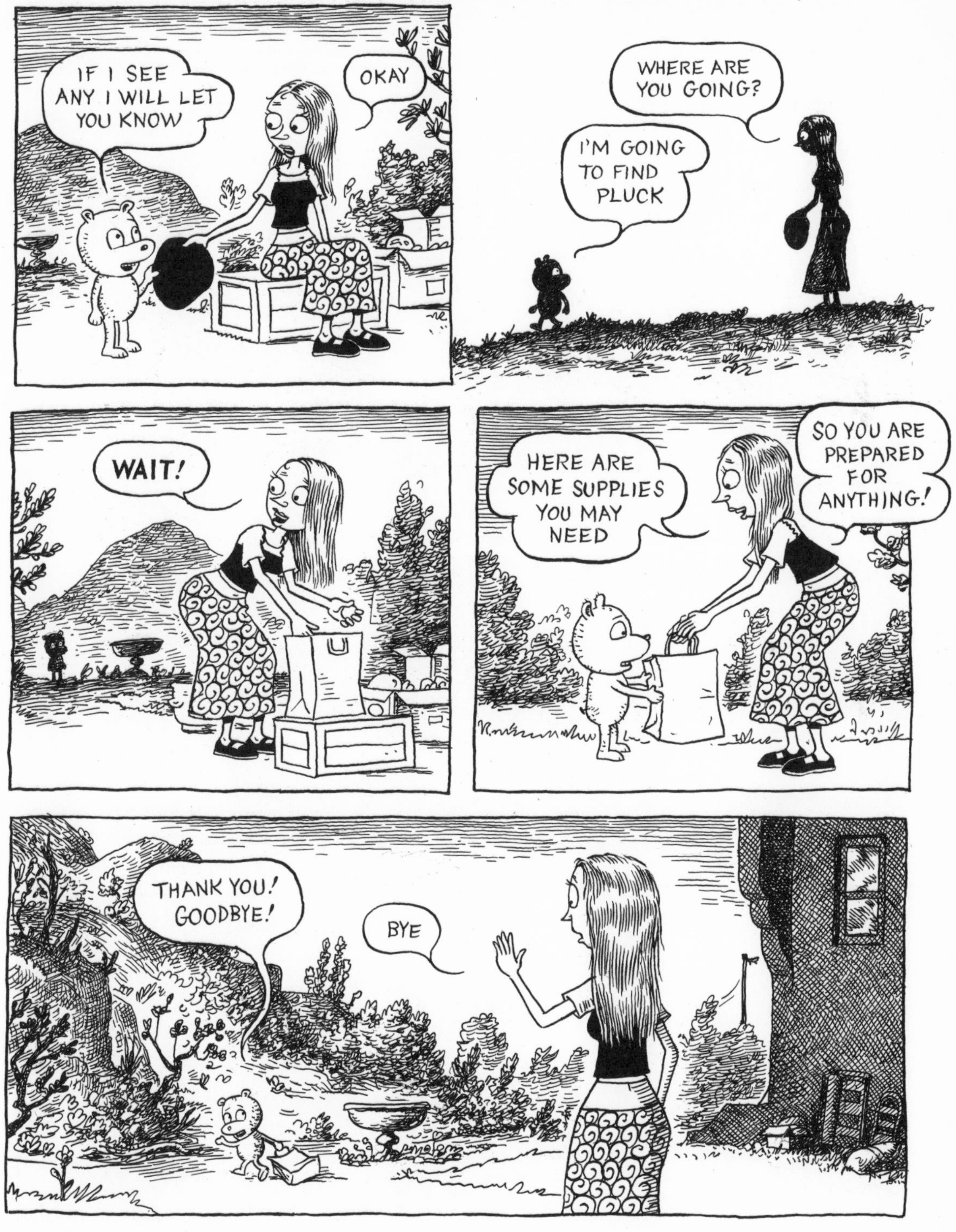
IF I SEE ANY I WILL LET YOU KNOW
OKAY
WHERE ARE YOU GOING?
I'M GOING TO FIND PLUCK
WAIT!
HERE ARE SOME SUPPLIES YOU MAY NEED
SO YOU ARE PREPARED FOR ANYTHING!
THANK YOU! GOODBYE!
BYE

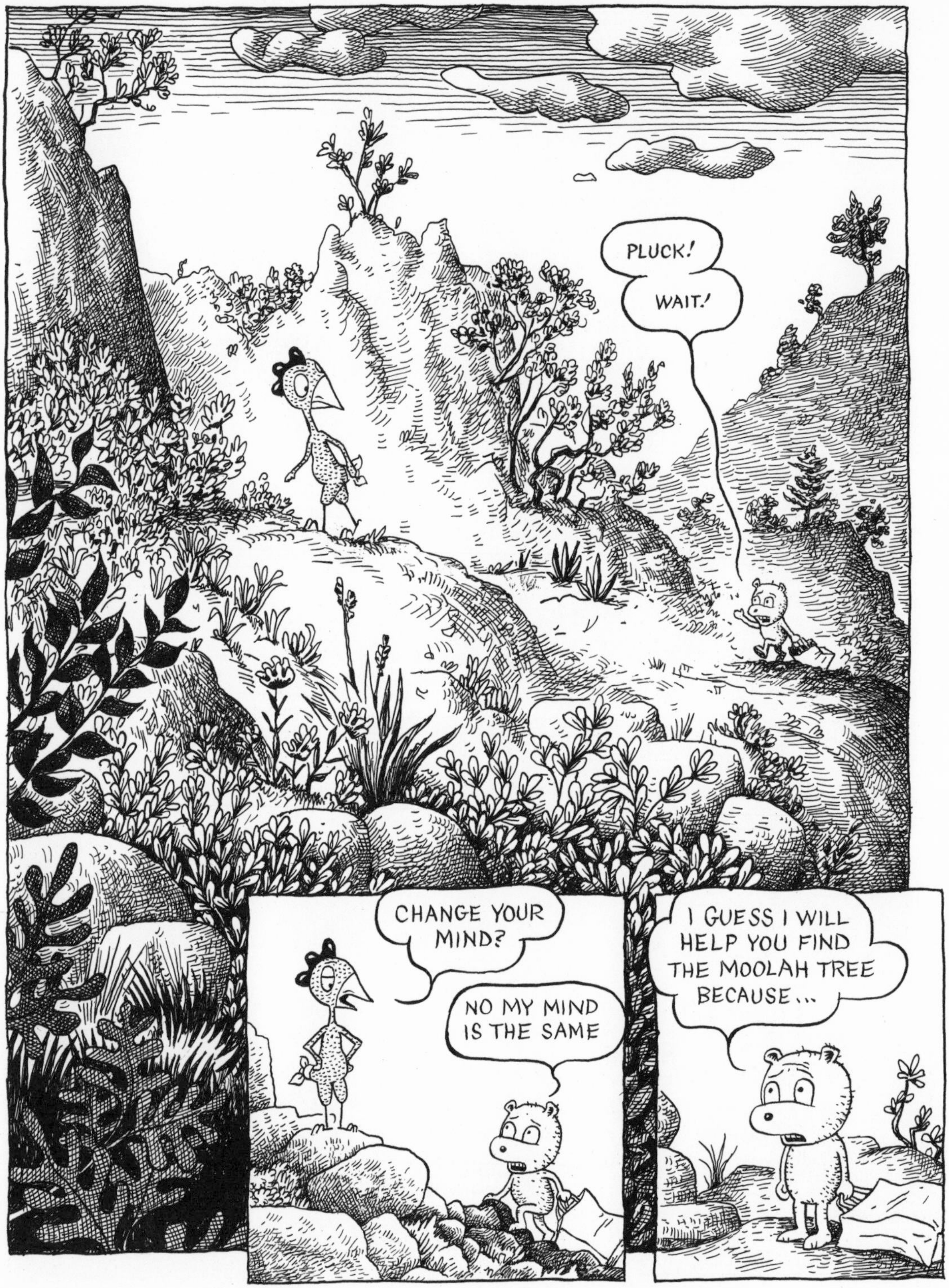
PLUCK!
WAIT!
CHANGE YOUR MIND?
NO MY MIND IS THE SAME
I GUESS I WILL HELP YOU FIND THE MOOLAH TREE BECAUSE...

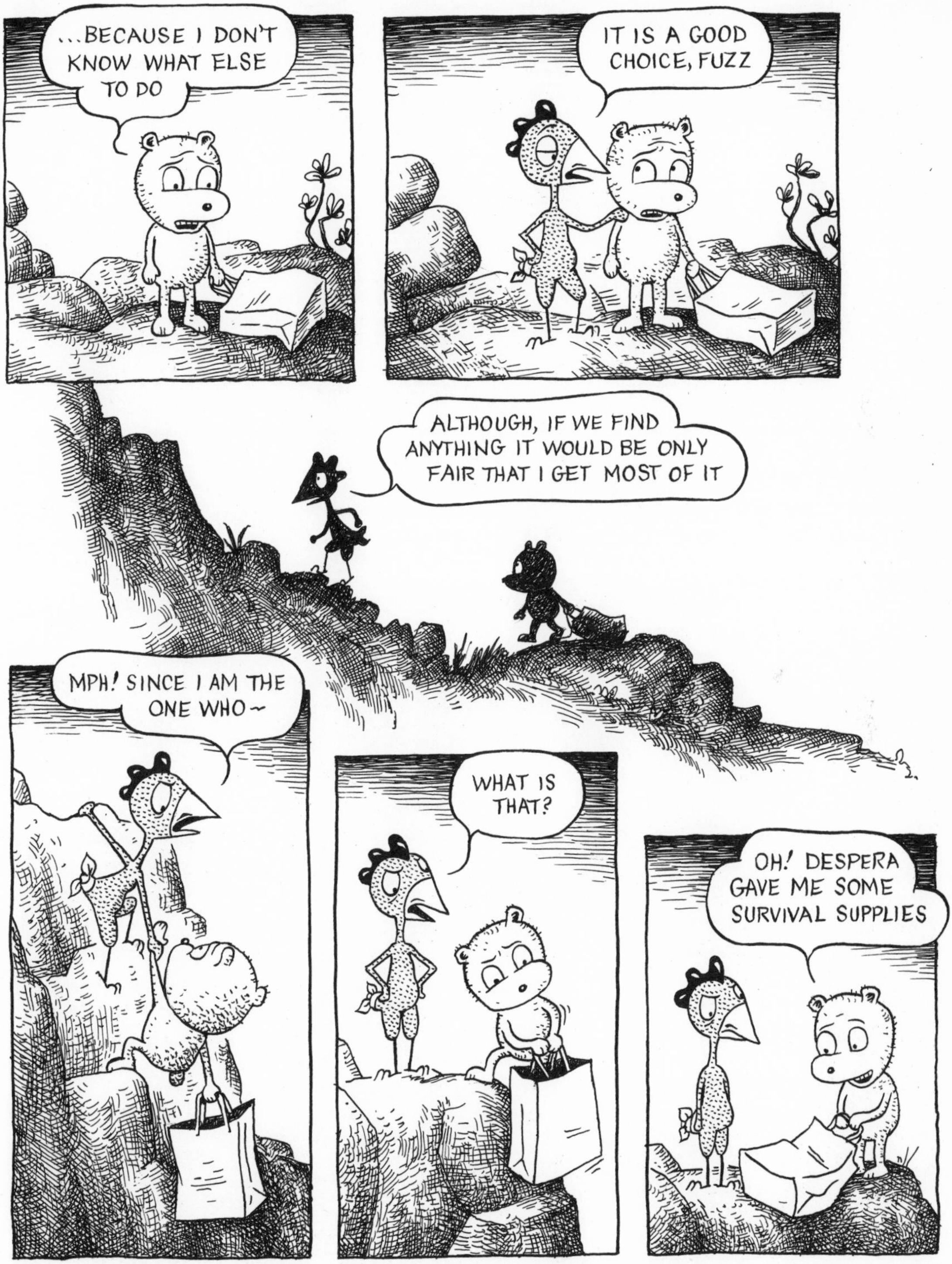
...BECAUSE I DON'T KNOW WHAT ELSE TO DO
IT IS A GOOD CHOICE, FUZZ
ALTHOUGH, IF WE FIND ANYTHING IT WOULD BE ONLY FAIR THAT I GET MOST OF IT
MPH! SINCE I AM THE ONE WHO~
WHAT IS THAT?
OH! DESPERA GAVE ME SOME SURVIVAL SUPPLIES

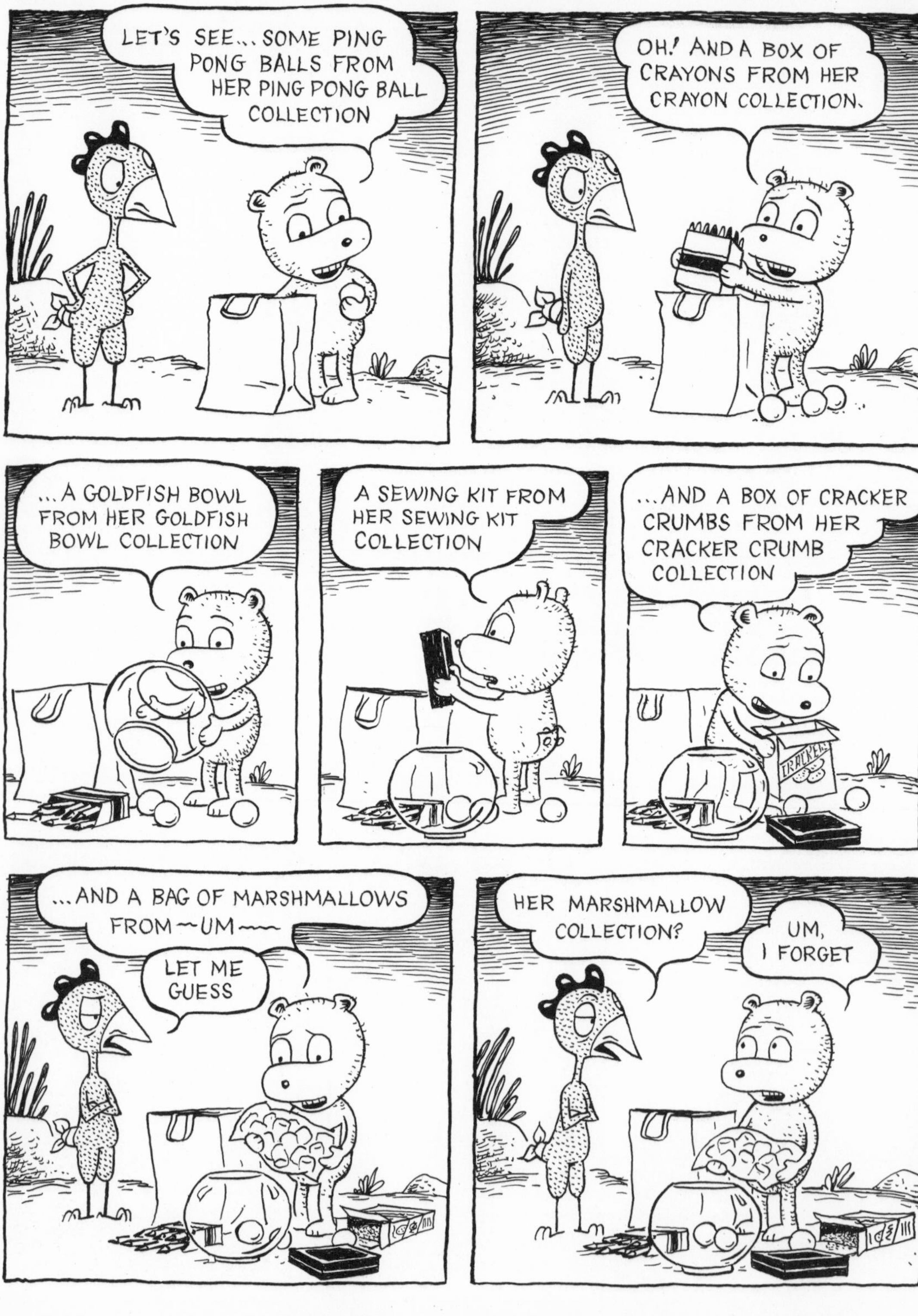
LET'S SEE... SOME PING PONG BALLS FROM HER PING PONG BALL COLLECTION
OH! AND A BOX OF CRAYONS FROM HER CRAYON COLLECTION.
...A GOLDFISH BOWL FROM HER GOLDFISH BOWL COLLECTION
A SEWING KIT FROM HER SEWING KIT COLLECTION
...AND A BOX OF CRACKER CRUMBS FROM HER CRACKER CRUMB COLLECTION
CRACKERS
...AND A BAG OF MARSHMALLOWS FROM ~UM~~
LET ME GUESS
HER MARSHMALLOW COLLECTION?
UM, I FORGET

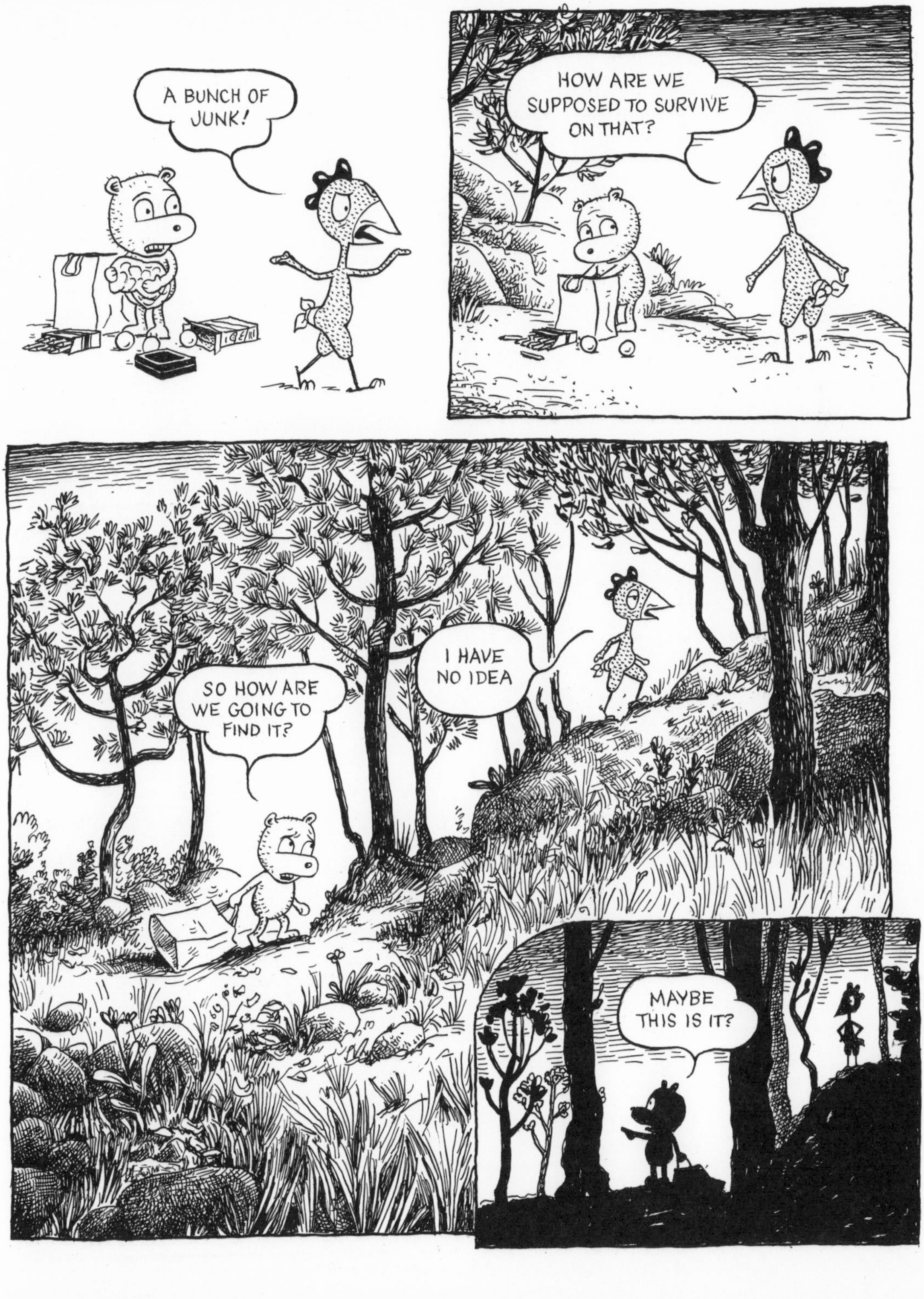
A BUNCH OF JUNK!
HOW ARE WE SUPPOSED TO SURVIVE ON THAT?
SO HOW ARE WE GOING TO FIND IT?
I HAVE NO IDEA
MAYBE THIS IS IT?

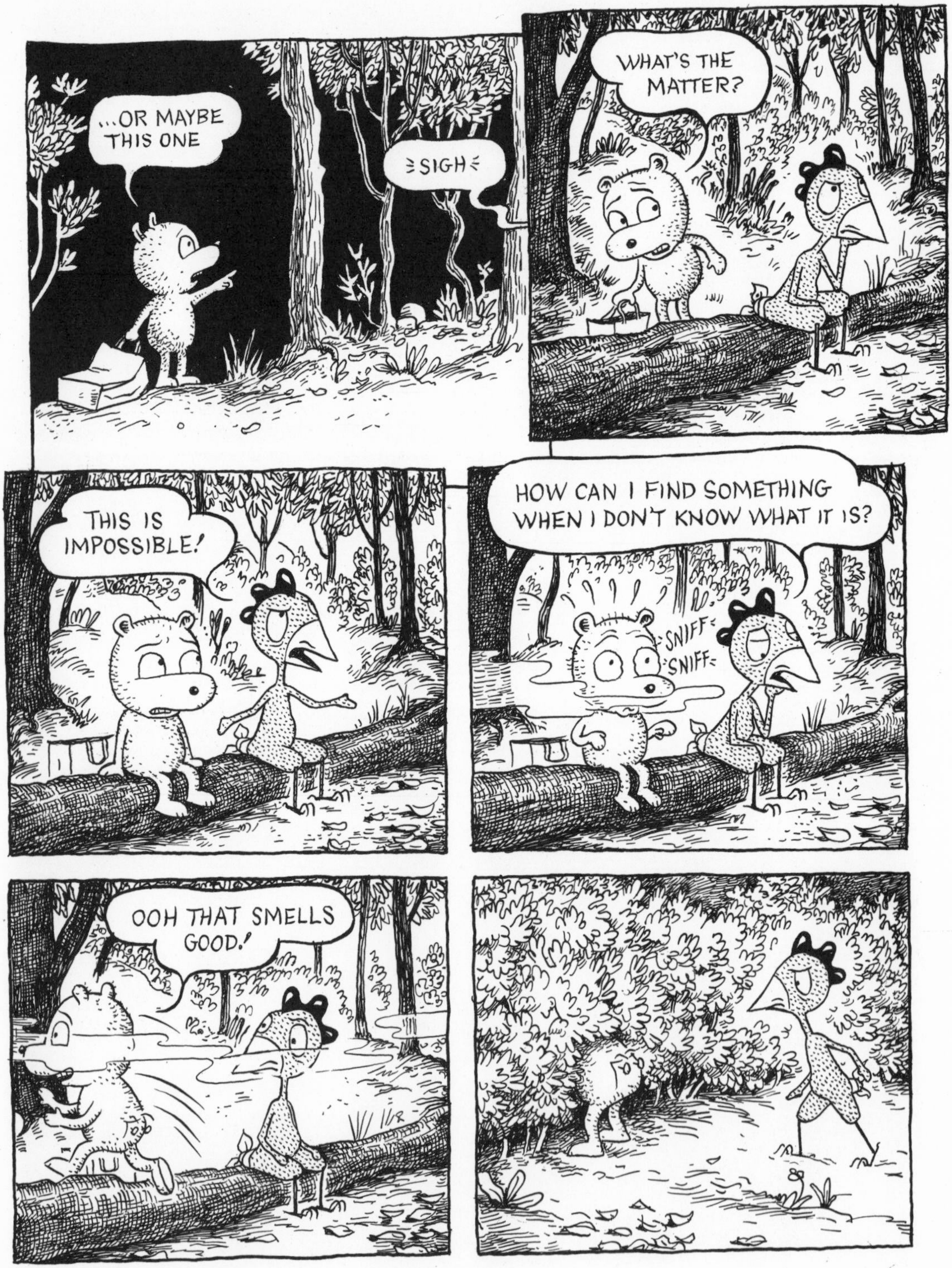
...OR MAYBE THIS ONE
SIGH
WHAT'S THE MATTER?
THIS IS IMPOSSIBLE!
HOW CAN I FIND SOMETHING WHEN I DON'T KNOW WHAT IT IS?
SNIFF
SNIFF
OOH THAT SMELLS GOOD!

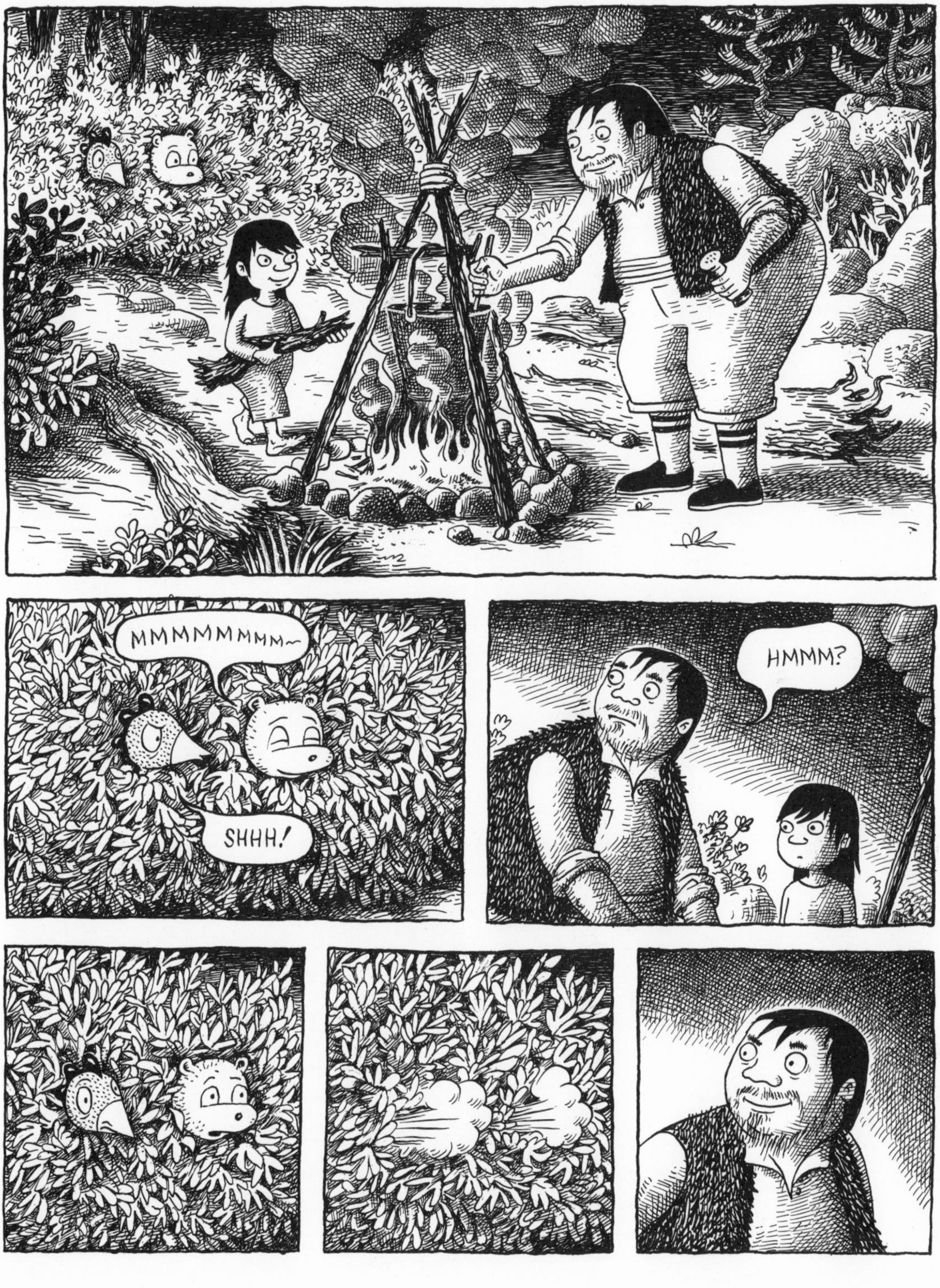
MMMMMMMMM~
SHHH!
HMMM?

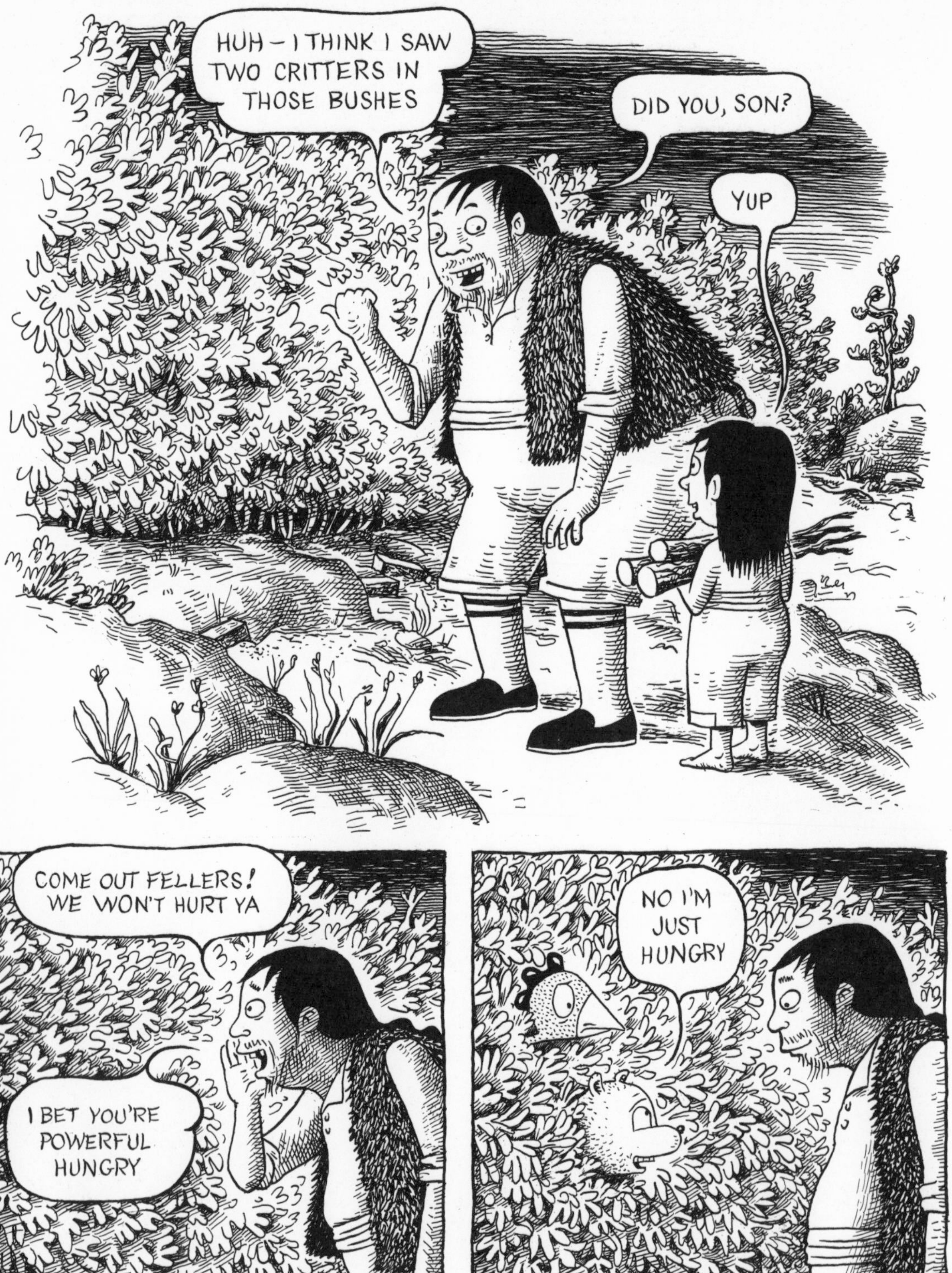
HUH – I THINK I SAW TWO CRITTERS IN THOSE BUSHES
DID YOU, SON?
YUP
COME OUT FELLERS! WE WON'T HURT YA
I BET YOU'RE POWERFUL HUNGRY
NO I'M JUST HUNGRY

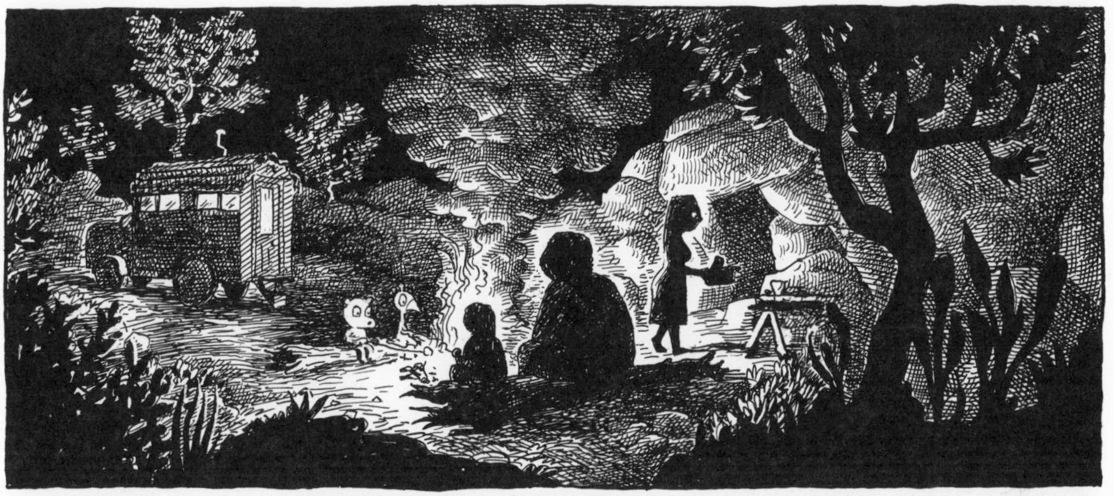

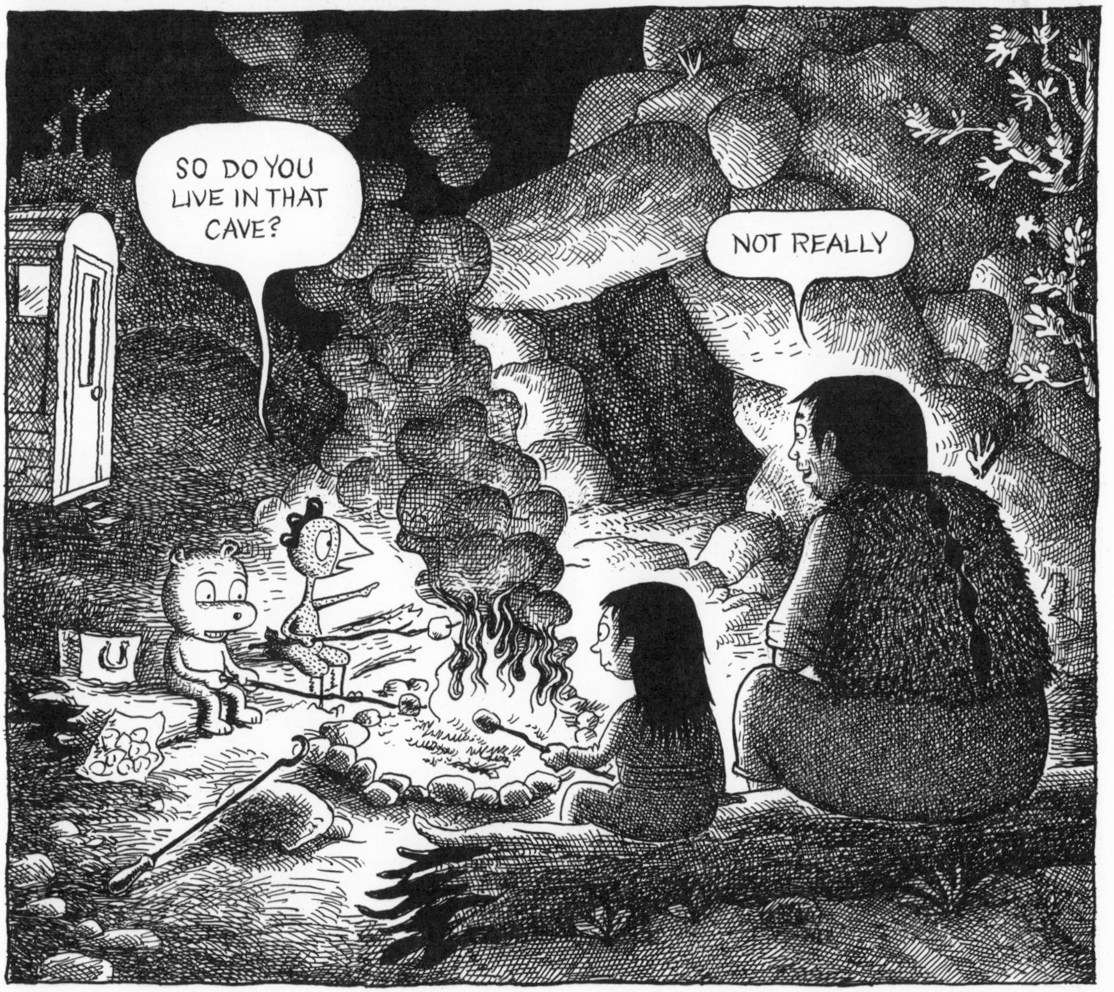
SO DO YOU LIVE IN THAT CAVE?
NOT REALLY

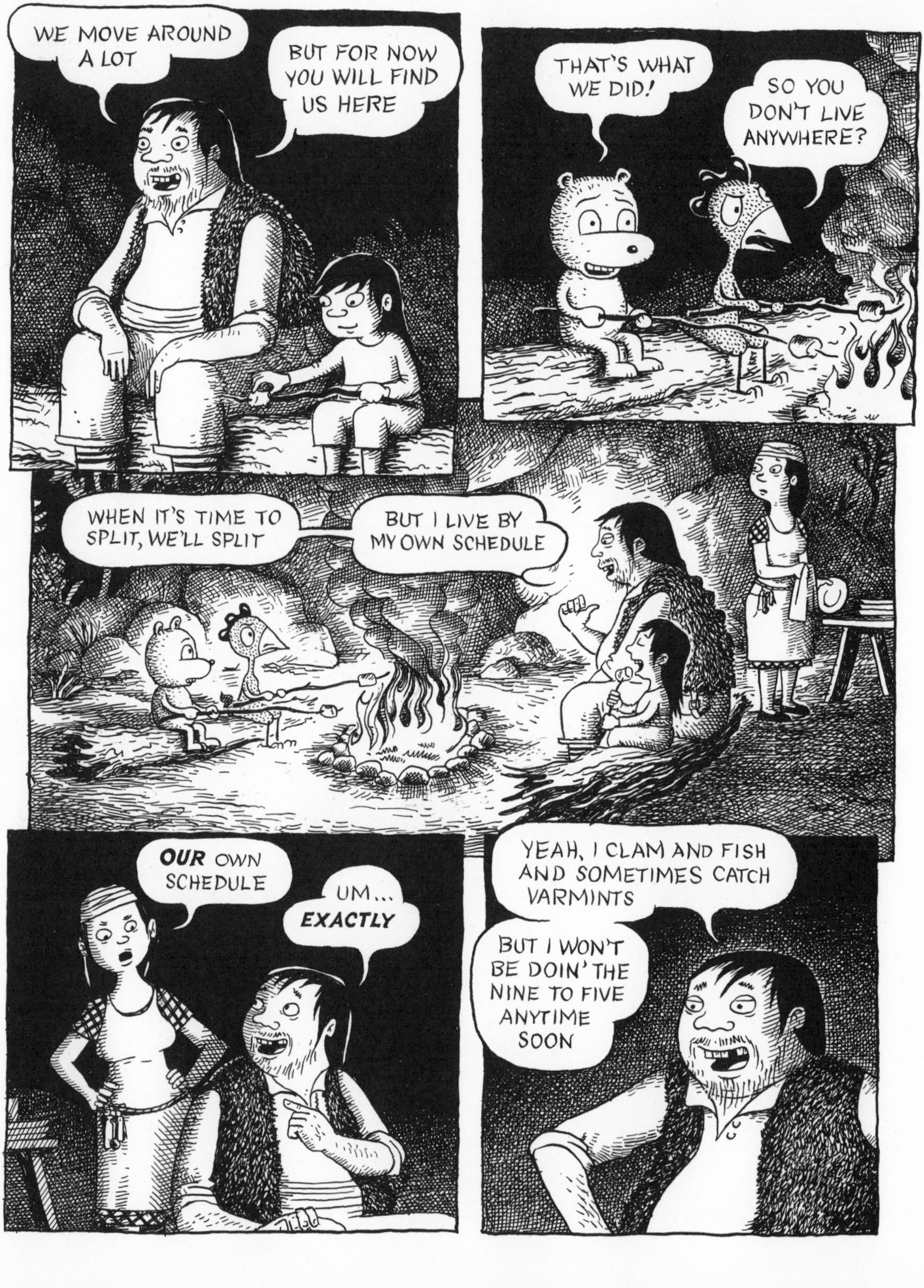
WE MOVE AROUND A LOT
BUT FOR NOW YOU WILL FIND US HERE
THAT'S WHAT WE DID!
SO YOU DON'T LIVE ANYWHERE?
WHEN IT'S TIME TO SPLIT, WE'LL SPLIT
BUT I LIVE BY MY OWN SCHEDULE
OUR OWN SCHEDULE
UM... EXACTLY
YEAH, I CLAM AND FISH AND SOMETIMES CATCH VARMINTS
BUT I WON'T BE DOIN' THE NINE TO FIVE ANYTIME SOON

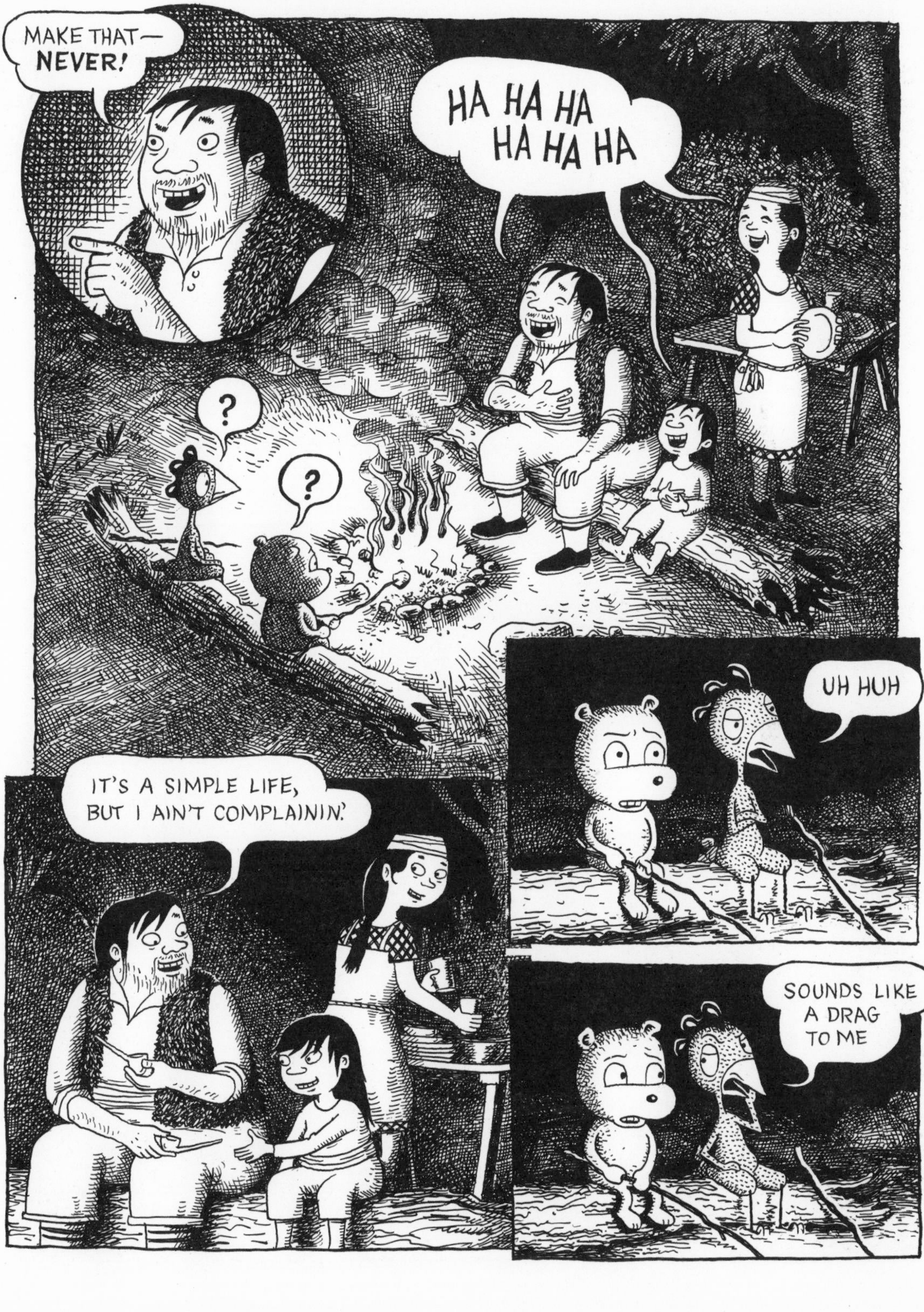
MAKE THAT—
NEVER!
HA HA HA
HA HA HA
?
?
UH HUH
IT'S A SIMPLE LIFE,
BUT I AIN'T COMPLAININ'.
SOUNDS LIKE
A DRAG
TO ME

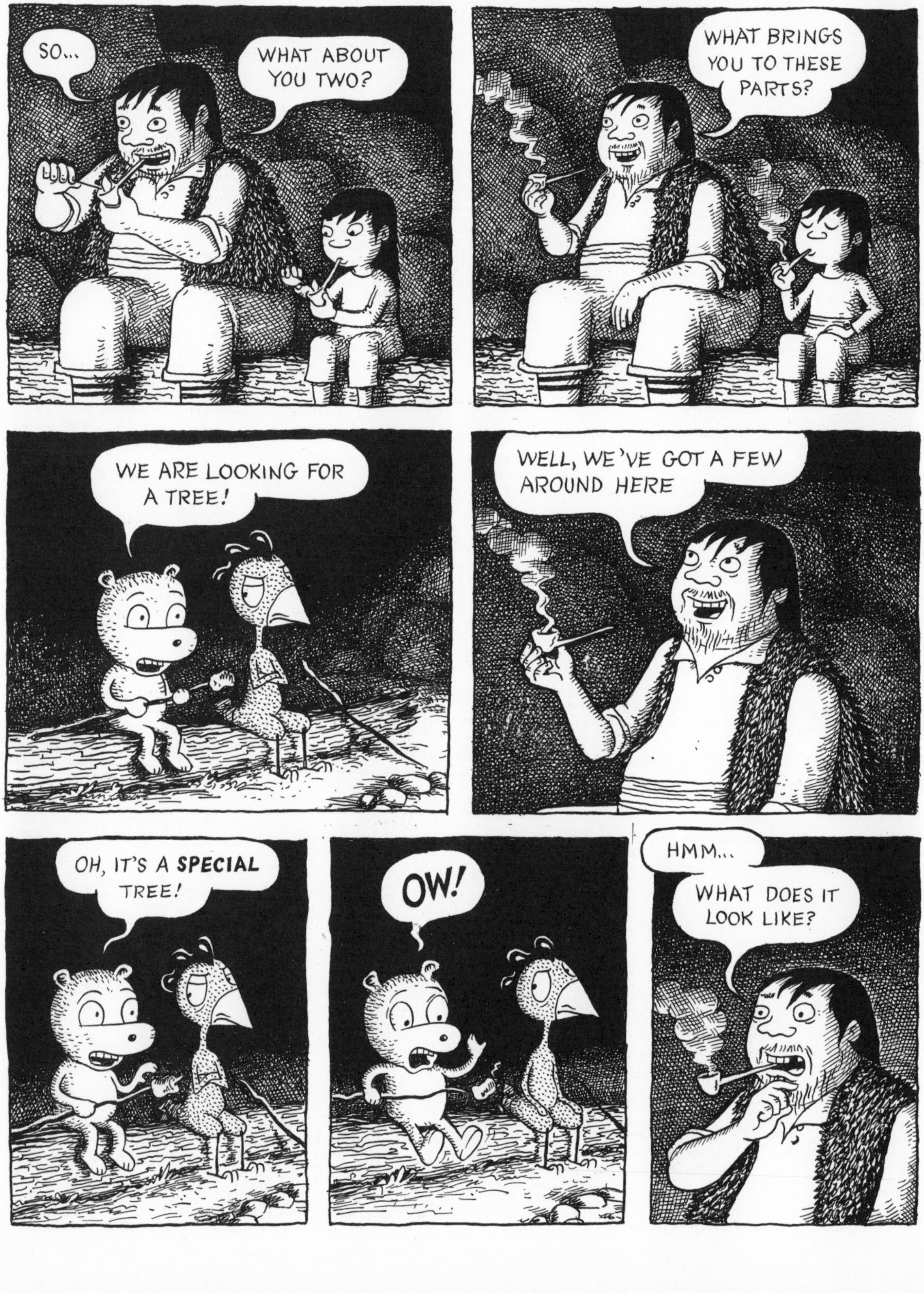
SO...
WHAT ABOUT YOU TWO?
WHAT BRINGS YOU TO THESE PARTS?
WE ARE LOOKING FOR A TREE!
WELL, WE'VE GOT A FEW AROUND HERE
OH, IT'S A **SPECIAL** TREE!
OW!
HMM...
WHAT DOES IT LOOK LIKE?

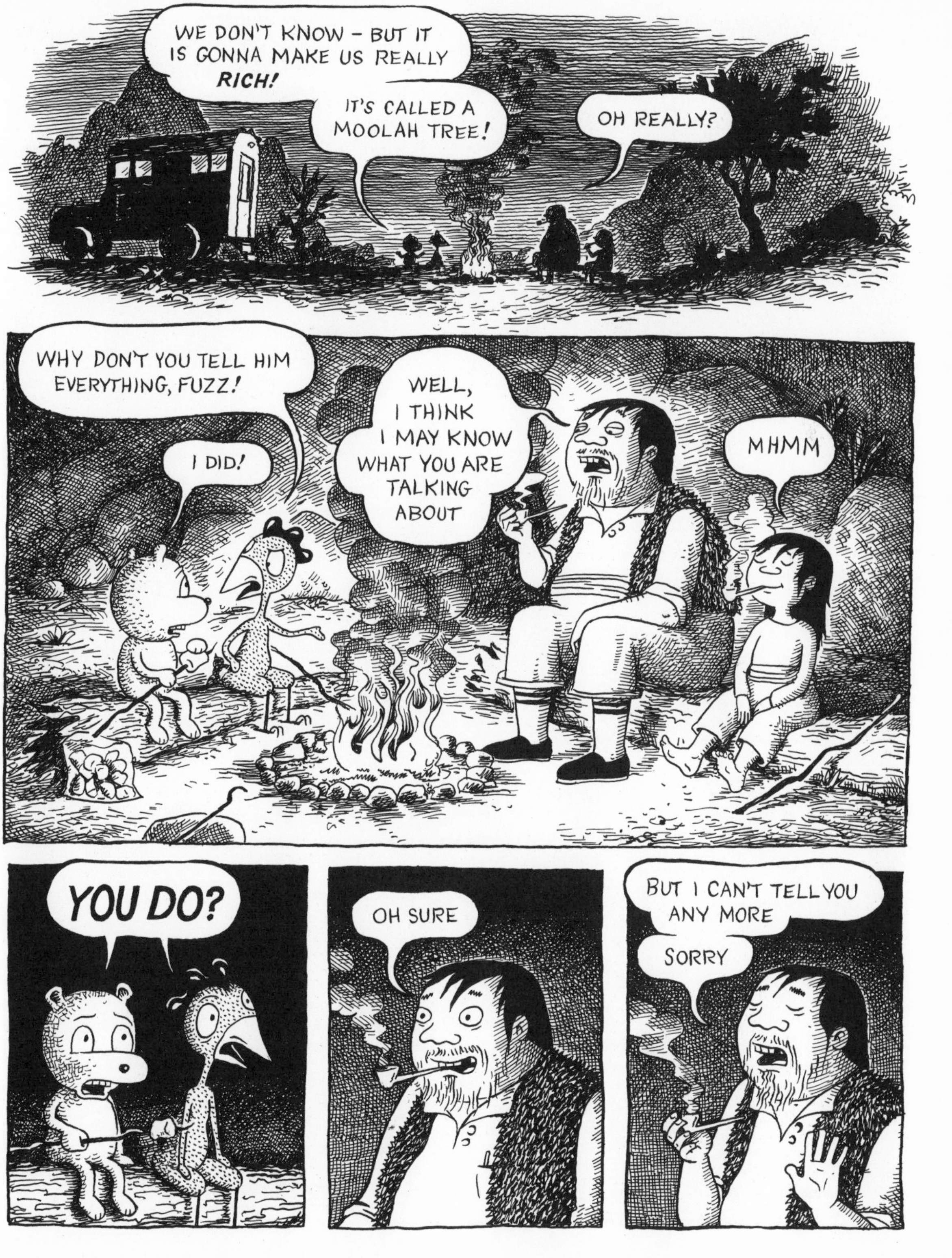
WE DON'T KNOW - BUT IT IS GONNA MAKE US REALLY RICH!
IT'S CALLED A MOOLAH TREE!
OH REALLY?
WHY DON'T YOU TELL HIM EVERYTHING, FUZZ!
I DID!
WELL, I THINK I MAY KNOW WHAT YOU ARE TALKING ABOUT
MHMM
YOU DO?
OH SURE
BUT I CAN'T TELL YOU ANY MORE
SORRY

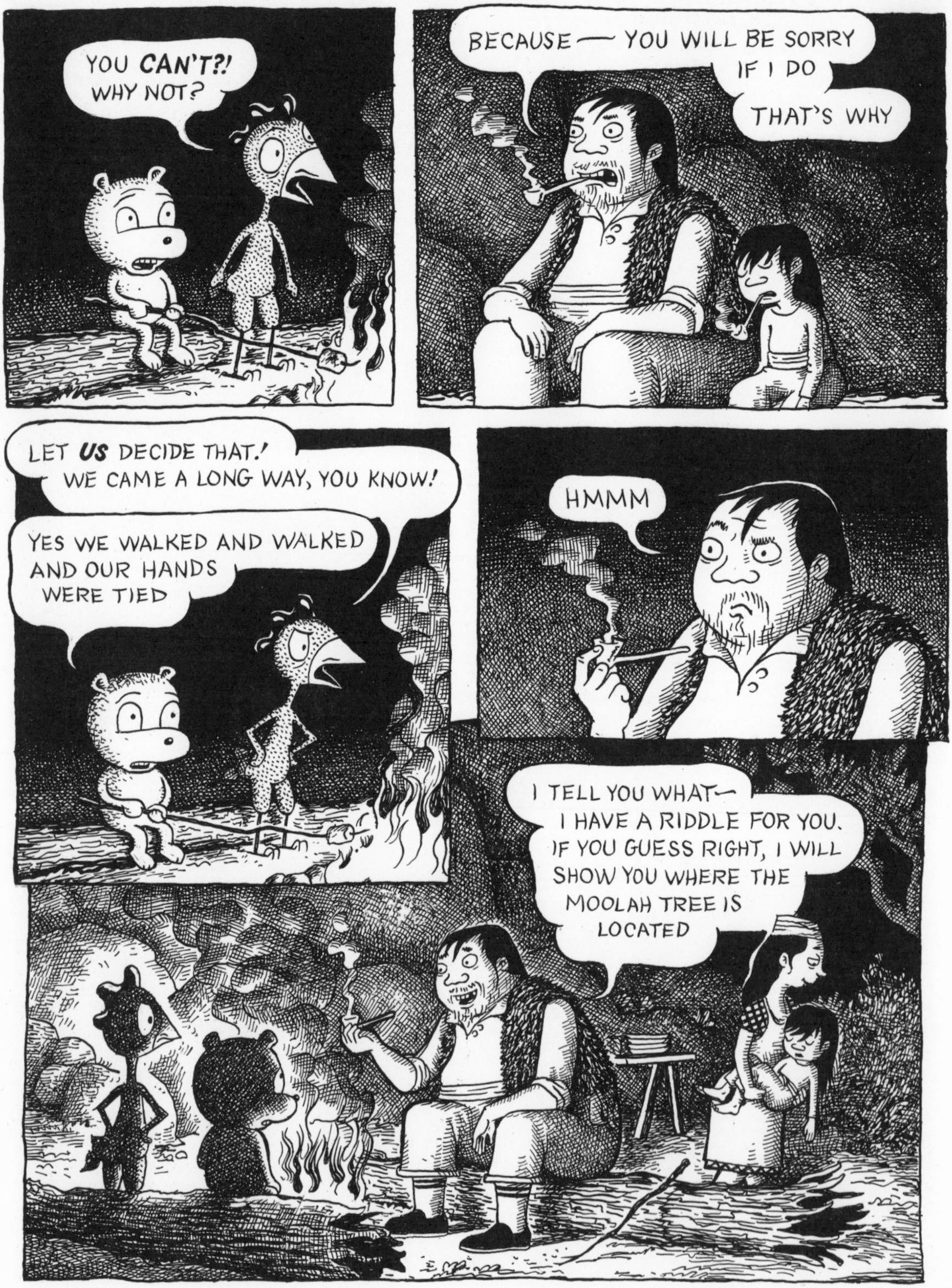
YOU CAN'T?! WHY NOT?
BECAUSE — YOU WILL BE SORRY IF I DO
THAT'S WHY
LET US DECIDE THAT! WE CAME A LONG WAY, YOU KNOW!
YES WE WALKED AND WALKED AND OUR HANDS WERE TIED
HMMM
I TELL YOU WHAT— I HAVE A RIDDLE FOR YOU. IF YOU GUESS RIGHT, I WILL SHOW YOU WHERE THE MOOLAH TREE IS LOCATED

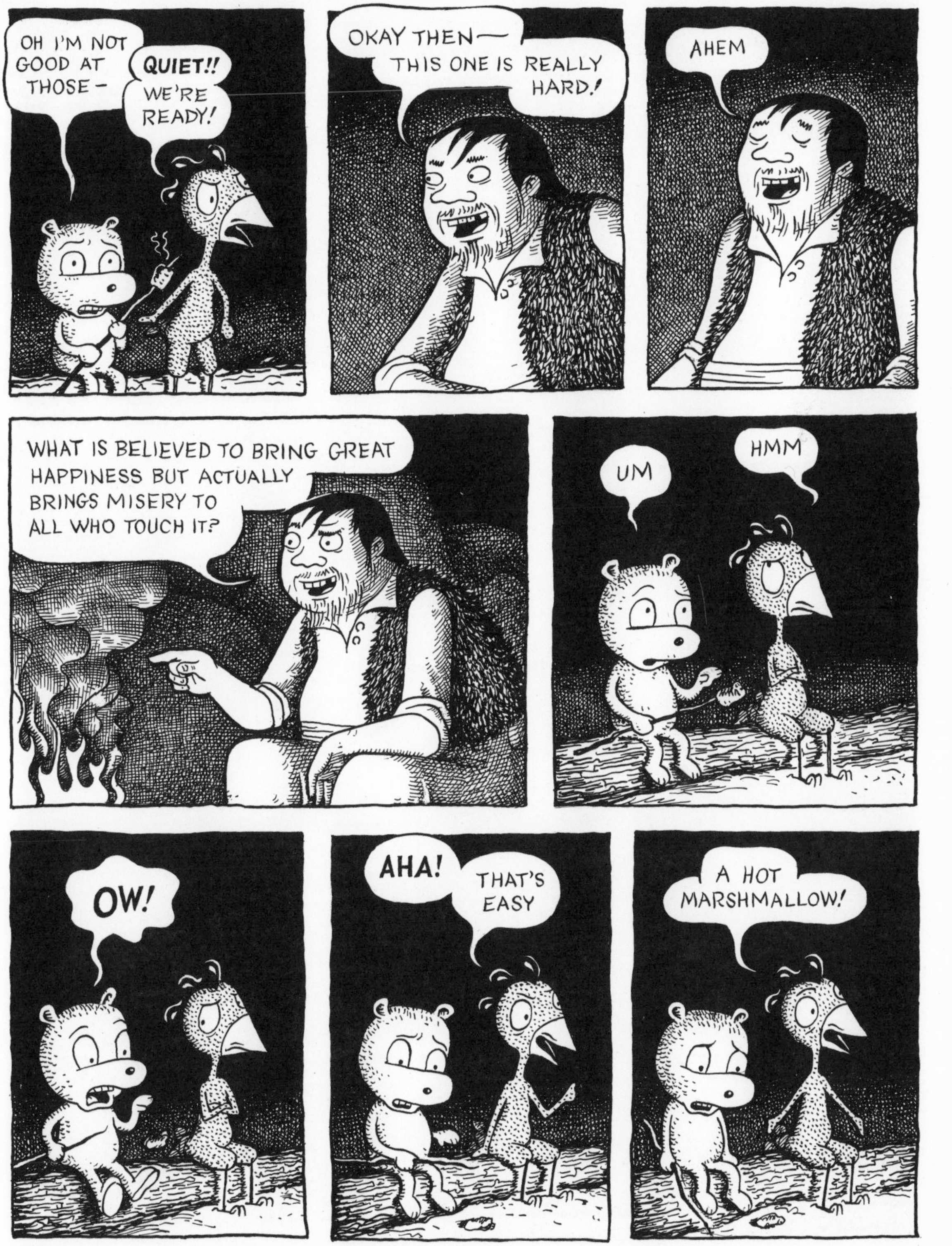
OH I'M NOT GOOD AT THOSE -
QUIET!! WE'RE READY!
OKAY THEN—
THIS ONE IS REALLY HARD!
AHEM
WHAT IS BELIEVED TO BRING GREAT HAPPINESS BUT ACTUALLY BRINGS MISERY TO ALL WHO TOUCH IT?
UM
HMM
OW!
AHA!
THAT'S EASY
A HOT MARSHMALLOW!

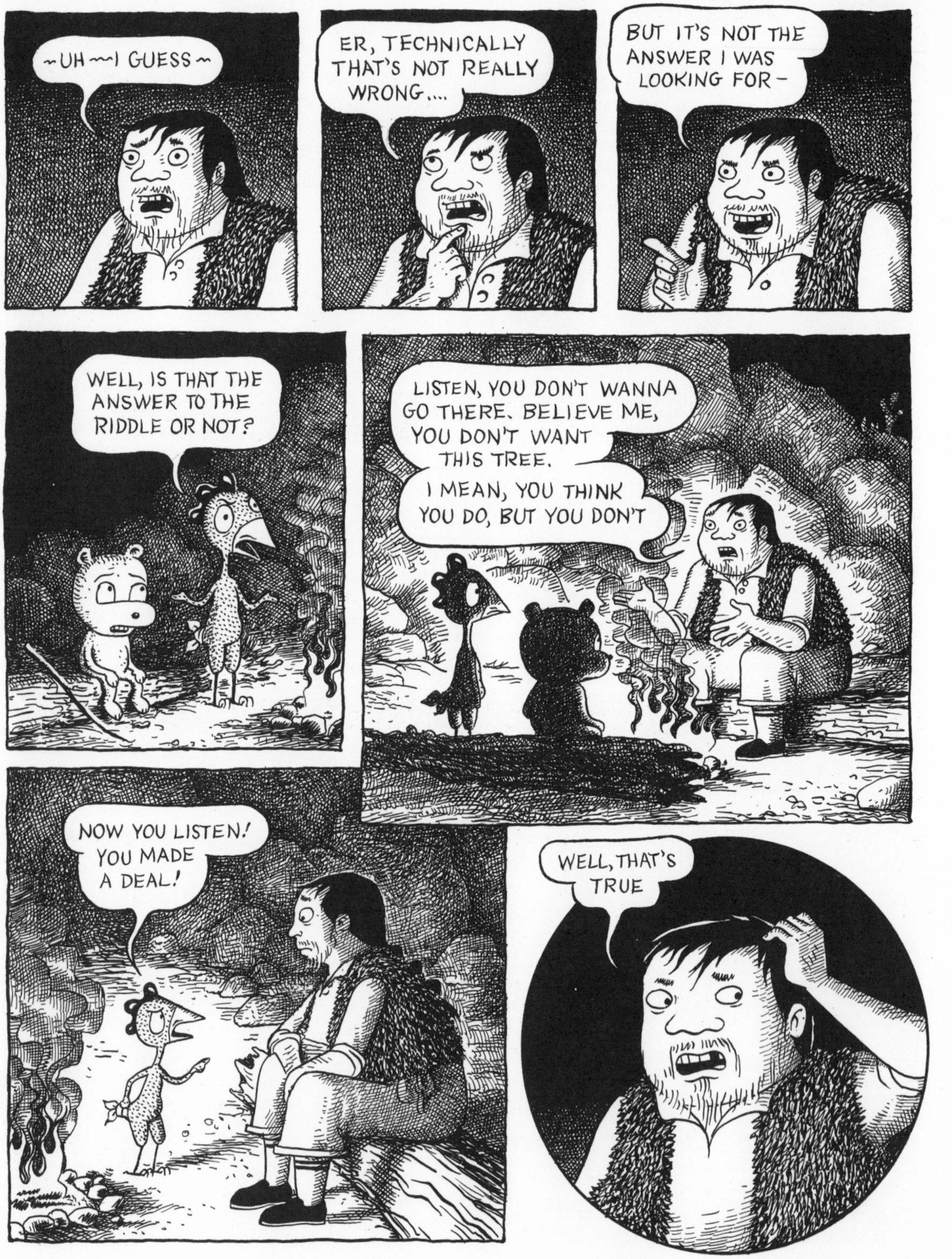
~UH~I GUESS~
ER, TECHNICALLY THAT'S NOT REALLY WRONG....
BUT IT'S NOT THE ANSWER I WAS LOOKING FOR-
WELL, IS THAT THE ANSWER TO THE RIDDLE OR NOT?
LISTEN, YOU DON'T WANNA GO THERE. BELIEVE ME, YOU DON'T WANT THIS TREE.
I MEAN, YOU THINK YOU DO, BUT YOU DON'T
NOW YOU LISTEN! YOU MADE A DEAL!
WELL, THAT'S TRUE

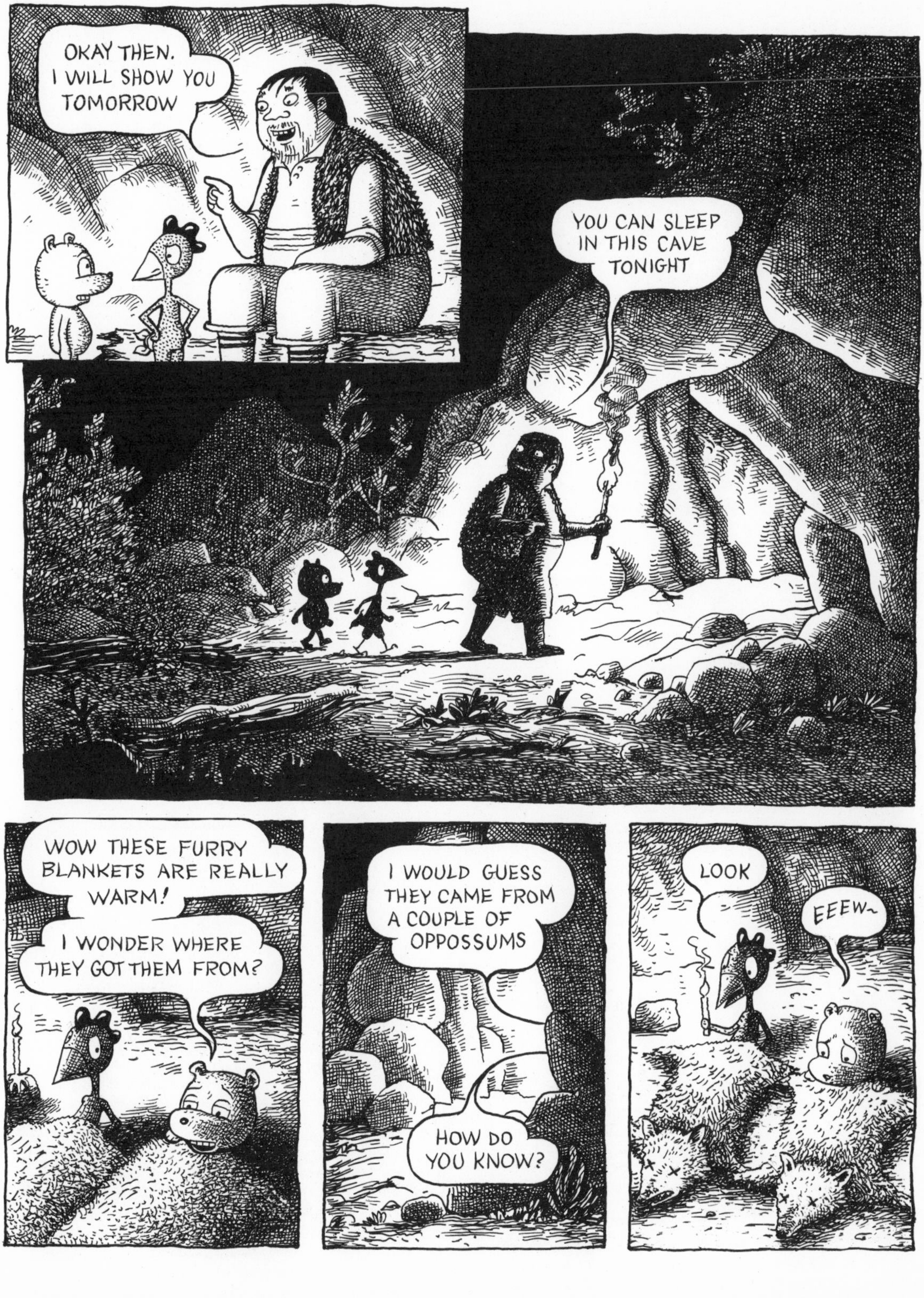

OKAY THEN. I WILL SHOW YOU TOMORROW
YOU CAN SLEEP IN THIS CAVE TONIGHT
WOW THESE FURRY BLANKETS ARE REALLY WARM!
I WONDER WHERE THEY GOT THEM FROM?
I WOULD GUESS THEY CAME FROM A COUPLE OF OPPOSSUMS
HOW DO YOU KNOW?
LOOK
EEEW~

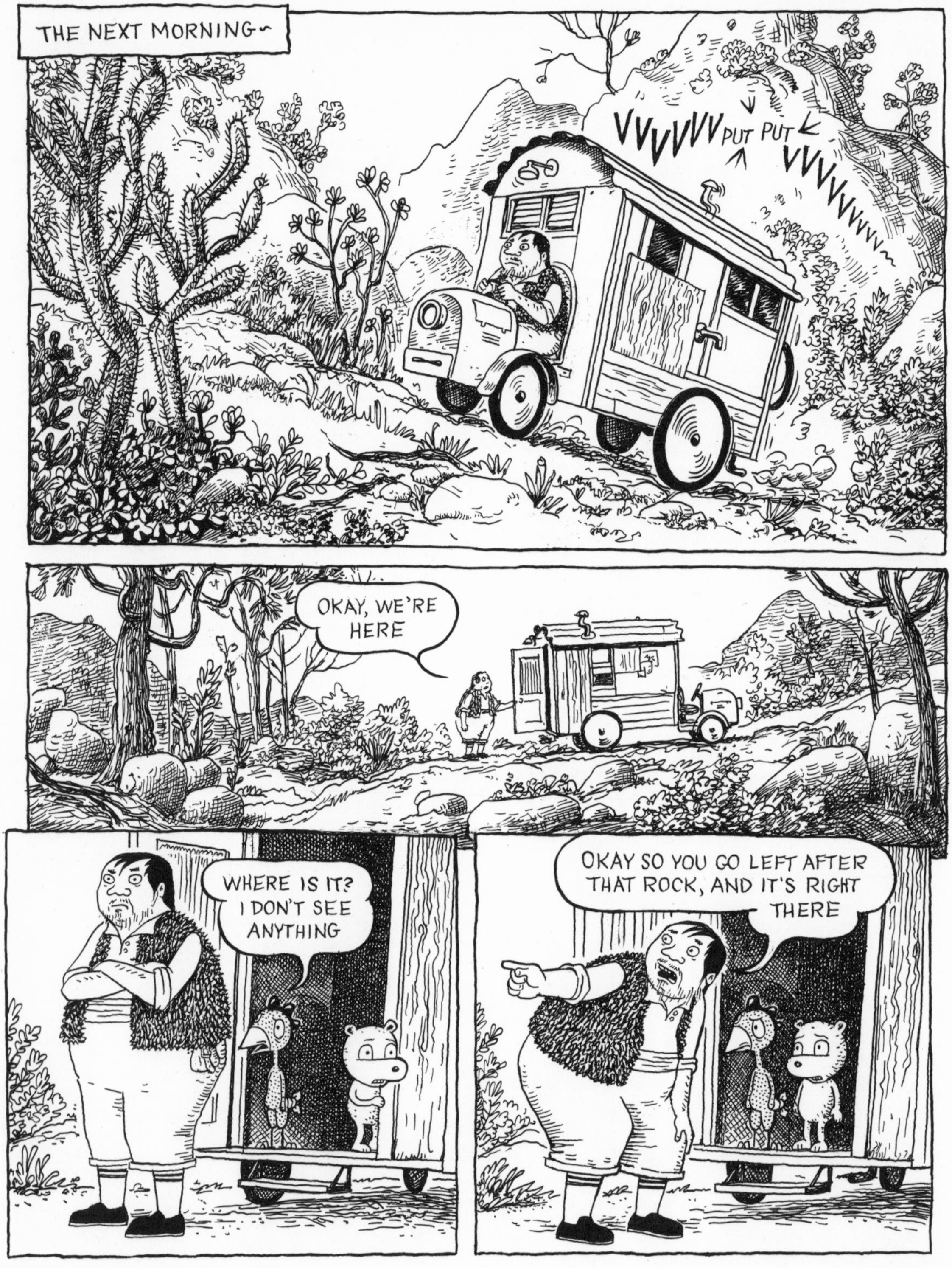
THE NEXT MORNING~
VVVVVV PUT PUT VVVVVVVVV
OKAY, WE'RE HERE
WHERE IS IT? I DON'T SEE ANYTHING
OKAY SO YOU GO LEFT AFTER THAT ROCK, AND IT'S RIGHT THERE

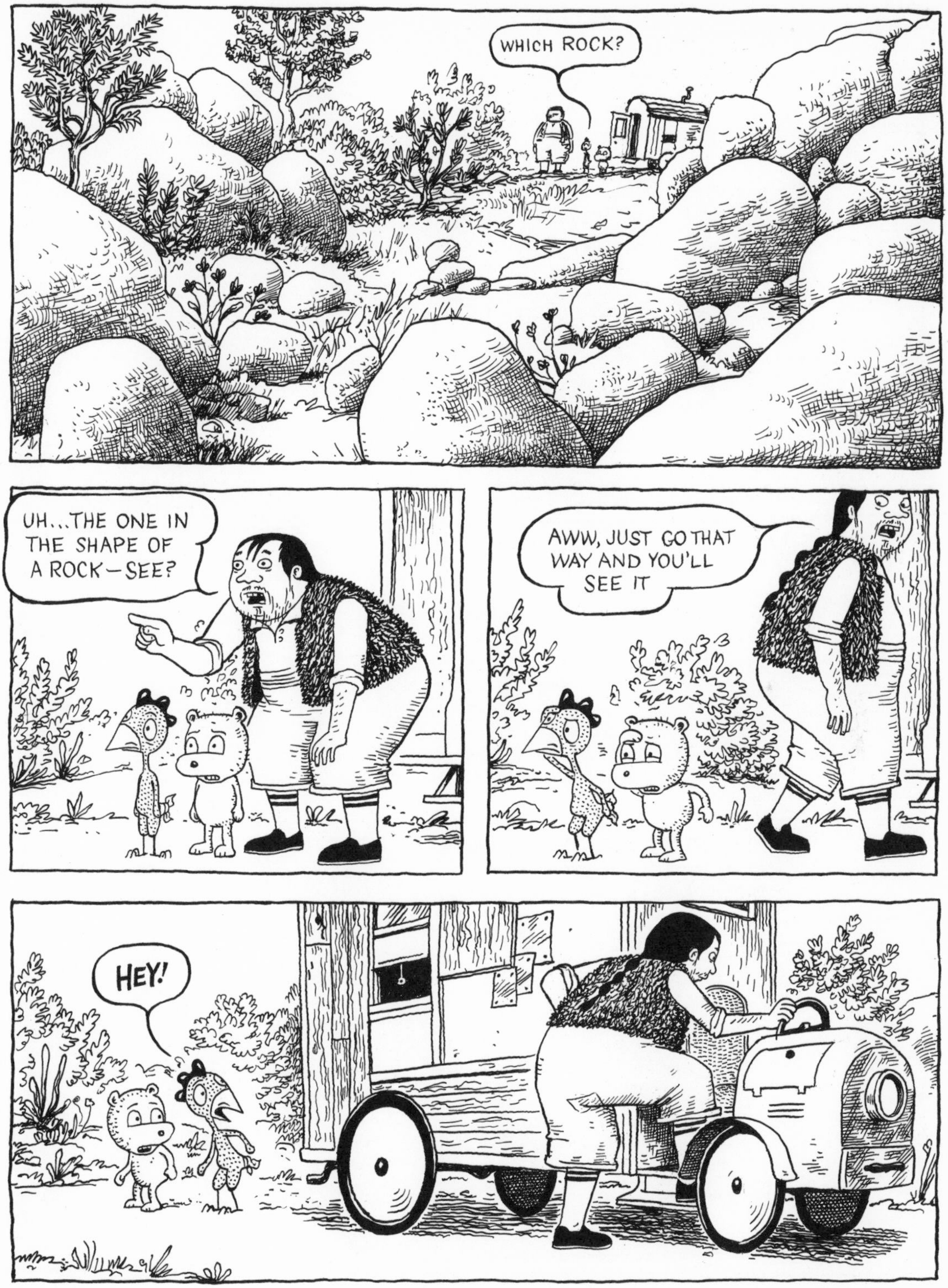
WHICH ROCK?
UH...THE ONE IN THE SHAPE OF A ROCK—SEE?
AWW, JUST GO THAT WAY AND YOU'LL SEE IT
HEY!

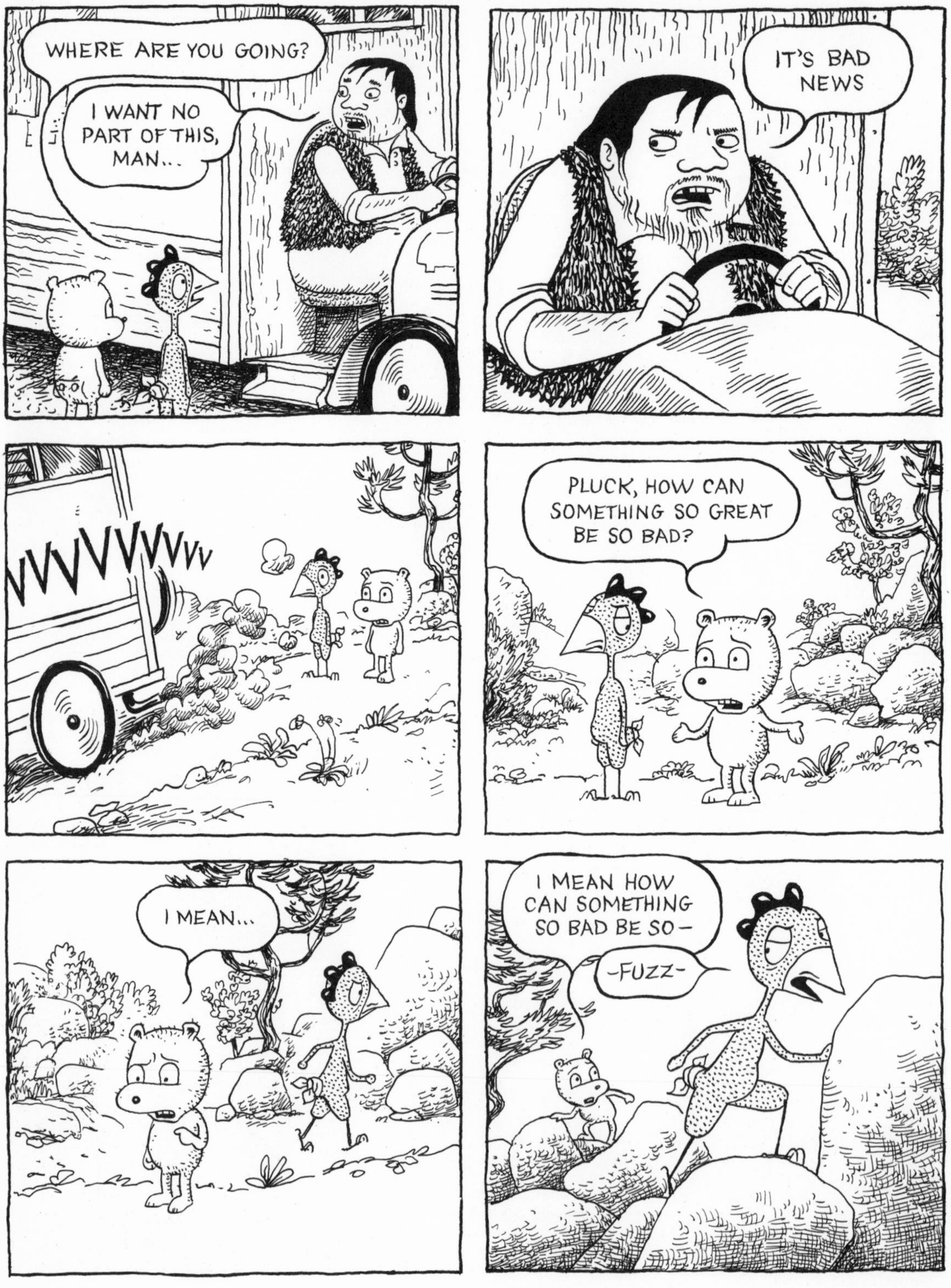
WHERE ARE YOU GOING?
I WANT NO PART OF THIS, MAN...
IT'S BAD NEWS
VVVVVVVvvv
PLUCK, HOW CAN SOMETHING SO GREAT BE SO BAD?
I MEAN...
I MEAN HOW CAN SOMETHING SO BAD BE SO—
-FUZZ-

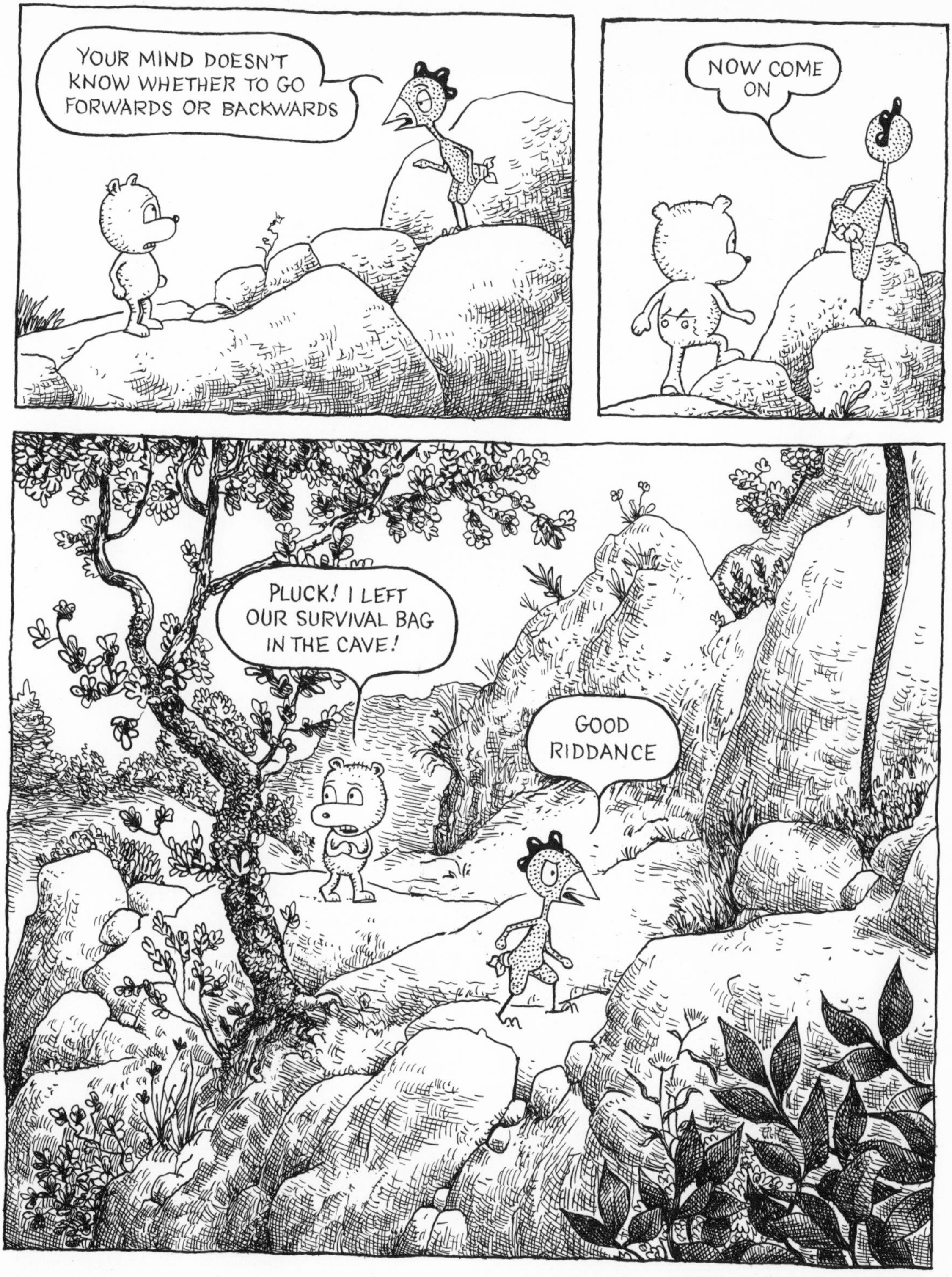
YOUR MIND DOESN'T KNOW WHETHER TO GO FORWARDS OR BACKWARDS
NOW COME ON
PLUCK! I LEFT OUR SURVIVAL BAG IN THE CAVE!
GOOD RIDDANCE

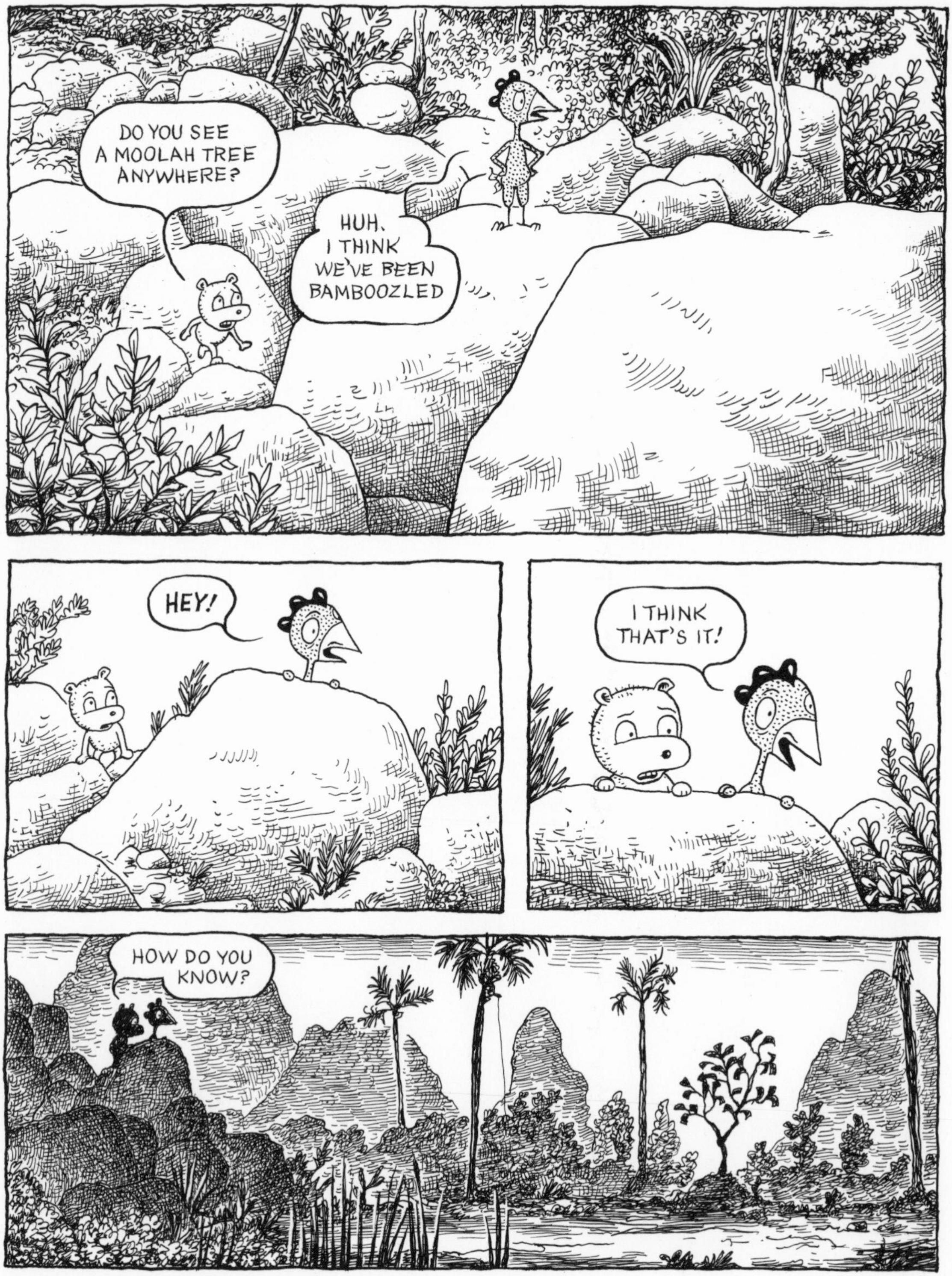
DO YOU SEE A MOOLAH TREE ANYWHERE?
HUH. I THINK WE'VE BEEN BAMBOOZLED
HEY!
I THINK THAT'S IT!
HOW DO YOU KNOW?

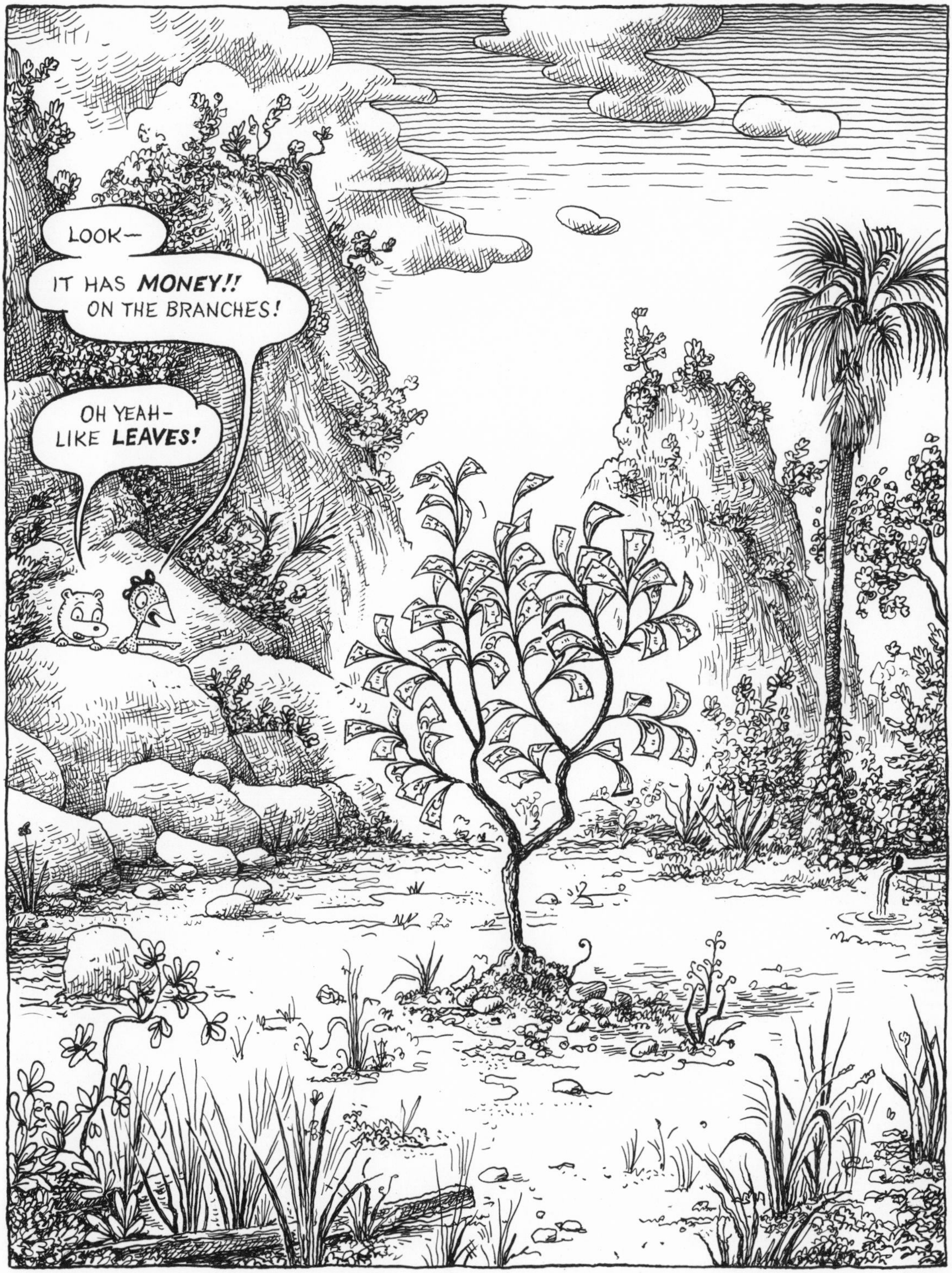
LOOK—
IT HAS **MONEY!!** ON THE BRANCHES!
OH YEAH- LIKE **LEAVES!**

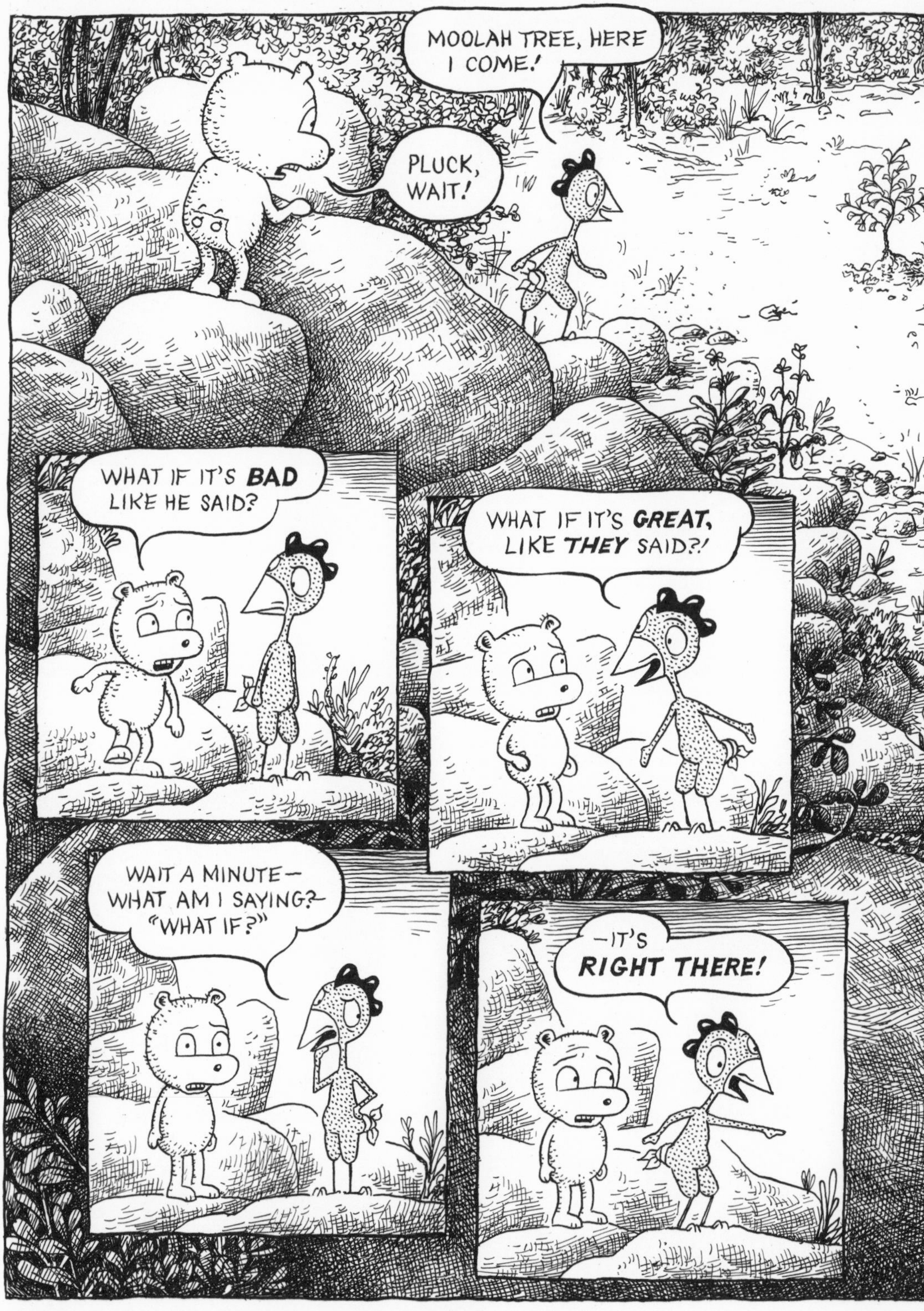
MOOLAH TREE, HERE I COME!
PLUCK, WAIT!
WHAT IF IT'S BAD LIKE HE SAID?
WHAT IF IT'S GREAT, LIKE THEY SAID?!
WAIT A MINUTE— WHAT AM I SAYING?— "WHAT IF?"
—IT'S RIGHT THERE!

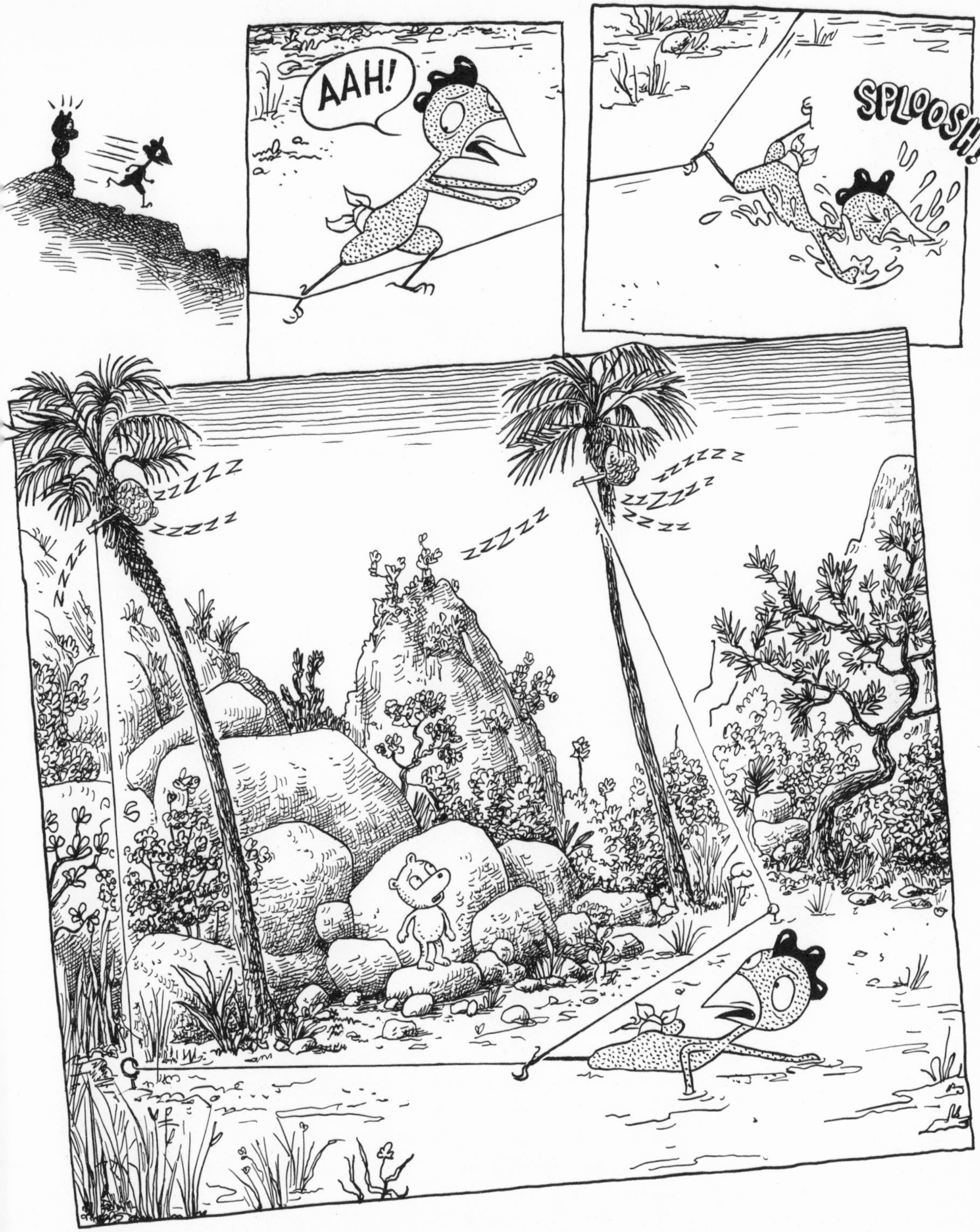
AAH!
SPLOOSH!

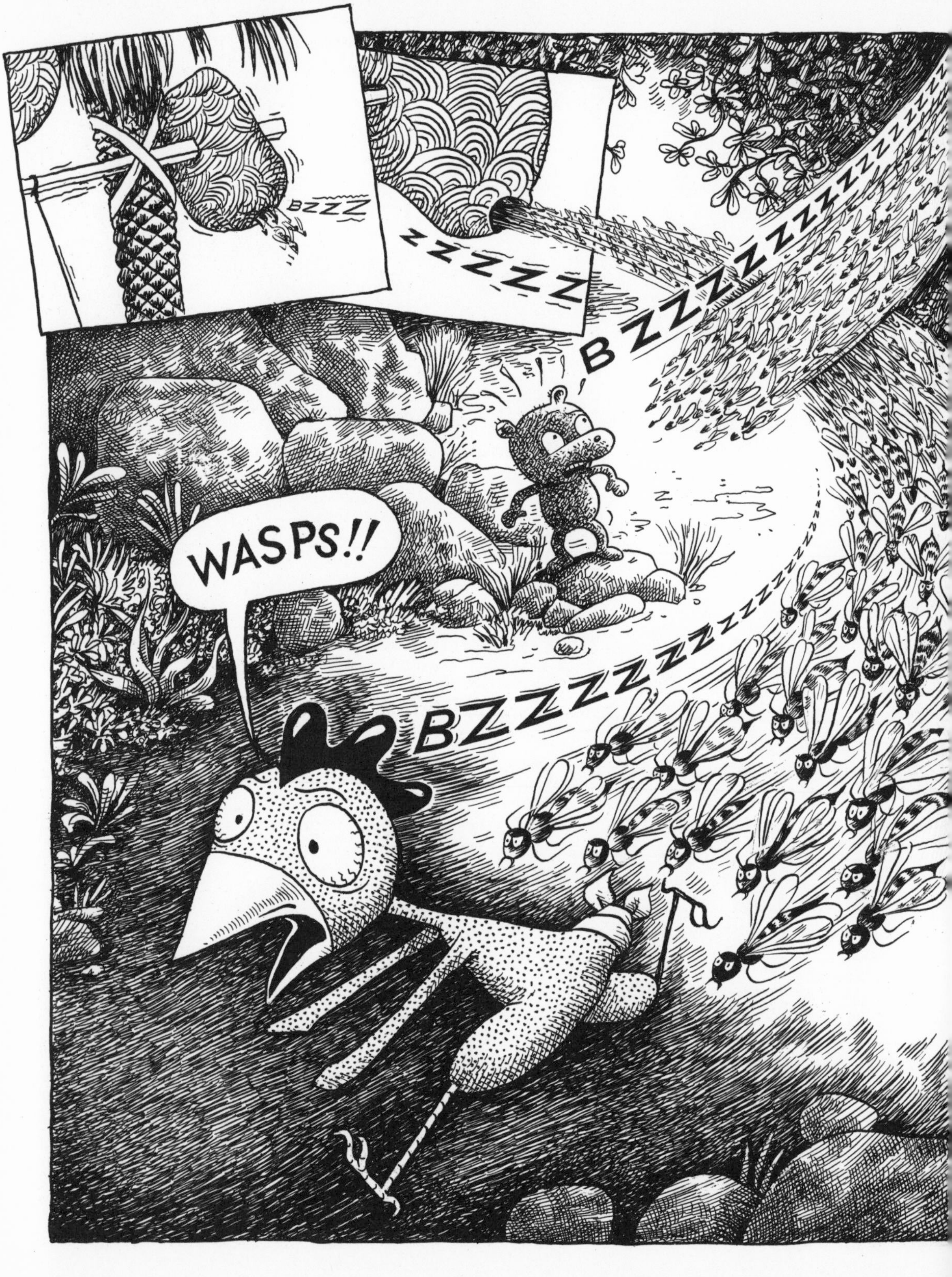
BZZZ
ZZZZZZ
BZZZZZZZZZZZZZZZZ
WASPS!!
BZZZZZZZZZZZZ

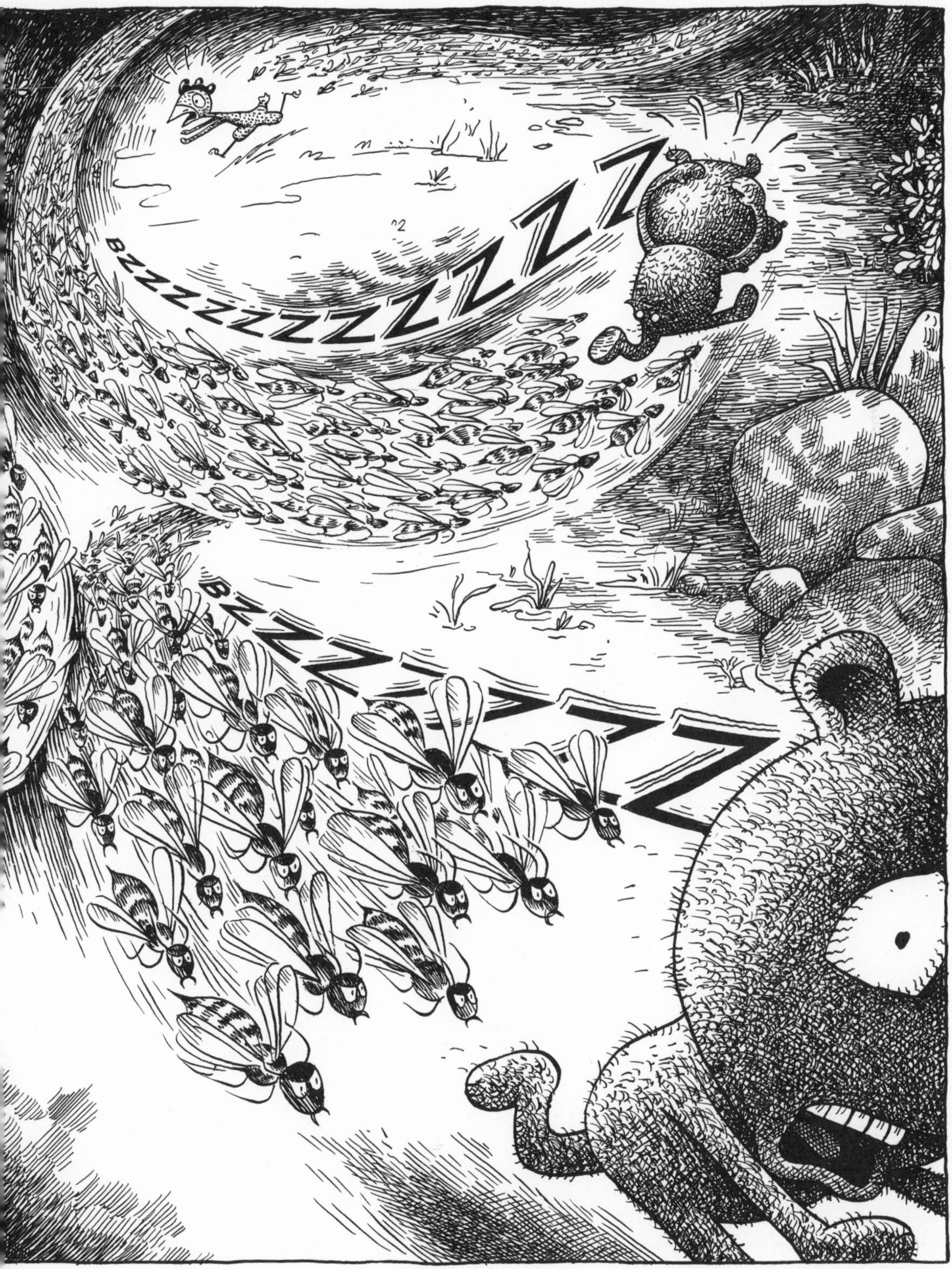

BZZZZZZZZZZZZZZZ
BZZZZZ

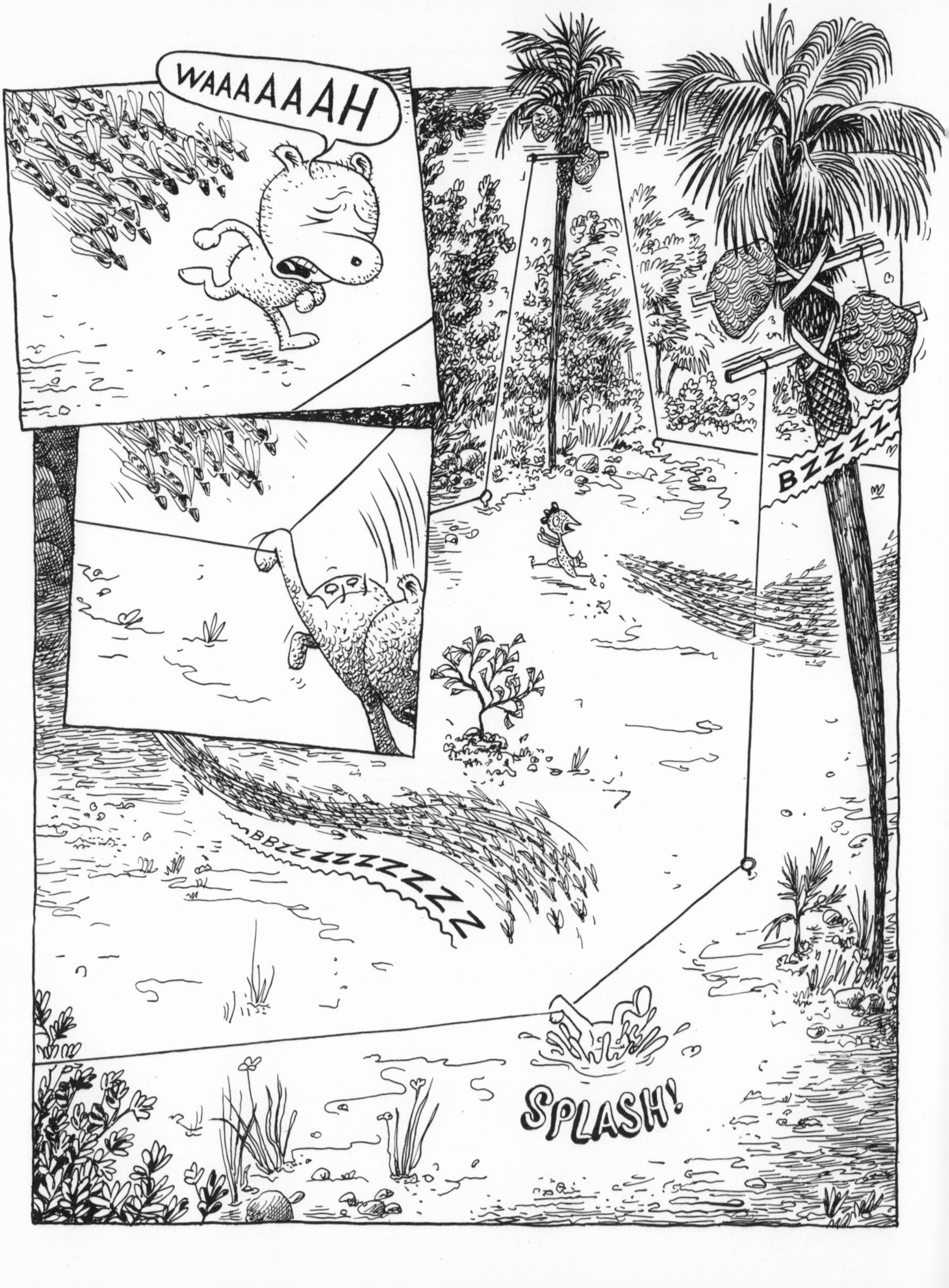
WAAAAAAH
BZZZZ
BBZZZZZZZZZZZZ
SPLASH!

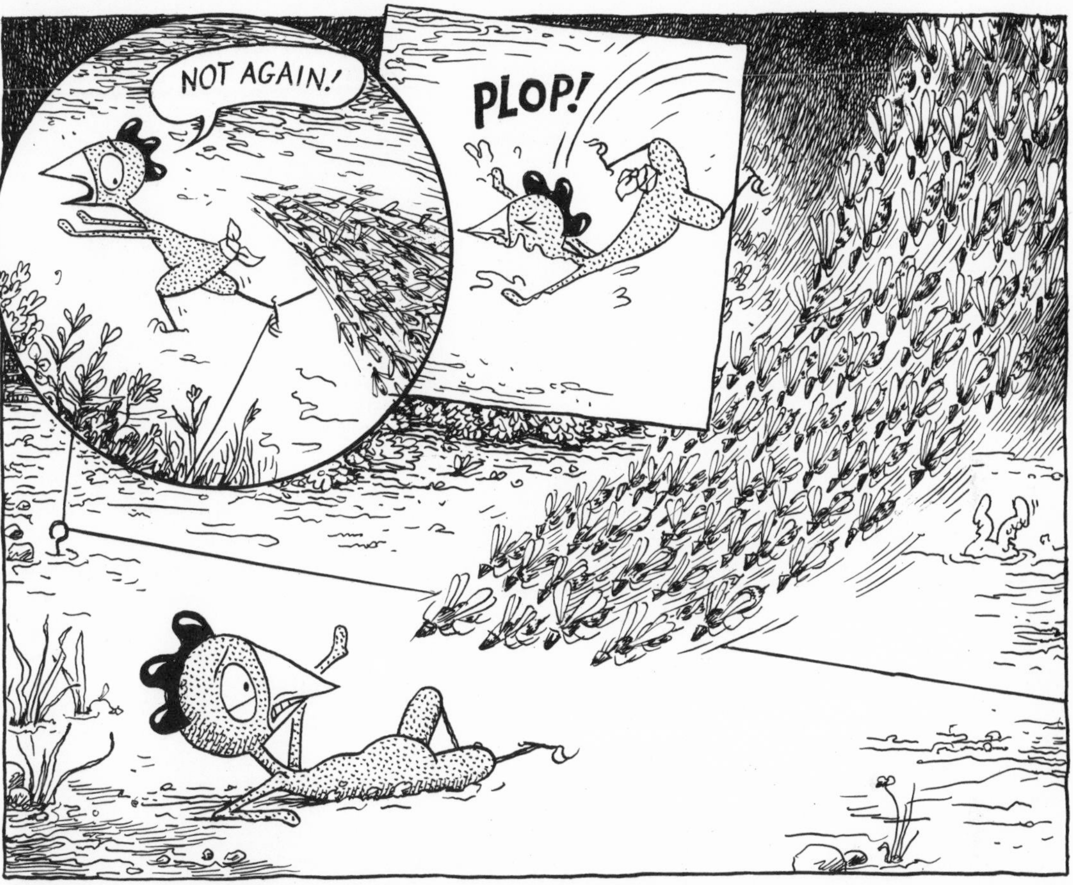
NOT AGAIN!
PLOP!

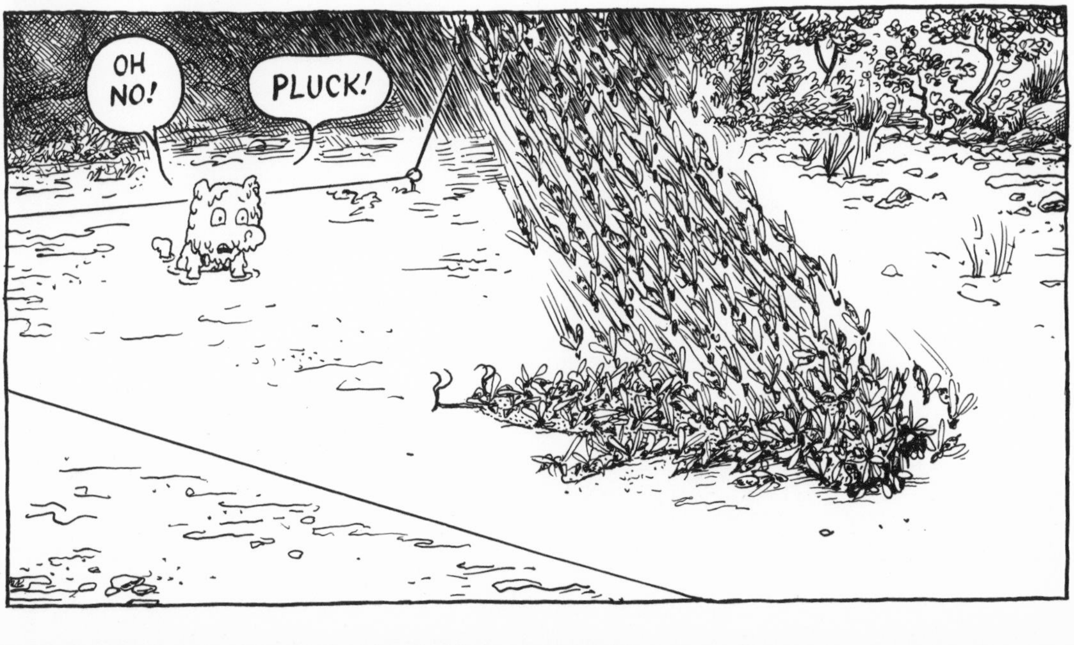
OH NO!
PLUCK!

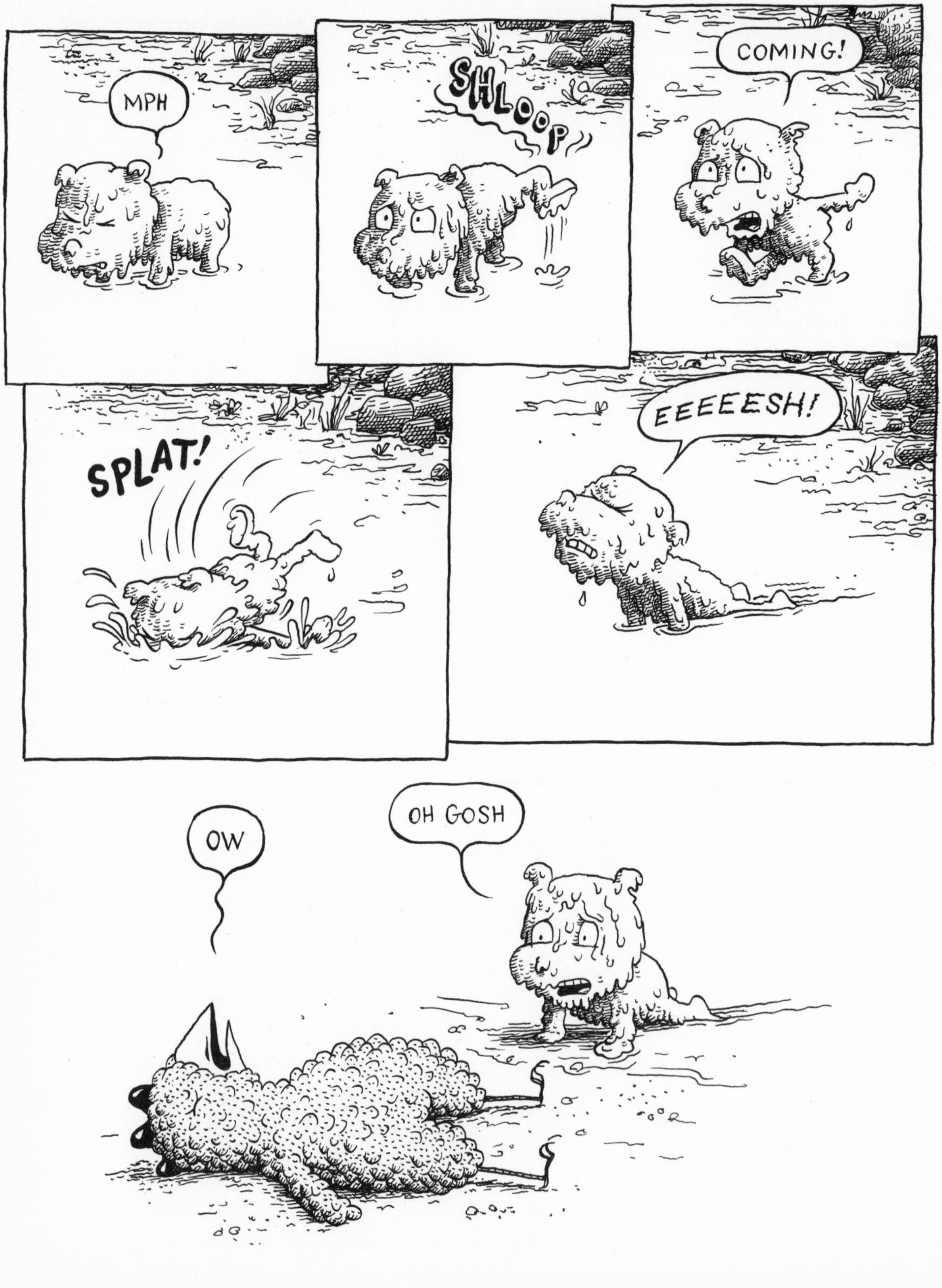
MPH
SHLOOP
COMING!
SPLAT!
EEEEEESH!
OW
OH GOSH

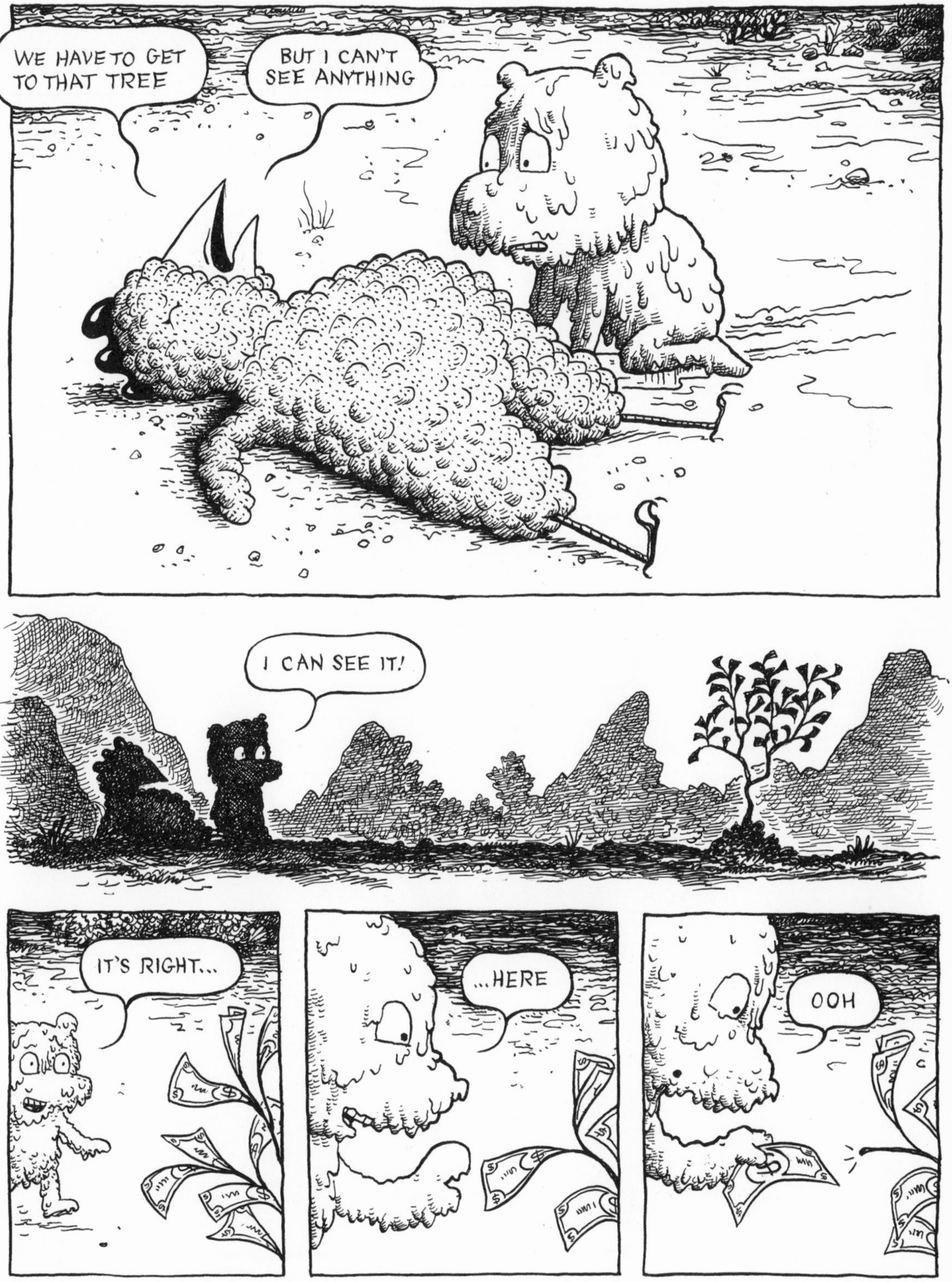
WE HAVE TO GET TO THAT TREE
BUT I CAN'T SEE ANYTHING
I CAN SEE IT!
IT'S RIGHT...
...HERE
OOH

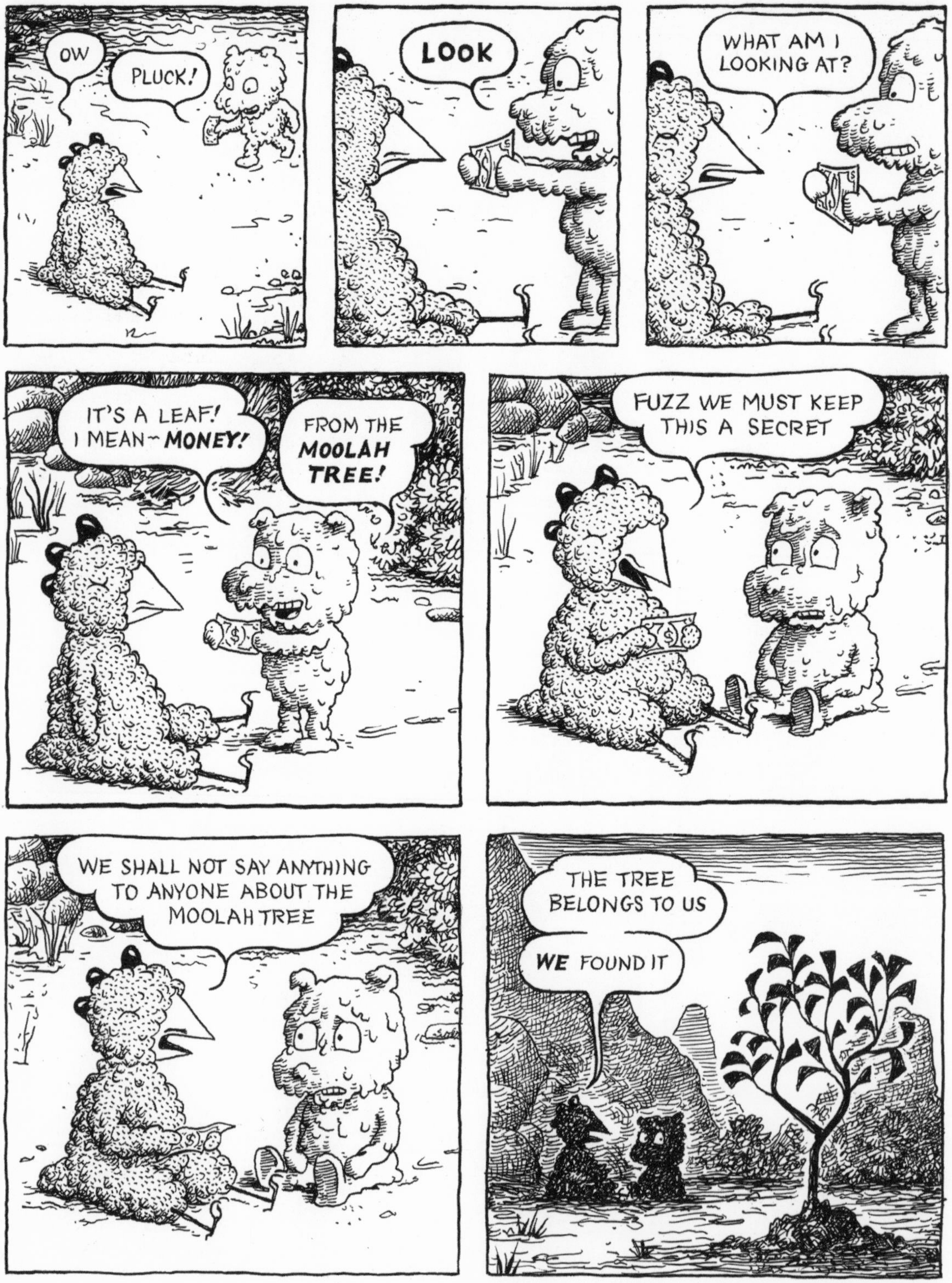
OW
PLUCK!
LOOK
WHAT AM I LOOKING AT?
IT'S A LEAF! I MEAN~MONEY!
FROM THE MOOLAH TREE!
FUZZ WE MUST KEEP THIS A SECRET
WE SHALL NOT SAY ANYTHING TO ANYONE ABOUT THE MOOLAH TREE
THE TREE BELONGS TO US
WE FOUND IT

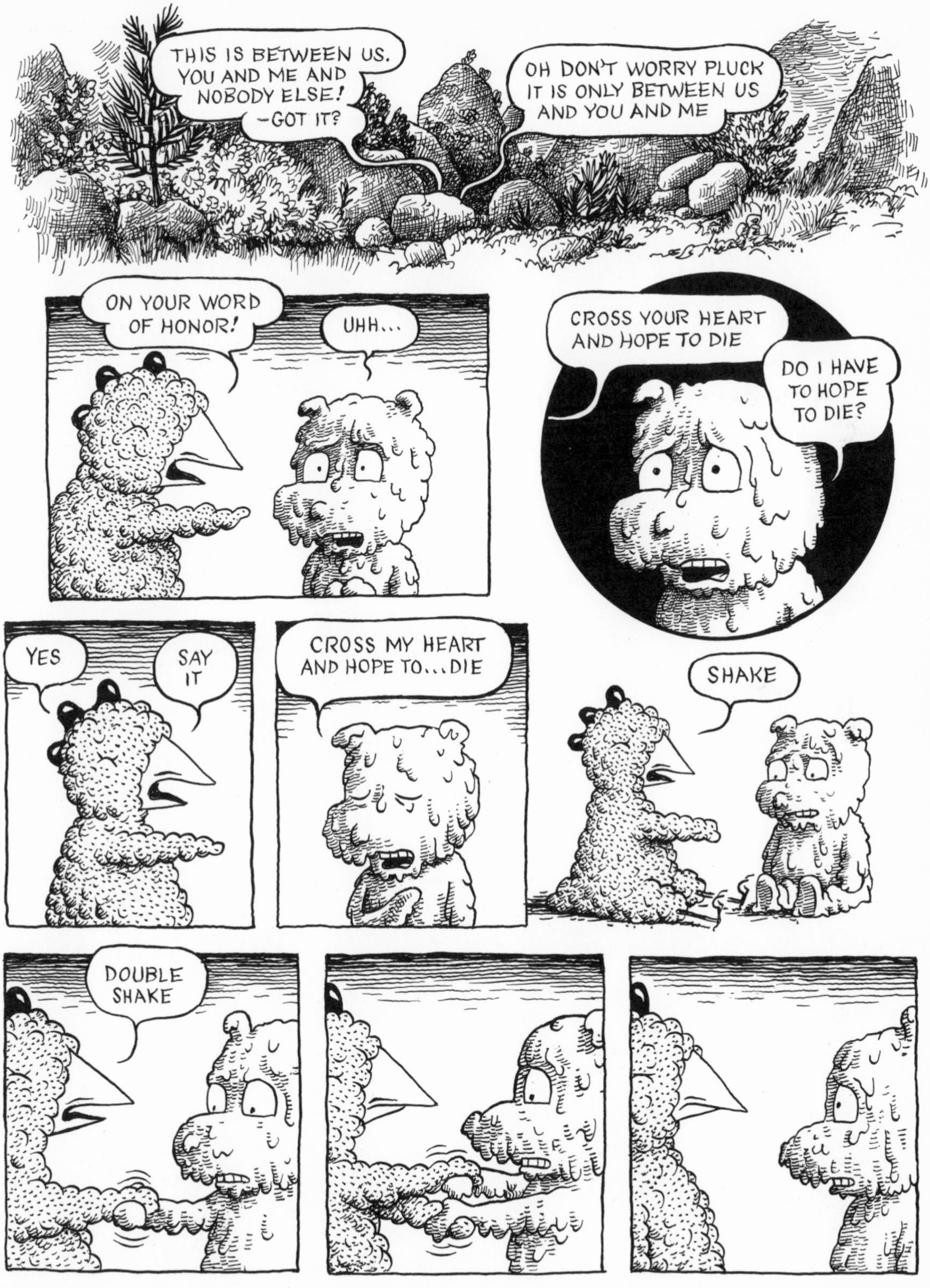
THIS IS BETWEEN US. YOU AND ME AND NOBODY ELSE! —GOT IT?
OH DON'T WORRY PLUCK IT IS ONLY BETWEEN US AND YOU AND ME
ON YOUR WORD OF HONOR!
UHH...
CROSS YOUR HEART AND HOPE TO DIE
DO I HAVE TO HOPE TO DIE?
YES
SAY IT
CROSS MY HEART AND HOPE TO...DIE
SHAKE
DOUBLE SHAKE

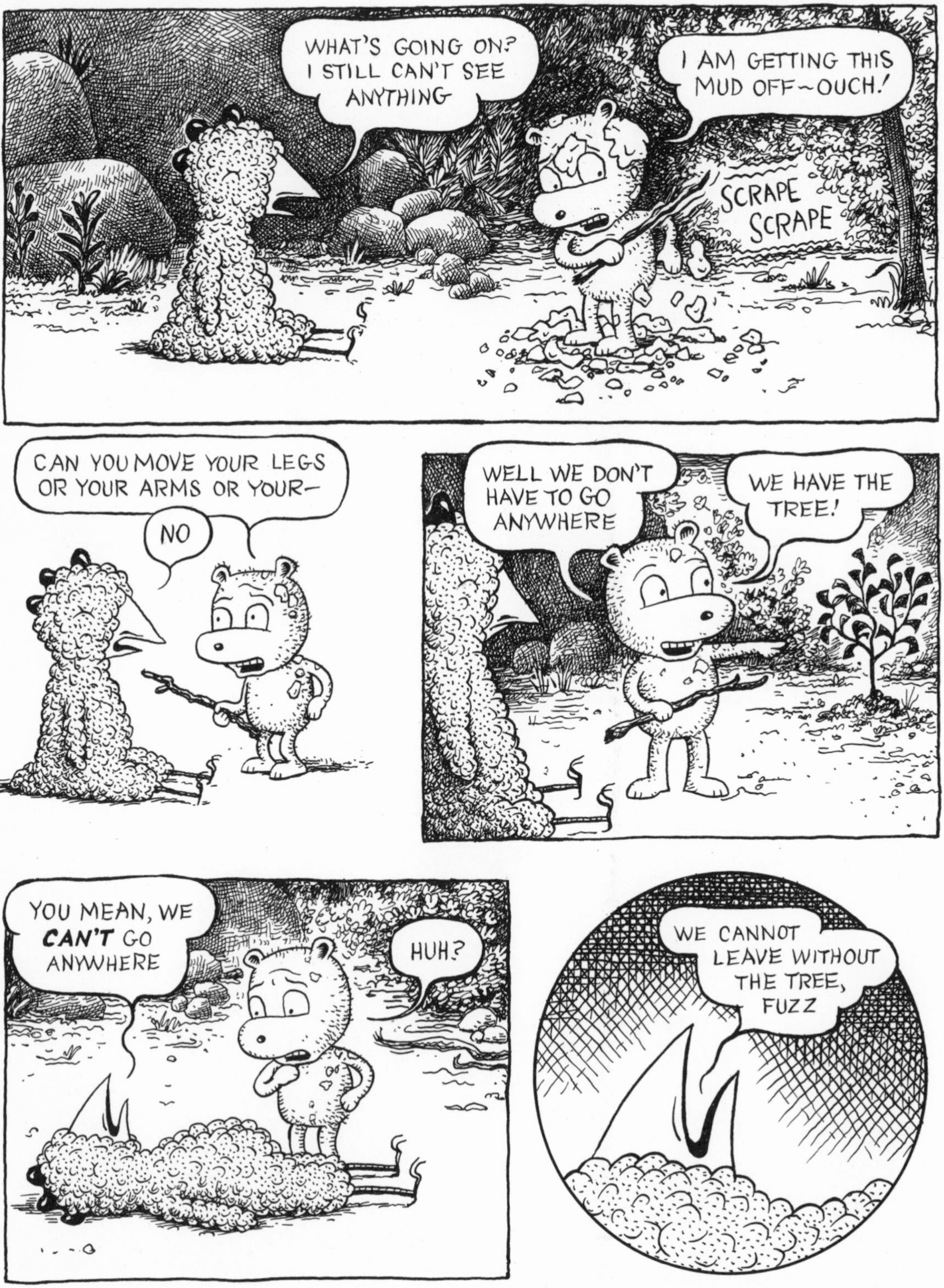
WHAT'S GOING ON? I STILL CAN'T SEE ANYTHING
I AM GETTING THIS MUD OFF~OUCH!
SCRAPE SCRAPE
CAN YOU MOVE YOUR LEGS OR YOUR ARMS OR YOUR–
NO
WELL WE DON'T HAVE TO GO ANYWHERE
WE HAVE THE TREE!
YOU MEAN, WE **CAN'T** GO ANYWHERE
HUH?
WE CANNOT LEAVE WITHOUT THE TREE, FUZZ

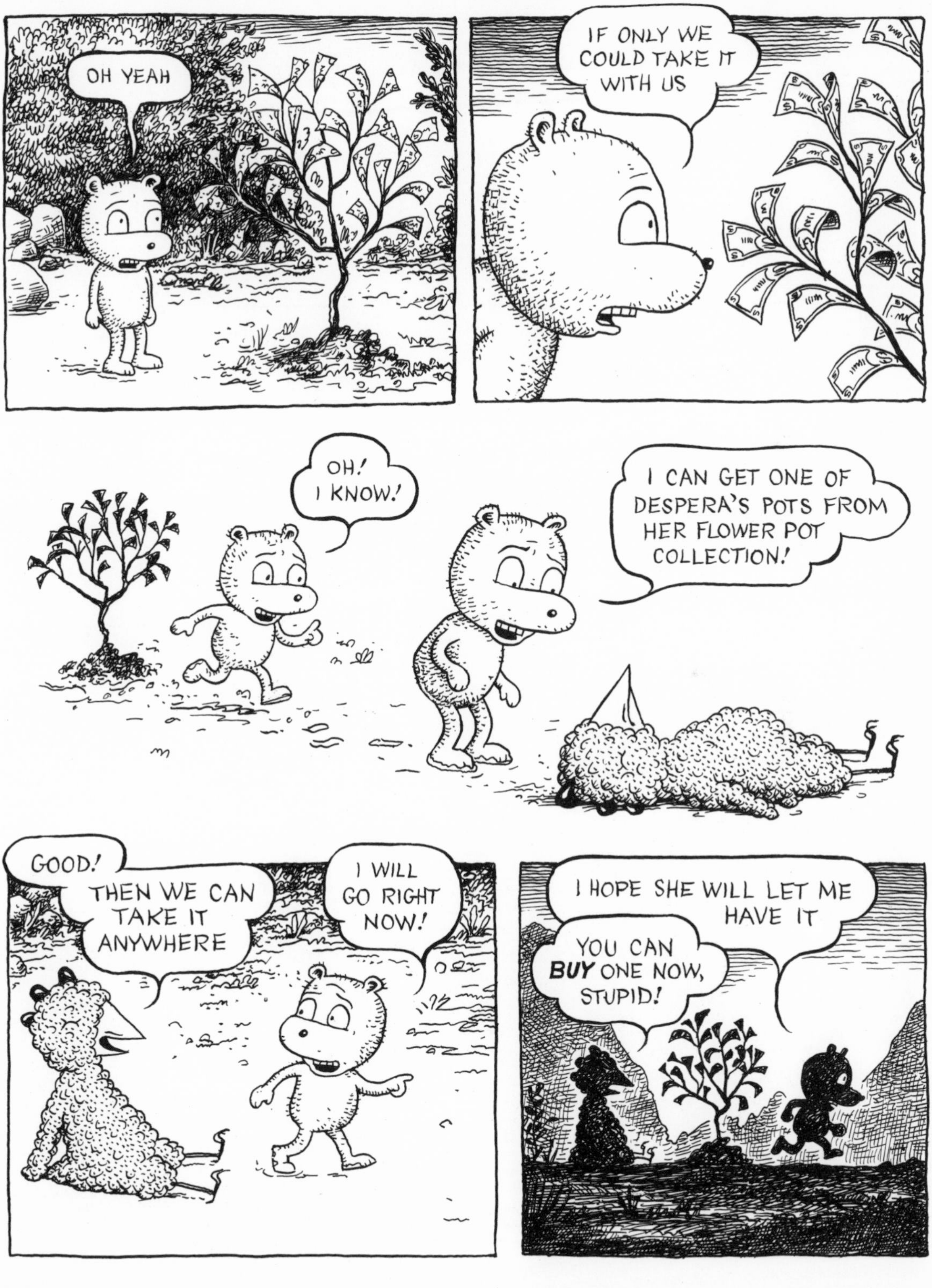
OH YEAH
IF ONLY WE COULD TAKE IT WITH US
OH! I KNOW!
I CAN GET ONE OF DESPERA'S POTS FROM HER FLOWER POT COLLECTION!
GOOD!
THEN WE CAN TAKE IT ANYWHERE
I WILL GO RIGHT NOW!
I HOPE SHE WILL LET ME HAVE IT
YOU CAN **BUY** ONE NOW, STUPID!

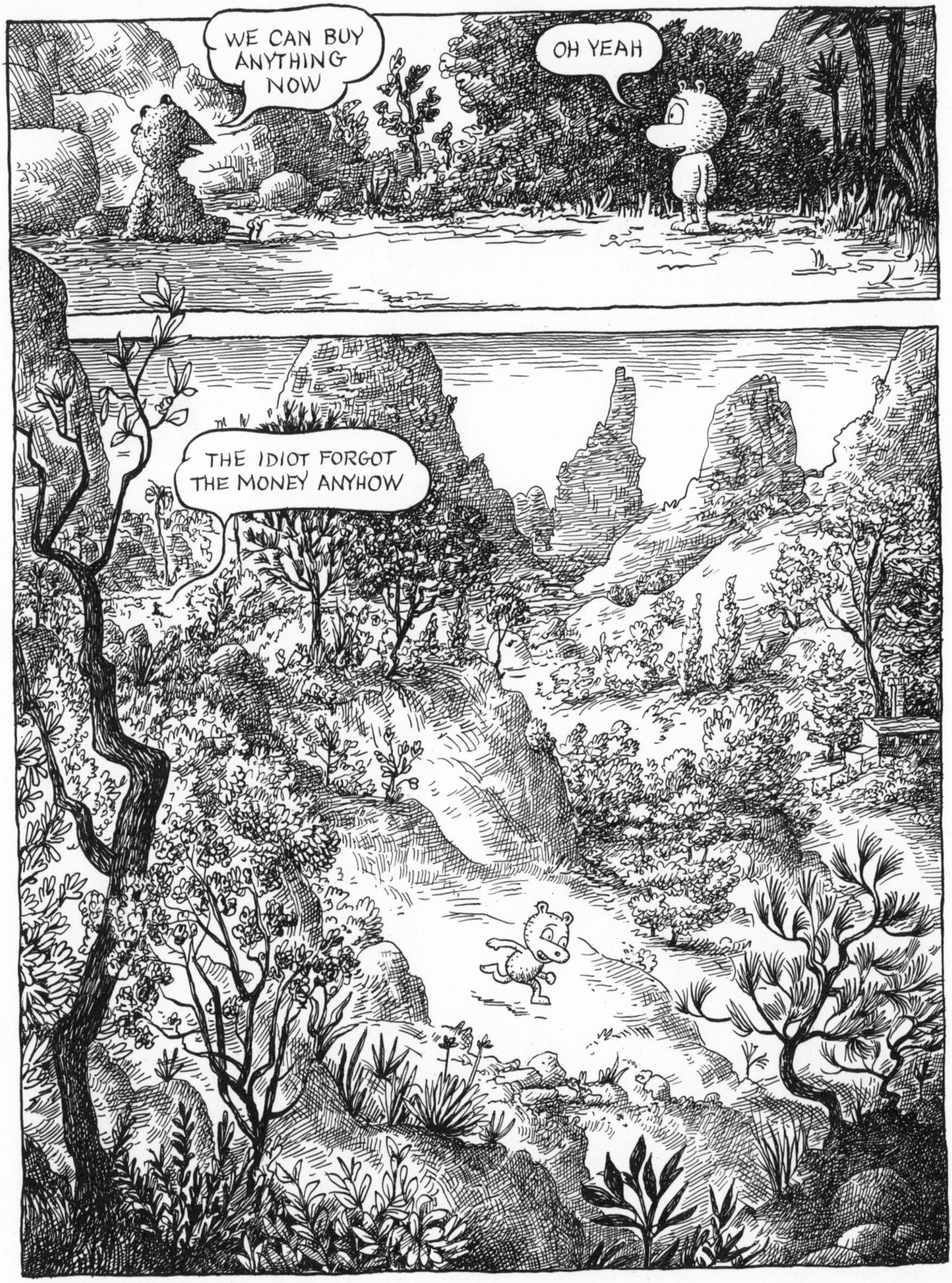
WE CAN BUY ANYTHING NOW
OH YEAH
THE IDIOT FORGOT THE MONEY ANYHOW

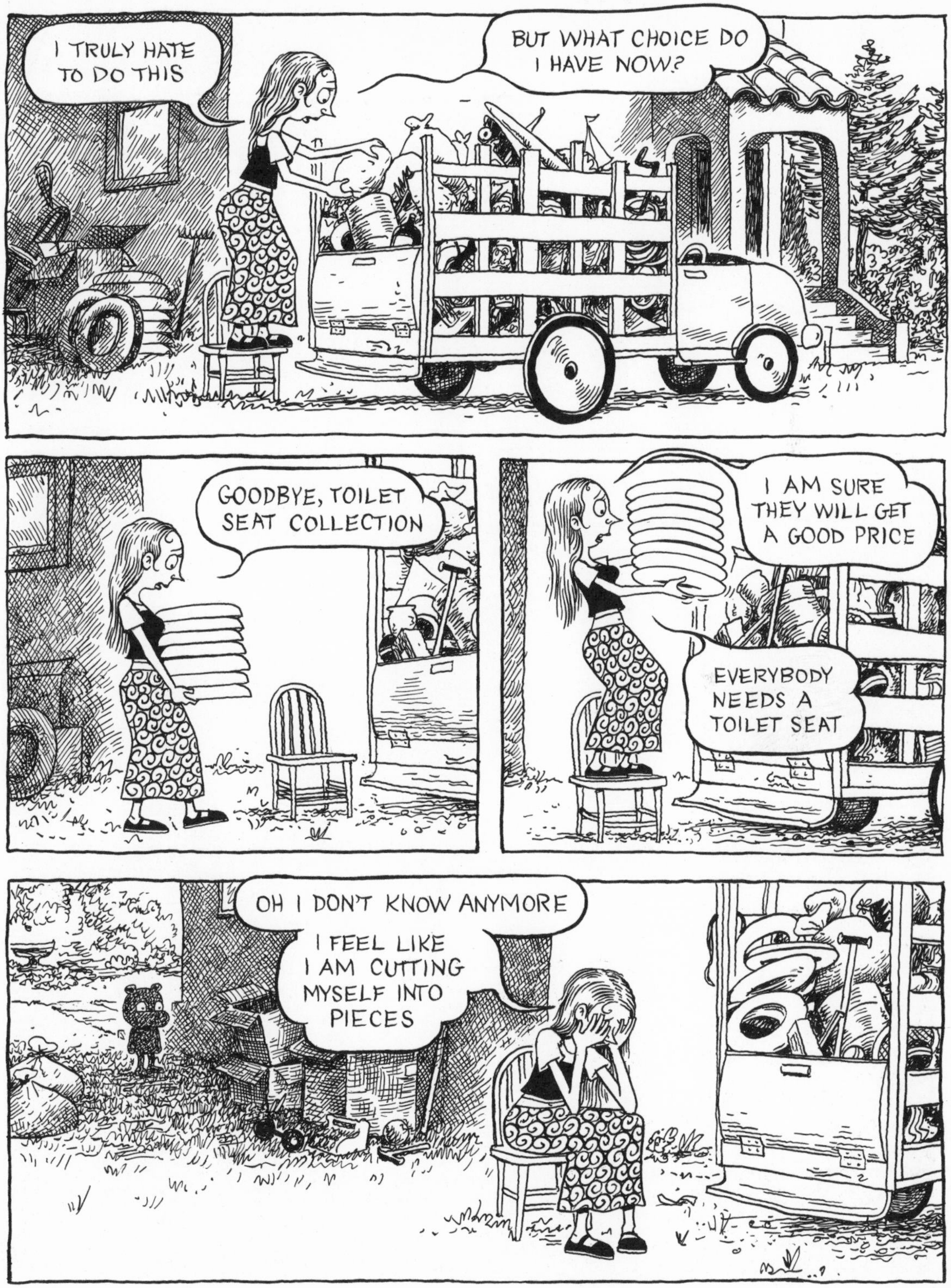
I TRULY HATE TO DO THIS
BUT WHAT CHOICE DO I HAVE NOW?
GOODBYE, TOILET SEAT COLLECTION
I AM SURE THEY WILL GET A GOOD PRICE
EVERYBODY NEEDS A TOILET SEAT
OH I DON'T KNOW ANYMORE
I FEEL LIKE I AM CUTTING MYSELF INTO PIECES

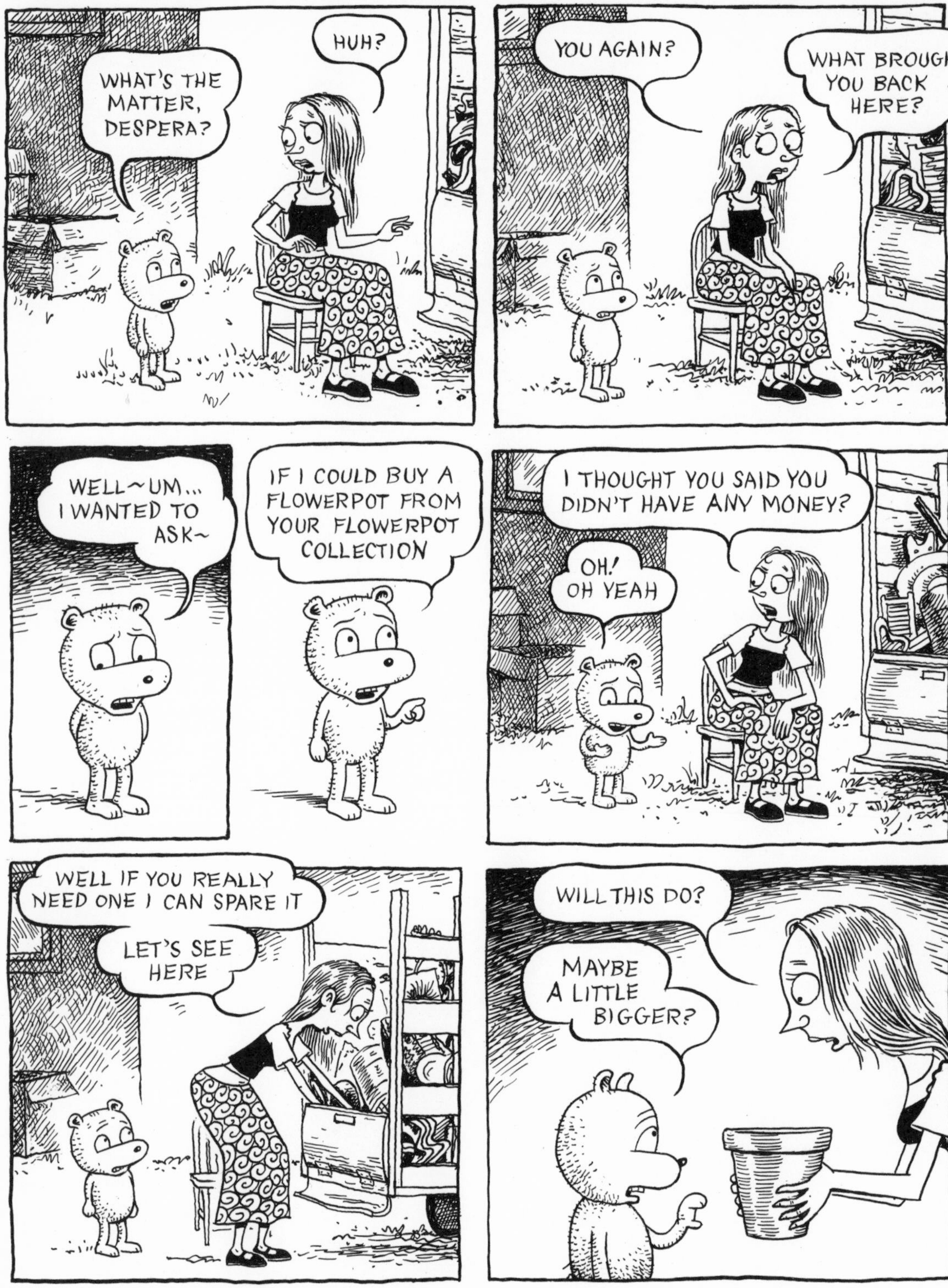
WHAT'S THE MATTER, DESPERA?
HUH?
YOU AGAIN?
WHAT BROUGHT YOU BACK HERE?
WELL~UM... I WANTED TO ASK~
IF I COULD BUY A FLOWERPOT FROM YOUR FLOWERPOT COLLECTION
I THOUGHT YOU SAID YOU DIDN'T HAVE ANY MONEY?
OH! OH YEAH
WELL IF YOU REALLY NEED ONE I CAN SPARE IT
LET'S SEE HERE
WILL THIS DO?
MAYBE A LITTLE BIGGER?

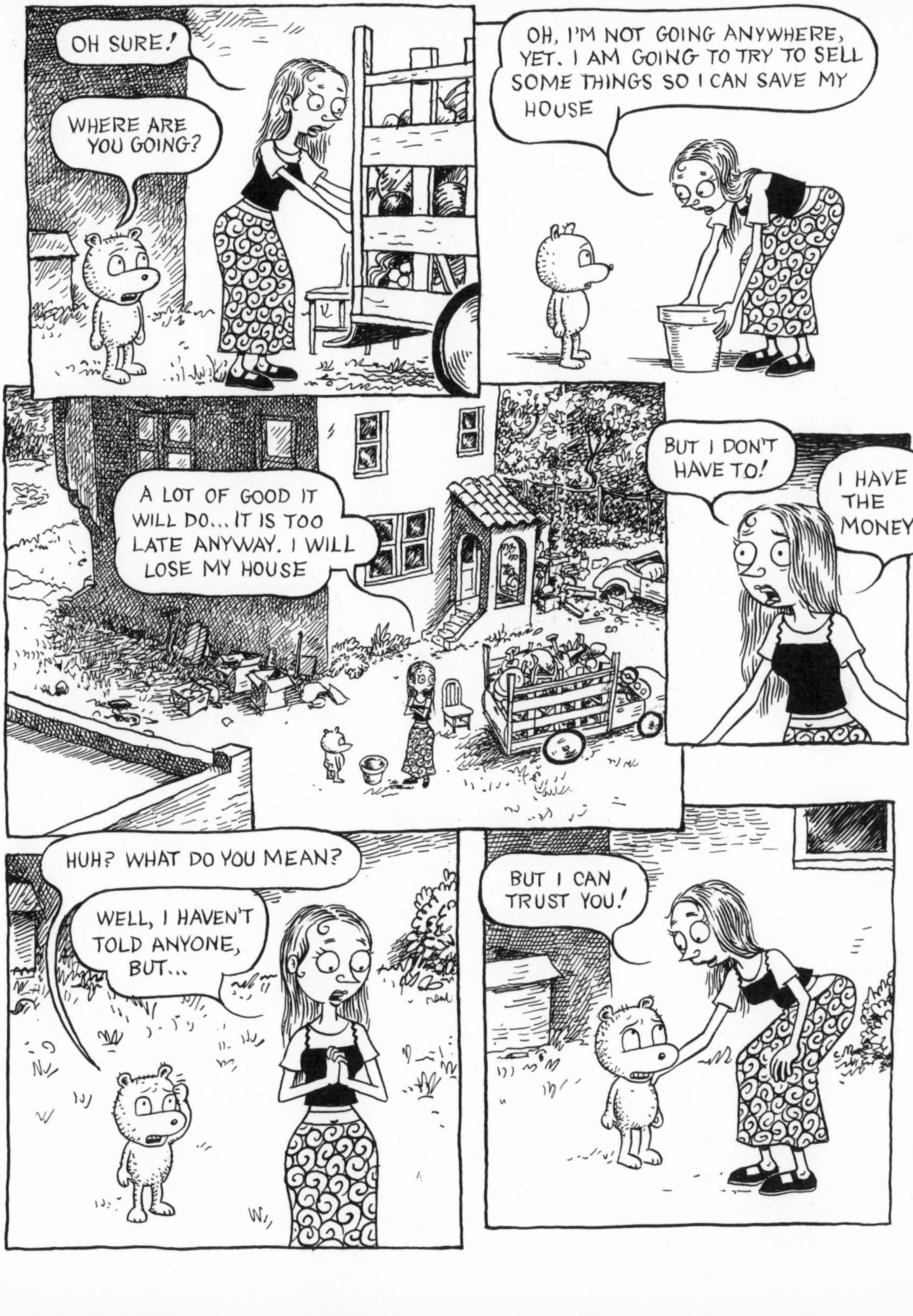

WHERE ARE YOU GOING?
OH SURE!
OH, I'M NOT GOING ANYWHERE, YET. I AM GOING TO TRY TO SELL SOME THINGS SO I CAN SAVE MY HOUSE
A LOT OF GOOD IT WILL DO... IT IS TOO LATE ANYWAY. I WILL LOSE MY HOUSE
BUT I DON'T HAVE TO!
I HAVE THE MONEY!
HUH? WHAT DO YOU MEAN?
WELL, I HAVEN'T TOLD ANYONE, BUT...
BUT I CAN TRUST YOU!

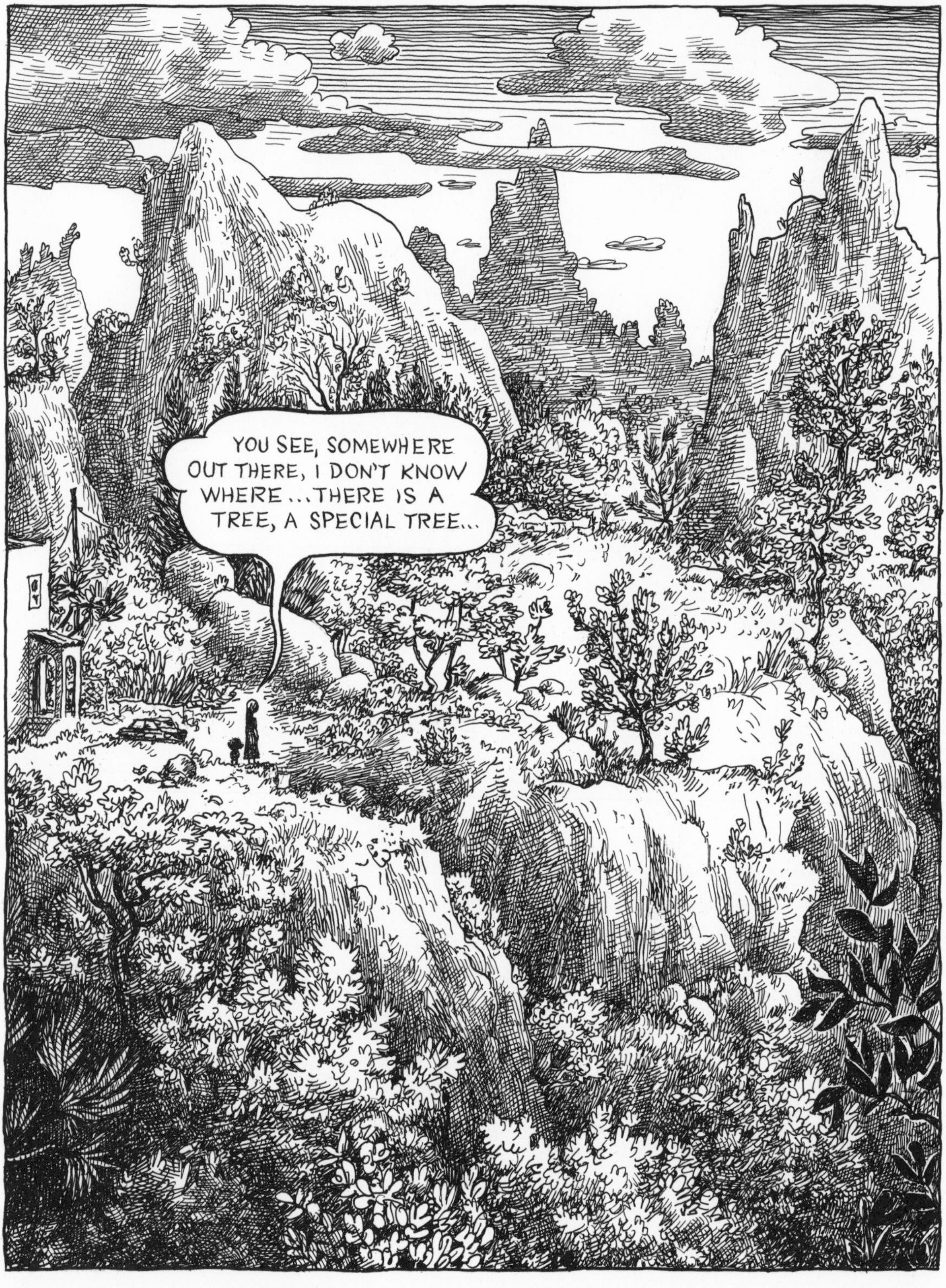
YOU SEE, SOMEWHERE OUT THERE, I DON'T KNOW WHERE... THERE IS A TREE, A SPECIAL TREE...

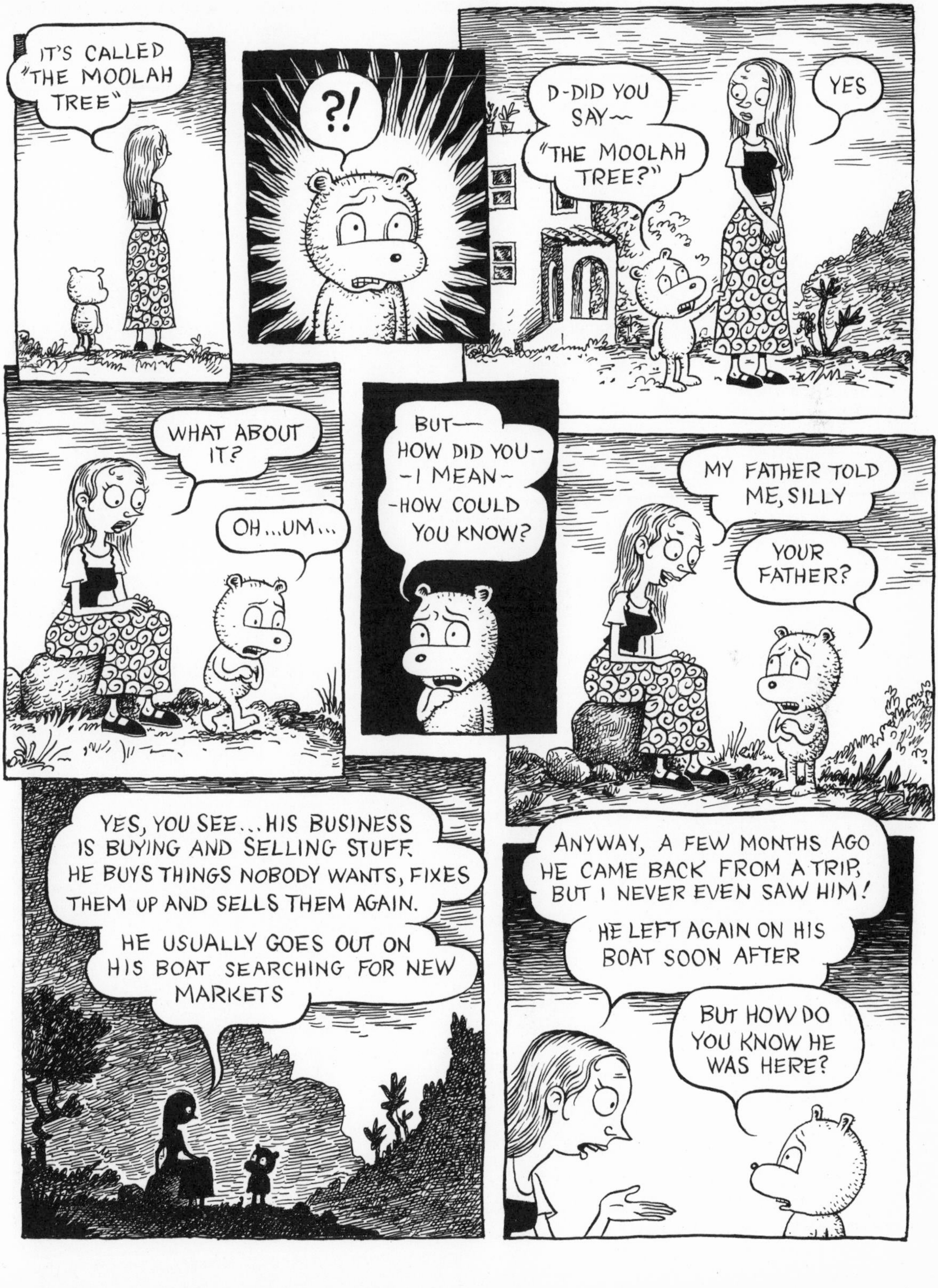
IT'S CALLED "THE MOOLAH TREE"
?!
D-DID YOU SAY~ "THE MOOLAH TREE?"
YES
WHAT ABOUT IT?
OH...UM...
BUT— HOW DID YOU- -I MEAN- -HOW COULD YOU KNOW?
MY FATHER TOLD ME, SILLY
YOUR FATHER?
YES, YOU SEE...HIS BUSINESS IS BUYING AND SELLING STUFF. HE BUYS THINGS NOBODY WANTS, FIXES THEM UP AND SELLS THEM AGAIN.
HE USUALLY GOES OUT ON HIS BOAT SEARCHING FOR NEW MARKETS
ANYWAY, A FEW MONTHS AGO HE CAME BACK FROM A TRIP, BUT I NEVER EVEN SAW HIM!
HE LEFT AGAIN ON HIS BOAT SOON AFTER
BUT HOW DO YOU KNOW HE WAS HERE?

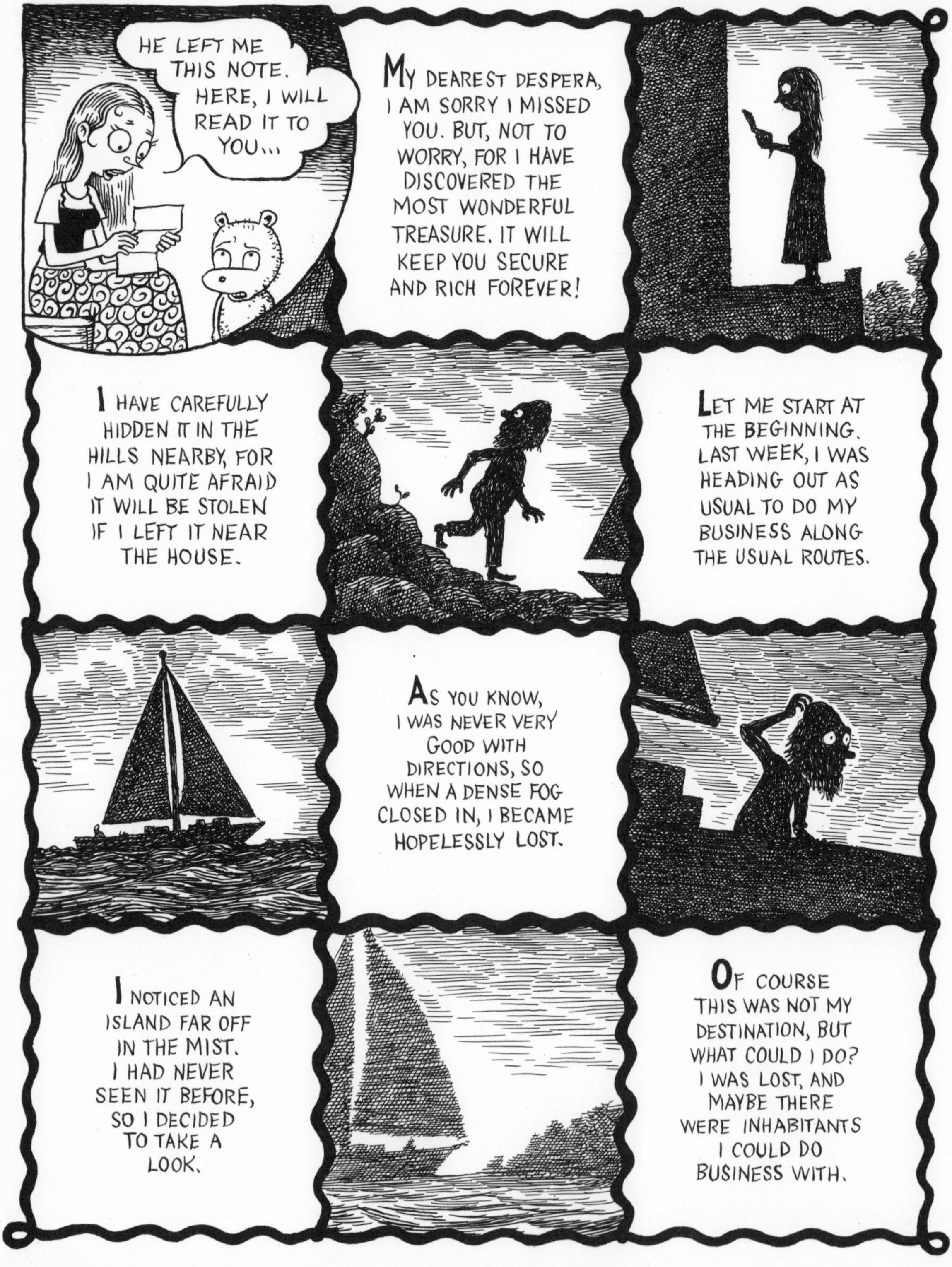
HE LEFT ME THIS NOTE. HERE, I WILL READ IT TO YOU...
MY DEAREST DESPERA, I AM SORRY I MISSED YOU. BUT, NOT TO WORRY, FOR I HAVE DISCOVERED THE MOST WONDERFUL TREASURE. IT WILL KEEP YOU SECURE AND RICH FOREVER!
I HAVE CAREFULLY HIDDEN IT IN THE HILLS NEARBY, FOR I AM QUITE AFRAID IT WILL BE STOLEN IF I LEFT IT NEAR THE HOUSE.
LET ME START AT THE BEGINNING. LAST WEEK, I WAS HEADING OUT AS USUAL TO DO MY BUSINESS ALONG THE USUAL ROUTES.
AS YOU KNOW, I WAS NEVER VERY GOOD WITH DIRECTIONS, SO WHEN A DENSE FOG CLOSED IN, I BECAME HOPELESSLY LOST.
I NOTICED AN ISLAND FAR OFF IN THE MIST. I HAD NEVER SEEN IT BEFORE, SO I DECIDED TO TAKE A LOOK.
OF COURSE THIS WAS NOT MY DESTINATION, BUT WHAT COULD I DO? I WAS LOST, AND MAYBE THERE WERE INHABITANTS I COULD DO BUSINESS WITH.

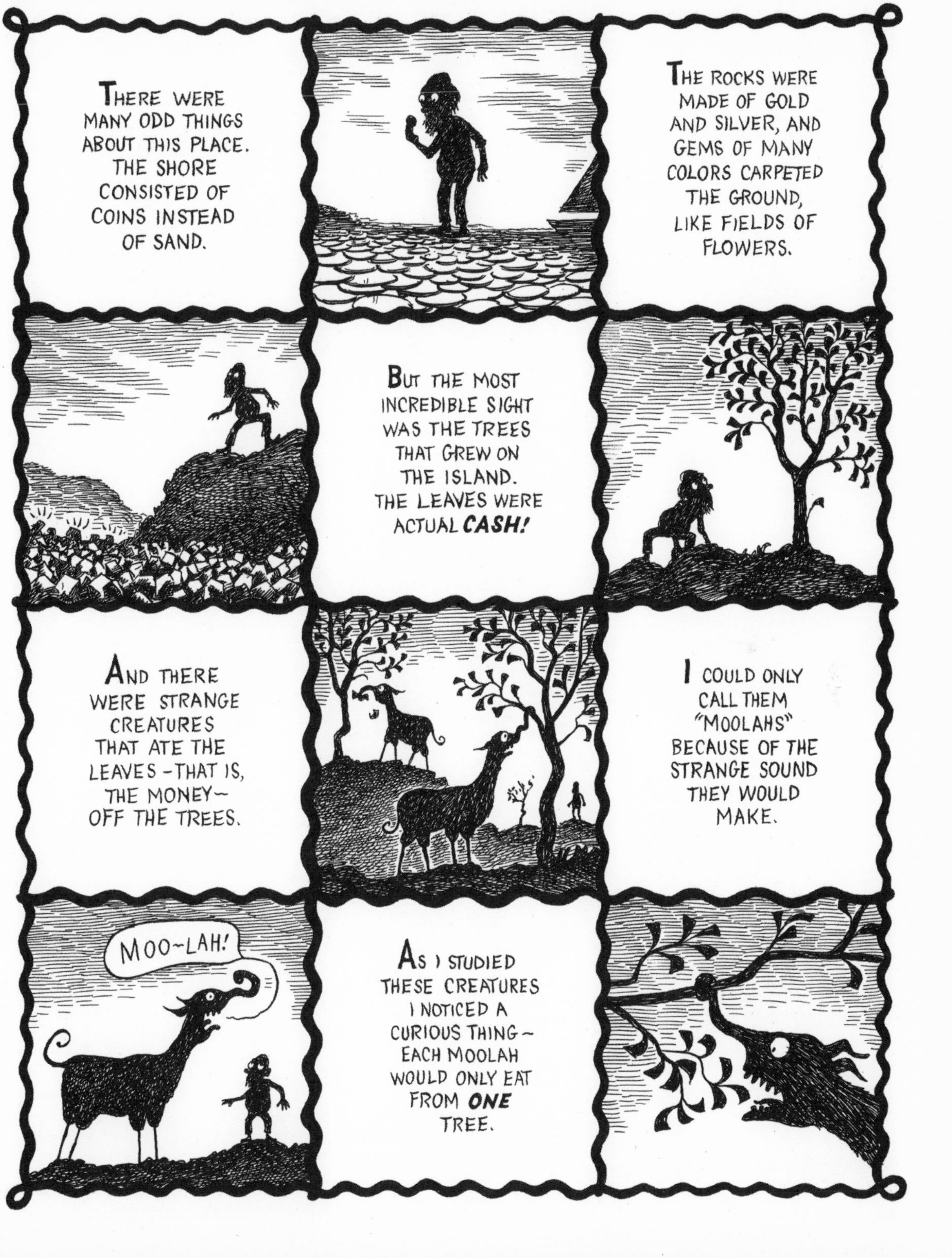
There were many odd things about this place. The shore consisted of coins instead of sand.
The rocks were made of gold and silver, and gems of many colors carpeted the ground, like fields of flowers.
But the most incredible sight was the trees that grew on the island. The leaves were actual *CASH!*
And there were strange creatures that ate the leaves - that is, the money - off the trees.
I could only call them "Moolahs" because of the strange sound they would make.
MOO-LAH!
As I studied these creatures I noticed a curious thing - each Moolah would only eat from *ONE* tree.

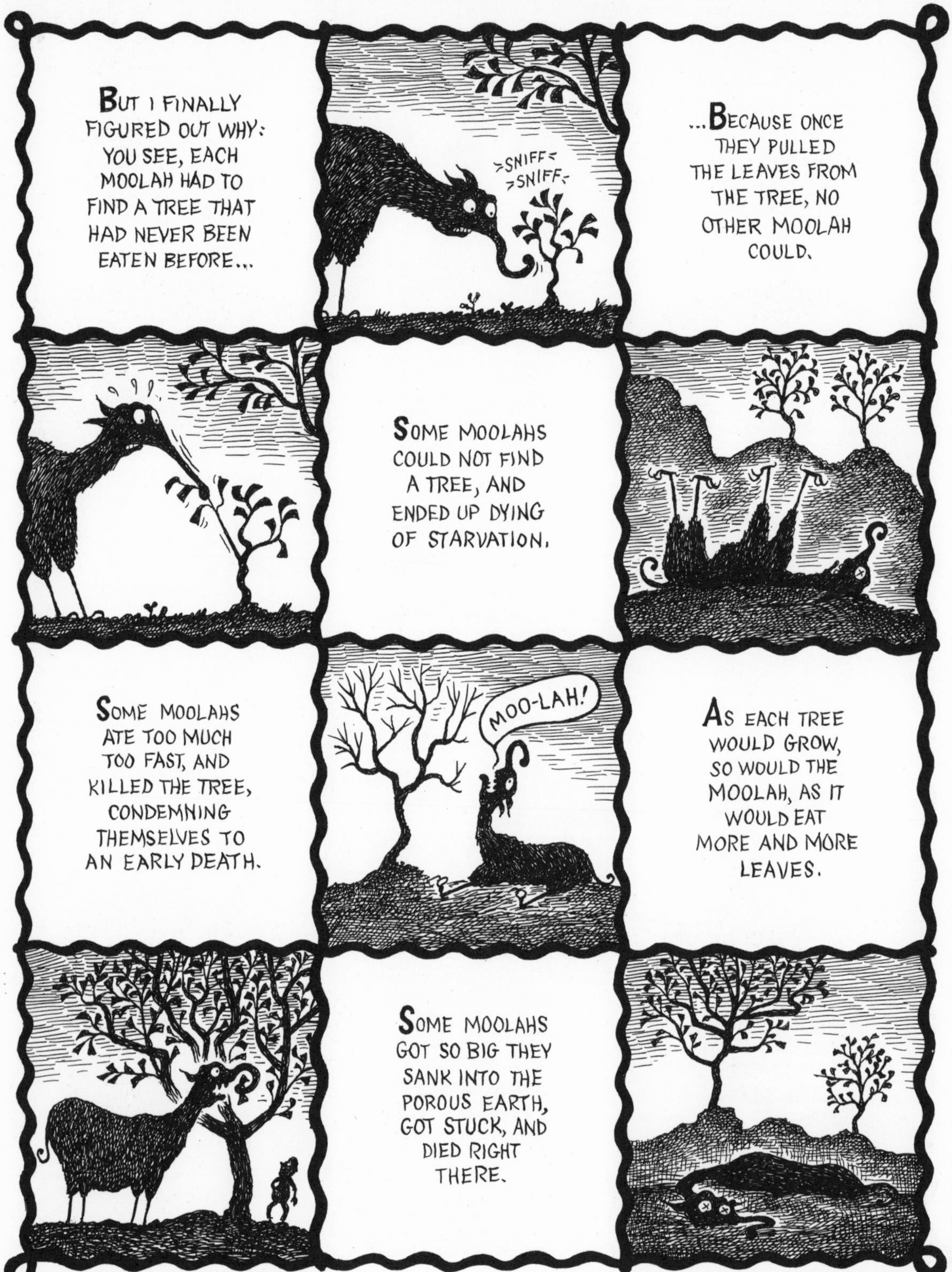
But I finally figured out why: you see, each moolah had to find a tree that had never been eaten before...
>SNIFF< >SNIFF<
...Because once they pulled the leaves from the tree, no other moolah could.
Some moolahs could not find a tree, and ended up dying of starvation.
Some moolahs ate too much too fast, and killed the tree, condemning themselves to an early death.
MOO-LAH!
As each tree would grow, so would the moolah, as it would eat more and more leaves.
Some moolahs got so big they sank into the porous earth, got stuck, and died right there.

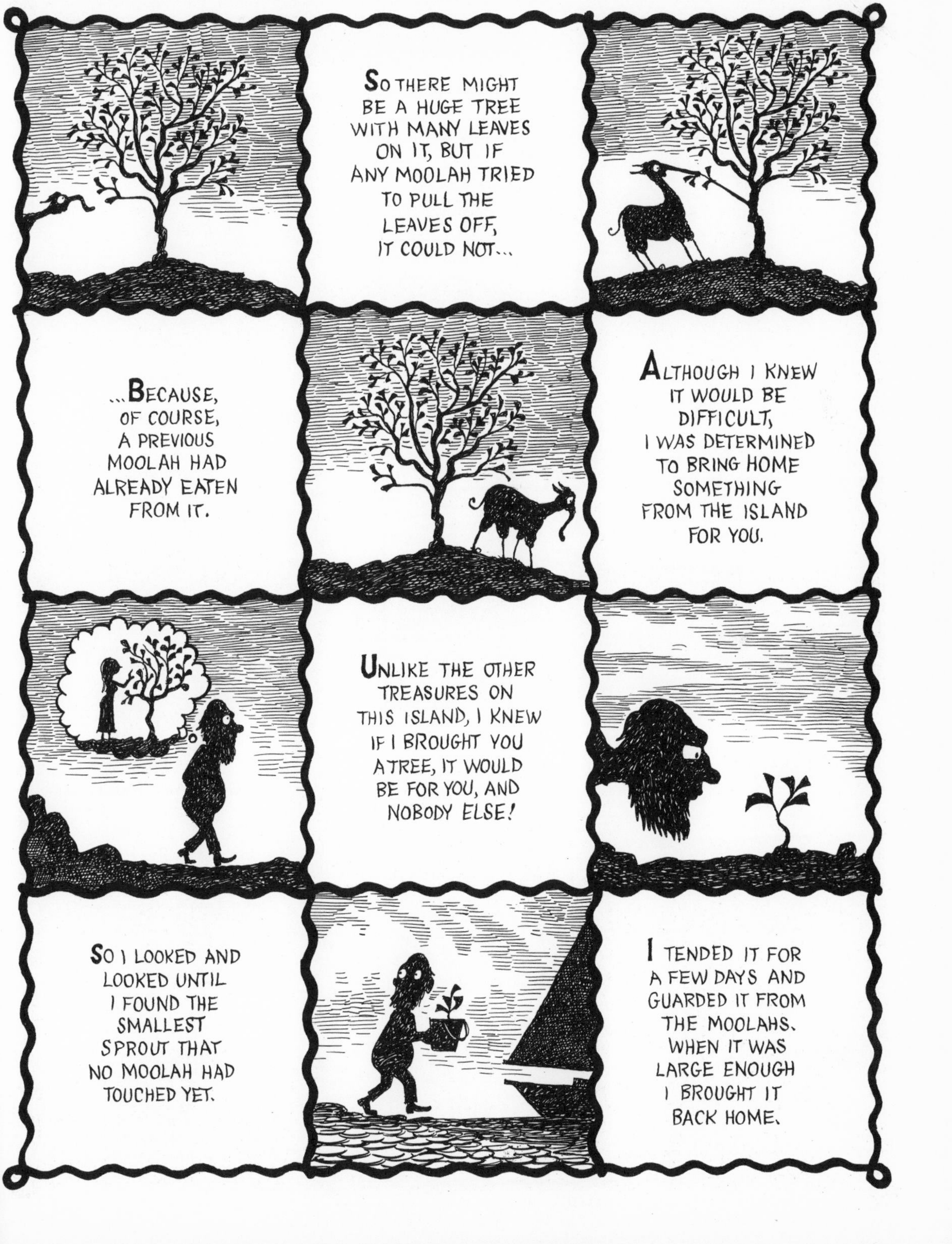
So there might be a huge tree with many leaves on it, but if any moolah tried to pull the leaves off, it could not...
...Because, of course, a previous moolah had already eaten from it.
Although I knew it would be difficult, I was determined to bring home something from the island for you.
Unlike the other treasures on this island, I knew if I brought you a tree, it would be for you, and nobody else!
So I looked and looked until I found the smallest sprout that no moolah had touched yet.
I tended it for a few days and guarded it from the moolahs. When it was large enough I brought it back home.

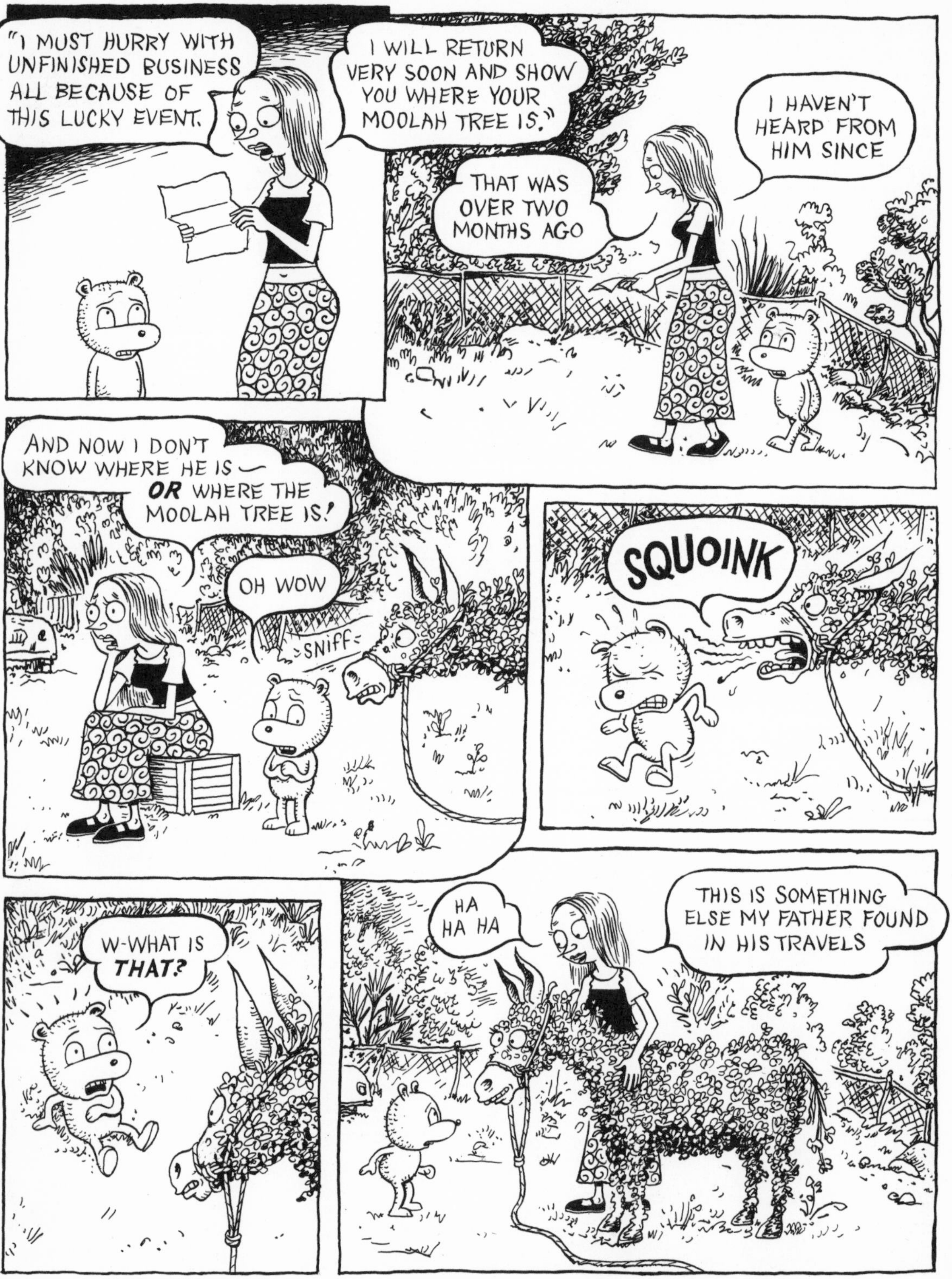
"I MUST HURRY WITH UNFINISHED BUSINESS ALL BECAUSE OF THIS LUCKY EVENT.
I WILL RETURN VERY SOON AND SHOW YOU WHERE YOUR MOOLAH TREE IS."
I HAVEN'T HEARD FROM HIM SINCE
THAT WAS OVER TWO MONTHS AGO
AND NOW I DON'T KNOW WHERE HE IS — OR WHERE THE MOOLAH TREE IS!
OH WOW
SNIFF
SQUOINK
W-WHAT IS THAT?
HA HA HA
THIS IS SOMETHING ELSE MY FATHER FOUND IN HIS TRAVELS

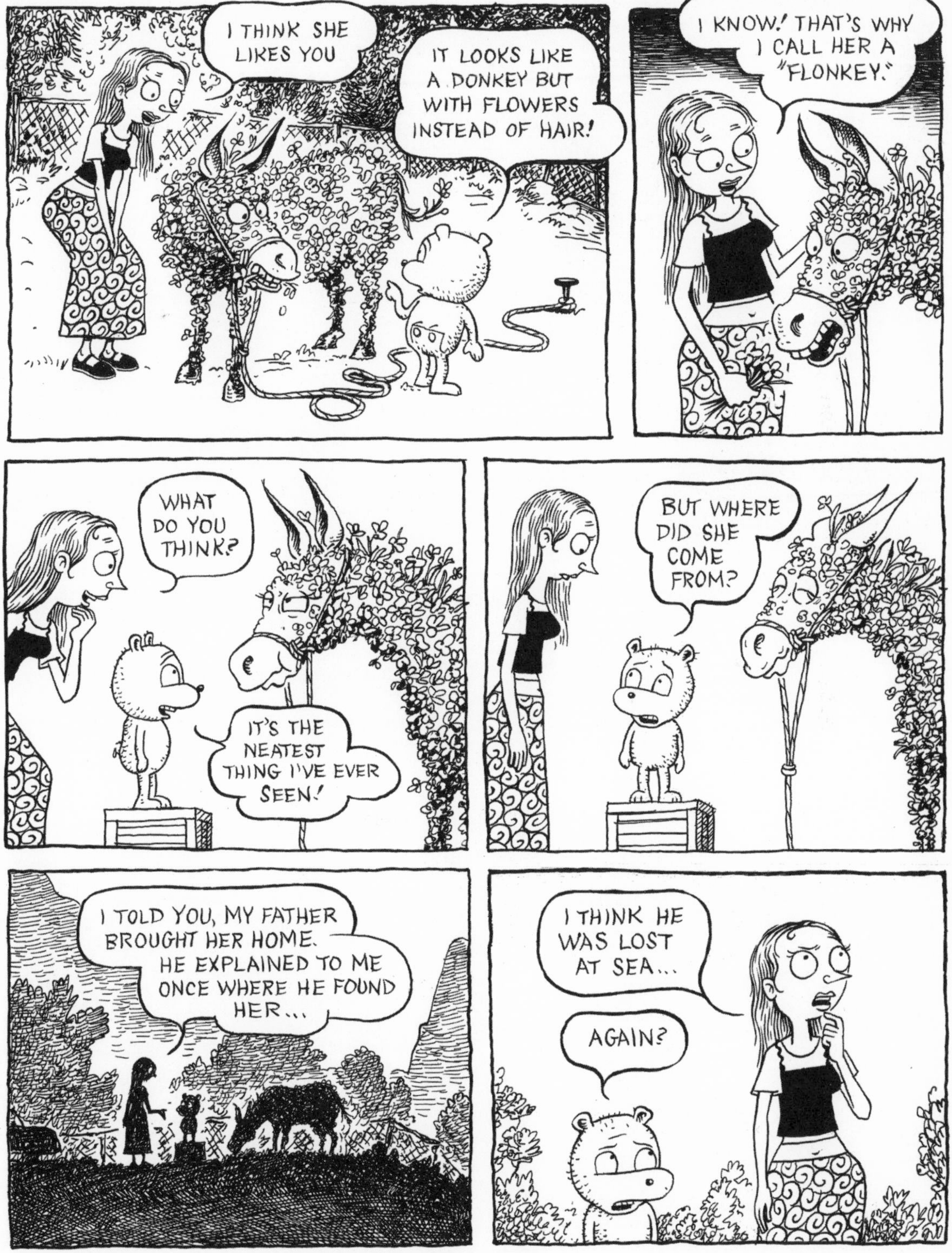
I THINK SHE LIKES YOU
IT LOOKS LIKE A DONKEY BUT WITH FLOWERS INSTEAD OF HAIR!
I KNOW! THAT'S WHY I CALL HER A "FLONKEY."
WHAT DO YOU THINK?
IT'S THE NEATEST THING I'VE EVER SEEN!
BUT WHERE DID SHE COME FROM?
I TOLD YOU, MY FATHER BROUGHT HER HOME.
HE EXPLAINED TO ME ONCE WHERE HE FOUND HER...
I THINK HE WAS LOST AT SEA...
AGAIN?

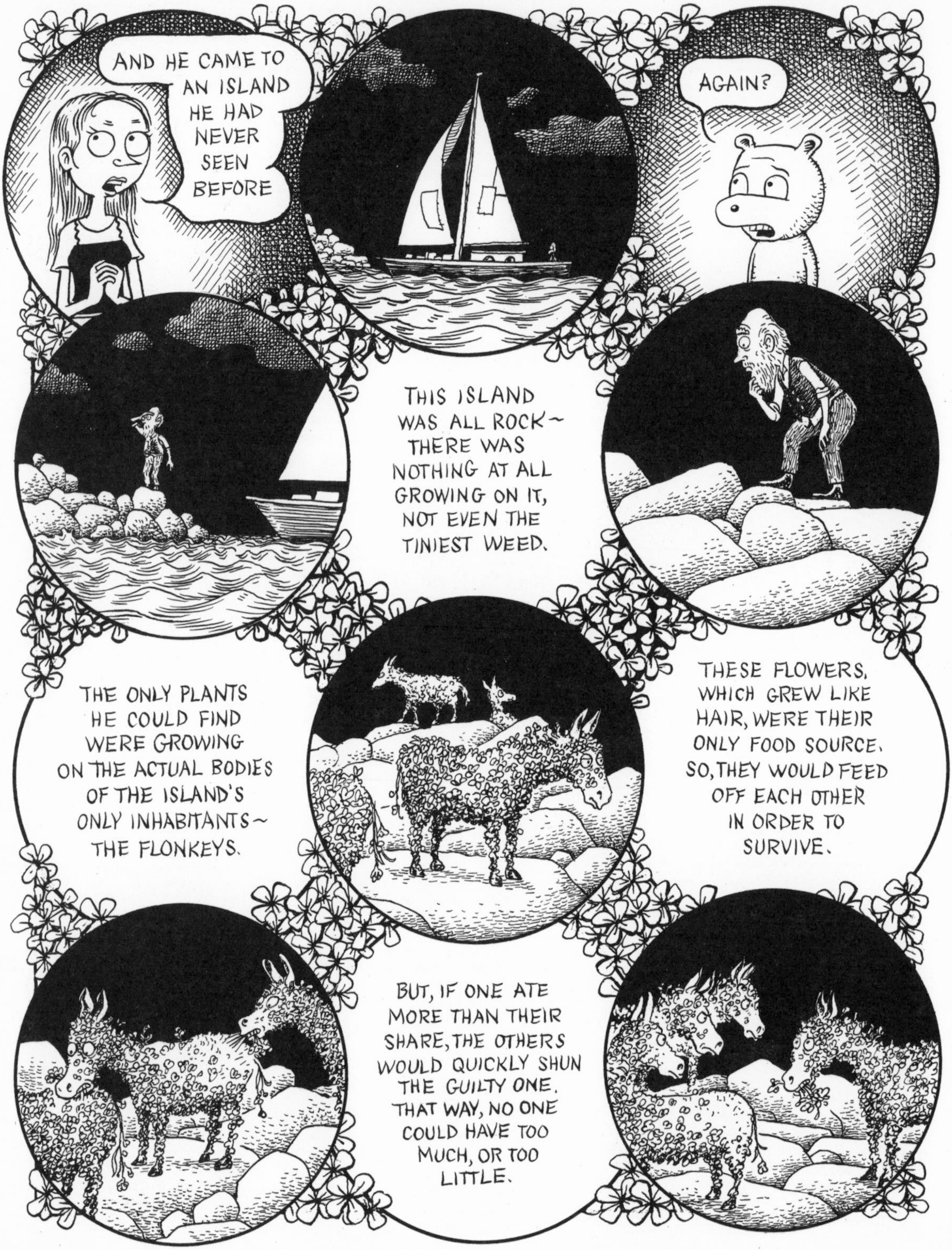
AND HE CAME TO AN ISLAND HE HAD NEVER SEEN BEFORE
AGAIN?
THIS ISLAND WAS ALL ROCK~ THERE WAS NOTHING AT ALL GROWING ON IT, NOT EVEN THE TINIEST WEED.
THE ONLY PLANTS HE COULD FIND WERE GROWING ON THE ACTUAL BODIES OF THE ISLAND'S ONLY INHABITANTS~ THE FLONKEYS.
THESE FLOWERS, WHICH GREW LIKE HAIR, WERE THEIR ONLY FOOD SOURCE. SO, THEY WOULD FEED OFF EACH OTHER IN ORDER TO SURVIVE.
BUT, IF ONE ATE MORE THAN THEIR SHARE, THE OTHERS WOULD QUICKLY SHUN THE GUILTY ONE. THAT WAY, NO ONE COULD HAVE TOO MUCH, OR TOO LITTLE.

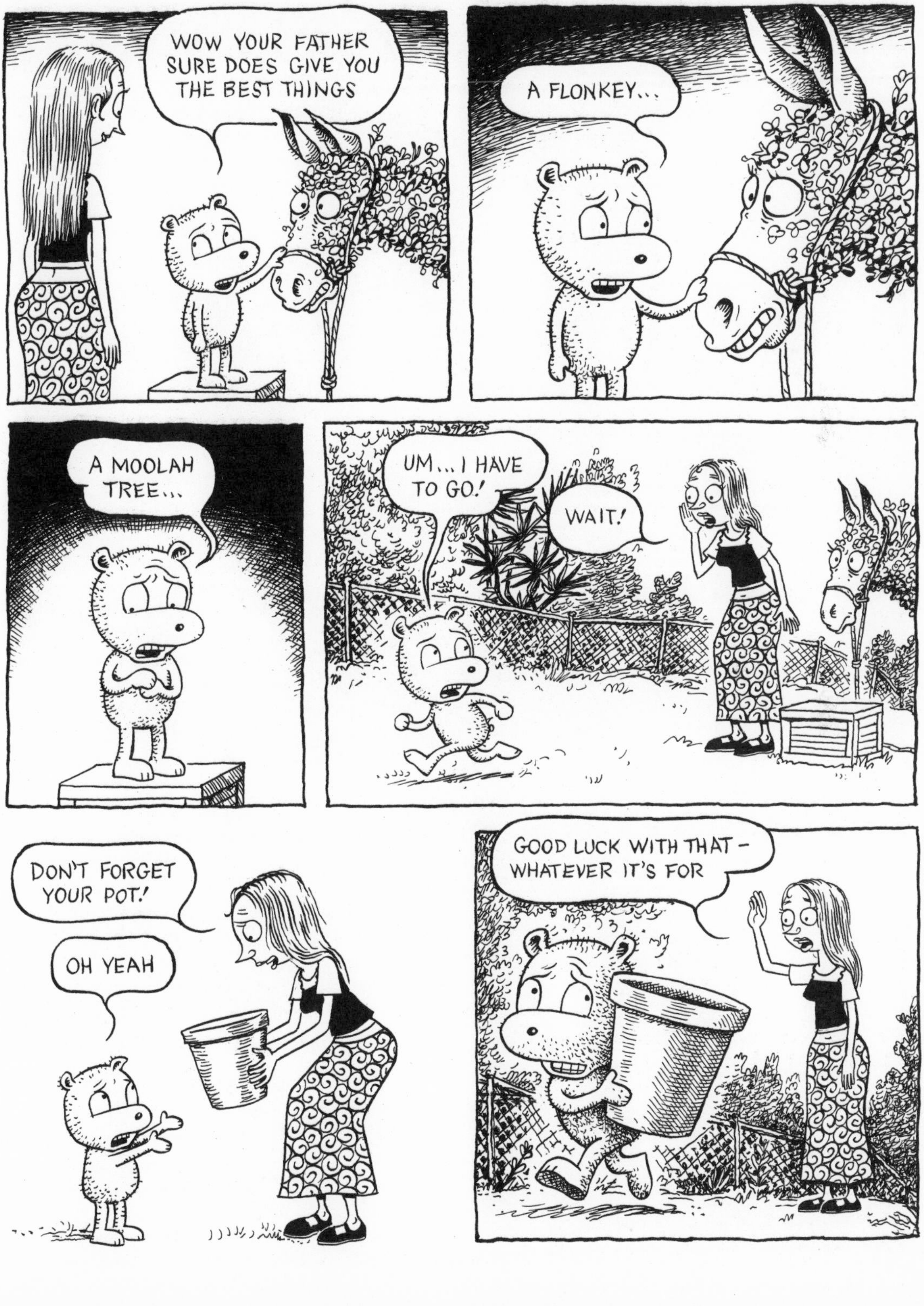
WOW YOUR FATHER SURE DOES GIVE YOU THE BEST THINGS
A FLONKEY...
A MOOLAH TREE...
UM... I HAVE TO GO!
WAIT!
DON'T FORGET YOUR POT!
OH YEAH
GOOD LUCK WITH THAT - WHATEVER IT'S FOR

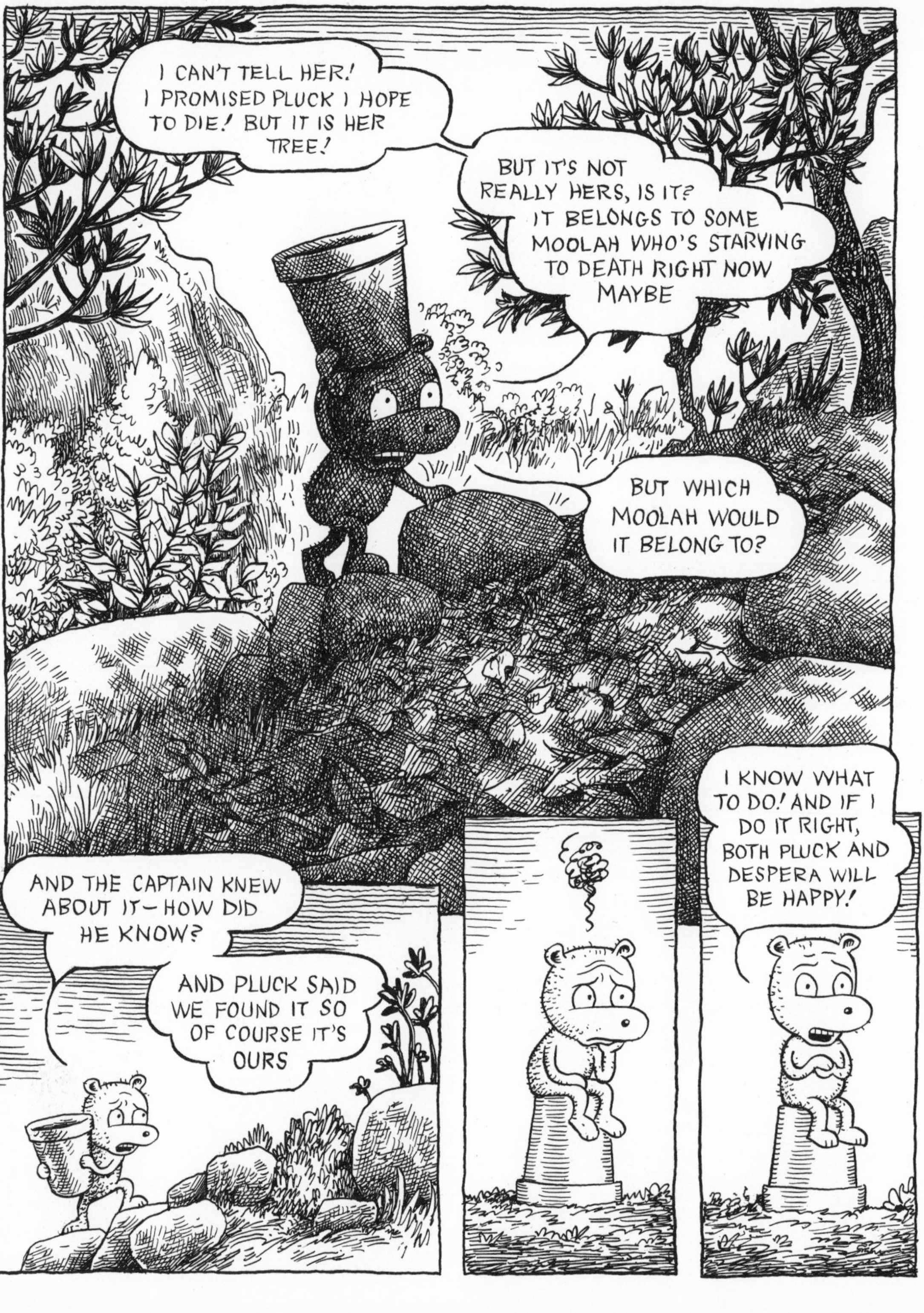

I CAN'T TELL HER! I PROMISED PLUCK I HOPE TO DIE! BUT IT IS HER TREE!
BUT IT'S NOT REALLY HERS, IS IT?
IT BELONGS TO SOME MOOLAH WHO'S STARVING TO DEATH RIGHT NOW MAYBE
BUT WHICH MOOLAH WOULD IT BELONG TO?
AND THE CAPTAIN KNEW ABOUT IT— HOW DID HE KNOW?
AND PLUCK SAID WE FOUND IT SO OF COURSE IT'S OURS
I KNOW WHAT TO DO! AND IF I DO IT RIGHT, BOTH PLUCK AND DESPERA WILL BE HAPPY!

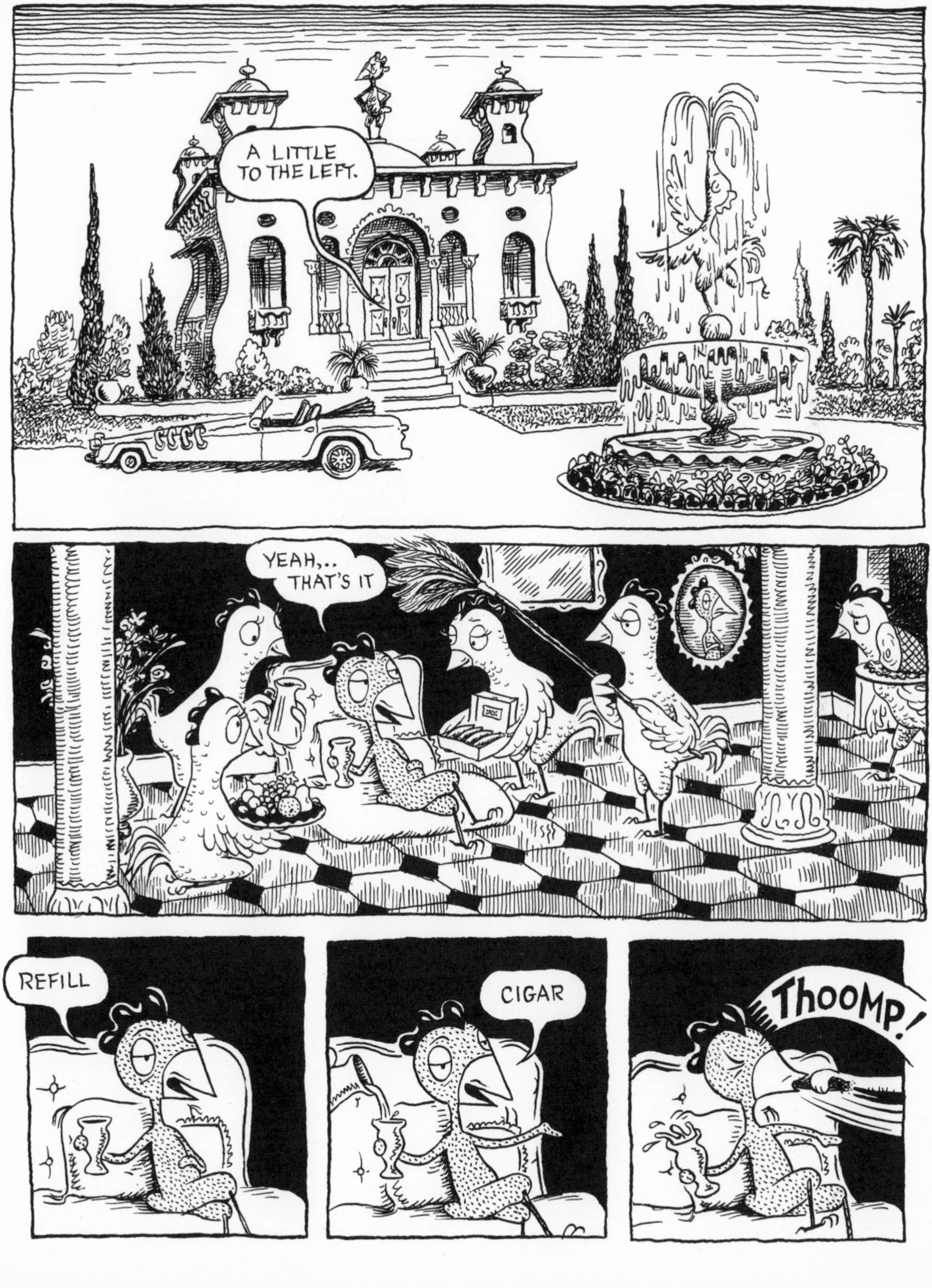
A LITTLE TO THE LEFT.
YEAH,.. THAT'S IT
REFILL
CIGAR
THOOMP!

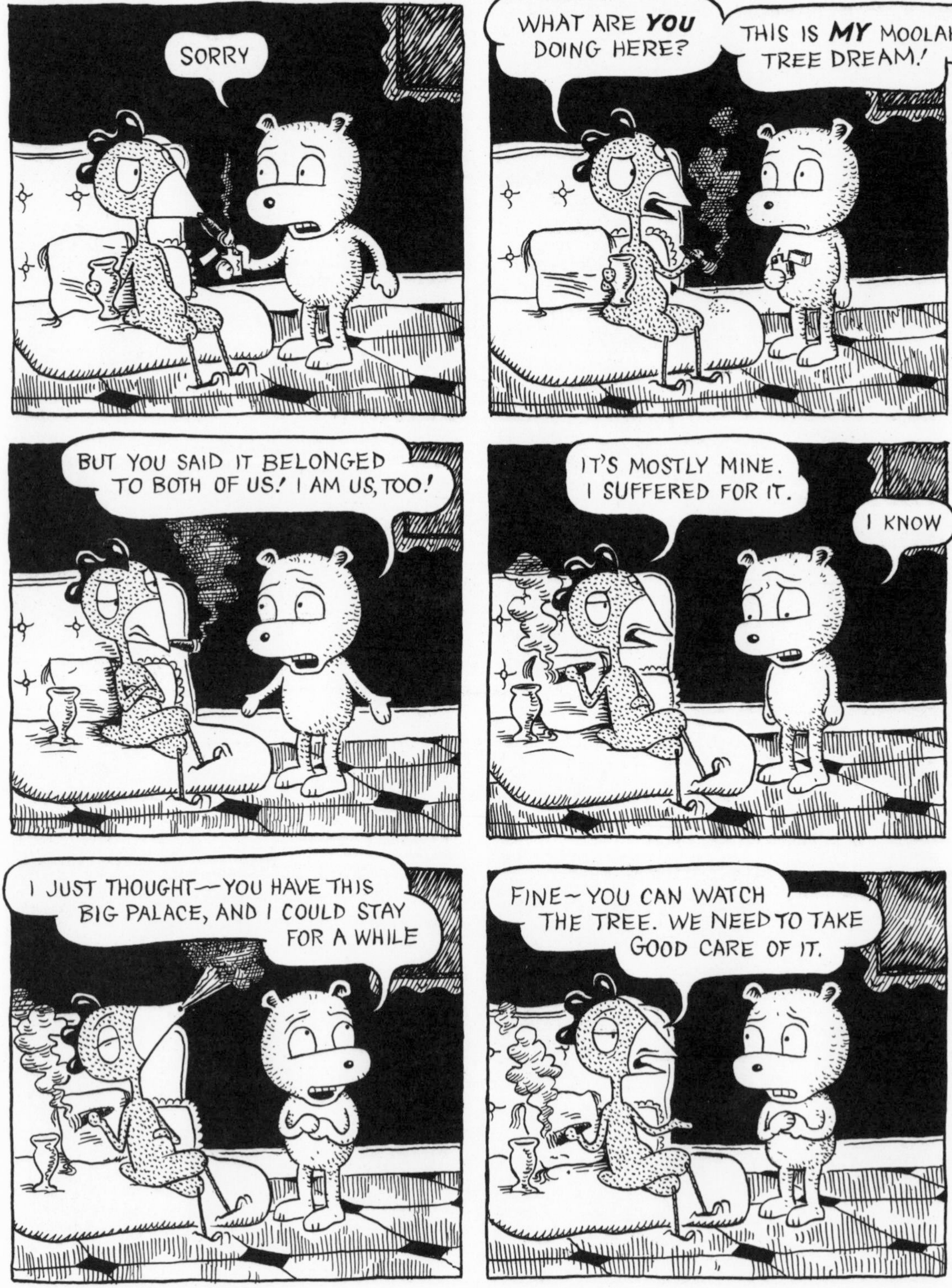
SORRY
WHAT ARE **YOU** DOING HERE?
THIS IS **MY** MOOLAH TREE DREAM!
BUT YOU SAID IT BELONGED TO BOTH OF US! I AM US, TOO!
IT'S MOSTLY MINE. I SUFFERED FOR IT.
I KNOW
I JUST THOUGHT— YOU HAVE THIS BIG PALACE, AND I COULD STAY FOR A WHILE
FINE~ YOU CAN WATCH THE TREE. WE NEED TO TAKE GOOD CARE OF IT.

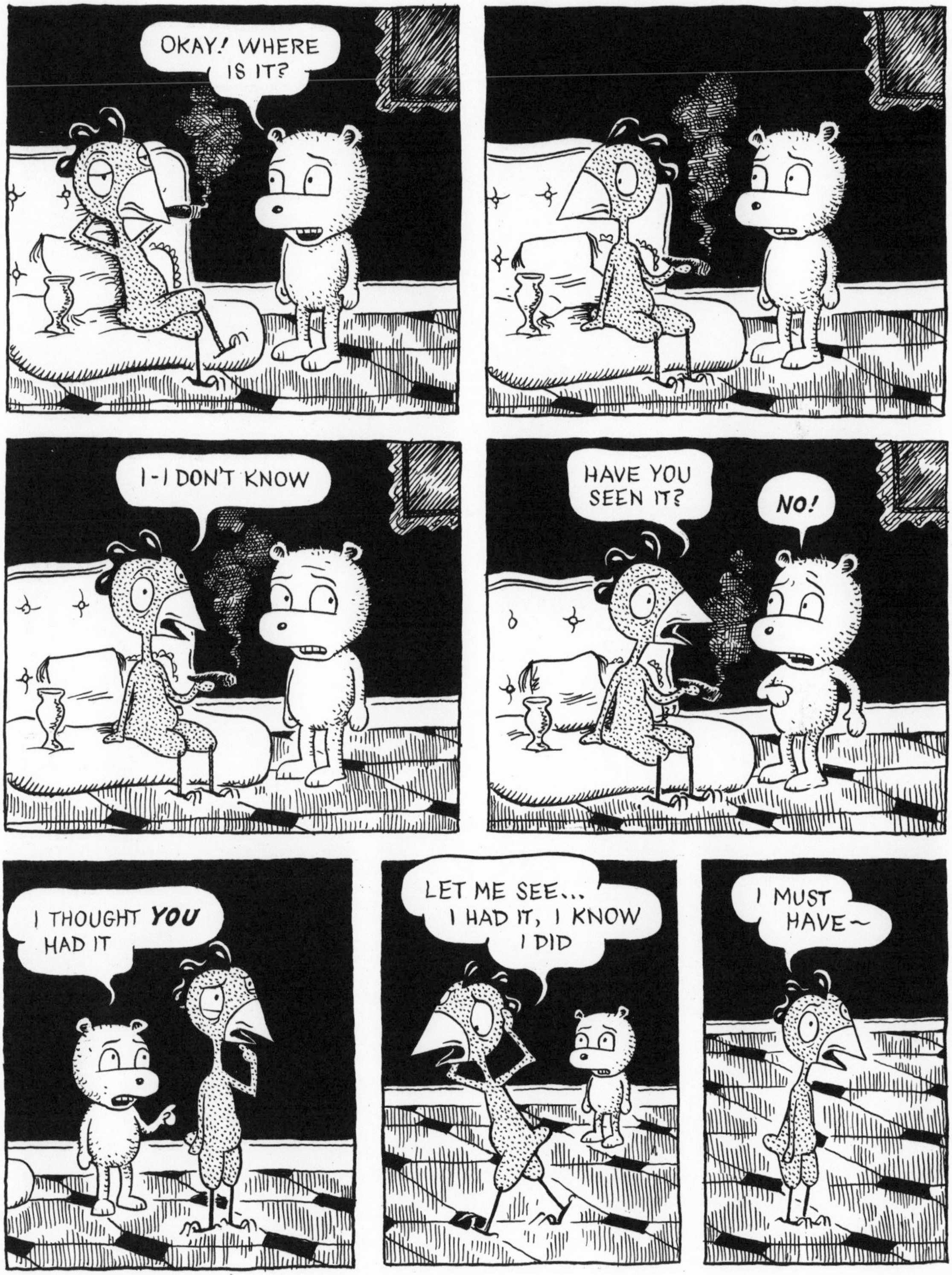
OKAY! WHERE IS IT?
I-I DON'T KNOW
HAVE YOU SEEN IT?
NO!
I THOUGHT **YOU** HAD IT
LET ME SEE... I HAD IT, I KNOW I DID
I MUST HAVE~

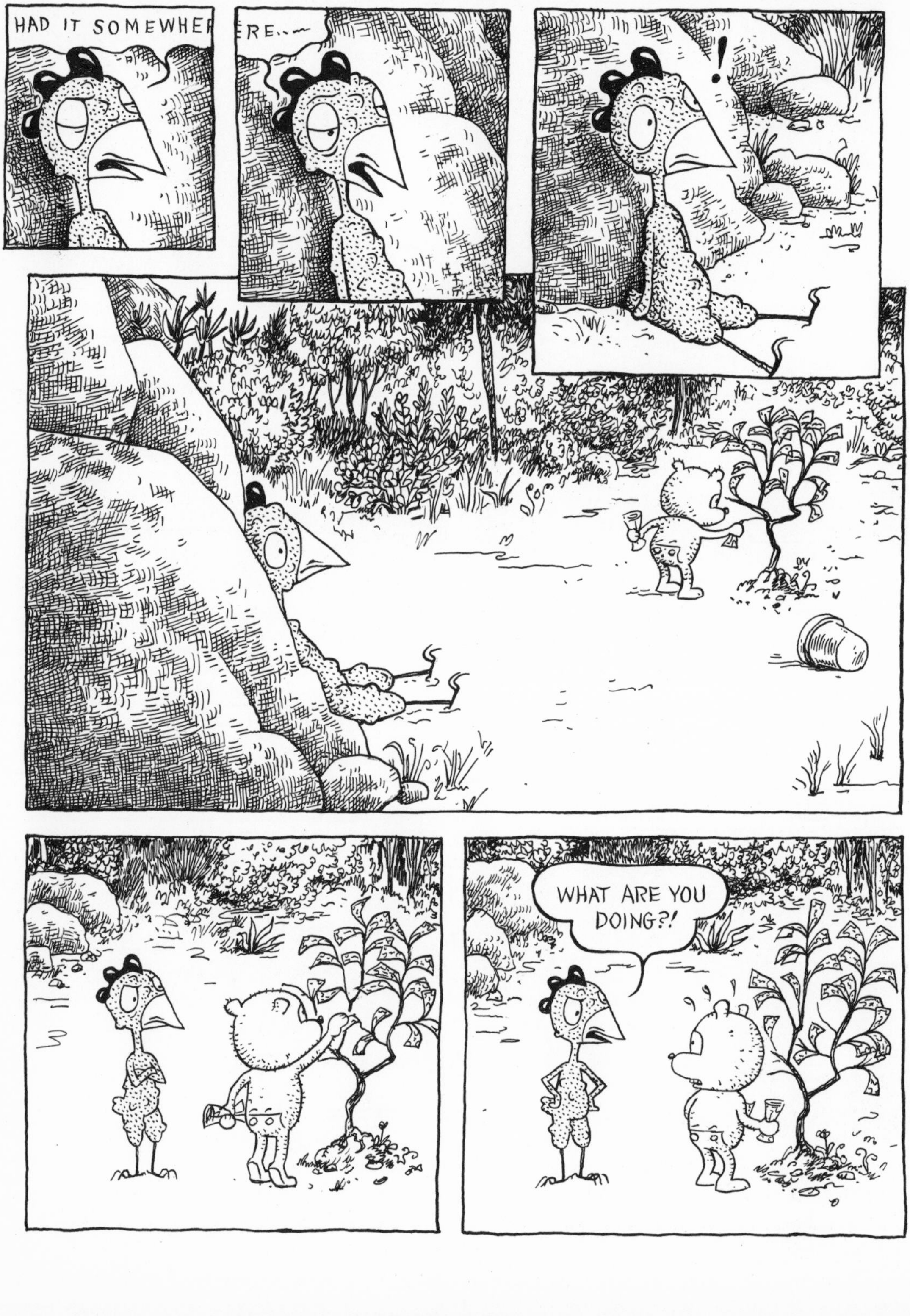
HAD IT SOMEWHERE...
!
WHAT ARE YOU DOING?!

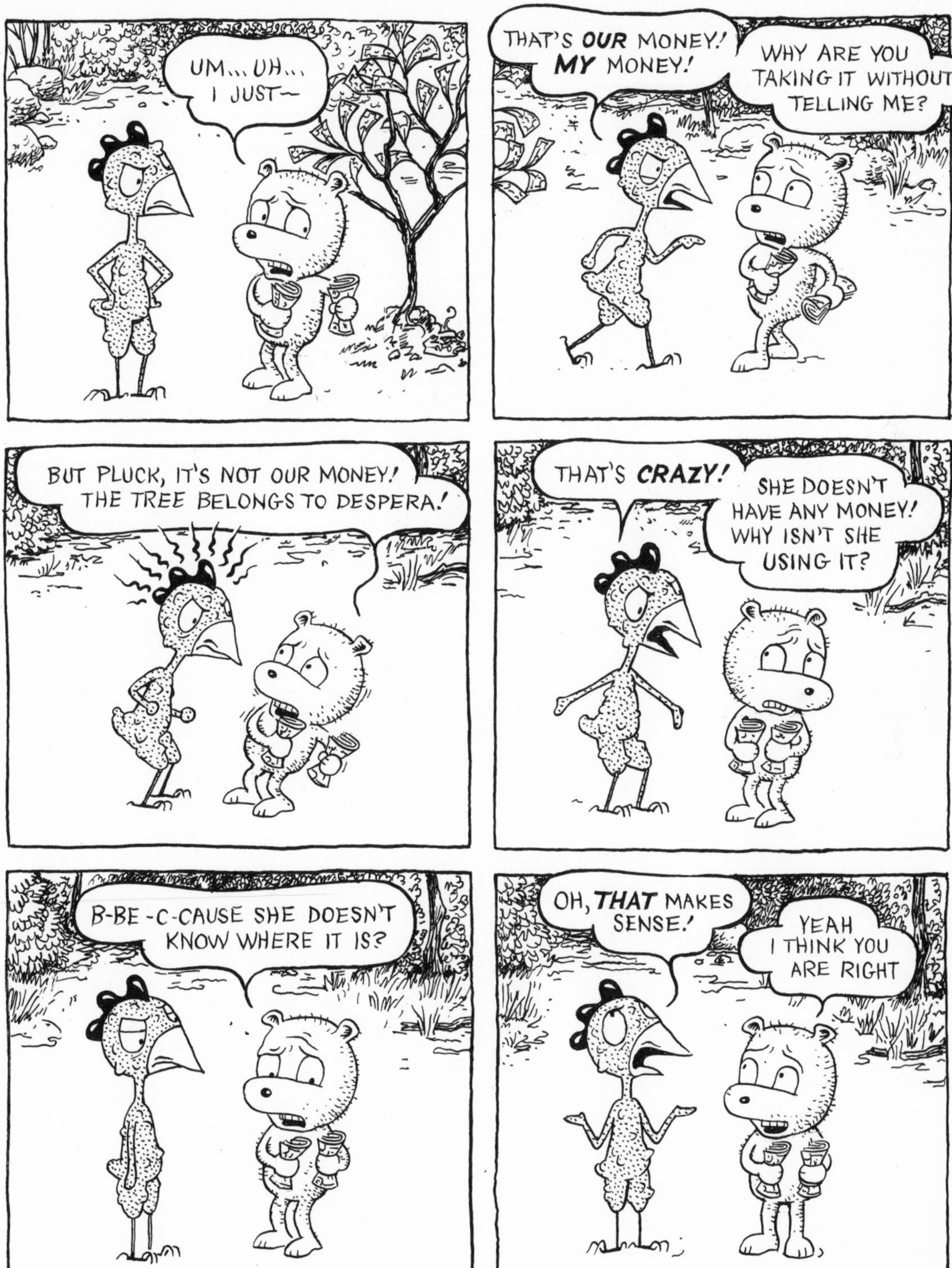
UM... UH... I JUST—
THAT'S **OUR** MONEY! **MY** MONEY!
WHY ARE YOU TAKING IT WITHOUT TELLING ME?
BUT PLUCK, IT'S NOT OUR MONEY! THE TREE BELONGS TO DESPERA!
THAT'S **CRAZY!**
SHE DOESN'T HAVE ANY MONEY! WHY ISN'T SHE USING IT?
B-BE-C-CAUSE SHE DOESN'T KNOW WHERE IT IS?
OH, **THAT** MAKES SENSE!
YEAH I THINK YOU ARE RIGHT

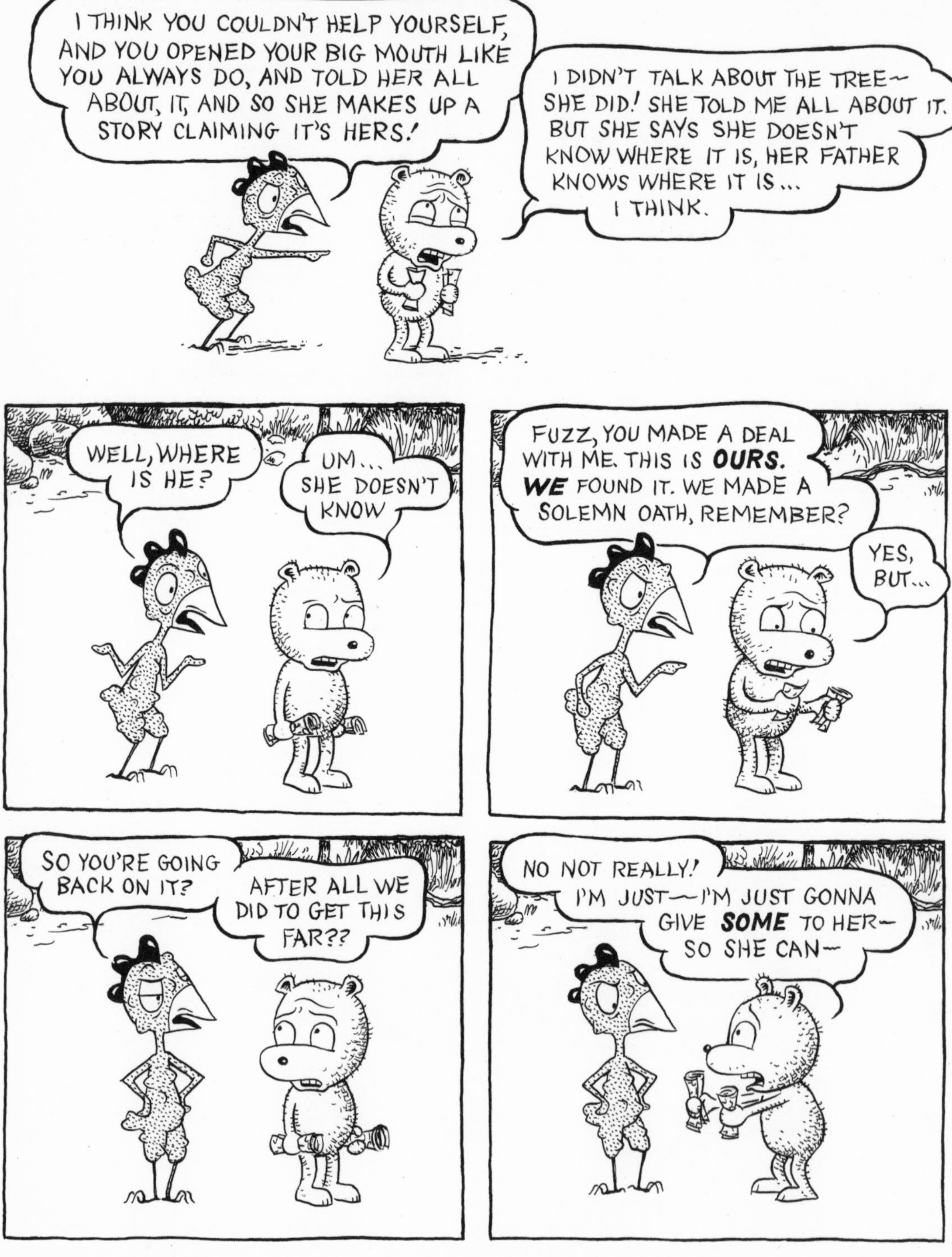
I THINK YOU COULDN'T HELP YOURSELF, AND YOU OPENED YOUR BIG MOUTH LIKE YOU ALWAYS DO, AND TOLD HER ALL ABOUT, IT, AND SO SHE MAKES UP A STORY CLAIMING IT'S HERS!
I DIDN'T TALK ABOUT THE TREE~ SHE DID! SHE TOLD ME ALL ABOUT IT. BUT SHE SAYS SHE DOESN'T KNOW WHERE IT IS, HER FATHER KNOWS WHERE IT IS... I THINK.
WELL, WHERE IS HE?
UM... SHE DOESN'T KNOW
FUZZ, YOU MADE A DEAL WITH ME. THIS IS **OURS.** **WE** FOUND IT. WE MADE A SOLEMN OATH, REMEMBER?
YES, BUT...
SO YOU'RE GOING BACK ON IT?
AFTER ALL WE DID TO GET THIS FAR??
NO NOT REALLY!
I'M JUST—I'M JUST GONNA GIVE **SOME** TO HER—SO SHE CAN—

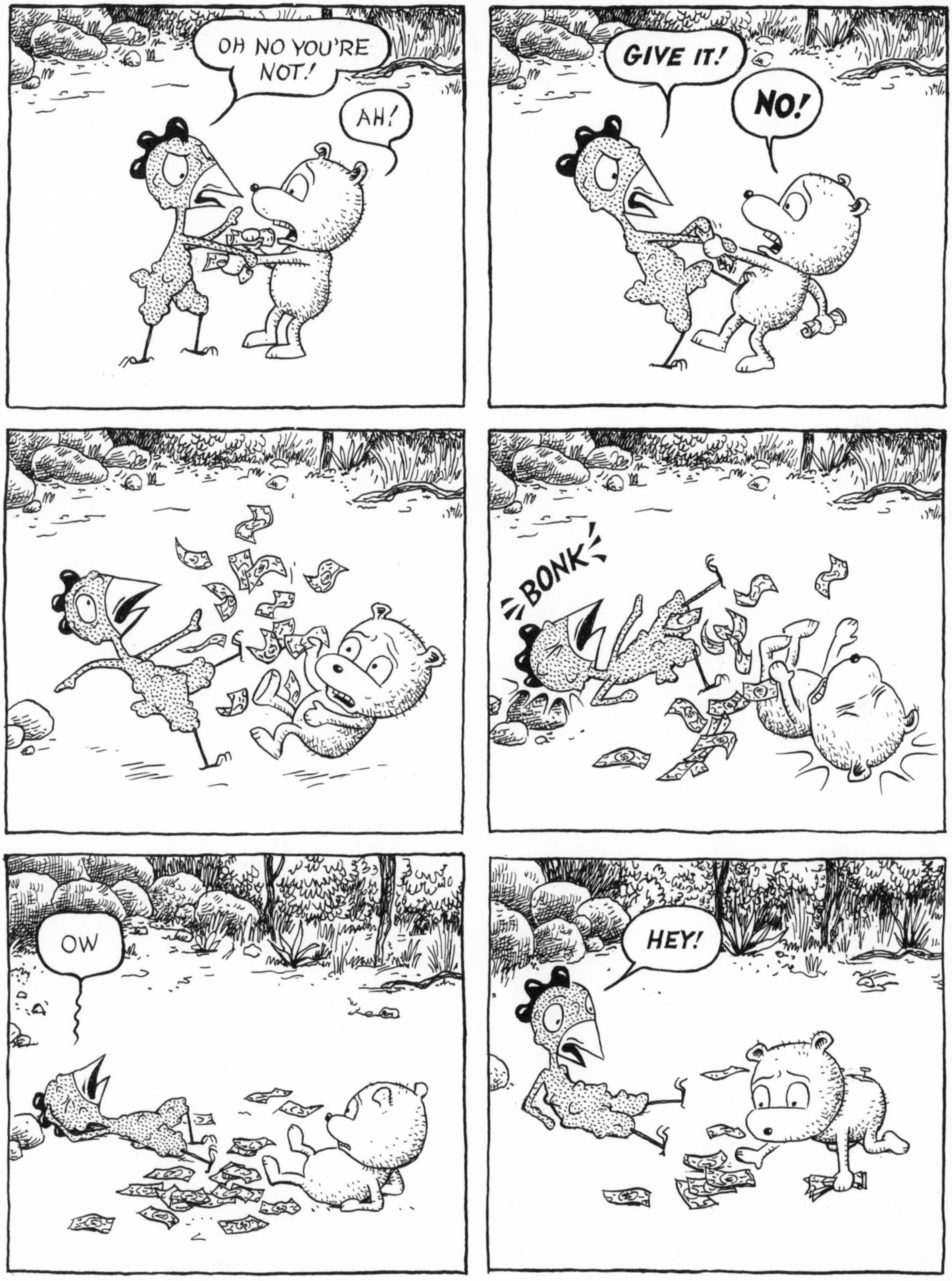
OH NO YOU'RE NOT!
AH!
GIVE IT!
NO!
BONK
OW
HEY!

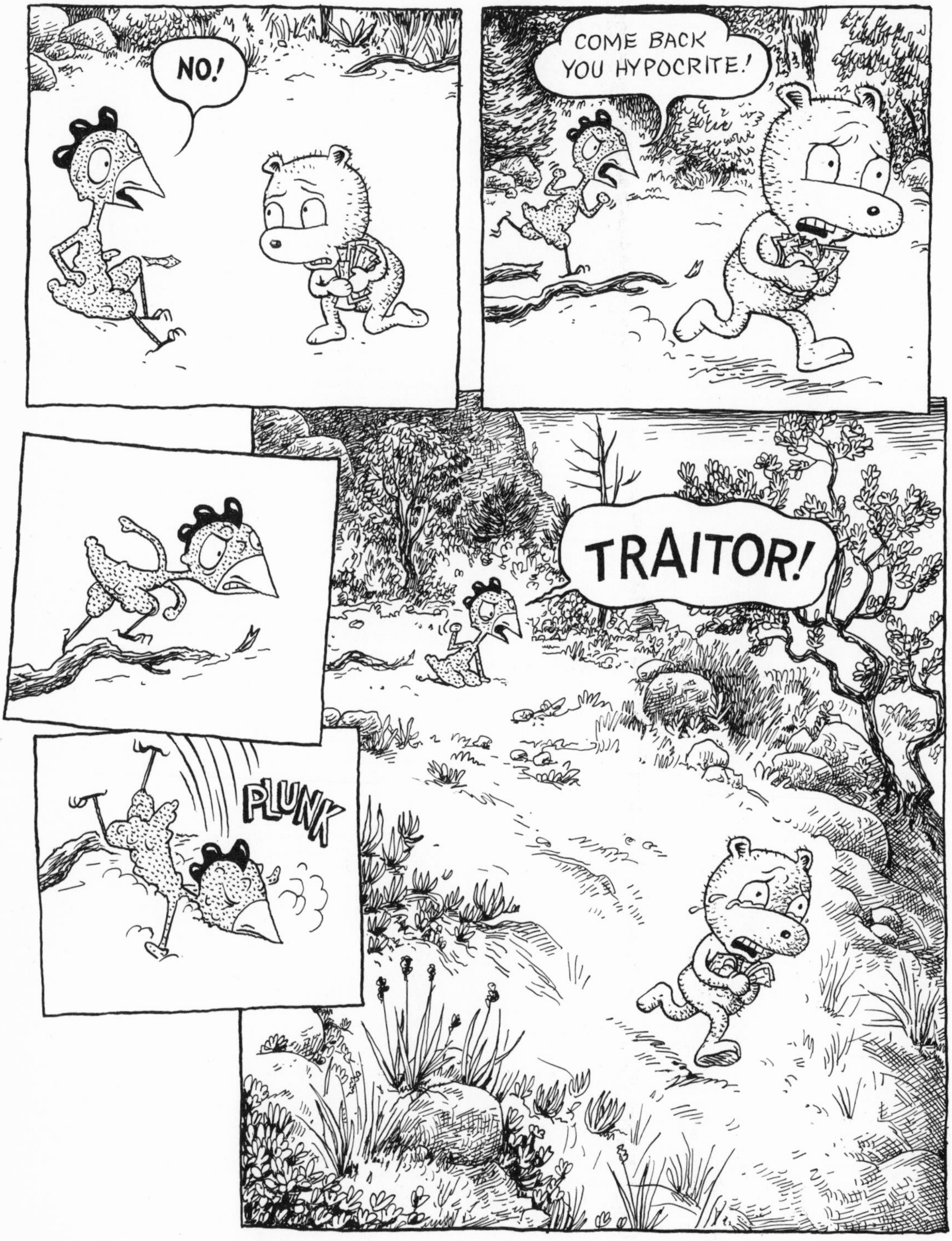
NO!
COME BACK YOU HYPOCRITE!
PLUNK
TRAITOR!

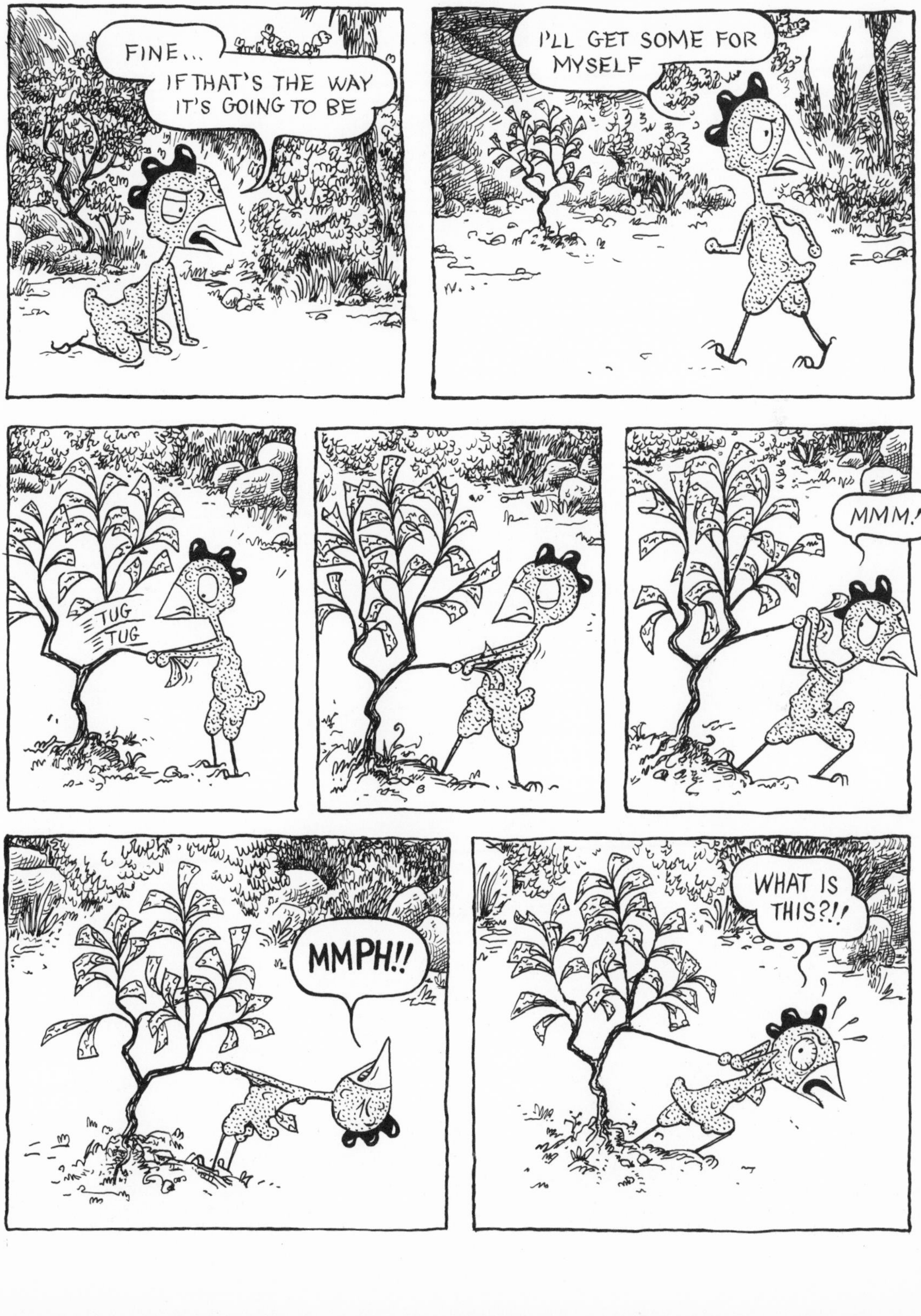
FINE...
IF THAT'S THE WAY IT'S GOING TO BE
I'LL GET SOME FOR MYSELF
TUG TUG
MMM!
MMPH!!
WHAT IS THIS?!!

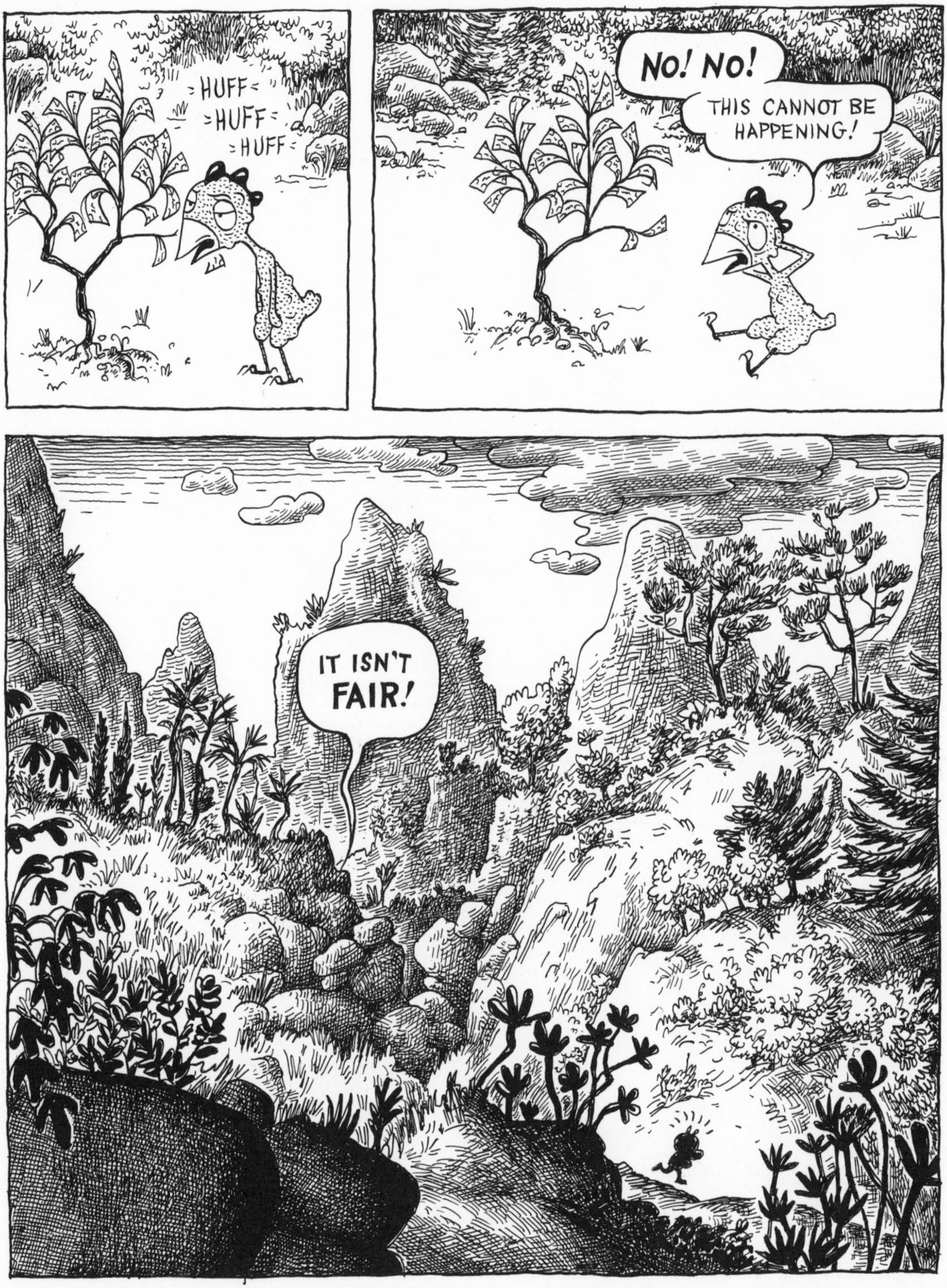
HUFF
HUFF
HUFF
NO! NO!
THIS CANNOT BE HAPPENING!
IT ISN'T FAIR!

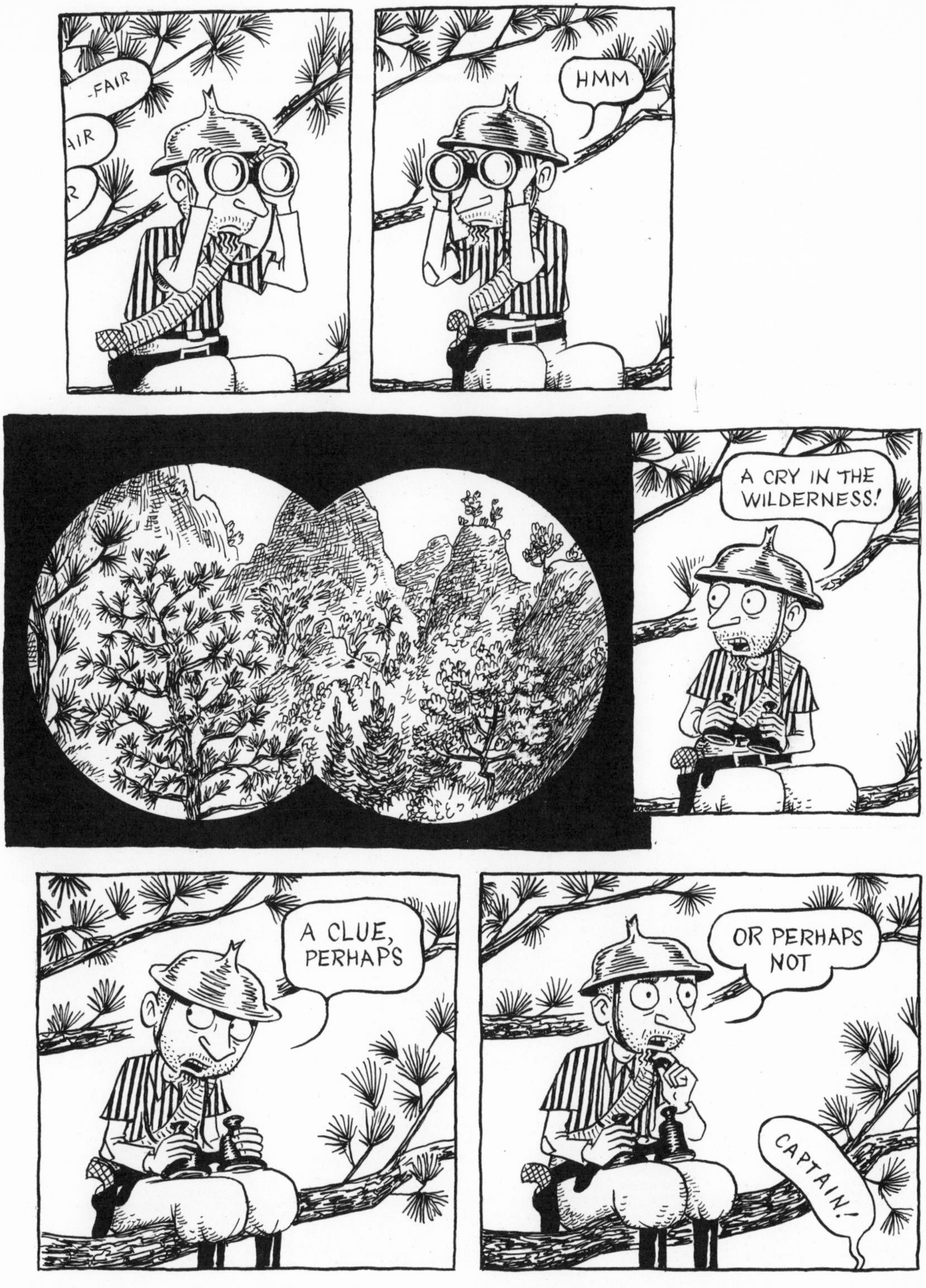
-FAIR
AIR
R
HMM
A CRY IN THE WILDERNESS!
A CLUE, PERHAPS
OR PERHAPS NOT
CAPTAIN!

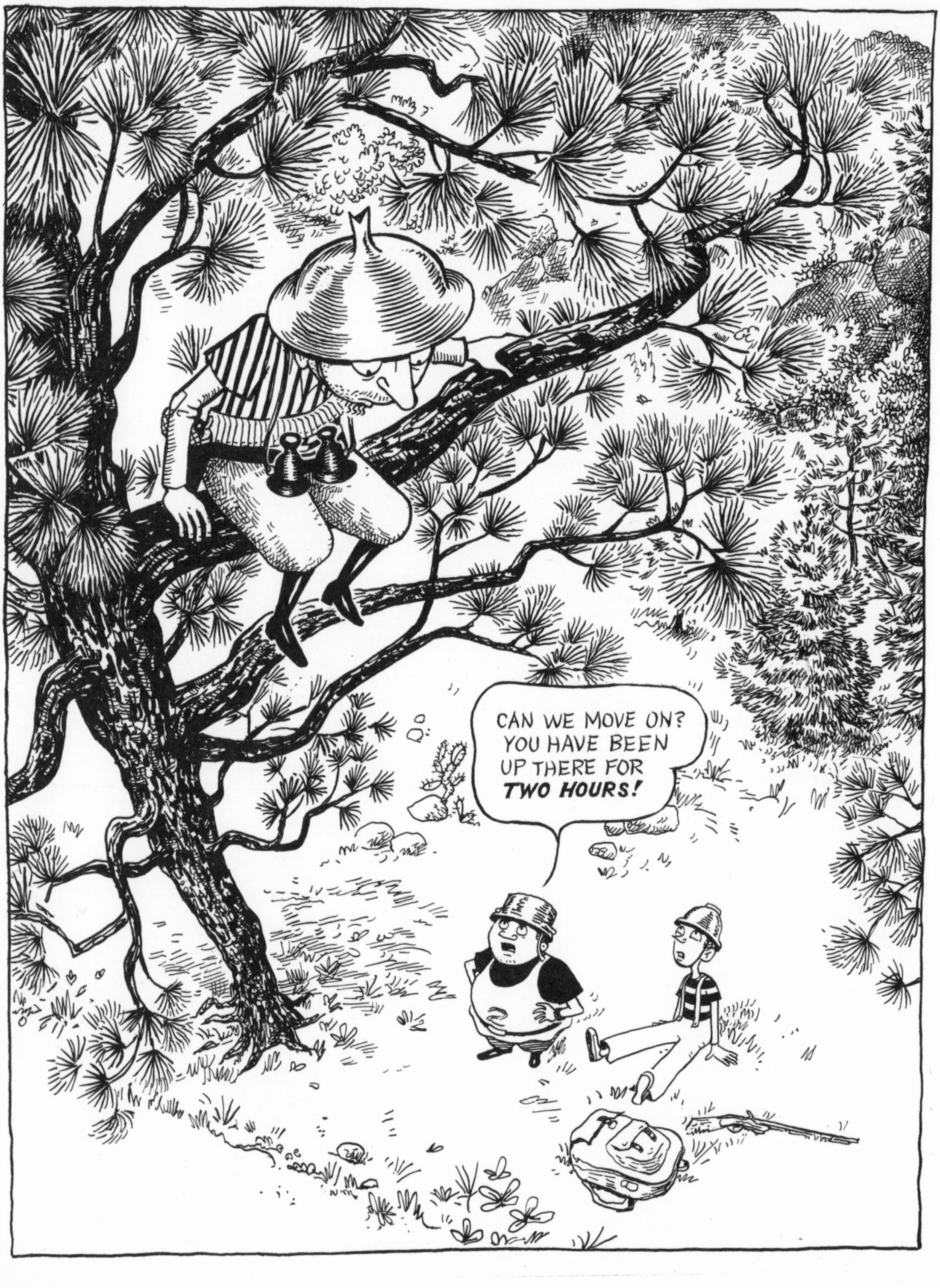
CAN WE MOVE ON? YOU HAVE BEEN UP THERE FOR **TWO HOURS!**

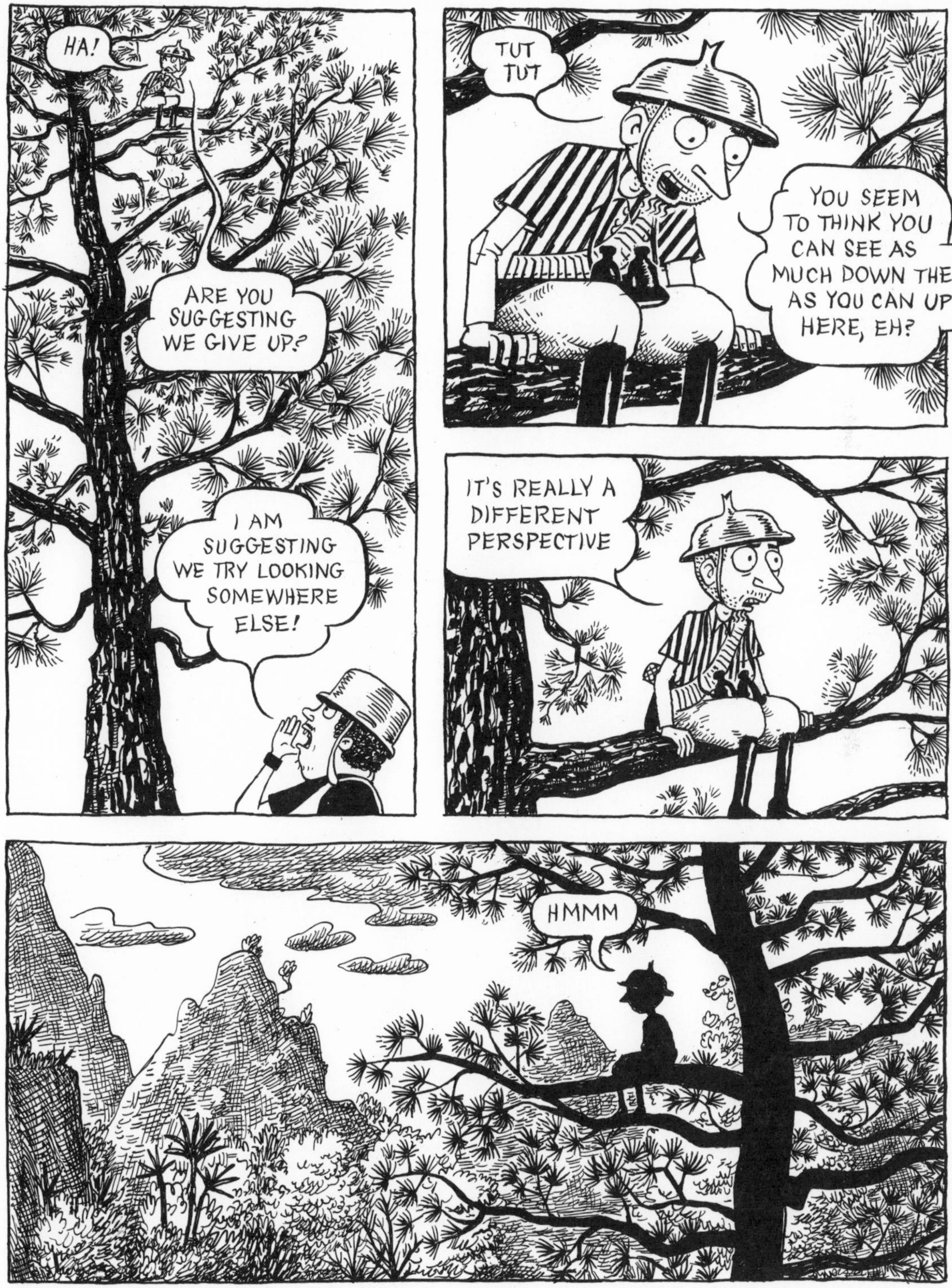
HA!
ARE YOU SUGGESTING WE GIVE UP?
I AM SUGGESTING WE TRY LOOKING SOMEWHERE ELSE!
TUT TUT
YOU SEEM TO THINK YOU CAN SEE AS MUCH DOWN THERE AS YOU CAN UP HERE, EH?
IT'S REALLY A DIFFERENT PERSPECTIVE
HMMM

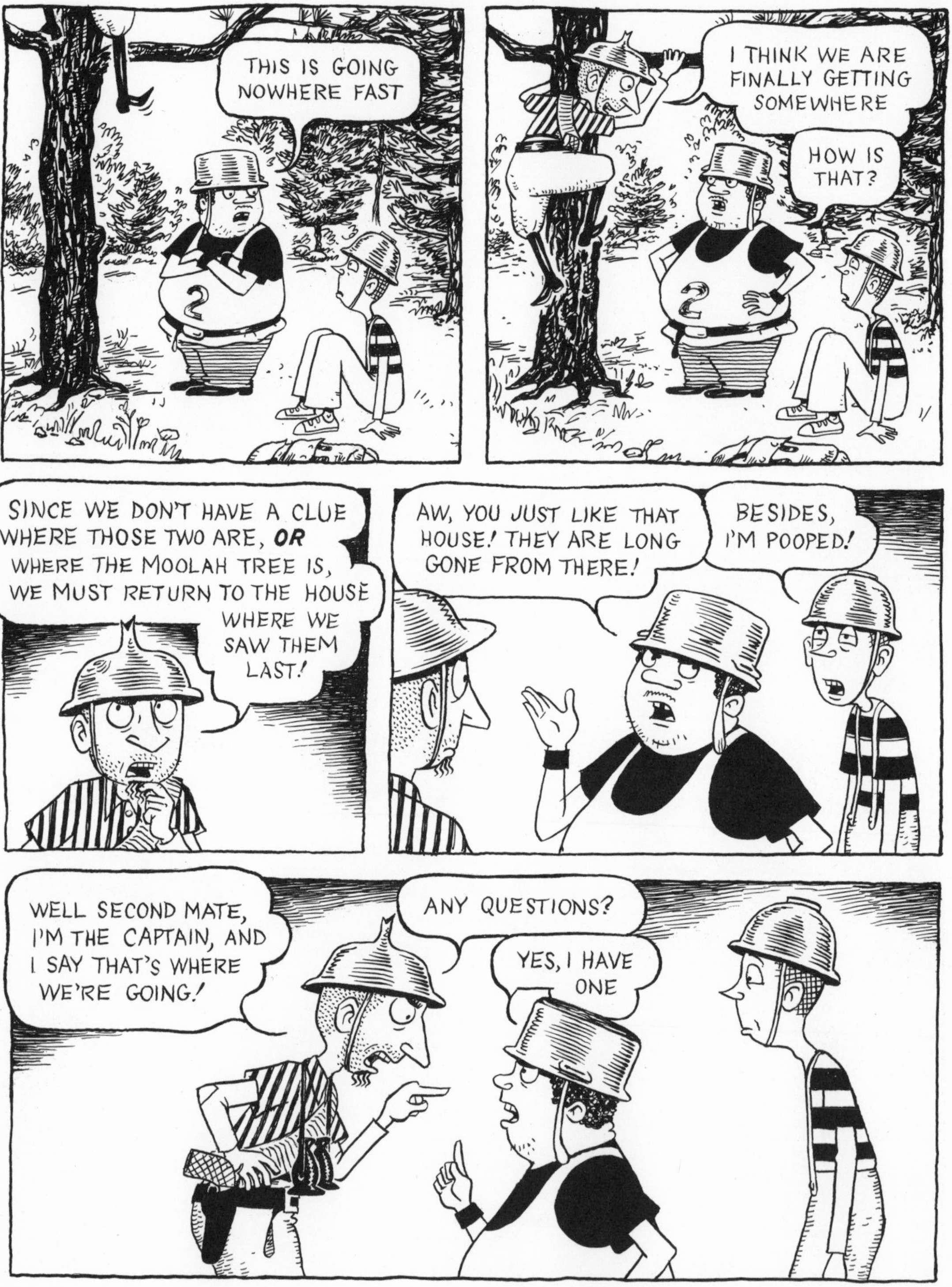
THIS IS GOING NOWHERE FAST
I THINK WE ARE FINALLY GETTING SOMEWHERE
HOW IS THAT?
SINCE WE DON'T HAVE A CLUE WHERE THOSE TWO ARE, **OR** WHERE THE MOOLAH TREE IS, WE MUST RETURN TO THE HOUSE WHERE WE SAW THEM LAST!
AW, YOU JUST LIKE THAT HOUSE! THEY ARE LONG GONE FROM THERE!
BESIDES, I'M POOPED!
WELL SECOND MATE, I'M THE CAPTAIN, AND I SAY THAT'S WHERE WE'RE GOING!
ANY QUESTIONS?
YES, I HAVE ONE

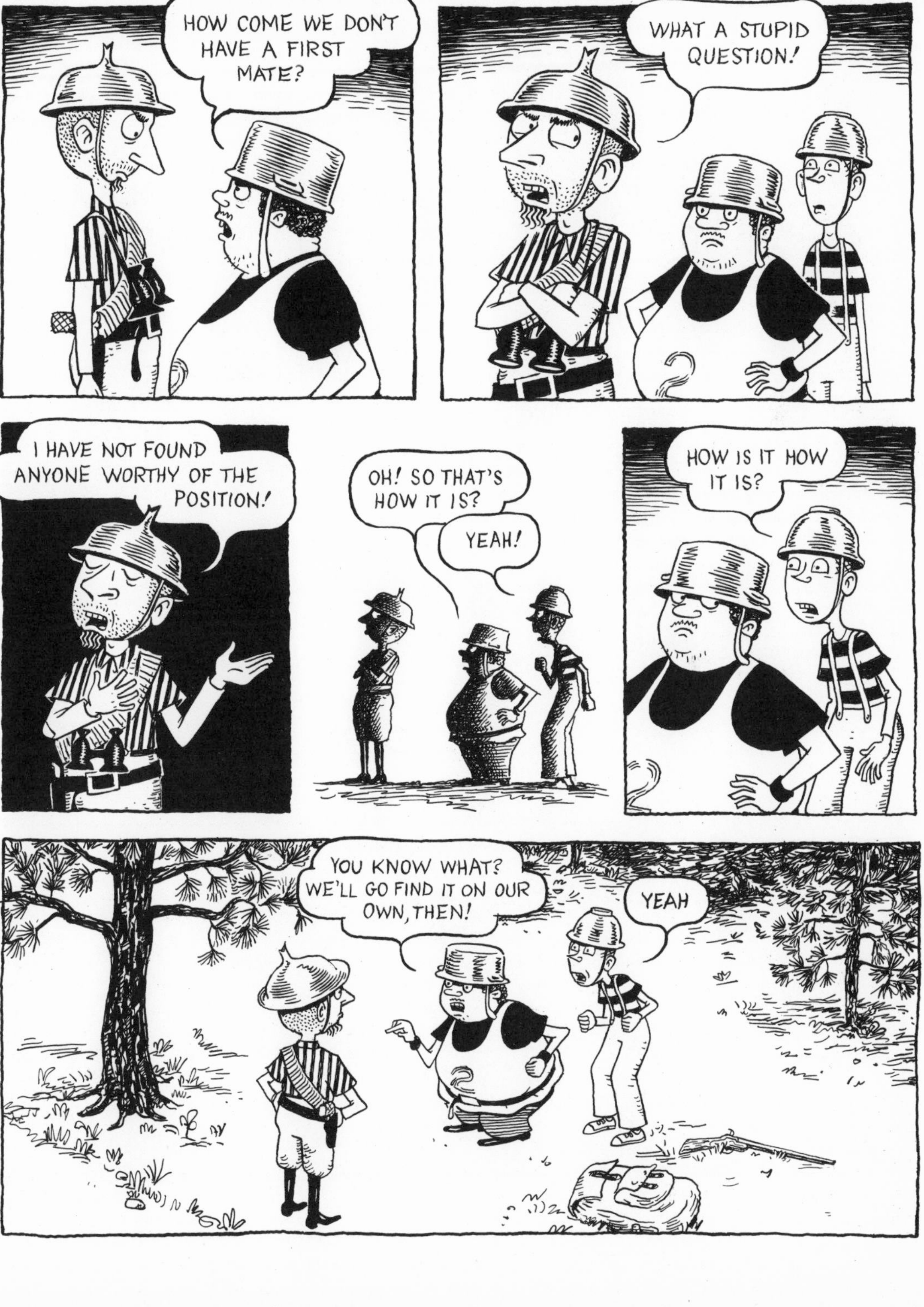
HOW COME WE DON'T HAVE A FIRST MATE?
WHAT A STUPID QUESTION!
I HAVE NOT FOUND ANYONE WORTHY OF THE POSITION!
OH! SO THAT'S HOW IT IS?
YEAH!
HOW IS IT HOW IT IS?
YOU KNOW WHAT? WE'LL GO FIND IT ON OUR OWN, THEN!
YEAH

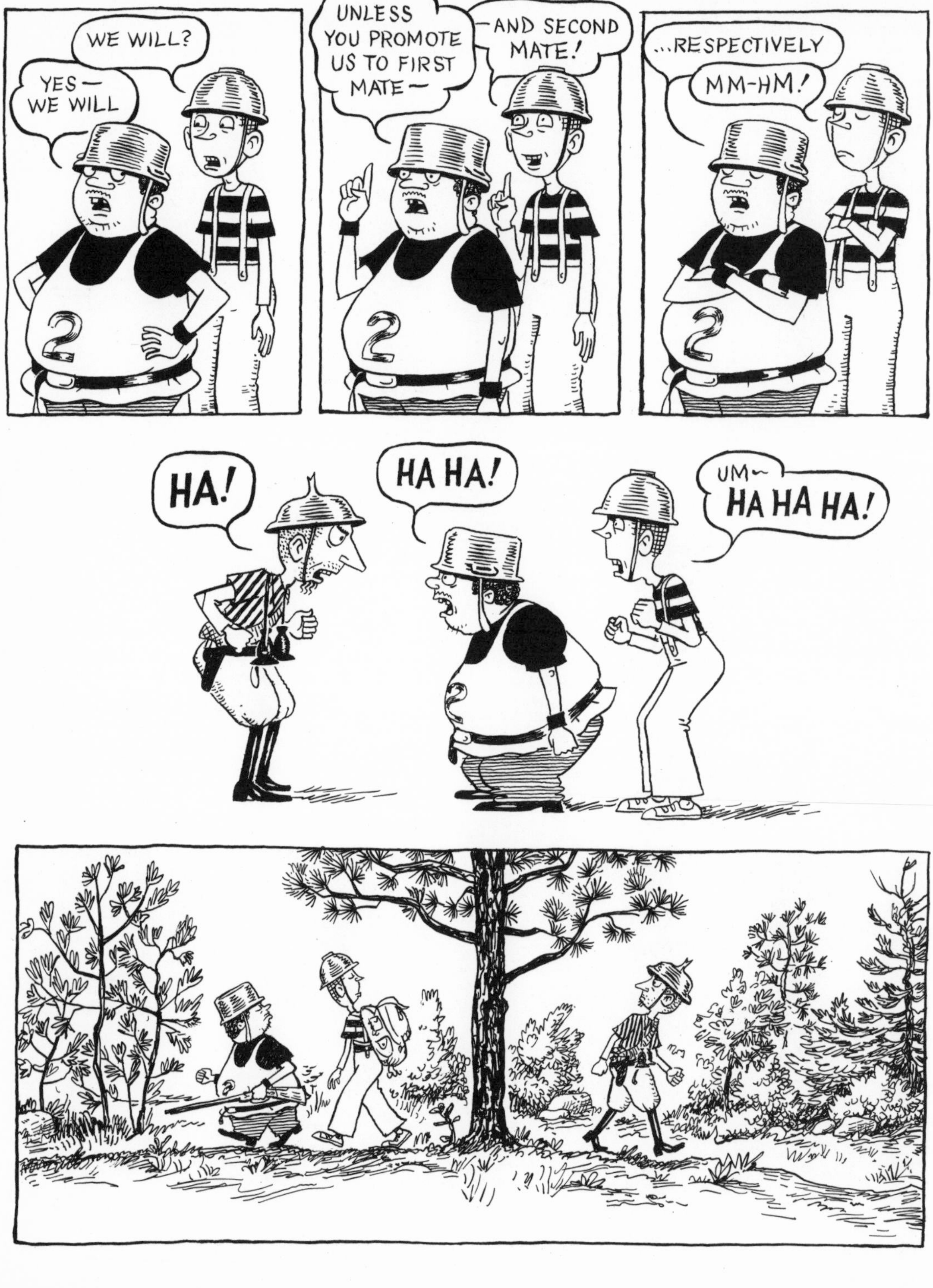
WE WILL?
YES— WE WILL
UNLESS YOU PROMOTE US TO FIRST MATE—
—AND SECOND MATE!
...RESPECTIVELY
MM-HM!
HA!
HA HA!
UM~ HA HA HA!

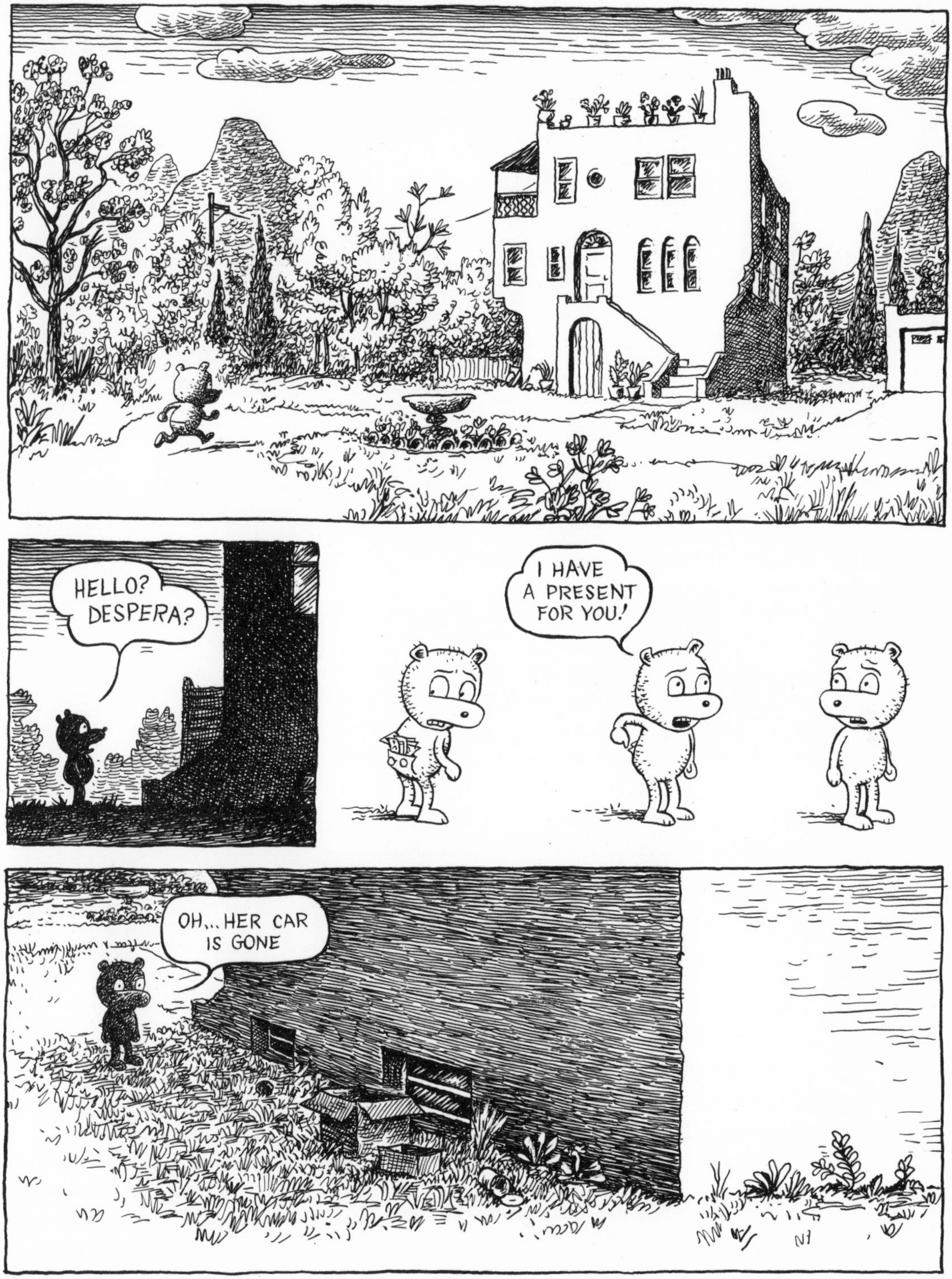
HELLO? DESPERA?
I HAVE A PRESENT FOR YOU!
OH... HER CAR IS GONE

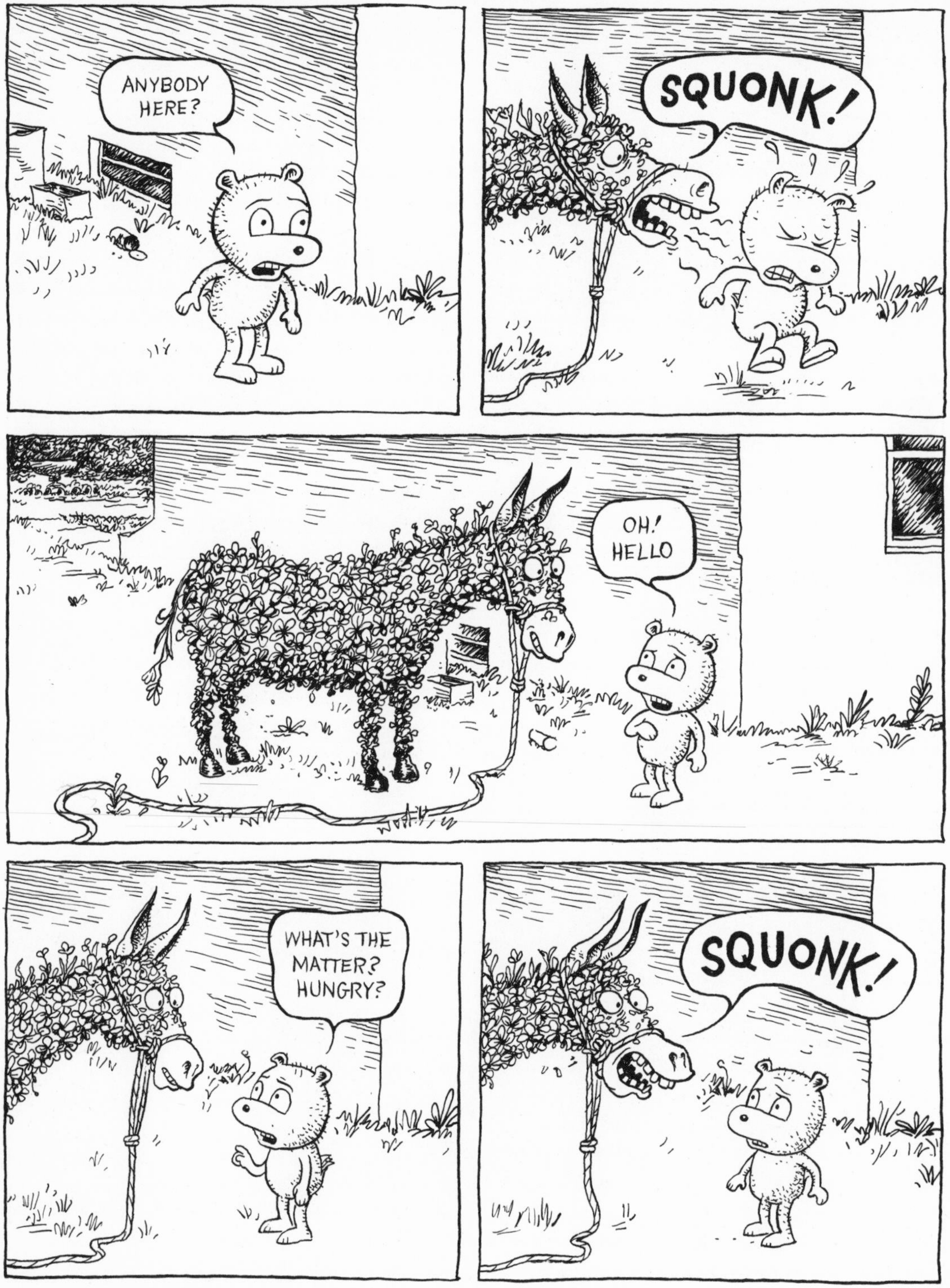
ANYBODY HERE?
SQUONK!
OH! HELLO
WHAT'S THE MATTER? HUNGRY?
SQUONK!

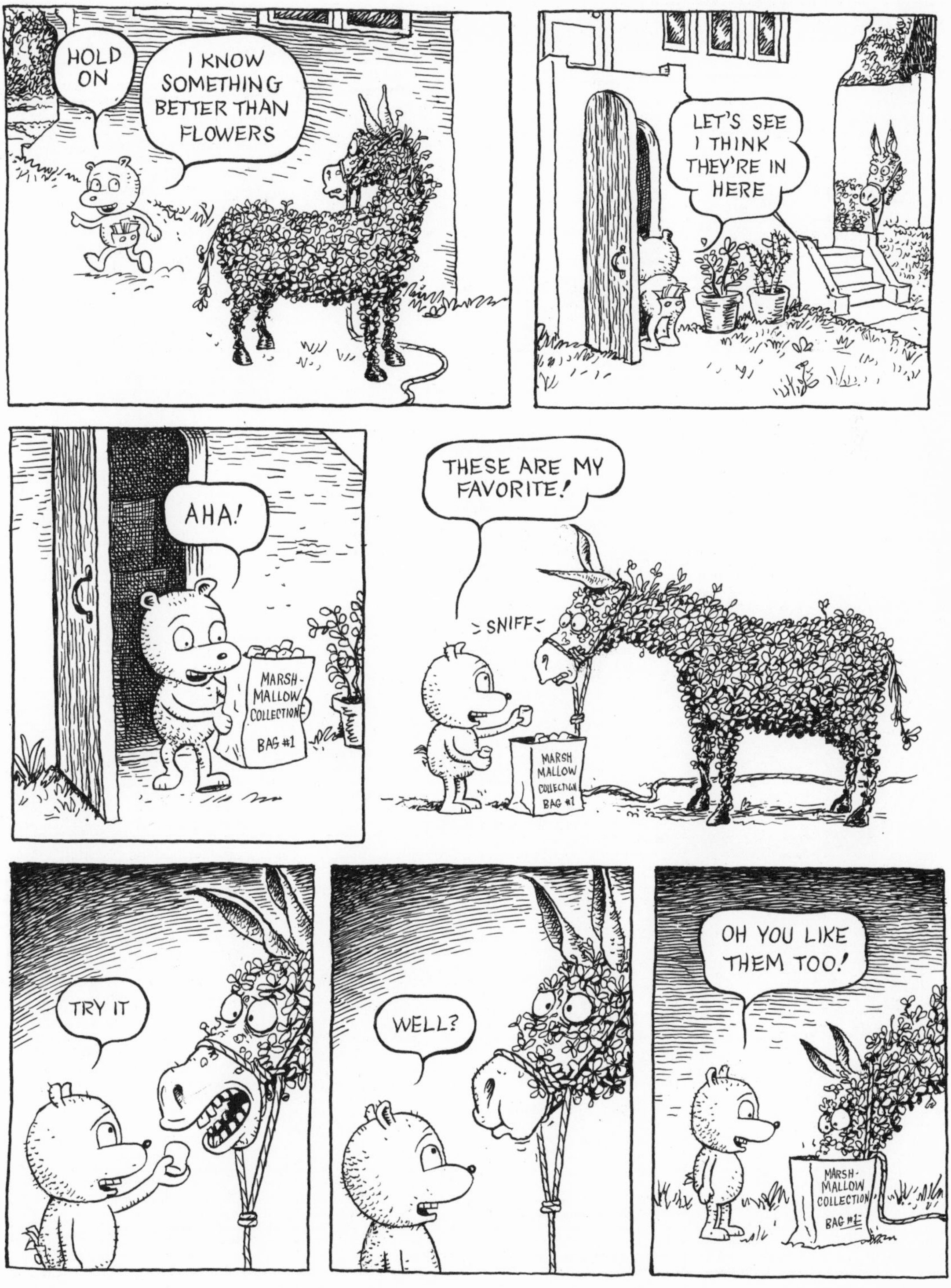
HOLD ON
I KNOW SOMETHING BETTER THAN FLOWERS
LET'S SEE I THINK THEY'RE IN HERE
AHA!
MARSH-MALLOW COLLECTION BAG #1
THESE ARE MY FAVORITE!
SNIFF
MARSH MALLOW COLLECTION BAG #1
TRY IT
WELL?
OH YOU LIKE THEM TOO!
MARSH-MALLOW COLLECTION BAG #1

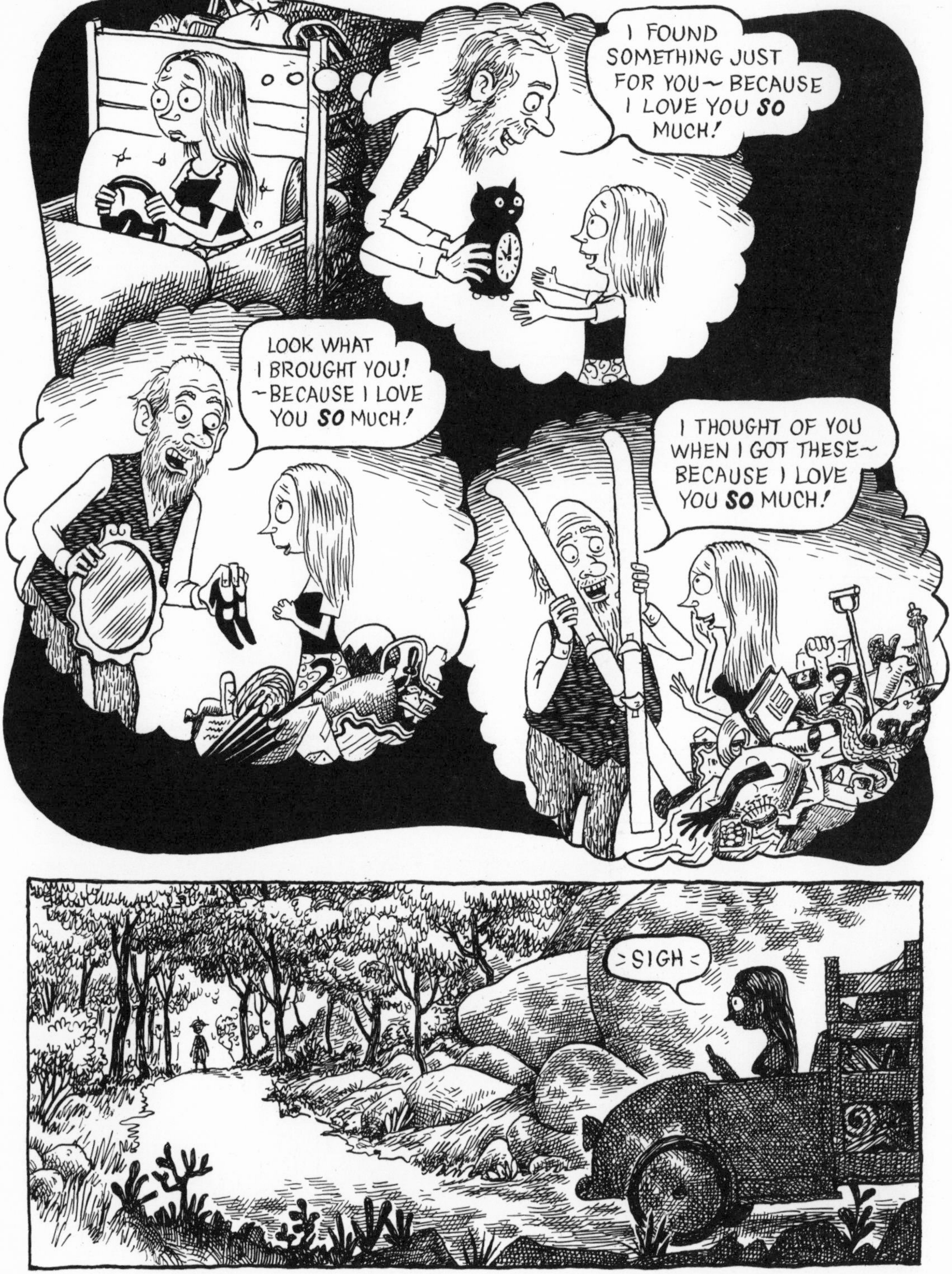
I FOUND SOMETHING JUST FOR YOU~ BECAUSE I LOVE YOU **SO** MUCH!
LOOK WHAT I BROUGHT YOU! ~BECAUSE I LOVE YOU **SO** MUCH!
I THOUGHT OF YOU WHEN I GOT THESE~ BECAUSE I LOVE YOU **SO** MUCH!
SIGH

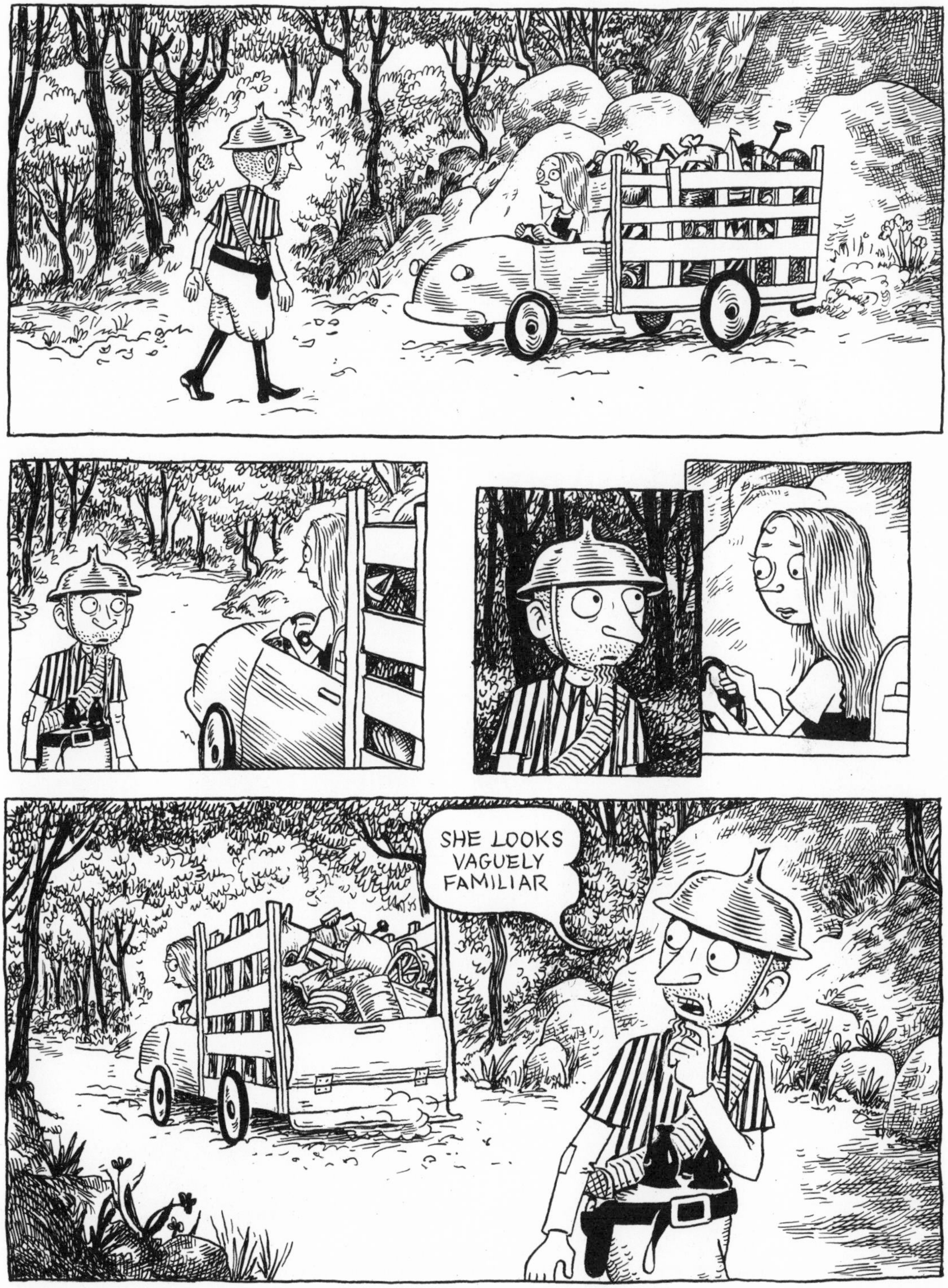
SHE LOOKS VAGUELY FAMILIAR

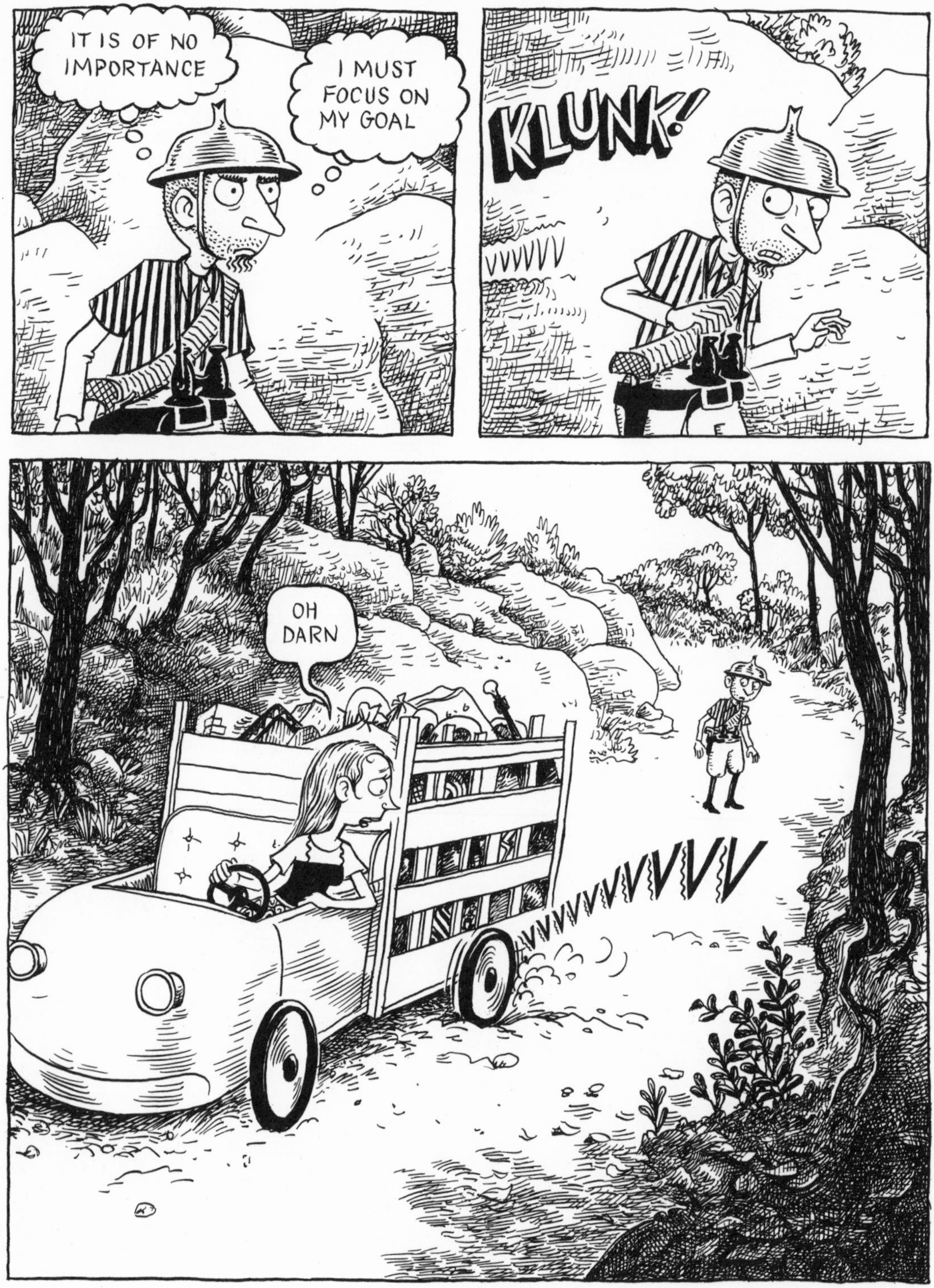
IT IS OF NO IMPORTANCE
I MUST FOCUS ON MY GOAL
KLUNK!
VVVVVV
OH DARN
VVVVVVVVVV

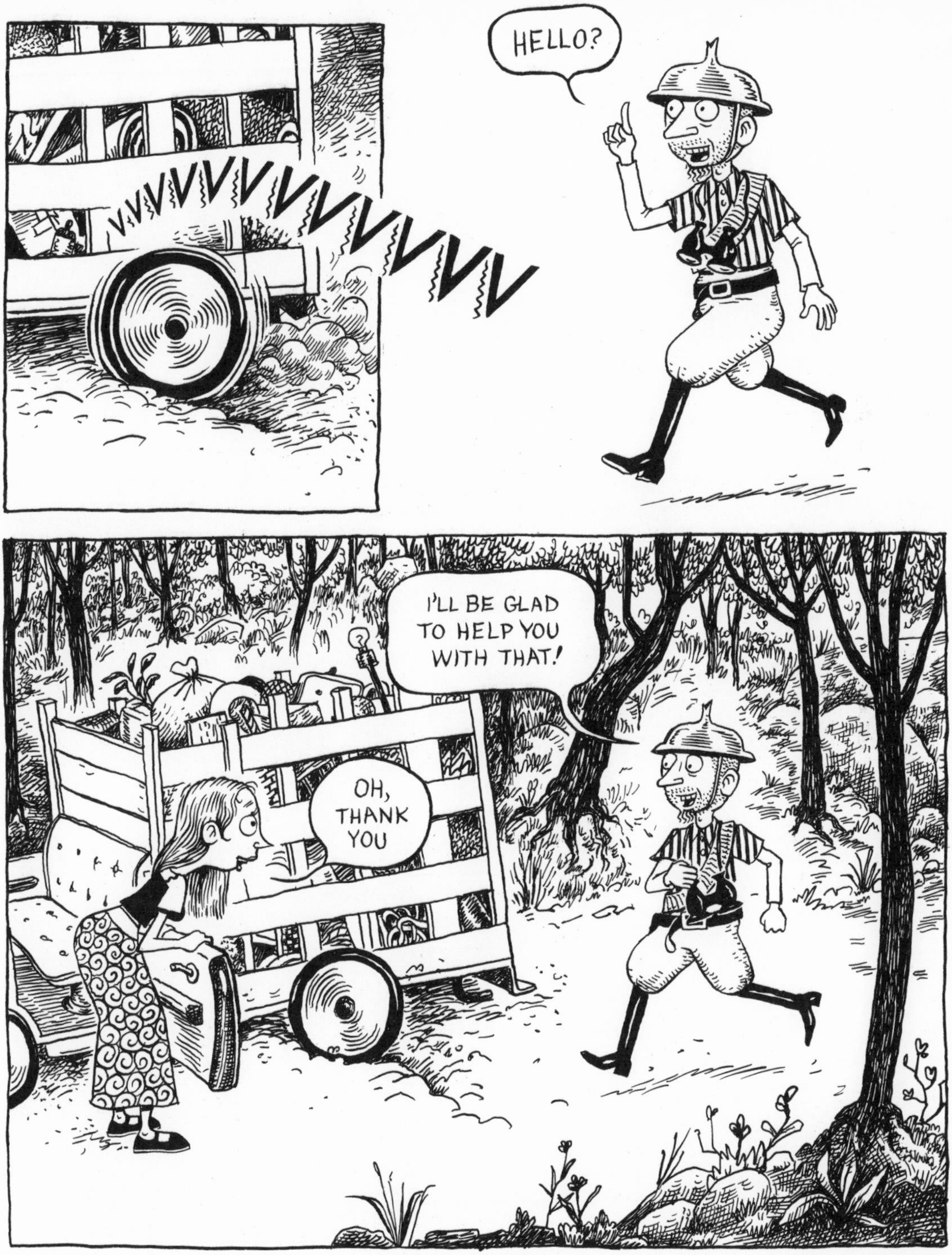
VVVVVVVVVVVVVVVVVV
HELLO?
I'LL BE GLAD TO HELP YOU WITH THAT!
OH, THANK YOU

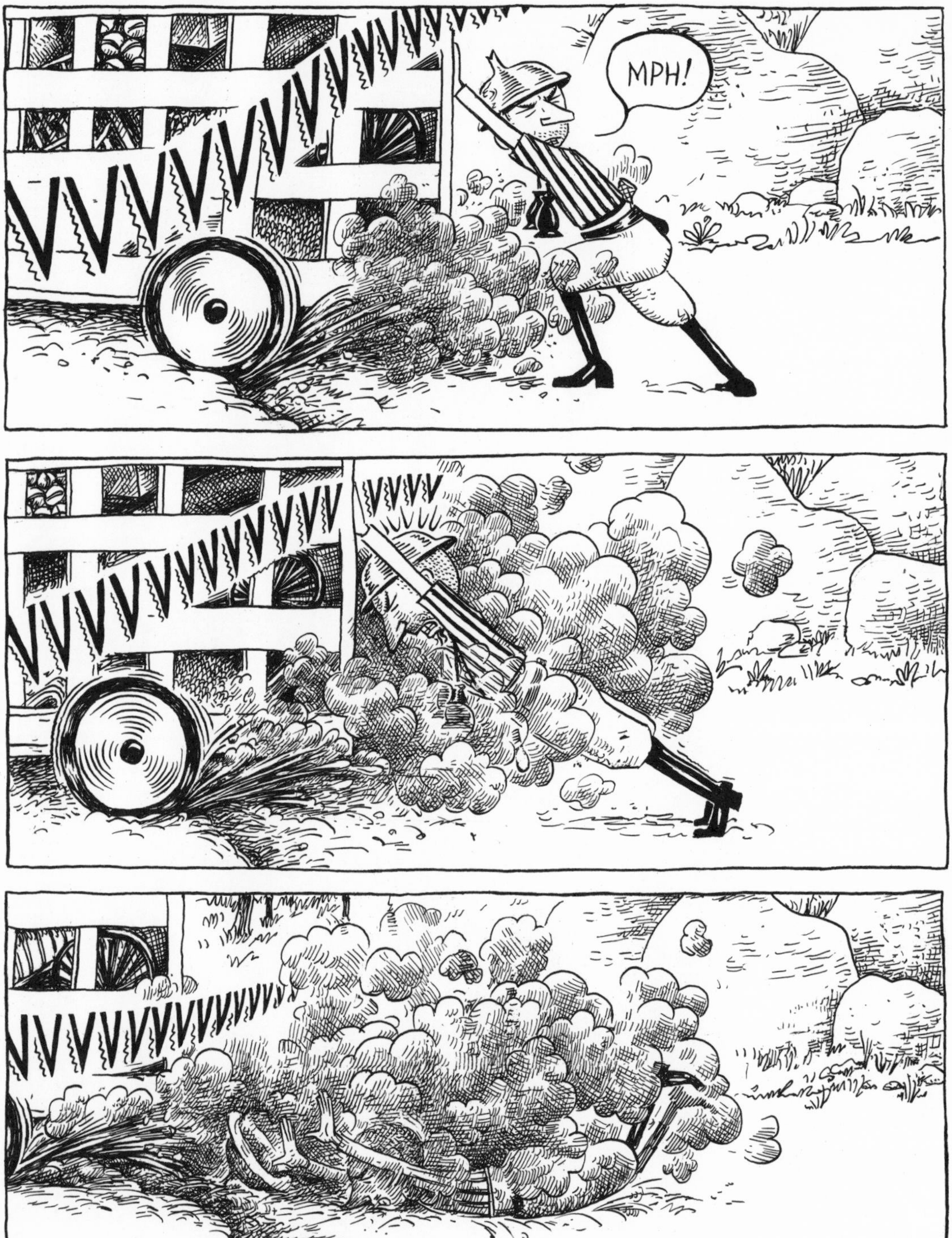
MPH!

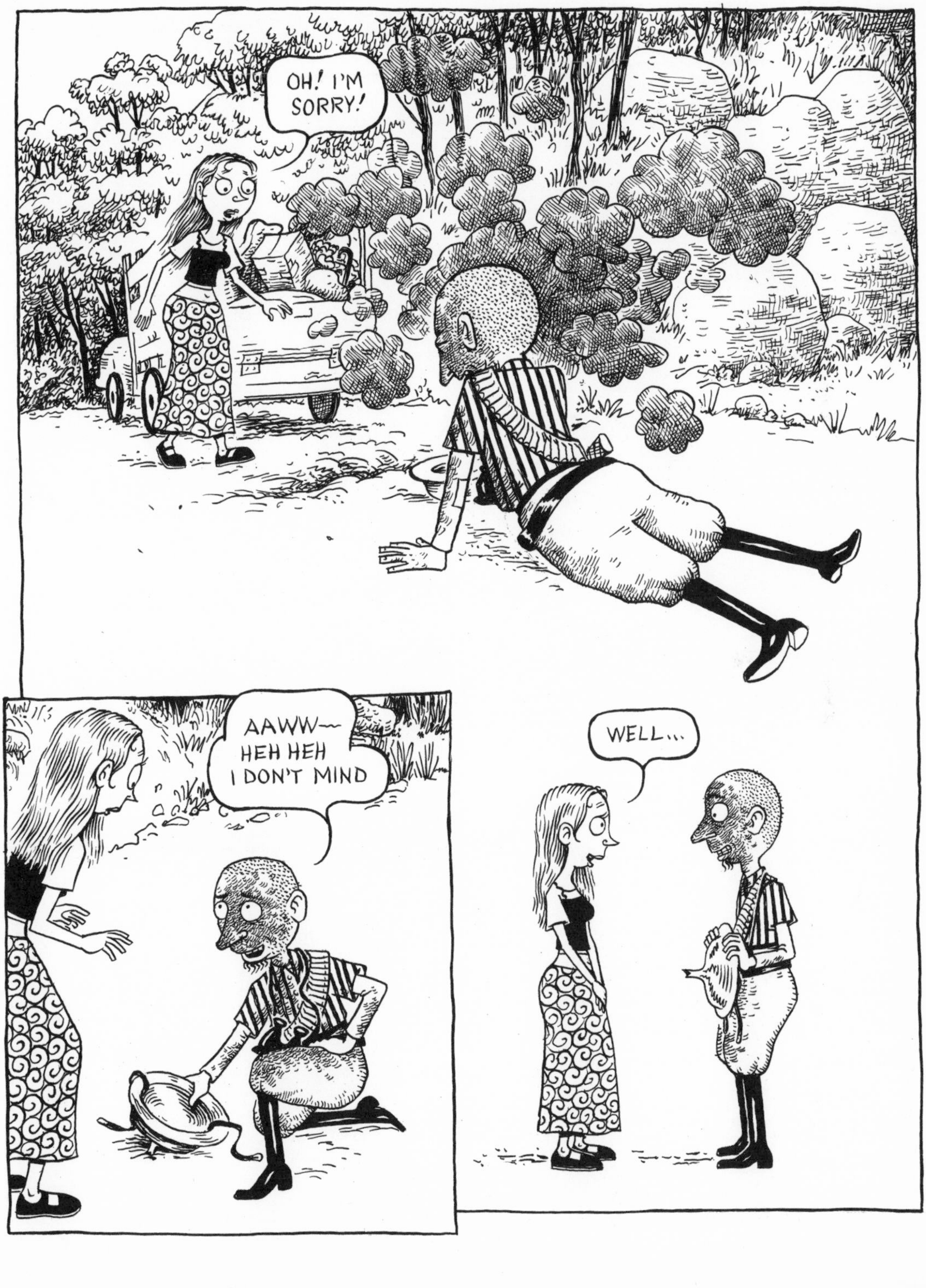
OH! I'M SORRY!
AAWW— HEH HEH I DON'T MIND
WELL...

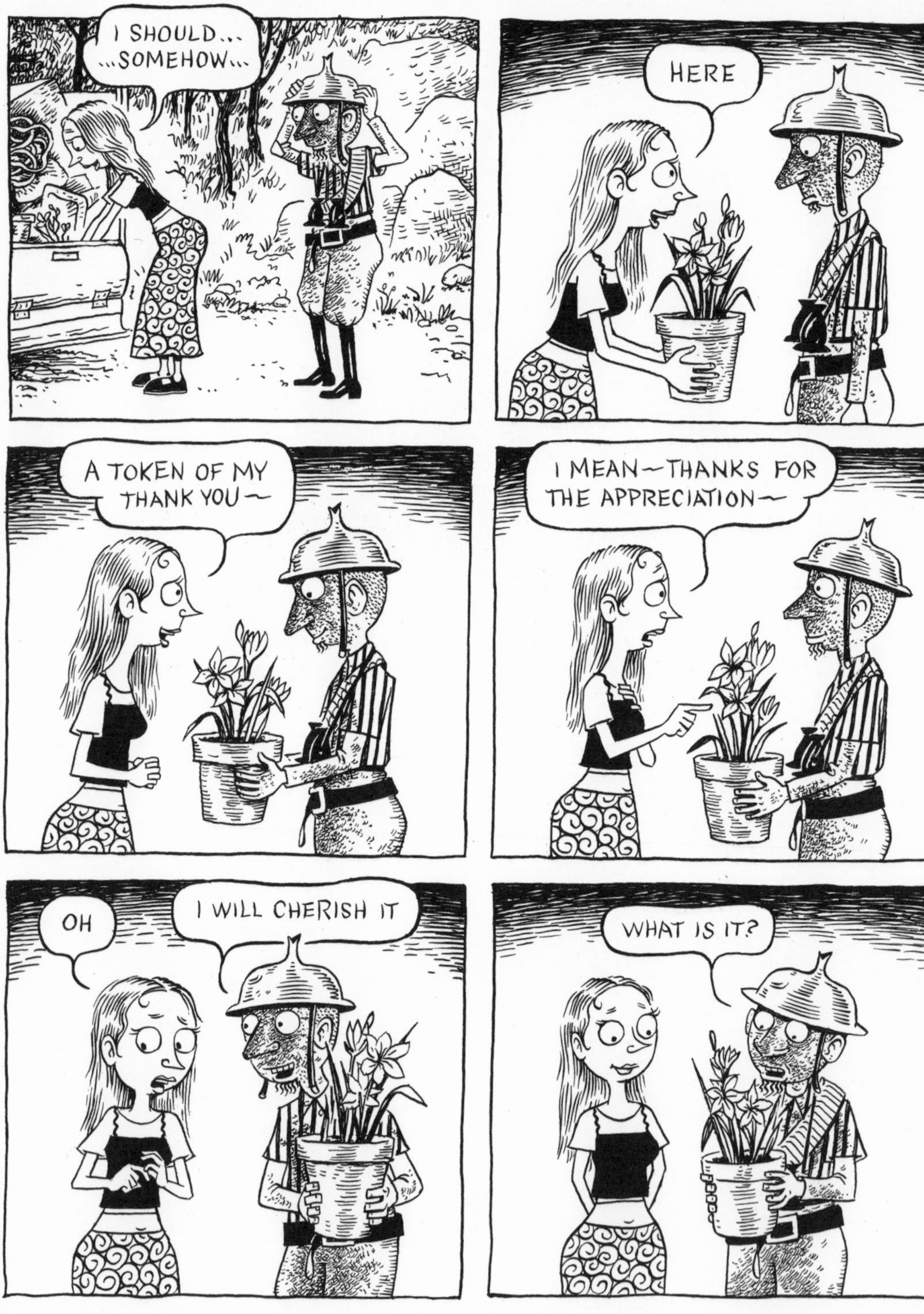
I SHOULD...
...SOMEHOW...
HERE
A TOKEN OF MY THANK YOU~
I MEAN~THANKS FOR THE APPRECIATION~
OH
I WILL CHERISH IT
WHAT IS IT?

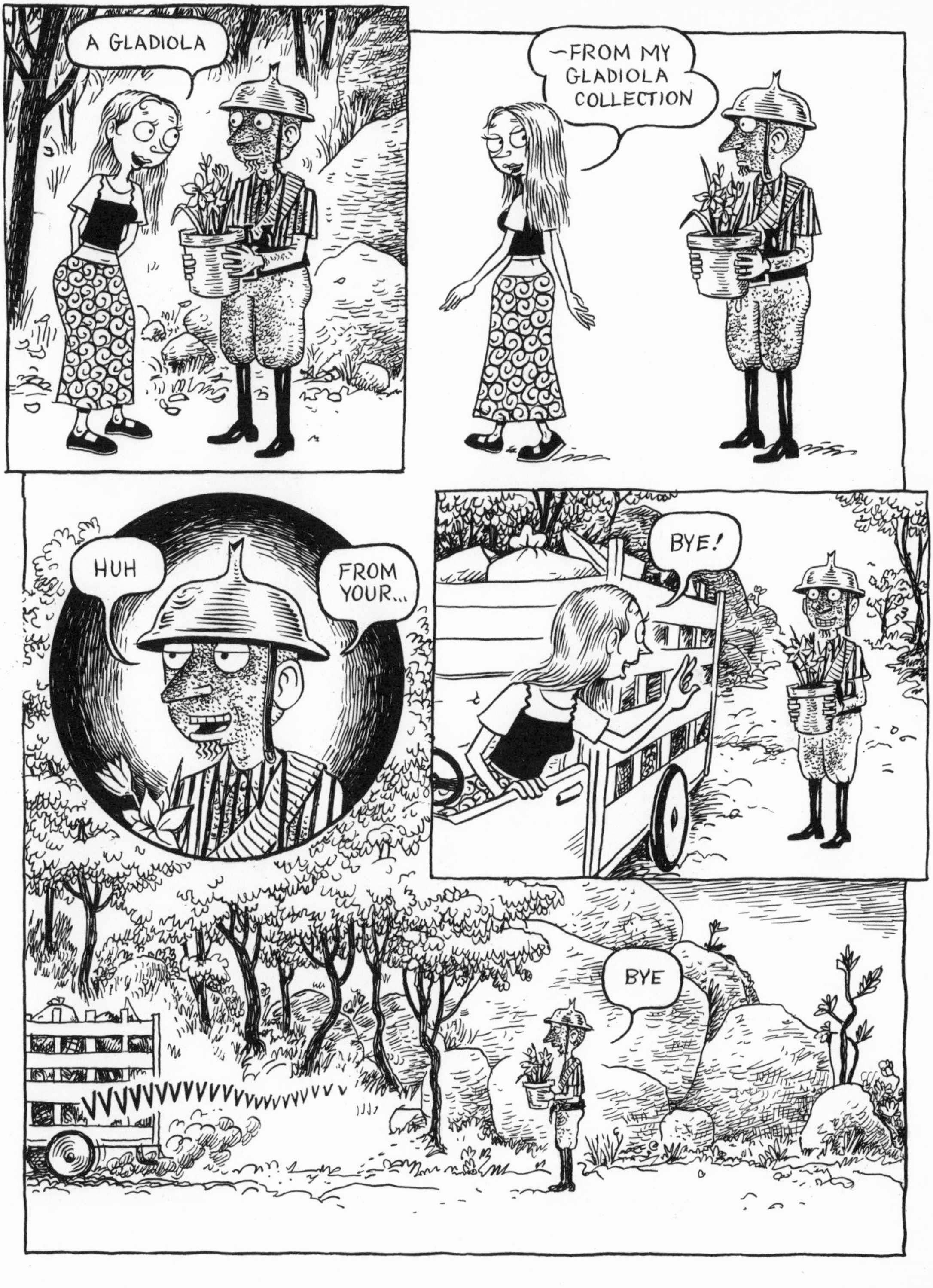
A GLADIOLA
—FROM MY GLADIOLA COLLECTION
HUH
FROM YOUR...
BYE!
BYE

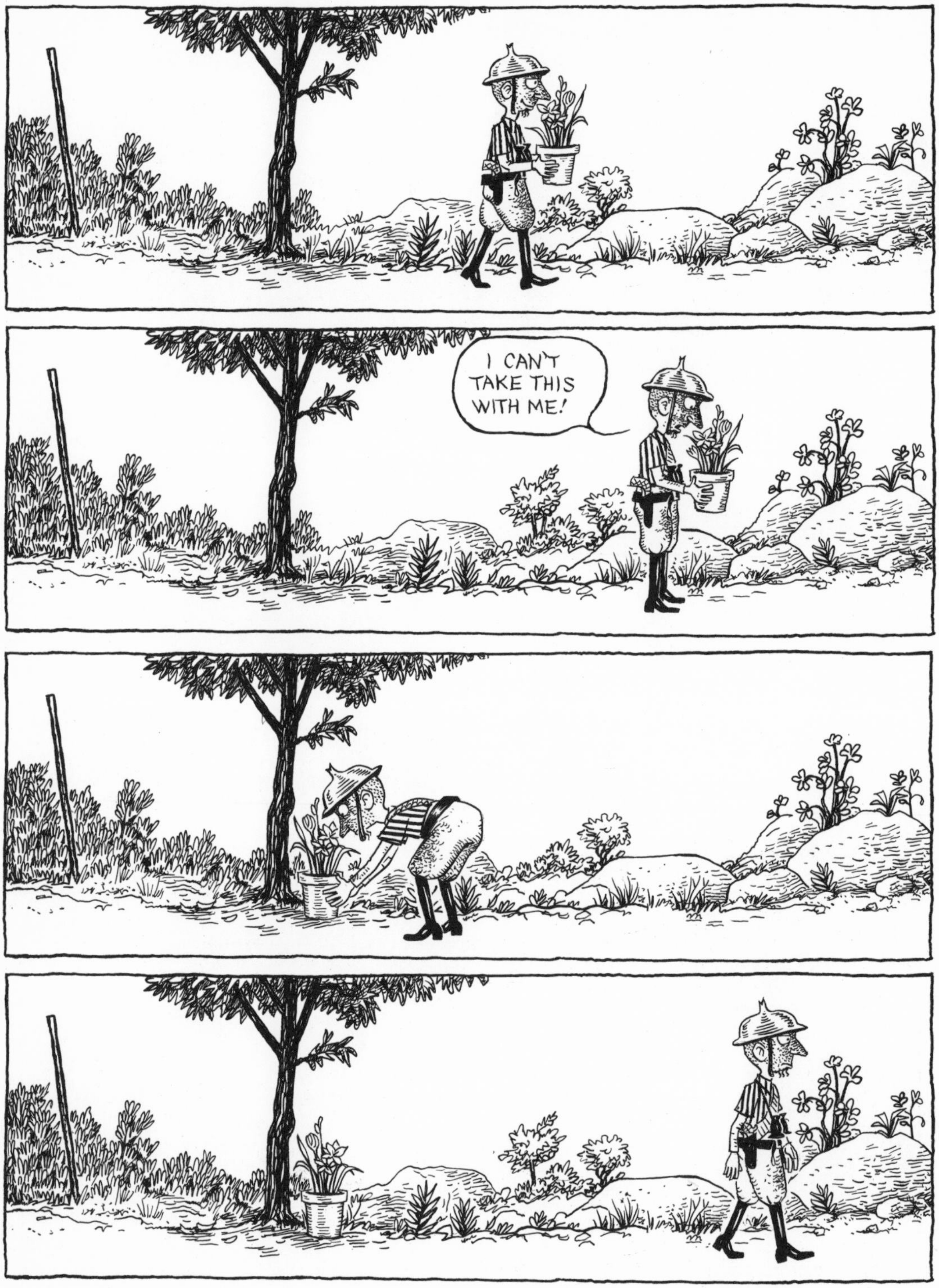
I CAN'T TAKE THIS WITH ME!

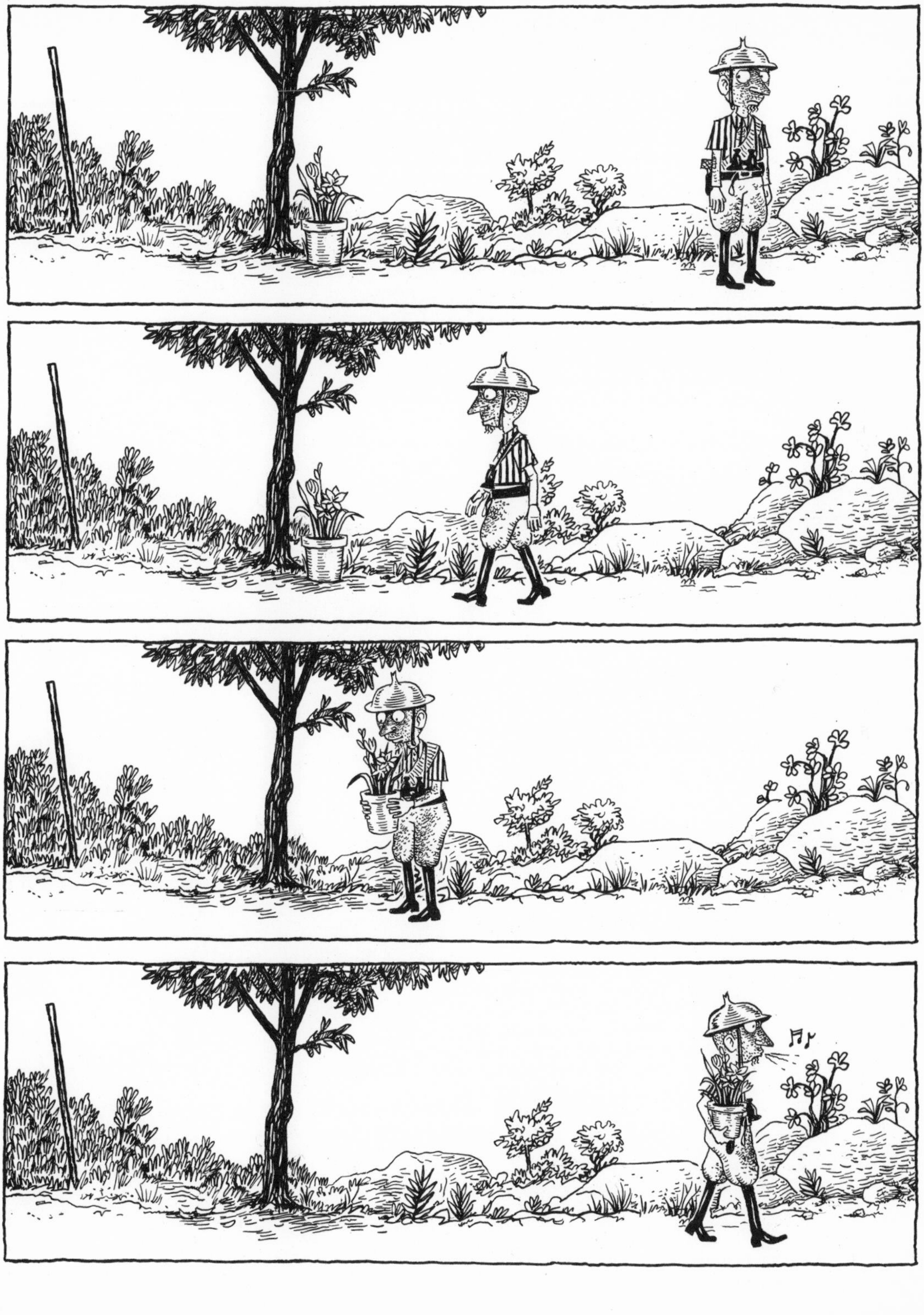

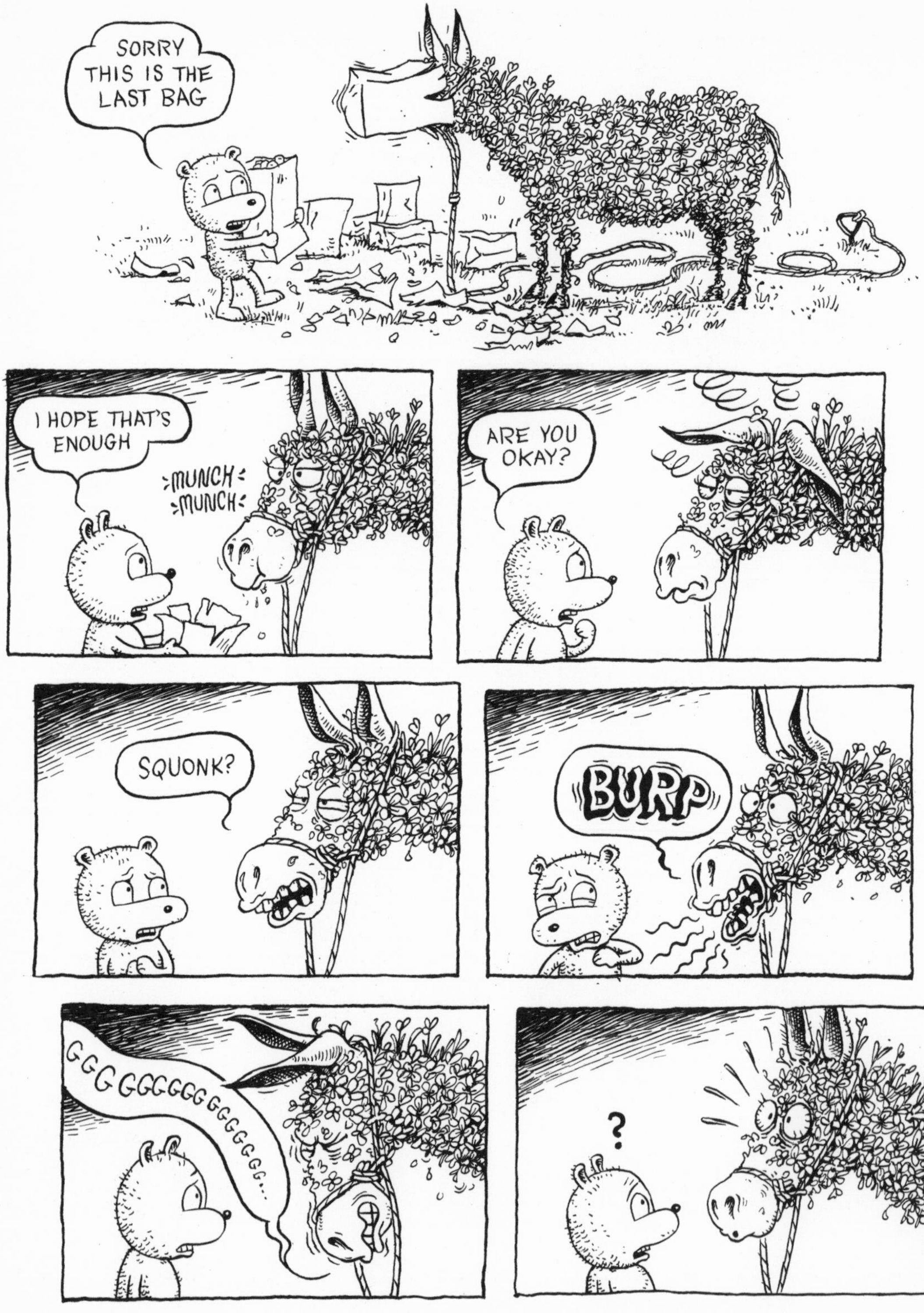

SORRY THIS IS THE LAST BAG
I HOPE THAT'S ENOUGH
MUNCH MUNCH
ARE YOU OKAY?
SQUONK?
BURP
GGGGGGGGGGGGGGGGG...
?

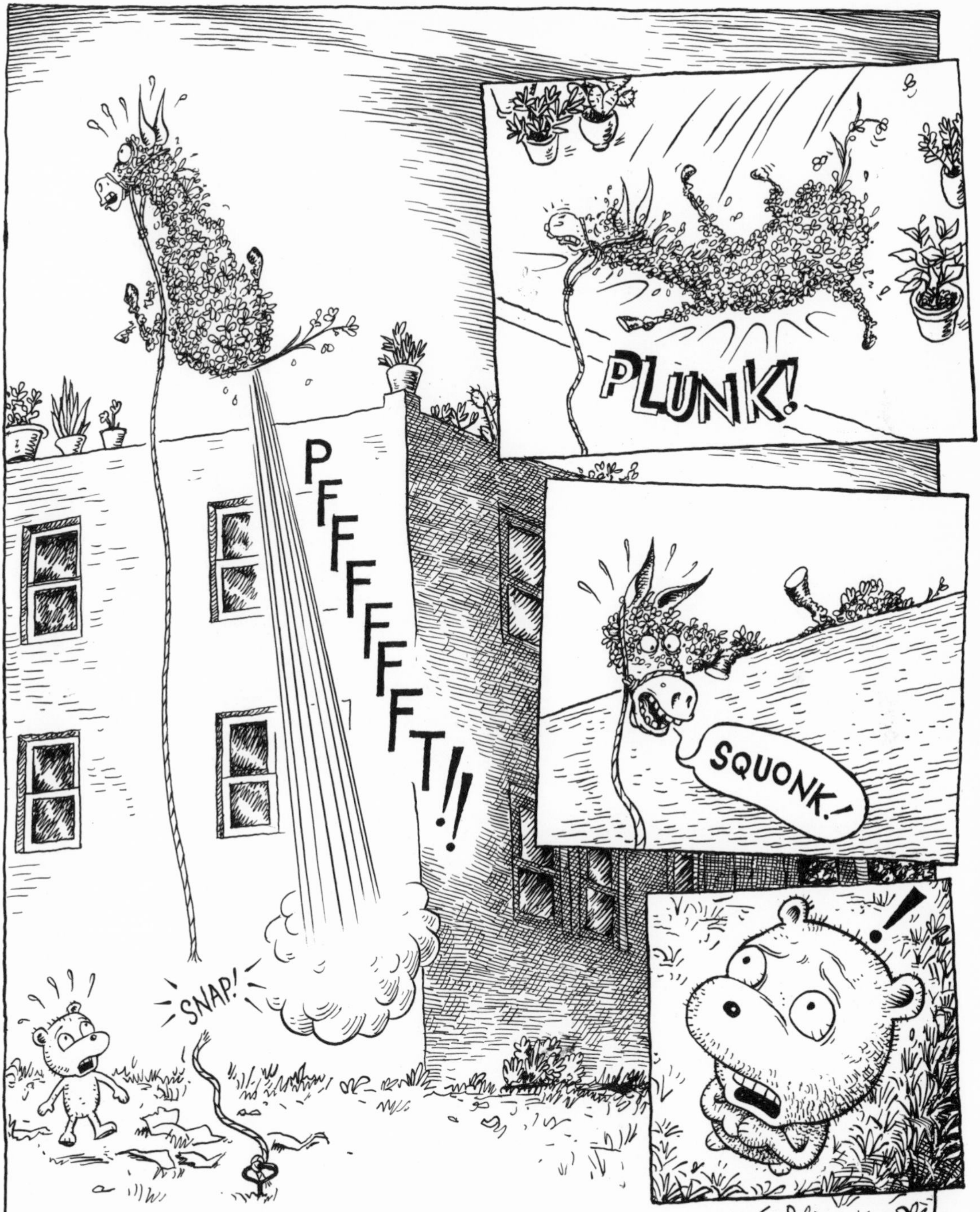
PFFFFFFFT!!
SNAP!
PLUNK!
SQUONK!
!

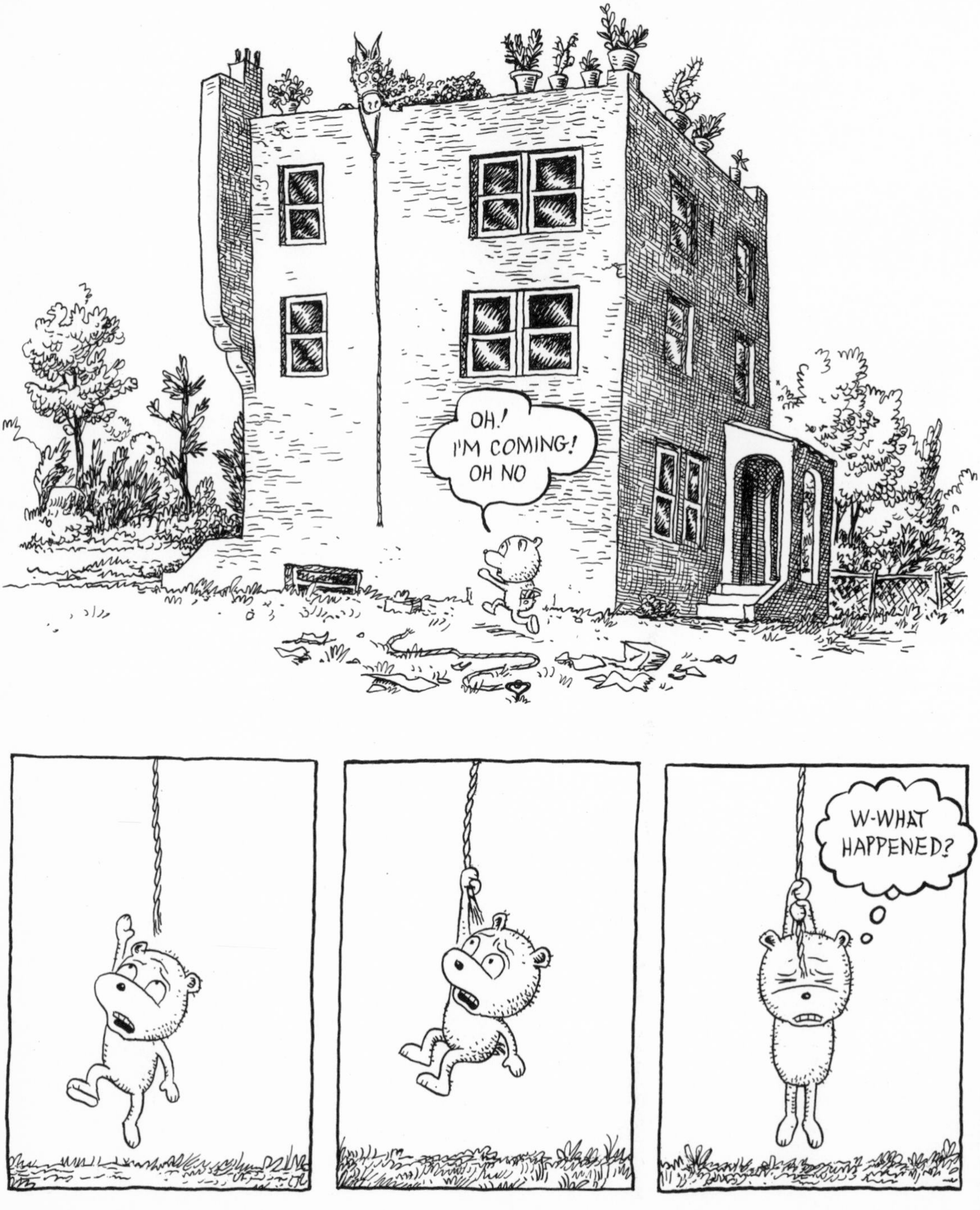
OH! I'M COMING! OH NO
W-WHAT HAPPENED?

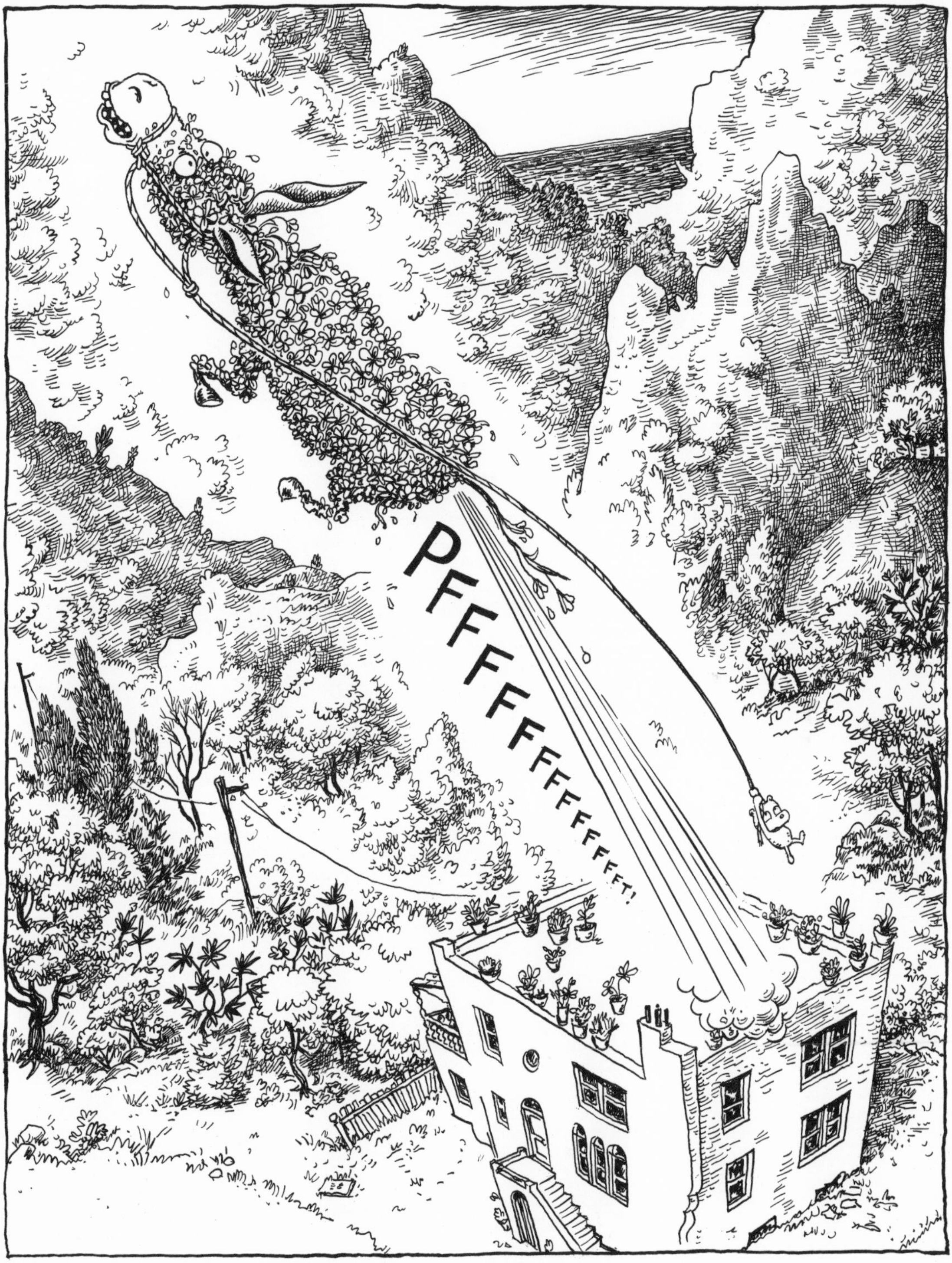
PFFFFFFFFFFFFFT!

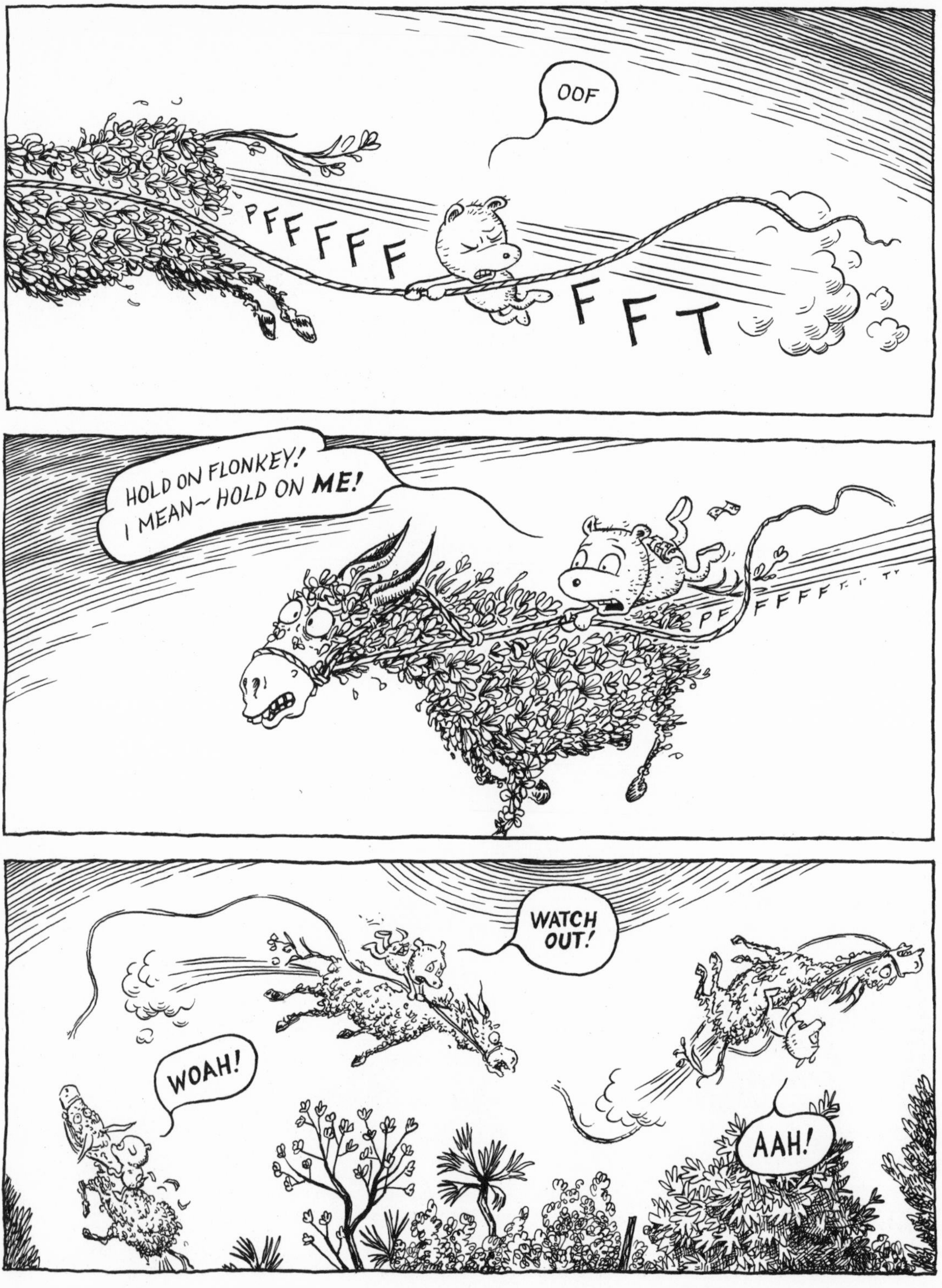
OOF
PFFFFFF
FFT
HOLD ON FLONKEY! I MEAN~ HOLD ON ME!
PFFFFFF
WATCH OUT!
WOAH!
AAH!

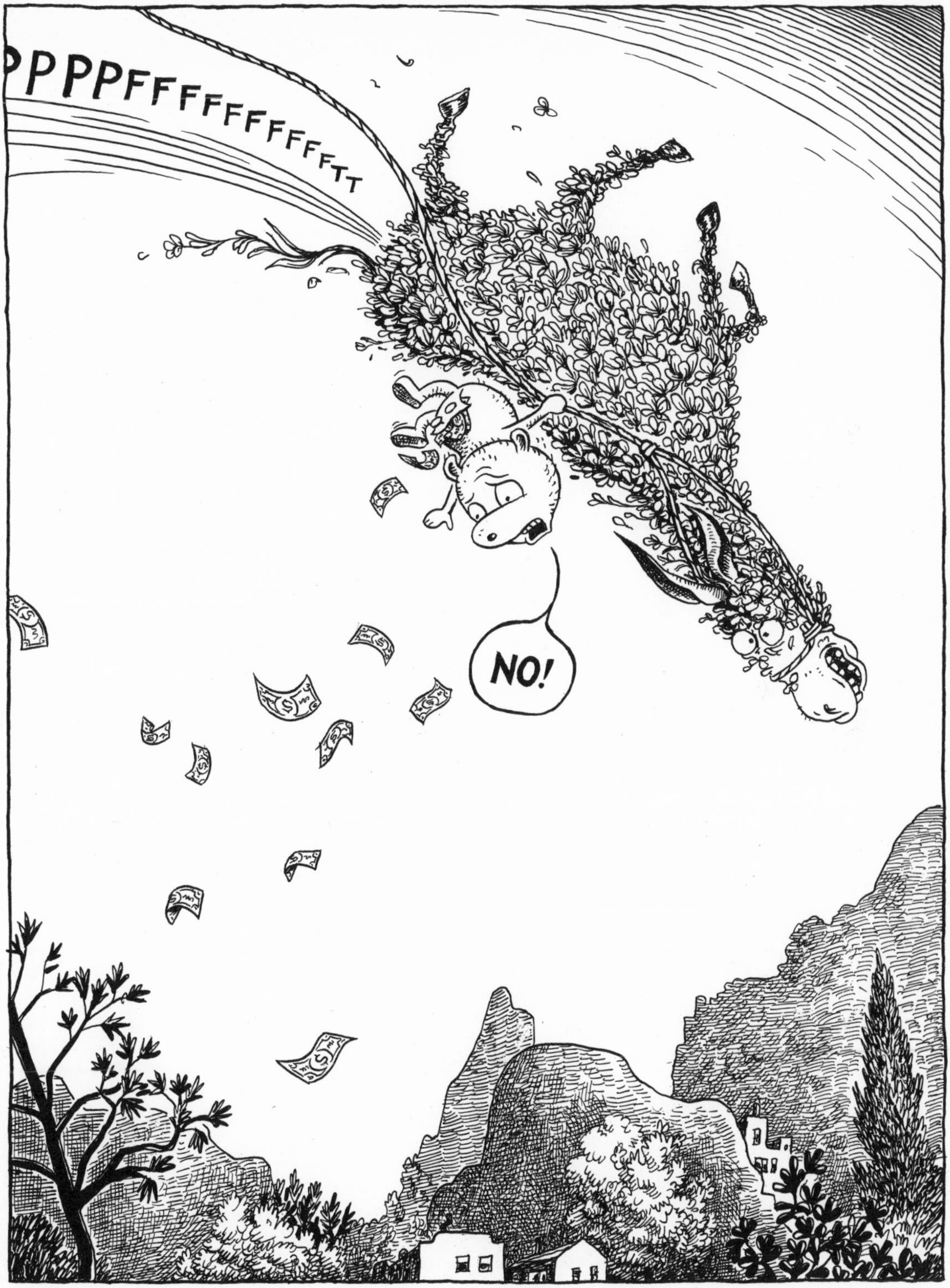
PPPPFFFFFFFFFFFFFFTTT
NO!

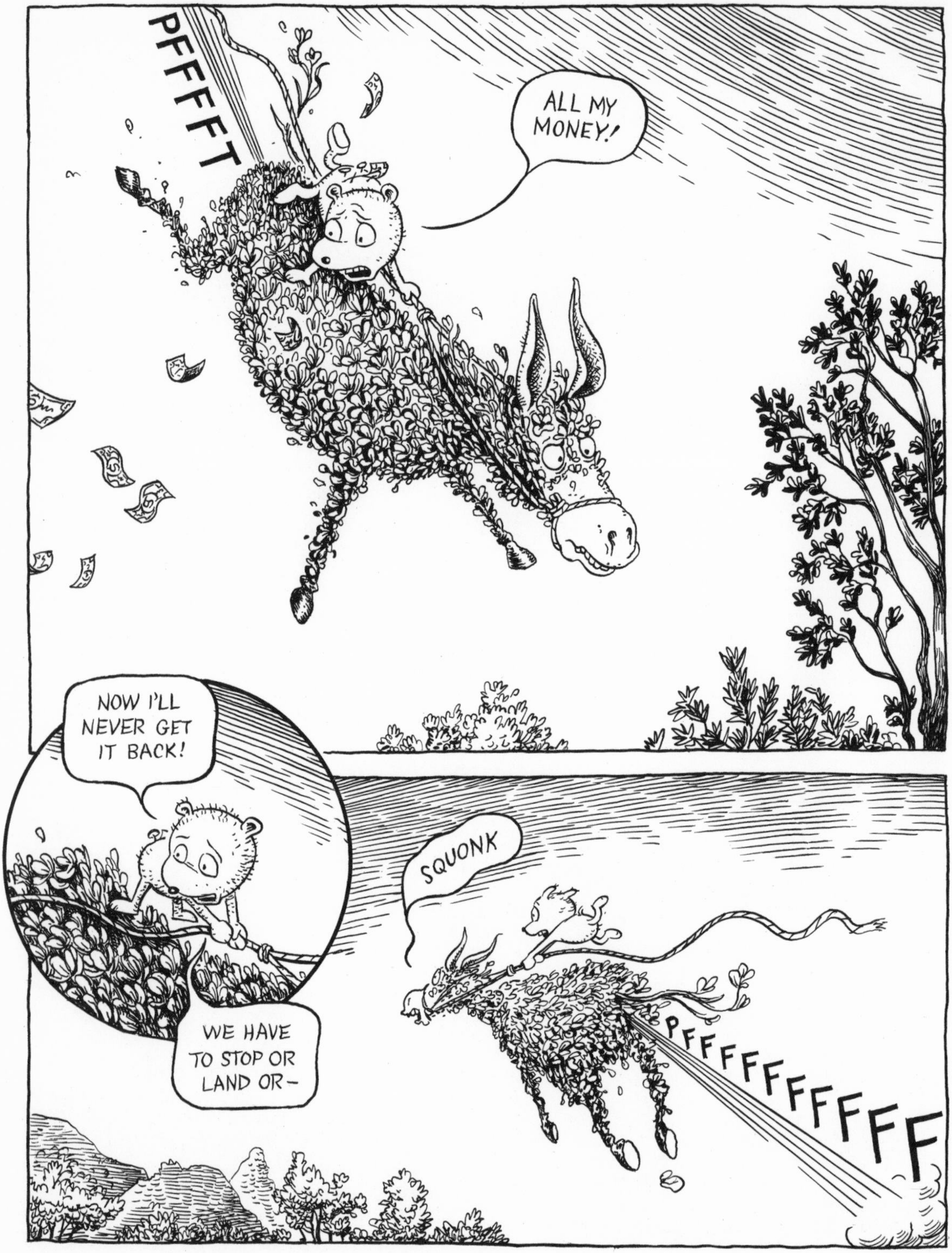
PFFFFFT
ALL MY MONEY!
NOW I'LL NEVER GET IT BACK!
WE HAVE TO STOP OR LAND OR—
SQUONK
PFFFFFFFFFFFF

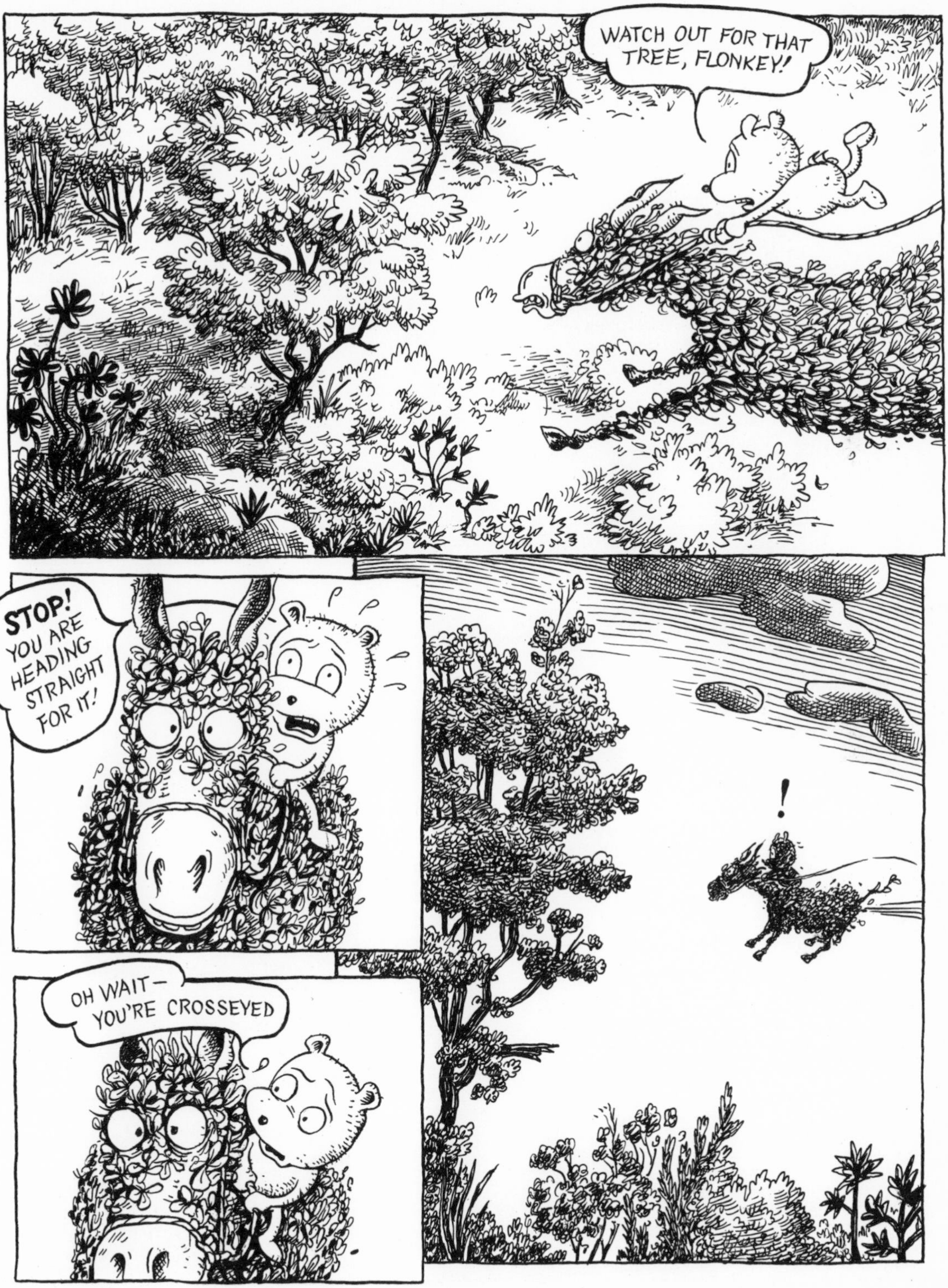
WATCH OUT FOR THAT TREE, FLONKEY!
STOP! YOU ARE HEADING STRAIGHT FOR IT!
OH WAIT— YOU'RE CROSSEYED
!

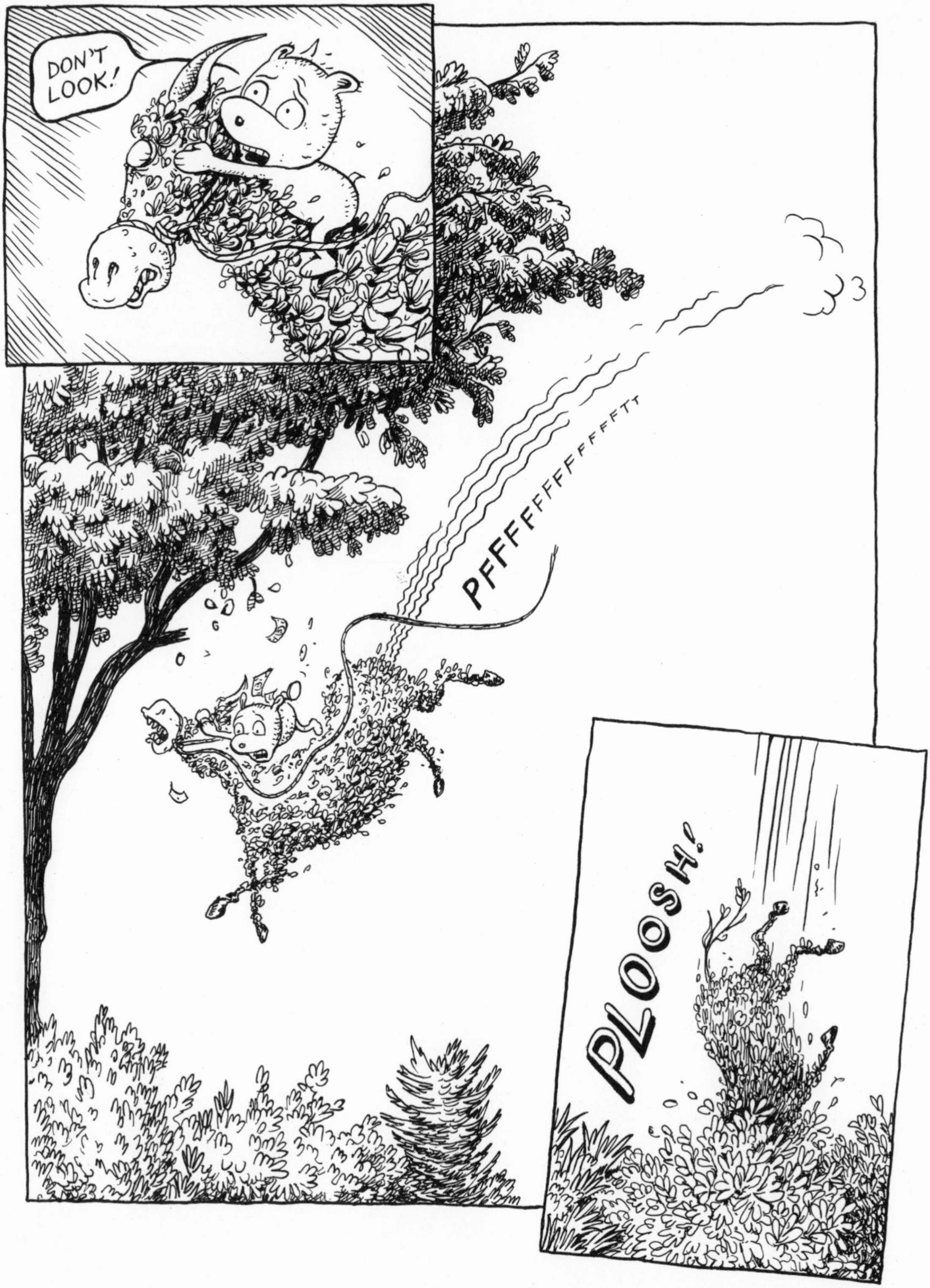
DON'T LOOK!
PFFFFFFFFFFFFFFTT
PLOOSH!

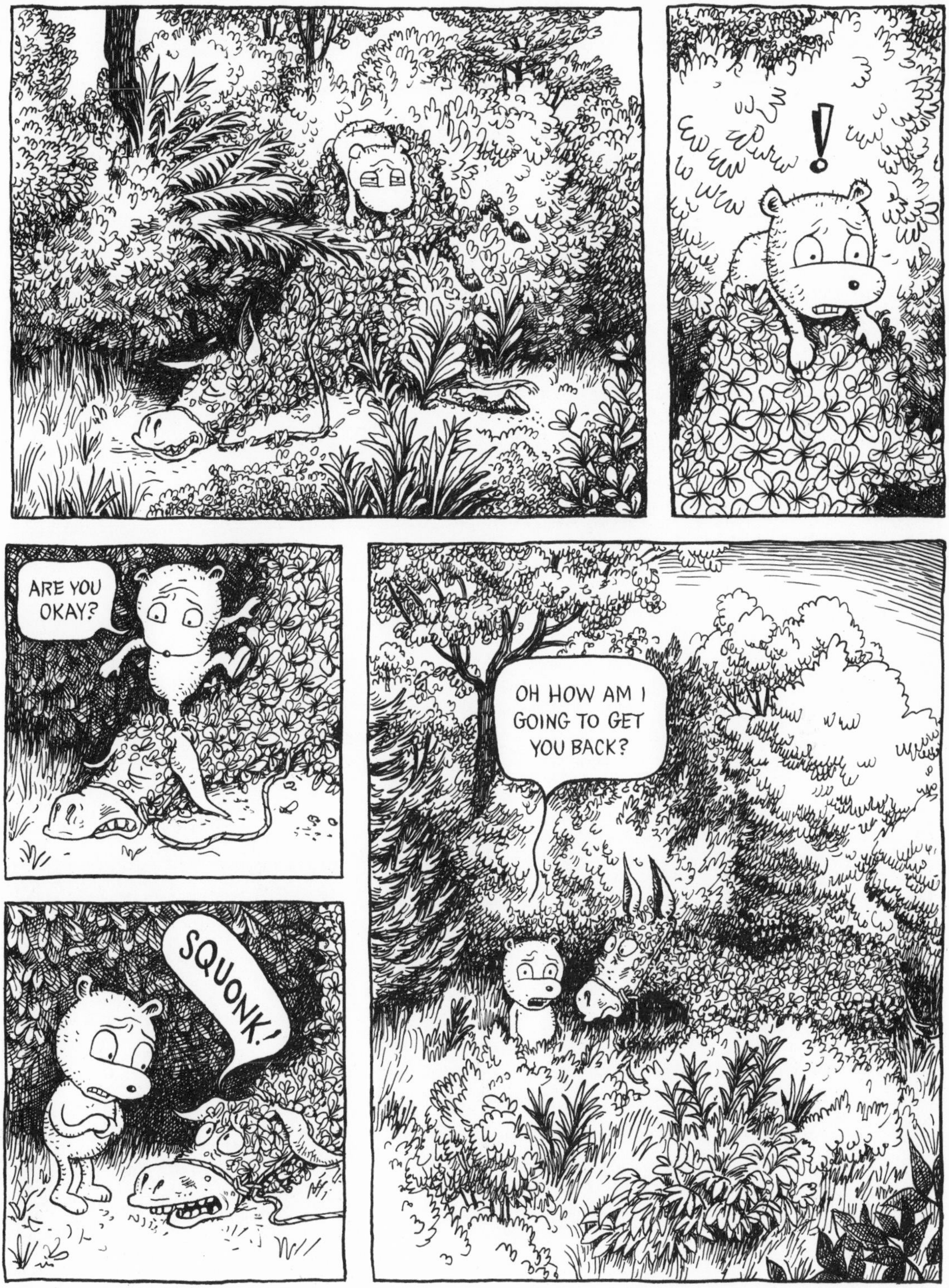
!
ARE YOU OKAY?
SQUONK!
OH HOW AM I GOING TO GET YOU BACK?

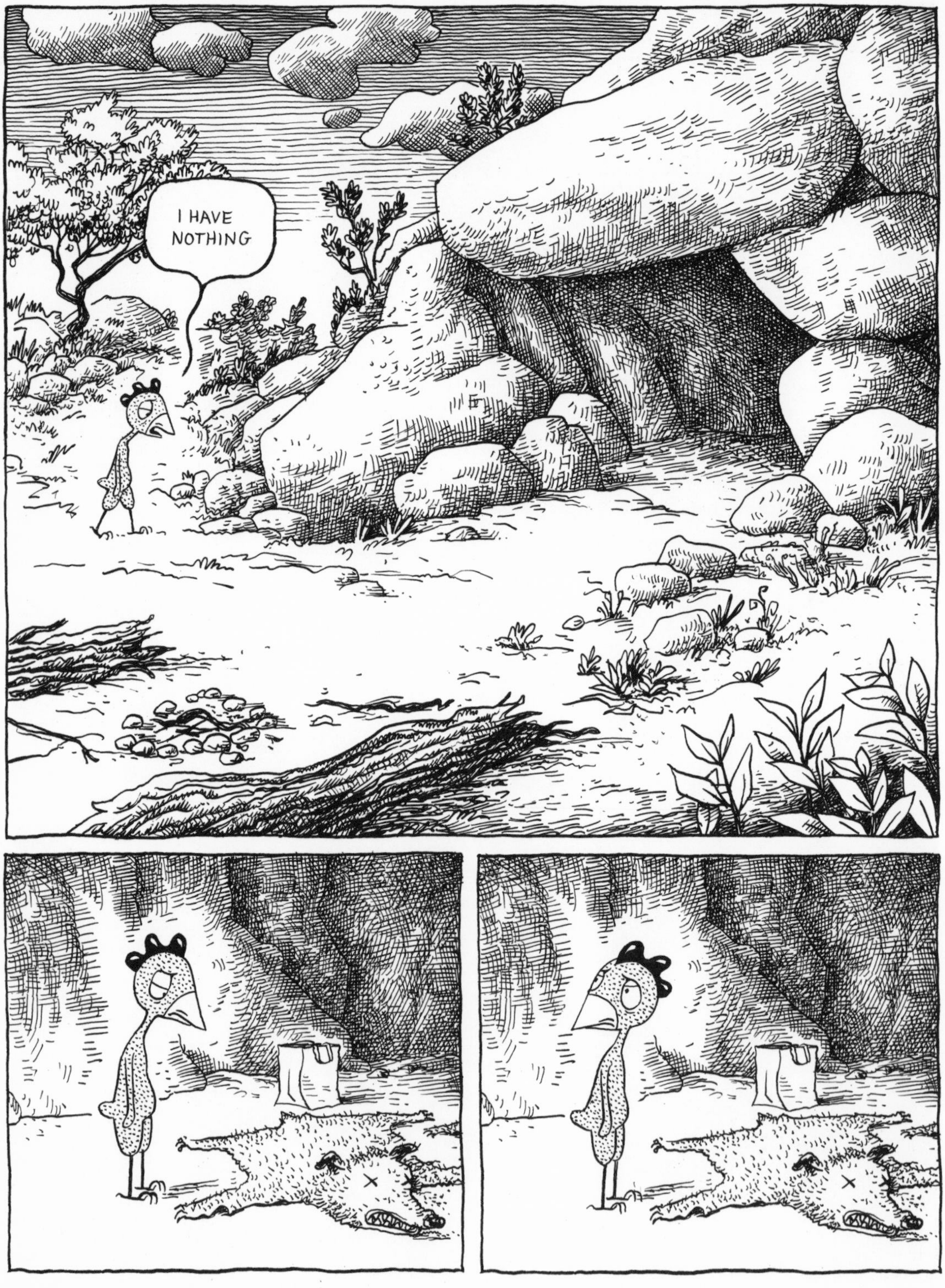
I HAVE NOTHING

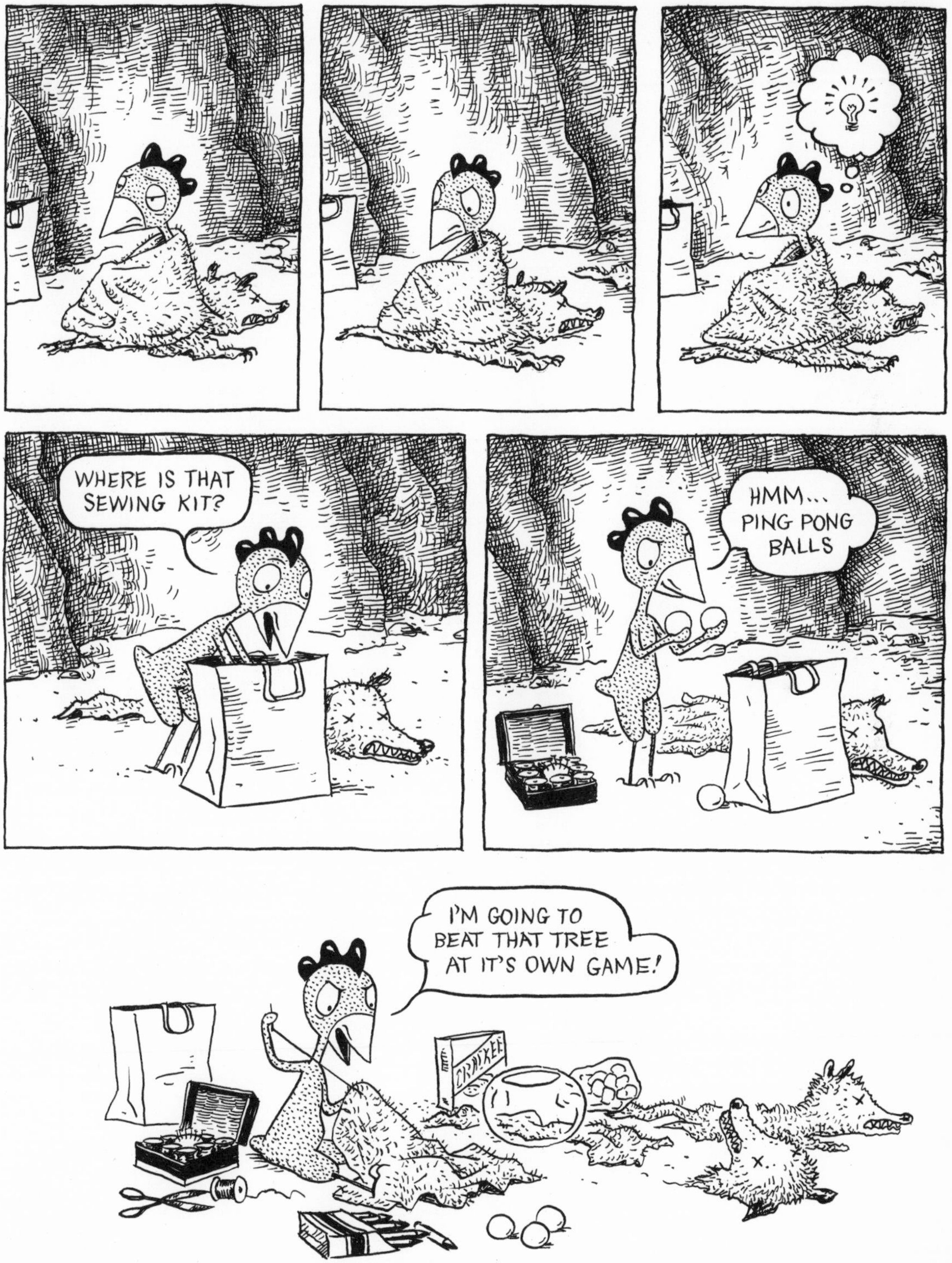
WHERE IS THAT SEWING KIT?
HMM... PING PONG BALLS
I'M GOING TO BEAT THAT TREE AT IT'S OWN GAME!

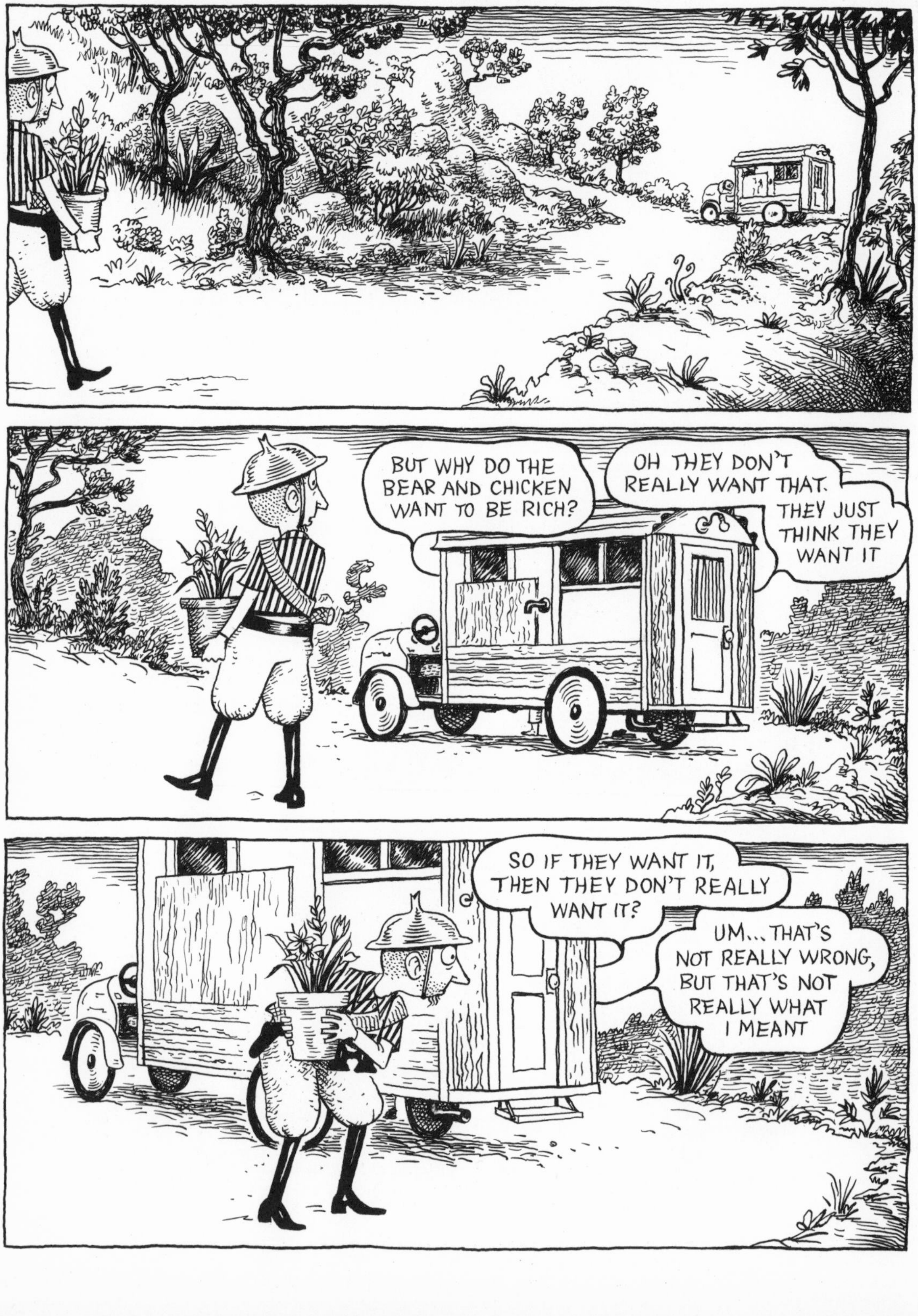
BUT WHY DO THE BEAR AND CHICKEN WANT TO BE RICH?
OH THEY DON'T REALLY WANT THAT.
THEY JUST THINK THEY WANT IT
SO IF THEY WANT IT, THEN THEY DON'T REALLY WANT IT?
UM... THAT'S NOT REALLY WRONG, BUT THAT'S NOT REALLY WHAT I MEANT

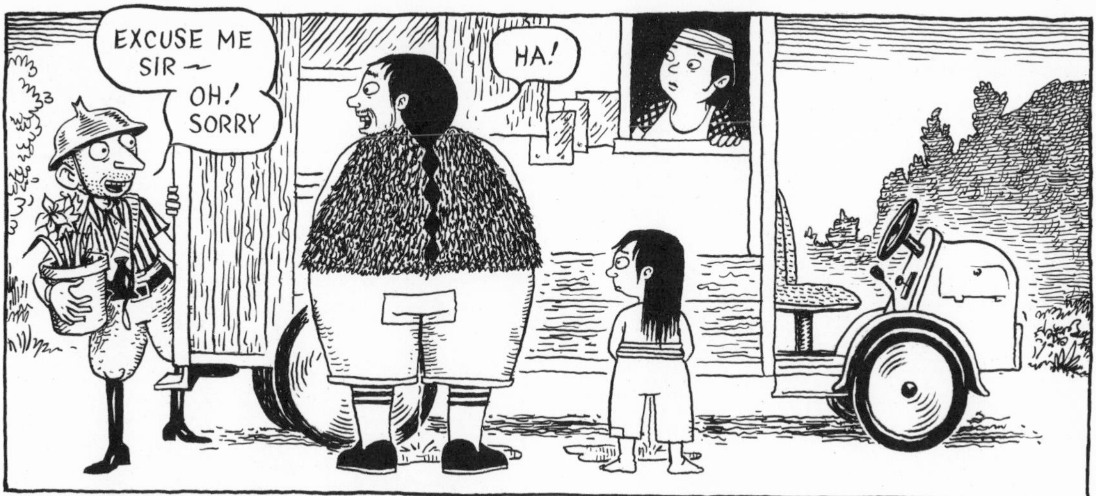
EXCUSE ME SIR—
OH! SORRY
HA!

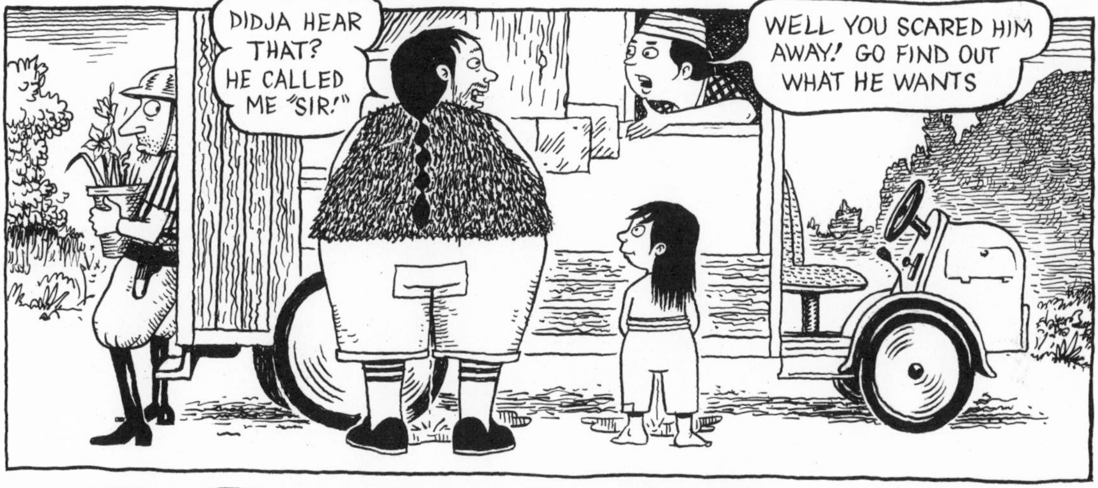
DIDJA HEAR THAT? HE CALLED ME "SIR!"
WELL YOU SCARED HIM AWAY! GO FIND OUT WHAT HE WANTS

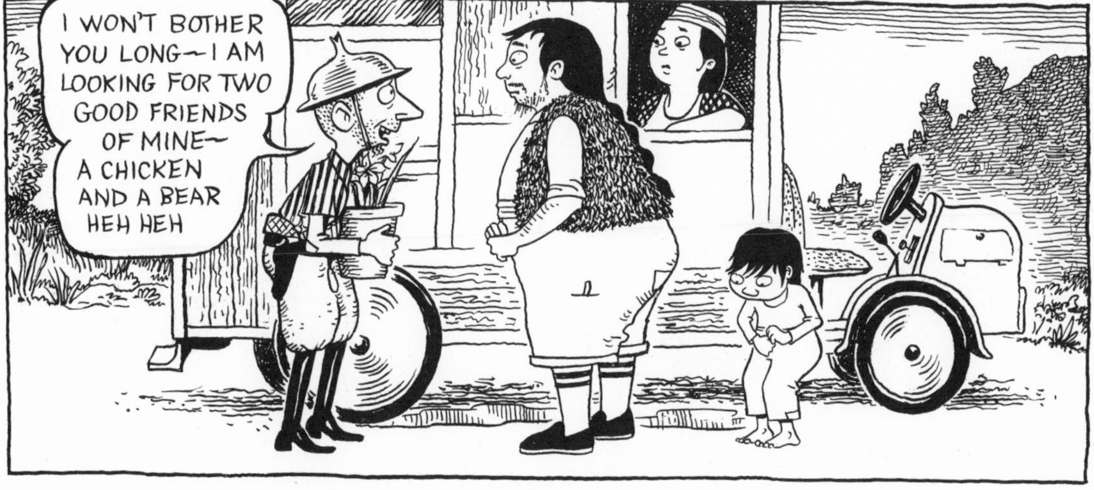
I WON'T BOTHER YOU LONG—I AM LOOKING FOR TWO GOOD FRIENDS OF MINE—A CHICKEN AND A BEAR HEH HEH

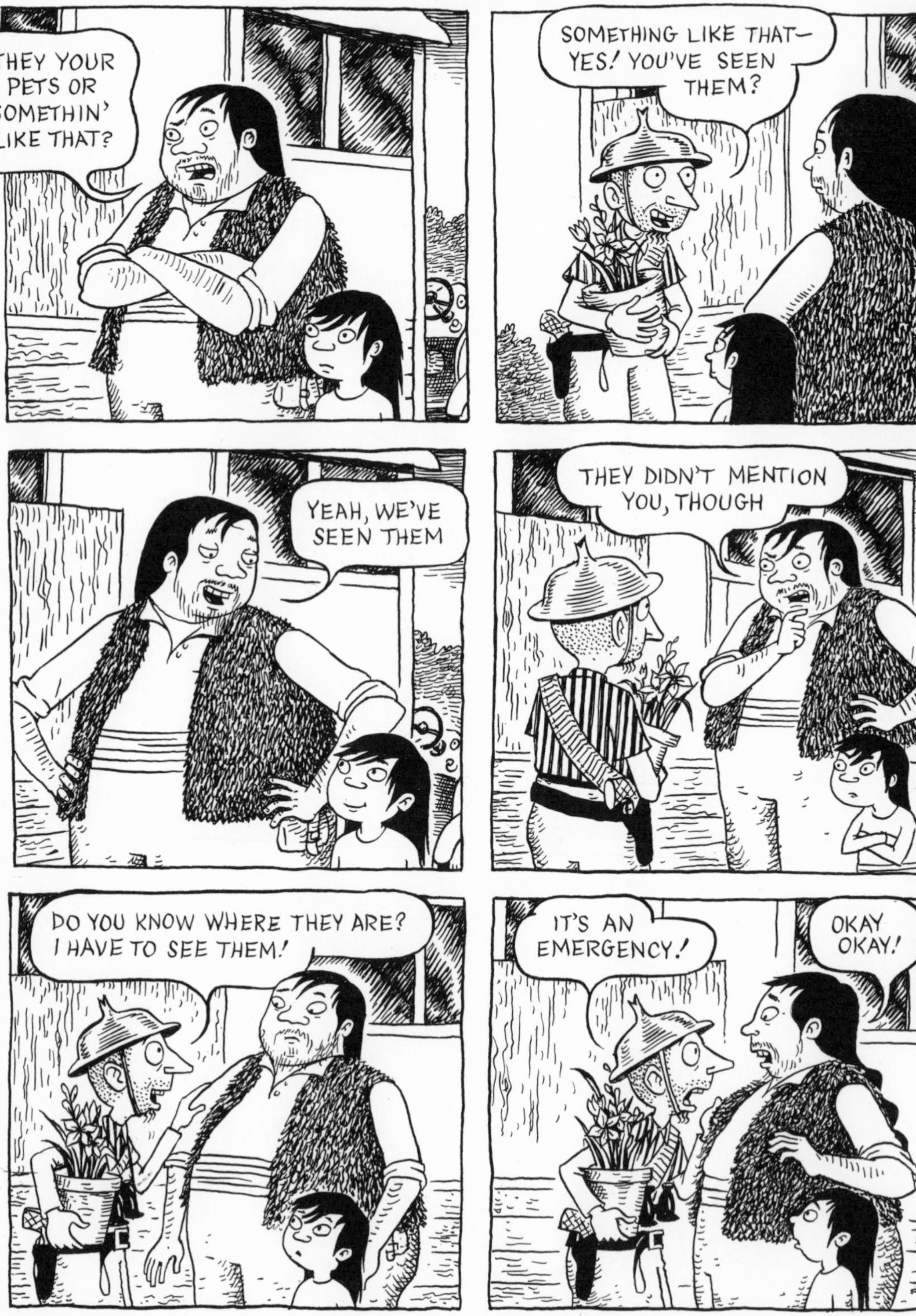
THEY YOUR PETS OR SOMETHIN' LIKE THAT?
SOMETHING LIKE THAT— YES! YOU'VE SEEN THEM?
YEAH, WE'VE SEEN THEM
THEY DIDN'T MENTION YOU, THOUGH
DO YOU KNOW WHERE THEY ARE? I HAVE TO SEE THEM!
IT'S AN EMERGENCY!
OKAY OKAY!

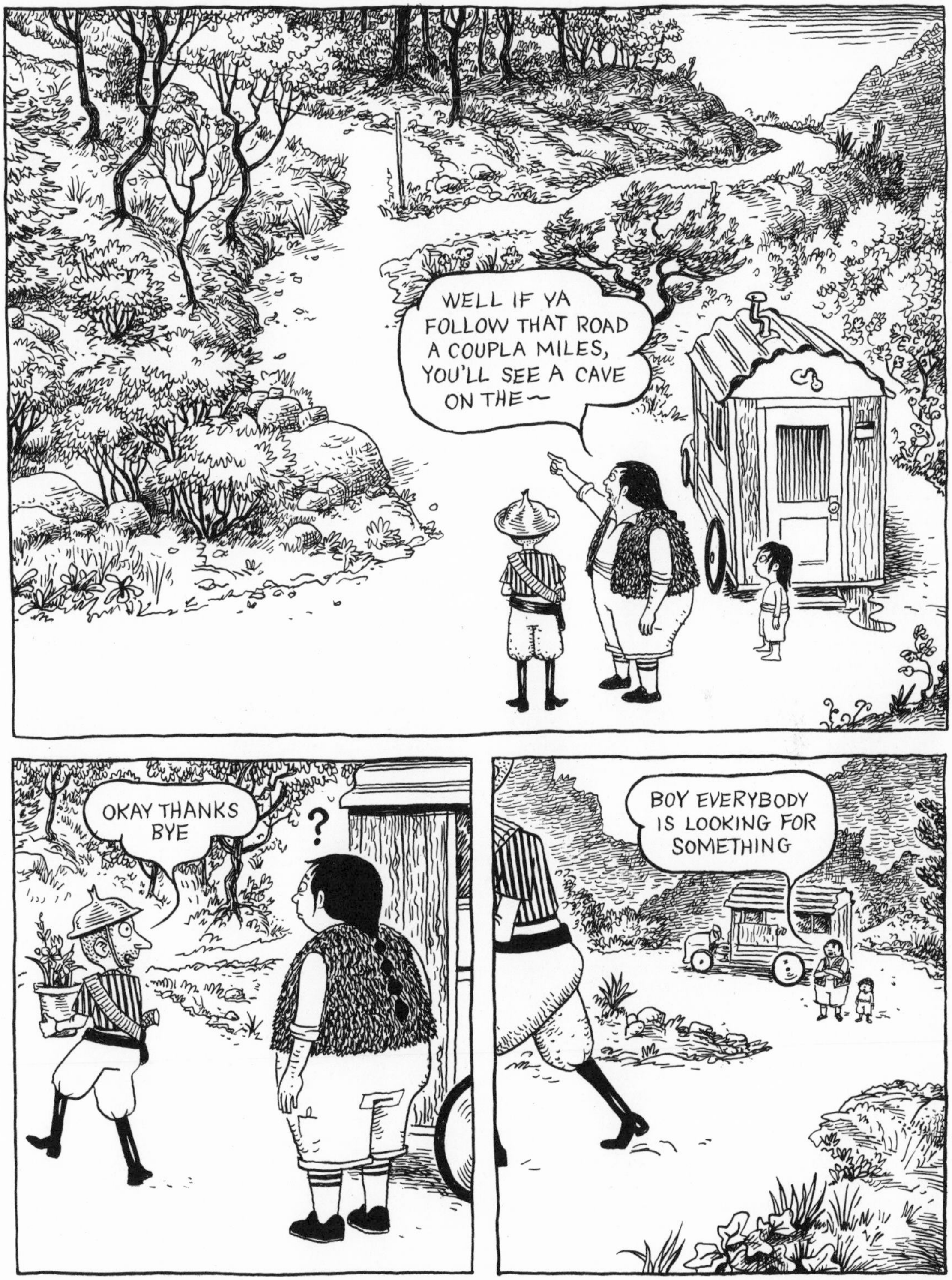
WELL IF YA FOLLOW THAT ROAD A COUPLA MILES, YOU'LL SEE A CAVE ON THE~
OKAY THANKS BYE
?
BOY EVERYBODY IS LOOKING FOR SOMETHING

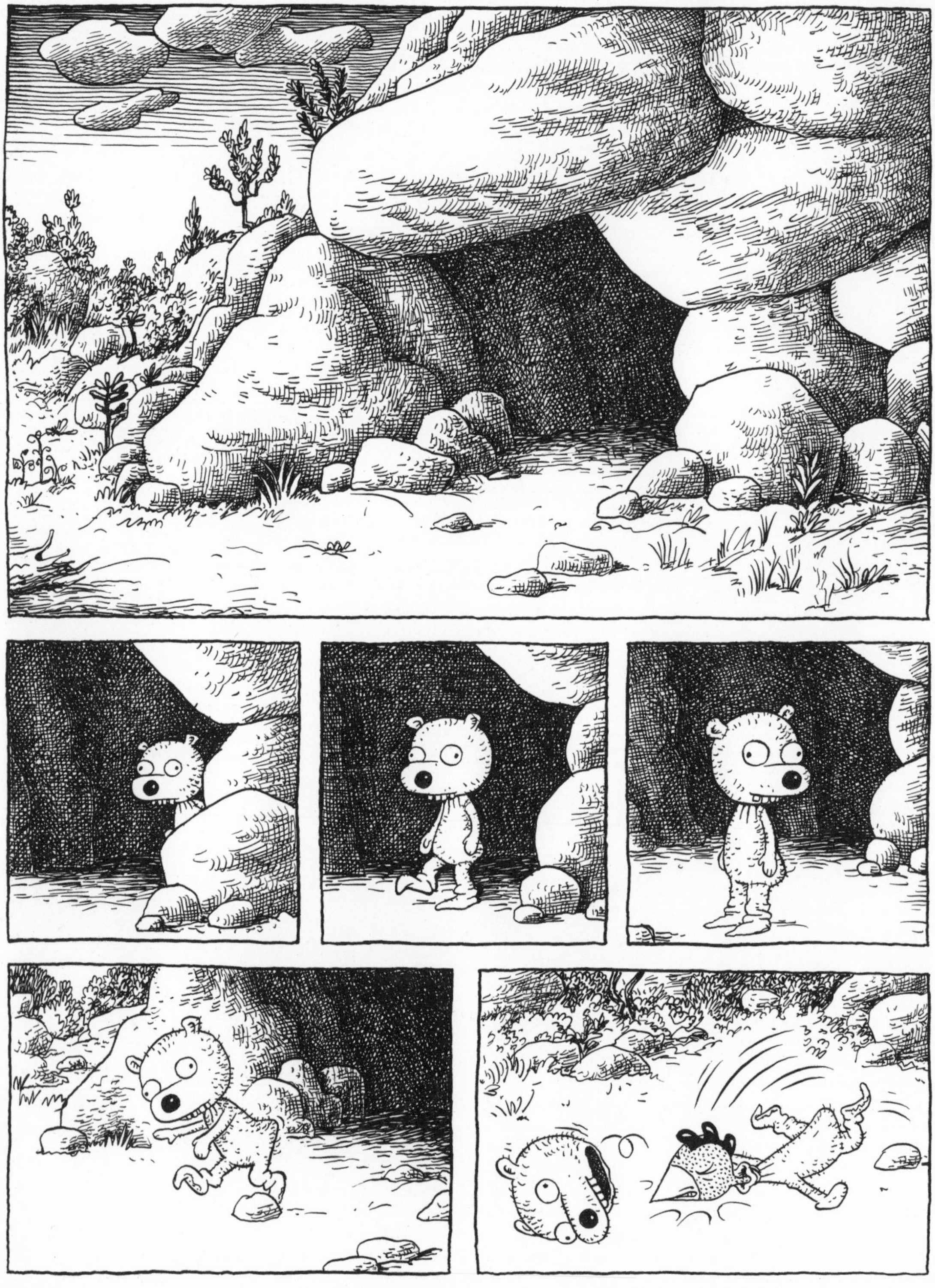

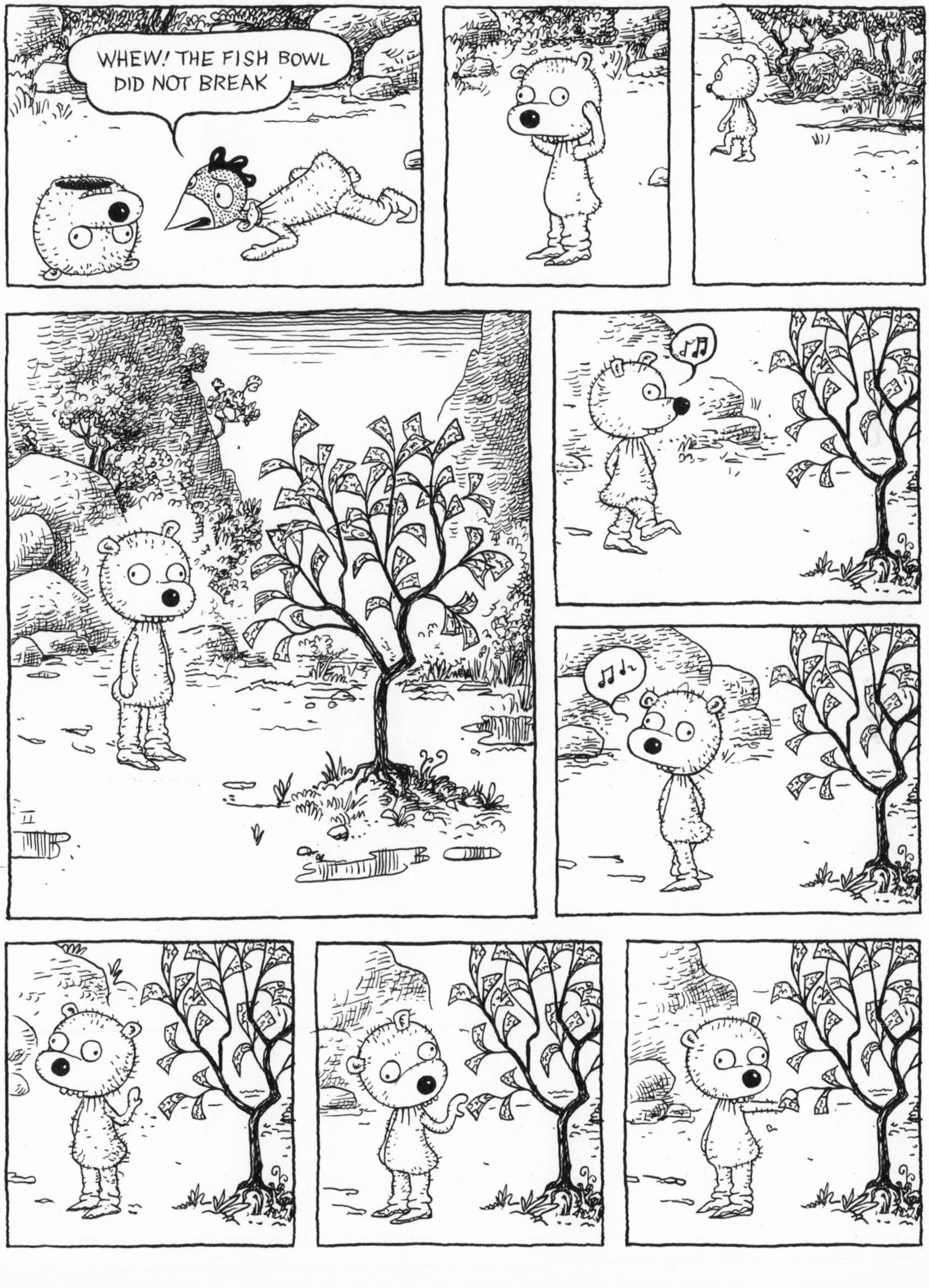
WHEW! THE FISH BOWL DID NOT BREAK

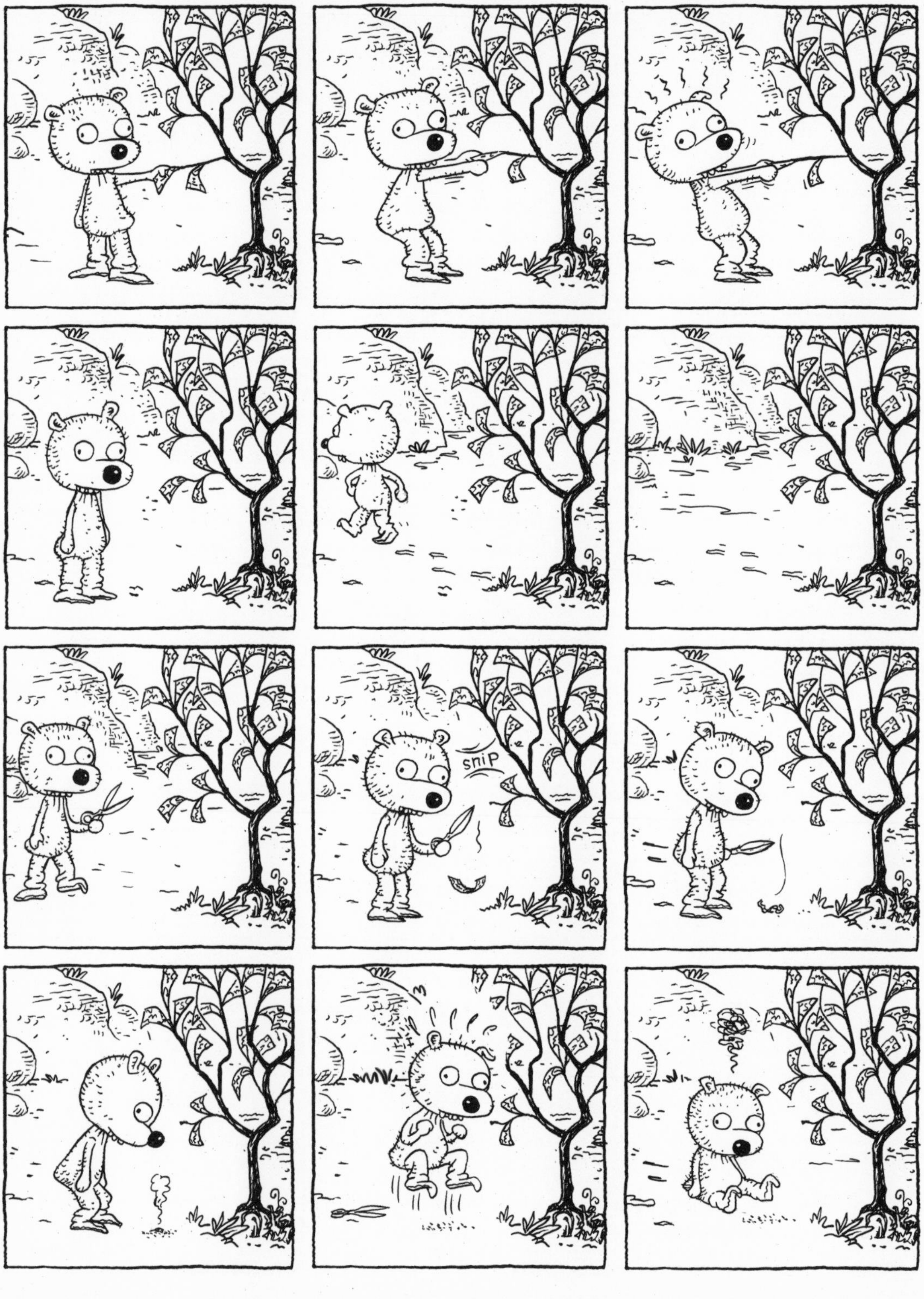
sniP

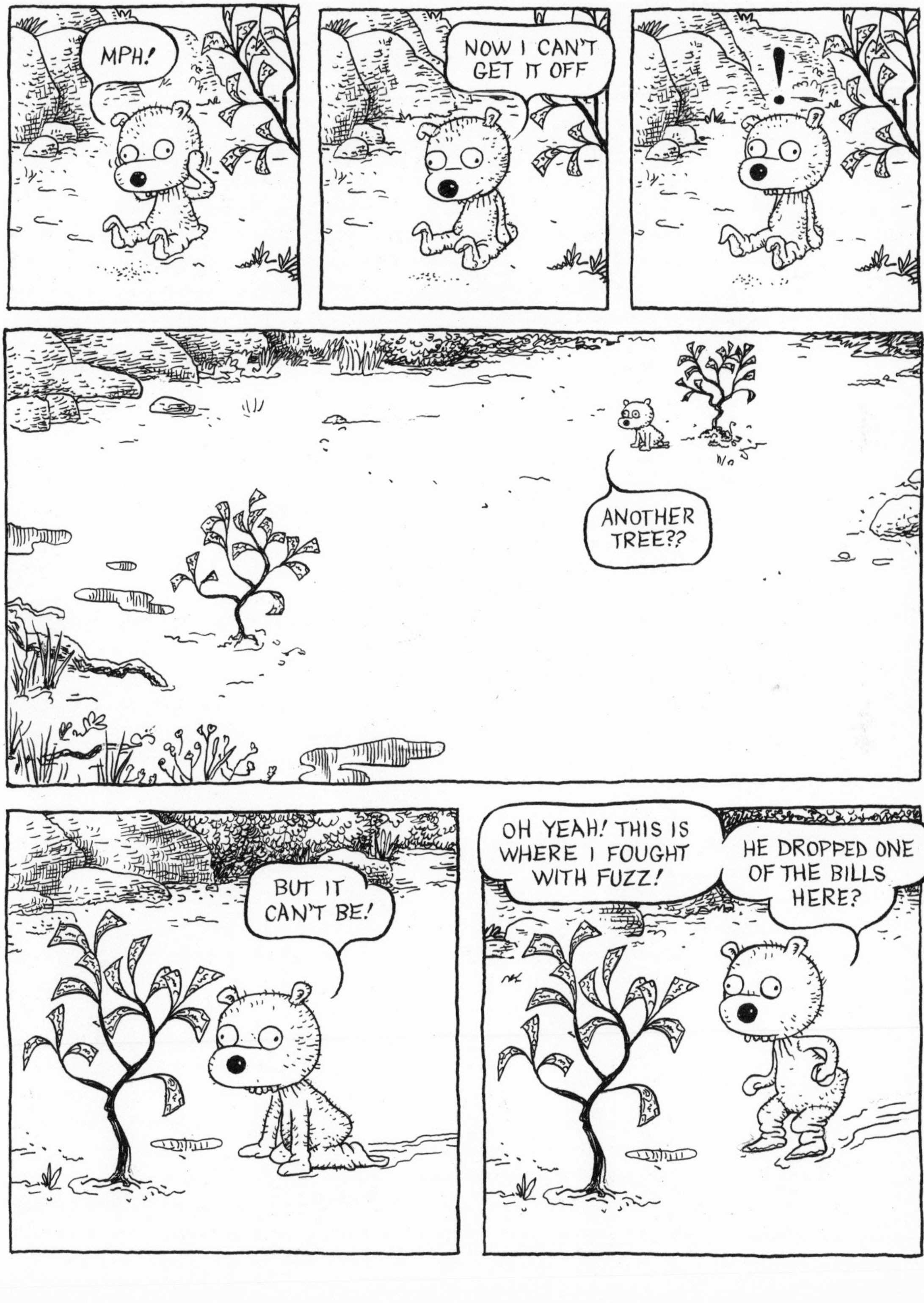
MPH!
NOW I CAN'T GET IT OFF
!
ANOTHER TREE??
BUT IT CAN'T BE!
OH YEAH! THIS IS WHERE I FOUGHT WITH FUZZ!
HE DROPPED ONE OF THE BILLS HERE?

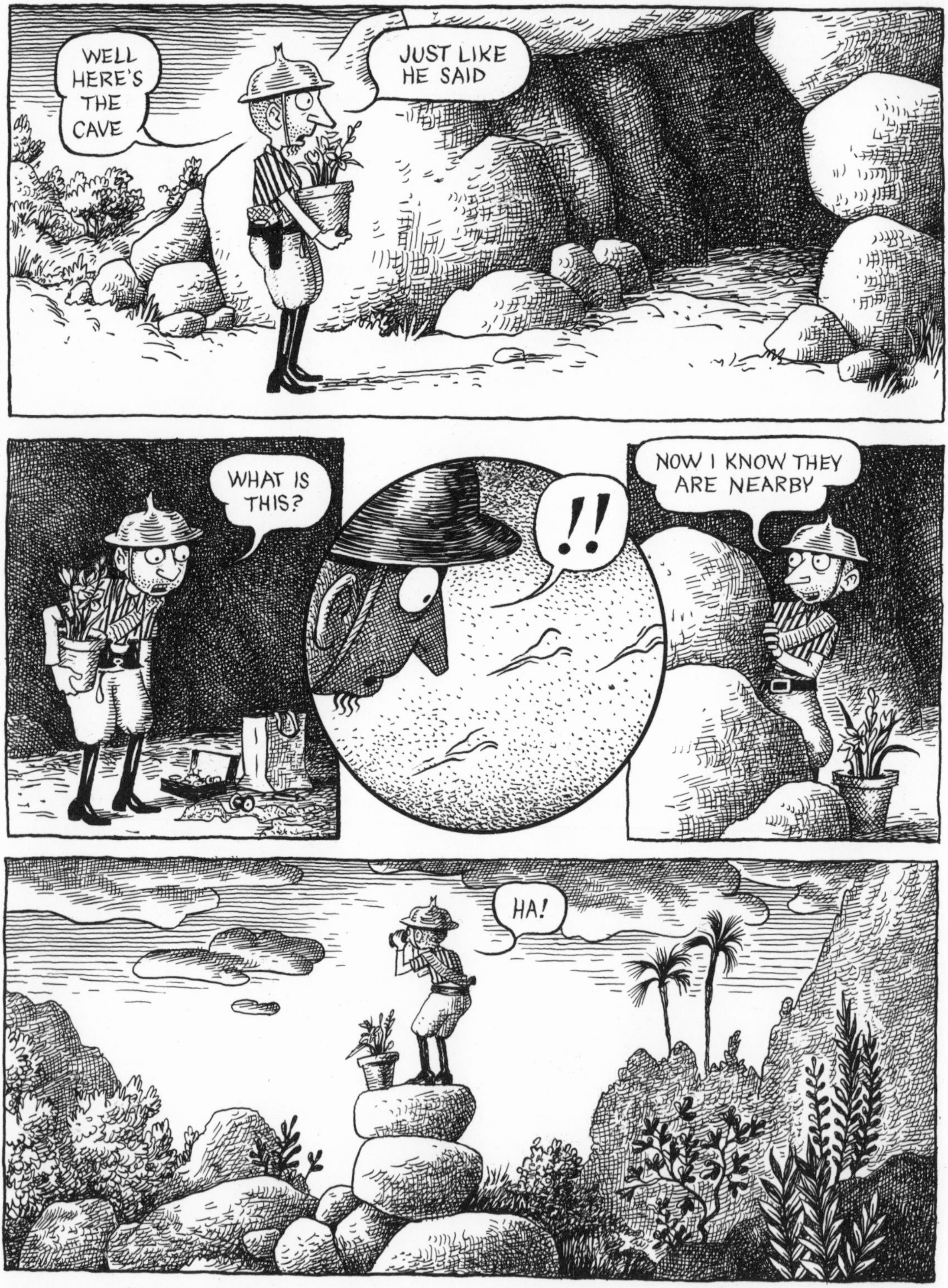
WELL HERE'S THE CAVE
JUST LIKE HE SAID
WHAT IS THIS?
!!
NOW I KNOW THEY ARE NEARBY
HA!

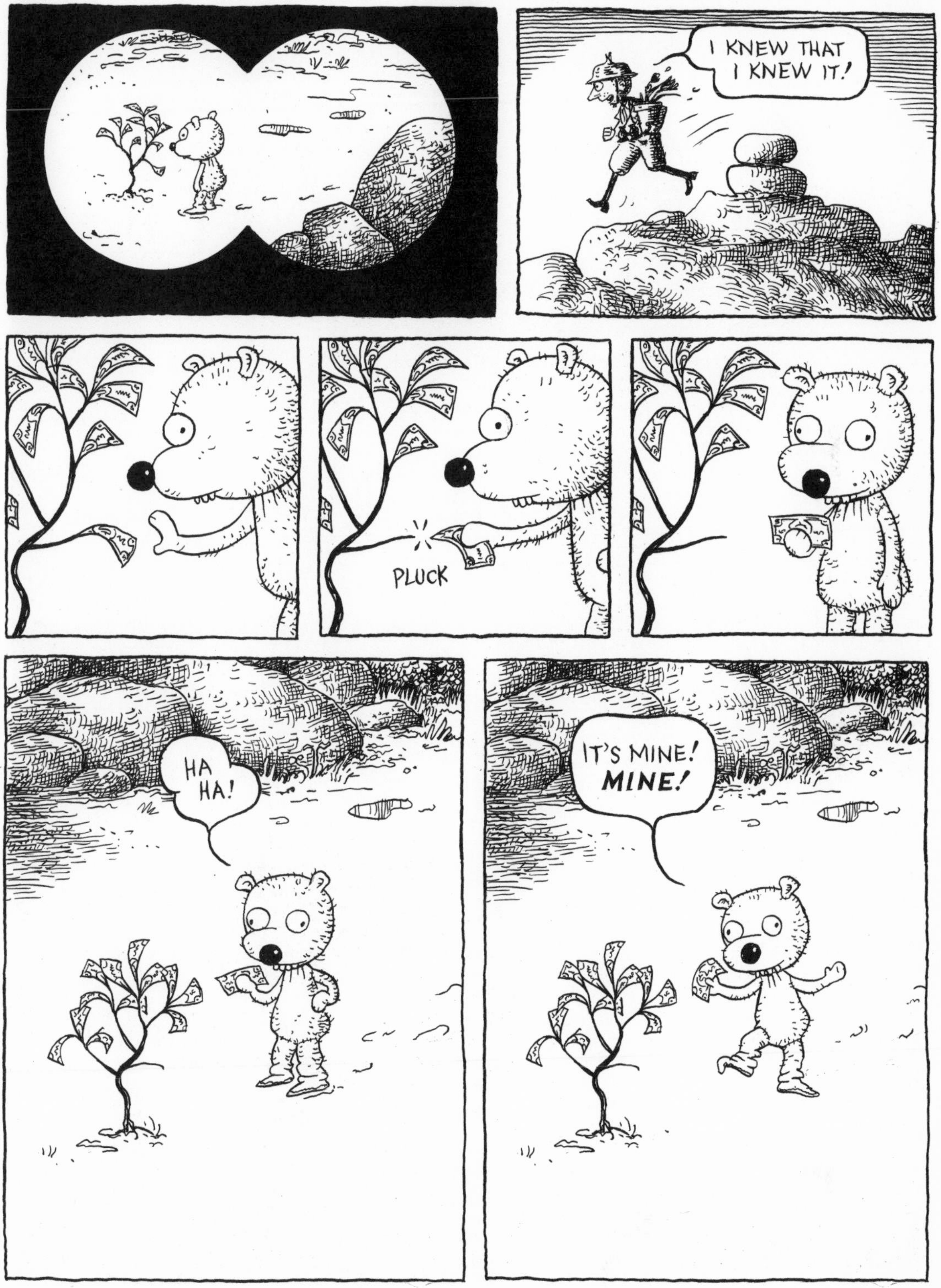
I KNEW THAT
I KNEW IT!
PLUCK
HA
HA!
IT'S MINE!
MINE!

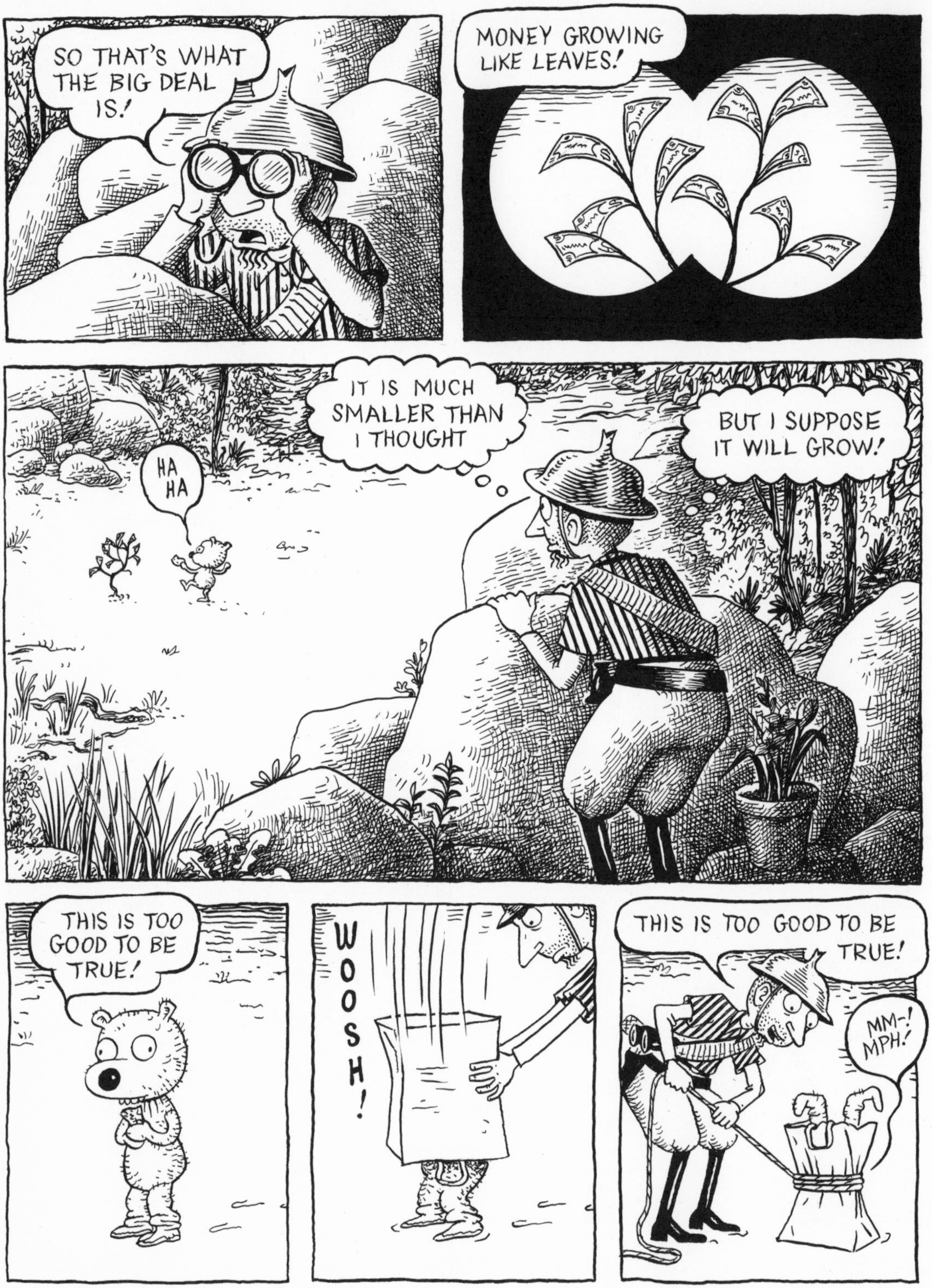
SO THAT'S WHAT THE BIG DEAL IS!
MONEY GROWING LIKE LEAVES!
HA HA
IT IS MUCH SMALLER THAN I THOUGHT
BUT I SUPPOSE IT WILL GROW!
THIS IS TOO GOOD TO BE TRUE!
WOOSH!
THIS IS TOO GOOD TO BE TRUE!
MM-! MPH!

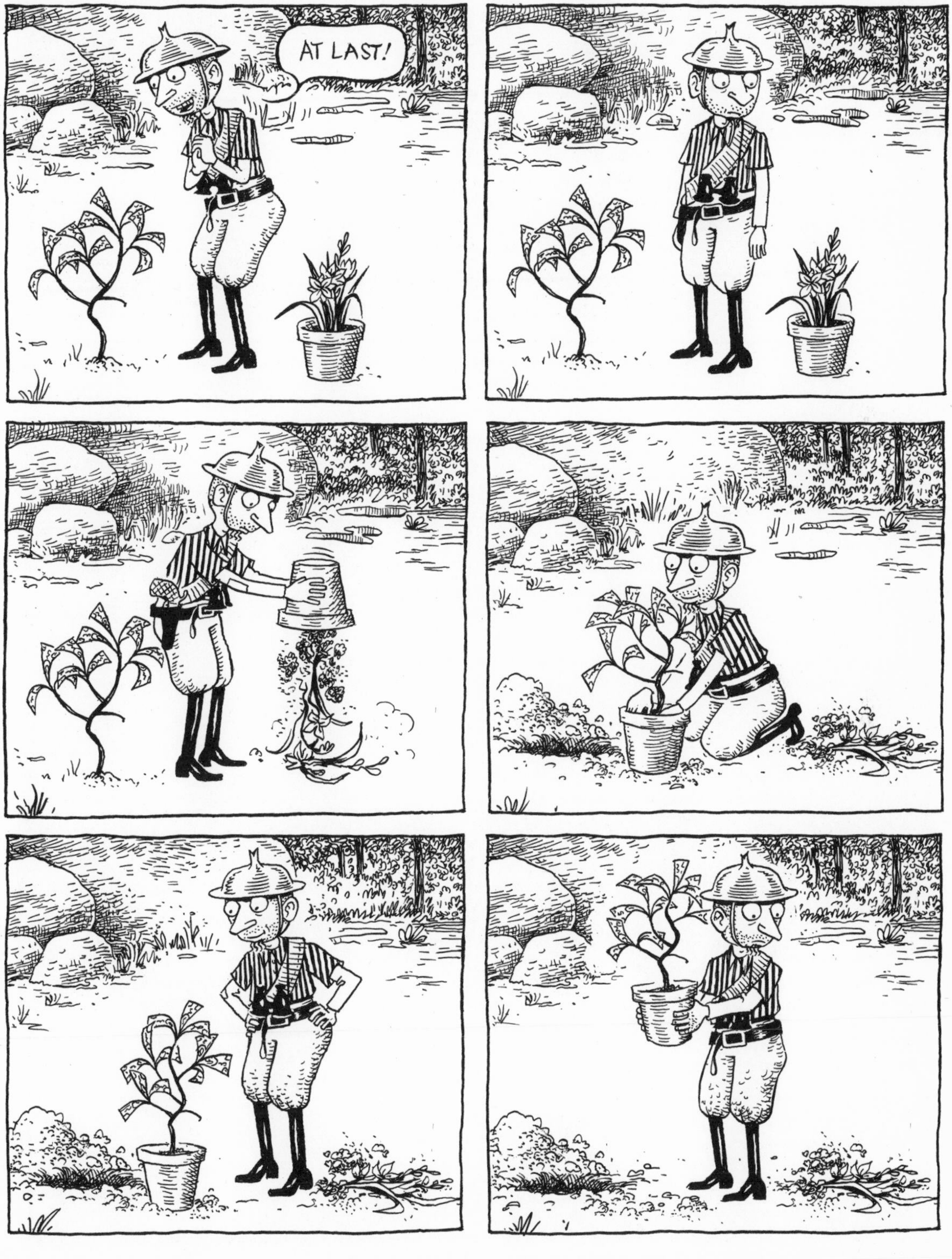
AT LAST!

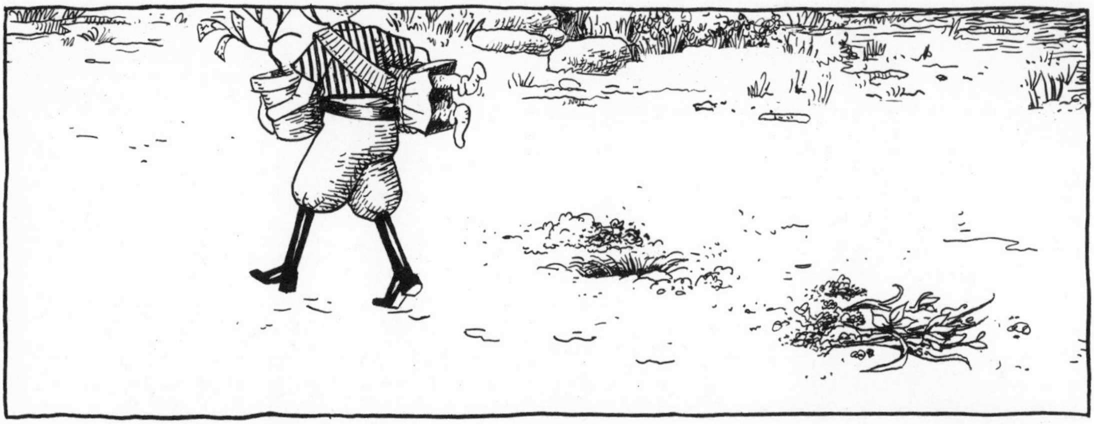
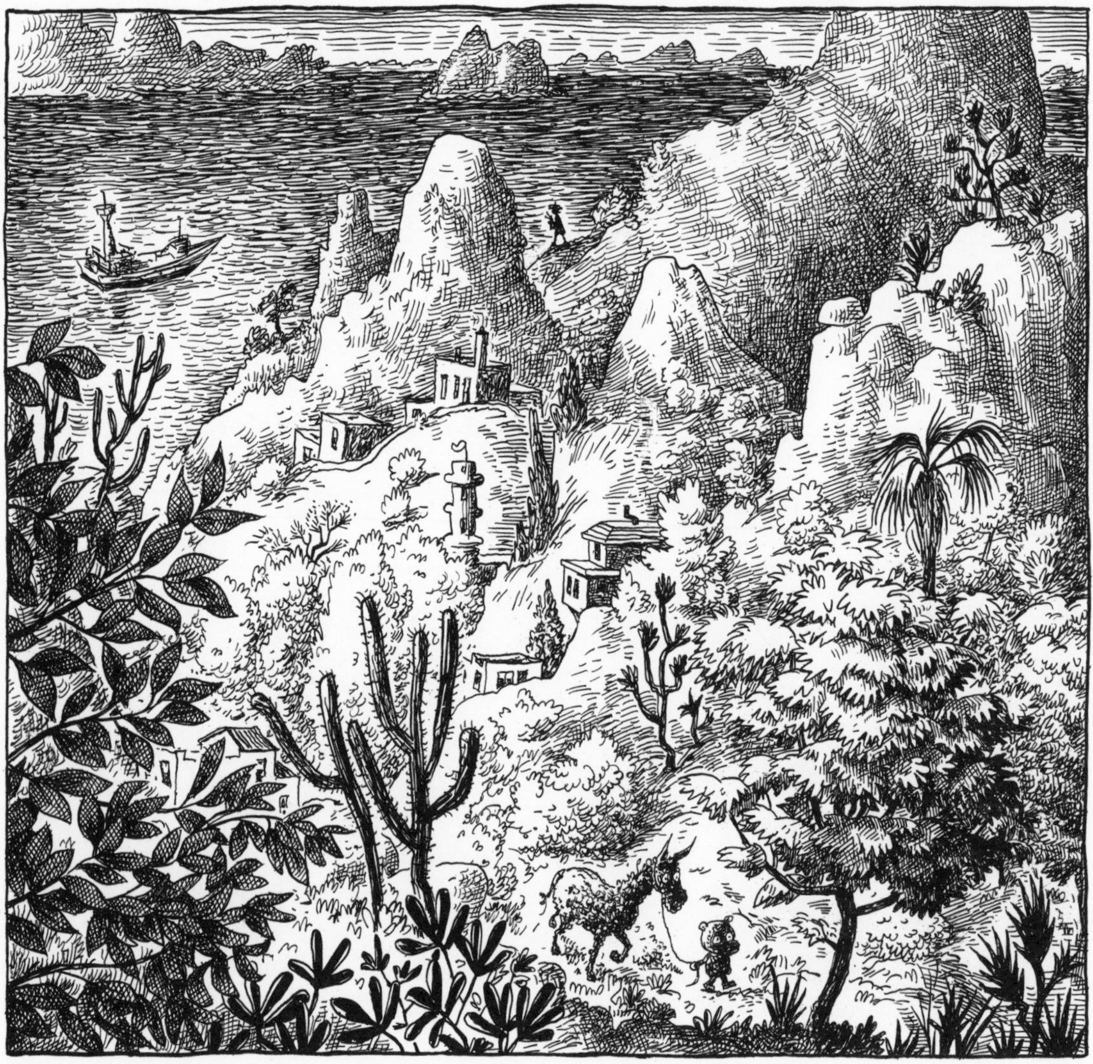

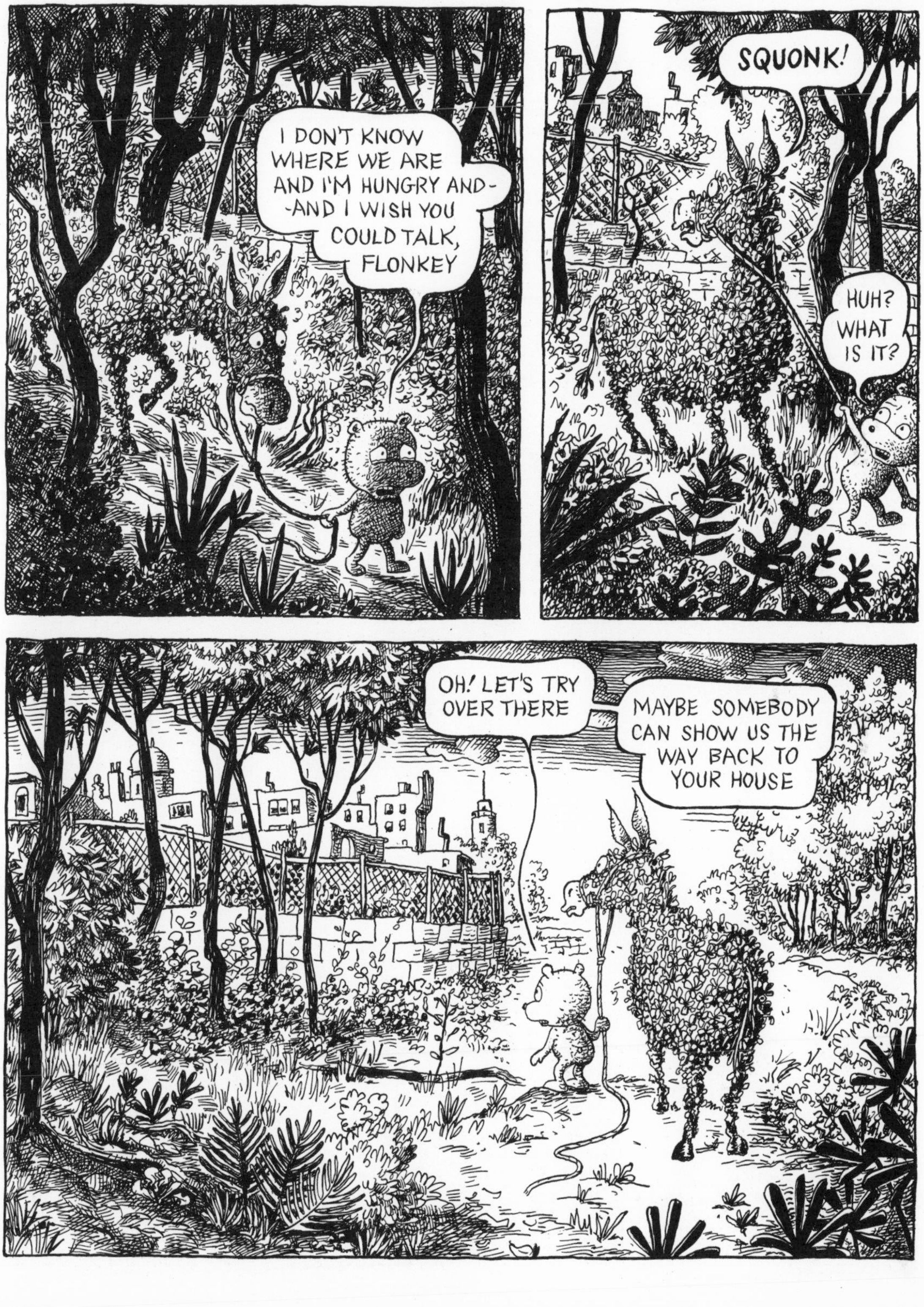
I DON'T KNOW WHERE WE ARE AND I'M HUNGRY AND-
-AND I WISH YOU COULD TALK, FLONKEY
SQUONK!
HUH? WHAT IS IT?
OH! LET'S TRY OVER THERE
MAYBE SOMEBODY CAN SHOW US THE WAY BACK TO YOUR HOUSE

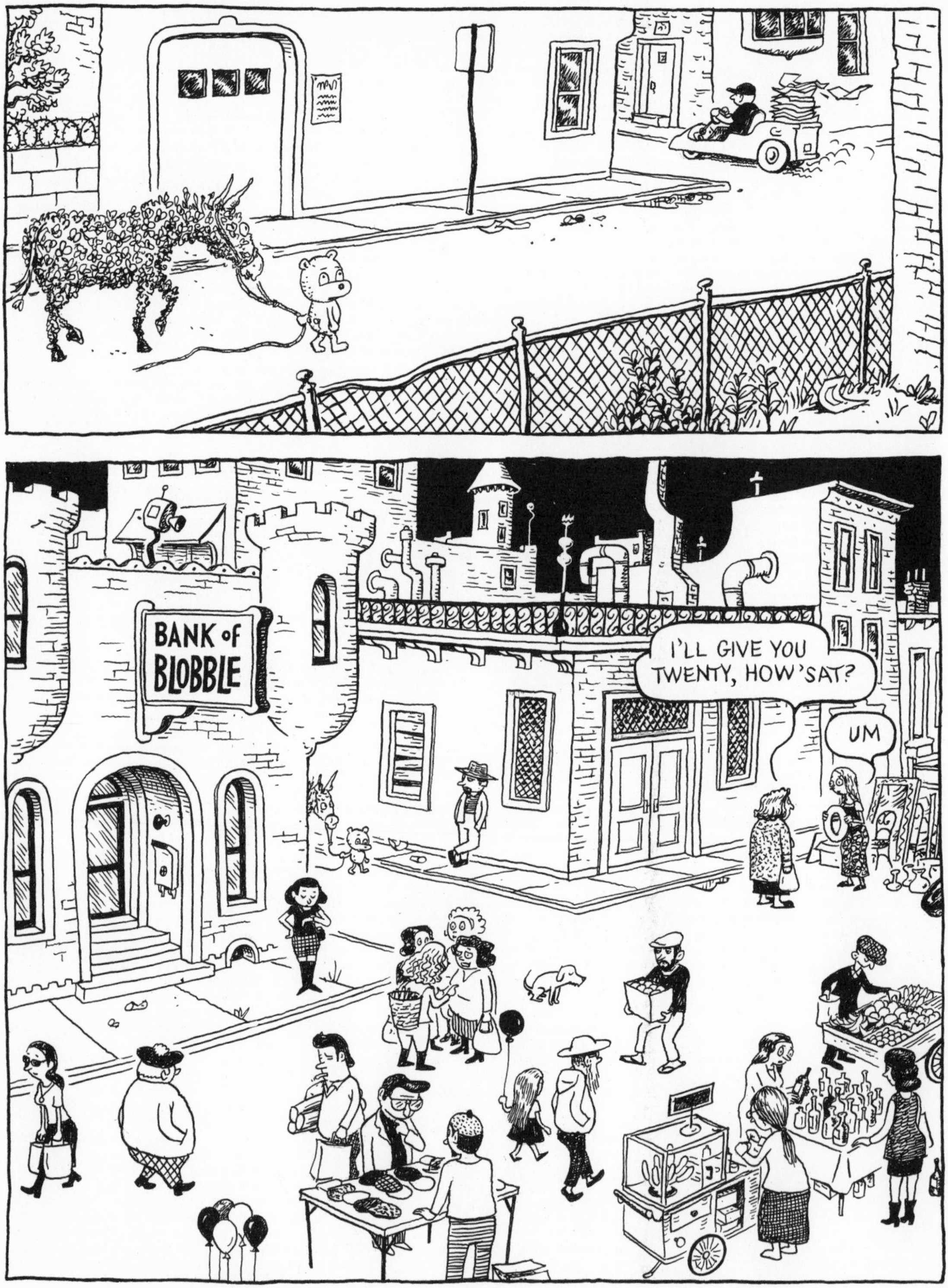
BANK of BLOBBLE
I'LL GIVE YOU TWENTY, HOW'SAT?
UM

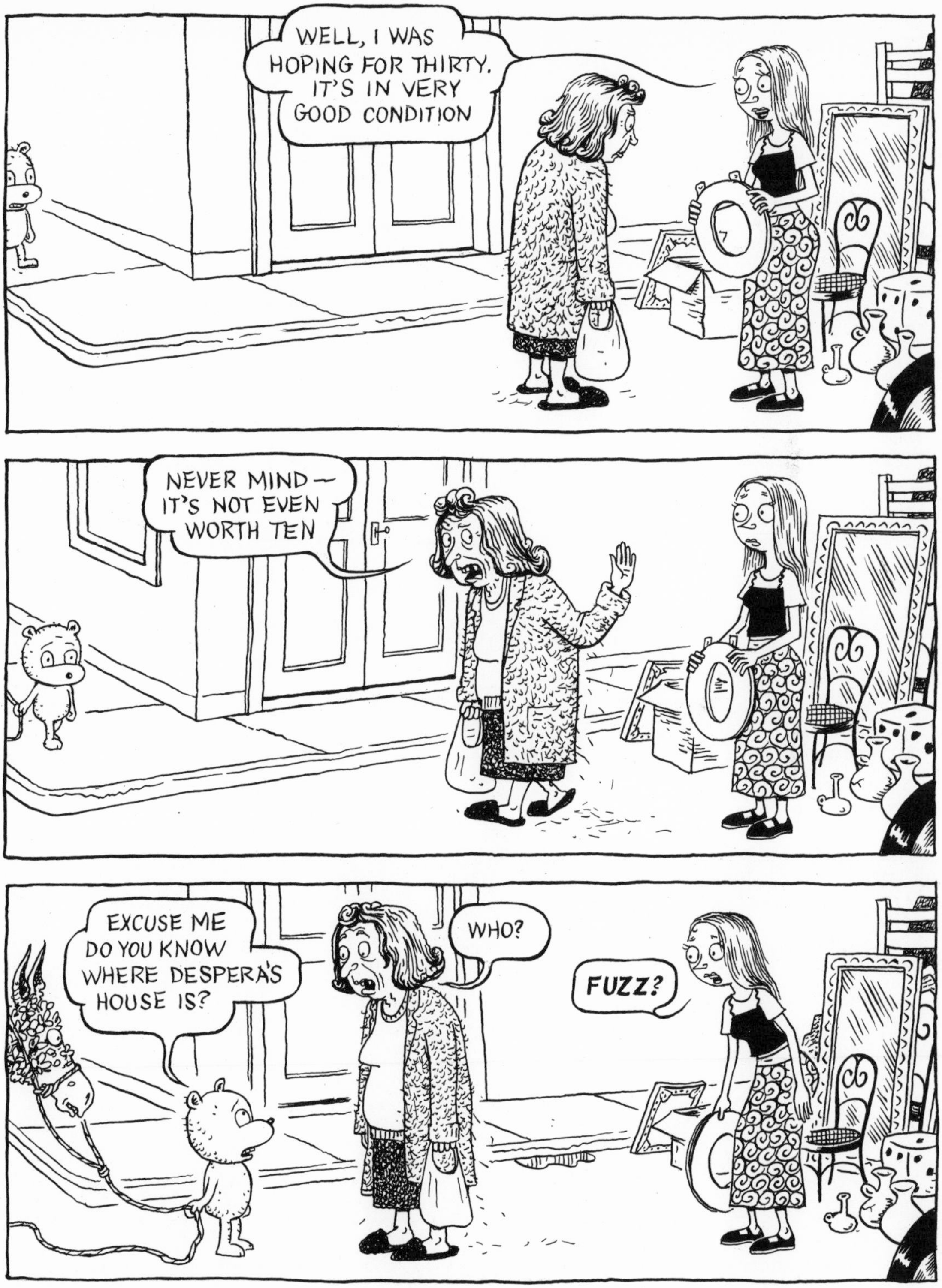
WELL, I WAS HOPING FOR THIRTY. IT'S IN VERY GOOD CONDITION
NEVER MIND— IT'S NOT EVEN WORTH TEN
EXCUSE ME DO YOU KNOW WHERE DESPERA'S HOUSE IS?
WHO?
FUZZ?

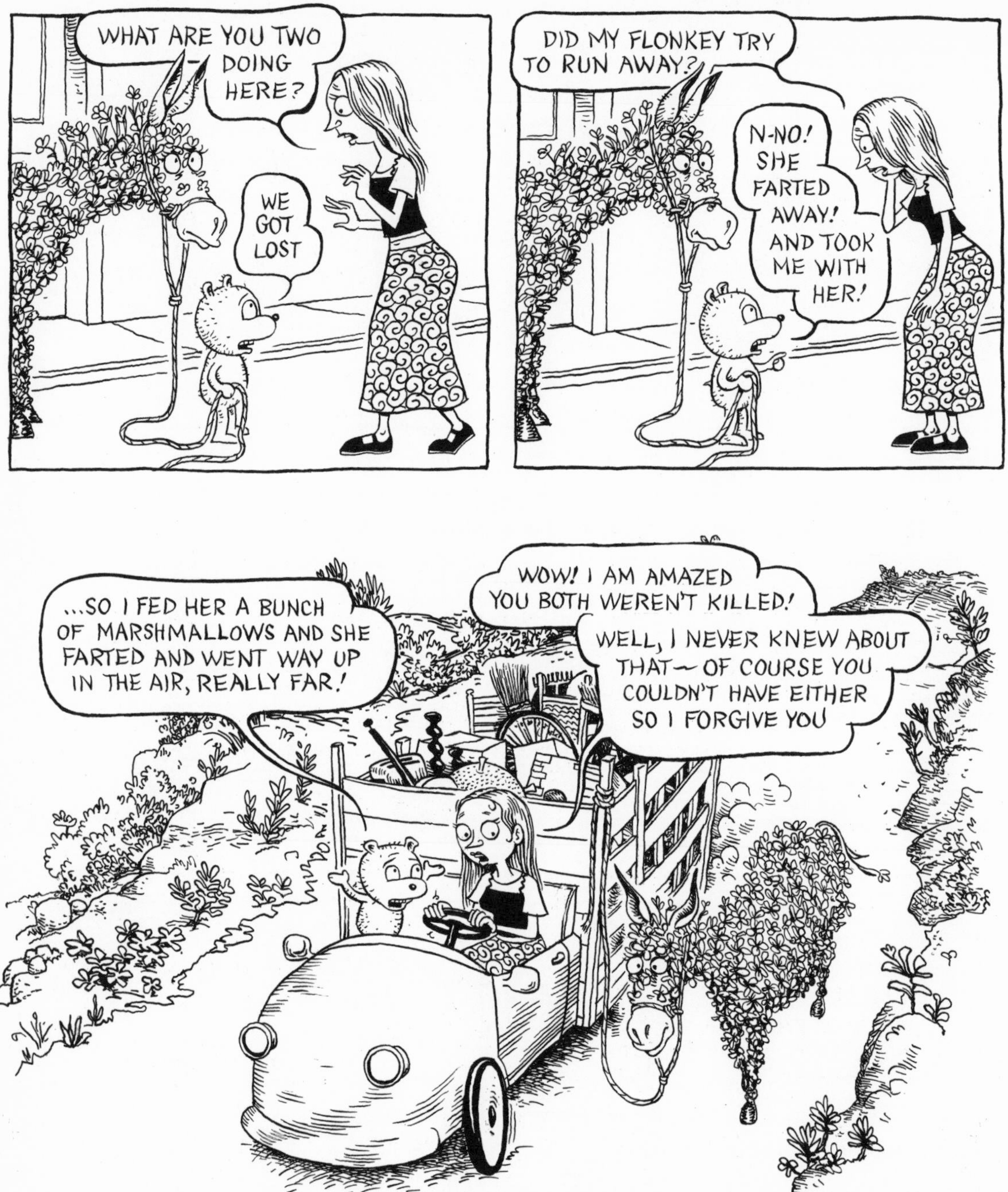
WHAT ARE YOU TWO DOING HERE?
WE GOT LOST
DID MY FLONKEY TRY TO RUN AWAY?
N-NO! SHE FARTED AWAY! AND TOOK ME WITH HER!
...SO I FED HER A BUNCH OF MARSHMALLOWS AND SHE FARTED AND WENT WAY UP IN THE AIR, REALLY FAR!
WOW! I AM AMAZED YOU BOTH WEREN'T KILLED!
WELL, I NEVER KNEW ABOUT THAT— OF COURSE YOU COULDN'T HAVE EITHER SO I FORGIVE YOU

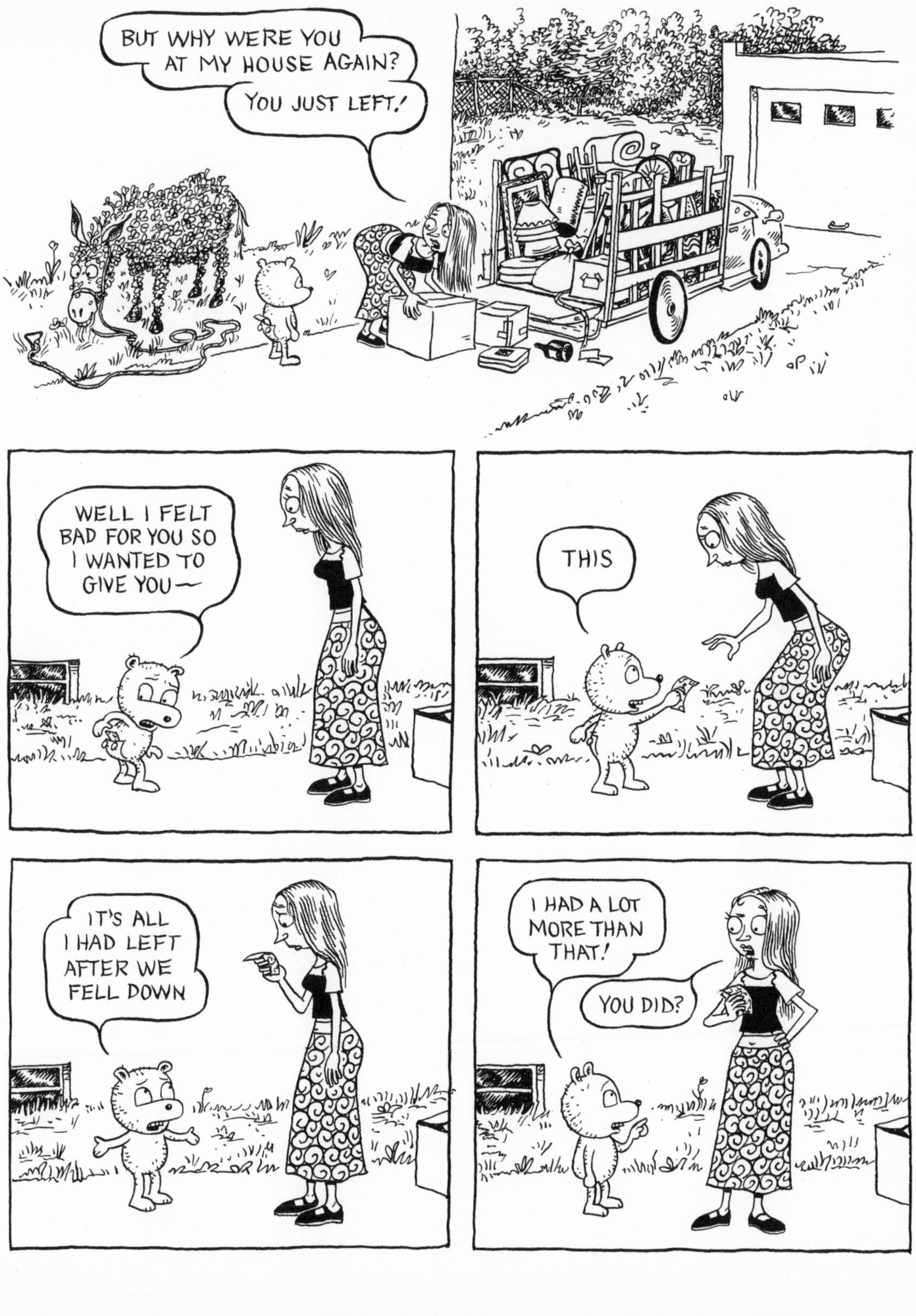
BUT WHY WERE YOU AT MY HOUSE AGAIN?
YOU JUST LEFT!
WELL I FELT BAD FOR YOU SO I WANTED TO GIVE YOU—
THIS
IT'S ALL I HAD LEFT AFTER WE FELL DOWN
I HAD A LOT MORE THAN THAT!
YOU DID?

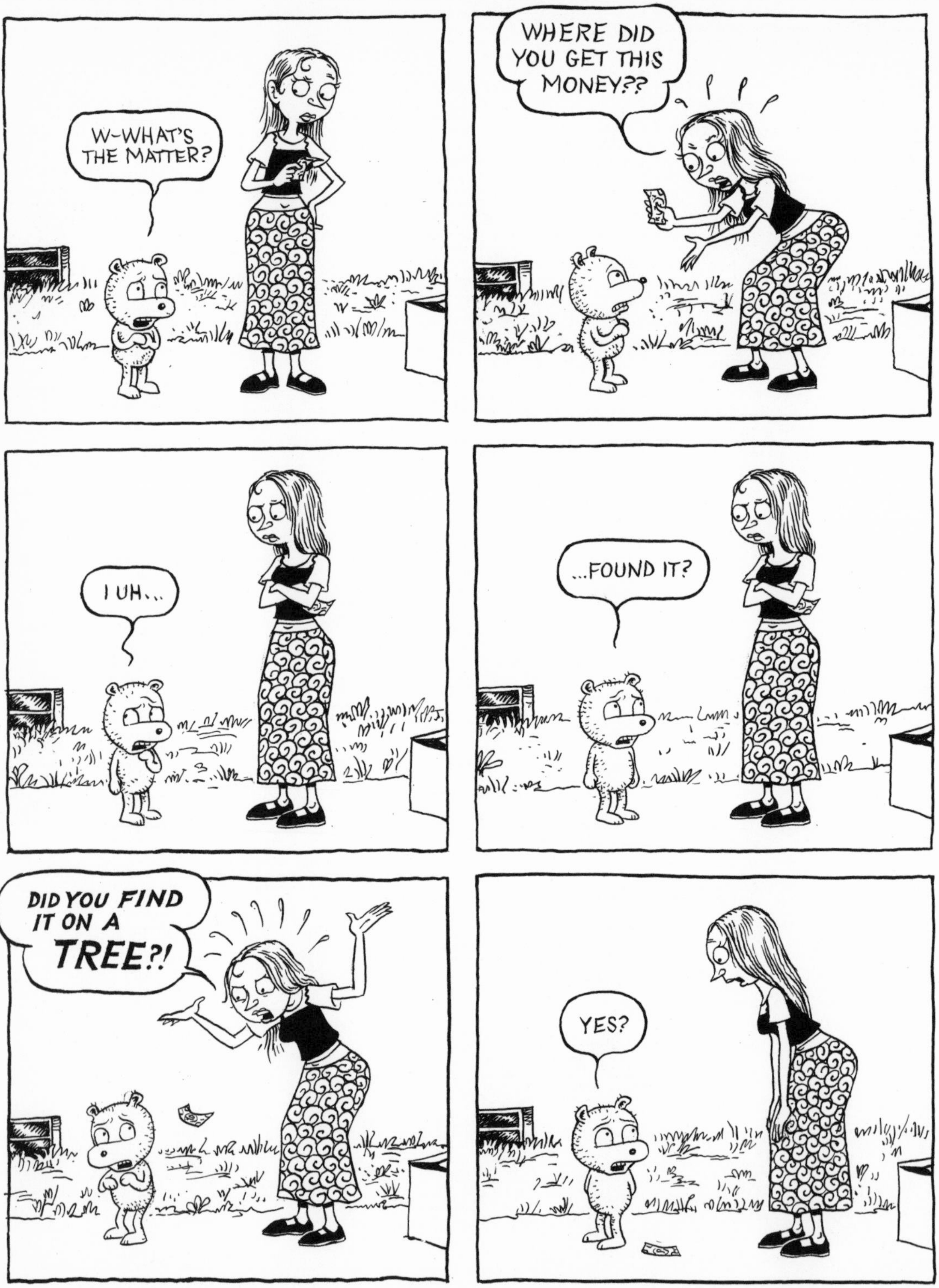
W-WHAT'S THE MATTER?
WHERE DID YOU GET THIS MONEY??
I UH...
...FOUND IT?
DID YOU FIND IT ON A TREE?!
YES?

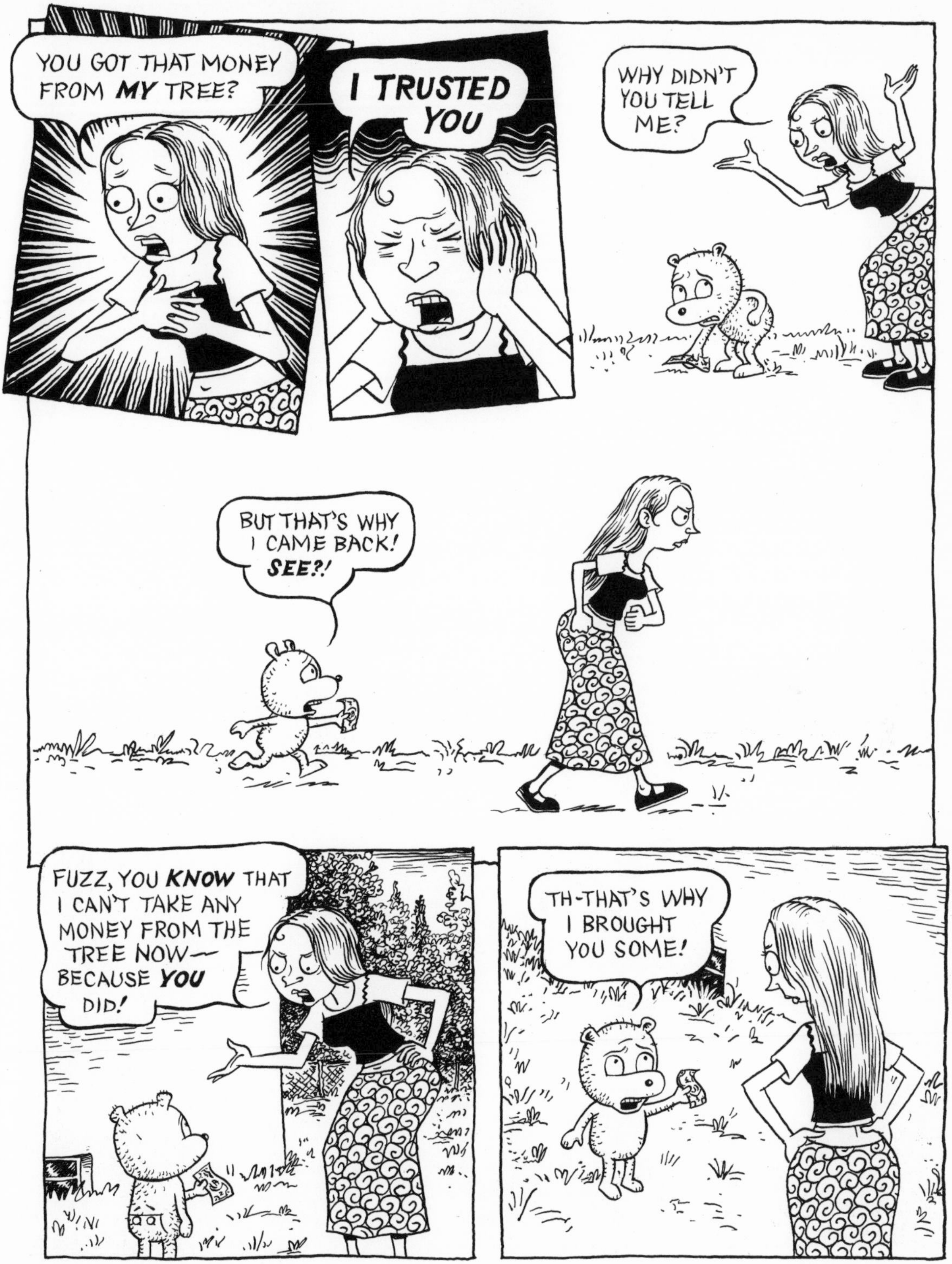

YOU GOT THAT MONEY FROM *MY* TREE?
I TRUSTED YOU
WHY DIDN'T YOU TELL ME?
BUT THAT'S WHY I CAME BACK! *SEE?!*
FUZZ, YOU *KNOW* THAT I CAN'T TAKE ANY MONEY FROM THE TREE NOW— BECAUSE *YOU* DID!
TH-THAT'S WHY I BROUGHT YOU SOME!

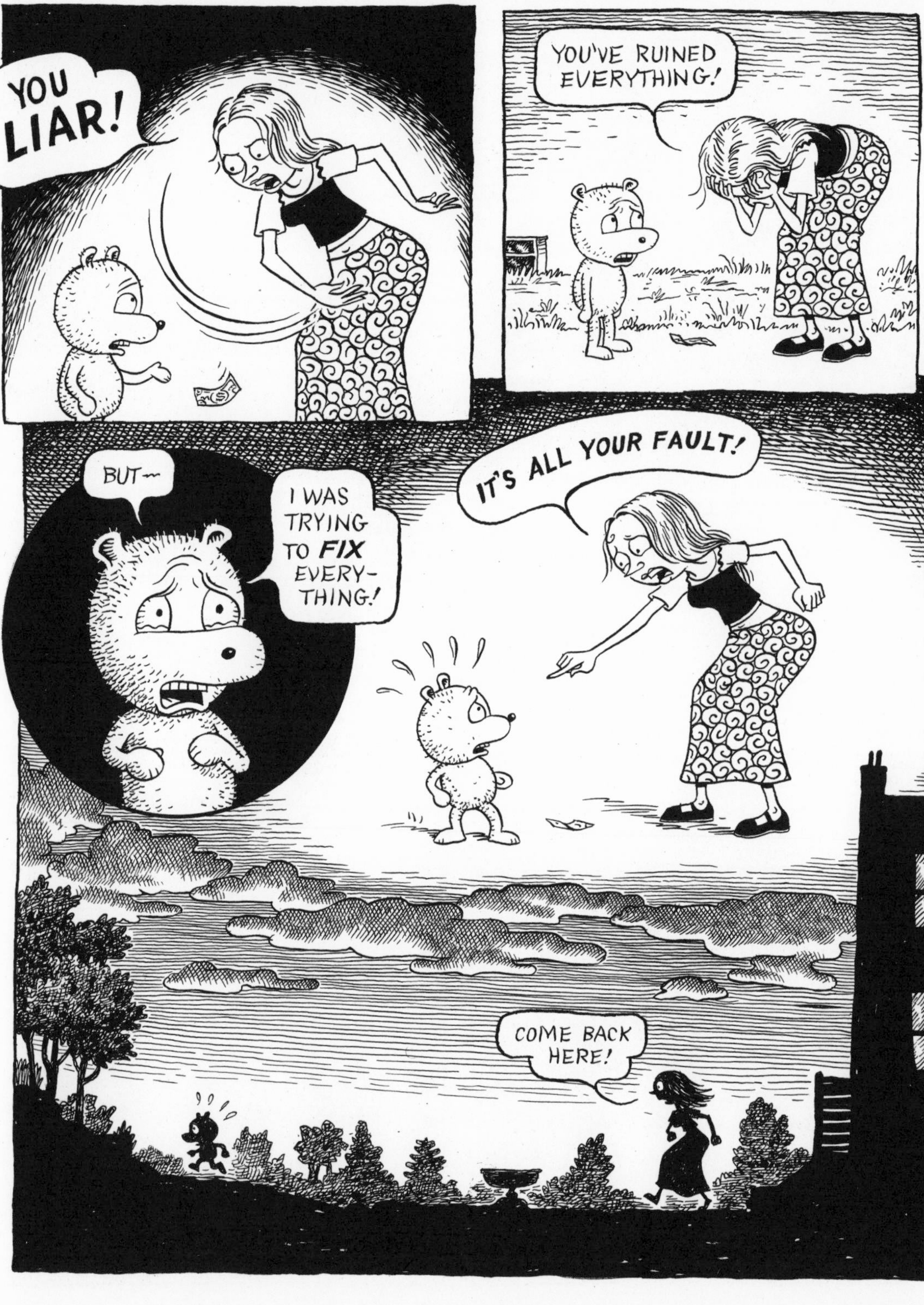
YOU LIAR!
YOU'VE RUINED EVERYTHING!
BUT—
I WAS TRYING TO FIX EVERYTHING!
IT'S ALL YOUR FAULT!
COME BACK HERE!

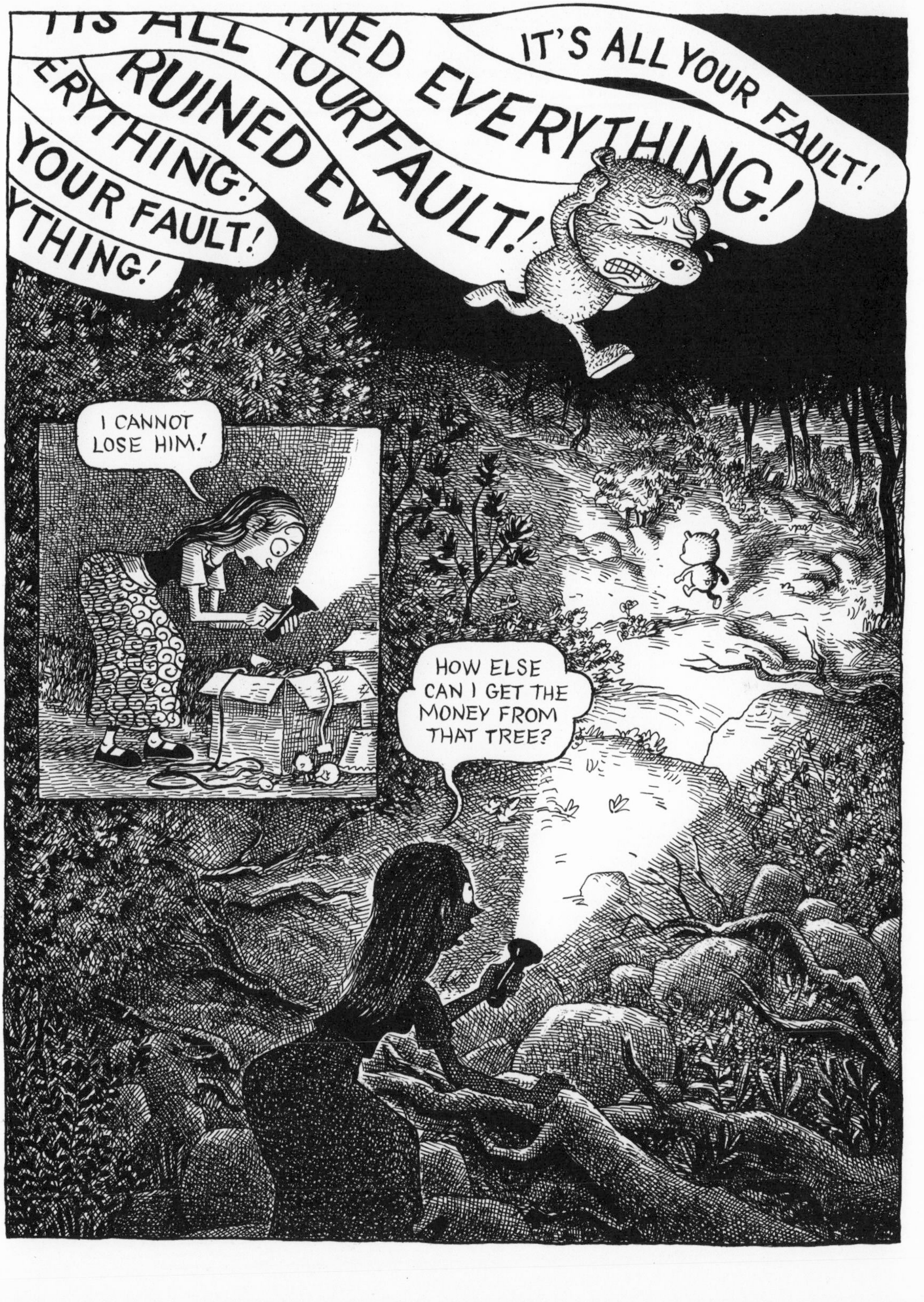
ALL
NED EVERYTHING!
ALL YOUR
RUINED EVERYTHING!
IT'S ALL YOUR FAULT!
YOURFAULT!
ERYTHING!
RUINED EVE
YOUR FAULT!
YTHING!
I CANNOT LOSE HIM!
HOW ELSE CAN I GET THE MONEY FROM THAT TREE?

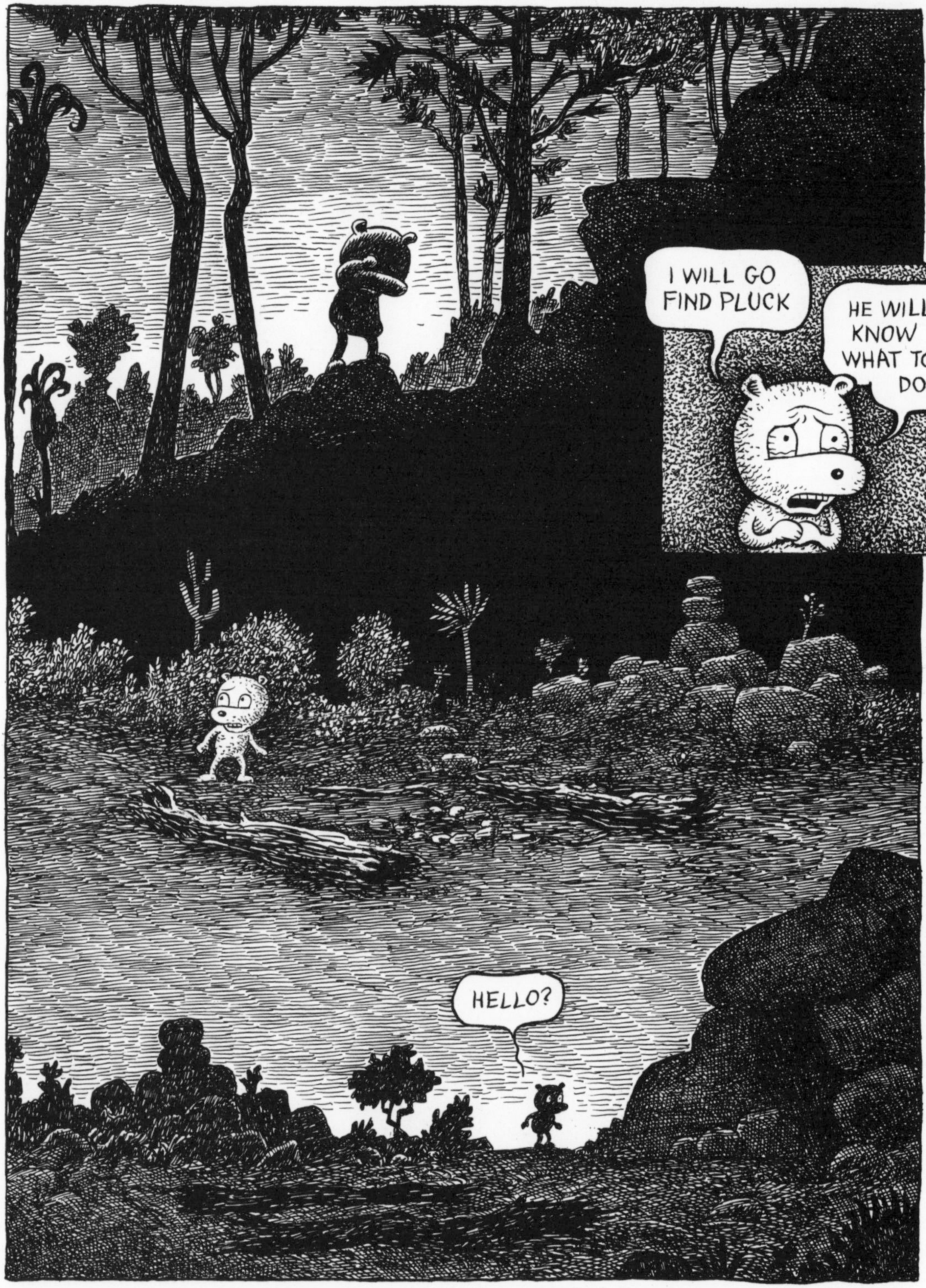
I WILL GO FIND PLUCK
HE WILL KNOW WHAT TO DO
HELLO?

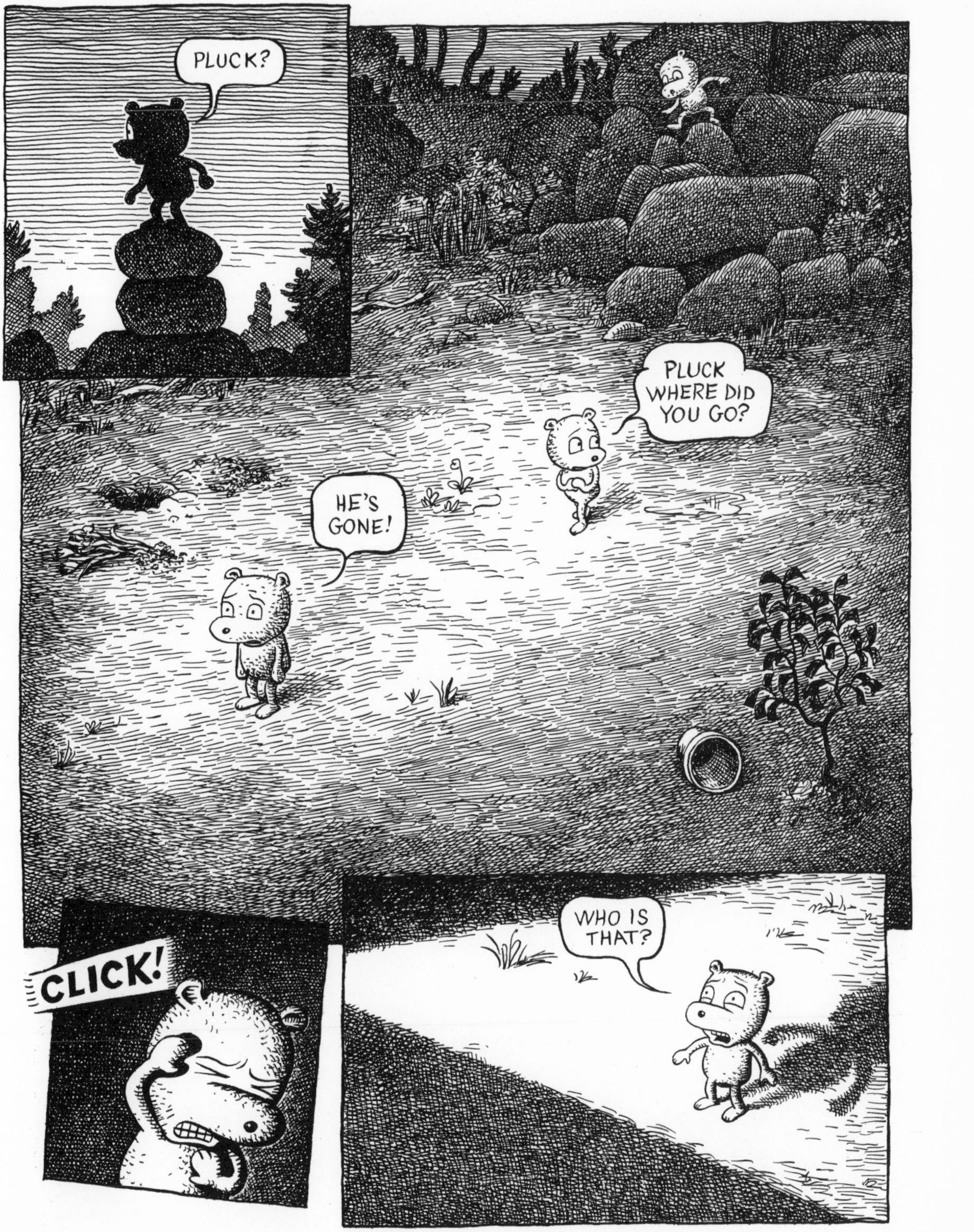
PLUCK?
PLUCK WHERE DID YOU GO?
HE'S GONE!
CLICK!
WHO IS THAT?

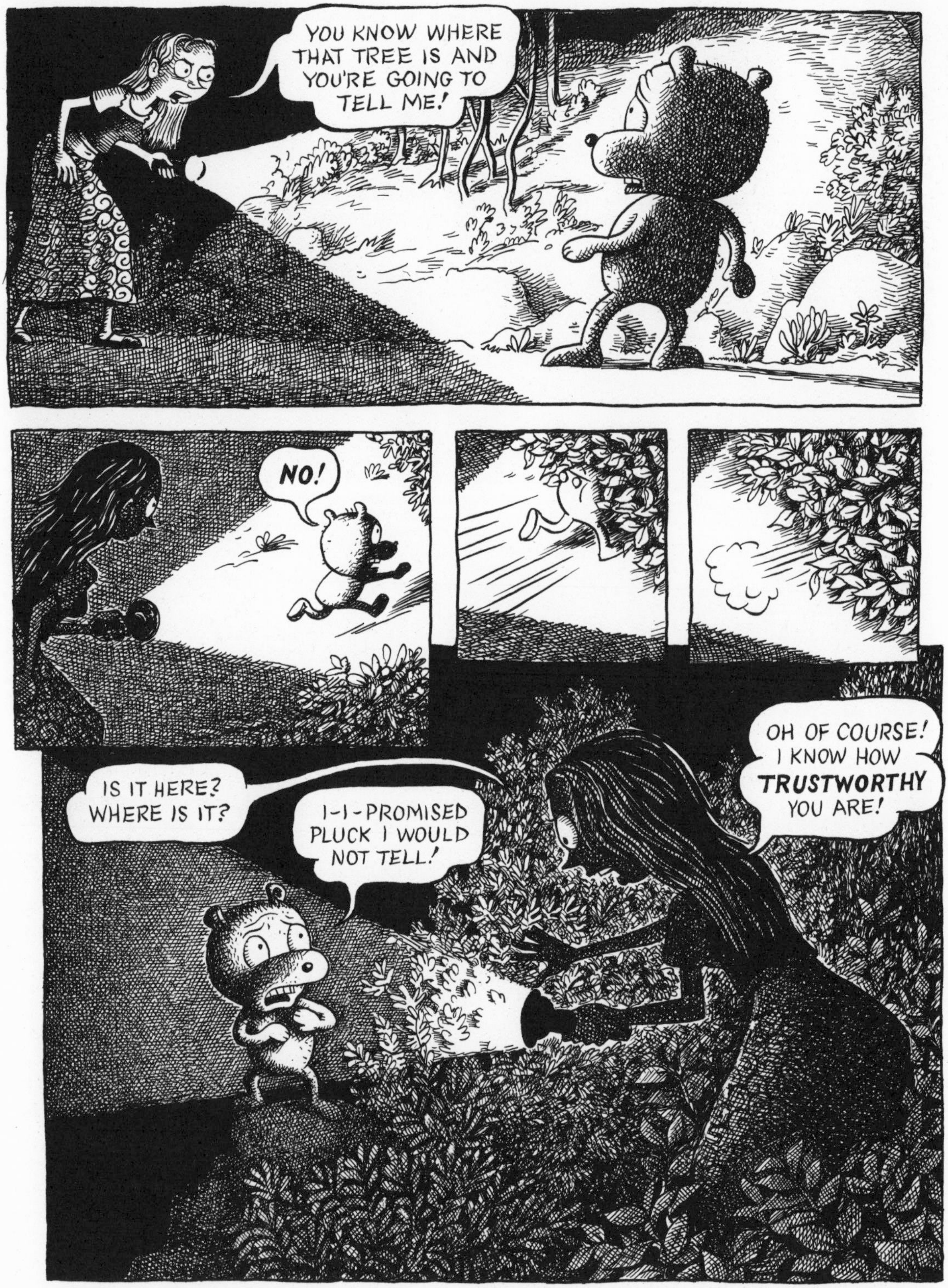
YOU KNOW WHERE THAT TREE IS AND YOU'RE GOING TO TELL ME!
NO!
IS IT HERE? WHERE IS IT?
I-I-PROMISED PLUCK I WOULD NOT TELL!
OH OF COURSE! I KNOW HOW TRUSTWORTHY YOU ARE!

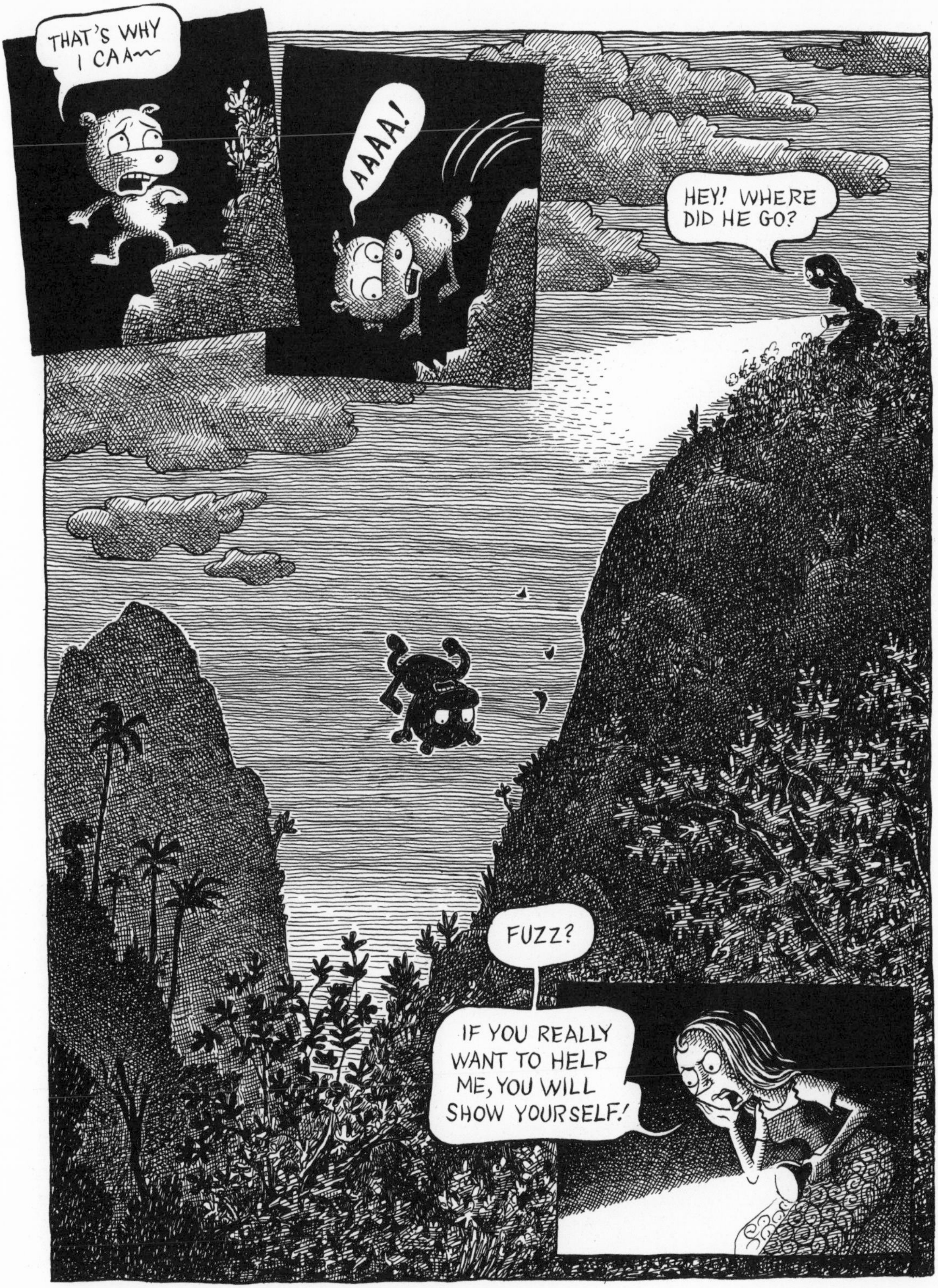
THAT'S WHY I CAA~
AAAA!
HEY! WHERE DID HE GO?
FUZZ?
IF YOU REALLY WANT TO HELP ME, YOU WILL SHOW YOURSELF!

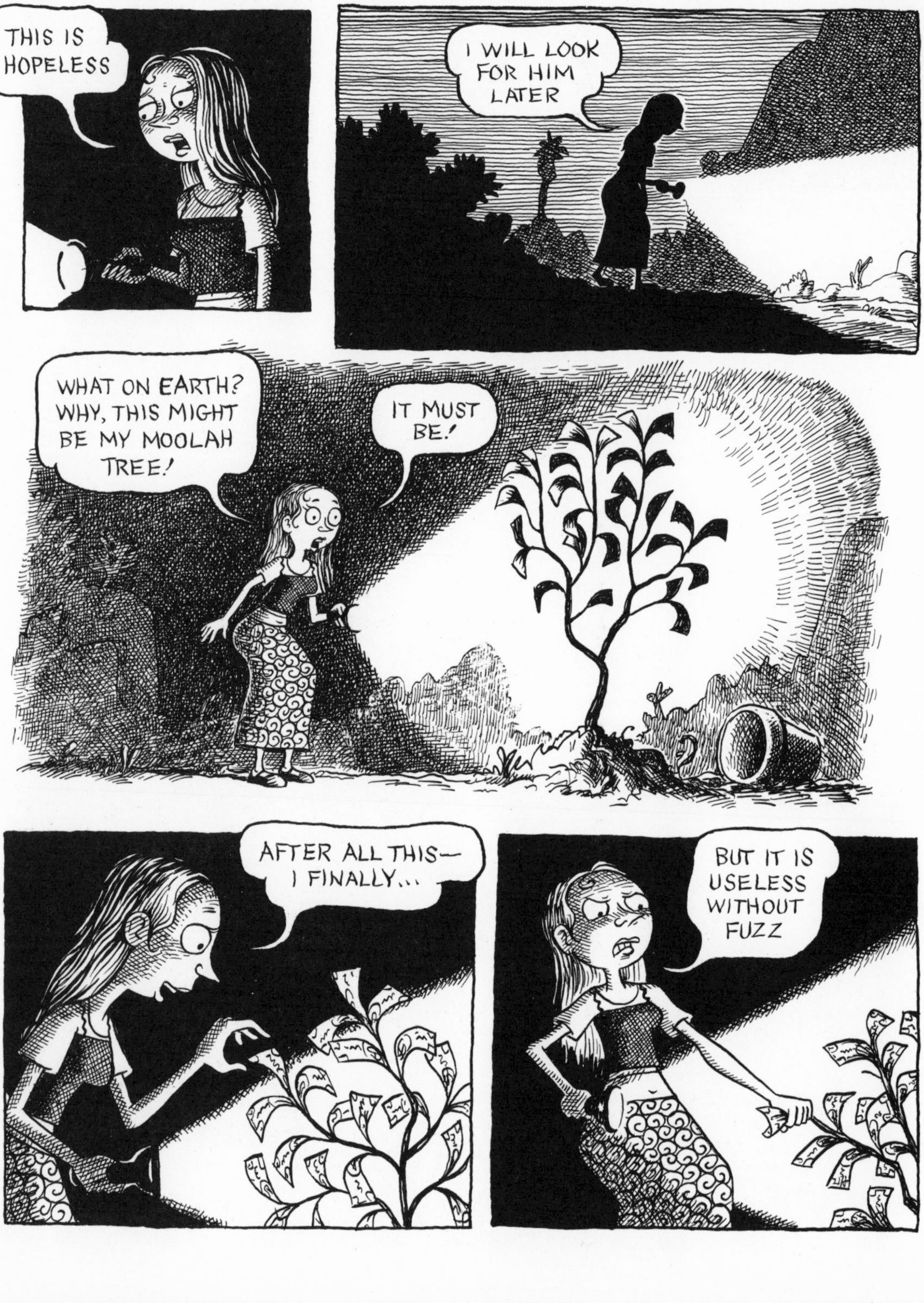
THIS IS HOPELESS
I WILL LOOK FOR HIM LATER
WHAT ON EARTH? WHY, THIS MIGHT BE MY MOOLAH TREE!
IT MUST BE!
AFTER ALL THIS— I FINALLY...
BUT IT IS USELESS WITHOUT FUZZ

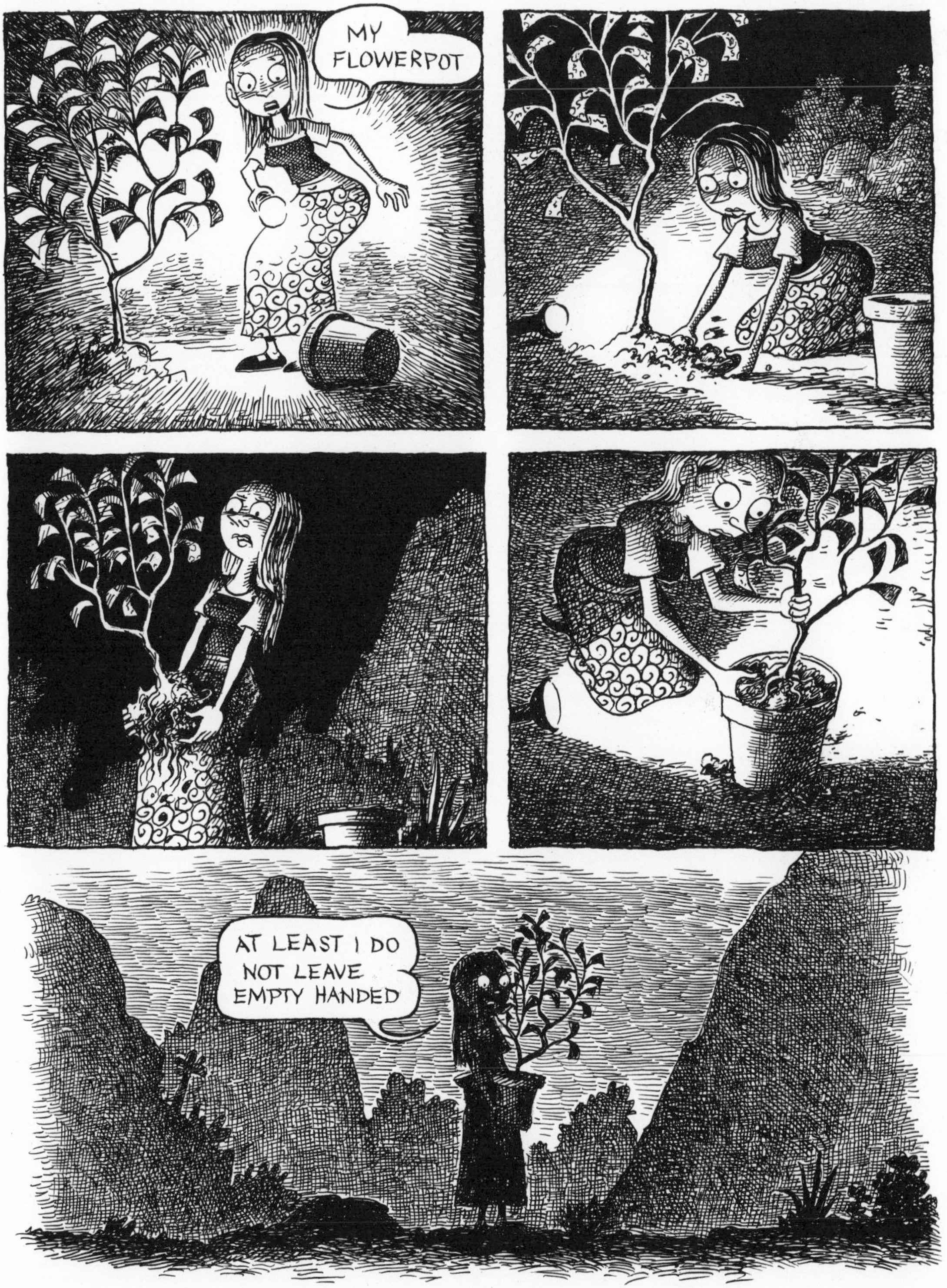
MY FLOWERPOT
AT LEAST I DO NOT LEAVE EMPTY HANDED

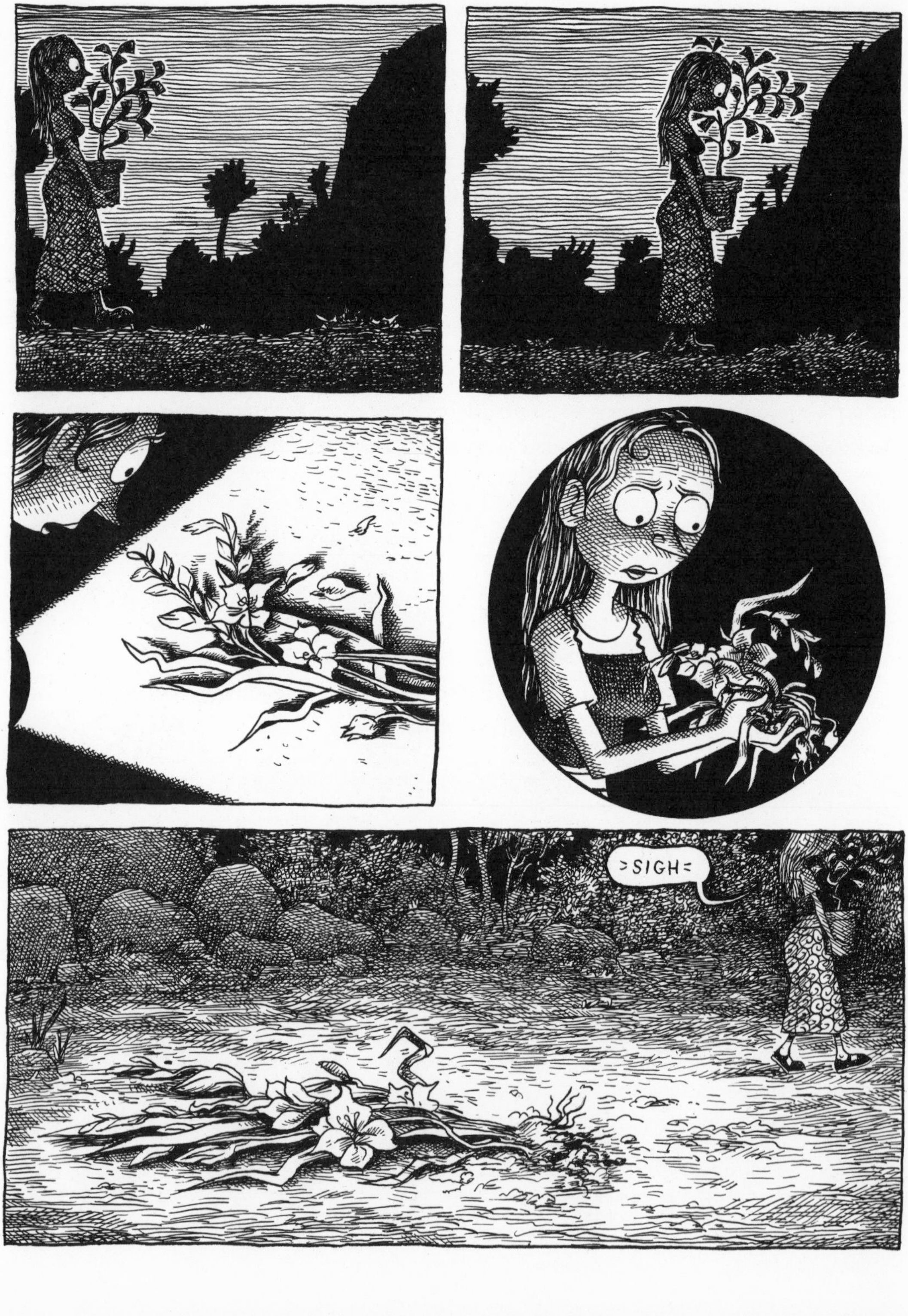
SIGH

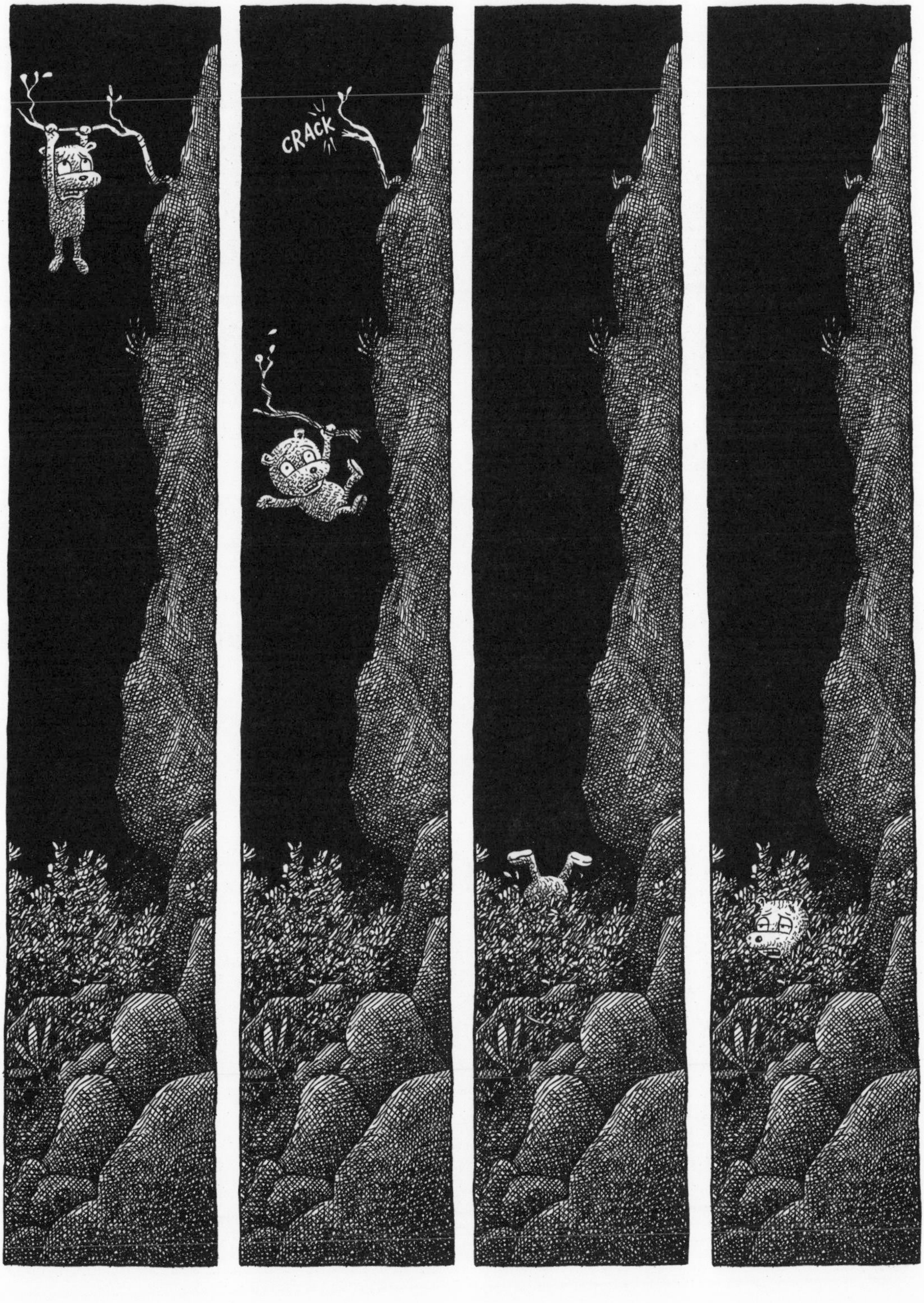
CRACK

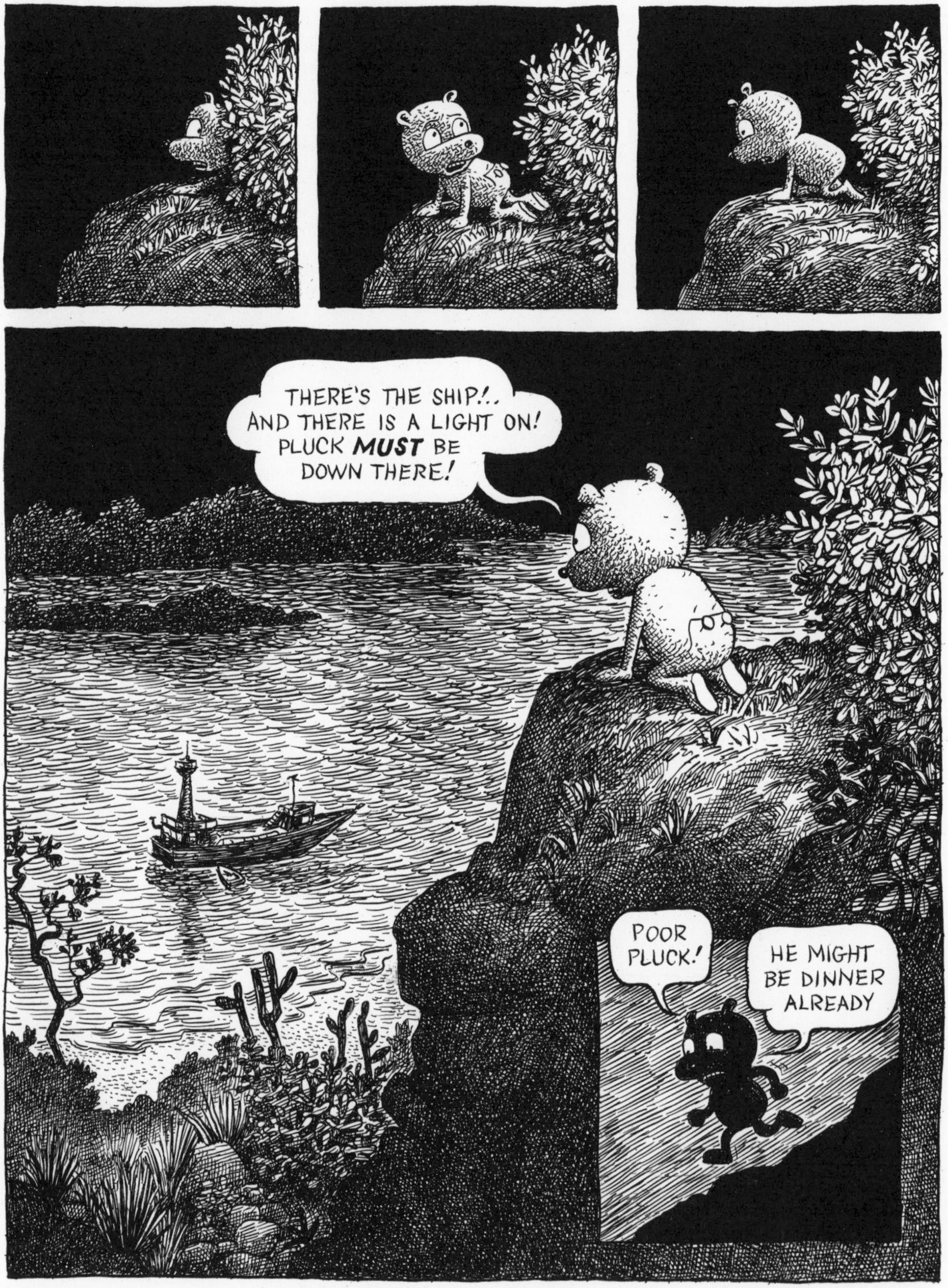
THERE'S THE SHIP!.. AND THERE IS A LIGHT ON! PLUCK **MUST** BE DOWN THERE!
POOR PLUCK!
HE MIGHT BE DINNER ALREADY

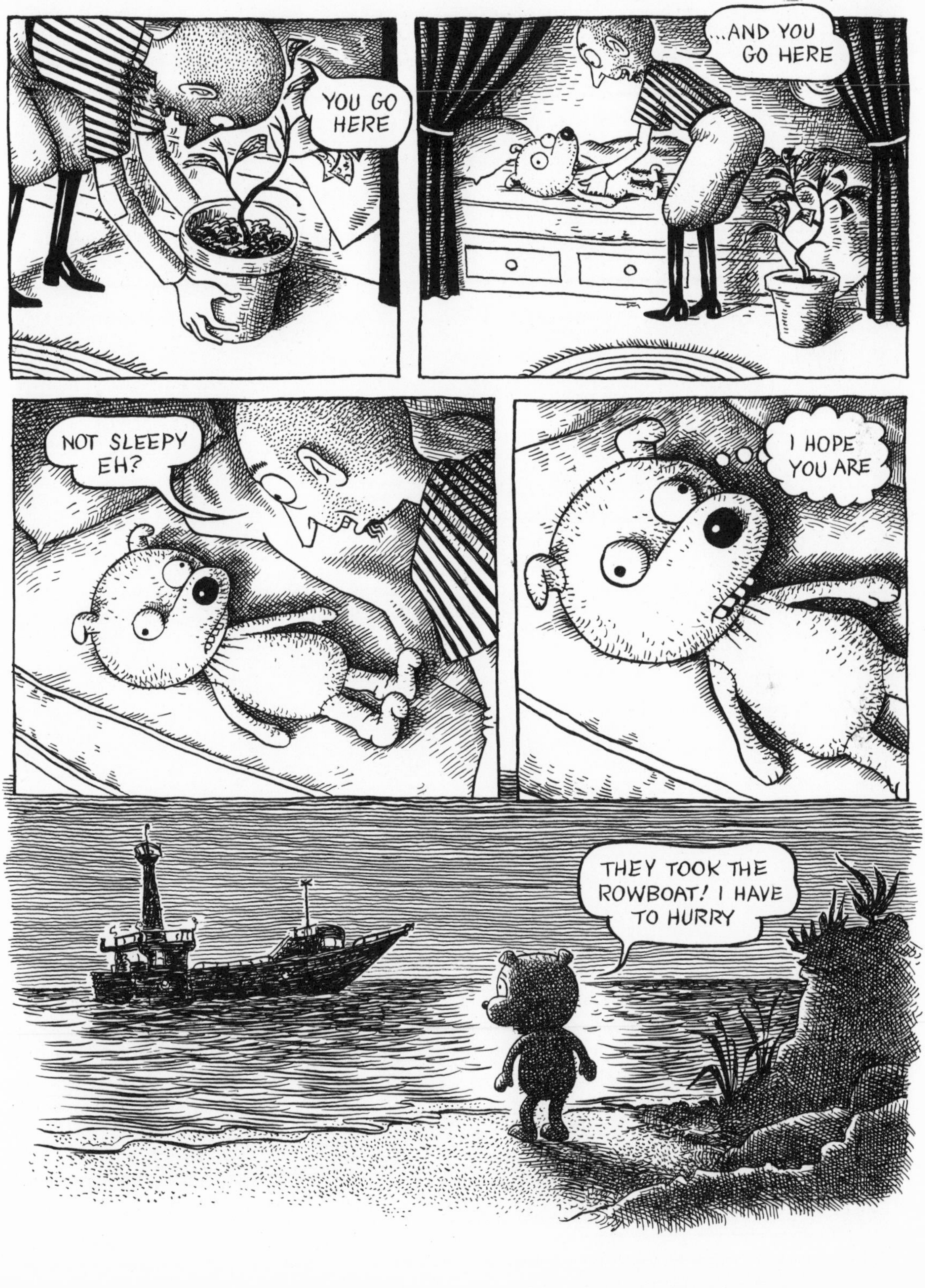
YOU GO HERE
...AND YOU GO HERE
NOT SLEEPY EH?
I HOPE YOU ARE
THEY TOOK THE ROWBOAT! I HAVE TO HURRY

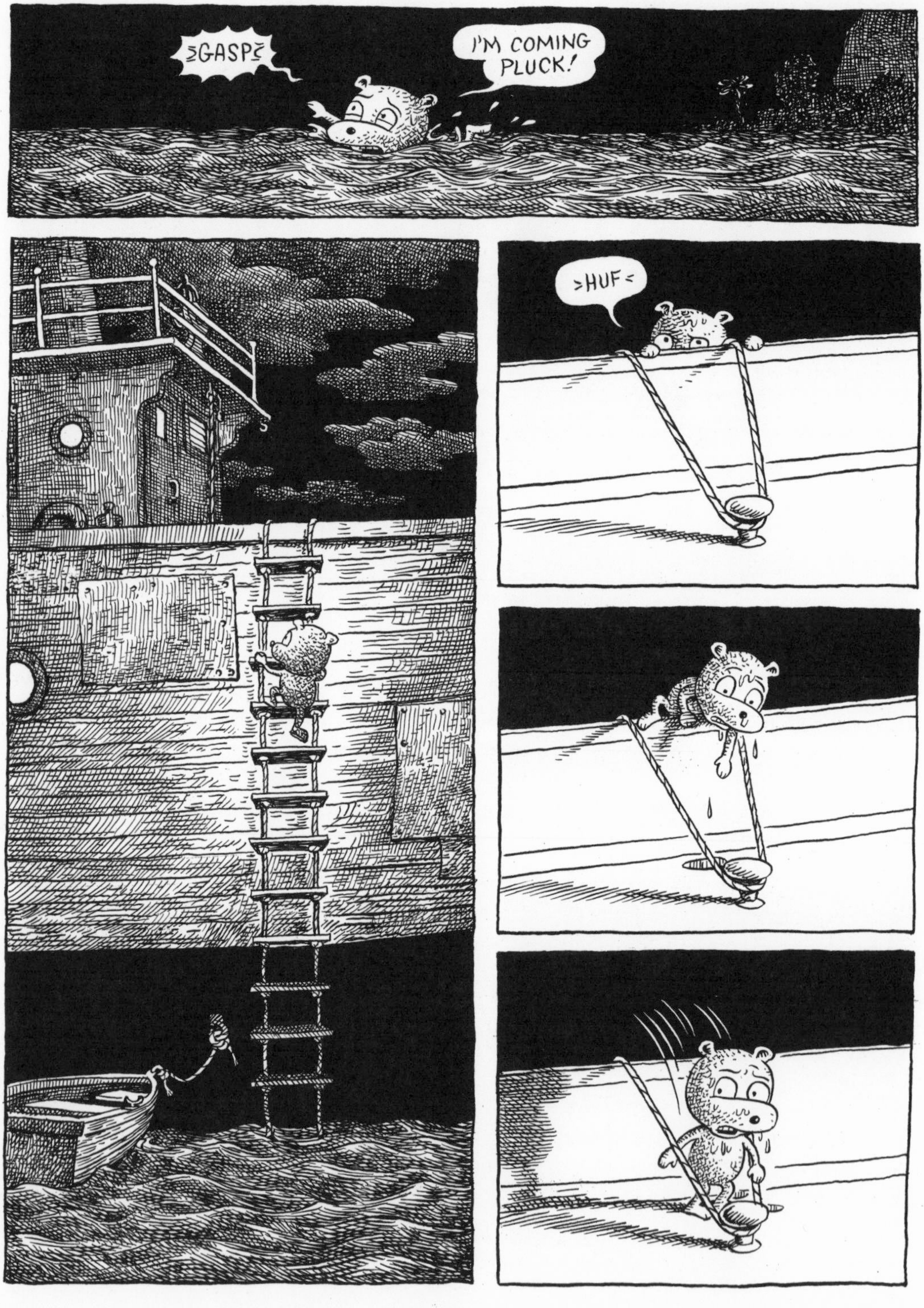
≥GASP≤
I'M COMING PLUCK!
>HUF<

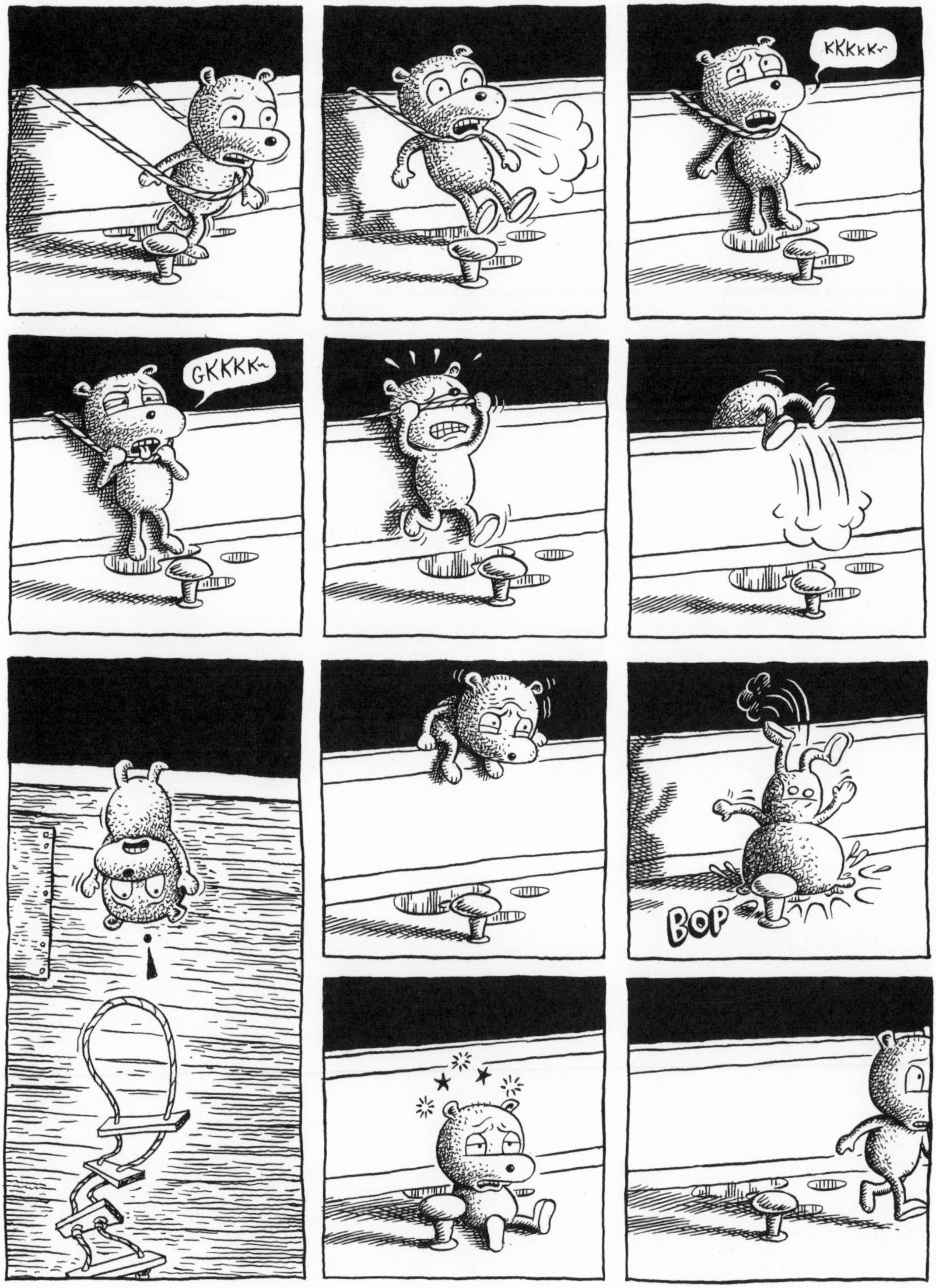
KKKKK~
GKKKK~
BOP

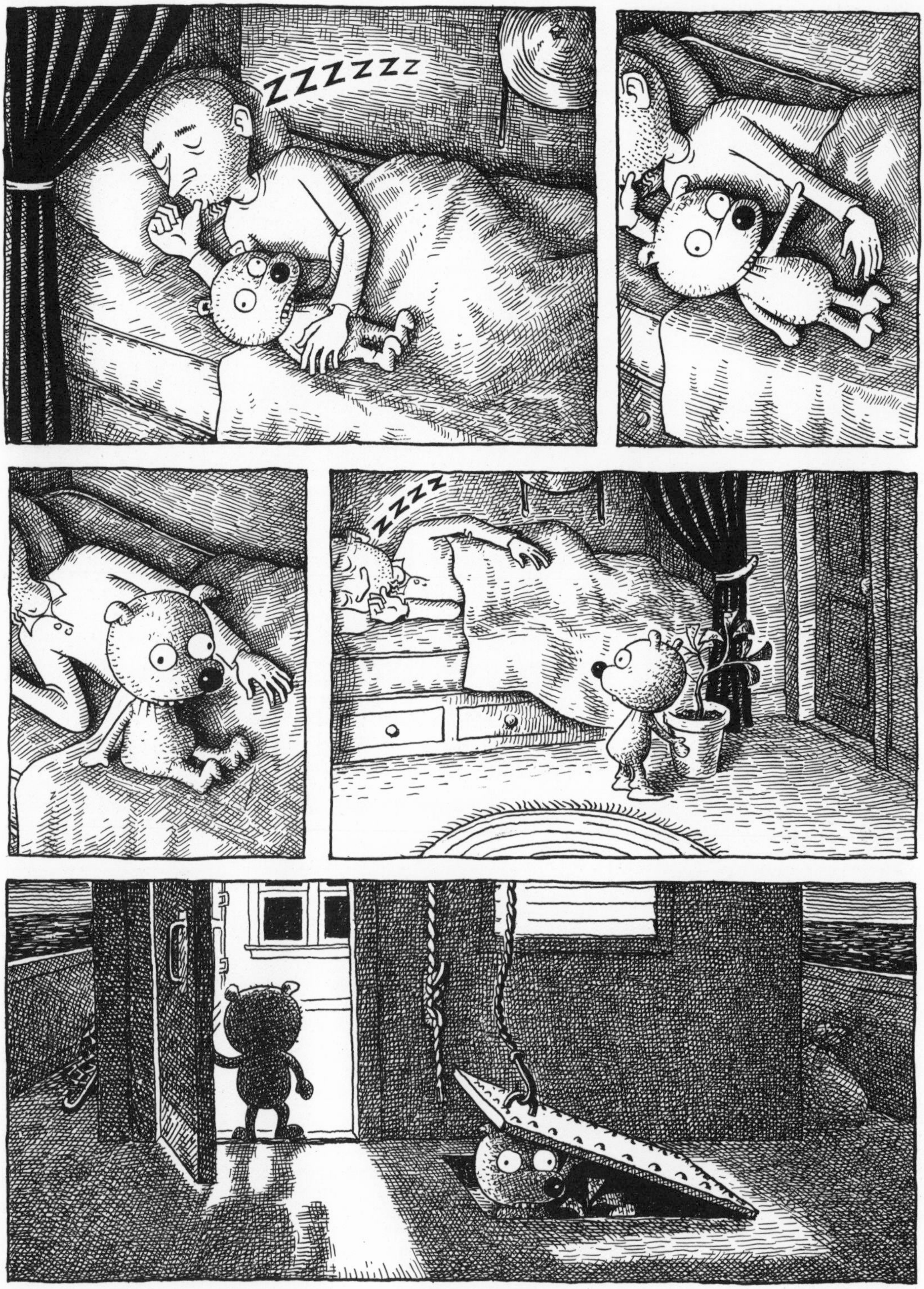
ZZZZZZz
ZZZZ

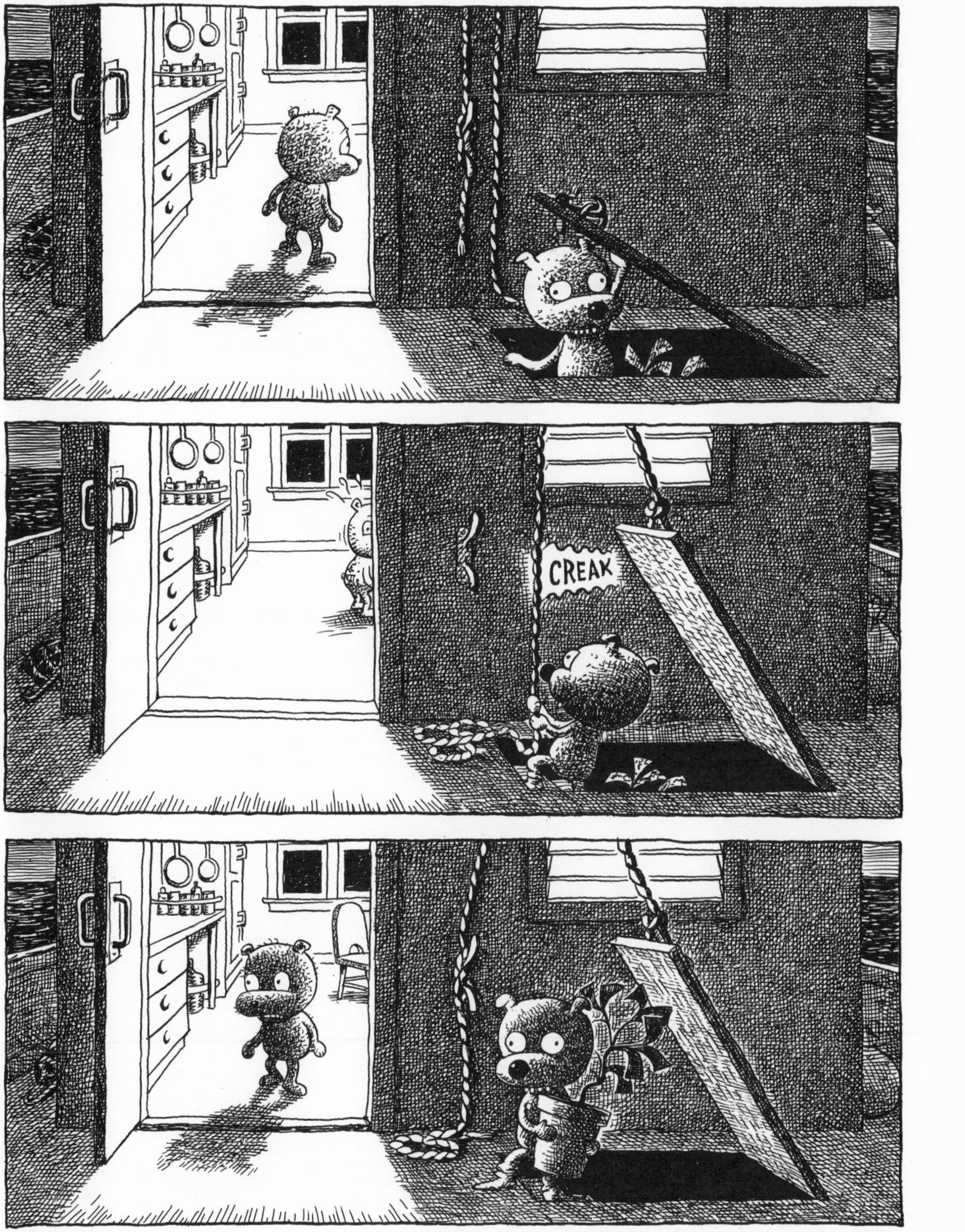
CREAK

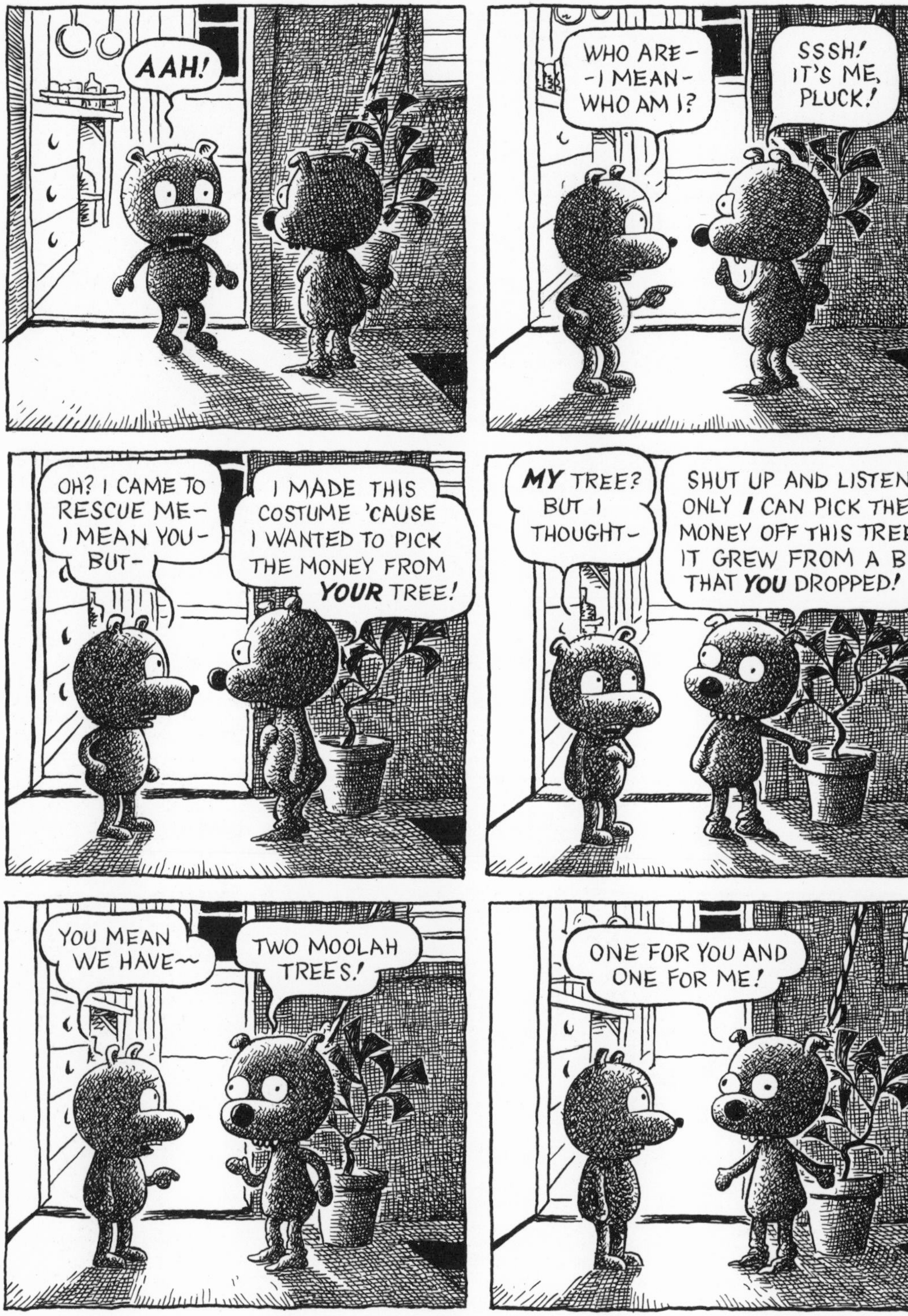
AAH!
WHO ARE- -I MEAN- WHO AM I?
SSSH! IT'S ME, PLUCK!
OH? I CAME TO RESCUE ME- I MEAN YOU- BUT-
I MADE THIS COSTUME 'CAUSE I WANTED TO PICK THE MONEY FROM YOUR TREE!
MY TREE? BUT I THOUGHT-
SHUT UP AND LISTEN! ONLY I CAN PICK THE MONEY OFF THIS TREE. IT GREW FROM A BILL THAT YOU DROPPED!
YOU MEAN WE HAVE~
TWO MOOLAH TREES!
ONE FOR YOU AND ONE FOR ME!

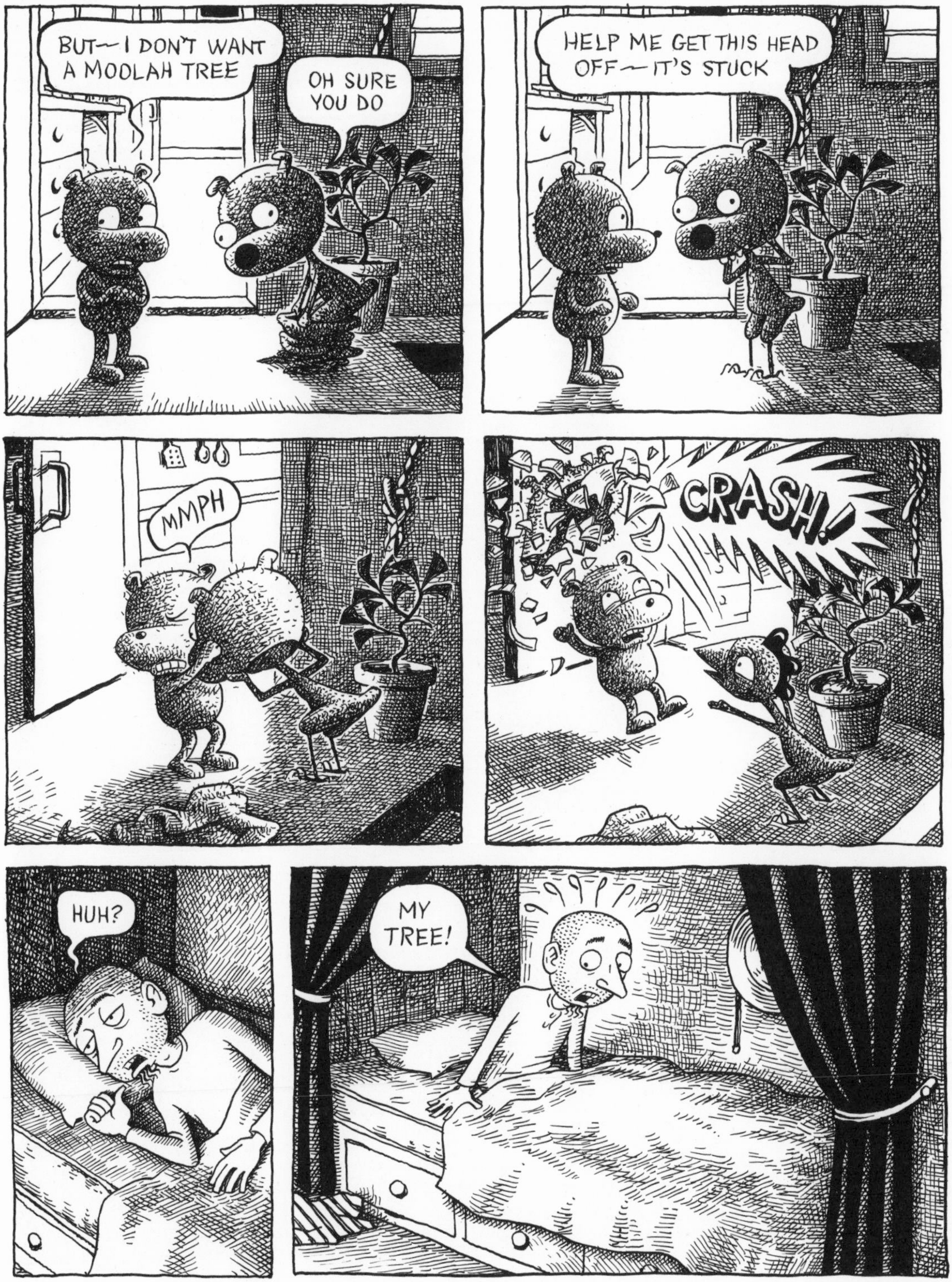
BUT— I DON'T WANT A MOOLAH TREE
OH SURE YOU DO
HELP ME GET THIS HEAD OFF— IT'S STUCK
MMPH
CRASH!
HUH?
MY TREE!

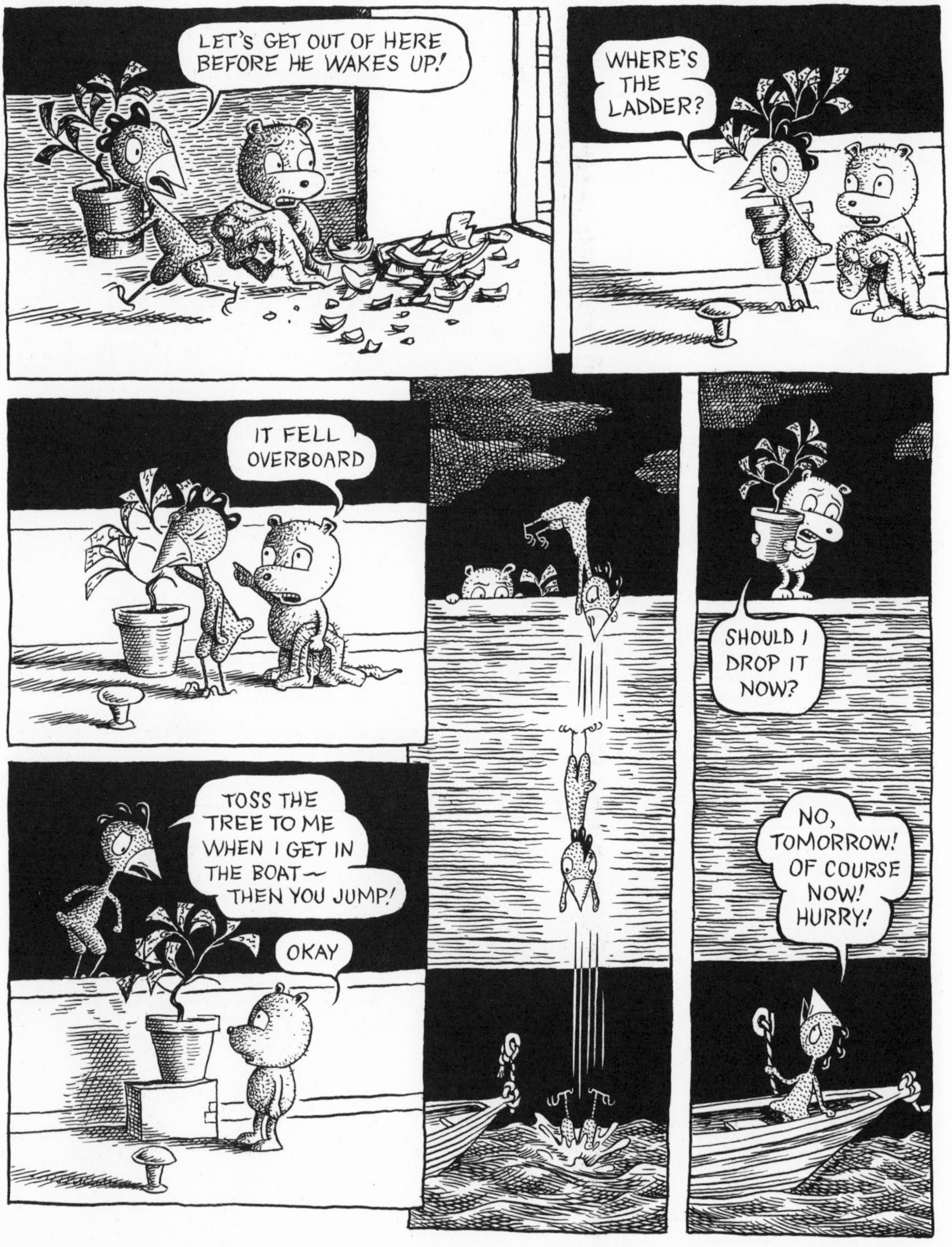
LET'S GET OUT OF HERE BEFORE HE WAKES UP!
WHERE'S THE LADDER?
IT FELL OVERBOARD
TOSS THE TREE TO ME WHEN I GET IN THE BOAT— THEN YOU JUMP!
OKAY
SHOULD I DROP IT NOW?
NO, TOMORROW! OF COURSE NOW! HURRY!

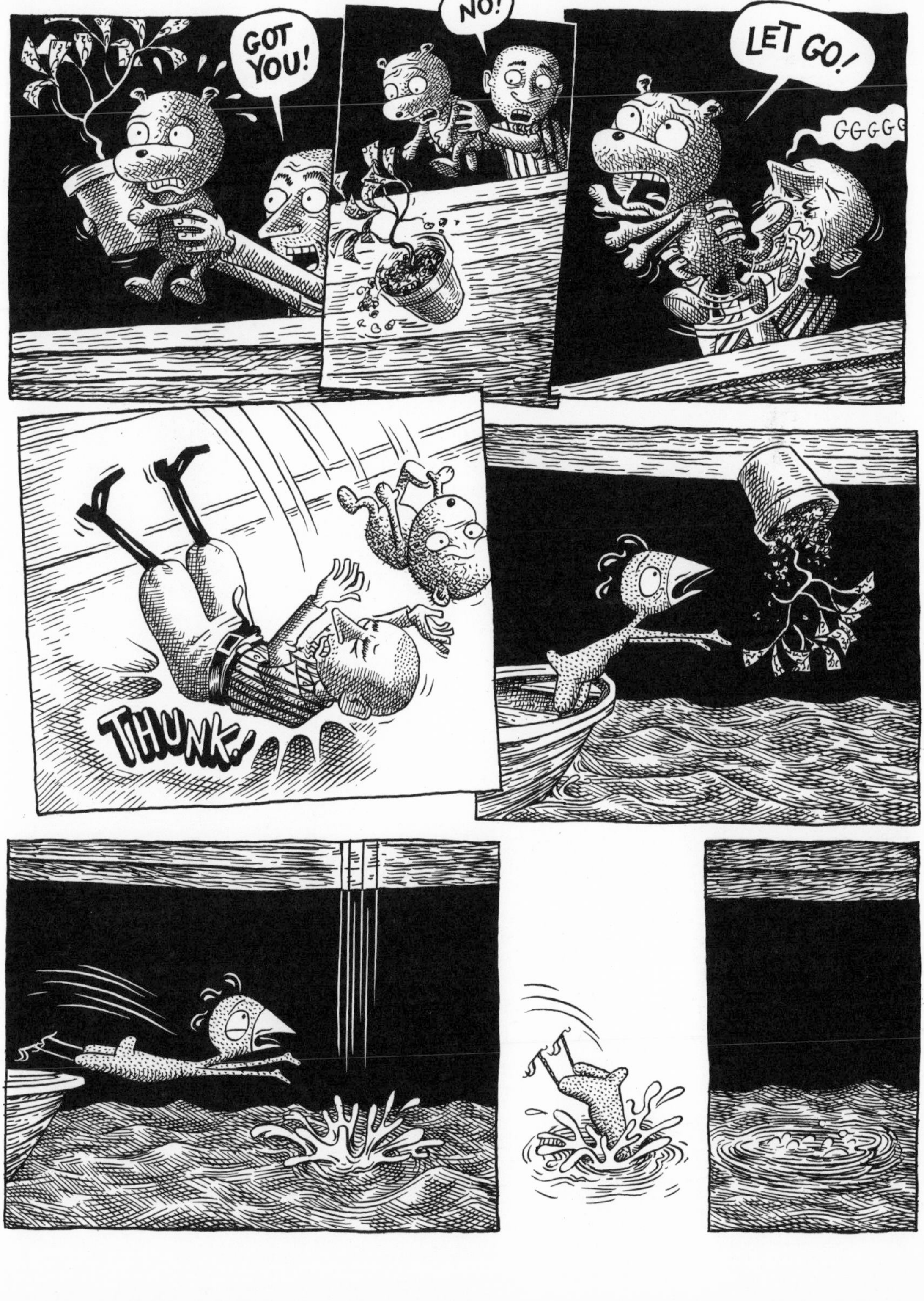
GOT YOU!
NO!
LET GO!
GGGGG
THUNK!

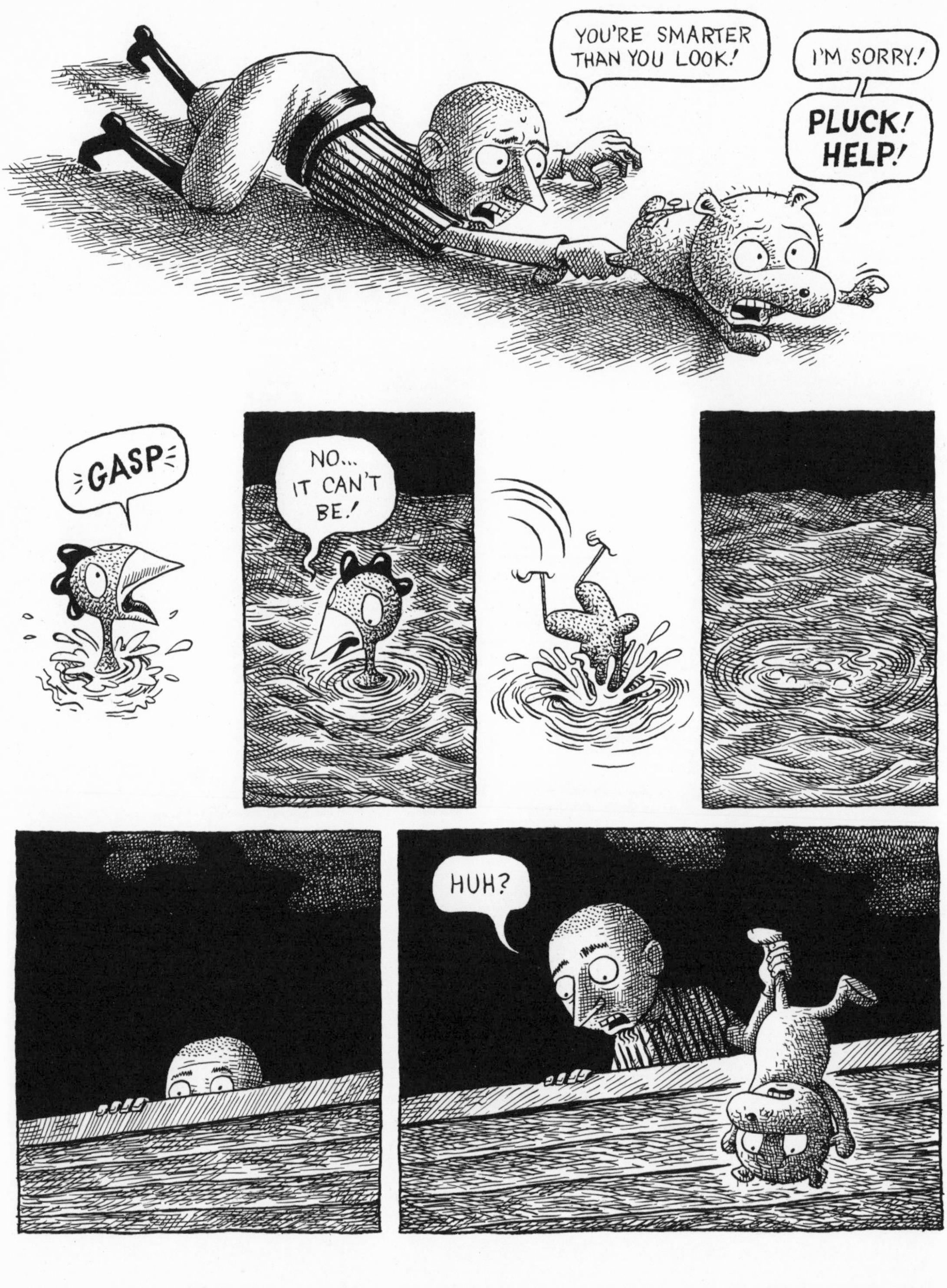
YOU'RE SMARTER THAN YOU LOOK!
I'M SORRY!
PLUCK! HELP!
GASP
NO... IT CAN'T BE!
HUH?

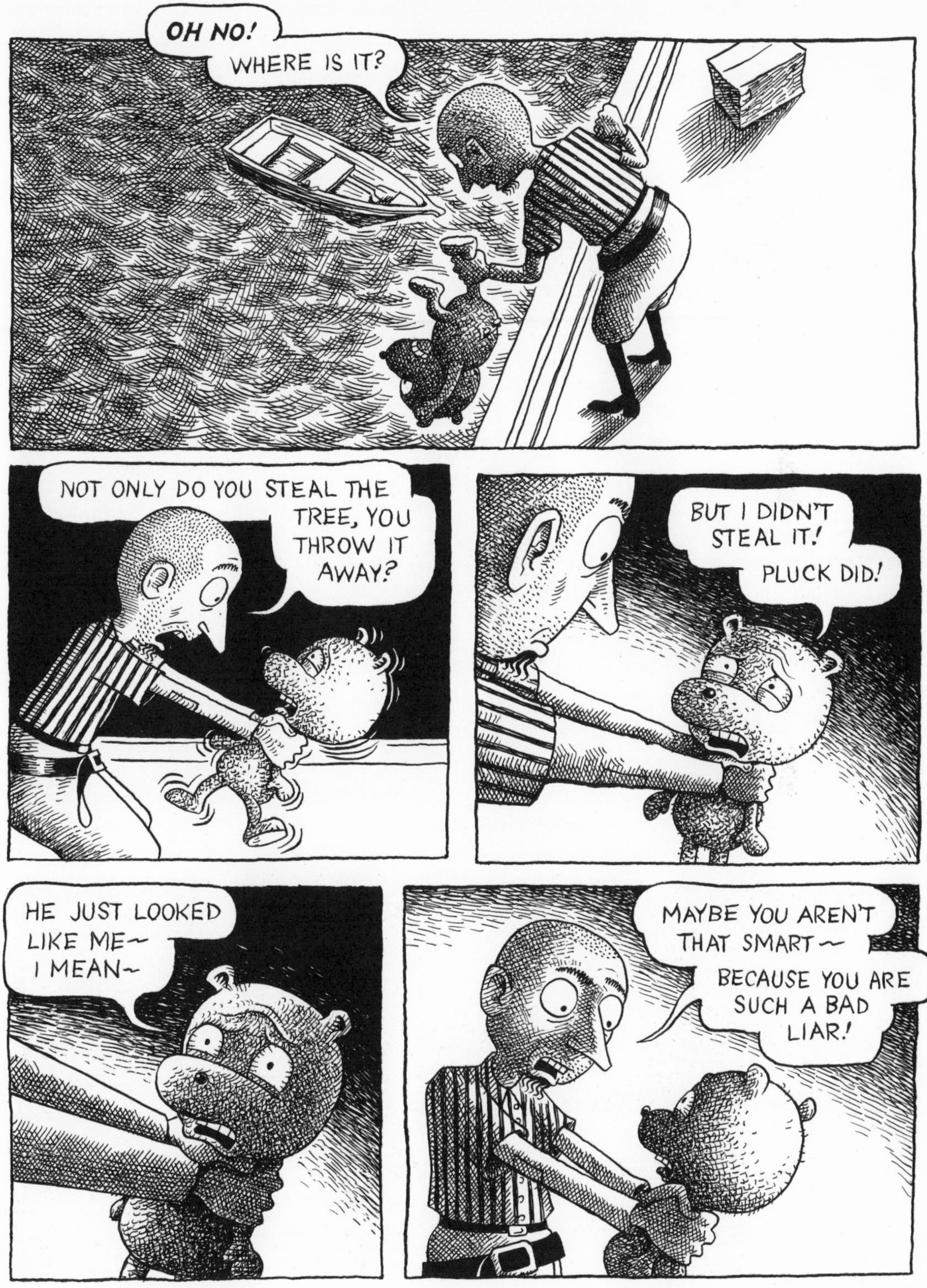
OH NO!
WHERE IS IT?
NOT ONLY DO YOU STEAL THE TREE, YOU THROW IT AWAY?
BUT I DIDN'T STEAL IT!
PLUCK DID!
HE JUST LOOKED LIKE ME~ I MEAN~
MAYBE YOU AREN'T THAT SMART~
BECAUSE YOU ARE SUCH A BAD LIAR!

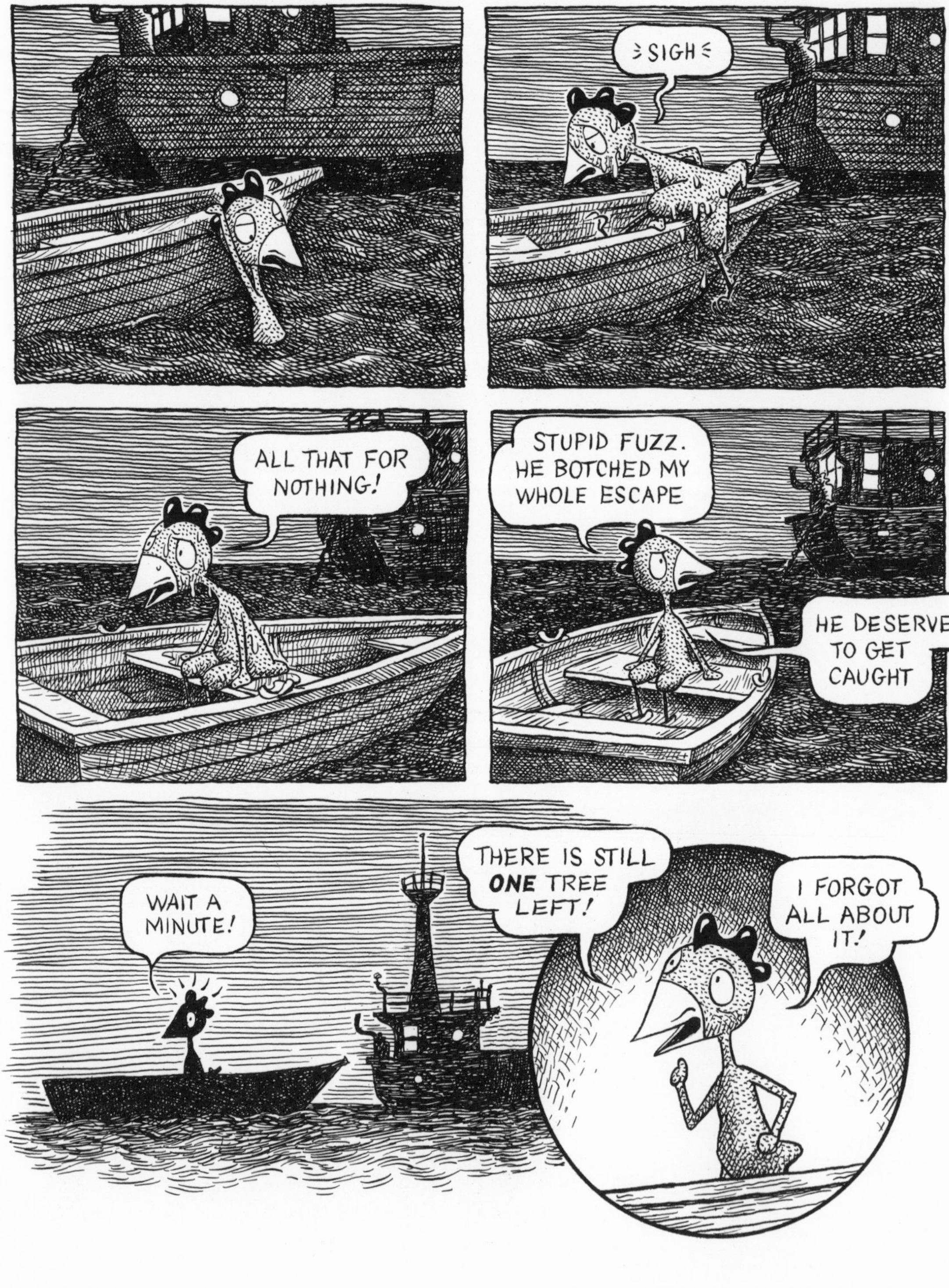
SIGH
ALL THAT FOR NOTHING!
STUPID FUZZ. HE BOTCHED MY WHOLE ESCAPE
HE DESERVES TO GET CAUGHT
WAIT A MINUTE!
THERE IS STILL **ONE** TREE LEFT!
I FORGOT ALL ABOUT IT!

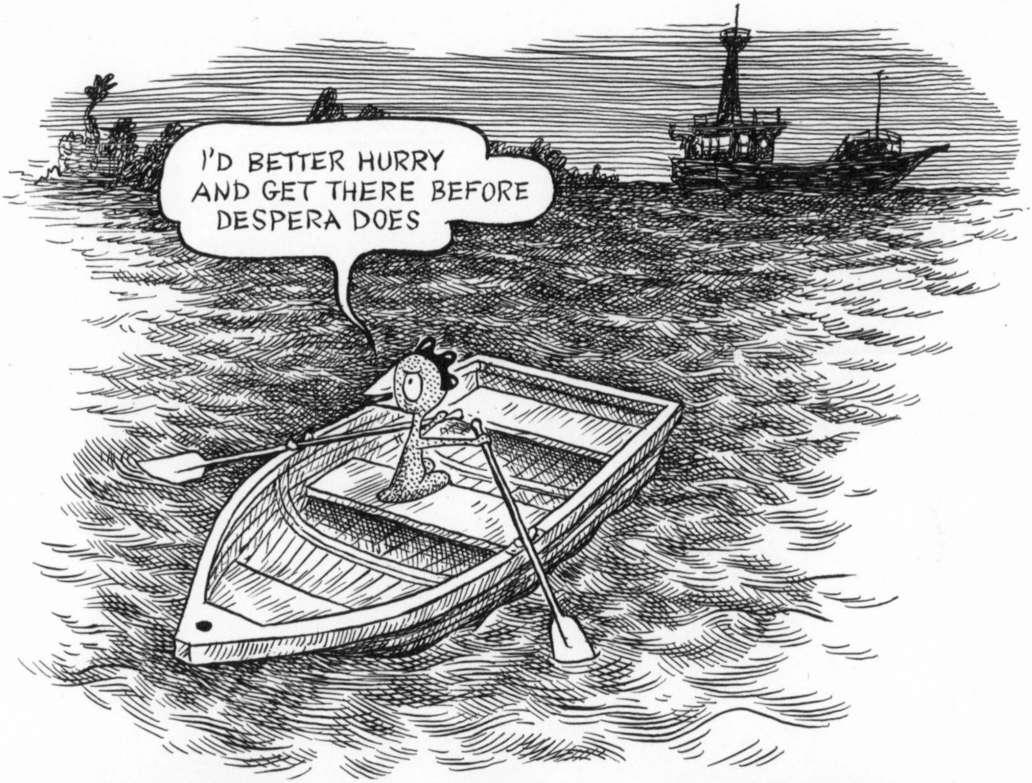
I'D BETTER HURRY AND GET THERE BEFORE DESPERA DOES

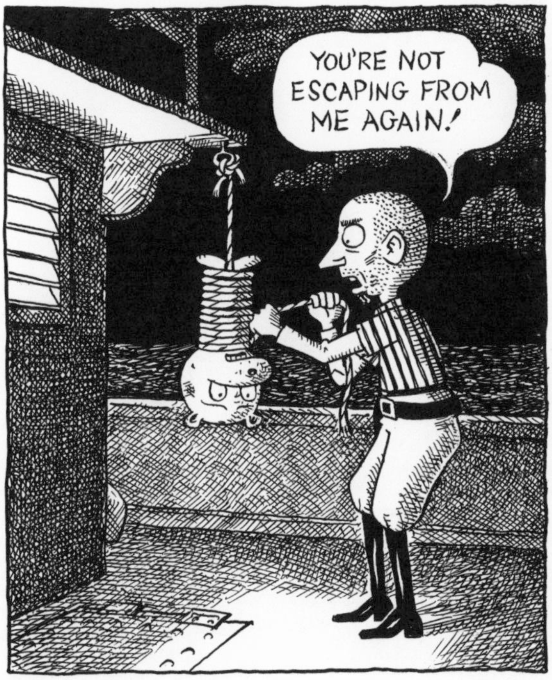
YOU'RE NOT ESCAPING FROM ME AGAIN!

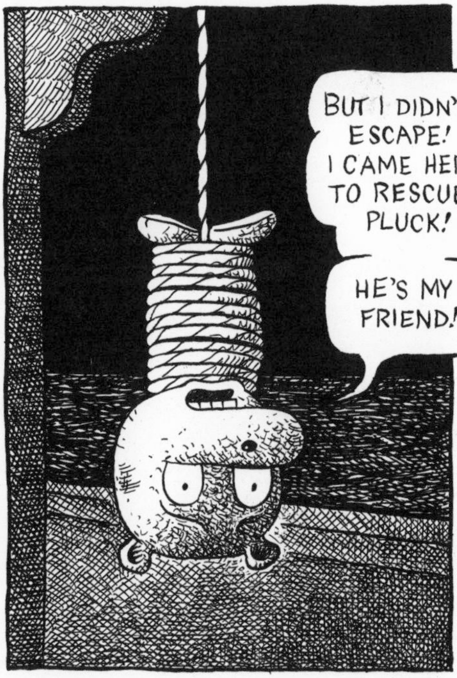
BUT I DIDN'T ESCAPE! I CAME HERE TO RESCUE PLUCK!
HE'S MY FRIEND!

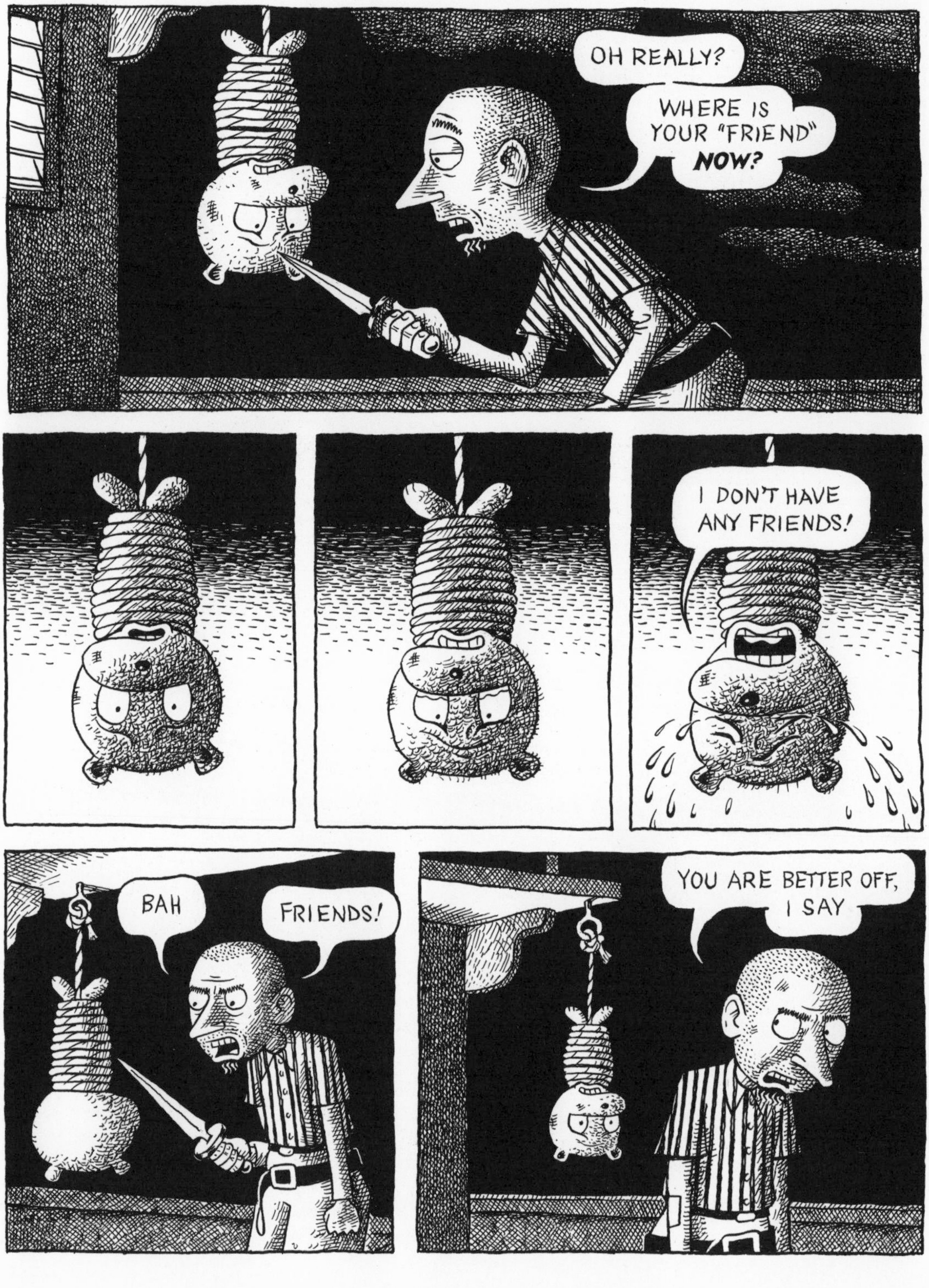
OH REALLY?
WHERE IS YOUR "FRIEND" **NOW?**
I DON'T HAVE ANY FRIENDS!
BAH
FRIENDS!
YOU ARE BETTER OFF, I SAY

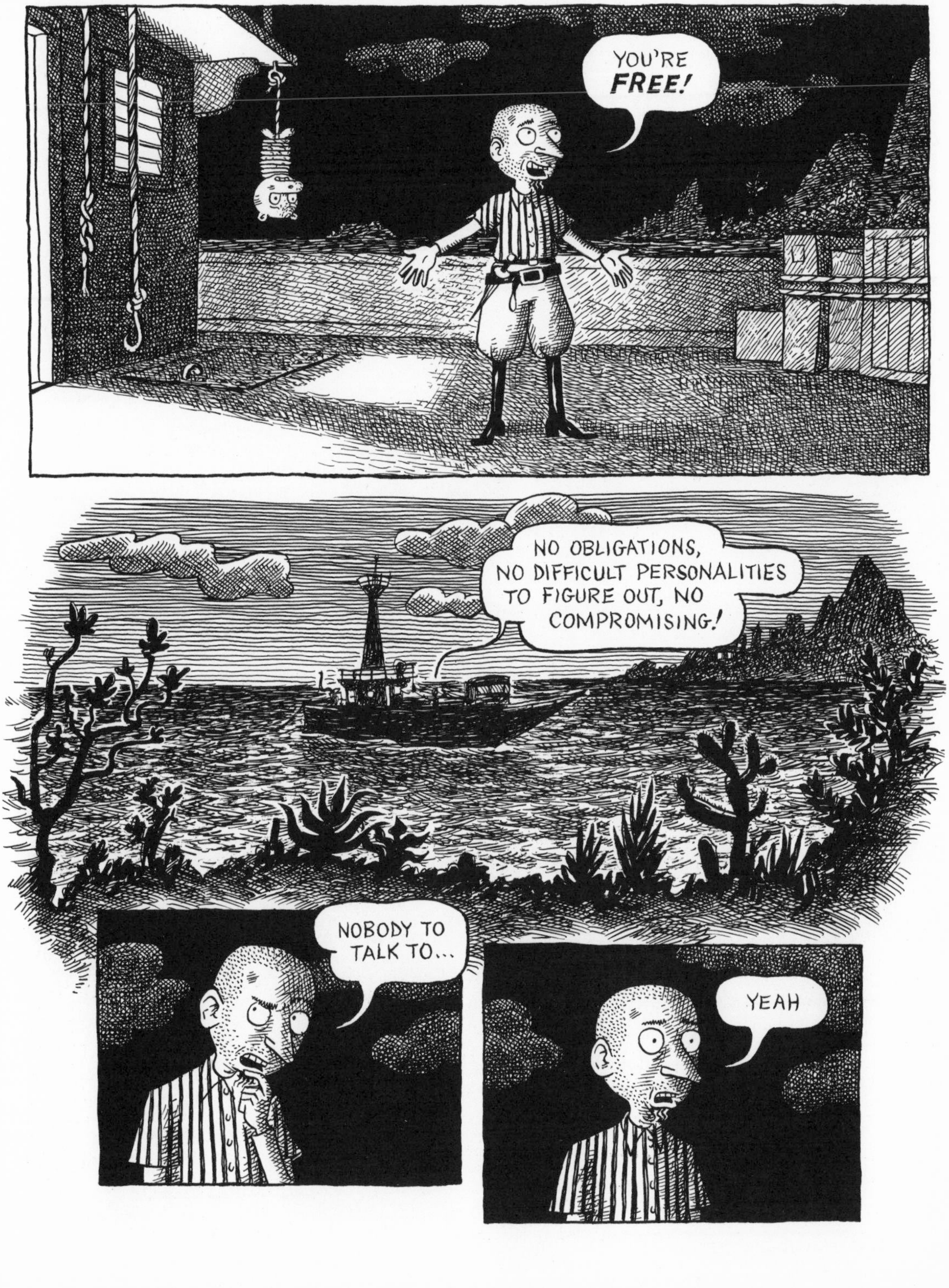
YOU'RE FREE!
NO OBLIGATIONS, NO DIFFICULT PERSONALITIES TO FIGURE OUT, NO COMPROMISING!
NOBODY TO TALK TO...
YEAH

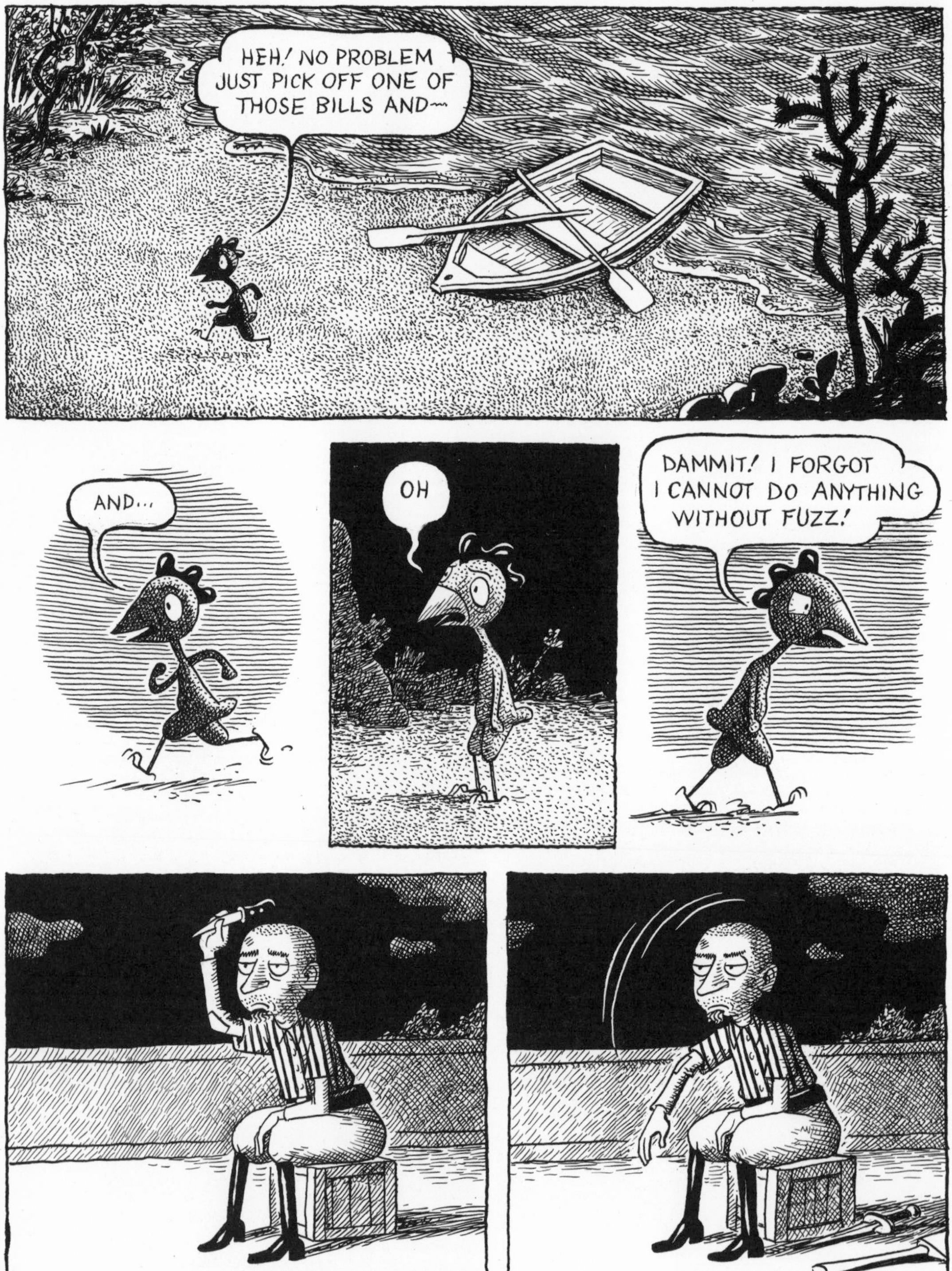
HEH! NO PROBLEM JUST PICK OFF ONE OF THOSE BILLS AND—
AND...
OH
DAMMIT! I FORGOT I CANNOT DO ANYTHING WITHOUT FUZZ!

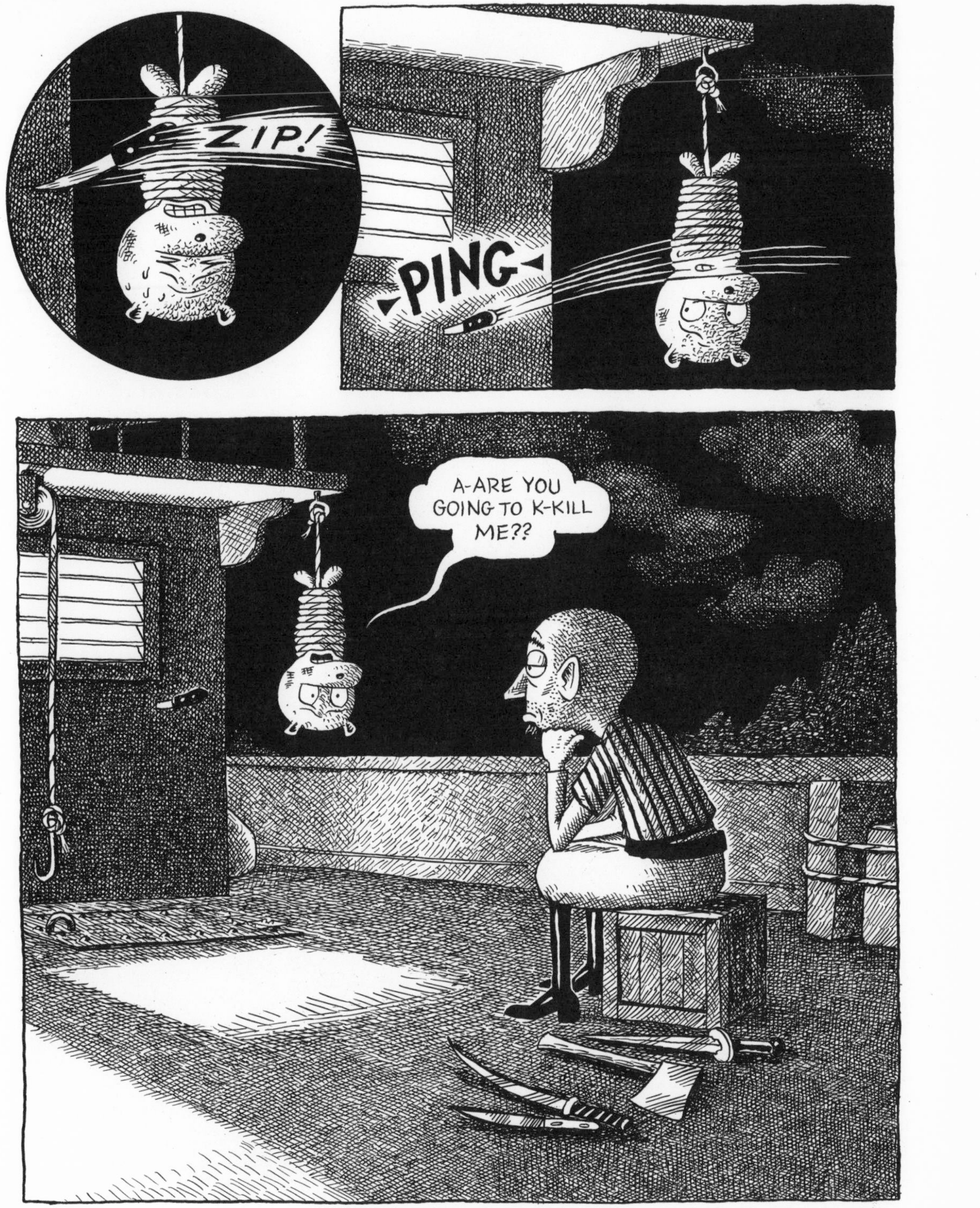
ZIP!
PING
A-ARE YOU GOING TO K-KILL ME??

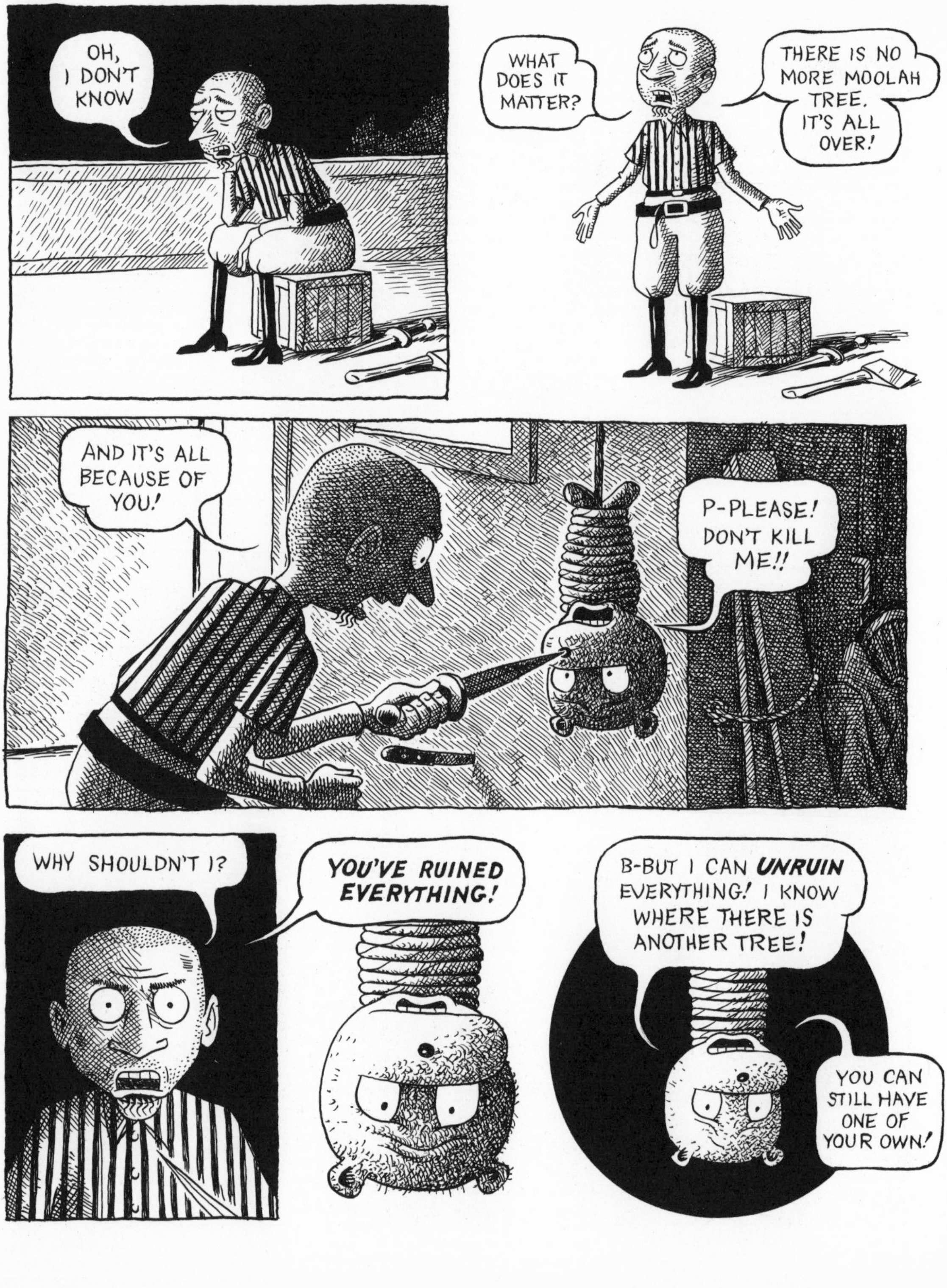

OH, I DON'T KNOW
WHAT DOES IT MATTER?
THERE IS NO MORE MOOLAH TREE. IT'S ALL OVER!
AND IT'S ALL BECAUSE OF YOU!
P-PLEASE! DON'T KILL ME!!
WHY SHOULDN'T I?
YOU'VE RUINED EVERYTHING!
B-BUT I CAN UNRUIN EVERYTHING! I KNOW WHERE THERE IS ANOTHER TREE!
YOU CAN STILL HAVE ONE OF YOUR OWN!

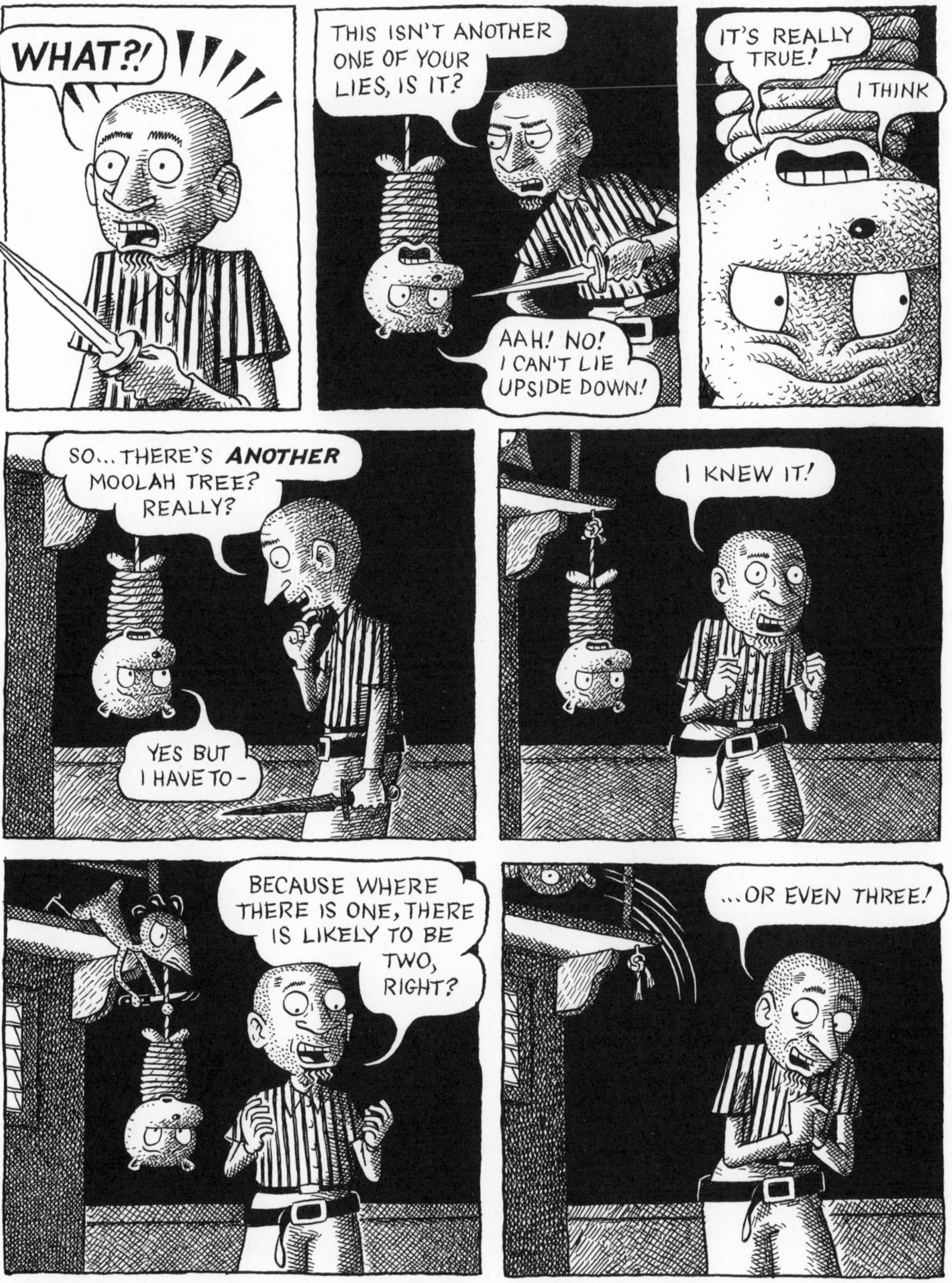
WHAT?!
THIS ISN'T ANOTHER ONE OF YOUR LIES, IS IT?
AAH! NO! I CAN'T LIE UPSIDE DOWN!
IT'S REALLY TRUE!
I THINK
SO... THERE'S **ANOTHER** MOOLAH TREE? REALLY?
YES BUT I HAVE TO-
I KNEW IT!
BECAUSE WHERE THERE IS ONE, THERE IS LIKELY TO BE TWO, RIGHT?
...OR EVEN THREE!

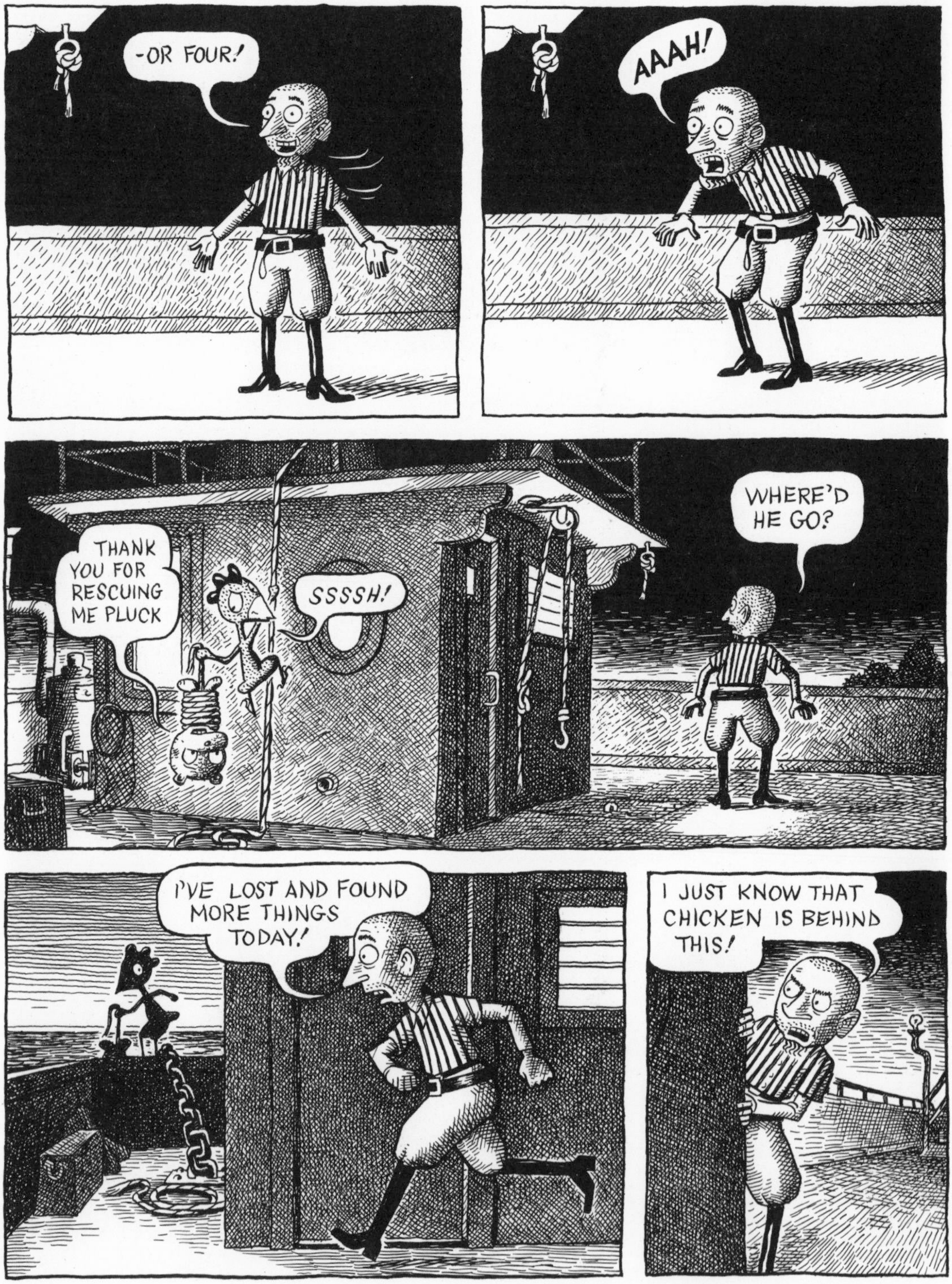
-OR FOUR!
AAAH!
THANK YOU FOR RESCUING ME PLUCK
SSSSH!
WHERE'D HE GO?
I'VE LOST AND FOUND MORE THINGS TODAY!
I JUST KNOW THAT CHICKEN IS BEHIND THIS!

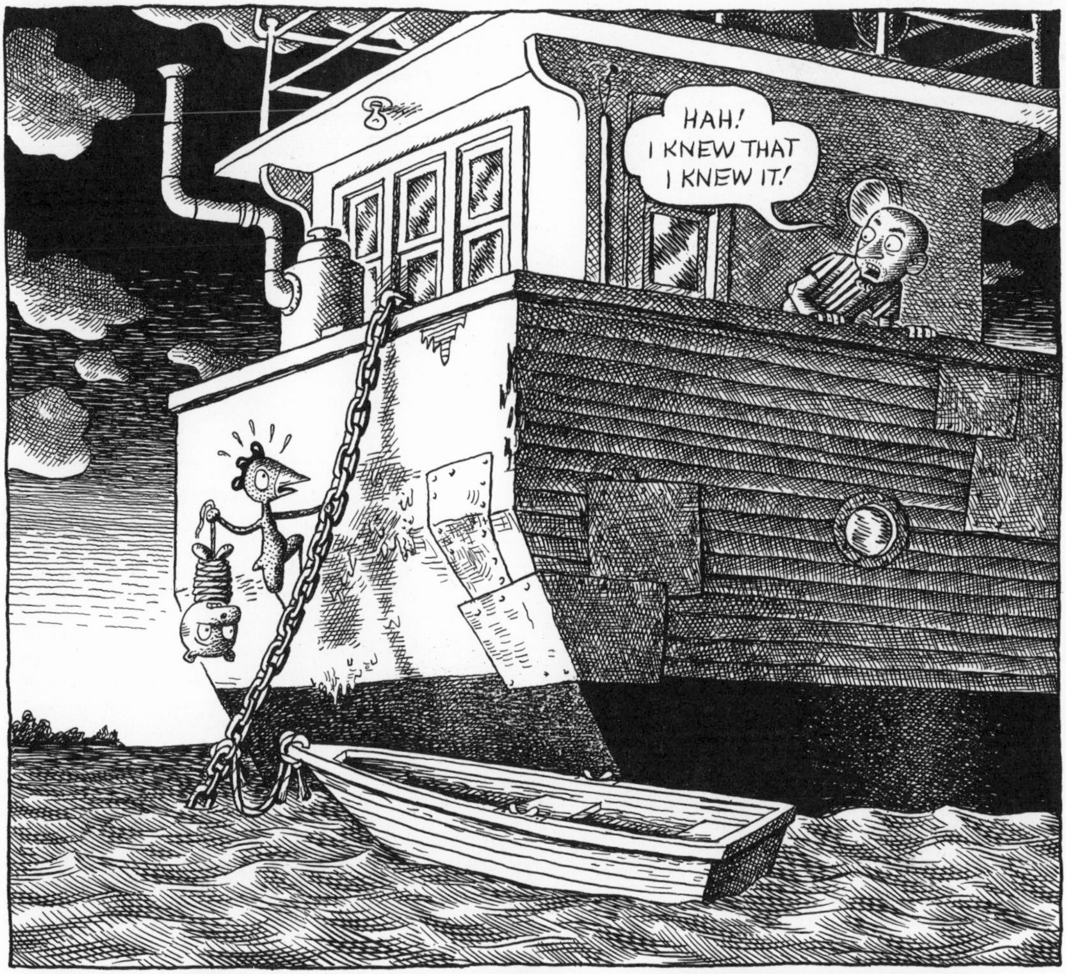
HAH!
I KNEW THAT
I KNEW IT!

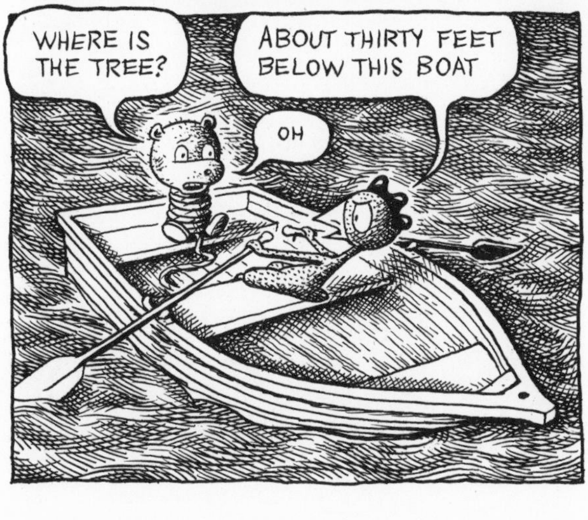
WHERE IS
THE TREE?
ABOUT THIRTY FEET
BELOW THIS BOAT
OH

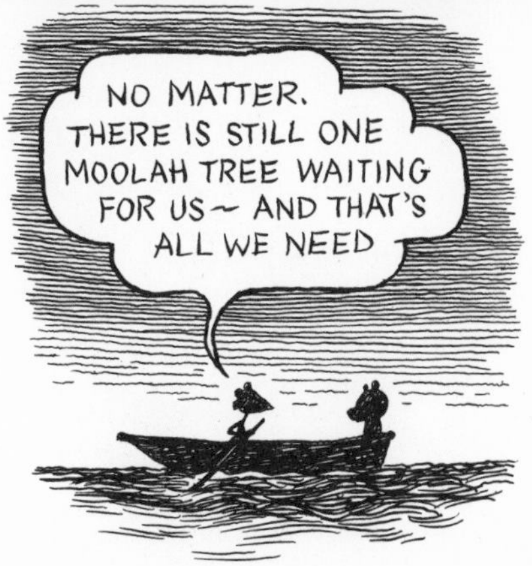
NO MATTER.
THERE IS STILL ONE
MOOLAH TREE WAITING
FOR US~ AND THAT'S
ALL WE NEED

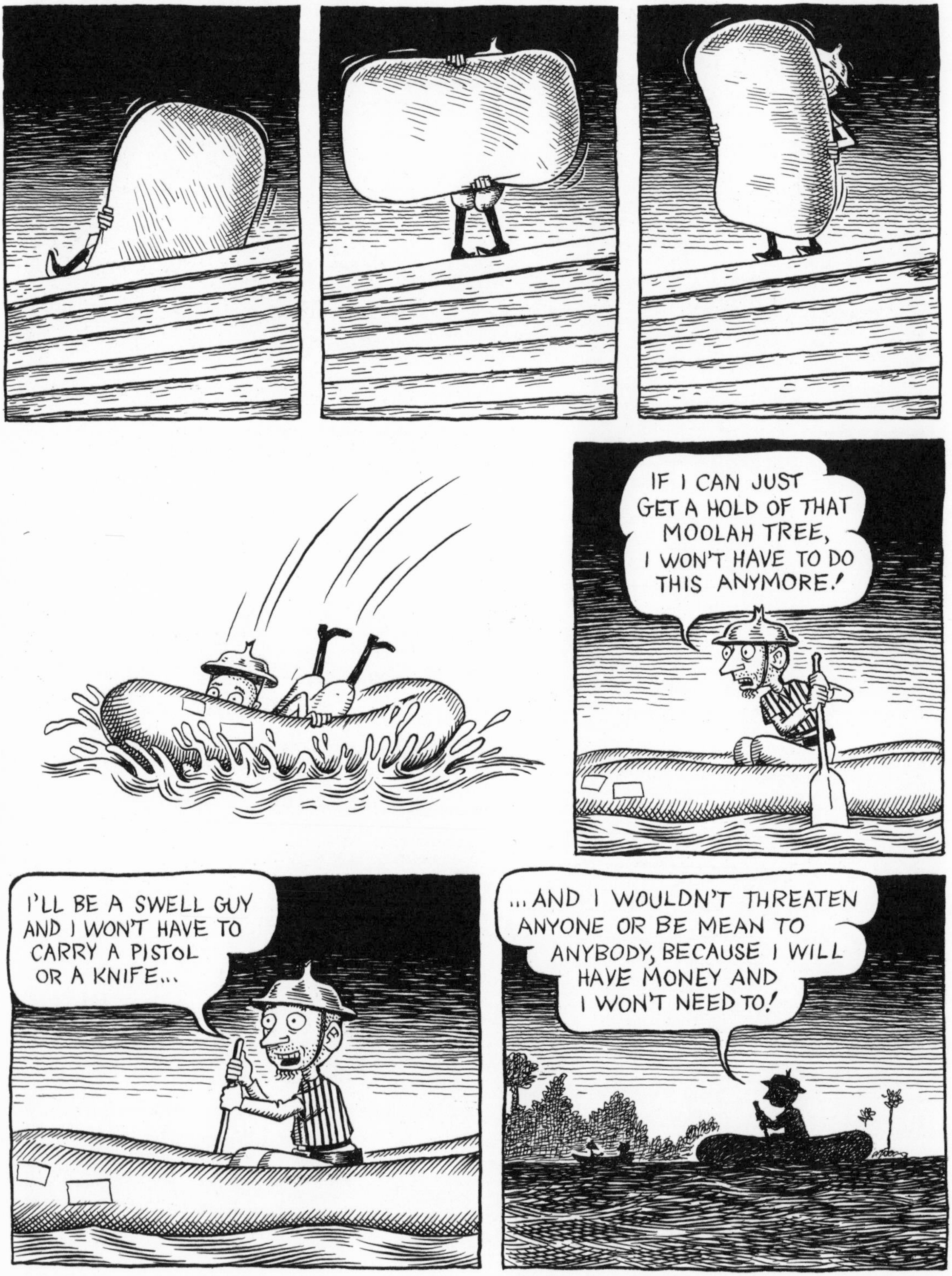
IF I CAN JUST GET A HOLD OF THAT MOOLAH TREE, I WON'T HAVE TO DO THIS ANYMORE!
I'LL BE A SWELL GUY AND I WON'T HAVE TO CARRY A PISTOL OR A KNIFE...
...AND I WOULDN'T THREATEN ANYONE OR BE MEAN TO ANYBODY, BECAUSE I WILL HAVE MONEY AND I WON'T NEED TO!

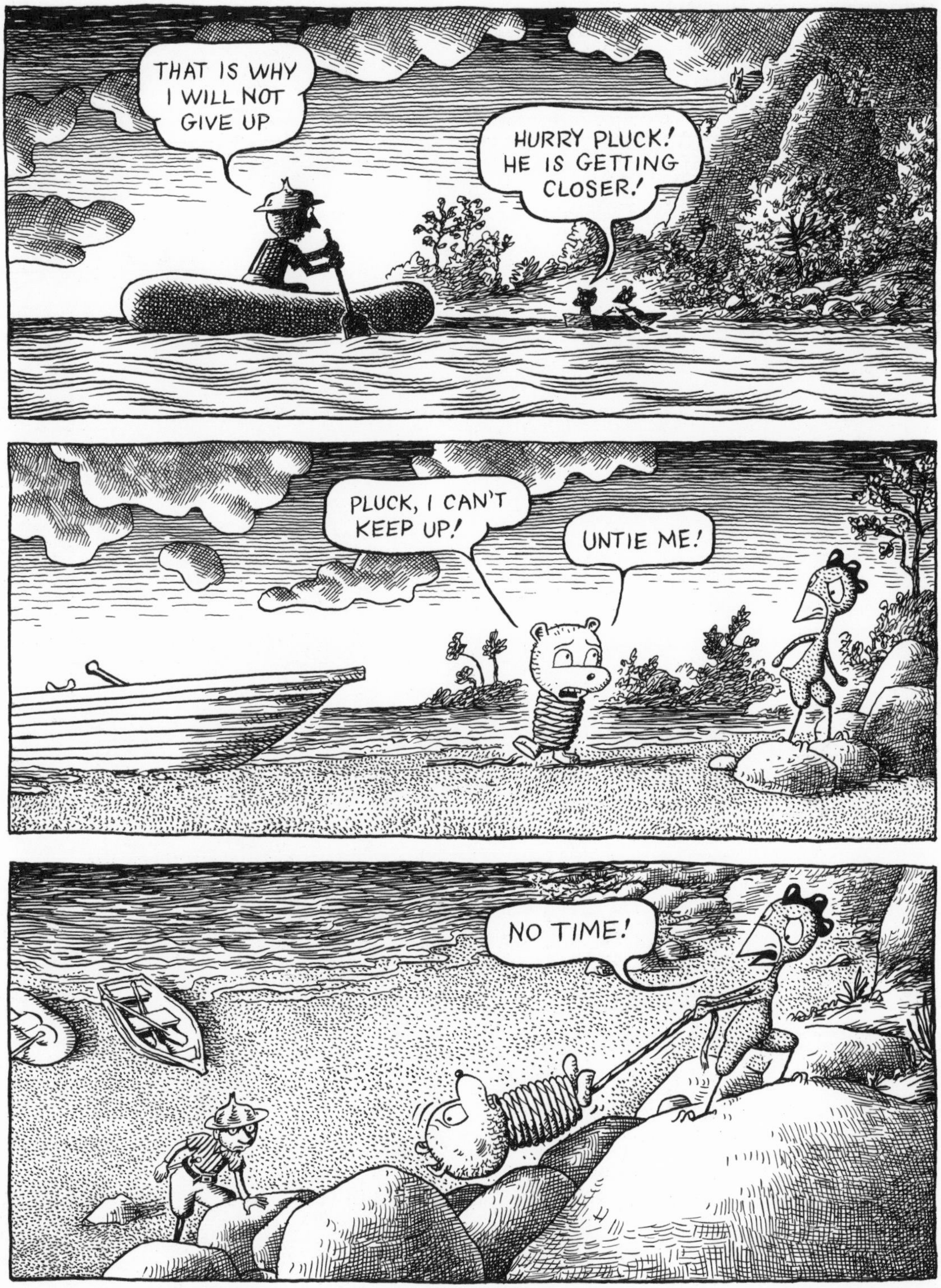
THAT IS WHY I WILL NOT GIVE UP
HURRY PLUCK! HE IS GETTING CLOSER!
PLUCK, I CAN'T KEEP UP!
UNTIE ME!
NO TIME!

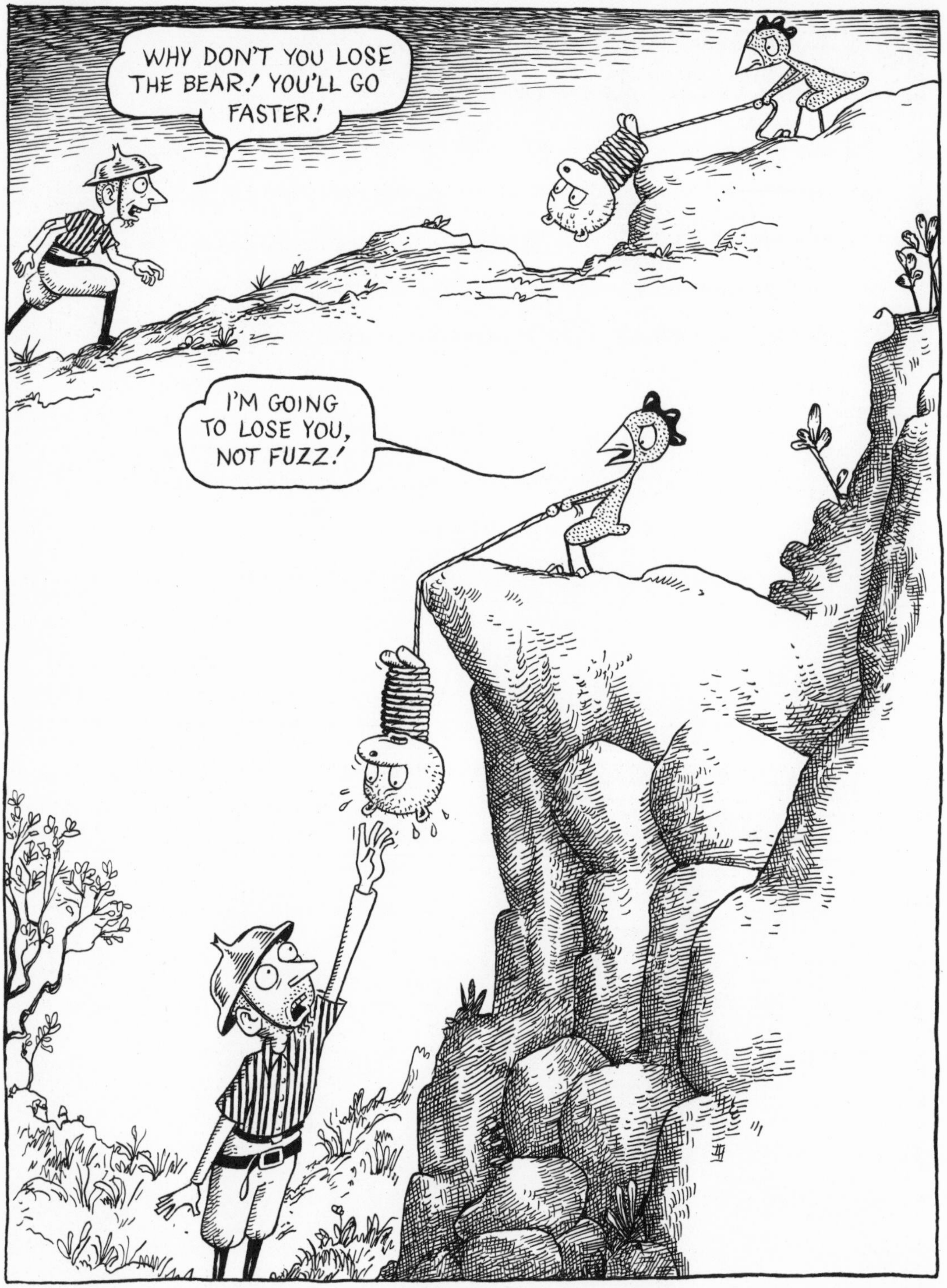
WHY DON'T YOU LOSE THE BEAR! YOU'LL GO FASTER!
I'M GOING TO LOSE YOU, NOT FUZZ!

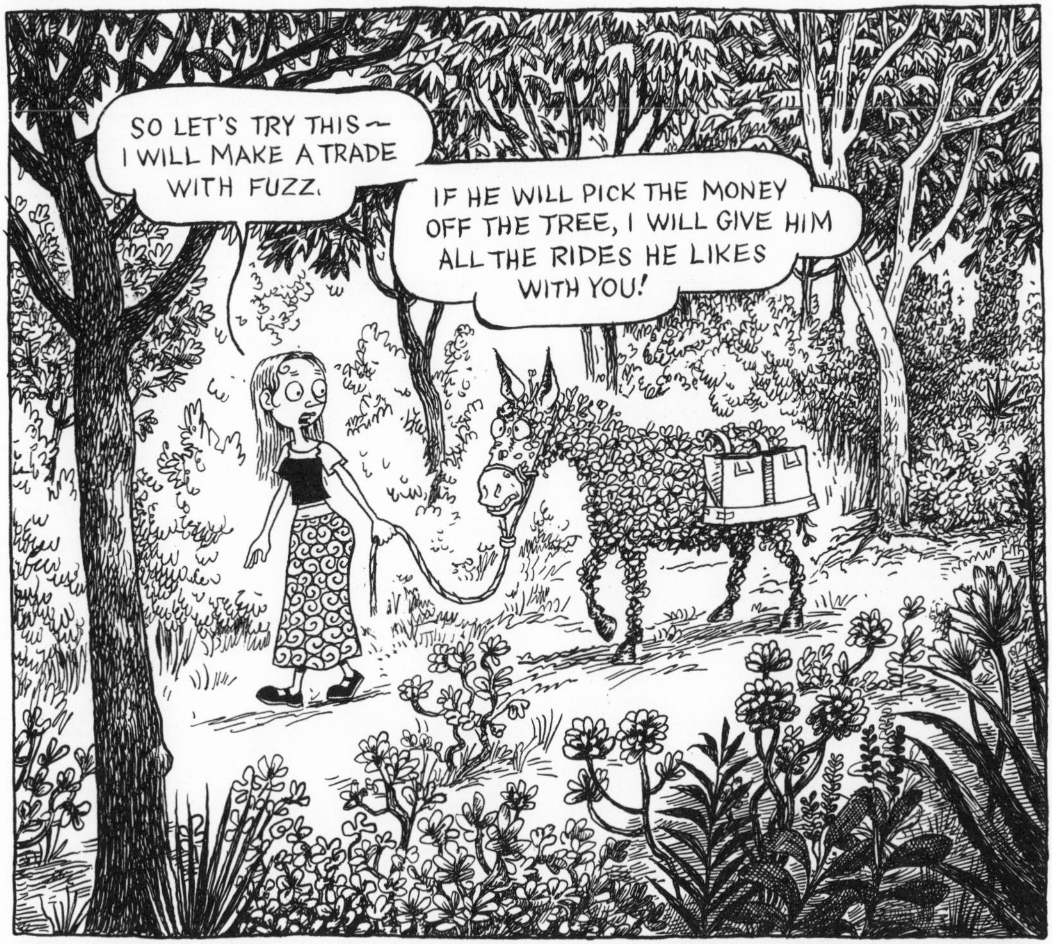
SO LET'S TRY THIS— I WILL MAKE A TRADE WITH FUZZ.
IF HE WILL PICK THE MONEY OFF THE TREE, I WILL GIVE HIM ALL THE RIDES HE LIKES WITH YOU!

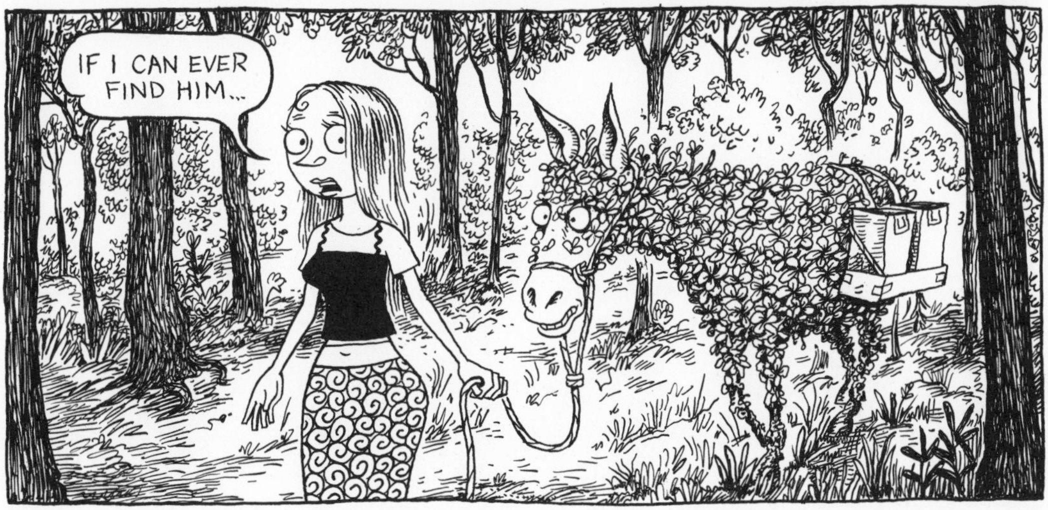
IF I CAN EVER FIND HIM...

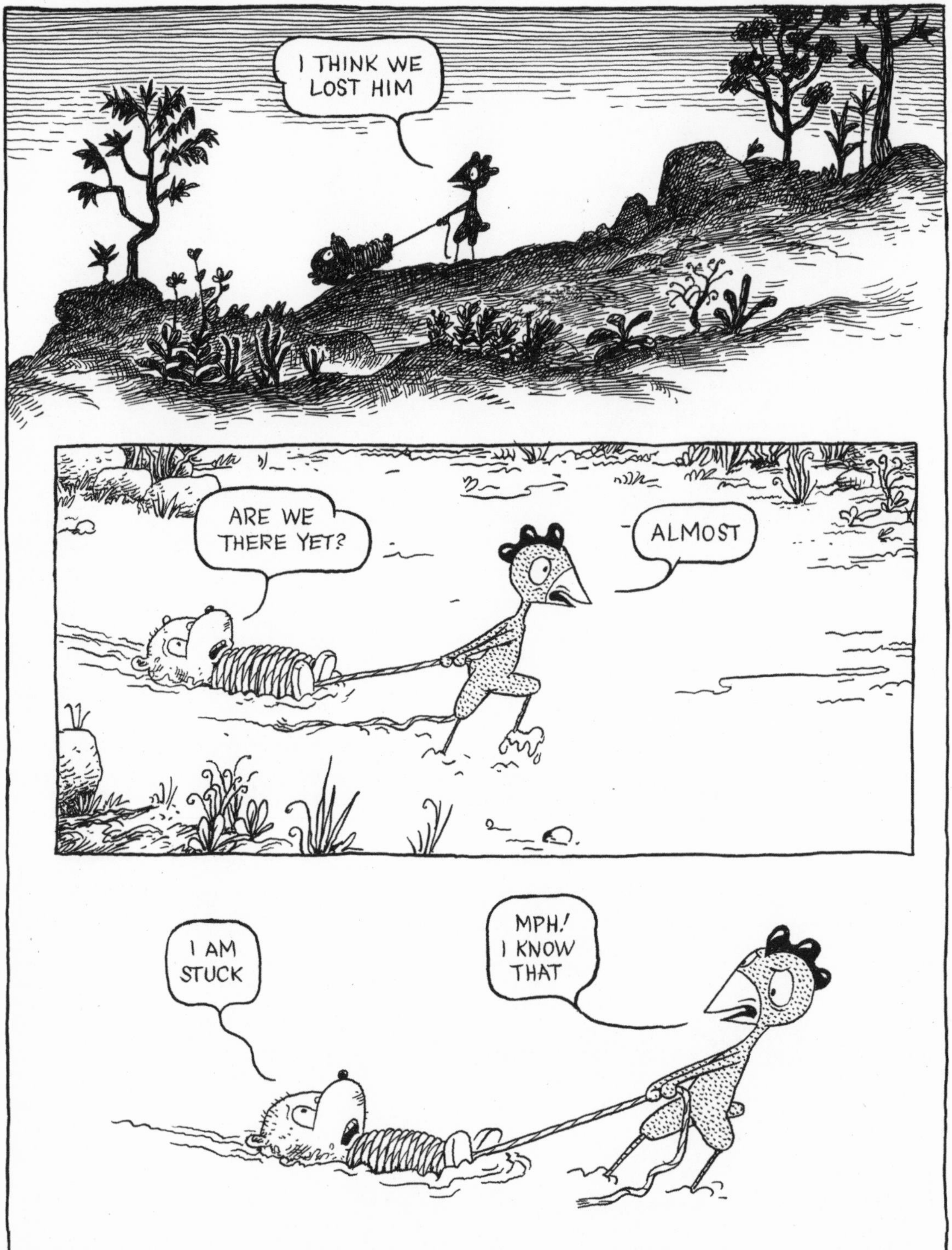
I THINK WE LOST HIM
ARE WE THERE YET?
ALMOST
I AM STUCK
MPH! I KNOW THAT

STAY THERE— DON'T MOVE!
OKAY
I'LL BE RIGHT BACK
DON'T FORGET ABOUT ME, PLUCK!
I KNOW THIS IS THE RIGHT PLACE—
RIGHT WHERE THIS HOLE IS!
SOMEONE MUST HAVE DUG IT UP AND TAKEN IT
THAT'S RIGHT
YOU!

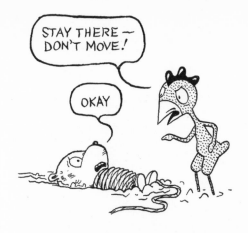

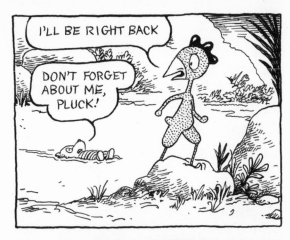

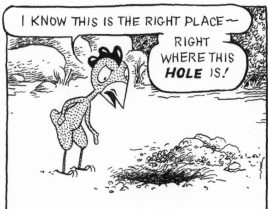

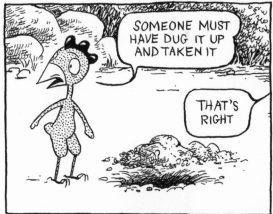

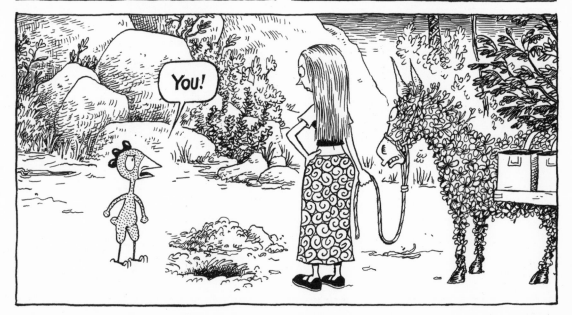

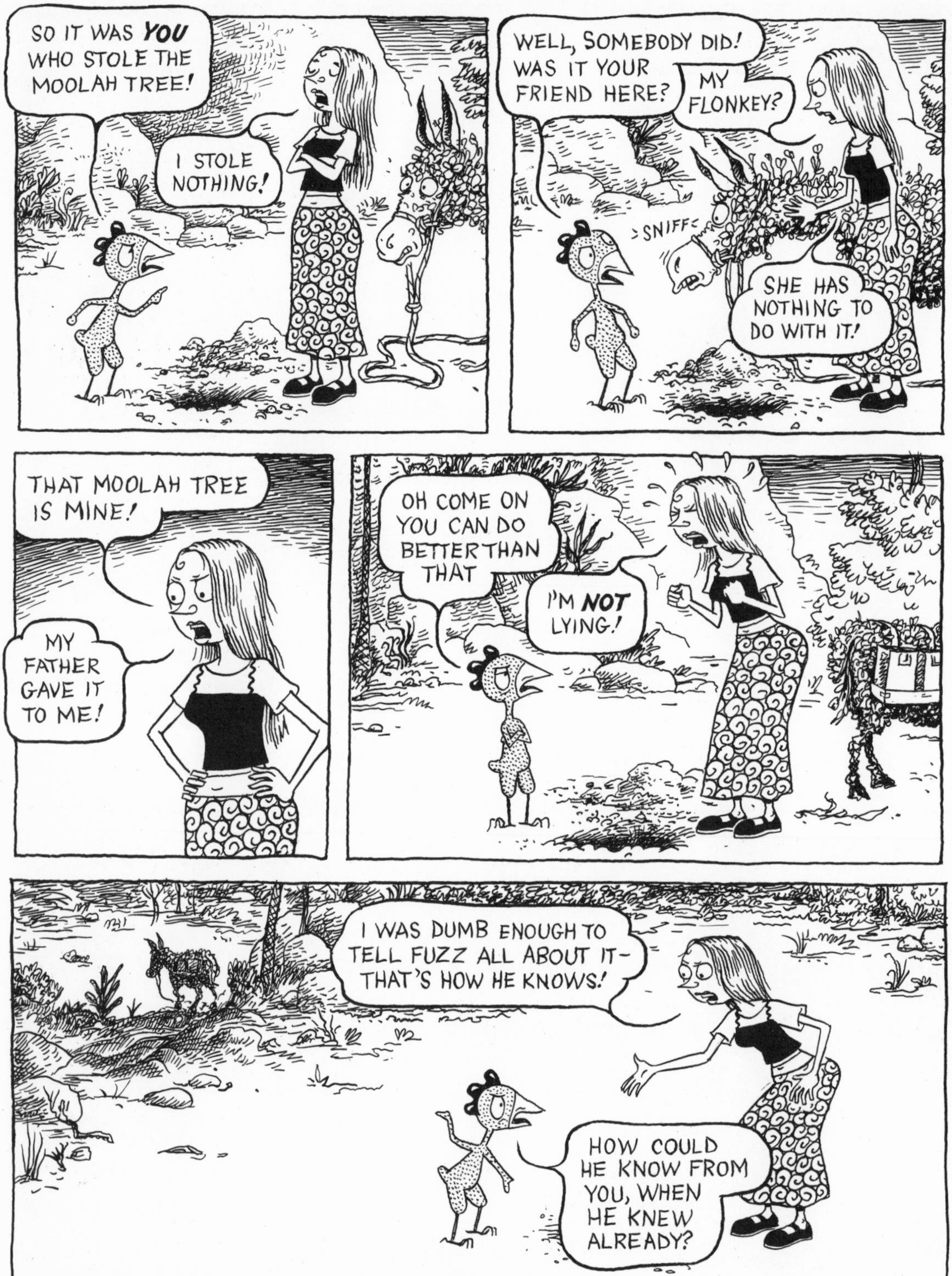
SO IT WAS **YOU** WHO STOLE THE MOOLAH TREE!
I STOLE NOTHING!
WELL, SOMEBODY DID! WAS IT YOUR FRIEND HERE?
MY FLONKEY?
SNIFF
SHE HAS NOTHING TO DO WITH IT!
THAT MOOLAH TREE IS MINE!
MY FATHER GAVE IT TO ME!
OH COME ON YOU CAN DO BETTER THAN THAT
I'M **NOT** LYING!
I WAS DUMB ENOUGH TO TELL FUZZ ALL ABOUT IT- THAT'S HOW HE KNOWS!
HOW COULD HE KNOW FROM YOU, WHEN HE KNEW ALREADY?

EEEAAFF~
HELLO FLONKEY
CAN YOU CHEW THESE ROPES OFF?
I CAN'T
HEE HEE THAT TICKLES
I DON'T HAVE TIME TO TALK TO YOU. I HAVE BUSINESS TO ATTEND TO!
HEE HEE

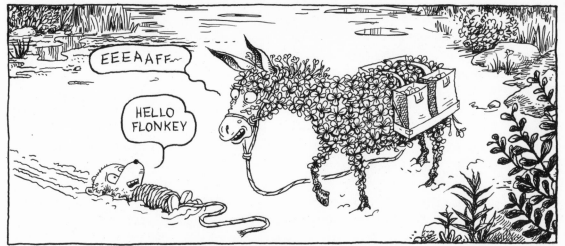

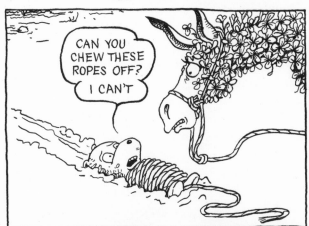

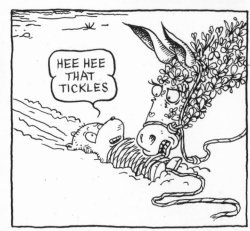

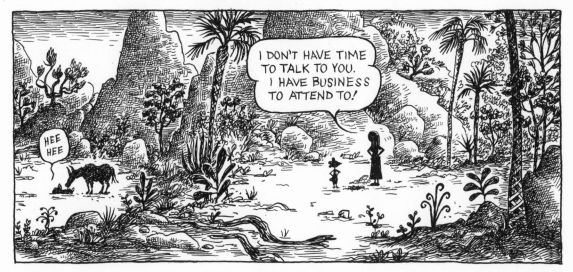

OH!
WHERE DID MY FLONKEY GO?
I HAVE TO GO-
WAIT A MINUTE! I'M NOT LOSING SIGHT OF YOU UNTIL YOU TELL ME WHERE YOU PUT THAT TREE-
I WILL NEVER EVER, EVER TELL YOU WHERE MY HOUSE-
I MEAN-
...WHERE MY TREE IS...
OKAY— BYE THEN

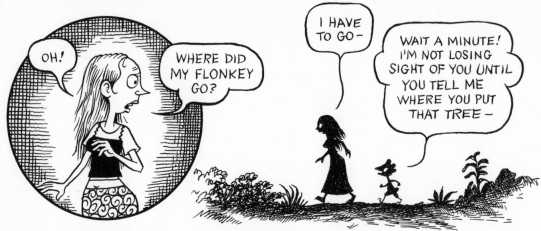

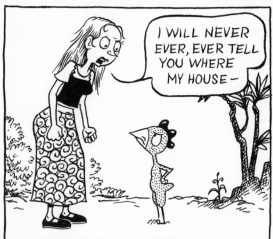

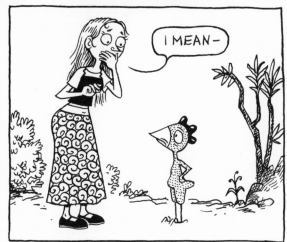

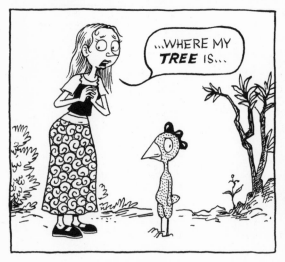

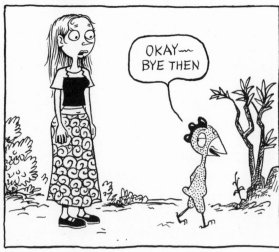

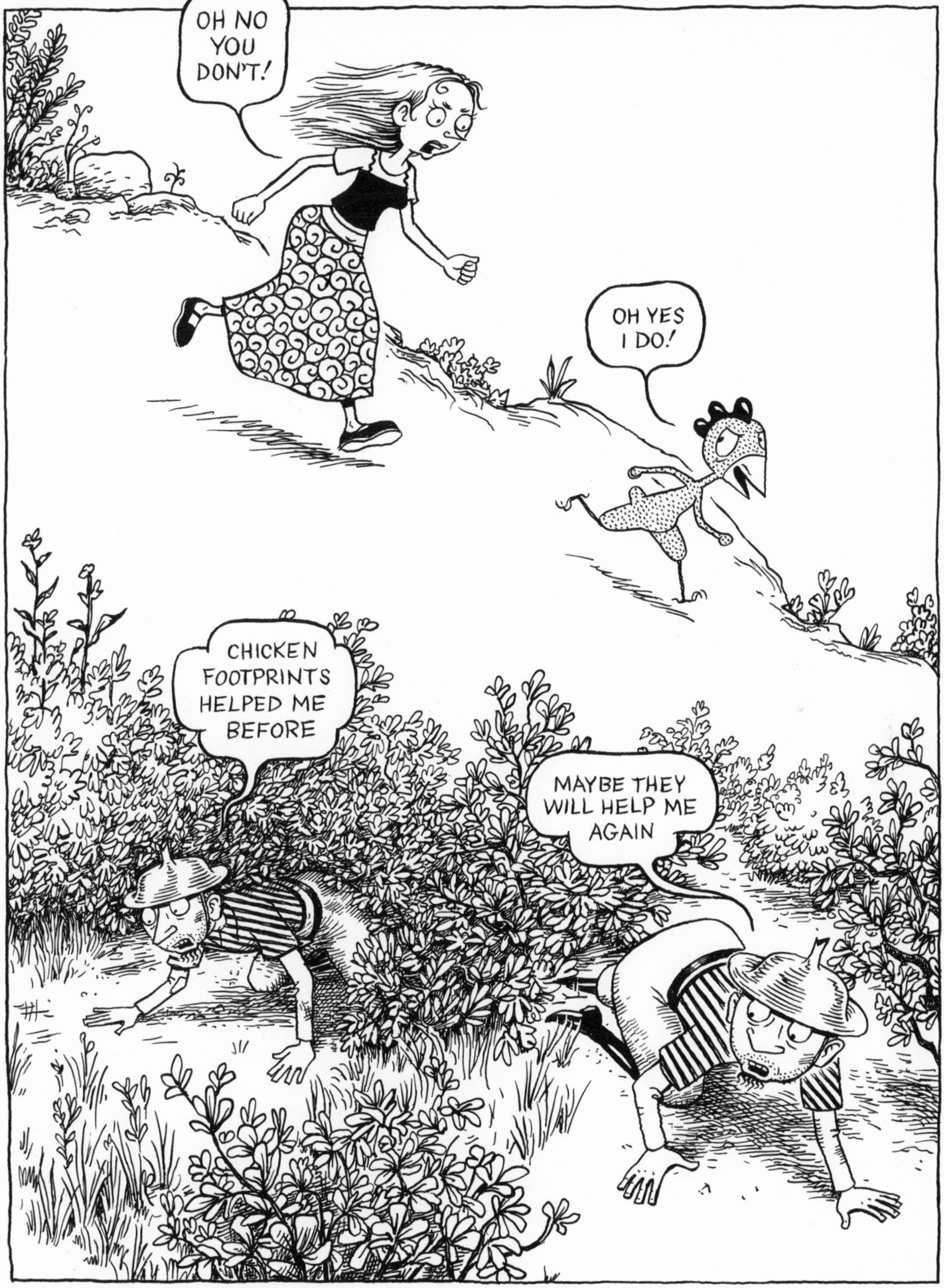
OH NO YOU DON'T!
OH YES I DO!
CHICKEN FOOTPRINTS HELPED ME BEFORE
MAYBE THEY WILL HELP ME AGAIN

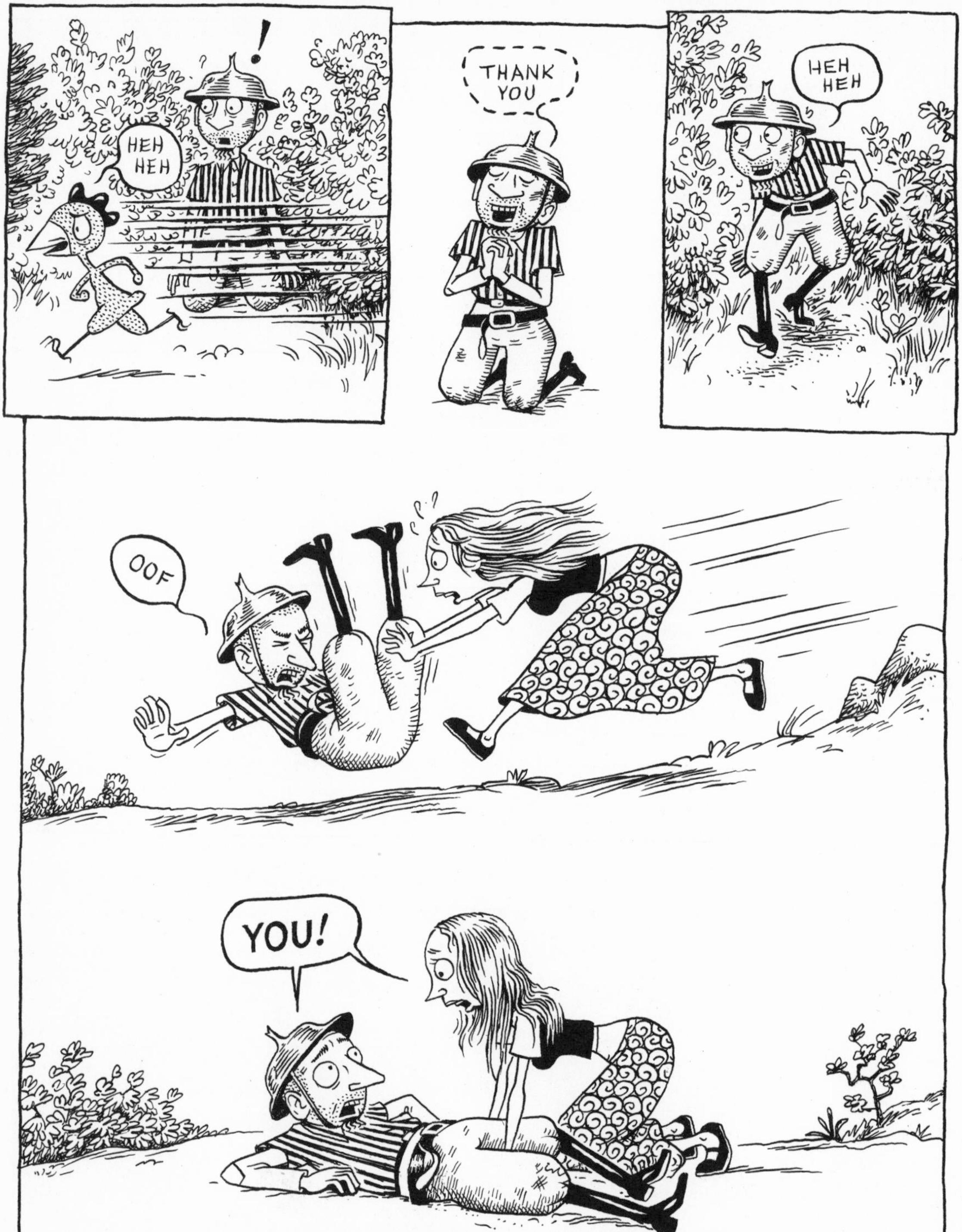
!
HEH HEH
THANK YOU
HEH HEH
OOF
YOU!

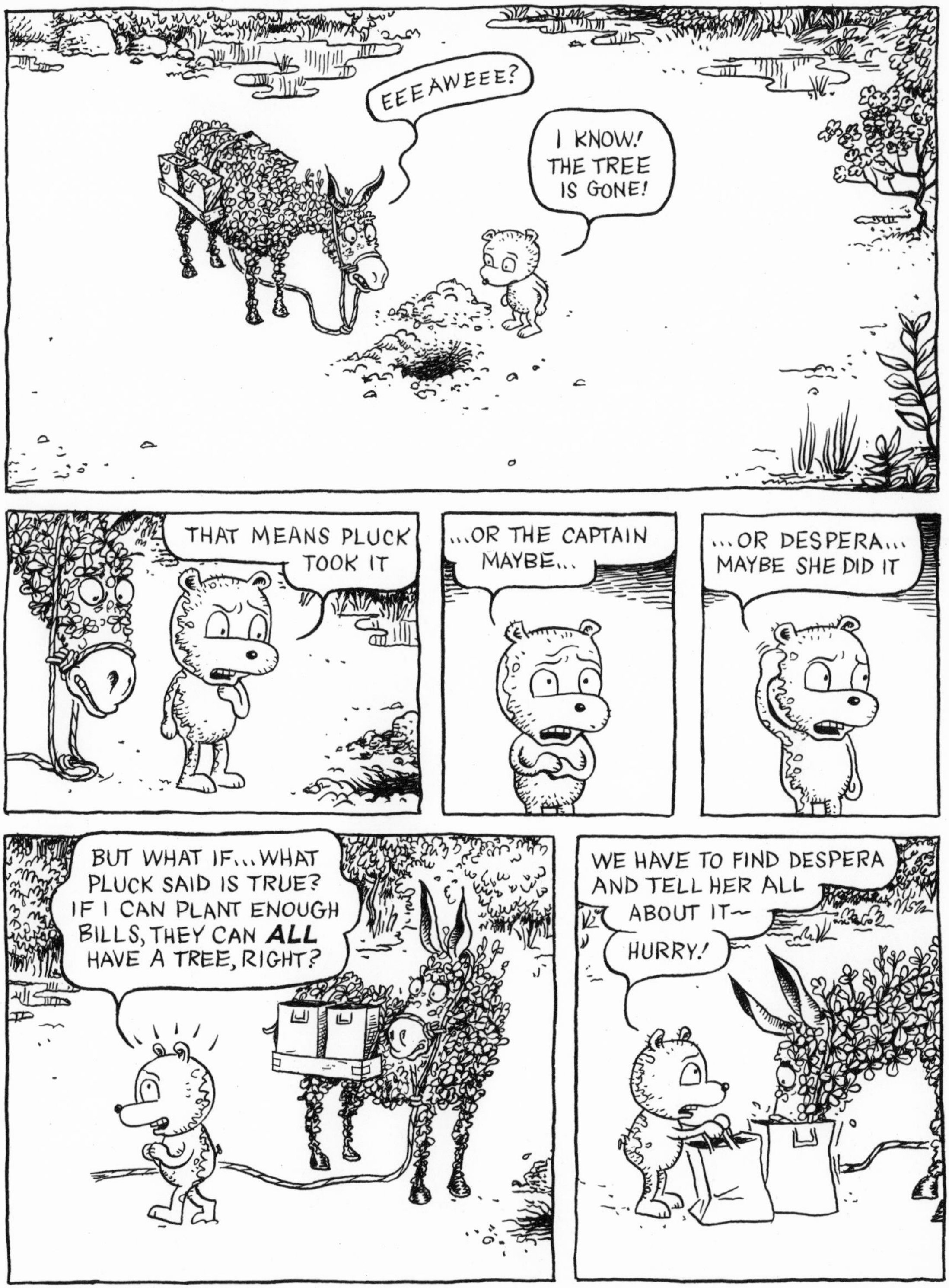
EEEAWEEE?
I KNOW! THE TREE IS GONE!
THAT MEANS PLUCK TOOK IT
...OR THE CAPTAIN MAYBE...
...OR DESPERA... MAYBE SHE DID IT
BUT WHAT IF... WHAT PLUCK SAID IS TRUE? IF I CAN PLANT ENOUGH BILLS, THEY CAN **ALL** HAVE A TREE, RIGHT?
WE HAVE TO FIND DESPERA AND TELL HER ALL ABOUT IT~
HURRY!

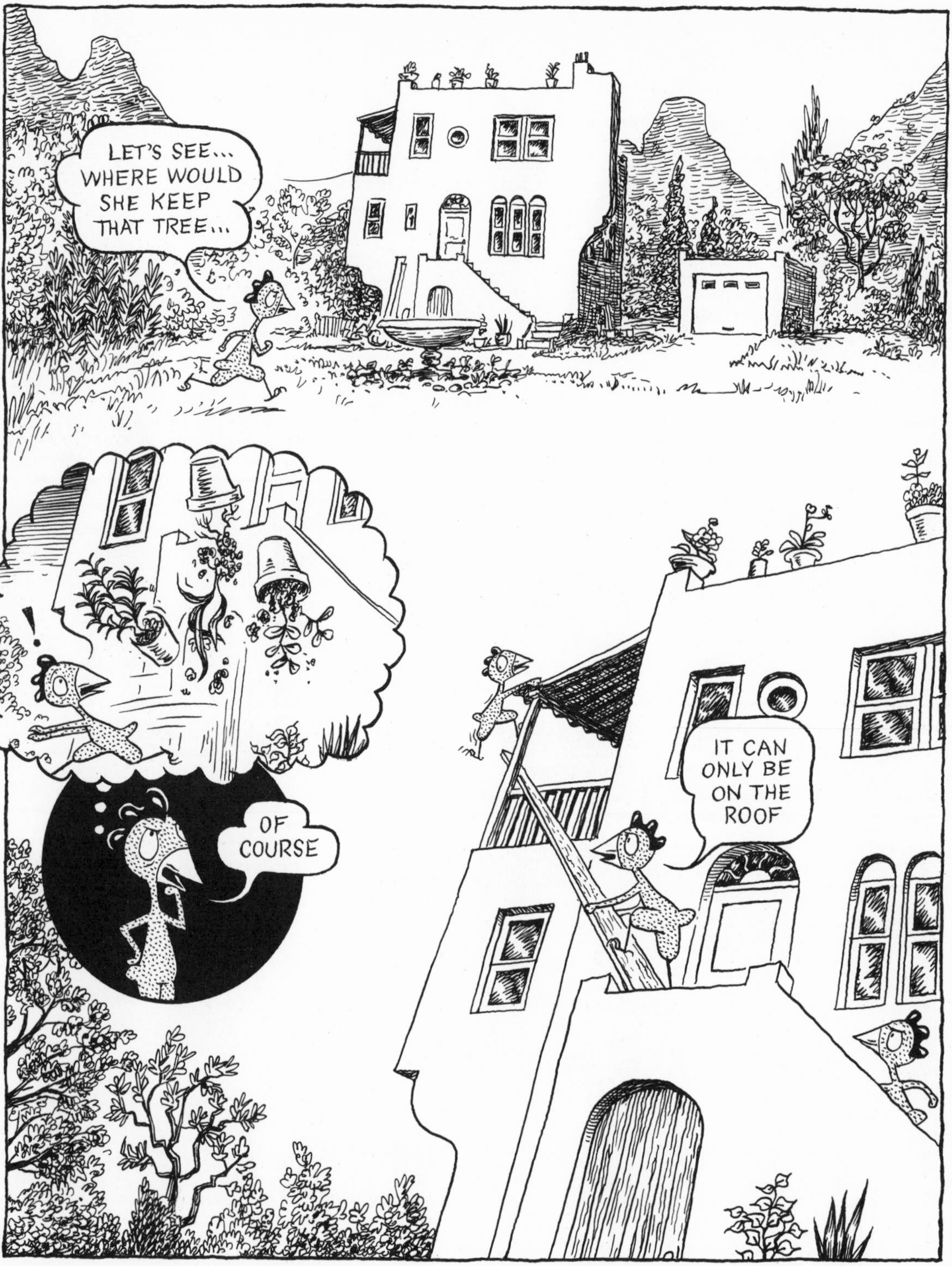
LET'S SEE... WHERE WOULD SHE KEEP THAT TREE...
!
OF COURSE
IT CAN ONLY BE ON THE ROOF

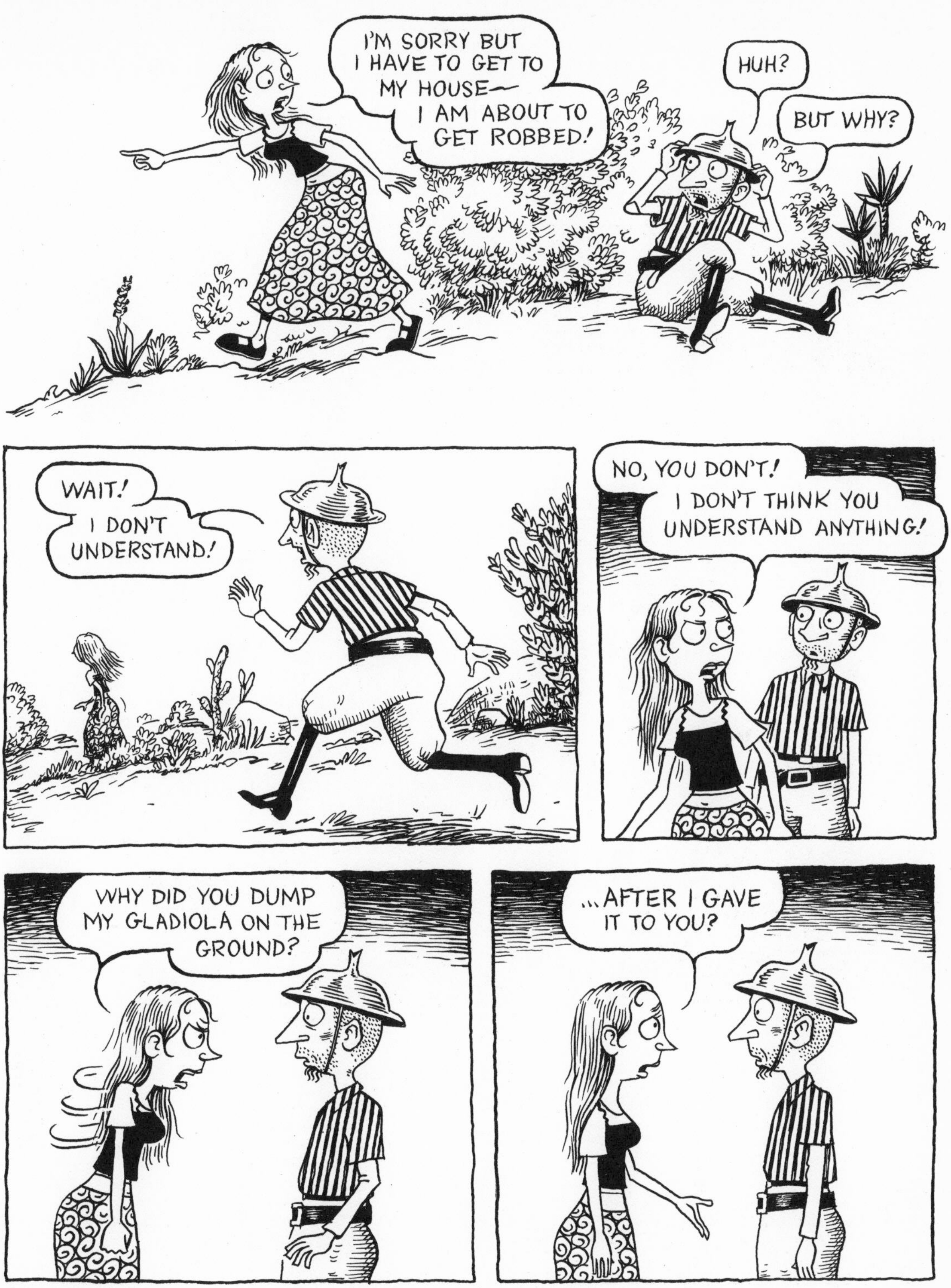
I'M SORRY BUT I HAVE TO GET TO MY HOUSE—
I AM ABOUT TO GET ROBBED!
HUH?
BUT WHY?
WAIT! I DON'T UNDERSTAND!
NO, YOU DON'T!
I DON'T THINK YOU UNDERSTAND ANYTHING!
WHY DID YOU DUMP MY GLADIOLA ON THE GROUND?
...AFTER I GAVE IT TO YOU?

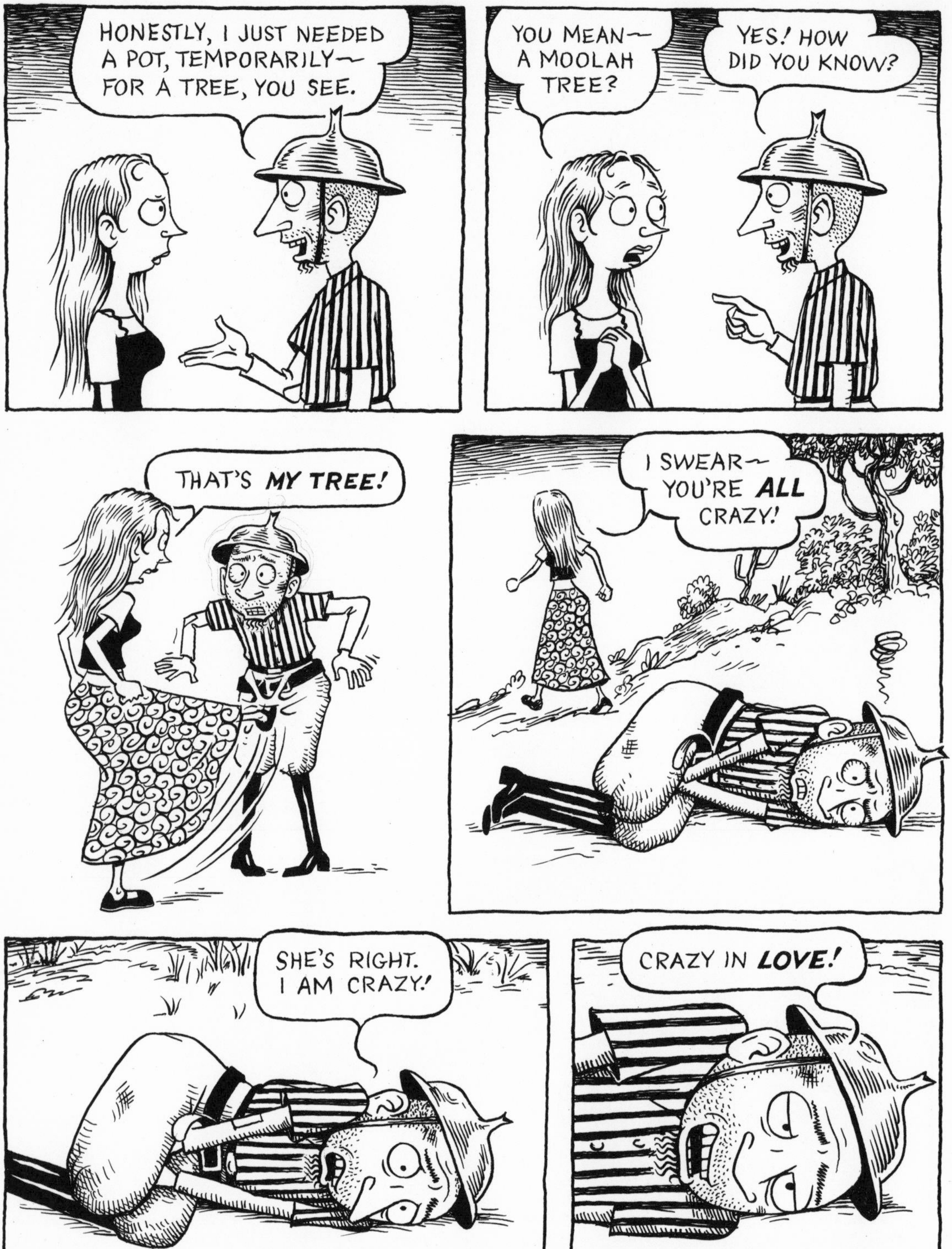
HONESTLY, I JUST NEEDED A POT, TEMPORARILY— FOR A TREE, YOU SEE.
YOU MEAN— A MOOLAH TREE?
YES! HOW DID YOU KNOW?
THAT'S MY TREE!
I SWEAR— YOU'RE ALL CRAZY!
SHE'S RIGHT. I AM CRAZY!
CRAZY IN LOVE!

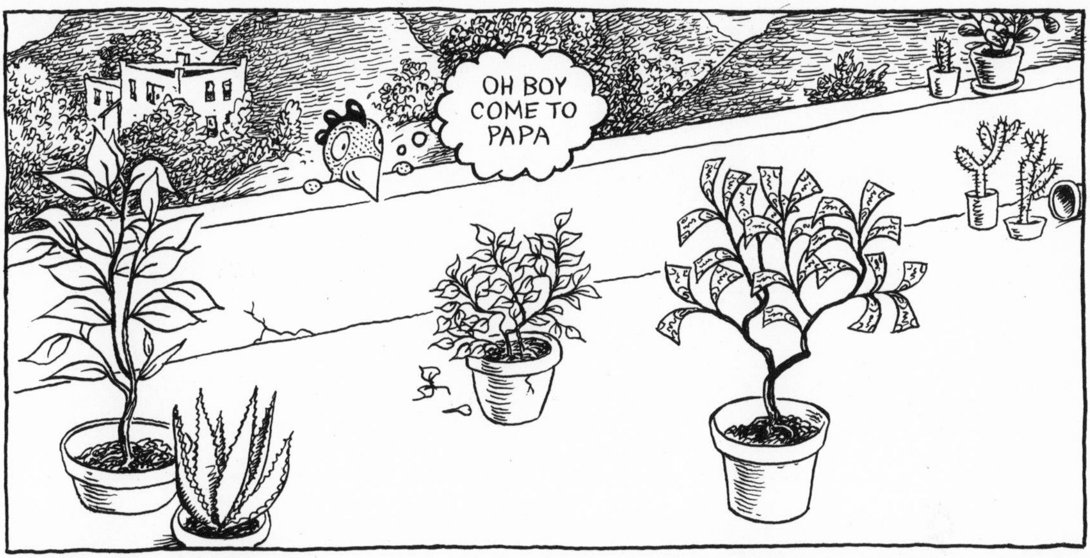
OH BOY COME TO PAPA

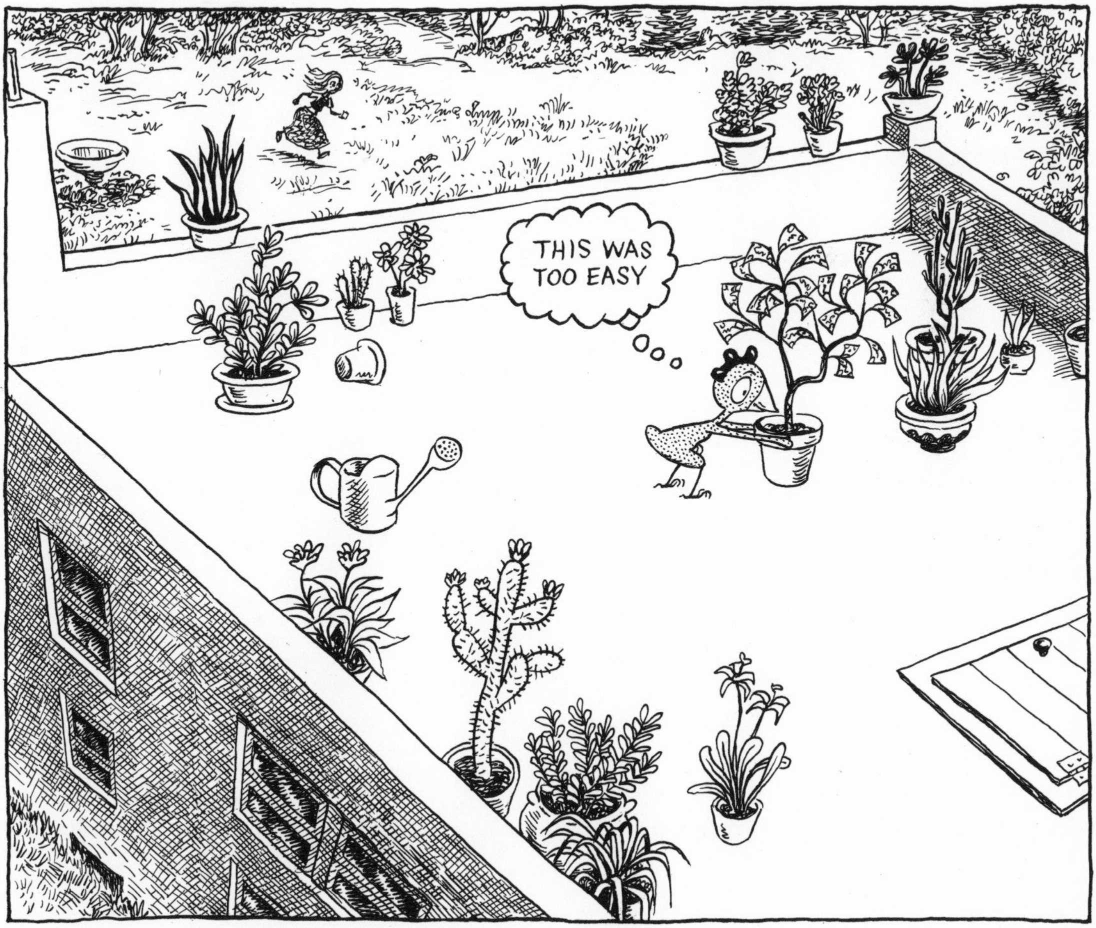
THIS WAS TOO EASY

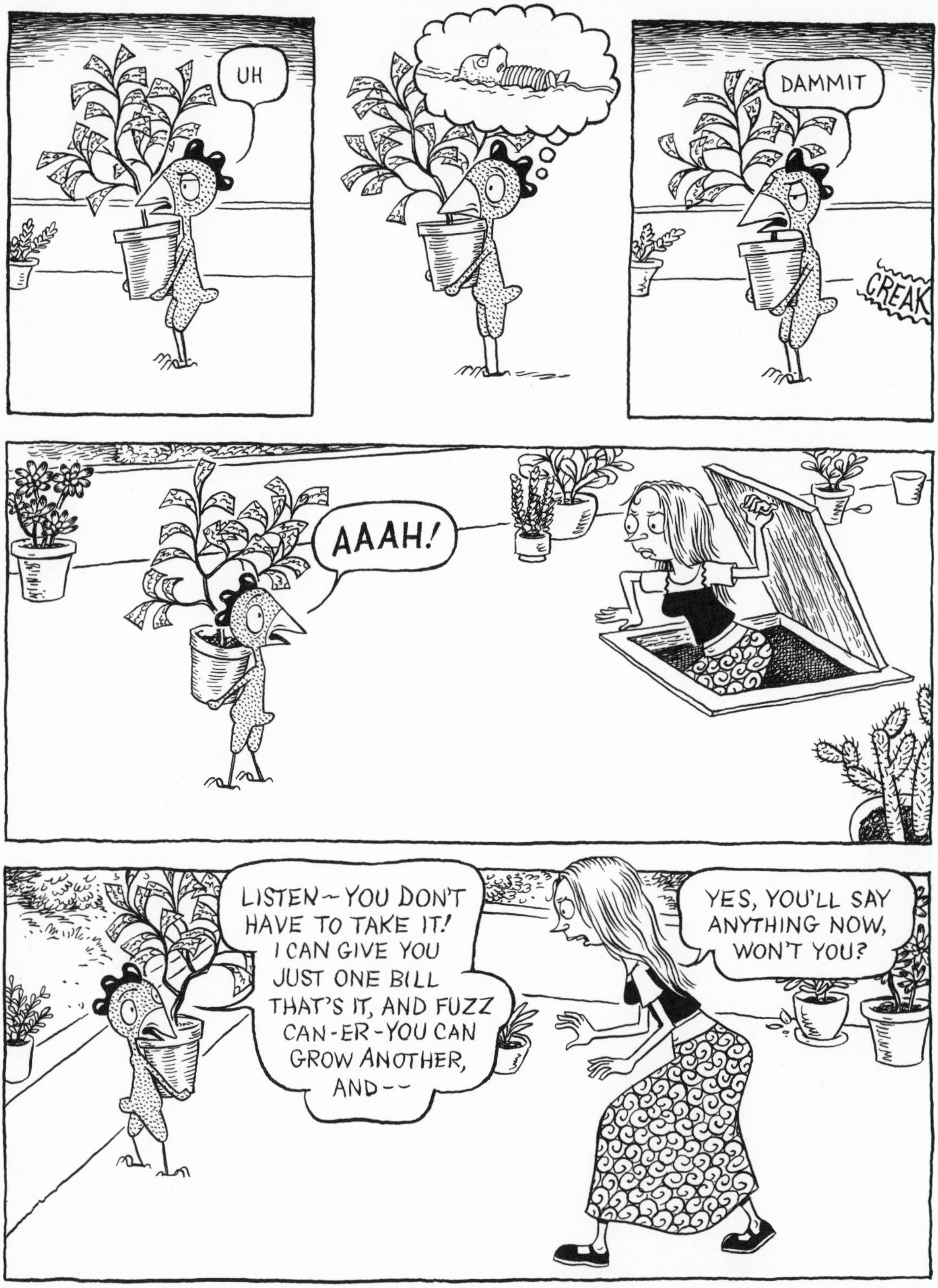
UH
DAMMIT
CREAK
AAAH!
LISTEN ~ YOU DON'T HAVE TO TAKE IT! I CAN GIVE YOU JUST ONE BILL THAT'S IT, AND FUZZ CAN-ER-YOU CAN GROW ANOTHER, AND--
YES, YOU'LL SAY ANYTHING NOW, WON'T YOU?

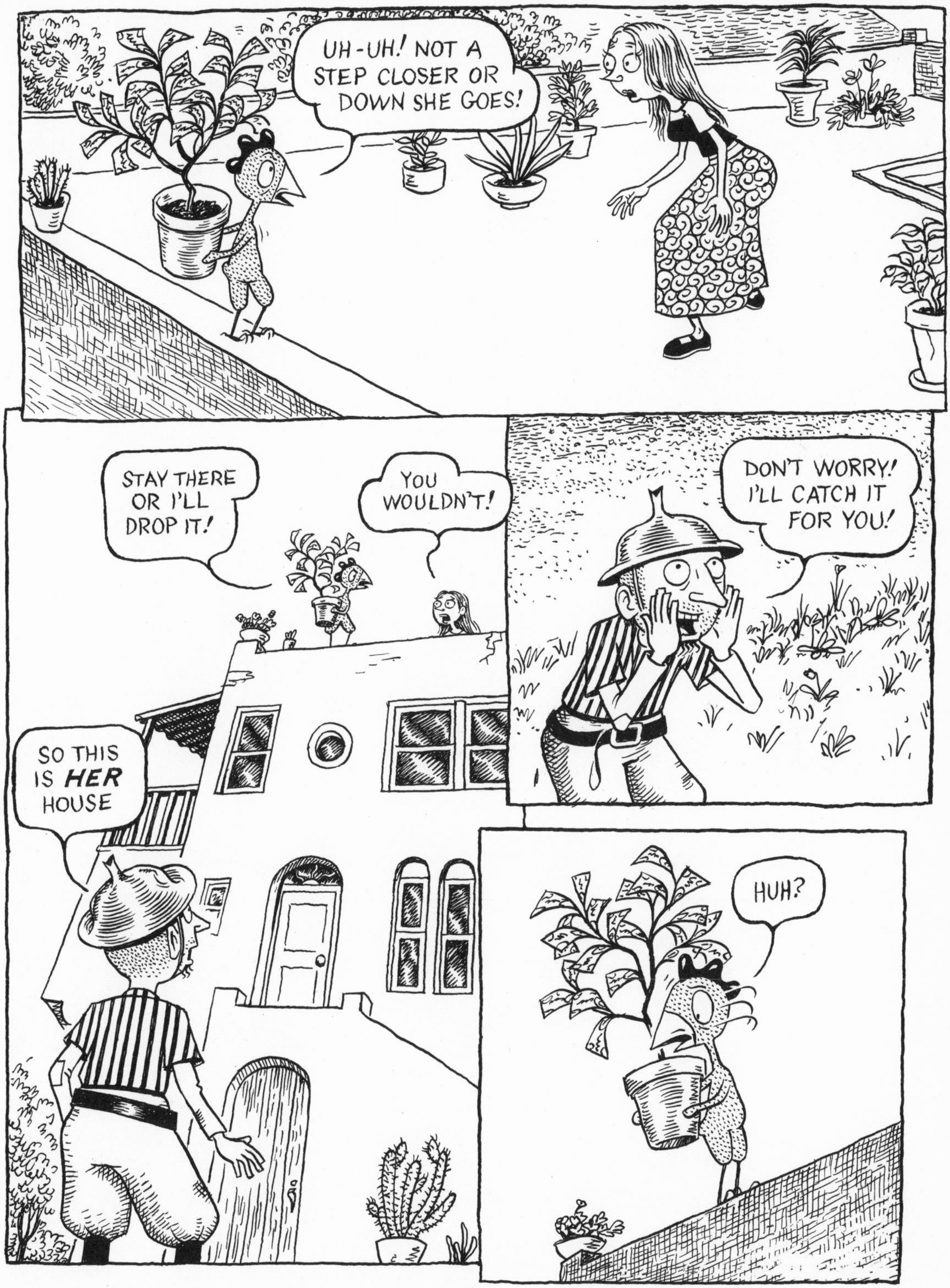
UH-UH! NOT A STEP CLOSER OR DOWN SHE GOES!
STAY THERE OR I'LL DROP IT!
YOU WOULDN'T!
DON'T WORRY! I'LL CATCH IT FOR YOU!
SO THIS IS **HER** HOUSE
HUH?

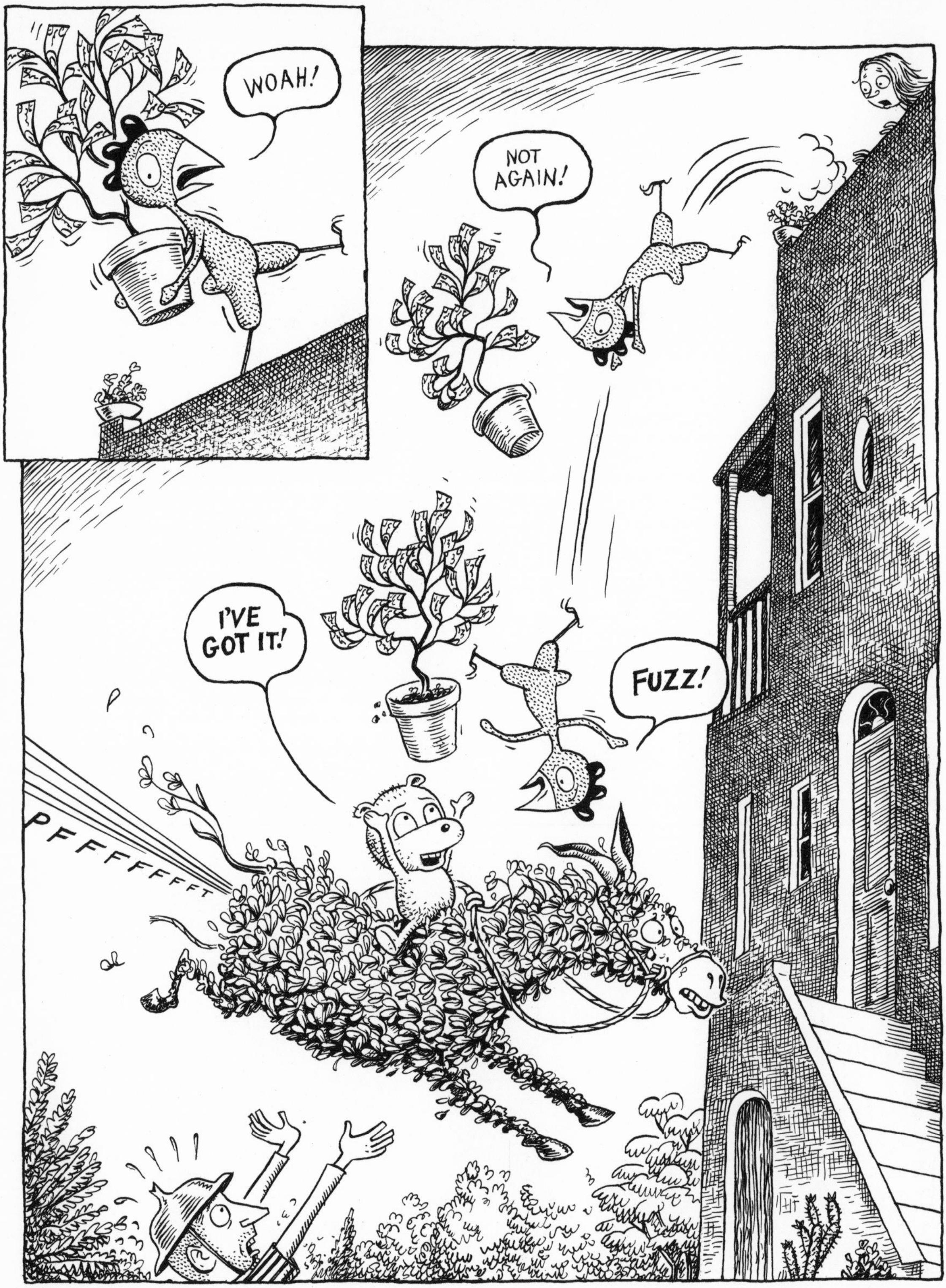
WOAH!
NOT AGAIN!
I'VE GOT IT!
FUZZ!
PFFFFFFFFFT

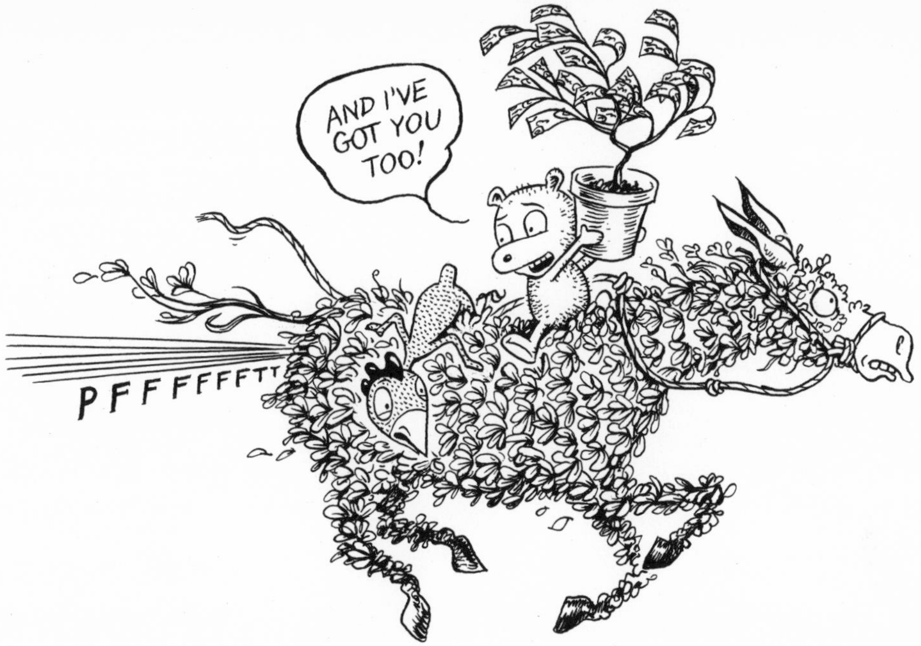
AND I'VE GOT YOU TOO!
PFFFFFFFTTT

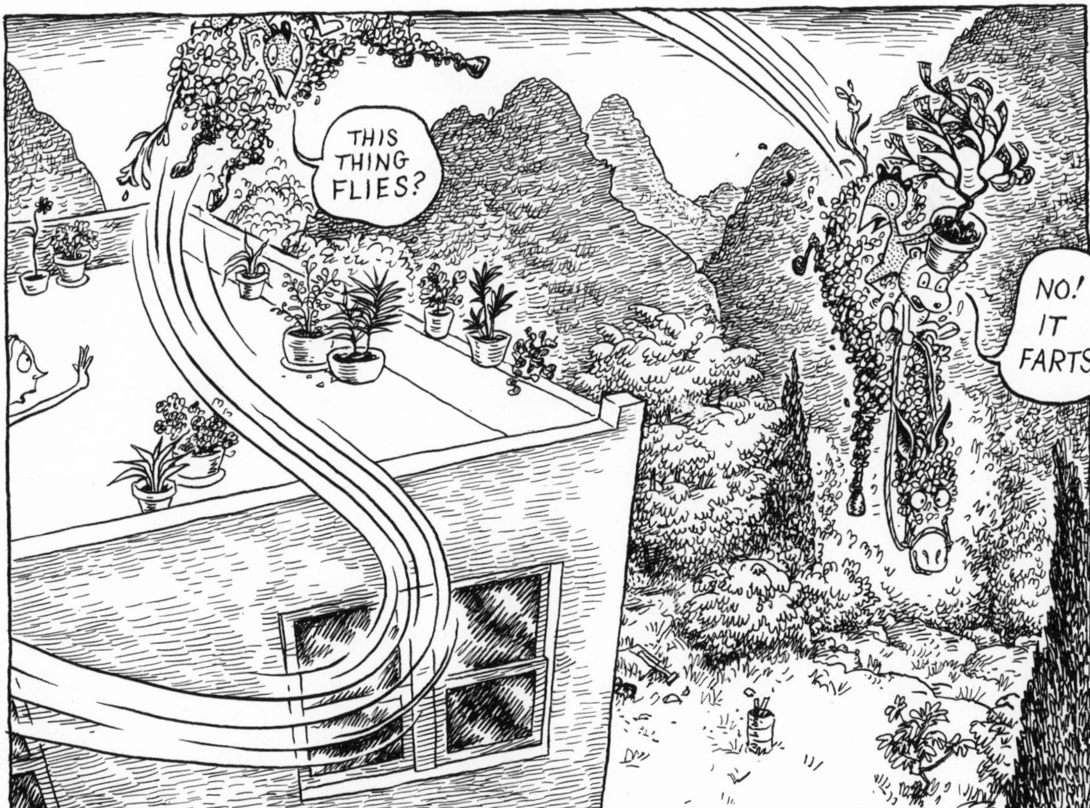
THIS THING FLIES?
NO! IT FARTS

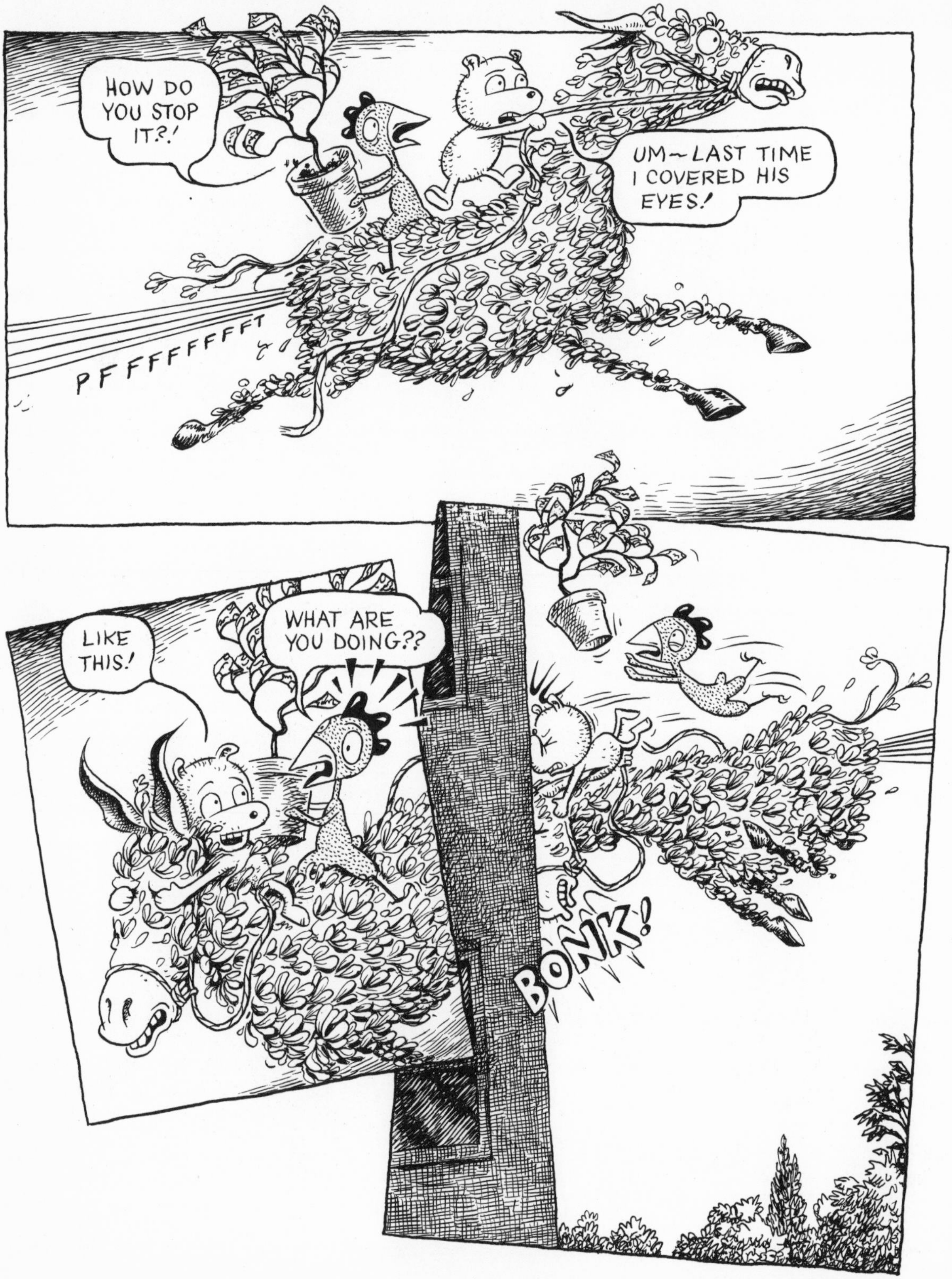
HOW DO YOU STOP IT?!
UM~LAST TIME I COVERED HIS EYES!
PFFFFFFFFT
LIKE THIS!
WHAT ARE YOU DOING??
BONK!

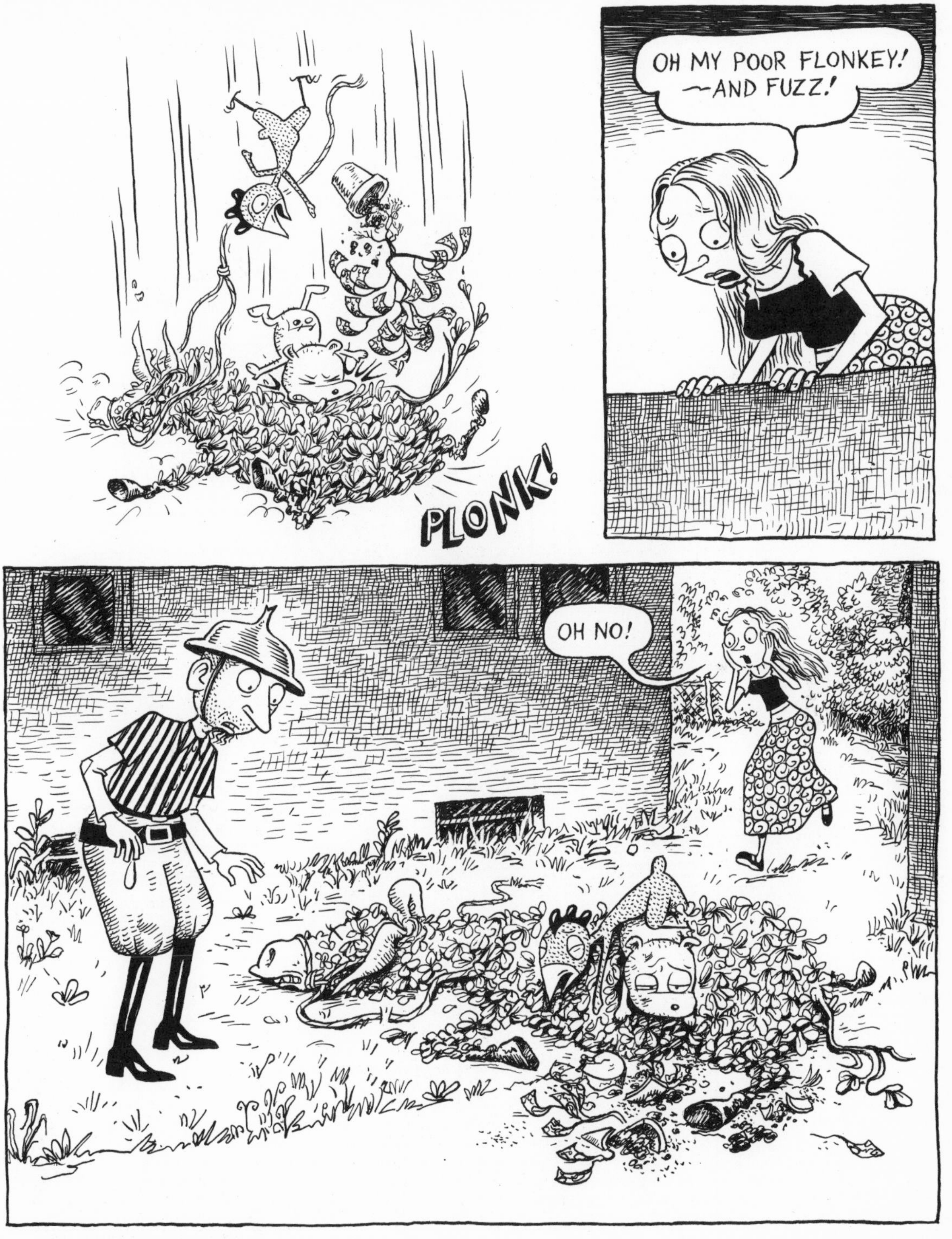
PLONK!
OH MY POOR FLONKEY! —AND FUZZ!
OH NO!

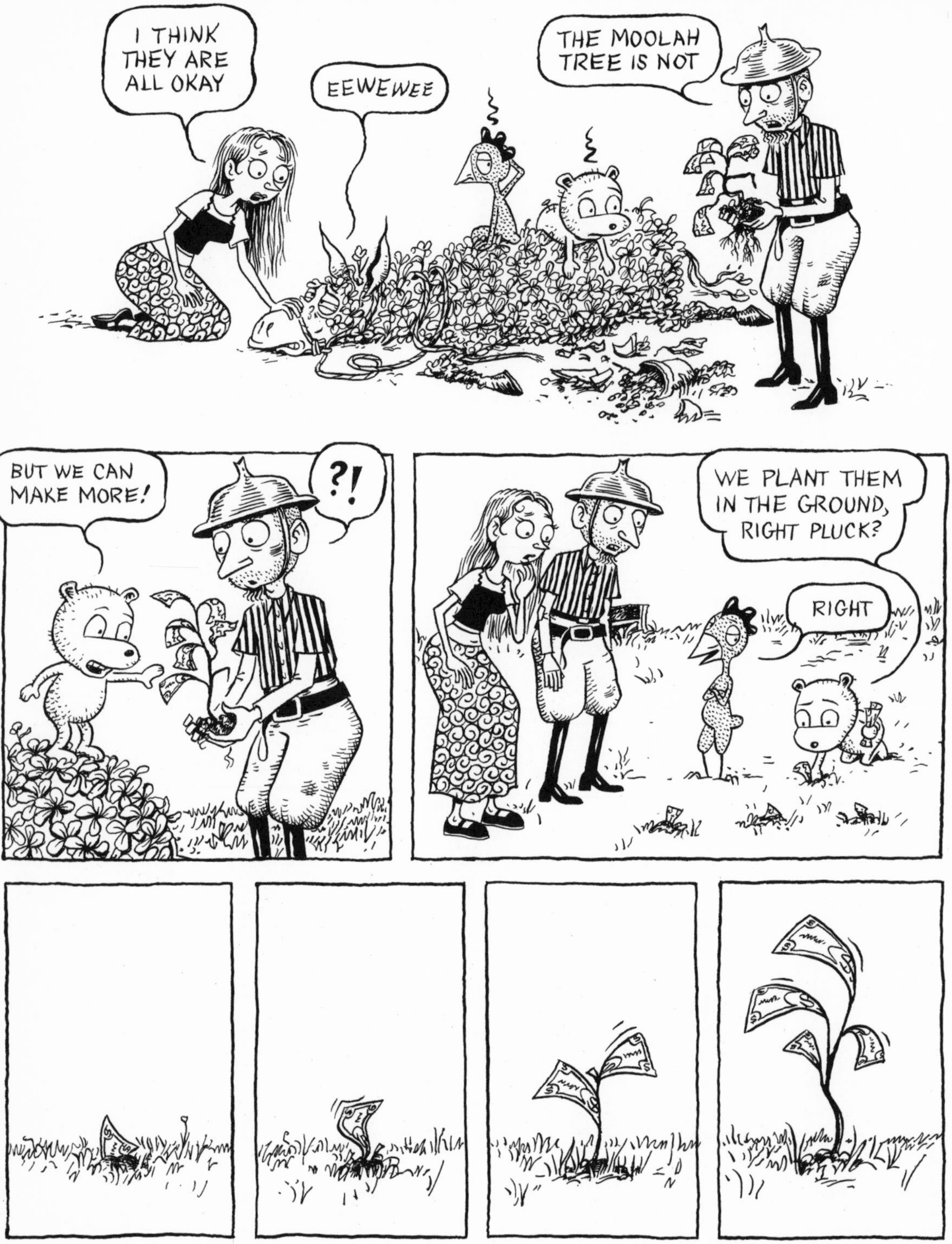
I THINK THEY ARE ALL OKAY
EEWEWEE
THE MOOLAH TREE IS NOT
BUT WE CAN MAKE MORE!
?!
WE PLANT THEM IN THE GROUND, RIGHT PLUCK?
RIGHT

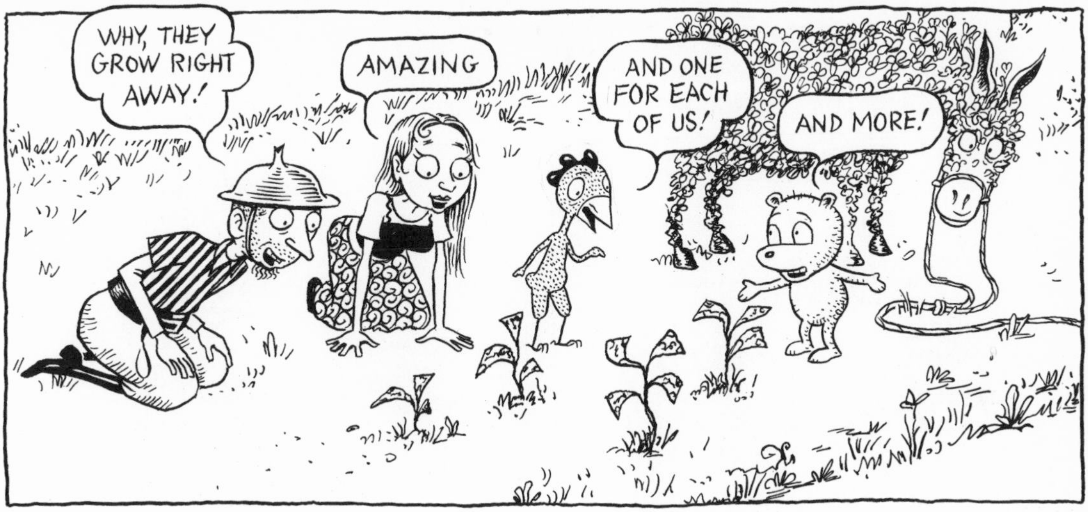
WHY, THEY GROW RIGHT AWAY!
AMAZING
AND ONE FOR EACH OF US!
AND MORE!

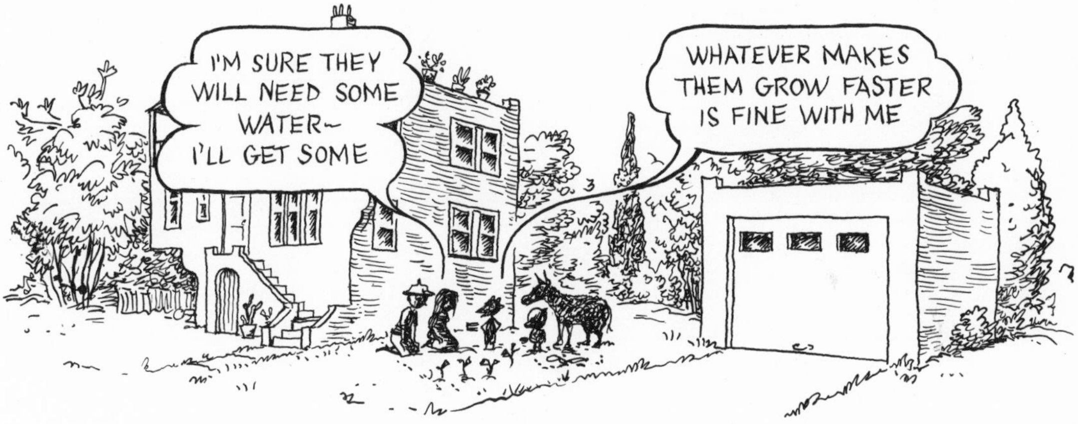
I'M SURE THEY WILL NEED SOME WATER– I'LL GET SOME
WHATEVER MAKES THEM GROW FASTER IS FINE WITH ME

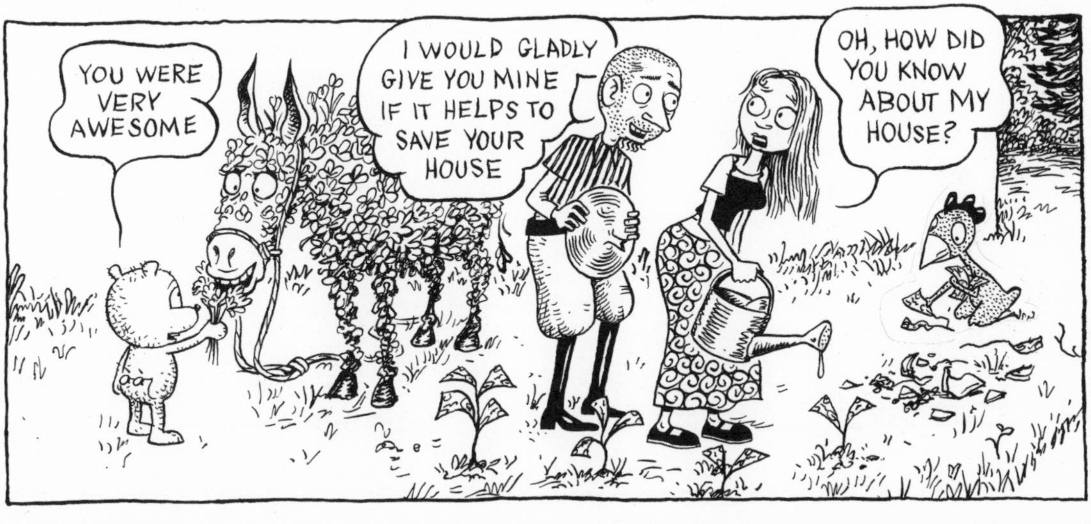
YOU WERE VERY AWESOME
I WOULD GLADLY GIVE YOU MINE IF IT HELPS TO SAVE YOUR HOUSE
OH, HOW DID YOU KNOW ABOUT MY HOUSE?

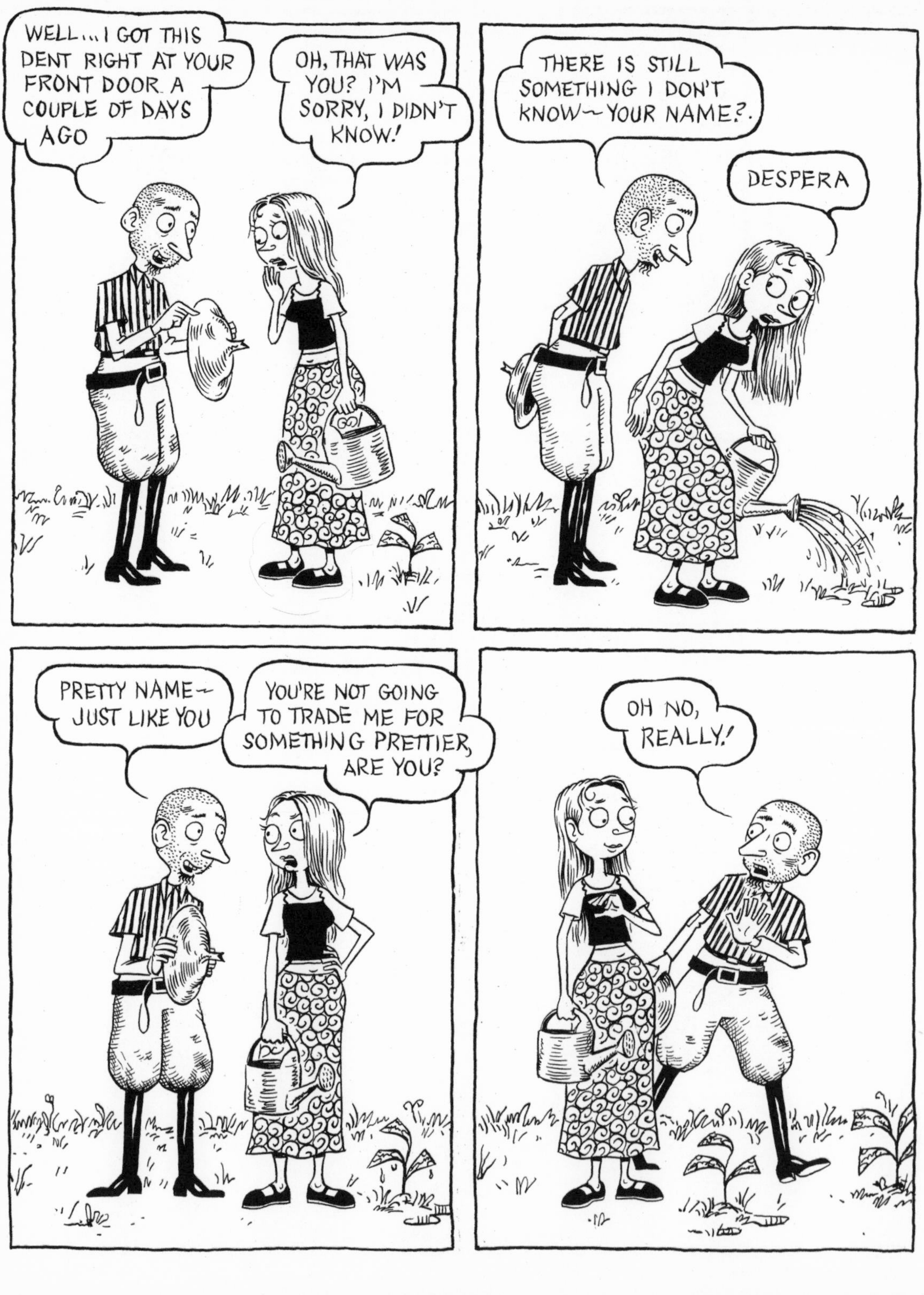
WELL... I GOT THIS DENT RIGHT AT YOUR FRONT DOOR A COUPLE OF DAYS AGO
OH, THAT WAS YOU? I'M SORRY, I DIDN'T KNOW!
THERE IS STILL SOMETHING I DON'T KNOW~ YOUR NAME?.
DESPERA
PRETTY NAME~ JUST LIKE YOU
YOU'RE NOT GOING TO TRADE ME FOR SOMETHING PRETTIER, ARE YOU?
OH NO, REALLY!

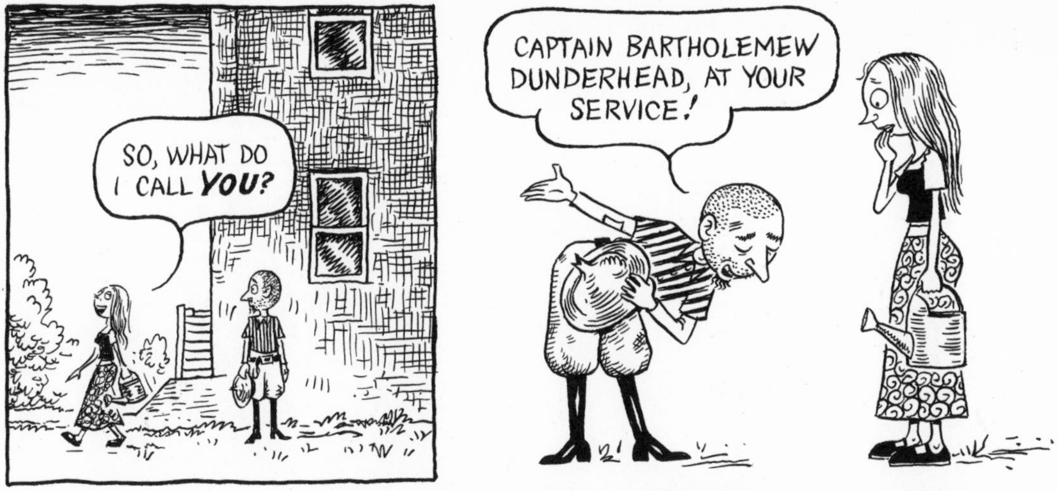
SO, WHAT DO I CALL YOU?
CAPTAIN BARTHOLEMEW DUNDERHEAD, AT YOUR SERVICE!
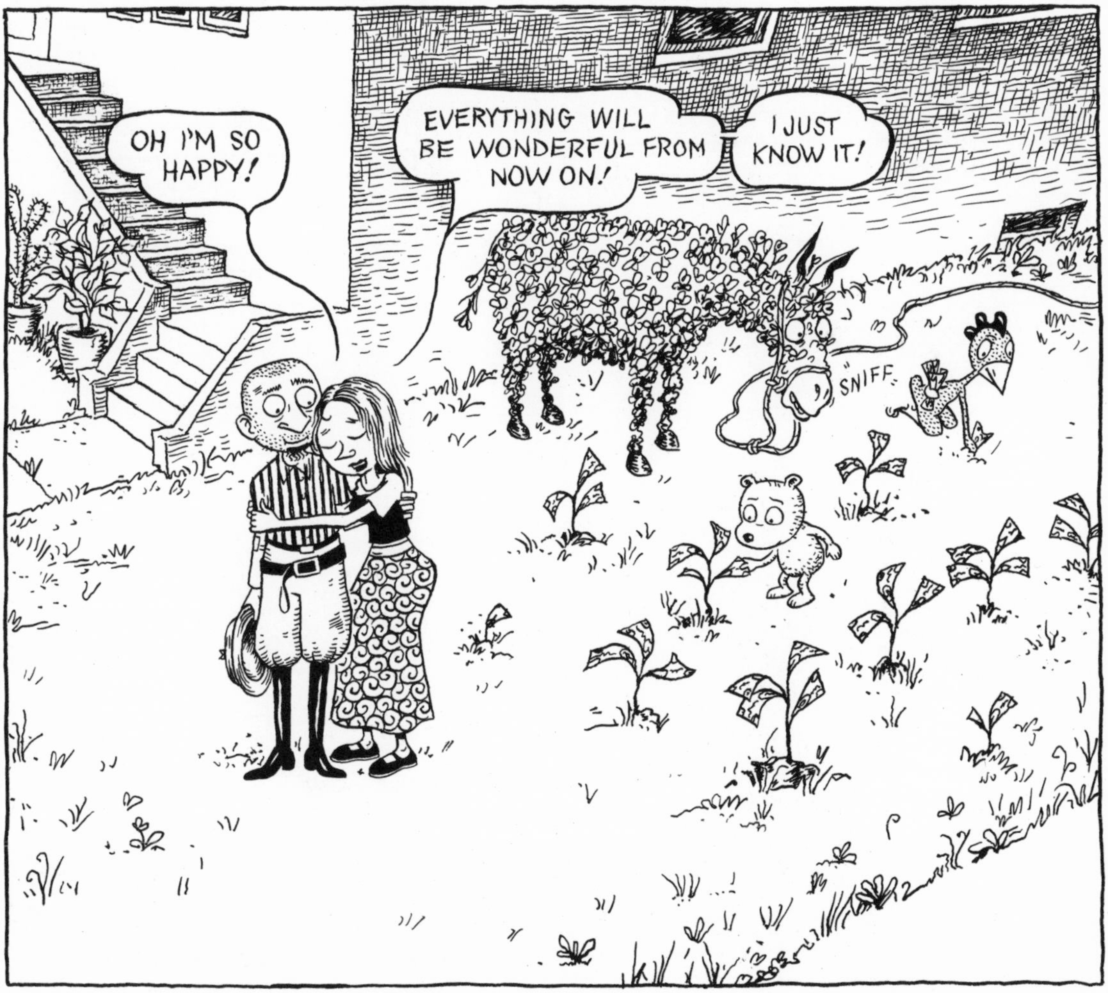
OH I'M SO HAPPY!
EVERYTHING WILL BE WONDERFUL FROM NOW ON!
I JUST KNOW IT!
SNIFF

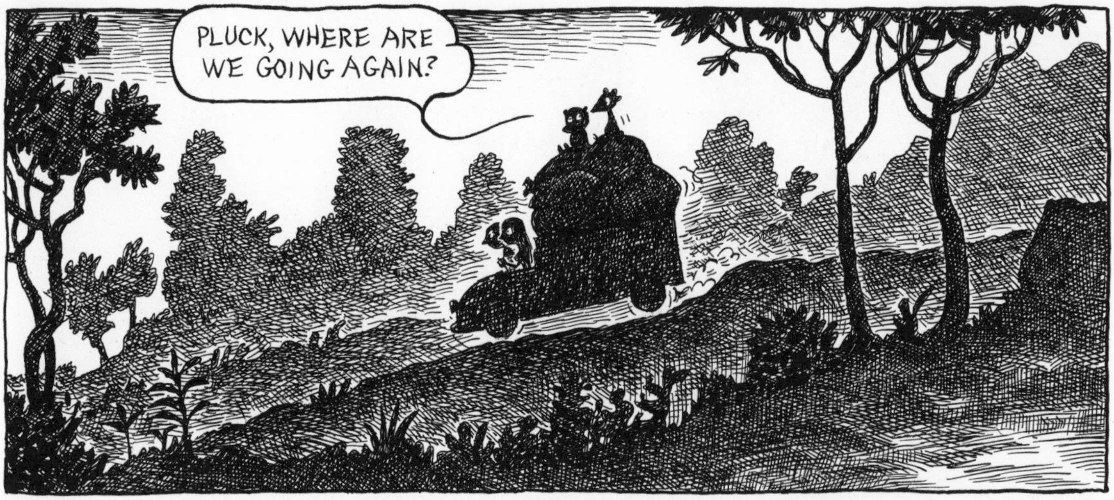
PLUCK, WHERE ARE WE GOING AGAIN?

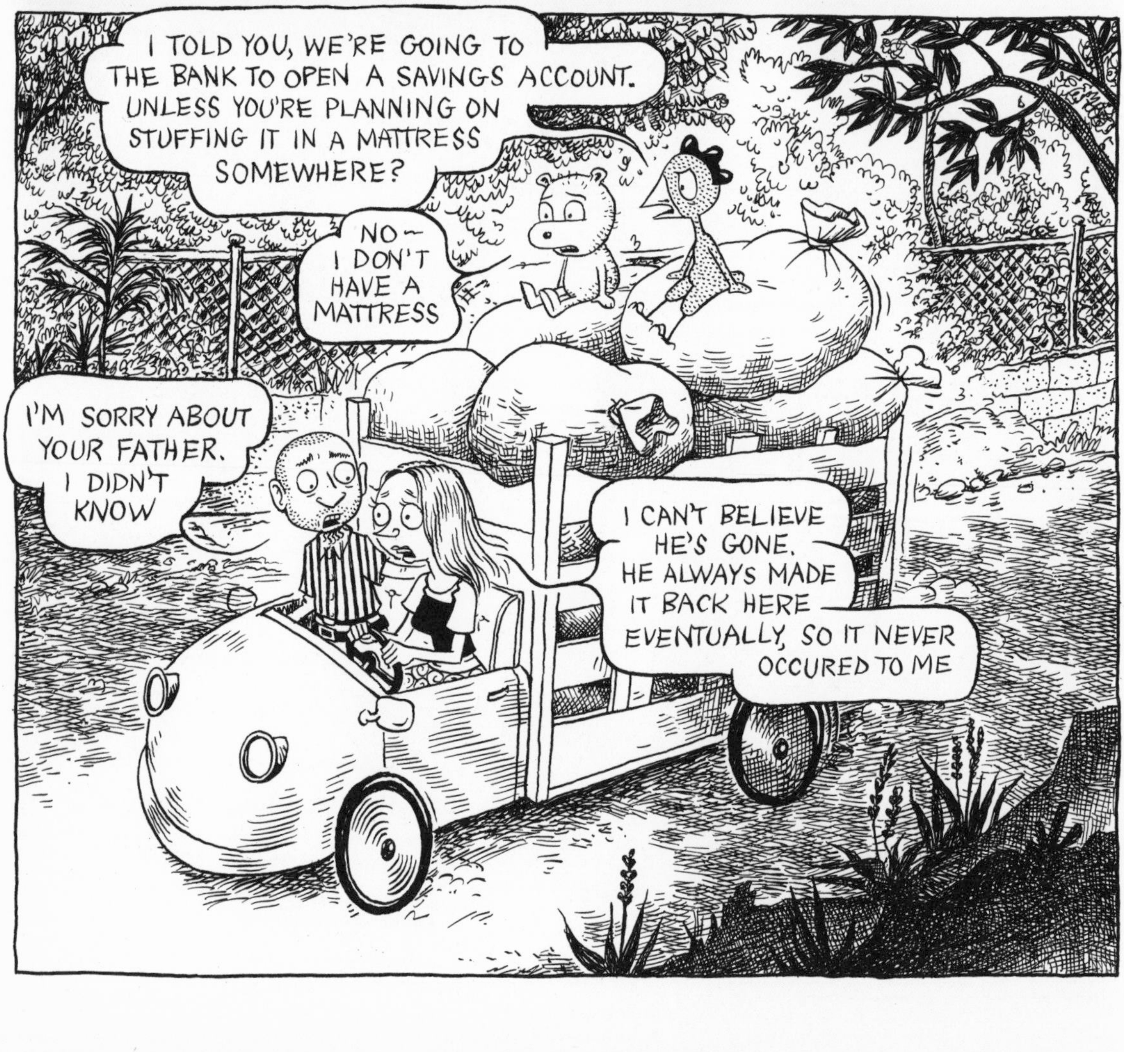
I TOLD YOU, WE'RE GOING TO THE BANK TO OPEN A SAVINGS ACCOUNT. UNLESS YOU'RE PLANNING ON STUFFING IT IN A MATTRESS SOMEWHERE?
NO~ I DON'T HAVE A MATTRESS
I'M SORRY ABOUT YOUR FATHER. I DIDN'T KNOW
I CAN'T BELIEVE HE'S GONE. HE ALWAYS MADE IT BACK HERE EVENTUALLY, SO IT NEVER OCCURED TO ME

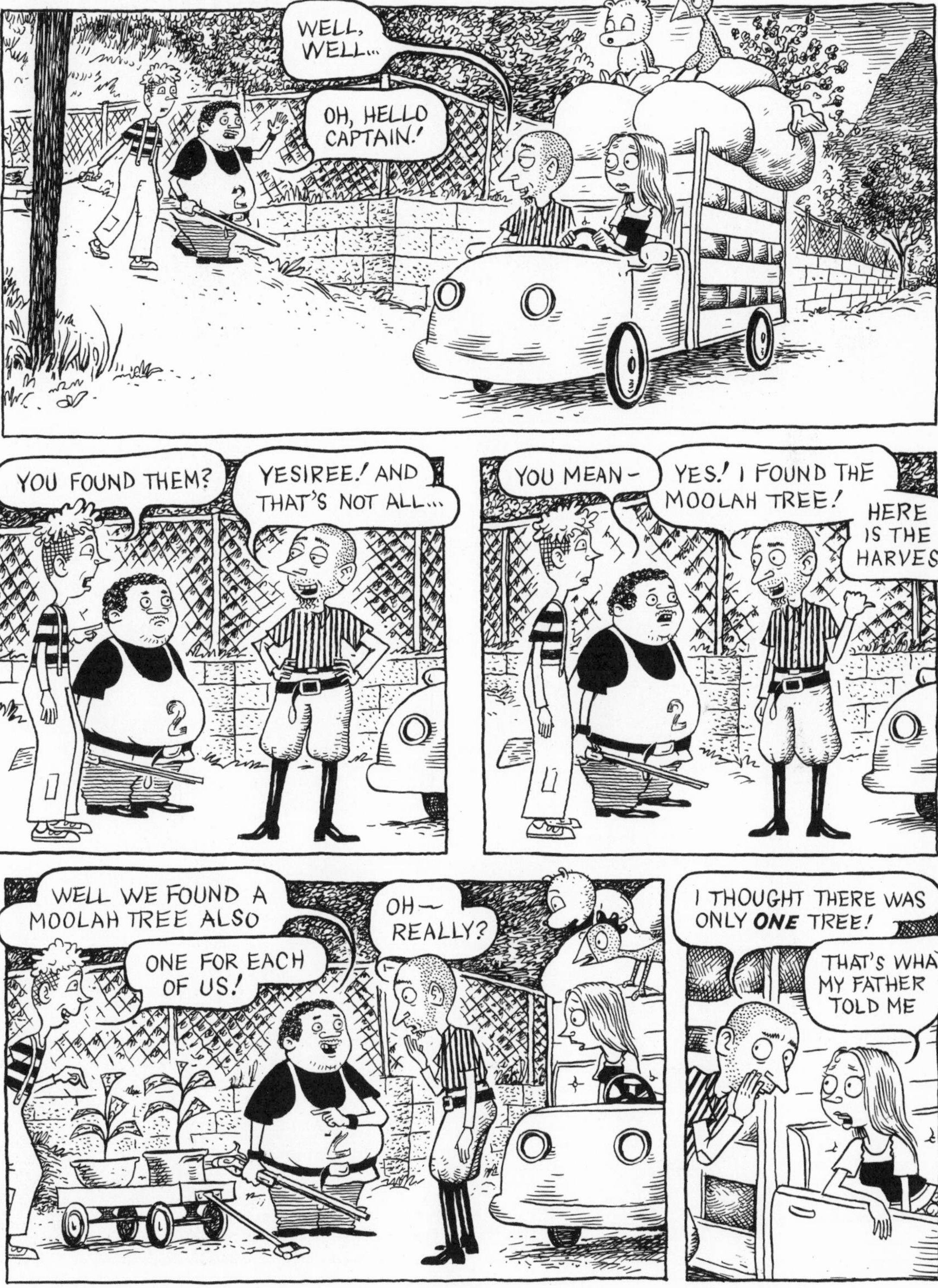
WELL, WELL...
OH, HELLO CAPTAIN!
YOU FOUND THEM?
YESIREE! AND THAT'S NOT ALL...
YOU MEAN-
YES! I FOUND THE MOOLAH TREE!
HERE IS THE HARVEST!
WELL WE FOUND A MOOLAH TREE ALSO
ONE FOR EACH OF US!
OH— REALLY?
I THOUGHT THERE WAS ONLY ONE TREE!
THAT'S WHAT MY FATHER TOLD ME

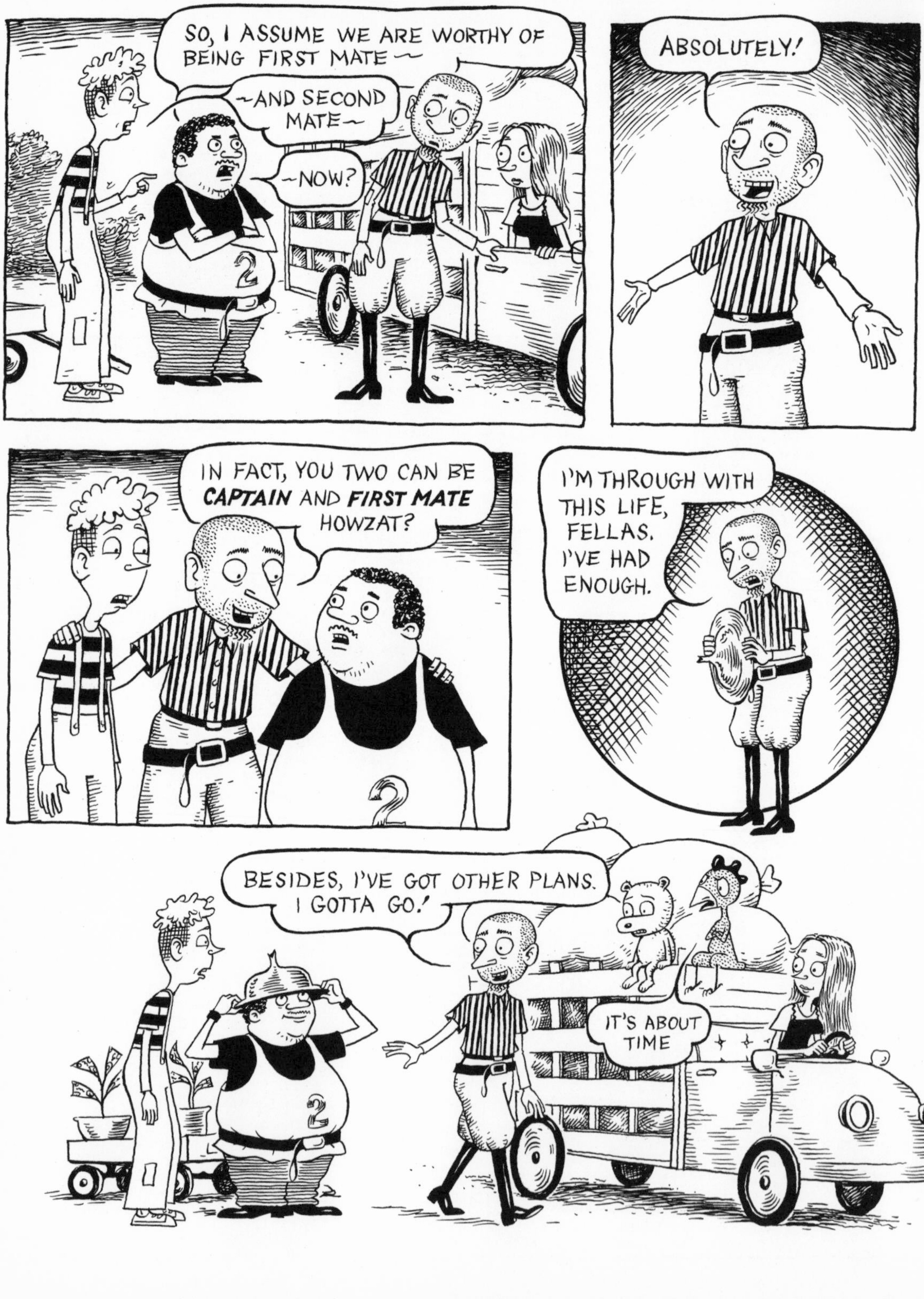
SO, I ASSUME WE ARE WORTHY OF BEING FIRST MATE~
~AND SECOND MATE~
~NOW?
ABSOLUTELY!
IN FACT, YOU TWO CAN BE **CAPTAIN** AND **FIRST MATE** HOWZAT?
I'M THROUGH WITH THIS LIFE, FELLAS. I'VE HAD ENOUGH.
BESIDES, I'VE GOT OTHER PLANS. I GOTTA GO!
IT'S ABOUT TIME

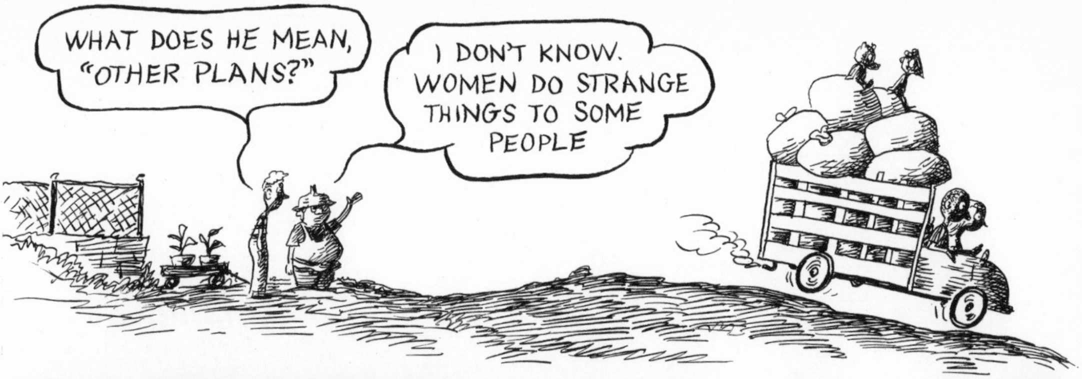
WHAT DOES HE MEAN, "OTHER PLANS?"
I DON'T KNOW. WOMEN DO STRANGE THINGS TO SOME PEOPLE

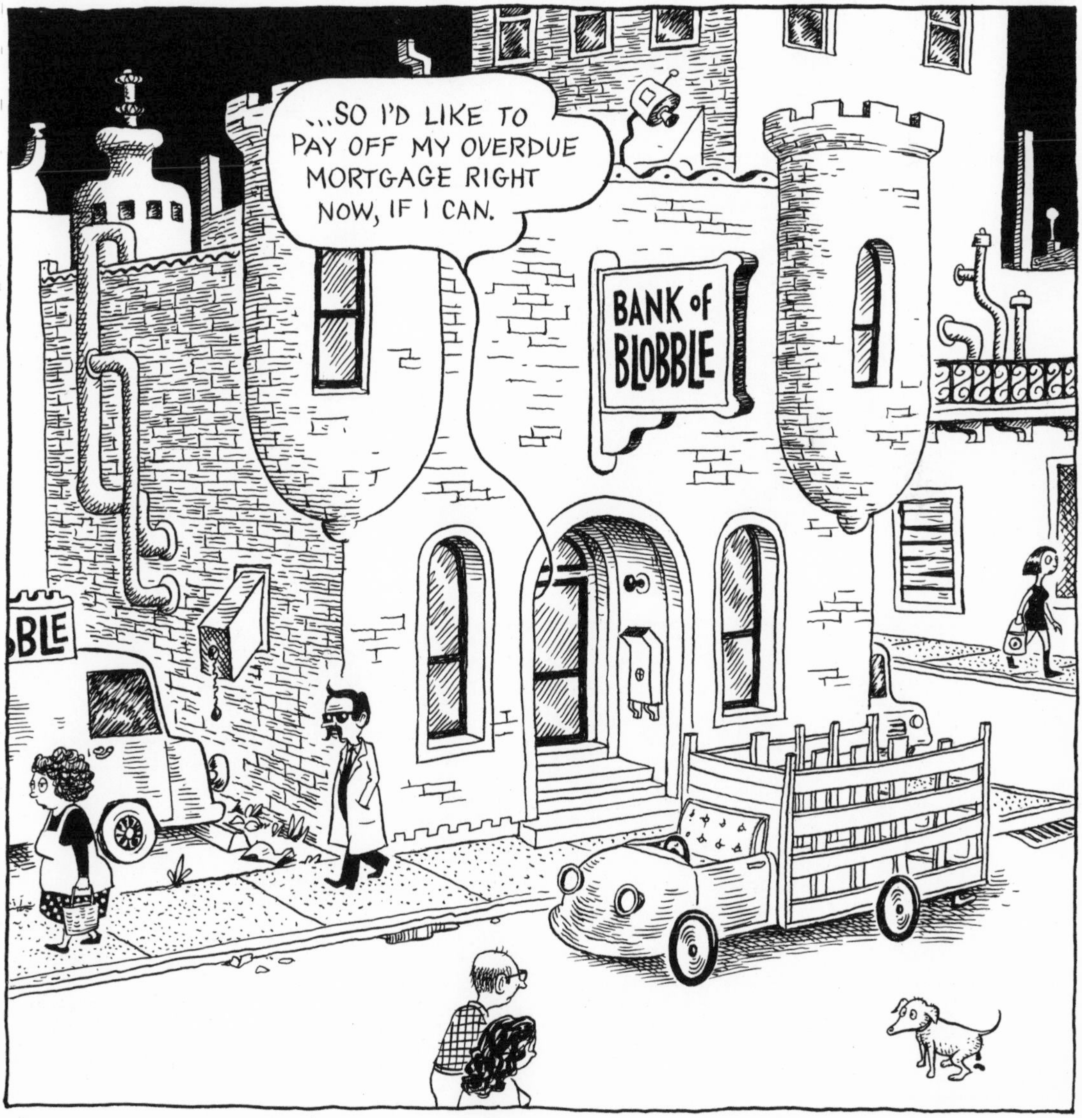
...SO I'D LIKE TO PAY OFF MY OVERDUE MORTGAGE RIGHT NOW, IF I CAN.
BANK of BLOBBLE
BLE

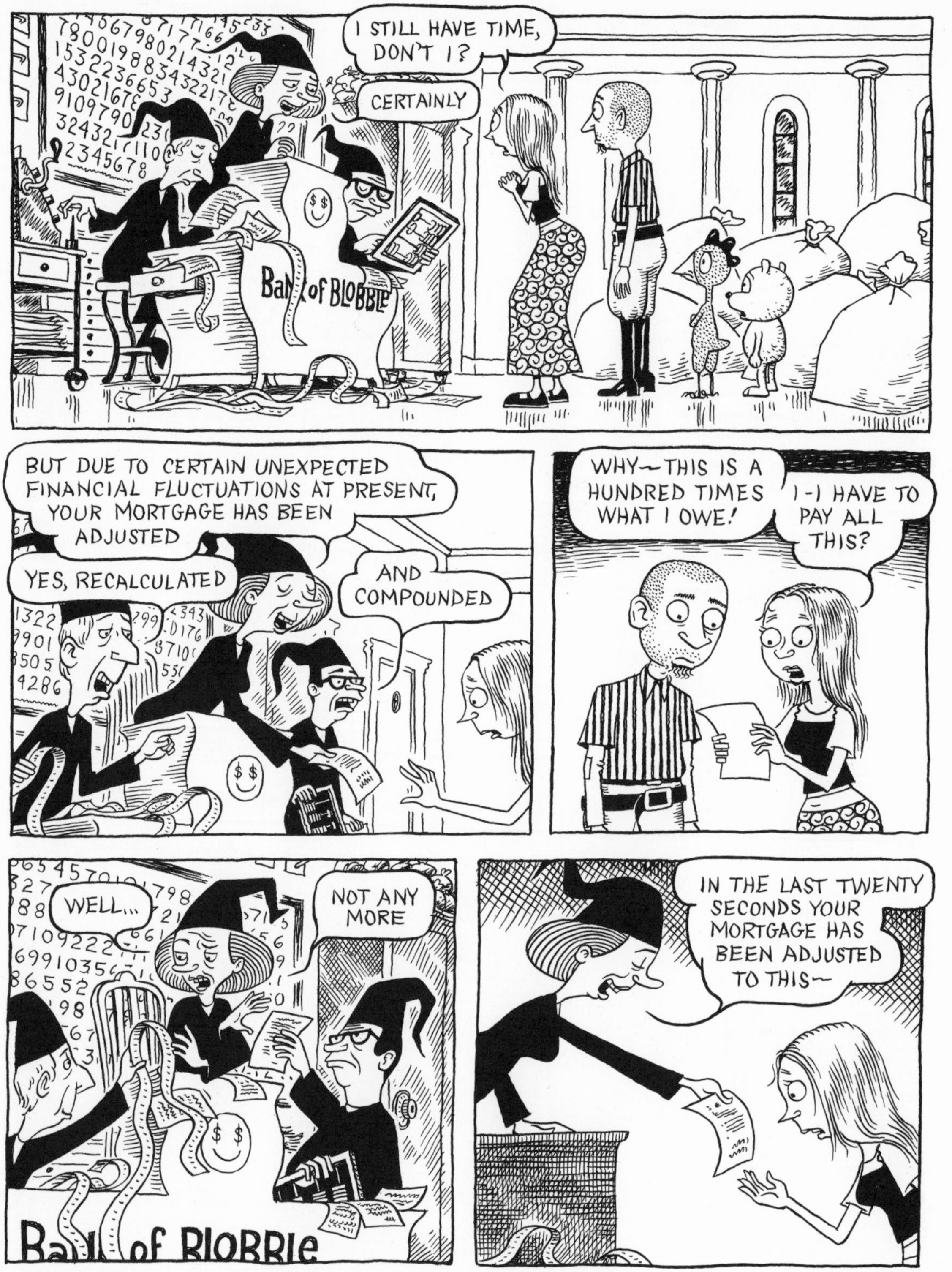

I STILL HAVE TIME, DON'T I?
CERTAINLY
Bank of BLOBBLE
BUT DUE TO CERTAIN UNEXPECTED FINANCIAL FLUCTUATIONS AT PRESENT, YOUR MORTGAGE HAS BEEN ADJUSTED
YES, RECALCULATED
AND COMPOUNDED
WHY—THIS IS A HUNDRED TIMES WHAT I OWE!
I-I HAVE TO PAY ALL THIS?
WELL...
NOT ANY MORE
Bank of BLOBBLE
IN THE LAST TWENTY SECONDS YOUR MORTGAGE HAS BEEN ADJUSTED TO THIS—

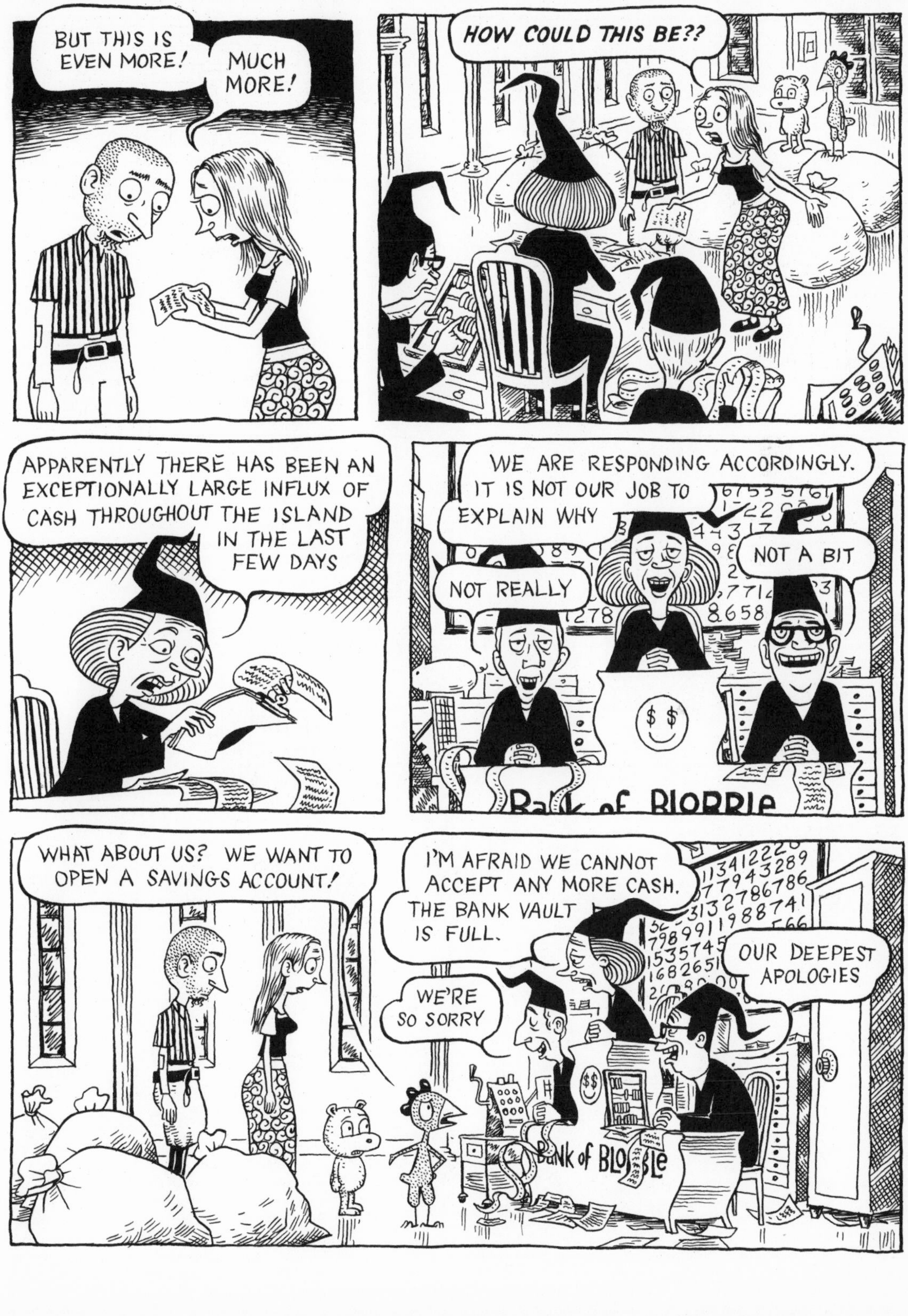

BUT THIS IS EVEN MORE!
MUCH MORE!
HOW COULD THIS BE??
APPARENTLY THERE HAS BEEN AN EXCEPTIONALLY LARGE INFLUX OF CASH THROUGHOUT THE ISLAND IN THE LAST FEW DAYS
WE ARE RESPONDING ACCORDINGLY.
IT IS NOT OUR JOB TO EXPLAIN WHY
NOT REALLY
NOT A BIT
BANK of BLORBLE
WHAT ABOUT US? WE WANT TO OPEN A SAVINGS ACCOUNT!
I'M AFRAID WE CANNOT ACCEPT ANY MORE CASH. THE BANK VAULT IS FULL.
WE'RE SO SORRY
OUR DEEPEST APOLOGIES
Bank of BLORBLE

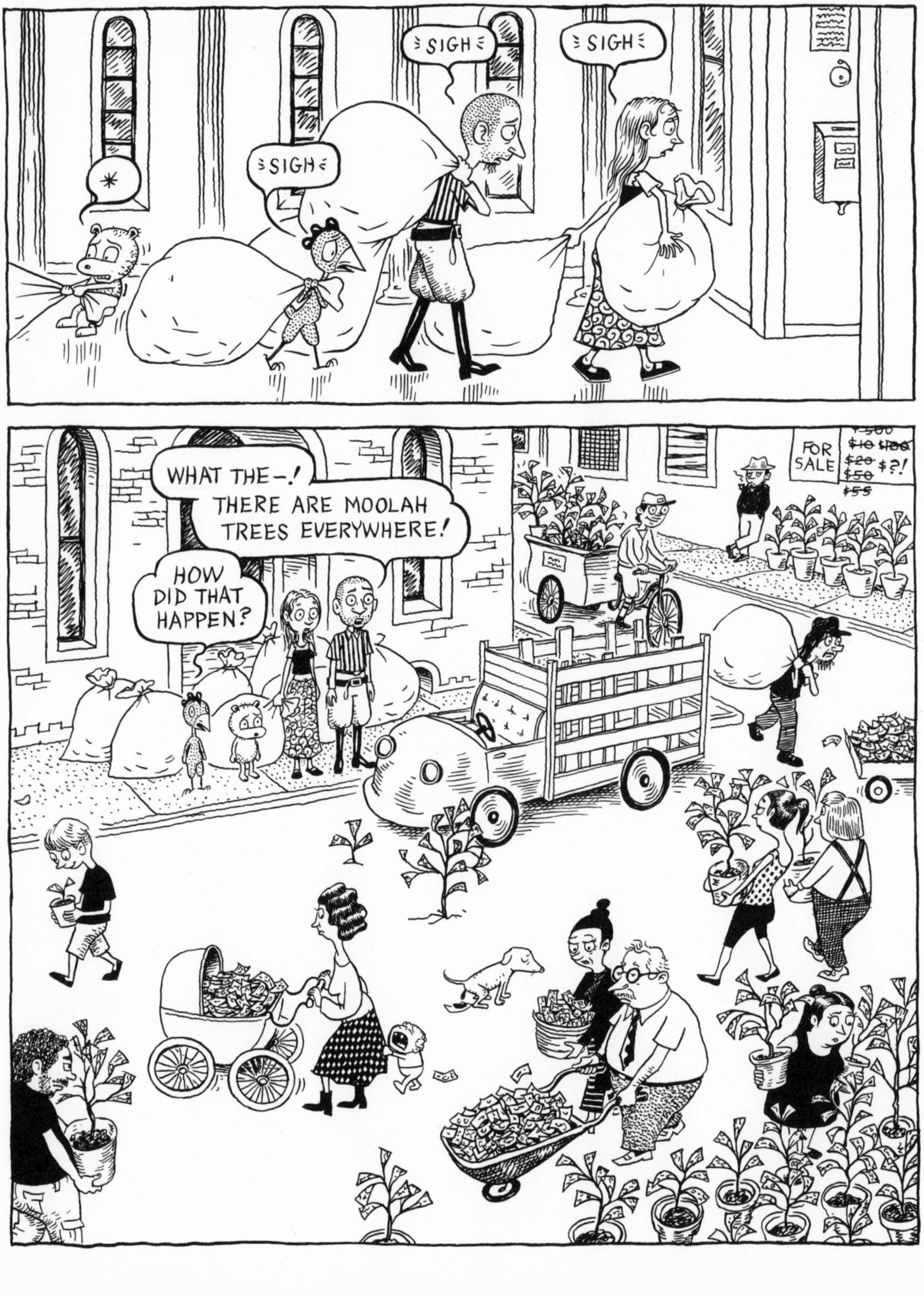
*
SIGH
SIGH
SIGH
WHAT THE–!
THERE ARE MOOLAH TREES EVERYWHERE!
HOW DID THAT HAPPEN?
FOR SALE
$10 $100 $20 $50 $55 $?!

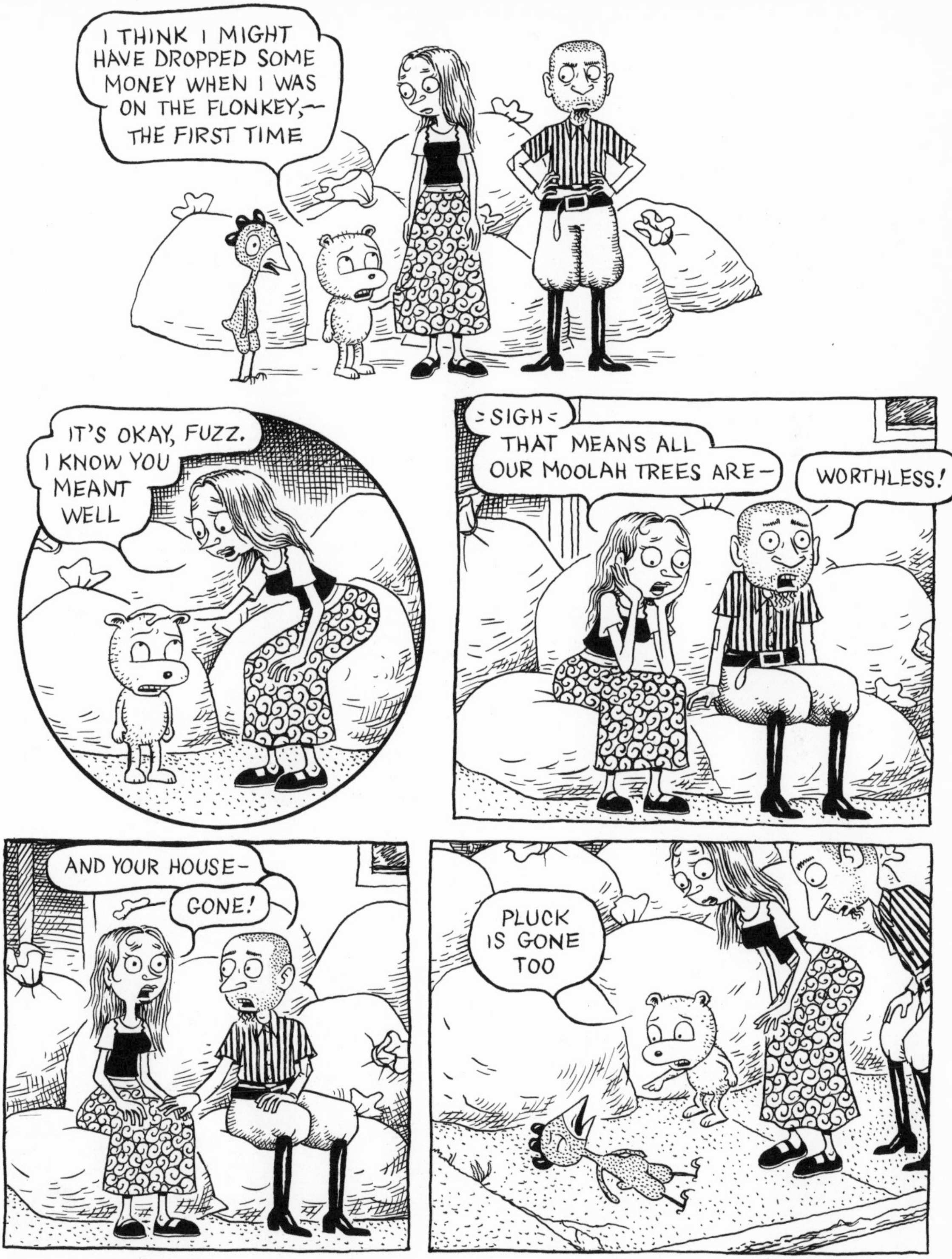
I THINK I MIGHT HAVE DROPPED SOME MONEY WHEN I WAS ON THE FLONKEY,— THE FIRST TIME
IT'S OKAY, FUZZ. I KNOW YOU MEANT WELL
=SIGH=
THAT MEANS ALL OUR MOOLAH TREES ARE—
WORTHLESS!
AND YOUR HOUSE—
GONE!
PLUCK IS GONE TOO

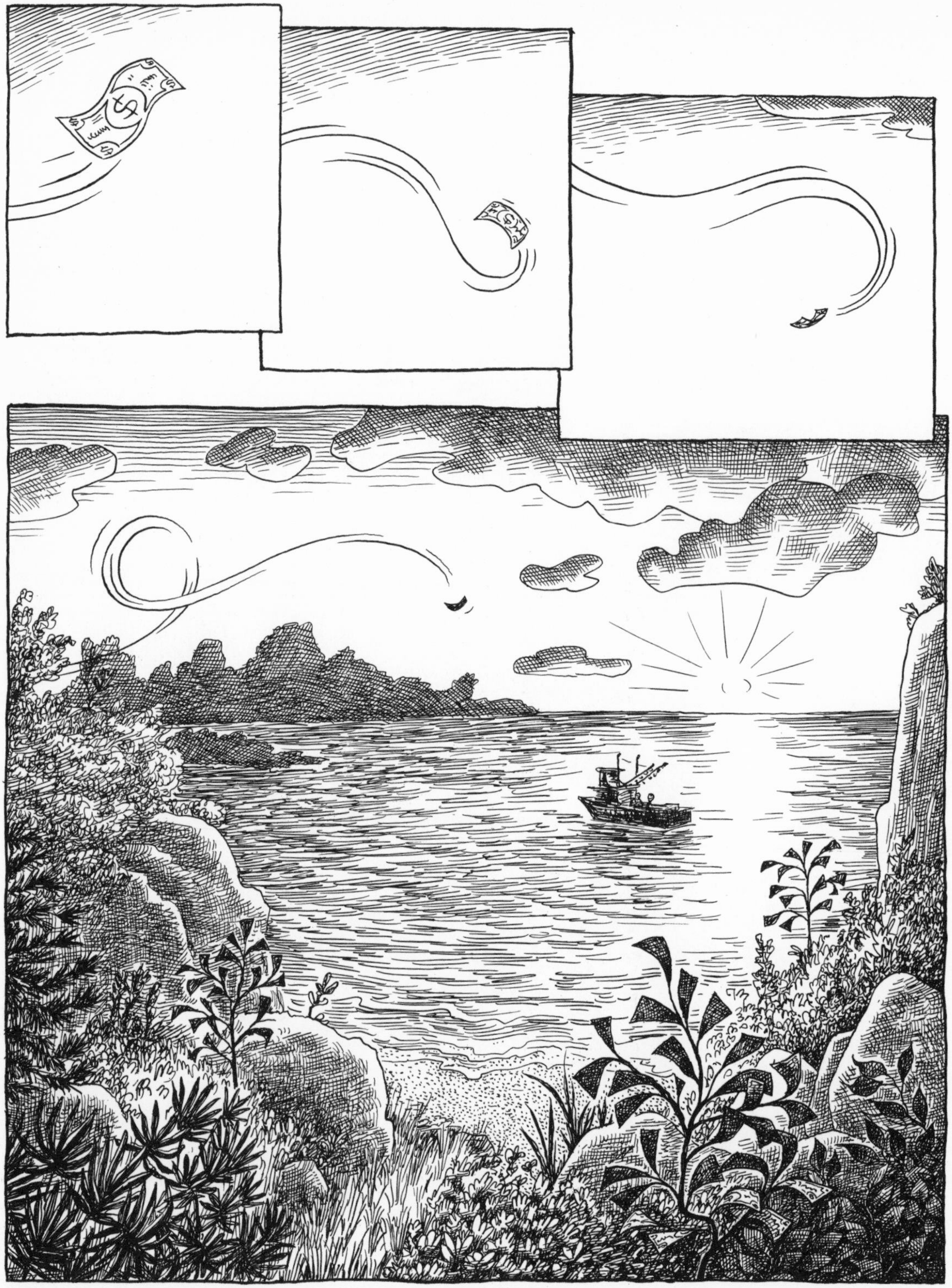

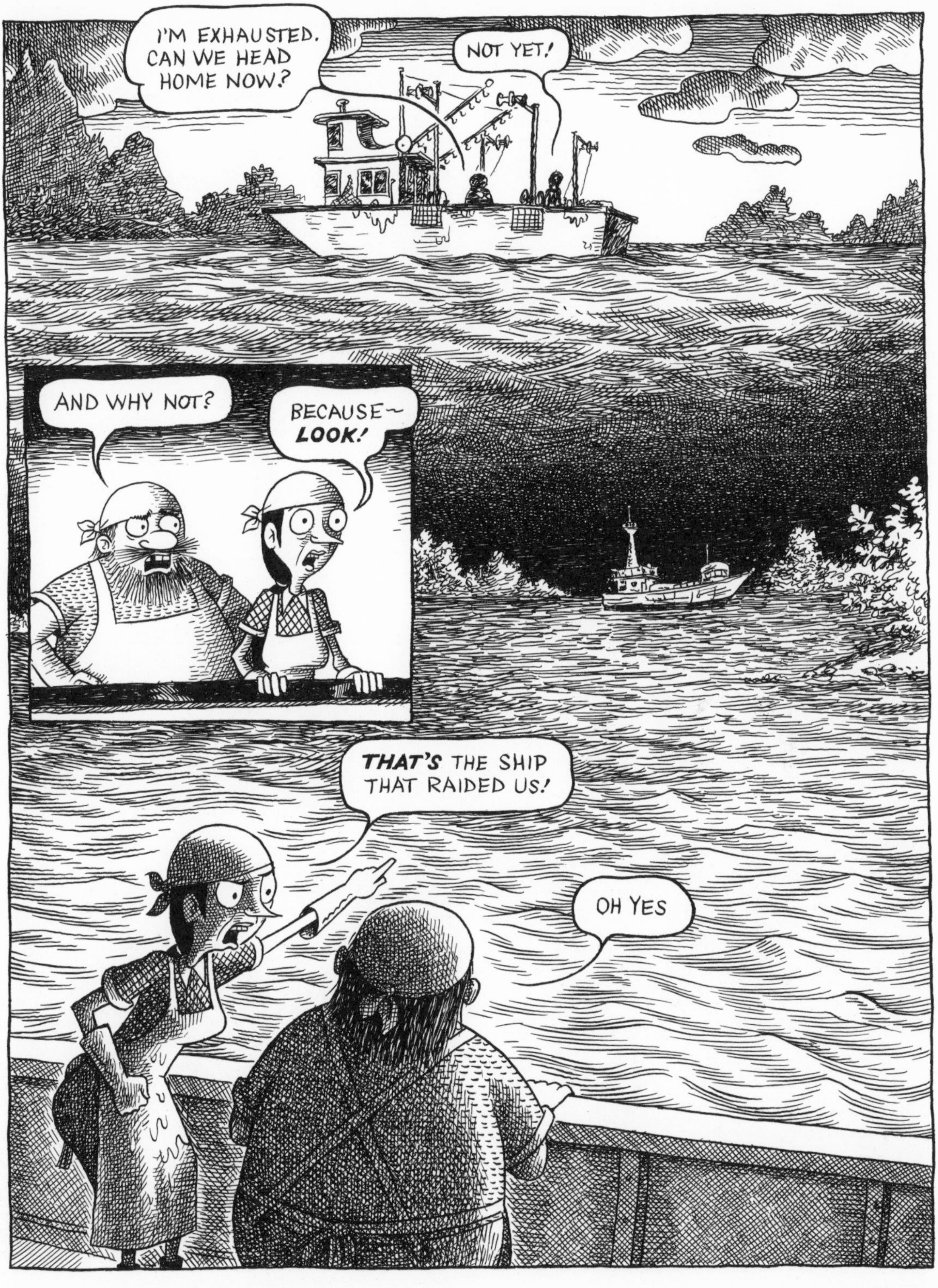
I'M EXHAUSTED. CAN WE HEAD HOME NOW?
NOT YET!
AND WHY NOT?
BECAUSE~ **LOOK!**
THAT'S THE SHIP THAT RAIDED US!
OH YES

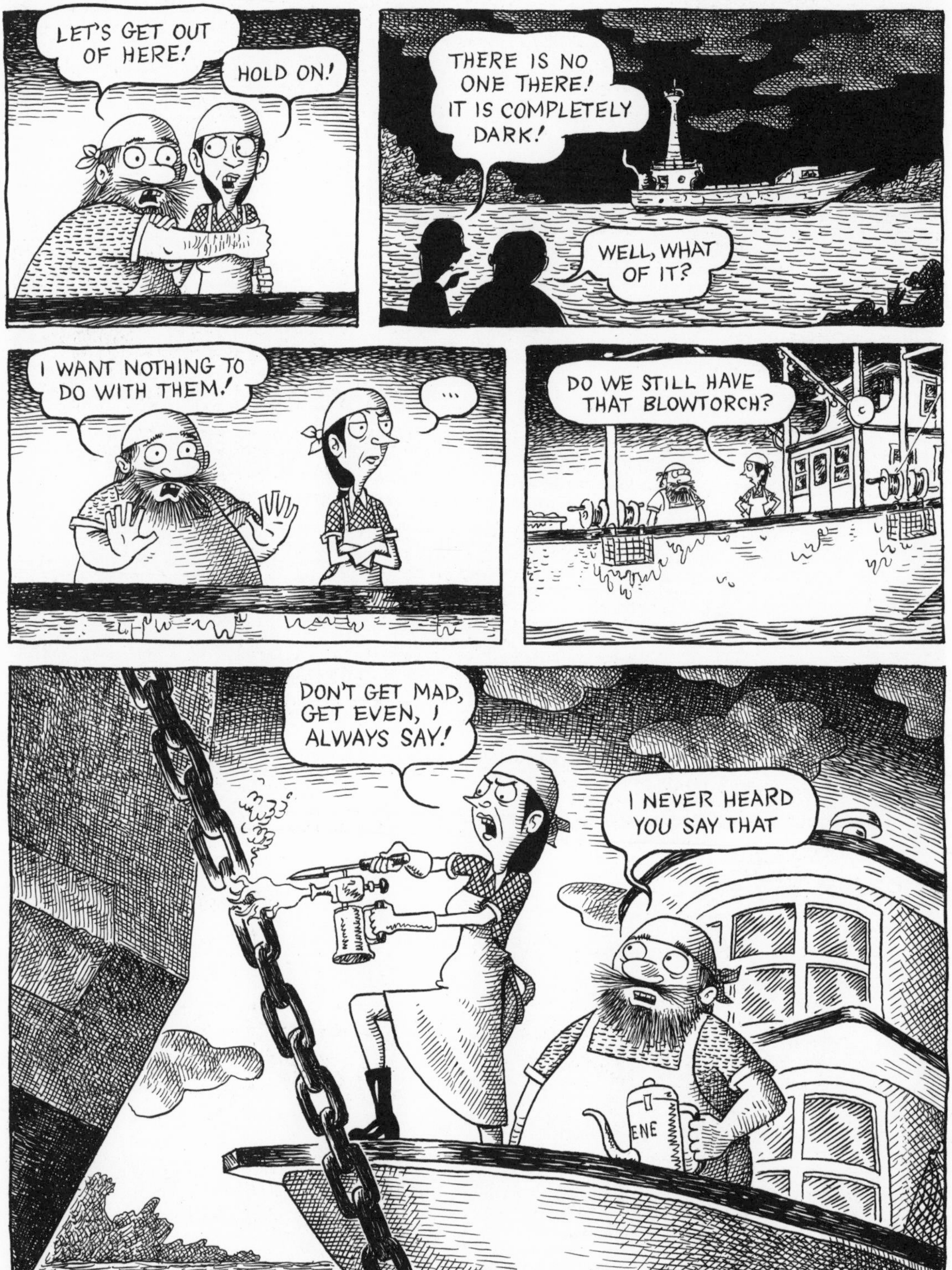
LET'S GET OUT OF HERE!
HOLD ON!
THERE IS NO ONE THERE! IT IS COMPLETELY DARK!
WELL, WHAT OF IT?
I WANT NOTHING TO DO WITH THEM!
...
DO WE STILL HAVE THAT BLOWTORCH?
DON'T GET MAD, GET EVEN, I ALWAYS SAY!
I NEVER HEARD YOU SAY THAT
ENE

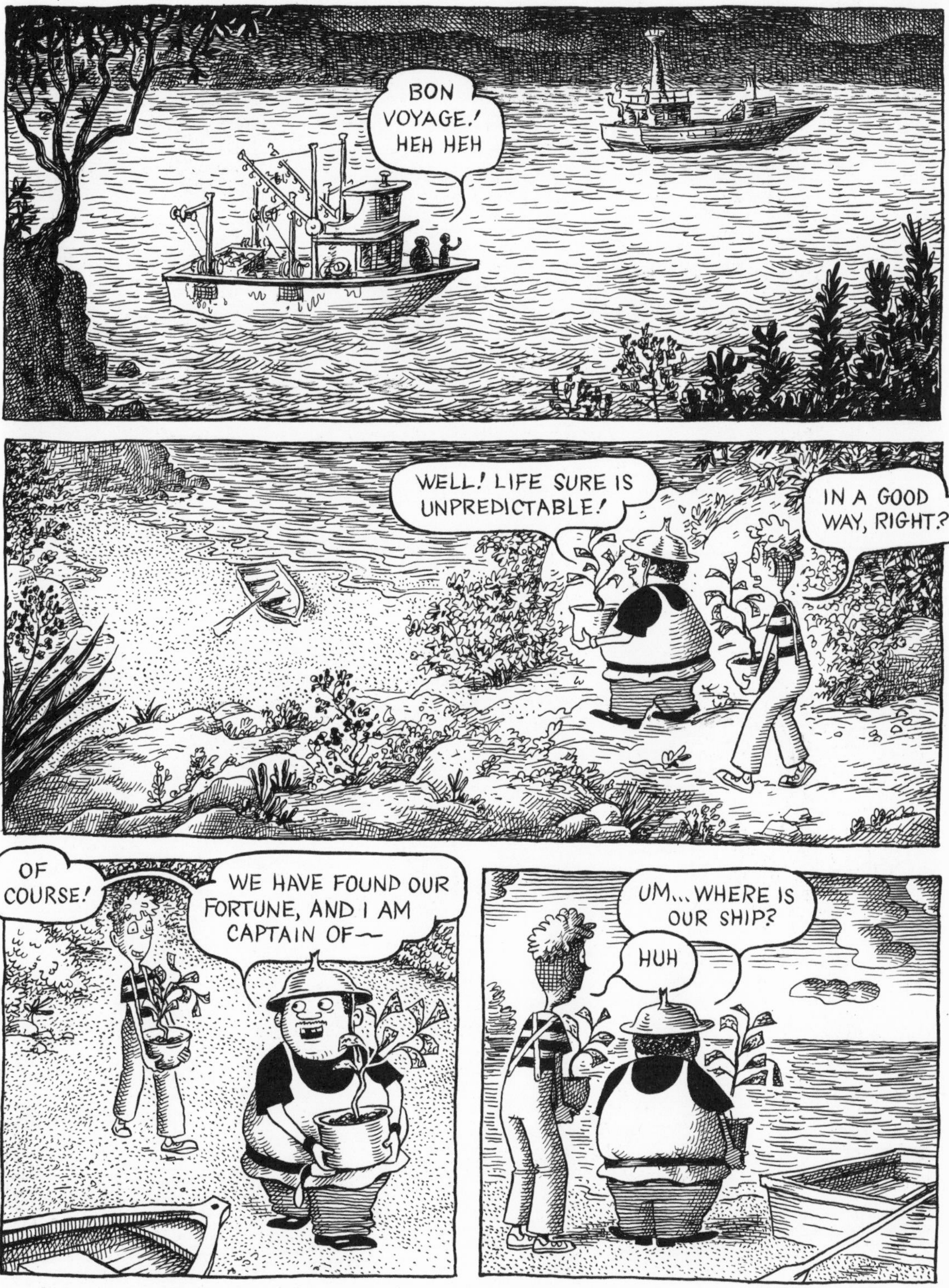
BON VOYAGE! HEH HEH
WELL! LIFE SURE IS UNPREDICTABLE!
IN A GOOD WAY, RIGHT?
OF COURSE!
WE HAVE FOUND OUR FORTUNE, AND I AM CAPTAIN OF—
UM... WHERE IS OUR SHIP?
HUH

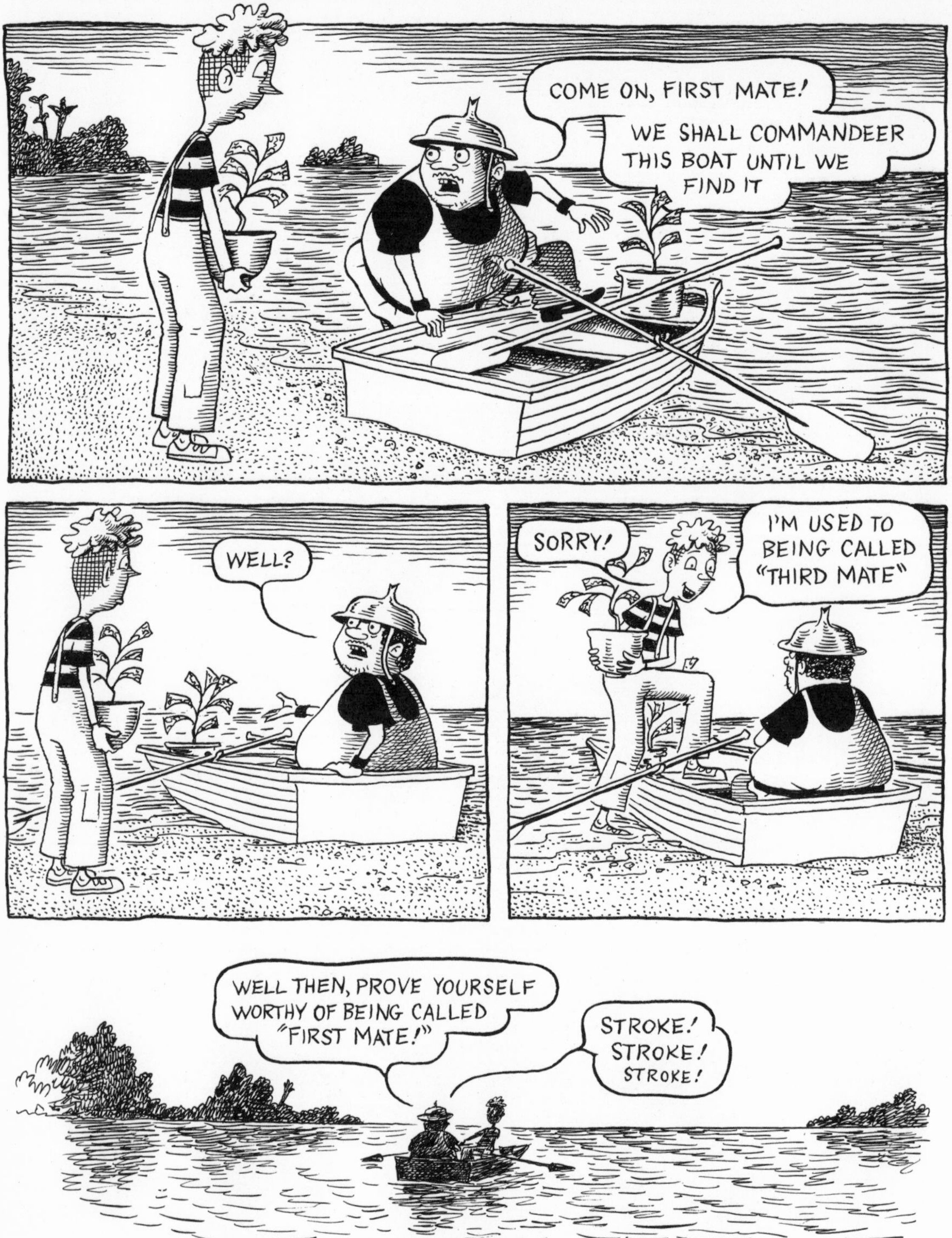
COME ON, FIRST MATE!
WE SHALL COMMANDEER THIS BOAT UNTIL WE FIND IT
WELL?
SORRY!
I'M USED TO BEING CALLED "THIRD MATE"
WELL THEN, PROVE YOURSELF WORTHY OF BEING CALLED "FIRST MATE!"
STROKE! STROKE! STROKE!

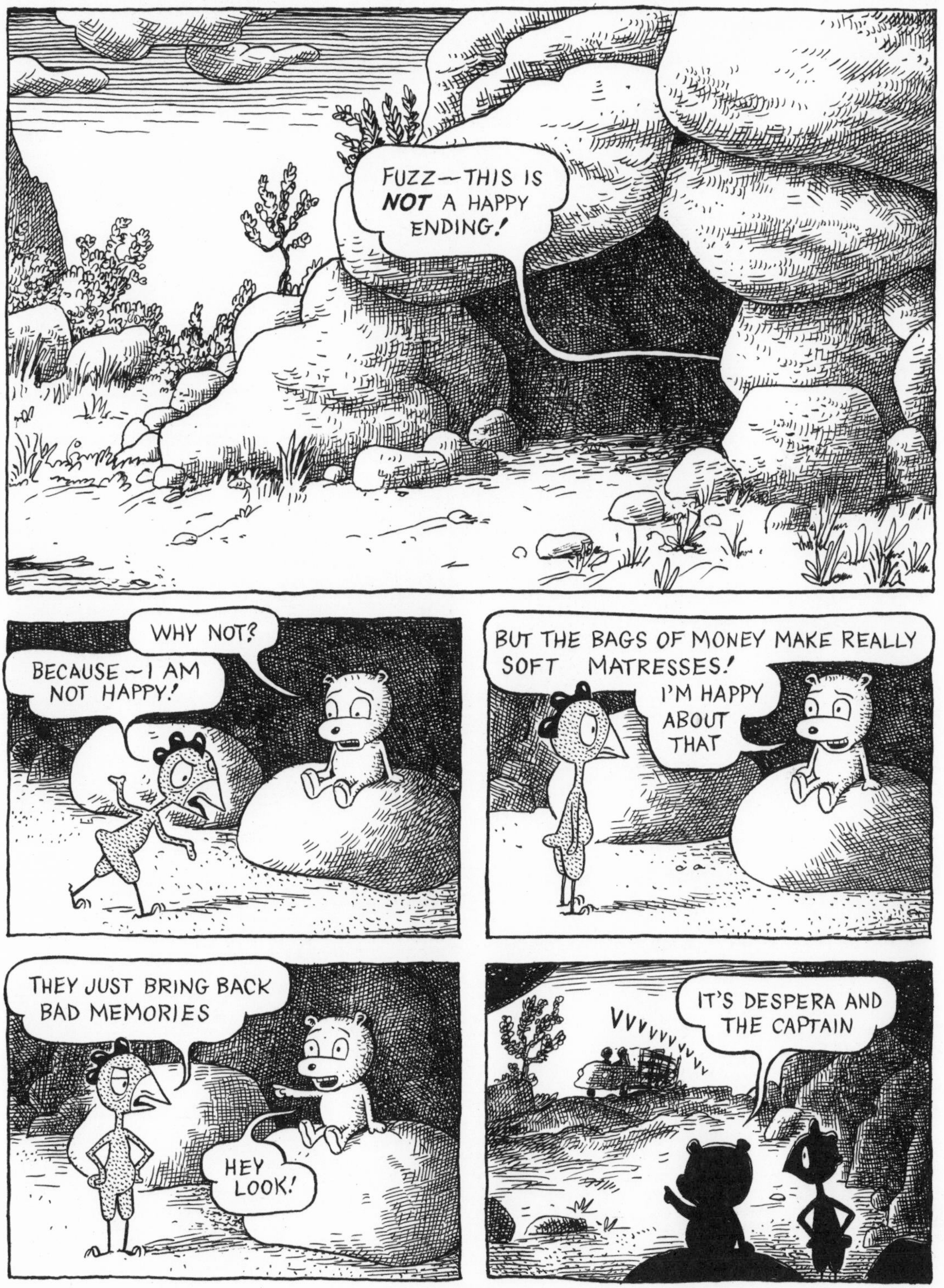

FUZZ—THIS IS **NOT** A HAPPY ENDING!
WHY NOT?
BECAUSE—I AM NOT HAPPY!
BUT THE BAGS OF MONEY MAKE REALLY SOFT MATRESSES!
I'M HAPPY ABOUT THAT
THEY JUST BRING BACK BAD MEMORIES
HEY LOOK!
VVVVVVVVVVV
IT'S DESPERA AND THE CAPTAIN

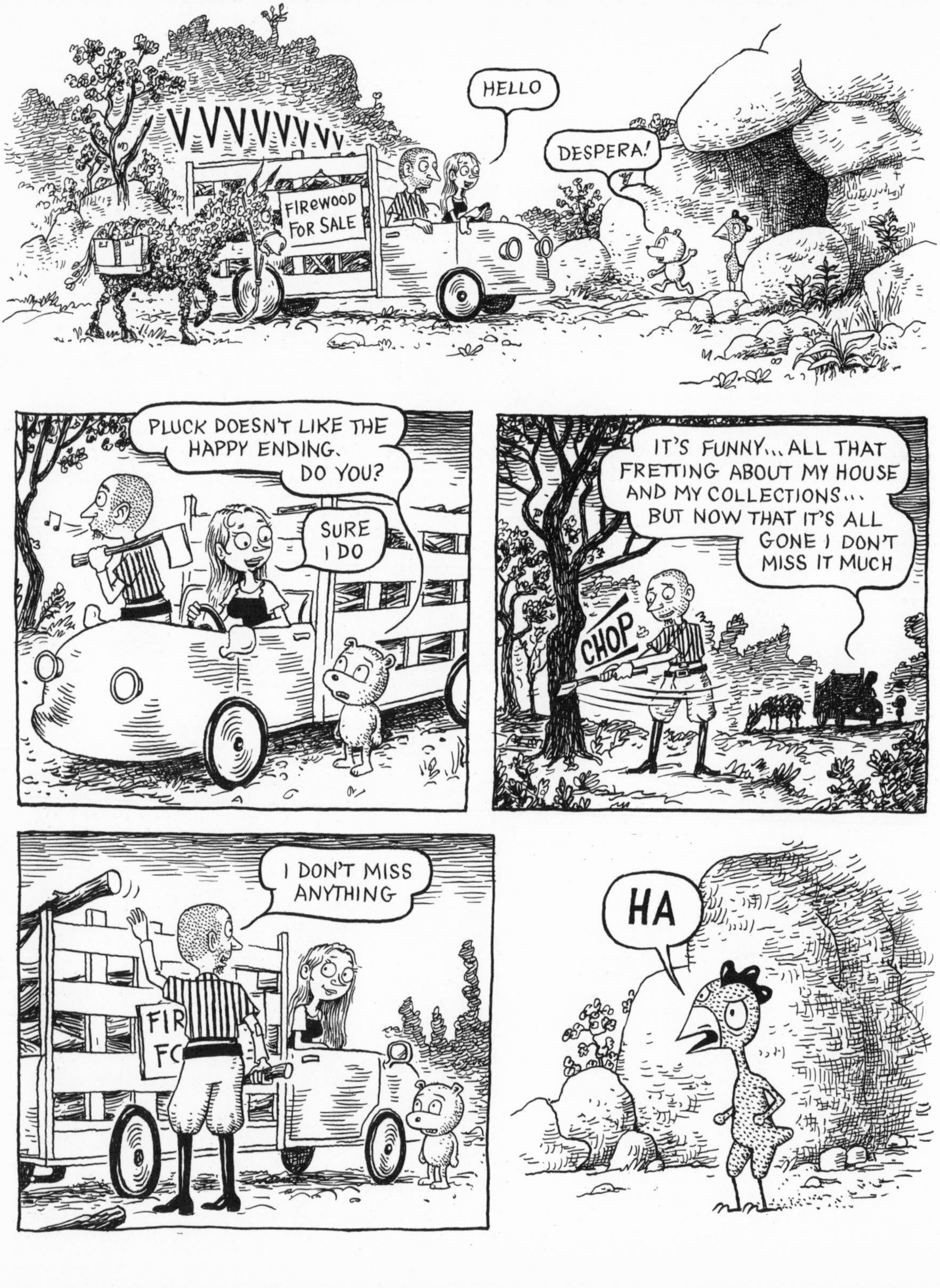
VVVVVVVVV
FIREWOOD FOR SALE
HELLO
DESPERA!
PLUCK DOESN'T LIKE THE HAPPY ENDING. DO YOU?
SURE I DO
IT'S FUNNY... ALL THAT FRETTING ABOUT MY HOUSE AND MY COLLECTIONS... BUT NOW THAT IT'S ALL GONE I DON'T MISS IT MUCH
CHOP
I DON'T MISS ANYTHING
HA

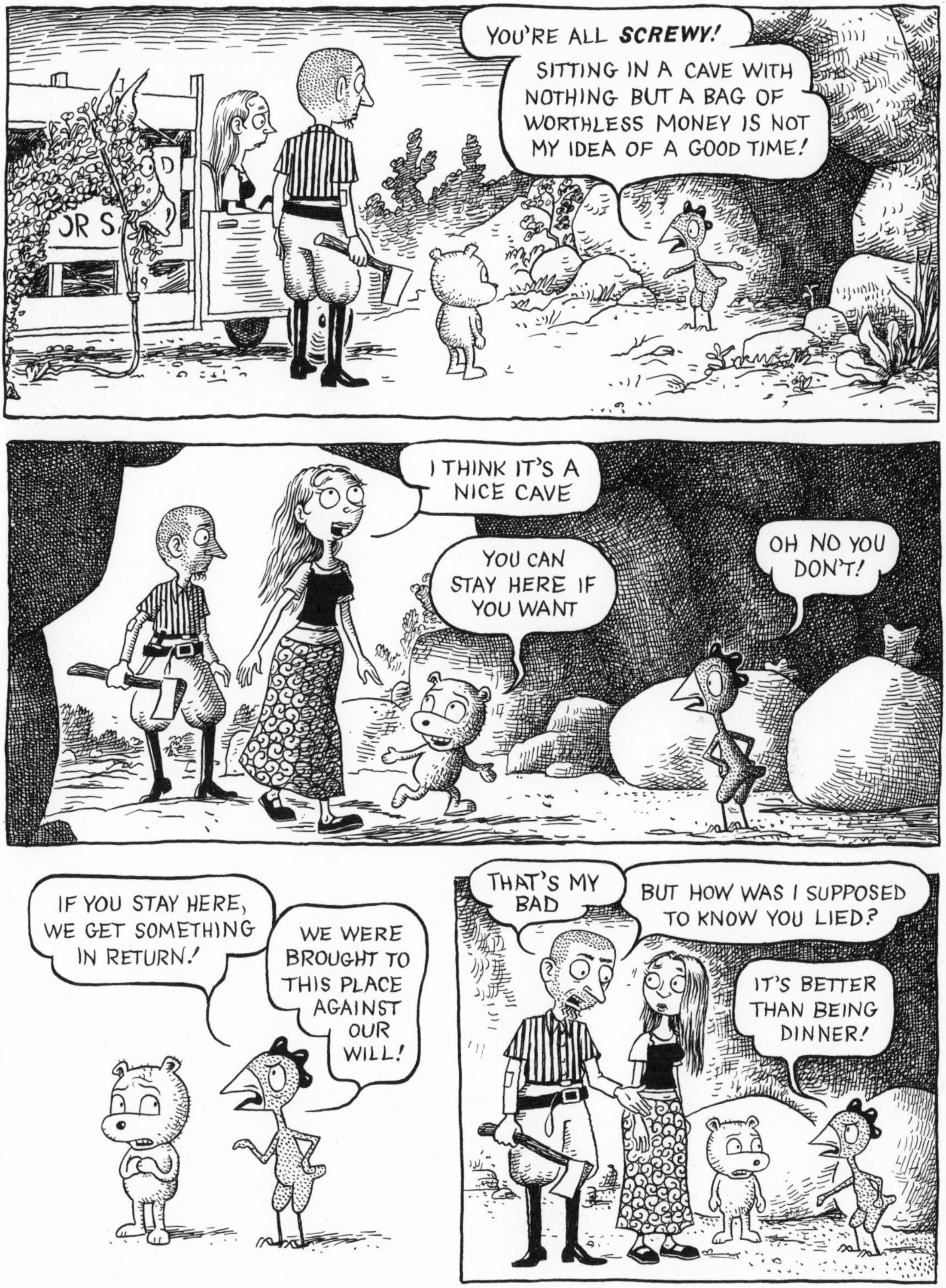
YOU'RE ALL SCREWY!
SITTING IN A CAVE WITH NOTHING BUT A BAG OF WORTHLESS MONEY IS NOT MY IDEA OF A GOOD TIME!
I THINK IT'S A NICE CAVE
YOU CAN STAY HERE IF YOU WANT
OH NO YOU DON'T!
IF YOU STAY HERE, WE GET SOMETHING IN RETURN!
WE WERE BROUGHT TO THIS PLACE AGAINST OUR WILL!
THAT'S MY BAD
BUT HOW WAS I SUPPOSED TO KNOW YOU LIED?
IT'S BETTER THAN BEING DINNER!

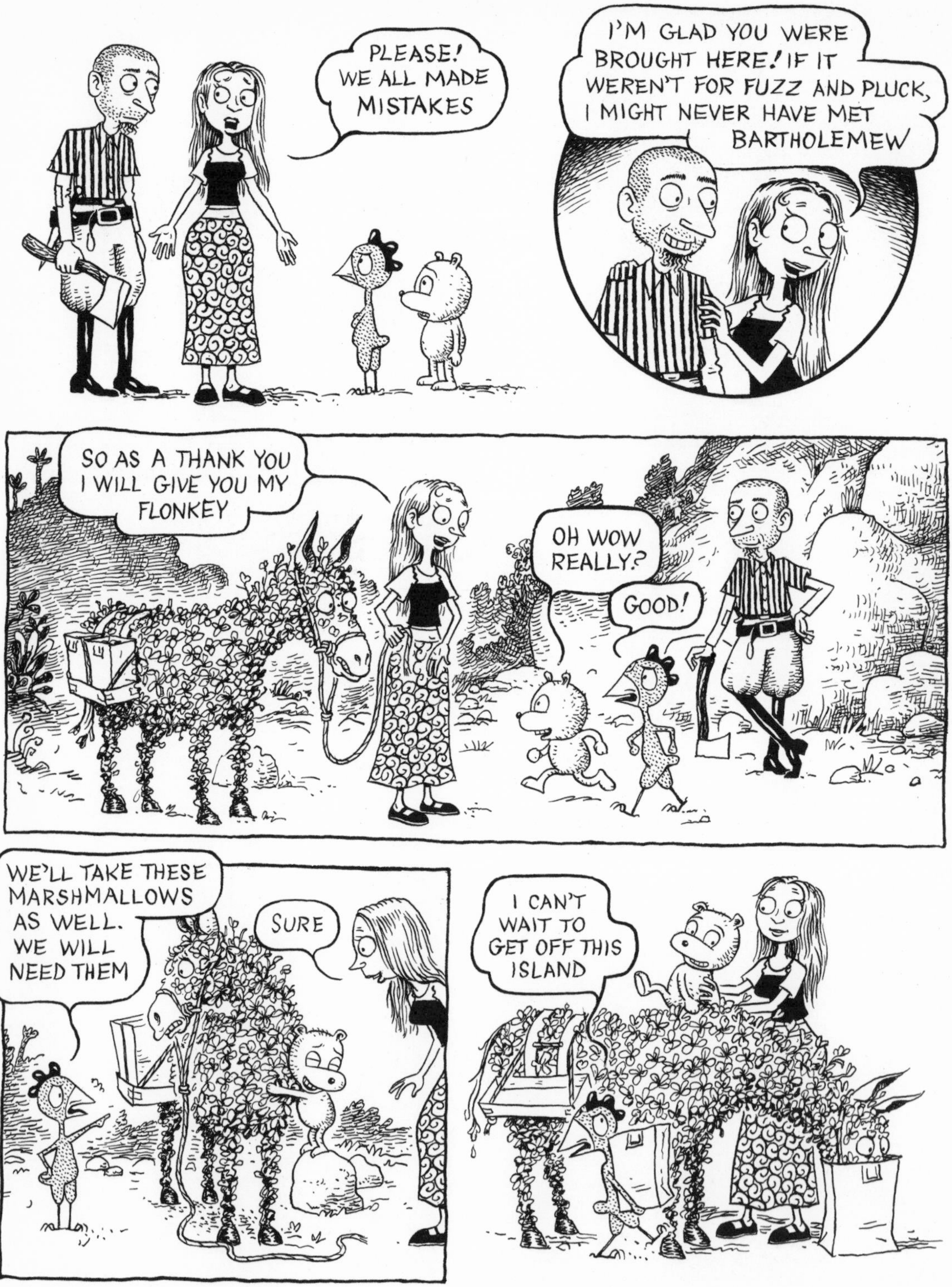
PLEASE! WE ALL MADE MISTAKES
I'M GLAD YOU WERE BROUGHT HERE! IF IT WEREN'T FOR FUZZ AND PLUCK, I MIGHT NEVER HAVE MET BARTHOLEMEW
SO AS A THANK YOU I WILL GIVE YOU MY FLONKEY
OH WOW REALLY?
GOOD!
WE'LL TAKE THESE MARSHMALLOWS AS WELL. WE WILL NEED THEM
SURE
I CAN'T WAIT TO GET OFF THIS ISLAND

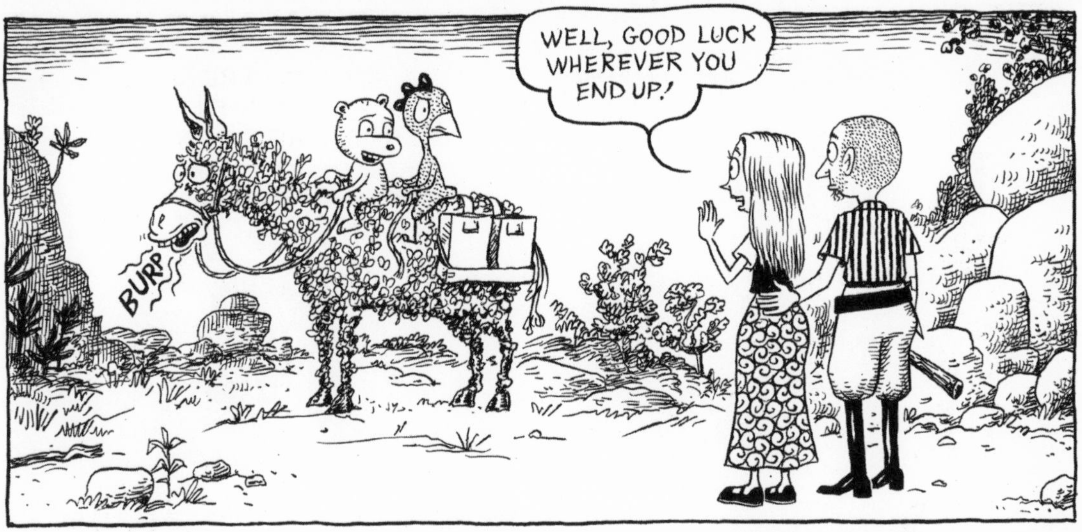
WELL, GOOD LUCK WHEREVER YOU END UP!
BURP

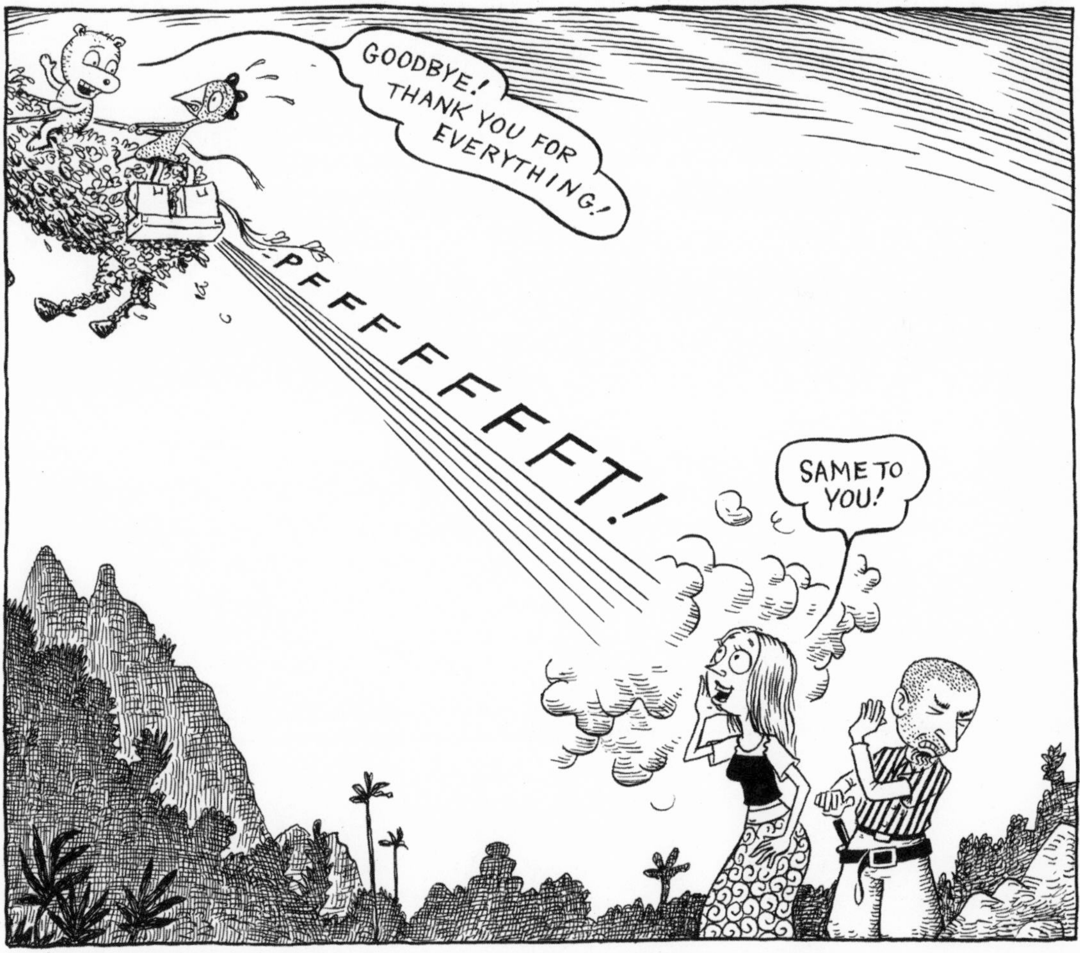
GOODBYE! THANK YOU FOR EVERYTHING!
PFFFFFFFFT!
SAME TO YOU!

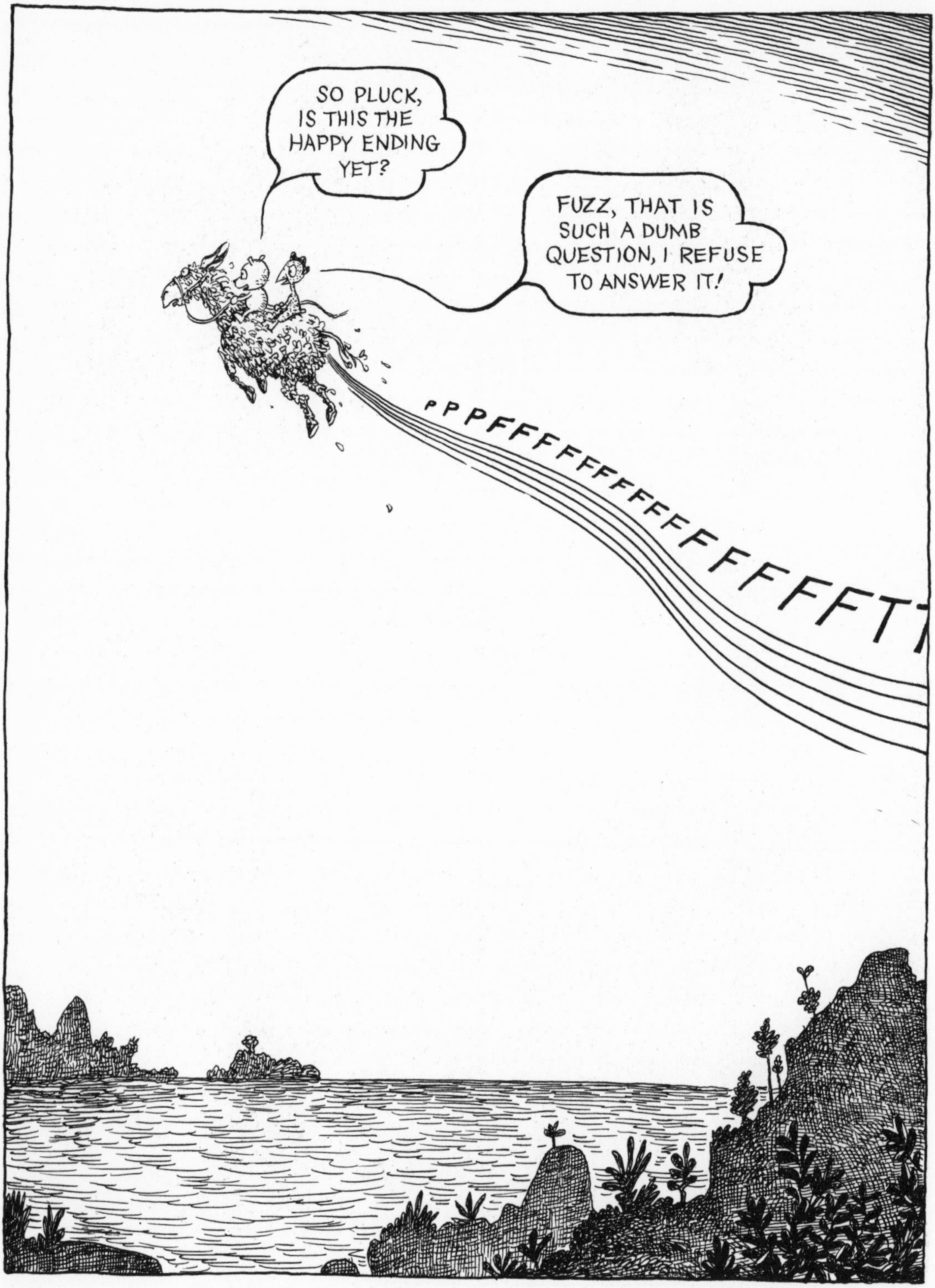
SO PLUCK, IS THIS THE HAPPY ENDING YET?
FUZZ, THAT IS SUCH A DUMB QUESTION, I REFUSE TO ANSWER IT!
PPPFFFFFFFFFFFFFFFFFFTT

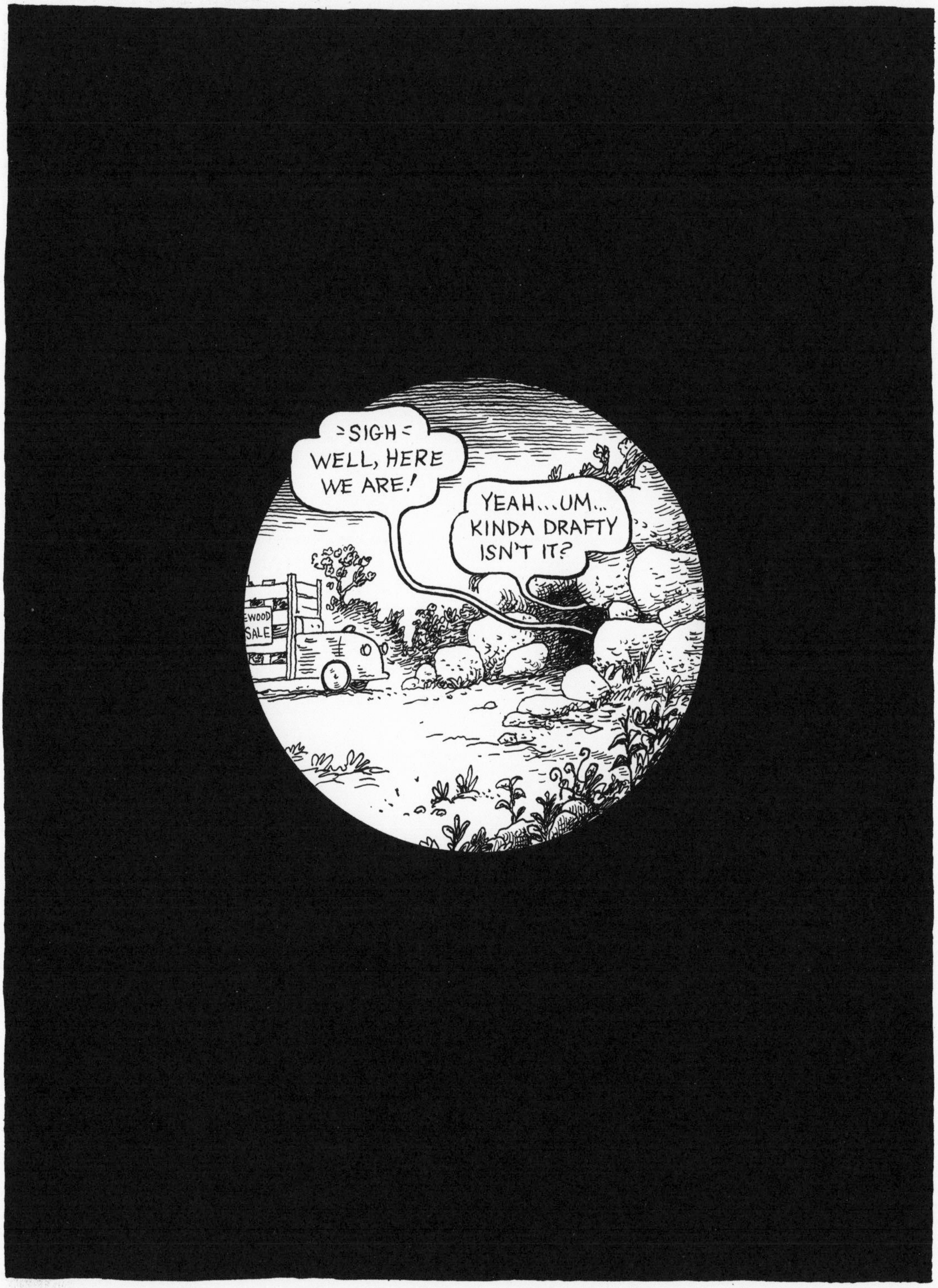
=SIGH=
WELL, HERE WE ARE!
YEAH...UM.. KINDA DRAFTY ISN'T IT?
EWOOD SALE

Also by Ted Stearn

and previously published by Fantagraphics Books:

FUZZ &
PLUCK
TED STEARN

FUZZ &
PLUCK
SPLITS-VILLE
Ted Stearn

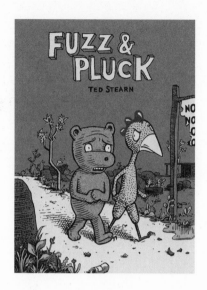

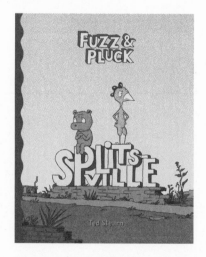